The Very First Lady

Steve Dunleavy

Simon and Schuster
NEW YORK

Published by Simon and Schuster
A Division of Gulf & Western Corporation
Simon & Schuster Building
Rockefeller Center
1230 Avenue of the Americas
New York, New York 10020
SIMON AND SCHUSTER and colophon are trademarks of Simon & Schuster

Designed by Irving Perkins
Manufactured in the United States of America
1 2 3 4 5 6 7 8 9 10

Library of Congress Cataloging in Publication Data
Dunleavy, Steve.
  The very first lady.
  I. Title
PZ4.D9198Ve [PS3554.U46974] 813'.54 80-14544
ISBN 0-671-24691-7

To an old man called Steve and a young man called Ted who have drunk all the booze in heaven. And to the Blake gang, Mick and Pete Brennan, Travis, and McGovern who have failed to do it on earth

The Very First Lady

Book
One

Chapter

1

AT FIVE o'clock on the morning of January 20, 1985, the magnificent white marble of the Lincoln Monument gave off an almost celestial glow as the predawn light washed across the city that determines the destiny of so many lives.

Outside—on the banks of the Potomac, around the Reflecting Pool, on the Washington Monument grounds and along the Mall—they had gathered in the thousands, clustered around oil-drum fires, huddled under blankets and standing in quiet but joyful bunches waiting for the sunlight hours that would include them all in a piece of history. The more awestruck among the men and women who thronged around the glistening white marble monument had sworn that the chiseled features of Lincoln could no longer be called brooding. The expression was that of a paternalistic pride that had come to fruition on this most important of days in the history of the United States.

Around the Tidal Basin, even the bald cherry-blossom trees had been blessed with beauty. At the tips of their tiny finger branches the dew had frozen, and they sparkled like delicate crystal balls.

Mike McGavin felt a surge of overwhelming emotion as he thrust his hands deep into the pockets of his Chesterfield coat and trudged the crisp white carpet of snow back to his car. He edged through smiling faces, flushed red by the wind that sailed off the Potomac, his breath making blue puffs in the air.

He opened the rear door of the limousine and told the chauffeur simply to drive. Even locked in the dark warmth of the limousine he could sense the smell of pleasant, harmless madness in the air. Everywhere there were people. The car circled the immaculate city and without asking for instructions the chauffeur turned onto Constitution Avenue, past the Senate Office Building and left onto Delaware Avenue. At the end of Delaware, in Union Station Plaza, the crowds were almost shoulder to shoulder, many of them with guitars and virtually all of them singing different songs in different accents from all parts of the country and in some languages from other countries. They all seemed to share the same air of anticipation, one of controlled excitement, as if they were about to be part of one of the greatest celebrations of the age.

As the car circled Union Station and headed up Massachusetts Avenue, he glanced at the thin gold face of his elegant watch. Five fifty A.M.

"Okay," he told the chauffeur, "let's head back."

The limousine purred down New York Avenue.

Mike McGavin straightened the immaculate dark blue silk tie. He glanced in the rearview mirror to make sure he was as faultlessly turned out as he had been when he rose from his bed at four that morning with his heart pounding with excitement.

The limousine turned from New York into Pennsylvania Avenue. He could see the crowds huddled against the cold, standing near where Pennsylvania becomes Fifteenth Street. The wooden horses that had been erected by police were quietly respected by the people who milled around the elegantly austere Blair House, the mansion that had hosted state visitors since McGavin was a child.

He stepped lightly from the limousine. Heads in the crowd turned. He must be important. There may even have been some in the crowd who knew he was the young press secretary.

A group of reporters, their fingers, blue with cold, coiled around pencils, approached him.

"Anything, Mike?" one of them asked familiarly.

"Nothing yet, fellas. Just a last-minute visit. More later," he said with a smile and a wave as the line of Secret Service men with transistorized two-way radios attached to their ears parted to allow him access.

He trotted past the ramrod-stiff uniformed guards, who clicked their heels with metallic precision as he went through the impressive entrance and into the chandeliered lobby.

He nodded to another contingent of Secret Service men inside and sprinted athletically up the giant staircase to the first-floor suites. He walked down the wide hallway, then stopped briefly in front of a giant brass-framed mirror to check himself out. Good.

He knocked gently on a huge double door. The ornate brass handle turned, and yet another Secret Service man smiled politely. He walked into the foyer of the elegant suite and knocked on the door presided over by the maid. The door opened. It wasn't the maid.

"Hi, Terrence." He warmly grabbed the hand of Terrence Keogh. Terrence was a slightly built youth of seventeen, pleasantly assertive, good-looking in a mildly intellectual sort of way. He wore thick-lensed dark glasses.

"Come in, Michael; sit down. Hmm—I can smell that you're wearing your best after-shave lotion," he said. He had his back turned to Mc-Gavin now. Mike never ceased to marvel at the young man's perception of the minutest detail.

"I thought this would be as good a day as any to make the best of myself."

The youth turned and smiled warmly. "How about some coffee?"

"Love some, although I don't think I need much more to pump the adrenaline in my body."

"Yes," the young man answered with the same even smile, "it's quite a day. What's it like outside?"

"Clear, crisp, cold and very crowded—very crowded." McGavin had a no-nonsense way of giving an accurate picture without wasting words. He continued: "It will certainly break all earlier attendance records. Perhaps a million."

The coffee appeared. Mike took off his coat and took a cup from a maid who seemed to materialize from nowhere.

Mike went on: "Just wanted to go over a few tiny details." He reached into his suit jacket and produced a neat sheaf of typewritten pages.

"The address the President will use is typed in large print. I've made a few small changes. Has the President risen yet?"

Before Terrence could answer, a voice came from the entrance of the living room.

"I certainly have. How are you, Mike? Well, you look like a member of the Cabinet, you're so well dressed."

Before him stood Rose Margaret Keogh.

The hairdresser would arrive soon. But now, without a touch of makeup and wearing a tastefully conservative house gown that was but-toned from the neck to the floor, the tiny, firm figure looked impressive. Rose Keogh had never been a beautiful woman, but she had attractively pert features. Her carriage was dignified but still very young. Her dark brown medium-length hair was lush and healthy, her skin smooth and flawless. She had an easy, ladylike smile that was never too self-conscious to burst into an attractive laugh.

McGavin stood up and returned her smile, giving her a brief hand-shake.

"I thought the speech you wrote was excellent, Michael," she said, taking a cup of coffee handed to her by her son, Terrence. "What did you think, Terrence?"

"Masterpiece, Mother."

"Just a few tiny changes, if I may," McGavin said, handing her the typewritten pages.

"Certainly," she said, taking the pages. She read at lightning speed, but she absorbed every word and noted immediately where the changes were. It was, as Rose Margaret Keogh said, an excellent speech. It would be the Inaugural Address she would deliver.

From this day on, she would be addressed as Madam President.

IT WAS exactly 10:35 A.M. Mike McGavin was in his temporary press office down the hallway from President-elect Rose Keogh. He had made all the last-minute telephone calls to the parade marshals, to the Capitol Building, to the Secret Service heads. He noticed that as the magic hour of 11 A.M. approached there was a slight quiver to his hands and his heart refused to stop pounding. He smiled to himself. Why wouldn't he be nervous?

Outside, Washington had given in to the madness that the early hours of the day had foreshadowed. People were tooting car horns. The skies were filled with balloons, thousands of them, in every color. The white winter sunshine bounced off the iced snow, and it gave a bright face to the immaculate but normally most serious of cities.

One million people had jammed the center of the city, gaily stretching it almost to bursting. But the crowds, the cars, the noise, the music only added to the breathless atmosphere of an early-season Mardi Gras. America was inaugurating its first woman President in history, and everyone felt proud, strong, happy and reassured that the country at last was working like no other place on earth.

Behind a phalanx of security men who operated like parts of a ticking watch, President-elect Rose Keogh emerged from Blair House flanked by her son, Terrence, and Mike McGavin. She smiled demurely as a huge roar split the air from the jammed humanity behind the police barricades. Then she gave them a wave and another roar exploded. The press cameras and television crews jostled in front of her. She posed briefly and then walked to a giant enclosed limousine that was part of the motorcade. Later she would use the open limousine. As she walked to the limousine, she kept her eyes slightly lowered. In front of her, across from Blair House, it stood. The White House.

Whether it was a childish superstition or a wish to savor the most important morsel last, her gaze avoided the proud sandstone structure which in 1985 had been the awesome seat of power for 184 years. She had been there many times before, but only as a guest, never the host. Soon the key to that stately mansion would be hers.

Mike McGavin hopped into the car in front of the President-elect's. Terrence Keogh, without the aid of the cane that guided his blindness, assisted his mother into the warm, dark luxury of the giant black limousine that followed.

In the left-hand corner of the back seat, Lionel Rawlins sat like a man suddenly awakened from sedation. Lionel Rawlins was about to be superseded as President of the United States. He attempted to mask his uneasiness with formality. It didn't work. It never does with losers who try too hard to lose graciously.

Rose Keogh, President-elect, flashed a warm smile. She had beaten this man. Yet her expression held warmth. Victors are warmer than losers.

Terrence Keogh could smell his mother's subtle perfume. He loved his mother. The scent conveyed to him a special sense of her love.

He nodded the head with sightless eyes toward Lionel Rawlins, the outgoing President. That was all he could do. He wasn't being rude. It was just that he was so caught up in the moment—and who could blame him? And who could blame the first woman President of the United States of America for being similarly awed?

President-elect Rose Margaret Keogh and her son, Terrence, did not speak to Lionel Rawlins after their formalities. The Secret Service cars pulled out first, then McGavin's, followed by the presidential limousine.

The motorcade took the same route as McGavin had taken earlier in the day. A semicircle around the parade route. Right on New York Avenue, right on Massachusetts, past Union Station and right again on Delaware to the Capitol dome and then to the Capitol steps, where the official swearing in would take place and the Inaugural address delivered.

At the sight of the official motorcade, the crowds milling along the route seemed to strike a note of beautiful insanity. The bystanders shouted themselves hoarse and many showered the motorcade with thousands of roses, flown from the West Coast—a floral tribute to the first President named Rose.

Once in the cloistered security of the limousine, the dark, petite woman, dressed immaculately in an elegantly cut form-fitting black coat with a fur-trimmed collar, flushed slightly with excitement.

Terrence Keogh gently squeezed her arm. "They love you out there, Mother. They love you."

"Thank you, Terrence . . . and I return their love . . . I return their love."

She breathed deeply as the limousine motorcade slowly slid past the screaming crowds onto the circle around the Capitol. The muscles of her body tensed like straining piano wires, almost as if in the moment before a climax.

The first cars of the motorcade had already arrived at the East Plaza of the Capitol. They had emptied their passengers, the Secret Service slithering into obscurity but ever watchful.

On the steps of the Capitol, a stand had been erected to seat two thousand of the country's and the world's most powerful. Across the plaza, another twenty thousand people would hear and see the swearing-in ceremonies.

The President-elect's car crawled slowly to the base of the steps, flanked by an honor guard of the armed services standing on a blood-red carpet. Inside the limousine, Rose Margaret Keogh put her hand on Terrence's forearm. She gripped it tightly. Terrence put a reassuring hand on his mother's.

"They love you, Mother. The world is all here for you. The world."

She stared straight ahead, then turned her head and smiled at him, looking into the darkness of the thick lenses. Terrence adored his mother, not only because she returned his love but also because he had felt she was the only true friend he had ever had since the first day of his life, when he was born blind. When she smiled, despite his sightless eyes, it was always the same. He knew.

He smiled at her. "Go on, Mother. Go out there and show them."

"I will, Terrence."

As she stepped lightly from the limousine, assisted by the Speaker of the House, the immaculate Marine Band, dressed in ceremonial blue and scarlet, played a subdued and muted version of the National Anthem. Daintily she ascended the red-carpeted steps.

Terrence was right. The world was all here for her. There were prime ministers and presidents from forty countries sitting in the stands. Many of them wore rosebuds in their lapels. To underscore the message of peace and unity, it had been arranged that representatives of countries with past animosities arrive together. The Prime Minister of England and the President of the Republic of Ireland had arrived arm in arm. Likewise the heads of state of Greece and Turkey. When Igor Kolotoc, the Soviet Premier, and Chinese Premier Hsu Peng-lai arrived together, they were greeted with approving applause. They both wore red rosebuds in their lapels. Mike McGavin had executed a masterstroke in public relations.

As President-elect Rose Margaret Keogh picked her way up the steps, the crowd in front of the Capitol let forth an almost frightening roar. The applause carried in the wind for a mile up Pennsylvania Avenue. Across from the Capitol's west face, in the parade-staging area on the Mall, flanked by Independence and Constitution Avenues, fifteen thousand paraders, bands, floats and state delegations seemed to strike a note of frenzy. Sixteen bands played different tunes and nobody cared.

Suddenly, as if by invisible signal, the raucous celebrants fell silent as the tiny form of Rose Keogh stood erect on the rostrum, in front of the dignified array of the Supreme Court Justices. She shook their hands one by one. Close behind followed her son, Terrence, who walked almost totally without reliance on the thin white cane which he held in his left hand. Already standing on the rostrum were the Vice President-elect, a man who had formed much history of his own; the Speaker of the House and an array of clergymen.

Mike McGavin fell behind into the ranks of the elite to observe history from a more obscure vantage point. The knots were still there in McGavin's stomach, and he wondered if perhaps his nervousness was genuine apprehension. He had to admit that he had real reservations about a woman of Rose Keogh's experience. Perhaps he was simply a crypto male chauvinist, for there was no question as to her overwhelming intellect or her power to grasp the emotion of a nation. More truthfully, perhaps, it was because he thought with a mysterious pang of guilt about Rose's husband, a man who had been almost a surrogate father to him.

He looked with an amused touch of cynicism as the President-elect shook hands with the clergymen on the podium. Joseph Cardinal O'Connor from Boston, Rabbi Cohen of New York, Episcopal Bishop Young from Atlanta. He smiled inwardly. They should indeed be there. The Keogh family had given enough money to the clergy to rebuild Canterbury, the Vatican and Jerusalem combined. Then there was the priest from South Boston to whom he had just waved. Father Velas Zeibatski, the Keogh family confessor, a deep, mysterious man with many secrets, an ageless man whose handsome face and deep-set, slanted Slavic eyes saw so much but betrayed so little. That was one man who deserved to be there, McGavin thought.

Rose Keogh sat with dignity to the side of the lectern on the rostrum. Behind her the giant dome of the Capitol looked down on the mortals below who had come to celebrate the ultimate ritual of politics. The inauguration.

She sat erect, her dark brown hair, arranged in a French twist, showing unselfconscious streaks of gray that glistened in the bright winter sun. She stared straight ahead, almost mesmerized by the mass of humanity that had come to adore and revere her.

As Joseph Cardinal O'Connor delivered the invocation, it was as if she were detached from reality. It was impossible to believe that so many people in such a small area could suddenly become so silent. After the invocation, a black Gospel singer gave a stirring rendition of "America the Beautiful." The wind starched the American flags stiff. A prayer was then offered by Rabbi Cohen, and another was led by Episcopal Bishop Young.

Through it all, Rose Keogh sat solemn and rigid. It was, as McGavin observed from behind the white heads and pink scalps of the gentlemen of the Supreme Court, how it should be.

Rose Keogh, despite her outward solemn control, could feel her heartbeat intensify until it was thumping in her nipples. The moment drew nearer as the Speaker of the House administered the oath of office to the Vice President. Then another prayer. Agony played in her body. This was the moment. Not a muscle moved as the Marine Band then struck up for the second time in fifty minutes the National Anthem.

As the last strains died in the air, United States Chief Justice James Rodgers walked slowly to the lectern at the edge of the red-carpeted rostrum, his robes rustling loudly in the stiff cold breeze. He gave a small nod.

Rose Margaret Keogh stepped forward. Slowly, from a polished cedar box, the Chief Justice lifted a gold-encrusted Bible. It was a Douay-Reims Bible. She was the second President in history to take the oath of office on a Catholic Bible; the first had been John Kennedy.

Suddenly everything seemed to freeze in time. Even the wind stood still and paid its respect. She raised her right hand and placed her left on the cool leather cover of the Bible. Her left hand trembled slightly. It was adorned by a simple wedding band, bought many years before in South Boston.

Across the land, as millions watched on television, people stopped breathing. In a small but clear voice, she spoke her name and thirty-four words in taking the oath of office as forty Presidents had before her.

"I, Rose Margaret Keogh, do solemnly swear that I will faithfully execute the office of President of the United States and will, to the best of my ability, preserve, protect and defend the Constitution of the United States."

The simplicity of the moment was majestic.

Chief Justice Rodgers stepped backward to join the dignitaries standing like marble. Mike McGavin watched riveted. Terrence Keogh stood with his shoulders pulled squarely back as if in a drill line. The eyes of the Lithuanian priest remained dark and impassive.

President Rose Keogh's delicate right hand pulled the microphone closer to her small mouth. Her words would be brief. They had been molded in inspired brevity forty-eight hours before by McGavin. The tiny voice, magnified many times by the public-address system, echoed across the huge crowd.

"I stand here before you as a representative of your faith in me, a faith I hold as sacred as life itself."

The dignitaries on the rostrum gave tiny nods of acknowledgment.

"I also stand here humbly as a representative, an extension, of the ideals of my beloved husband, whose illness at this time prevents his sharing this moment in person, but it is one which I promise you he is sharing with us today.

"This is for me a moment of overwhelming personal joy—a joy, however, that is overshadowed by the awesome responsibility which you have invested in me and which in turn I have invested in you, the people of this country, and even to some degree other countries that look to the United States for compassion, understanding and an inspiration of freedom. It is a responsibility underwritten by my oath of office."

She paused. Her hand trembled slightly, but her voice was infused with confidence and sincerity.

"Both personally and as an American, I, together with you, have endured tragic times. While those times should never disappear from our consciousness and while those times must be sagely learned from, we must not sink in self-pity and recrimination. Globally our compassion has been misread as weakness. Nationally our divergence of cultures and opinion has been misread as disunity. For us and others to believe we are both weak and without unity is an error.

"It is now a time to show our moral strength and our committed unity. We must show it to ourselves and to others.

"But as we have endured together, we must now celebrate together, celebrate in all tongues and accents of this great land. A celebration of harmony.

"It will be a harmony to celebrate true equality, not just token equality; true prosperity, not just temporary financial good times; true peace, not just an absence of hostility.

"The goals are not easy. Our worlds of commerce and industry and the labor movement must work together as they have never worked before; our cultural and geographic differences must be dramatically forged in a common purpose; our executive, legislative and judiciary branches of government must work as equal parts of a great machine committed to work for togetherness and not divisiveness. I am confident it can be done. We must see ourselves as one.

"As Chief Executive of this nation, I shall administer what the people decree; the people govern, not I. And you, as the people, should demand to be served by me as I have never served before. And I pray that you serve one another as you have never served before.

"Twenty-four years ago a brave young man stood where I stand today and exhorted a nation to ask not what your country could do for you but what you could do for your country. With humility I once again invoke this request and add, ask what you can do for one another."

The masses seemed spellbound by this tiny woman as she continued: "One human being, no matter how dedicated, cannot do the job alone. So I pray for your help so that I can serve as a Chief Executive has never served before.

"With your help and the help of the Almighty, I will accomplish and you will accomplish our shared ambition. Let this day, as I stand before you, signal a celebration of an era which we can proudly call 'The Beginning of the New World.'

"Thank you, and God bless you."

There was a moment of silence as the people stood mesmerized by this small woman. It was 12:23 P.M.

Then pandemonium, glorious pandemonium, as the brilliant blue sky was again colored by thousands of balloons. The cheers from the crowd would never be forgotten as President Keogh, that January day, stood with humility and dignity on that rostrum.

The reporters raced for the telephones and dictated thousands of words. The Waterbury Drum Band from Connecticut was the first to strike up "Hail to the Chief." At another moment in history, President Ulysses Grant had said of the band, "It makes a helluva racket for a few doggone drums." Today it was at its loudest. The cheers continued like a series of encores.

She looked out into the thousands before her almost in total disbelief. Rose Margaret Keogh, the former Rose Sweeney from South Boston. Could all that love and adulation be for her? she thought as her mind raced. The tension that had torn at her body was disappearing as the waves of love washed over her. On both sides and behind and in front of her were humans singing and cheering, and music was playing. It was all for her. Was it really happening?

As she looked out in bewilderment, she felt Terrence's touch at her arm. She held his hand. He squeezed it.

"That's all for you, Mother," he said amid the tumult.

And it was. Her face flushed ever so slightly. Her breathing became quicker. The pores of her scalp began to prickle with emotion. She could feel a dampness, and her small breasts heaved ever so slightly under the tight-fitting coat.

Her heart pounded as the waves of idolatry washed over her. No man could give her this kind of love. No man.

Mike McGavin watched from behind. There was no question she had handled herself magnificently. And then he thought about Sean Keogh, her husband.

President Keogh's eyes glazed, and she was in a world of her own.

THE PRESIDENT had chosen to eliminate the traditional lunch at the Capitol and start the Inaugural Parade immediately after the ceremony. Against the advice of the Secret Service, she had chosen an open limousine.

She entered the limousine, and Terrence took his place by her side. She ordered the chauffeur to drive at a snail's pace.

The Presidential limousine crawled from the Capitol plaza, and suddenly she was among the people who had come from Iowa and Alabama —old men, young girls, veterans and homemakers who had come by Greyhound bus and station wagon. The hysteria was not so much for the event as for her . . . for her.

Slowly the open limousine crawled along Independence Avenue, then Third Street. To her left on the Mall, the participants in the official parade, like the cast of a giant Barnum & Bailey Circus, champed at the bit to get into the act. The moment the limousine and the official motorcade passed by, the excitement reached fever point. There were marshals and cops blowing whistles as the giant floats and marching bands lined up behind their flag bearers, readying to march along Pennsylvania Avenue.

The Marine Band strode out at a snappy step of a hundred and twenty paces to the minute. They would arrive at the official reviewing stand a long time before President Keogh. After the motorcade edged into Pennsylvania Avenue, forty floats, fifteen equestrian units and seventy-two marching bands readied themselves.

The wind had picked up again, and it played games with the President's hair. Only a fraction of the crowd could be seen because of the inordinate glare of the sun bouncing off the snow. But she could hear their cheers, their shouts of encouragement and their pledges of loyalty. Past the Federal Trade Commission, the National Archives building, the Department of Justice, it was all the same. Simple people, with a message of love and respect, telling her she was the best in the land.

The limousine cruised past Pershing Square, where she and Terrence had stayed the night before. The whole trip was only a mile and a half, but it took thirty-seven minutes. She had stood in the back waving and throwing an occasional ladylike kiss. And as the limousine passed the Treasury building she allowed herself to look squarely at the East Wing of the White House. She turned to Terrence. "We're there . . . we're there."

The limousine arrived at the official viewing stands. The Presidential stand was a triangular wooden rostrum constructed three days earlier. It was shared by the Cabinet. On the right were the members of the U.S. Senate, the Republican National Committee and official family guests. In the case of President Rose Keogh, the last stand bulged with the faces of men and women from South Boston. There was an unfamiliar look to them. Most of them, with the exception of Edward Wilson, had never been to Washington. Many of them cared little for downtown Boston. They were from Southie.

Opposite, on the other side of Pennsylvania Avenue, facing the White House, were the stands reserved for the Diplomatic Corps, Vice Presidential guests, the Inaugural Committee, the press, the House of Representatives, governors, mayors and the military brass.

Again the cheers came as she alighted from the car. This time they came from the powerful, the politicians and the diplomats. No matter how many times she heard the roars of adulation, they did not lose the impact of excitement. Russia's Premier, Igor Kolotoc, handed the U.S. Ambassador to Moscow a large cigar. Everybody was at the party.

She stepped into the reviewing stand.

The Knickerbocker Boys Band strutted by, followed by the South Bronx Boys Club of New York. With each band came a new wave of applause. President Keogh's face was lit with a special happiness.

Mike McGavin had done an incredible job. He turned to the priest, Father Zeibatski. They were sitting on the presidential reviewing stand.

"What do you think, Father? Impressive?"

"Very impressive. Very. You did a wonderful job, Mike." He smiled and applauded as a float from Puerto Rico edged by. Some of the women on the float were wearing bare-shouldered Caribbean costumes. And the temperature was thirty-one degrees.

"I think they need a cheer," the priest said, and Mike McGavin fell silent. He thought of the man at the Naval Hospital. Sean Keogh.

It was ninety minutes before the Virginia Boys Marching Band, a group of three hundred, marched by. They were followed by the last group, a band from Los Angeles. They were dressed in clothes that could be worn only for such a glorious occasion as this, with plumed hats and gold braid.

President Rose Keogh stood throughout the entire parade.

It was 2:30 P.M. when the last bands were heard still playing as they turned into Seventeenth Street. As the sounds faded and the noise of the reviewing stands was reduced to chatter among the politicians and organizers, the air was rent by a massive blast. It was a twenty-one-gun salute that signaled the end of the ceremonies.

President Rose Keogh, encircled by Cabinet members and security men, moved closer to her son, Terrence, and kissed him lightly on the cheek.

"It was a very stirring experience, Terrence."

"I know, Mother," said the good-looking lad behind the thick dark glasses. "In my own way, I saw it all."

Despite the security, the officialdom, the Cabinet members and the host of people in the inauguration party, President Keogh felt slightly ill at ease walking up the drive toward the stately mansion. They looked like a gaggle of tourists, she thought.

She rebuked herself. There was no need to feel that way anymore. This was her house.

There would be a late buffet lunch, and Mike McGavin told her who would be there.

"Thank you, Michael," she said, slightly breathless. "Your arrangements were marvelous."

"Madam President," he said, inwardly wincing at the unfamiliarity of the address, "There is no question this was the grandest and most emotional inauguration in history."

"It would be nice to think that, Michael."

The buffet lunch was held in the East Room.

Rose Keogh stood in the room as the guests and some of the 478 staff members approached the buffet. This, she knew, was where another Republican President, Abraham Lincoln, had received the public on New Year's Day, 1863. What had once belonged to Abraham Lincoln now belonged to her. And she didn't feel ashamed to permit herself to be squarely thrilled by the feeling. She knew the White House backward. She knew that the East Room, where the last reception would be held that night after seven Inaugural Balls, measured eight hundred feet by forty feet and had a twenty-two-foot-high ceiling. Presidents Lincoln and Kennedy had lain in state there. President Nixon had said an emotional farewell to his staff and aides there after Watergate. She knew also that Franklin Roosevelt's grandchildren had roller-skated in that room. And she knew that President Truman had played his Steinway piano there.

The guests were now pouring into the giant room. Later that night they would be wearing tails and designer evening gowns. Flanked by security men and her son, she wandered among the guests, greeting them with warm formality. She was now the President, and this was her house. Although she had walked through the beautiful rooms many times before, she did so now with a special pride of ownership. Through the Green Room, with its Sheraton-style furniture made by Duncan Phyfe in the early 1800s, the walls covered with green silk. She touched it and thrilled as she felt the luxury under her fingertips. She could feel Terrence at her elbow. Then into the Blue Room with its French Empire furniture. She knew this had been President James Monroe's favorite room. It was now hers. Into the Red Room and then on to the State Dining Room, which she noted could hold a hundred and forty people at fourteen round tables. It was magnificent. She then returned to the East Room and the buffet. The power in that huge room was awesome.

At 4:30 P.M. the reception wound to a respectable end. The men and women would need many hours to prepare for the balls that night.

Mike McGavin touched her lightly on the elbow. "I've just called the hospital," he said.

"When will the Senator be here, Michael?"

"Half an hour."

"Then we'd better get ready. Terrence, your father will be here in half an hour. Everything in the room organized, Michael?"

"Perfectly. The nurses and doctors are there now, and a doctor is traveling with him."

"The press?" she asked.

"They have been cleared. They may get a shot of the ambulance coming in at the gate. But that's all."

"Good," she said with crisp finality.

At 5 P.M. a large ambulance rounded the Ellipse, turned right through the gate and pulled to a halt at the Executive Mansion. A cluster of nurses and doctors in starched white uniforms stood by as the ambulance attendants opened the doors of the vehicle. Working with swift efficiency, they then lifted out a large stretcher.

On the stretcher was the still form of Senator Sean Keogh. His gaunt, ash-white face was partially covered with a large oxygen mask. Attached to his arm and under his armpits were the life-giving tubes that held him back from oblivion.

Father Zeibatski looked grave as the stretcher and the attendant paraphernalia were whisked inside the White House and to the third floor.

President Rose Keogh hurried behind as the stretcher was taken to a large, freshly painted room with huge windows facing onto West Executive Avenue.

Inside, the room looked like a giant operating theater. A television monitor was mounted against one wall. It had a computerized link to the office of the White House doctor. Three oxygen tanks and a nitrogen tank stood by the large bed.

Gently the attendants laid the limp form on the bed. President Rose

Keogh, Terrence, Edward Wilson, Mike McGavin and the priest watched silently.

The chief White House physician approached her.

"Well, Madam President, we have done everything to make him comfortable. Everything."

"Thank you," she said slowly.

Mike looked at her anxiously. She was close to tears.

She walked across to the bedside. The nurses stood aside. Her eyes glistened as she leaned over the form staring upward at the ceiling. She ran her hands through his thick black-gray hair and then kissed him gently on the forehead.

"This day was for you, darling . . . this day was for you."

The eyes of Senator Sean Keogh were fixed like marble. Mike Mc-Gavin could feel his throat thickening. The others approached the bedside. They all felt awkward.

Mike McGavin stayed in the room long after the others had left. He stared in disbelief. He had seen the lifeless body so many times in the last months, and still he couldn't grasp the fact that this once-vital human was now reduced to a vegetable.

"I suppose it's wrong to hope for miracles," McGavin said abstractly to the nurse who was attending the monitor.

She looked up, gave him a professional smile and said, "Unfortunately, it is."

The voice screamed in silence inside Sean Keogh's body. "There will be miracles, Michael. Pray for them. Pray for them," the voice yelled noiselessly.

Senator Sean Keogh's body might have been reduced to a motionless hulk, but his thought processes had remained untouched. For six months he had lain there without moving so much as a single muscle, his body atrophying at a steady rate. But his mind was still as alert and sharp as it had ever been. And it rebelled as he listened to numbskull doctors telling anyone who cared to listen that Senator Sean Keogh was all but clinically dead. The fools, he thought bitterly. If only they could understand; if only they knew.

As he sadly watched the handsome Mike McGavin, Sean Keogh felt the twisted pain of a convict in a prison where all the walls had fallen and freedom was only one step away, but each time the convict tried to move toward freedom he was hurled back by an invisible barrier. It was a cruel and recurring real-life nightmare. He could see, even though his eyes could move only slightly, and he could hear. It was just that his body refused to obey any orders, and the only voice that worked was the silent one that screamed inside his body.

Was this the ultimate punishment meted out by God? To be left a living dead person? Could God be that cruel? Was this retribution for an overly ambitious life, a life marked by so much violence and bloodshed?

All that was left him inside the prison of his body was his daily mental diary as he went over every detail of his struggle to the top. And each day as he went over his diary, new moments surfaced until his life had become an intricate canvas before his mind's eye.

He thought far back to when it all had started, so many years ago . . . so many years ago. . . .

Chapter

2

THE AIR hung like a wet blanket. It was August, 1957, in "Southie," the Irish working-class section of South Boston.

The clock struck ten, but still there was no move to bring in the kids off the streets of Southie. It was Friday night. There was no school tomorrow, and it was too hot to sleep anyway. From Dorchester Avenue to Carson Beach and Pleasure Bay, Southie celebrated Friday the way some people celebrated News Year's Eve. Saloons with names like McHenry's, Toolan's, The Emerald and Blarney Stone were packed with the sons of Sligo and Kerry and Wexford. On McDonough Street, you could hear the singing coming from the saloons. The boys were in full throat. They proudly sang "I Belong to Southie," to the tune of "I Belong to Glasgow," although a Scotsman would not necessarily be welcome there. They were a tough, honest bunch, beer in the bellies, calluses on their hands and red veins on their noses. There were very few nondrinkers among the men of Southie. It was serious business to have fun.

The men who were not in the saloons sat on the steps of their old but squeaky-clean wood-frame houses, watching their kids play in the street. The young family men talked about the Korean War; the older ones, with thinner hair and thicker middles, talked the Second War—"the big one," they would say to the younger men, as if Korea had only been a picnic.

Southie had always paid dearly when it came to wars.

South Boston, a place you can get to by car in as long a time as it takes you to smoke two cigarettes, is no great distance from where the Boston Brahmins take tea on Beacon Hill.

But to this day—even to this day—it could be a thousand miles away.

The Irish had come to Boston because it was the big American city closest to their homeland, and had chosen to live in this tiny area of 560 acres, originally settled by two families, which had become part of Boston in 1804.

There were potato famines. And there were "the Troubles" on three occasions. A small chunk of land that jutted out into Boston's inner harbor was a haven both for the bewildered Irish farmer, rejected by the ungiving soil of his homeland, and for the firebrand who knew another adversary called the "Black-and-Tan."

It was where the Irish immigrant ships had dropped anchor, and scores of their families refused to be moved. To this day there are children who live no more than one hundred feet from where their grandfathers or great-grandfathers dumped their baggage.

Some of the Irish had gone to Charlestown, but "Southie" had remained the wellspring of the Boston Irish. At first they were shunned by the more sophisticated Protestants, and that simply drove them closer together. Even today there are men in saloons who talk of blowing up the bridges that join Southie and Boston proper. There is still talk of "Blowin' the fuckin' things up."

If they are separate, they have never been elite. Almost in the shadow of Boston's downtown skyscrapers the men and women of the Southie welcome newcomers—as long as the newcomers do not try to change their ways.

In later years working-class Lithuanians and Germans came to live there, and the new arrivals, once welcomed, would wear the emerald on their windbreakers, swill beer with the boys, watch hockey games and lose on football games with the same neighborhood arrogance of ownership as if their fathers had been born in Sligo.

They were always the first to enlist in the Army, these boys and men from Southie, and often the talk would turn to war and "doin' yer duty."

The hockey season was a long way off, and the Red Sox weren't going to win the Series, so they talked the talk of soldiers and they drank cool beer from bottles and they enjoyed the beer and they enjoyed the talk. In front of No. 15 McDonough Street, the kids were playing catch in the dimly lit street. They hung on to the moments in the street before their fathers and mothers would call them in to sleep in beds rarely cooled by a breeze from Dorchester Bay.

On the tiny porch at No. 15 McDonough Street, the tired body of Molly Keogh sat motionless in a rickety cane chair. She fanned herself with a copy of the *Boston Record*. She sipped lemonade and watched with satisfaction as her fifteen-year-old son, Sean, hurled the baseball under the dim street lamp. Her thoughts ran to her big bear of a husband, Joe Keogh. He would be proud of Sean if he could see him now. That same coal-black hair. The clear, honest blue eyes that looked right into your body. They shone out of a face of alabaster skin. Black Irish. Big Joe had joined the Second Marines before Sean was born and before he could build his family to a respectable South Boston size. The men in his unit said he was swinging his rifle like a baseball bat at the Japs who charged out of the jungle on Saipan with their bayonets thrusting at his belly. Old Joe would have been proud of Sean.

Little Eddie Wilson, his red hair flopping over his freckled face like a big mop, joined her boy Sean and his friends. Funny little guy Eddie Wilson. Molly liked him. He was a bright little boy. Often helped Sean with his homework. But Molly knew Sean often helped Eddie out in the schoolyard scrapes he would get into at Sacred Heart. Sean was the boxing champion for his age at Sacred Heart. Old Joe would have been proud.

"Sean." Eddie motioned to him to come closer. He lowered his voice.

"Yeah, Eddie boy."

"Paddy Devlin and Frankie Burke wanna see you down at the club."

"Me, Eddie?"

"Yeah, down at the club." They spoke in that flat, harsh burr of the Southie accent that never quite made Southie a colony of Ireland but always set it apart from the rest of New England.

"Ma," Sean called, "just goin' to Eddie's place fer a minute. Back soon."

"And so ye better, young 'un, or 'twill be the back o' me hand fer ye."

"Sure, Ma." The both boys sprinted toward Quinlan Square, where the Erin Social Club was situated. They stood outside the door. The locals frowned on fifteen-year-olds' coming to the club unless they were with adults.

"Yer sure they wanna see me, Eddie?"

"Damn right, Sean."

Sean was flattered.

They stood outside the big batwing doors. Just inside, they could see Paddy Devlin and Frankie Burke sitting at a battered, cigarette-scarred table. They were drinking John Jameson with beer chasers. Devlin and Burke were both twenty-two. They had run away to Korea when they were seventeen and joined the Eighty-second Airborne. The rest was all in the newspapers. They had won the Congressional Medal of Honor in Pusan by wiping out a Chinese gun emplacement. They were heroes in Southie in their own right. Their bodies were the bodies of twenty-two-year-olds, but their eyes were old. They had seen much, and killed many. Now Bernie McLaughlin, aged fifty-five, who was the benign boss of the rackets, had parlayed their popularity for them. They worked for him, collecting numbers and bookie debts and organizing the card games. Bernie thought of himself as a social director and not a racketeer, and the boys helped out.

Devlin and Burke had not noticed the teen-age boys standing outside like little urchins awaiting an approving command to enter. Sean looked with unbridled admiration. These were real stand-up guys. And in the seconds to come, Sean saw at first hand just how tough these two young men with the old eyes were. Invariably on Friday nights, there was a brawl at the Erin Social Club. Tonight would be no exception.

Two burly longshoremen from Charlestown, the other strong Irish section of Boston, were looking for trouble. There was no love lost between Charlestown and Southie.

"Effin' heroes," the bigger one spat at Devlin and Burke as he lurched toward them. "Some friggin' heroes." He prodded his forefinger at them. "Friggin' heroes with a gun, but a pair of fags without 'em." The other big longshoreman lurched toward Burke. Both men were standing over Devlin and Burke, who looked resplendent in their drape suits and sharp shirts and ties. The younger men simply sat there. Then Burke spoke: "I think ya better go home before ya get a kick in the ass." Devlin and Burke exchanged quick glances, because they knew that last comment would do it.

The big guy picked up the bottle of whiskey from the table and swung it at Burke's head. It was like watching bullets in slow motion. Burke ducked, and the momentum of the big guy's swing turned him a full circle. Burke calmly waited for his face to come his way again and drove a left jab far into it. That was all. Nothing more. There was no fight left in the man after that. He crashed through three tables and lay there a long while. Devlin had measured his quarry with a hook to the head and a withering right rip that seemed to disappear into his victim's solar plexus. The air hissed from the man and he seemed to crumple in slow motion.

They sat down again at their table as if a minor irritation had interrupted a pleasant conversation. Burke shook his head in disbelief at the sprawled victims.

"Ya know drunks never learn; ya have to give 'em an occasional spankin'."

Both men looked with indifference as their victims were carried from the club. The buzz of conversation rose again at the bar. Devlin shouted to the bartender, "Another bottle, Pat."

Sean and Eddie Wilson stood frozen as they watched the expertise in the split-second explosion of violence. It was over. There would be no cops, no complaints, no recriminations. Not in Southie.

Devlin adjusted the knot in his silk tie and ran a comb through his hair. He glanced out the door, to see Sean and Eddie standing outside like statues.

"Hey, Sean, come in. . . . Eddie, we'll see ya tomorrow." Devlin waved Sean inside; Eddie, with disappointment, backed away from the door. Sean was the chosen one. It had always been like that.

Burke smiled at the white-faced teen-ager. "Glass of lemonade for the champ of Sacred Heart."

Sean filled with pride as he sat down with the men. Devlin pulled out the comb again. He parted his straight black hair slightly off center. That was how Robert Taylor combed his hair. Devlin thought of himself as a ladies' man. No question he was good-looking, even if the long sideburns and thin face made him a trifle seedy-looking. He was a ladies' man. Burke wasn't. Heavyset, he had tightly curled blond hair, a flat nose that had stopped too many punches and a thin scar that ran the length of the left side of his jaw. But for all the earmarks of the street, he had an open face. It was a face that could have been almost lovable had it not screamed that it was the face of a Southie street guy on his way up. He had, however, a gentlemanly manner, despite his appearance. Devlin? Devlin was something else again. Too much swagger.

Devlin spoke first: "We heard a lot about ya, son. Big heart. Boxing champ at old Sacred Heart. Might have been one myself—if they hadn't kicked me out . . . ha, ha." He was congratulating himself on his mastery of mischief.

Sean smiled self-consciously. Burke pushed a glass of lemonade toward him. For about the third time in as many minutes, Devlin adjusted the knot in his tie and glanced at himself in the mirror over the bar. He spoke again.

"Wanna earn yerself a hat?"

"A hat?" Sean queried.

"Yeah, a hat—a twenty-dollar bill." Sean flushed at his ignorance of underworld slang.

"Well, if you want me to do something, no need to pay me. Anything you want, Paddy—I mean, Mr. Devlin."

"Paddy—call me Paddy. No, no, we ain't bums; we want everyone to earn. Twenty."

"Well, sure."

"Atta boy."

Burke did a good job of masking his uneasiness. "Look, Sean boy-o, meet us down at Carson Beach tomorrow night at eight o'clock. Tell yer ma ya goin' fer a swim. Then we want ya to run a little message fer us —okay?"

"Sure thing." Sean stood up. It showed respect not to hang around with the big guys when not invited. "Sure thing, Paddy. Frankie. See you tomorrow down at Carson. Eight. Sure. See ya."

He ran excitedly back to his home on McDonough Street. His ma was in bed.

"Sean? That you, son?"

"Yeah, Ma. Going to bed."

"Bless you, boy."

He stripped to his underpants and lay on top of the bed. There was no breeze from the bay. He sweated as he dreamed. Paddy and Frankie —they're Mr. McLaughlin's boys. He's a big man. He's a good man. But important. He runs the crap games and the book and the numbers, and everybody calls him "Mr. Mac" because he's important. Paddy and Frankie were two of "the boys," and to a fifteen-year-old in Southie, that was more important than getting to college. He wanted to be one of "the boys." And with a bit of luck, he thought, I just might be.

BACK AT the club, Frankie Burke looked at Devlin quizzically. "Why the kid, Paddy? Don't let's complicate things."

"Why the kid, Frankie? I'll tell ya why. We bring another sap into this and they are gonna want a third of the hundred an' fifty bucks Old Man McLaughlin gave us. We give him twenty bucks, and he's a stand-up kid, he'll keep his mouth shut."

"Fer what?—just because Jimmy Rooney is gonna catch a beating? Look, why don't we just wait fer him—bam, bam, bust his jaw, crack a few ribs and call it quits? Jimmy knows he got it comin' fer tippin' off those Guineas in the North End about the crap game. Mr. Mac lost three thousand bucks on that heist those spaghetti benders pulled on the game. Jimmy knows it's comin'. He shouldn't do things like that to Mr. Mac."

Devlin's eyes narrowed. "Ya know, Frankie, yer a tough guy, but yer a dumb shit."

Burke's face registered hurt.

"C'mon, Frankie—just jokin'. But Christ, boy-o, whaddya wanna do with yer life?"

"Not the world, Paddy—just a few bucks so me an' Teresa can get married. Been goin' together since we was fourteen, ya know that. Just wanna few bucks; that's why I'm workin' fer Mr. Mac."

Devlin wanted to laugh out loud, but he knew better than to make light of Frankie Burke's relationship with Teresa Mullins. Burke would hit back.

"Frankie boy, listen. Now, listen good, pal. Ya listenin'?"

"I'm listenin', yeah."

"Ya gotta get people to notice ya. You know these big-time doctors an' lawyers an' politicians. How d'ya think they get to the top? Huh? I'll tell ya. Not because they're such hot shit; no, it's because people think they're hot shit. And ya know why they think that? I'll tell ya why. Because they are told to think that. Publicity, boy-o, publicity. Everybody needs publicity. People gotta know about ya. Ya gotta get noticed, Frankie; we gotta get noticed."

Frankie Burke still wasn't getting any message.

Paddy Devlin ordered another bottle and laid out plans to make Burke drink more than he wanted to.

They were plans that started in motion a chain of events that would change the course of the nation.

PADDY DEVLIN got up from the table. Burke was silent. Devlin looked pleased with himself.

"C'mon, Frankie, let's celebrate our future. Let's go down to Willie's. He's got a whole new bunch of French broads in from Montreal."

"No, thanks, Paddy. Teresa gets off the night shift at the factory. I wanna go home, get cleaned up and meet her fer breakfast." Burke wanted no part of Willie's whorehouse with the French broads and the Irish broads and the soundproofed rooms. He was no virgin, but it had always happened in the whorehouses of Tokyo and Hong Kong when he was on leave from combat in Korea. He hated the places but had been scared not to go to them when Paddy and the rest of the outfit went. Then he would go to confession. It was different between him and Teresa.

At seven in the morning, Frankie Burke stood outside the Cazro Knitting Mills on Athens Street behind West Broadway. A minute later Teresa Mullins emerged with the night shift and trotted toward him, her fresh face wreathed in smiles. She kissed him on the cheek.

"Frank." She never called him Frankie; it sounded too common. "You look tired, hon."

"Bit tired. Been up last night with Paddy and the boys."

Teresa frowned. "It's your business, Frank darling, but I wish you would stay away from that Devlin."

"Na, he's all right. He goes on with a lot of blarney about Korea, but he's a good guy. He's regular."

"No, Frank, Paddy Devlin is a mean man."

Burke felt a shudder go up his spine.

AT SEVEN forty-five on Saturday night, with the August light still high in the air, Devlin picked up Burke in his pink convertible. They drove toward Carson Beach for their rendezvous with Sean Keogh, their teen-age messenger boy.

Devlin spoke with elation of the night before at Willie's whorehouse. "They got this new broad there, Jenny Bryant. She's from Charlestown. Man, she is nuts. I'll tell ya all about it later. Wild broad."

Burke listened but heard nothing. He was feeling sick.

At Carson Beach, young Sean stood at the end of the park. He was dressed in his Saturday-night best—black pegged pants, salmon-pink shirt, crepe-soled shoes. Devlin smiled. The car eased to a stop.

"Hop in, Sean." Young Keogh respectfully greeted them both. Burke smiled and nodded.

"Here, kid. A debt is a debt. Here's yer twenty."

Self-consciously, Sean put the bill in his pocket. The car drove off. Sean felt like a million, riding in a pink convertible. His heart was racing.

"Now, son, here's what we want ya to do. All ya gotta do is this. We're gonna drop ya off at Colbrook Street, near Thomas Park. Now, go to 185 E. Jimmy Rooney lives there. You've seen Jimmy around. You know him—works for Mr. Mac." Sean nodded his head obediently. He knew Jimmy Rooney, and he knew he was in trouble with the boys. It was something to do with the Italians in the North End.

"Now, knock on his door and see Jimmy and tell him that Mr. Mc-Laughlin needs him to work the game tonight. Tell him he wants him to deal at the game at Fort Independence—you know, at Castle Island. Just tell him to be there at ten o'clock tonight. Go to the pink convertible —that's this car; it belongs to Mr. Mac, see. Then he will be taken to the game nearby. He knows the place where the game will be. Tell him Mr. Mac needs him because there ain't nobody else to work it. Frankie and me have got dates tonight. Okay?"

Devlin saw the inquisitive look on Sean's face.

"Why don't we tell him, yer askin' yerself? Well, first of all the bum don't have no telephone, and second of all, his wife, Jane, she's pregnant and she don't like Jimmy dealin', though he makes good bucks. An' besides, if we go there she knows what Jimmy is doin'; so we stay outa there—see?"

Sean nodded. He didn't buy it. Jimmy Rooney was in trouble, and he was going to get a beating from Paddy and Frankie, that was for sure. But hell, he shouldn't have done those things with those Italians in the North End. Mr. Mac had been good. He was a good man, and Paddy and Frankie were going to give Jimmy Rooney a beating for not being a stand-up guy. Sean knew the rules, and he abided by them. Jimmy Rooney deserved a crack in the jaw.

They dropped him off at the corner of Colbrook. He trotted up to 185 E. It was a small frame house. He knocked on the door. It was still half light.

Jimmy Rooney opened the door. A screen door separated them. He was dressed in an undershirt and undershorts. He was small and thin. He had mousy blond hair.

"Yeah?"

"Mr. Rooney."

"Yeah. Oh, hi. Yeah, you're the Keogh boy. Young Sean, ain't it? What can I do fer ya?

"Just a message, Mr. Rooney."

"A message?"

"Yes. Mr. McLaughlin couldn't get in touch with ya, but he wants ya to work the game tonight. Ten o'clock."

Jimmy put his forefinger to his lips to tell him to lower his voice.

"The old lady," he explained with a wink. Sean nodded his apology.

"Wants you to be at Fort Independence."

"Oh, the game off the boulevard at Castle Island. Yeah. Well, sure could use the scratch."

"Mr. Mac said he'll be in a pink convertible. Just go there. Okay?"

"Pink convertible," Rooney mused. "The old man is getting in the groove. Yeah, well, thanks, son." He reached onto a table inside the door. "Here, son. Thanks." He flipped young Keogh a quarter. "Thanks, son."

As Sean attempted to return the quarter, he could hear a female voice from inside: "Who is it, honey?"

"Just a buddy. Won't take a second," he called back inside as he winked a goodbye to Sean and closed the door. Sean Keogh ran down the street. The quarter and the twenty-dollar bill rubbed together inside his pocket of his pegged black gabardine pants. Sean Keogh had been in on a job for "the boys." Jimmy Rooney was gonna get a beatin', and Jimmy Rooney deserved it.

He was late getting down to Carson Beach to meet Eddie Wilson and his friends. They were going to a movie.

"C'mon, let's go, Sean. We're gonna be late." Eddie Wilson was always on time, never late. He had a precise mind even at fifteen.

Sean Keogh never knew what had made him say it, but he heard the words come from his lips: "Na, not tonight, Eddie. Just came down to tell ya, I'm goin' to the gym tonight. Gotta train."

Eddie scowled. "All right, Joe Louis. Well, we're takin' off. Yer mad. See ya."

For a long while he sat on the park bench as the light faded off the water. God, South Boston was beautiful! Calcutta is beautiful if you have never been anywhere else. It was dark now, and the breeze came.

He was deep in thought and knew as a fifteen-year-old kid he shouldn't have been thinking the thoughts going through his mind. Nobody would know, he thought. Who would know? I never seen the boys workin' anyone over. Jimmy Rooney deserves what's comin', I'm sure, but how do they do it? Do they tell him, 'Now, listen, Jimmy, we're gonna give you a crack on the jaw fer what ya did"? Then they crack him. Would Jimmy fight back? He'd been crazy. He would just take it until they stopped. Then they would say, "Well, Jimmy, it's over now, no hard feelin's, but ya had it comin'." Then Jimmy would go back home and get himself patched up. Next week he would call Mr. Mac and say he was awful sorry. Yeah, that was how it would go.

JIMMY ROONEY was smoking a Lucky Strike. He had been leaning up against the parked pink convertible, which was where young Keogh had said it would be. Nobody was there. He dragged heavily on the cigarette. Shit, I sure need this bread, what with the baby comin', he thought. But Jesus, I feel bad. Old Mac, he's a stand-up guy. Shit, I sure feel bad about steerin' those Guineas to the crap game. Needed the fuckin' money, that's why I did it. Still, it was wrong. I'll make it up to the old man as soon as I get the scratch together. I'll tell him straight out, then give him the three grand, pay him back. I'll make it up. . . . Where the fuck is everybody? Not like Mac to be late.

Sean Keogh was thinking the exact same thing. It had been only a short run from Carson Beach Park to Fort Independence. He just had to see Devlin and Burke at work. Perhaps it was wrong, but he just had to see it. He was down behind the short hedge, not twenty yards from where Rooney was leaning up against the convertible. He could see through the thin hedge. He was on his hands and knees, getting his pegged pants dirty, but he had to see it.

Suddenly he could see the powder-blue suit of Devlin. He moved like an angry little kitten, this Devlin. Burke must be hiding.

Rooney lit another cigarette. Where the fuck was everyone? He heard light footsteps.

"That you, Mac? Where the fuck ya—" he started to say as he turned around. "Oh, fuck, no, no!"

"Yours, Jimmy." That was all Devlin said. Young Keogh could see the ice pick flash as it slithered into Rooney's liver. Rooney's eyes bulged in disbelief, and he was still saying, "No, Paddy! No, pal!" It flashed again, and Rooney let out a little scream, like a baby that was frightened by a big dog. Rooney wasn't going to die easy.

Devlin kicked Rooney in the groin and as the head lowered slugged him hard with a blackjack.

Sean Keogh could feel the hot urine running down his thighs.

Rooney was not dead. Devlin looked around. Nobody in sight. He dragged the limp, thin form of Rooney from the side of Fort Independence where he had stuck him with the long ice pick and clubbed him into unconsciousness. Watching through the break in the hedge, Sean flattened out. If Devlin had looked hard in the darkness, he would have seen the salmon-pink shirt.

Devlin dragged Rooney toward a work shed on the Castle Island side of the Peninsula. He dumped him around the other side of the shed where Sean couldn't see. Devlin was about twenty yards away now.

Sean wanted to run, but he couldn't. His legs were jelly. He was terrified. He dug his face deeper into the dirt. He would wait till Devlin left and pray to God that he wouldn't be seen. But where is Burke? Maybe he's keeping watch on the other side. Maybe he can see me now. He couldn't run now. He might run smack bang into Burke keeping watch.

Then his heart leaped into his throat as suddenly the heavy silence was broken by a loud ugly noise. It sounded like the revving of a broken-down car engine. Sean felt his sphincter tighten as a muffled scream was heard over the noise of the engine. Then there were no more screams.

After about five minutes the revving noise stopped. His eyes lifted out of the dirt. He could see Devlin again now. He was carrying something. Shit, it's Jimmy Rooney. Oh, my God! Something is wrong.

He couldn't quite see it. Then Devlin was caught in the light of the low moon reflected off the water. There was a splash.

Oh, Jesus, he has dumped poor Rooney in the harbor. Oh, Jesus Christ! Sean's heart was exploding and he was certain he had stopped breathing.

Where's Burke? He'll come up behind me any moment. And then I'll get it.

Devlin was coming diagonally toward him. He was walking quickly. Sean squirmed sideways crab fashion to be partly hidden by the short, sparse hedge. He ate dirt and dared not breathe. Devlin's quick footsteps passed within about five feet of him. If he turns back toward the harbor, he'll sure as hell see me. Sure as hell.

He could hear the car door open and then it slammed shut. The engine started. Where is Burke? He had heard no voices. Burke may hang around after Devlin goes. Anything could be going on.

He heard the car slip away from the side of Fort Independence. The pink convertible had the top up, and it slithered onto the boulevard into the mainstream of traffic. He lifted his head up a tiny bit to see its rear lights disappearing.

He stayed there at least half an hour to convince himself that Burke was not in hiding to catch him. Young Keogh could feel dry, racking sobs tearing at his stomach. The legs of his black pegged pants were soaking. Oh, Jesus, I pissed myself. Oh, Jesus.

Gradually he could hear himself breathing again. He was now shaking despite the warm breeze coming from the ocean. He felt cold. His mind was a blur. What to do now?

Nobody must see me.

Nobody. He got up and ran to the water line, half expecting Frankie Burke to emerge from the shadows. He would run along the waterline.

He was starting to think clearly now. The only people he could bump into would be couples necking. Along the waterline there was a better chance he would not be seen.

The urine-soaked pant legs chafed against his skin. Please God, don't let me meet up with anyone I know.

It was ten forty-five. He could see the big clock overlooking Carson Beach in the distance. Damn it, the movies will be out at 11 P.M. I have to get home before the streets fill up.

He ran to the tip of Carson Beach Park. There were couples lying on the grass in the warm moonlight and sitting on the benches, but nobody took any notice of him. He bit his lip as he figured on how he would get across the well-lit boulevard. He lingered at water's edge and worked out the route he would take home through the back streets to McDonough Street. Despite the horror, right now he was thinking of survival. If he saw anyone he knew, they would know something was wrong, what with his face and pants and dirt all over his knees. He examined his shirt. It was dirty. He brushed his knees hard. Anybody would have to look hard to see the urine stains on the black gabardine. He wouldn't cross the boulevard at the pedestrian crossing. Traffic was light. The movies weren't out yet.

He waited for a break in the traffic and ran across the boulevard. His heart pounded as he expected one of his many friends to yell out his name from a street corner. After all, it was Saturday night.

He got to the other side of the boulevard, heeled sharp left and then a right down Watson Street. It was a narrow street and not many street lights. He walked fast, but not fast enough to attract attention.

He shook his head several times to come to grips with the reality of what he had just seen. Sean Keogh never swore, but he could feel rage in his throat and he heard himself whispering, "Fuckin' cowards . . . Devlin, Burke—heroes. Fuckin' cowards. Rooney might have deserved a crack on the jaw, but no, he didn't deserve that. Nobody deserves that. Maybe Bernie McLaughlin ordered them. Shit, and I thought Mr. Mac was a good guy. No, he wouldn't order that. He's no killer. But Devlin and Burke, damn right they're killers. Ain't that what they got their medals for? Killing. But that was wartime. Fuckin' cowards. Why did they do it to the poor bastard? He has a wife. And she's pregnant, too. Why did they do it?

No, Sean, he addressed himself, why did *you* do it? You wanted to be one of "the boys." Well, they sure as hell made you one of the boys. You saw it in the movies all the time. Me, Sean Keogh, I was the finger man. They made me one of their cowardly killers. Fight like a man. Don't stick an ice pick into someone. He saw Jimmy Rooney's eyes bulge. He wanted to vomit. He coughed hard and retched. Nothing came. It just made his eyes redder and his face puffier.

At the bottom of Watson Street he turned into Billings Lane.

Could they put you in jail for seeing a murder? No, but they could put him in jail for setting Jimmy Rooney up. Sure as hell they could, Sean. You're in it with Devlin and Burke. They would send you away—away from Ma, away from Southie. You would be an old man when you came out.

He got to the end of Billings Lane and then he turned into McDonough Street. The adults who weren't at the movies or in the saloons would be sitting outside on their front steps. Okay, now: deep breath, walk quickly and just wave to them, look like you're in a hurry so nobody stops you to talk. Thank God, there were no kids outside. Just adults. Thank you, God. He waved to a few families.

Now Ma. She's gone to bingo, but she could be home now. It breaks up at eleven. She might have left early. Lights aren't on. Oh, thank you God, thank you.

He sprinted up the five wooden steps onto the tiny porch and opened the front door with the key he had had since his fifteenth birthday. Ma isn't home. She probably went over to Eddie Wilson's mother's place for tea. Now the pants. Quickly he opened the icebox. Milk—get the milk. He spilled it over his pant legs. That would be his excuse for dumping them into the hamper to be cleaned. He stripped them off and padded upstairs in his underwear and salmon-pink shirt. He hung it up and threw himself on his bed in his underpants. He was sweating. But it didn't come from the warm breeze. It was a sticky sweat that smelled.

Okay, think, think. Think, fer Chrissake. No, don't swear. God has been good to you so far. Don't offend Him. What to do? Well, it's obvious. As soon as Ma comes home, you tell her everything—everything. Nobody goes wrong by tellin' the truth. Then you wake up Jack Crockford, the detective; you go there with your ma and you tell him everything. He's a fair man, friend of the family. Tell it to him exactly as it happened.

He heard the front door open and his mother saying good night to Mrs. Wilson. The door closed; then he heard the heavy steps of his mother coming up the creaky wooden staircase.

She stopped outside the door. "You there, Sean?"

Okay, this is when I'll tell her.

"Yeah, Ma."

"Home early, ain't ya, boy?"

"Yeah. But tired, Ma."

"See ye in the mornin', lovely."

"Right, Ma."

See, you didn't tell her. Now it's going to be harder to tell her. I'll tell her in the morning. Oh, yeah? Then Detective Crockford will ask, Why didn't you come here straightaway? Well, I was scared. Scared? Or something to hide? he'll say. No, I will tell him everything.

Yeah, and then you will have to go to court and point the finger at Devlin and Burke and everyone will say that Sean Keogh was a rat. And then Ma and me will have to move away from McDonough Street and Southie. I will have to leave my friend, Eddie Wilson, and she will have to leave Mrs. Wilson and all the people she grew up with and she'll be lonely, and it will be my fault because I wanted to be one of the boys instead of minding my own business and then I became a rat. No. No way. I'm no rat.

Maybe the police will never find the body. It will float out to sea and never be seen again, and when his wife tells the police Jimmy Rooney is missing they will think he ran away from his wife. Oh, Jesus, his wife. Gonna have a kid and it ain't gonna have no father and it's all my fault. Okay, then I'll run away and never be seen again. Run away? What with? No money. The money, the money. There's a twenty-dollar bill that Devlin gave me, and it's still in my pocket downstairs with the quarter that Rooney gave me. I've gotta get it. If Ma finds it going through my pockets, she'll know.

Sean Keogh got up and padded downstairs. If Molly Keogh heard him, she would think he was going to the bathroom downstairs. Hurriedly he retrieved the money. Then he flushed the toilet for effect and bounced upstairs again and lay on his bed. And the agonizing process started all over again until, like any fifteen-year-old, he found himself crying tears, and he cried softly for two hours until his nose ran and his eyes were slits.

As the quiet sobs stabbed through his body, he found himself praying to God to please make it yesterday. Make it Friday—please make it yesterday. At 4 A.M. he heard the first sounds of birds, and the black night turned blue-gray and a light breeze cooled his burning face and body. He got up to look at himself in the mirror. He looked as if he had been in a fifteen-round fight.

The breeze swept across his bare chest, and he looked away from the mirror in shame. This was not the act of a man. He lay quietly down in bed again. His tears dried; his nose cleared and dragged in the early-morning air wafting through his open window.

Now, let's think it again. He was not going to tell his mother; he was not going to go to the police; he was not going to do a darn thing. If boyhood hero worship had got him into this, then he was going to think his way out of it like a man. Now, let's go back over it all again. All the angles. Where was I last night? I wasn't at the movies. I told Eddie I was going to the gym. Well, nobody saw me at the gym. No, I jogged around Carson Beach Park for a while for exercise instead of going to the gym. Then I came home and listened to the radio. What did I listen to? Oh, that *Hit Parade* show. I've heard it before. Right? Right. Now I'll go downstairs again, wash my face, come up here and wait until Ma calls me for breakfast.

He washed his face. The cold water felt good. He returned to his room, closed the door and lay on his bed rigid, reinforcing his resolve to meet this horror head on—the way a man would. His eyes stared straight up at the ceiling, and the fear and teen-age emotion had finally drained from his body. He tried to push out the thought of Rooney's wife. Right now, all he thought of was to get through all this. He would think about the other later.

The blue eyes continued to stare upward, and as they did someone might say if they watched that the eyes lost that special color of blue. Suddenly they seemed old. They were the same kind of eyes as Paddy Devlin and Frankie Burke's. They were the eyes of a man, even if Sean Keogh didn't like what sort of man those eyes signaled.

It was 7 A.M., and the Sunday-morning sun streamed through his window, white, clean, warm and decent. He hadn't closed his eyes in what was the longest night of his life. He heard his mother stirring, and then Molly Keogh was knocking on the door.

"Out of bed, lovely, and I'll fix ye a whoppin' breakfast."

"Right, Ma." He felt like eating the way he felt like a dentist's needle. But no, he would eat. He had to act normal.

He came downstairs to the tiny kitchen.

"Faith, you look awful. You feelin' okay?" Molly looked at the boy's face.

"Couldn't sleep, Ma, too hot, Just couldn't sleep."

"Then go back to sleep and I'll call ye fer breakfast later, son."

"No, Ma. I'm up now. What's fer breakfast?"

"Great fat eggs, some blood sausage and some soda bread. Now, how about that?"

"Great, Ma."

She put on the kettle for tea, then waddled outside to pick the papers off the porch where the delivery boy had thrown them. She was humming quietly to herself.

She threw the papers, still rolled up, on the table. Sean resisted the impulse to open them. She poured herself a cup of tea, sat down at the end of the tiny table and opened up the papers.

"Oh, glory be, glory be. Oh, no. My God, oh, no," she gasped.

Sean clamped his jaw. That's it. Jimmy Rooney. His heart fluttered, but he looked up at his mother. "Ma, what's the matter—World War Three?"

"Oh, Sean boy, oh, it's terrible." She read on and gasped.

"Hey, Ma, what's the matter?" He got up and walked to look over her shoulder. He told his stomach to stay still. He hated this part of the lie —lying to his mother.

Across the front page of the *Boston American* the headline said it all. It also explained to Sean the revving sound the night before. HOODLUM FOUND CUT TO PIECES.

The story, below a photograph, told it with staccato succinctness:

> The bloodied torso of small-time South Boston hoodlum James Liam Rooney, 22, was found floating in Boston's Inner Harbor late last night.
> Police say Rooney's arms and legs had been severed from his body with what appeared to be a buzz saw.
> The Medical Examiner said the body contained two puncture wounds. However, he asserted, "Preliminary examinations show that neither the puncture wounds nor the dismemberment were the immediate cause of death." He added, "It appears Rooney was still alive when he was thrown into the harbor and that he drowned before his injuries proved fatal."

Sean felt a volcano inside his stomach. He said in a shocked voice, "Ma —oh, Ma, that's awful!"

"Awful it is. The poor baby darlin'. Yer dad knew his dad real well. I saw him about two months ago. My God, what savages would do a thing like that?"

"Oh, Ma, it's so hard to believe I can't imagine it."

He felt filthy putting on the act, but he was at last in control of himself. He looked at the photograph and noticed a blanket covering the body of Rooney. It was only a little lump.

"Oh, Sean, son, I'll just take a breather. I don't feel like makin' breakfast right now, boy."

"Let me pour you another cup of tea, Ma."

"Fine, boy, fine. Glory, that poor lad!"

He poured his mother another cup of tea. Minutes later she went up to her room. Sean rushed to the bathroom and threw up. Mother of God, Devlin and Burke. What kind of men are you? He gasped as he poured his stomach into the toilet bowl.

That day he skipped Mass. He would never be able to take Communion without having gone to confession.

How he got through school the next day he would never know. It was the talk of his class. Gang murders always were. But he managed. At four o'clock he disappeared from in front of the school. He didn't hang around, as was his practice, to talk to girls. He went home. His mother was out.

He felt himself gaining strength as he lived longer with the lie. But he did decide to see Father Zeibatski. He would risk confession. Could he trust Father Zeibatski? He thought for only a split second. Absolutely.

Nervously he approached the church. Slowly he walked up the steps. There was no need to be nervous. He often went to confession on a Monday. He peeked inside the door. There were three women in the pews. He waited and walked across the street and leaned up against the corner. The three women came out. Nobody else went in.

He trotted quickly up the steps, went inside, looked around. Swiftly he approached the confessional box on the left-hand side of the church in the corner, about fifteen feet away from the altar.

He pulled back the curtain. He sat there for a few seconds. Did he really want to? Fear was in his stomach. He rang the bell for Father Zeibatski. A minute passed and he could hear the rustle of the priest's cassock.

The priest settled into the box opposite and the little wooden partition which separated him from the priest was partly opened.

"Father, I have . . ."

Suddenly Sean didn't know what he was doing. But he threw the curtain back and strode around to where the priest was sitting on the opposite side of the confessional. He fought back the tears. But his voice cracked.

"Father, Father. God knows what I have done. I want a human to know. Jimmy Rooney, Jimmy Rooney . . ." His nails gripped into the priest's arms. "I was there . . . it was all my fault."

The high-cheekboned face of the priest remained impassive. There was not the slightest trace of emotion.

"Okay, Sean. Now calm down, Sean. As we have always done it. Go back into the confessional, son. It's all right. It's all right. Come on. Let's start over."

Sean Keogh felt new strength. He didn't know whether it was from God or from the deep-eyed priest. And he confessed all.

After confession, the priest said almost lightly, "Well, Sean, Communion tomorrow?"

"I . . . I . . . Sure, Father."

His cassock rustling, the priest with a thousand secrets disappeared, and Sean prayed that the mysterious man would never be far from him.

PADDY DEVLIN had gone to Willie's, the whorehouse with the sound-proofed walls, on that Saturday night after Rooney had been fished from the harbor. He had staggered into Willie's about three in the morning. Jenny Bryant was at the bar. Her lips parted with expectation as she saw Devlin swagger in. He was drunk.

"Ah, there, Jenny. Ain't seen ya for at least twenty-four hours, stranger."

"Good to see you anytime, Paddy."

Willie, the owner, pushed him a shot glass.

"Now, Jenny, in the words of my old sergeant of the Eighty-second, how about a fuck?"

Willie laughed. "Shit, Paddy, who writes your material? You should be at Harvard."

Devlin chuckled and threw down his shot. Wordlessly, he took Jenny Bryant by the hand and led her into one of the rooms.

"Always makes me feel I'm in some kind of nuthouse with these padded soundproof walls," he said.

"It's so people can do what they want to do, Paddy. You know about that." Already her breathing had quickened as she tore at her clothes to be naked. She ripped her stockings in her haste. Jenny Bryant had an exquisitely slim and tightly muscled body, even if her brains were where they would be safe forever, between her legs.

She threw herself backward onto the bed. She opened her legs and pulled her knees grotesquely back to her shoulders. Damp pinkness glistened in the half-light.

Devlin slopped out of his jacket. His movements were deliberately slow. He was teasing.

"Paddy—Jesus, Paddy, come on. Do it to me, Paddy, like the other night. I'm open for you. Paddy, I've been waiting. Christ, I couldn't forget the other night."

Devlin smiled inwardly. He fumbled with the strap of his shoulder holster. He hung it on the wall.

By the time he had thrown his pants carelessly on the floor, Jenny Bryant was a whimpering, twitching mass of nerves. As she sobbed for servicing, he slowly slid himself to his full length into the broiling, tight heat that made Jenny Bryant an exquisite conquest. She screeched out loud, and Devlin knew why Willie had soundproofed the walls.

"Go on, baby, get it in farther, farther. Stick it in as far as it can go . . . harder, baby, farther. Christ, Paddy . . . oh . . . oh . . . oh . . . right in . . . oh."

There had been a time when Devlin thought Jenny Bryant might have been a faker. But it was true she came with about every five thrusts.

"You like that, Jenny baby? Right up you, right into your stomach . . . harder, faster, right into your stomach . . . faster, harder . . . fuck, you little bitch . . . fuck."

She was in a world punctuated by muscle spasms, screams, orgasms and tooth grinding. She screeched as if she were being tortured. And in a way she was, because Devlin knew she wanted something.

Her eyes begged as she dug her nails deep into Devlin's back. She gasped, "Paddy, you know what I want . . . you know. . . . Come on, Paddy, give it to me."

Inwardly Devlin smiled. He knew. It was always the same with Jenny Bryant.

He pulled himself from her quivering body. She sobbed with expectation. This was the part that amused Devlin. There was no sex in it for him, but it amused him. As his penis stood out from his body ready to explode, he reached inside his shoulder holster.

"Yes, yes, Paddy, don't wait, now . . . now."

She screamed the scream of the agonized or the exorcised as he brutally thrust the long, gray steel barrel of his .38-caliber revolver far inside her. He pumped it with little regard for the result as the gun barrel tore at her quivering insides.

"Yes, Paddy, now . . . go on . . . I'm ready . . . I'm going to come now."

He had difficulty stifling a chuckle.

He pulled the trigger and there was a loud mechanical click. Her scream told him she had reached the climax of all climaxes.

The rest was perfunctory. She knew she owed him as she thrust her full mouth on Devlin's penis to give him one of the most expert jobs of oral gratification. They both lay there spent.

Devlin got to his feet. He reached toward the dresser and started reloading his revolver.

He laughed a sordid laugh. "Ya know, kid, one day I'm gonna be really drunk and fergit to take the slugs out playing that little game."

The eyes of Jenny Bryant misted over with a dark desire that she quickly banished from her mind.

Chapter

3

YOUNG SEAN KEOGH had been left with the most indelible of human scars: guilt. Till those clear blue eyes grew old, he would never erase from his mind that cruel headline which screamed that he had had a part in the most brutal mob hit in Boston history. Devlin's buzz saw had altered the course of young Keogh's life, and there was no going back.

They were only kids—even Devlin and Burke, both twenty-two. But around them was slowly growing an organization that commanded every racket in South Boston. Devlin got what he wanted: notoriety. And among the other Irish and Italian mobs, he was known as a man to be let alone.

For Sean Keogh the die was cast. To the horror of his mother, Molly Keogh, he dropped out of school and immediately went to work for the big, bluff Irishman Bernie McLaughlin, who had come from Dublin in 1920 to escape the British Government's hangman's noose for his activities in the I.R.A. But for all the brutality and misery that the heavy-jowled face of McLaughlin had seen, having the likes of Paddy Devlin around didn't add up to a strong organization to make money. All it did was cover Devlin with ugly gang glory. He didn't like Devlin, but McLaughlin knew there was plenty of mileage in having him as one of his boys to keep the other gangs off his back. The Rooney hit had sickened him, and he, like Sean, suffered no small burden of guilt.

Keogh threw himself into his new job working for Mr. Mac with a fury of energy and organization. His first job as a teen-ager was to pick up the numbers from the various collection points throughout Southie. Within his first three months as a numbers runner for Mr. Mac's policy bank, he had recruited almost every candy store, bar and barbershop in the area. By working out a generous deal for the proprietors, young Keogh had tripled the amount of people playing the numbers in South Boston. Mr. Mac liked the young, energetic Keogh, and the brown envelopes he gave him every Saturday night at the Erin Social Club on Quinlan Square were always bulging.

After making the numbers operation into a well-oiled machine, he moved next onto Mr. Mac's bookie operation. By the time he was sixteen, he was handling huge amounts of money for Mr. Mac. His integrity was unquestioned. Here too, he streamlined the organization, noting that it took too much physical "running" of the bets. He instituted a system of tape-recorded telephone bets. The bettor would have a number, not a name. He would telephone the bookie headquarters, give his identity number and then his bet. This eliminated the physical handling of paper, and there was an undisputed record of the bet. Mr. Mac was nothing short of amazed that the rackets had been brought into the twentieth century by a handsome young teen-ager.

The young man had a certain style about him. The black pegged pants had long since been discarded, and when he bought his first suit, it didn't come within a bull's roar of what Devlin thought was the organization's uniform—the padded gabardine drape suit. Young Keogh went downtown to Brooks Brothers and chose a well-cut dark blue serge three-piece number. It wasn't long before Eddie Wilson was dressing almost identically, and even Frank Burke slid his generous bulk into a gray flannel suit. Sean Keogh clearly had the marks of leadership.

As the baby of the organization, he worked under Devlin and Burke. But Devlin was too busy chasing women, drinking in whorehouses and forgetting business for swagger.

It gave young Keogh a chance to get close to Burke, a closeness that would never be widened all their lives. And it also gave Keogh the chance to like Burke when the curly-headed, broken-nosed young man took Keogh aside one day to simply say, "This is the only time I will say it. Sean, I had nothing to do with the Rooney hit. I knew about it, but it wasn't my handiwork." Young Keogh smiled, nodded and slapped Burke on the back. He had wanted to hear that.

By the time he was nineteen, Sean Keogh was firmly entrenched in the group as the main organization man. The first thing he did was eliminate the floating crap game.

"We're too vulnerable, Mr. Mac," he told the old man.

"I dunno what vulnerable means, son, but if ye got a better idea, I'm listenin'!"

"We're open to busts and cowboy heists from small-time stickup men," Sean said coolly. "We're too far away from the mainstream of our population."

Young Keogh then started to organize regular games in the many bars throughout Southie. The games would always be after hours.

Above all, the new system gave bar owners more money, and it regularized payoffs to the cops. Sean Keogh had always reasoned that if the Devlins of Southie rode around in big cars and operated as if they were the elite of Southie, they would never get the support of the people. He brought the rackets into every level of Southie life, and everyone got a slice—the Church, the community centers, the Little League, the hockey clubs. By the time Sean Keogh was twenty, he had made Bernie McLaughlin not a racketeer, but a community leader. Mac loved it, and so did everyone else.

Well, not everyone else.

Despite the fact that he was under twenty-one, young Keogh had been accorded the honor of membership in the Erin Social Club. As it had been the headquarters of Devlin, it was fast becoming Keogh's headquarters. For Keogh it was not for boozing and swaggering, it was for talking to the mainstream of men who drank there. Devlin clearly didn't like the student outpacing the master.

It was 5 P.M., Monday, June 11, 1962, at the Erin Social Club. Sean Keogh nursed a single Scotch, water, no ice. That was the way they drank their Scotch on Beacon Hill. Frankie Burke was in an expansive mood. A beer sat before him, and a shot glass full of Jameson stood next to it. Soon Sean would be off on the bookie rounds, paying out and collecting. Monday night was settling time, as it was for all bookies throughout the country.

Sean sipped sparingly at his drink. Burke threw one down after another as if he were celebrating winning the lottery.

"You look like a cat that's swallowed a mouse, Frank," Sean said with an even smile.

"Just a tiny thirst, Sean boy."

"You keep that up and you won't have a tiny head tomorrow."

"I admit, I'm feeling pretty good."

"What's the occasion?"

Burke reddened slightly. It was hard to tell when he reddened, because his big round face started that way.

"If I didn't know you better, you big ugly mug, I could have sworn I saw a blush."

"Yer crazy, Sean boy." And he reddened some more.

"Frank, you're holding out on me."

"Me? Hold out on ya? Never. No secrets between us, Sean boy."

"C'mon, Frank out with it. You're about as good a liar as you are a brain surgeon."

"Ferchrissake, can't a fella pop down a few drinks without ya thinking I'm sittin' on the secrets o' the hydrogen bomb?"

"Frank, simply the answer is no. Now, out with it."

He reddened some more. Took another slug of Jameson's, took a breath and in one long quick-fire sentence let it all tumble out.

"Well, on Friday I put some money in the bank and I found out I had three thousand bucks in the bank so I put the deposit on a house in Carson Beach."

"That's plenty. When I bought the house for Ma on McDonough Street, I only had to put down fifteen hundred. Is that all?"

"Okay," he said quickly. "Well, on Saturday night . . . I . . . I asked Teresa to marry me and she said yes and I saw Father Zeibatski and he's gonna to marry us on the eighth and we're gonna have a big reception here . . . and nobody knows about it and if you open yer big Irish mouth I'll bust ya in the melon. So now, fuck it, ya know. Satisfied?" He took a long swig of beer as if the admission were the worst ordeal he had undergone since having a tooth pulled.

"Ha," Sean yelled in a voice that was ten decibels louder than he normally talked.

Burke reddened again. "Shhh, fer Chrissake, I don't want the damn world to know."

Sean's face broke into a big smile. He ruffled Burke's short, tight curly hair. "You big mug, got wise at last. Ah, gee, Frank, what can I say— except say Poor Teresa. No, seriously, Frank, I . . . well, damn it, I'm as happy as you are . . . you big ugly lucky mug . . . you big mug." He grabbed him around his thick, wide shoulders and unselfconsciously gave him a hug. "That really is the best news I've heard since the Red Sox drafted a new pitcher. Where's Teresa now? I got to give her my good wishes."

"You do that and she'll crack my skull. She made me promise I wouldn't tell anyone. But I guess she knew I would tell you. But I wasn't going to. It's just that yer such a sneaky sonofabitch, you tortured it out of me."

"Okay, I won't call. I'm just so damn happy for you. I thought this was going to be the longest engagement since Nathan Detroit. You got smart at last. She's a queen, Teresa, a real queen."

"Don't I know it, boy! Whatta gal."

"This will be some wedding. Nothing is too good for you, Frank. Nothing."

"Aww, shuddup." Burke was like a little child. "Now, not a word to anyone."

Paddy Devlin swaggered through the door. He moved toward Burke and Keogh.

Burke looked up. "Not a word."

"'Course not," Sean replied.

"Well, here they are now. Whatcha plottin', Einstein?" Devlin said with a not-too-soft jab to Keogh's ribs.

"Nothing, Paddy, just a drink before I go on my rounds. Monday is settling day for Mr. Mac. Got to go and do a bit of paying out. The book didn't do too well this week. Lot's of long shots."

"Ahhh, you an' yer rounds. Have a drink."

"Thanks, Paddy, no, I got to get going. Business before pleasure."

"Yeah, well, when do you have any pleasure?"

"I manage. See you fellas. Bye, Frankie, see you tomorrow."

"See ya, Sean boy," Frank said with a friendly smile.

Devlin ordered a shot and a beer. He slugged them down silently, then looked up. "Another snap and a gaff," he said, using the Southie language for a round of drinks. He slugged it down again without a word.

"What's eatin' ya, Paddy boy?"

"Ahh, that Keogh kid."

"Kid—yer only seven years older yerself."

"Bullshit, he's a kid and he gives me the screamin' shits."

"Hey, hey, whatcha got a burr up yer ass fer?"

"I ain't got no burr up my ass. It's just him, snotty little prick. Him and his fuckin' banker's suits and his goin' to Mass and his educated friend Eddie Wilson. Why doesn't he be a fuckin' priest or a fuckin' banker? There's no room for him in the streets."

"Listen, Paddy, he's just about tripled Mr. Mac's take, and he's done it without no trouble."

"Ahhh, few crazy fuckin' ideas and McLaughlin thinks the sun shines out of his asshole. I think the old man is goin' soft in the head."

"I wouldn't say that, Paddy," Burke said cautiously.

"Oh, no, of course ya wouldn't. He makes more money from Mc-Laughlin than you do. Doesn't that burn yer ass?"

"None o' my business. All I know is that I'm makin' more money than I ever have. He's been the fella who's got the money comin' in."

"Bullshit. Has he ever taken anyone out fer Mac?"

"Mac has never asked anyone to take anyone out fer him. Who says ya have to bust heads to make bucks?"

"It's the only way."

"No, it ain't. I like no trouble and I like the money. If there's trouble, fine, but I ain't goin' lookin' fer it."

"Frankie, tell me, boy, when was the last time ya had any fun?"

Burke knew just what that meant, and he said coldly, "I have plenty of fun, but Jenny Bryant and her girls ain't my kind of fun. Get it?"

Burke's face was serious, and Devlin caught his meaning. You could do anything to Burke and he would ride with it. But an insinuation that his union with Teresa Mullins bordered on being dull would stir an anger in the big curly-haired guy that nobody could contain.

Devlin laughed nervously. "Hey, calm down. No offense, boy-o."

"No offense, Paddy," he said unsmilingly.

"It's just that little bastard gets me goin', ya know. I don't dislike him, really. It's just that he wouldn't have known old McLaughlin if it hadn't been for me."

"Ya mean Mr. Mac, don't ya, Paddy?"

"Yeah, Mr. Mac. Hey, another snap and a gaff."

Burke drank his drink, and Devlin changed the subject. But Burke in his mind hadn't changed the subject. He was talking about something else, but he was thinking only one thing: Look out, Sean, Paddy is goin' to cause trouble.

IN THE wood-paneled room behind the altar at Sacred Heart Church, Sean Keogh enjoyed the quiet, austere coolness of Father Zeibatski's quarters. There was much peace there, and there was much peace just talking to the high-cheekboned priest with those eyes and the raggedy crew cut.

"Drink, Sean?"

"No, thanks, Father, today is a working day, as they say."

The priest nodded his head and then shook it from side to side in mock scold.

"I might have one myself if you promise not to talk."

"Lips are sealed."

"How have you been, Sean? You're looking good. Saw your mother today, struggling down the street with a load of groceries. Good woman, Sean, good woman."

"Don't I know it, Father. Hey, I heard."

"Heard what?"

"About Frankie and Teresa."

"Oh, Lord, can you imagine the confessional after that party? They'll be lined up to the Boston Common."

They both laughed. They loved Frankie Burke.

"He's a bit wild," the priest said with a half smile, "but that Teresa Mullins, she'll tame him."

The good-looking priest with a secret past threw down a straight vodka. Sean always marveled that Father Velas Zeibatski was a foreigner. It was only in these moments that he realized he spoke with a heavy accent and drank a kind of liquor that he personally had never tasted.

Nobody drank vodka in Southie. Sean liked being near the priest. Not for religious reasons. There was so much serenity in his presence, so much sanity, so much quiet decency. Somebody said there were many secrets behind that handsome face. But nobody really wanted to know what they were. But the eyes said that suffering was not new.

"So, Father, now, anything myself and Mr. Mac can do for the wedding?"

"It's a bit like me saying 'Anything I can do for you boys in a crap game?' Marrying people is a thing I do quite well, and please tell Mr. McLaughlin to stick to his business and I'll stick to mine." They both laughed. It was right from the belly.

There was silence for a moment. Then Sean said, "Mr. Mac said to give you this." It was a large envelope. Both men knew the contents.

"Ahh, the wages of sin," said the priest with a smile. "I would gladly forfeit Bernie's contributions to see him contribute himself personally at Mass one Sunday. You know we have a three P.M. Mass for late risers. But tell the dear man thank you so much, he's very kind."

"And Father?"

"Hmm, huh?"

Sean slid across a smaller brown envelope.

"From me, Father."

"I'll see it reaches its destination as usual."

"I . . . er Father . . . is it impossible to know where they are?"

"I've told you before. It is not impossible, but if I may be so arrogant, I suggest it is not prudent for you to know where they are. The woman Rooney and her child are very well and far from here. They are happy, Sean. She is a good woman."

Sean clamped his teeth hard. "I wish you hadn't said that, Father."

"Sean, you can lie as much by not saying something as you can by screaming it from Beacon Hill."

"Now, about the wedding," Sean said hastily. "Mr. Mac is going to look after the reception. He'll pay for that, and of course, the cost of the wedding here."

"And so the old rascal should," he said with a laugh.

"So, Father, I'll see you. No doubt Ma will see you tonight at the bingo game."

"Heavenly Father, what skill that woman has."

"Okay, I'll be going."

"Goodbye, young fellow. See you soon. And get Bernie to Mass, will you . . . please."

YOUNG SEAN and Bernie McLaughlin had planned the wedding to the last detail. Sacred Heart was crowded that Saturday. Teresa Mullins looked serene and beautiful in white as Bernie McLaughlin walked her down the aisle. Frankie Burke looked uncomfortable and terrified. He mentioned in an aside to Sean, his best man, "Korea was easier."

Predictably, Burke fumbled the whole moment. When Sean produced the ring, Burke dropped it, and it rolled under Bernie McLaughlin's feet. McLaughlin let out a loud roar of laughter until a sharp look from Father Zeibatski silenced him and the gigglers in the body of the church. But it did go off beautifully.

Burke suddenly wanted to take charge, and he organized everyone into limousines for the reception at the Erin Social Club.

Eddie Wilson looked at Sean with a smile. "He has put ten people in one limousine and one person in another. Frankie is so nervous he couldn't organize a free lunch." They laughed. In the end Burke had organized everyone for transport. Then he found he was on the curbside without transport himself. He caught a taxi to his own reception and was greeted with applause as the last person to walk in.

The Erin Social Club was bursting at the seams with five hundred people. More than one tenth of the population of Southie, men, women and children, were there.

The Club, with its dun-colored walls, rickety tables and beat-up bar was hardly the Copley Plaza, particularly as it only had a single rest room. But the place buzzed with laughter, shouting and singing. They were happy for Frankie Burke, they were happy for Teresa and they were happy for themselves. The men, in their suits that no longer fit them as they had ten years ago, gathered around the bar and sang songs their forebears had sung for generations. They drank beer and Jameson. The women, in their print dresses and beehive hairdos, which all emanated from the same beauty salon on that Saturday morning, drank tea, and the more adventurous drank a single glass of sherry or maybe two. The boys would get drunk and everyone would laugh. If a woman got drunk it would be the talk of the neighborhood for at least a week. While the men crowded around Mr. Mac and Frankie Burke, the women crowded around Father Zeibatski. It was a point of honor for the priest to know you by your first name.

Teresa Mullins rustled in her stiff white dress to Sean's side. "Sean, I can't thank you enough for the way you've worked all this out. Sometimes I think he loves you more than he loves me."

Sean laughed. "Grounds for divorce already. Well, I don't think that, Teresa."

"I heard that, ya double-dealin' bum." It was Burke with a big smile on his face. He had a bottle of champagne in one hand and a bottle of beer in the other. His tie was undone, and he was swigging alternately from both bottles.

"Ahhh, Sean. God bless, fella."

Sean smiled, looked at Teresa and smiled again. "You're going to be in great shape for your honeymoon." He looked across at Bernie Mc-Laughlin. "Look what state our great romantic is in. Great honeymoon."

"What honeymoon? We're stayin' at Teresa's mother's place."

"The hell ye are," Bernie McLaughlin roared. "Now, look, take this, and fer cryin' out loud, when the reception is over get out of our bloody hair."

He handed him tickets from Logan Airport and a paid reservation for a week at the Harborside Inn in Martha's Vineyard. Burke had been to Korea, but he had never been to the Cape.

"Oh, Jesus, fellas."

"I caught that," said a smiling Father Zeibatski.

"I mean, what can I say? Teresa, fer cryin' out loud, say thanks."

She beamed. "Really, you have been so good to us. Really."

At that second Sean winked to the barman, who disappeared outside.

Suddenly the small club was filled with a roaring sound from outside.

"Faith be to God, now, who is that outside tryin' to ruin this reception?" Bernie McLaughlin was yelling with outrage. He had his arm around Molly Keogh, and she was surpressing a smile.

"Now, c'mon, Frankie boy. Go out there and see who is causin' that awful racket. Go on, Frankie, it's your party. Go and bust him in the bleedin' mouth."

The sound got louder, and it reverberated around the club. Burke frowned. He didn't want a brawl on his wedding day. But he lurched outside. Sean, Mr. Mac, Molly Keogh, Father Zeibatski and Eddie Wilson followed.

Burke was yelling blindly. "Who in the hell do ya think ya are?" he was screaming at the driver of a big truck. He walked up to the cabin to see it was Dan McCauley, the bartender.

"C'mon, Dan, ya gone mad or somethin'? Stop revvin' that motor or I'll jam yer head in the damn thing."

"Gotta keep the engine goin'," Dan said with a smile.

By this time the crowd was in the street, laughing.

"What are you bunch of idiots laughin' at?" He hadn't seen the neat gold lettering on the side of the big green truck. Then he noticed it. He seemed to be focusing his eyes.

Burke Trucking Company, the letters said simply. Sean Keogh walked over to Burke.

Burke was agape. "What's goin' on?"

Sean simply threw him the keys on a chain. "It's about time you made an honest living, you bum."

The crowd spilling into Quinlan Square cheered and clapped.

It finally sank through that Sean's wedding present was the huge truck. Sean followed it up with a union card for Teamsters Local 109 with Burke's name clearly printed on it. FRANCIS XAVIER BURKE.

Burke stood there wide-eyed. And then his eyes began to blur with tears. Suddenly his face flushed, and he forced a cough to mask the tears. Teresa ran to Sean and hugged him. Then she ran and threw her arms around Burke. Molly Keogh beamed. Old Joe Keogh would be mighty proud of his son if he were here today.

Burke tried to speak, but his voice cracked. His face reddened, and he charged self-consciously inside to the bar, and everybody cheered. They understood. When the emotion subsided, Burke swilled a beer from the bottle and simply said above the noise of the party, "I love ya, boy . . . and I'll never leave ya . . . never."

To save Burke the embarrassment of any more tears, Sean changed the subject.

"Holy hell, is that Edward George Wilson, the brain trust of South Boston, over there talking to a girl? Yes, it is. Well, look at old Eddie."

Eddie Wilson, in a corner of the club, was busily engaged in a conversation with a small-boned girl of about nineteen who was perhaps not even five feet two inches tall. Her diminutive stature made her look younger than however old she might be, a child-woman. Sean Keogh looked at her with curious interest. Even from a distance, she seemed to be nervous and extremely shy. The rest of the women from Southie were busily gossiping about their menfolk, or their kids, or their last operation. Somehow she seemed to stand apart. Not from aloofness, but from downright fear. Her nut-brown hair was parted in the middle, pulled severely back and rolled simply in a bun. There had been no attempt to achieve a beehive hairdo like the rest of the women.

For an instant Sean Keogh's attention seemed to drift from the scenes of revelry around him. His eyes narrowed as he inconspicuously studied the frail-looking girl. It was as if she were in dire need of a friend but too frightened to allow anyone too close to her. Her eyes darted nervously around the room as she talked to Eddie Wilson. They were nice eyes, big and brown. But frightened. She was dressed simply and economically in a light, pale gray sun dress. A simple belt with a little ornate clasp clung to her tiny waist. He couldn't tell for sure, but apart from a light application of lipstick, she appeared to have on no makeup. She was certainly Irish, but not like the rest of the warm, outgoing women of Southie.

Keogh studied her some more. Was it a certain style she had? Hardly; the dress was bargain-basement and nobody wore her hair like that. There was no sophistication there. She looked like a pretty, frail little rabbit who was afraid of her own shadow. Interesting kid. His brief inspection was interrupted by a loud slap on the back.

It was Burke. "Ain't this something?"

"It's the best for the best, Frankie."

"Ahh, yer the salt of the earth, Sean boy." Burke took a long guzzle from a champagne bottle. And Keogh found his eyes drifting back to her. Wilson was standing there in a gentlemanly way, talking with earnestness.

"Frankie, that girl over there talking to Eddie. I can't place her. She a neighborhood girl?"

"Sure, ya musta seen her around."

"Think so, but I just can't place her. Face is familiar."

"Ya know her, ferchrissake. The Sweeney girl—Rose Sweeney. Her old man, Pat Sweeney, and her brother Billy work on the docks fer Mr. Mac."

"Yes, I have seen her in the neighborhood, but I never see her around."

"She works as a nurse at Boston General. Great little lady. Looks after the old man and her brother like she was their ma. There was a whole bunch of the kids—five others, I think—but they've all taken off; living all over the place."

"Why is that?"

"Don't you remember? About eight, nine years ago, her ma went nuts. Stark ravin' mad. They took her away, they did. She looks after the old man and her brother. Hardworkin' little girl. Works as a nurse, then looks after the old man and the brother." Burke indicated the bar. The Sweeney men were a thirsty pair.

Sean tried not to show too much interest. "She hasn't been in Southie all the time, has she?" Sean wanted to know.

"Dunno. Think she's been down in New York. Came back about six months ago to work at the hospital. Just wanted to come back to take care of her old man and brother."

"She's a friend of Eddie's?"

"Think he knows her through her old man. Might have even taken her out a few times, the sly old dog."

Sean studied the glass in his hand. He had asked more questions than he intended to. Then he added: "Yes, I think I remember the time with her mother. Tragic." And he left it at that.

"It was a bad case, the poor kid," Burke said distractedly as he ordered another beer from Dan McCauley, the bartender.

Father Zeibatski came up to Sean and Burke.

"Now all we have to do is get a promise from Mr. Mac to come to Mass and it will have been a perfect day," he said with a grin.

"Not bloody likely, Father," McLaughlin roared as he swallowed a shot of Jameson. "I'll tell ye what; I'll go when ye get ya brother, Vinnie, to go."

Vinnie "the Chin" Zeibatski grinned sheepishly. His elder brother scowled.

Sean laughed along with the raucous banter, but his eyes always returned to the small-boned girl in the corner talking to Eddie Wilson. She was sipping lemonade. Her eyes blinked nervously and she seemed uncomfortable.

Eddie Wilson was engaged in quiet and polite small talk with the frail-looking young girl. "You prefer being back here in Boston, rather than New York?"

Her face flushed ever so lightly. Even the most casual conversation with a man gave hints of red in her cheeks. "Yes . . . yes I do. I went to school down in New York. But I like being here with Dad and Billy. And I like my job as a nurse."

"Bad hours, I guess."

"You get used to them, you really do." She sipped again at her soft drink.

"Rose, how about next Tuesday. You working?"

"Ah, no. No, I don't think so. I'm free."

"Like to take in a movie?"

"Well . . . I . . . er, I would have to check that Dad doesn't need anything."

"Come on, Rose. I know your father well. He isn't a slave driver."

They both smiled and she said, "Okay, fine. Tuesday." She seemed to say yes to avoid any more talk. She embarrassed easily.

Rose Sweeney looked hard at her father, Pat Sweeney. She could see only his big broad back. Billy, as always, was at his side. Sean Keogh caught her eye momentarily, but she didn't seem to notice him.

She looked around the room. She hated crowds. They are all here, she thought. There is Dan McCauley, and Teresa, who got married today. She was older than me, a class ahead of me. Dan was there and so was Teresa. And there is Jack Crockford. He was just a patrolman in those days. Now he is in plainclothes. He was there that day with Dan and Teresa. And Tim Matheson. Yes, he was there that day. And Joan Courtney. They were all there that day and now they are here.

Yes, there they are and they all feel sorry for me. They feel sorry for young Rose, and when they aren't feeling sorry, they are laughing at me, just like the kids at school did. They are laughing at me over what happened. And there is Pat Sweeney, he is my father, and there is Billy Sweeney, he is my brother, and they are drinking as usual and everyone else is laughing at me. Her upper lip broke out in a sweat.

Eddie Wilson discreetly peered into her eyes. Her eyes didn't see him.

"Rose, Rose. Are you all right? You're looking a little pale. Do you want to sit down?"

"Sit down?" It was as if she were awaking from a trance, "Oh, yes, thank you. Ahh, no, don't worry, really. I think I better go now. I worked the overnight shift at the hospital and I have had the flu. I'm very tired. I'm terribly sorry, I don't mean to be rude, but I think I better go now. Tell my dad and my brother I have gone. I don't want to spoil their fun. Thank you, Mr. Wilson. Thank you. Goodbye."

Eddie Wilson looked a little mystified. Just tired. It's hard being a nurse.

She quickly put down her glass of lemonade and eased her way through the crowd along the wall to avoid being noticed by the revelers.

Sean Keogh, standing at the bar in a large semicircle, watched her as she weaved her way urgently through the crowd.

He unobtrusively stood up straighter and craned his neck to get a glimpse of her. Although she was on the other side of the club, he could see that her face was flushed, and her movements seemed unsure, as if she wanted to avoid any further embarrassment. My, she is a shy young thing! He watched her with interest as she moved urgently through the crowd. Pretty little thing, he thought. It's almost like she needs a big protective arm around her.

"Sean, yer dragging yer feet," someone yelled. "Come on, lad, drink up." And once again he was caught up in the maelstrom of heady celebration. Pretty little thing, he thought, before he found himself swigging down a drink of which he had no earthly idea what it contained. Well, this was Frankie's wedding, and today he would have a few drinks.

They're all laughing at me in there, I have to get out. The faces of her friends seemed to get bigger, and the noise of the crowd came in waves like a shortwave radio broadcast.

That day, that day. There was Jack Crockford the policeman. Put that axe down, Margaret, now, come on. Yes, that was what Jack said. He was scared to go near her.

Rose Sweeney hit the fresh air. She started to walk fast until she almost broke into a run. Put the axe down, Margaret, we're not going to hurt you. Jack Crockford was scared that day so long ago. Then the other police arrived. Then all the neighbors came out. They were craning their necks to get a good look. And Margaret Sweeney was there on the porch, her face all twisted and awful, her hair everywhere. She had lost control of her bladder and she was standing barefoot in a big pool and her nose was running and she was growling like an animal.

"You're all trying to kill me," she kept screaming, and then she swung an axe at anyone who got near her. And all of us kids were there, and she was swinging the axe.

Then Dad came home and ran through the front gate toward her and she let out this horrible screech and fell on the ground and the ambulance men came quickly. Jack Crockford moved fast and grabbed the axe. She just kept sobbing. Then she started to throw her arms around, and they put her in a straitjacket, and all the neighbors saw it and they were craning their necks to get a better look.

Rose Sweeney had run all the way home, and her head was bursting from that terrible day which flashed in her brain. She opened the front door of the house on Dorchester Street. It was the same door that her mother had burst through hacking away with the axe. Quickly Rose pulled her hand in horror from the doorknob as if it were contaminated by some terrible disease. She ran upstairs and threw herself on the bed. Her head was bursting, and all those faces at the reception had been laughing, and the faces had all looked as though they were made out of rubber and their noses and chins had stretched. They were the same faces. They were the faces of Southie. The same faces that had been there that day when Margaret Sweeney had been taken away.

Her head was exploding. It was as if someone had put too much blood in her head and the vessels were bursting at the seams, like too much water in a balloon. God, won't it stop. She tried desperately to focus her eyes. The vision was blurred and she could feel her throat dry and constricting and the only way she could breathe was in short soblike gasps. What is happening to me? It happened once before, a memory flashed to her through the pain. The second day after she had come back to the house in Dorchester Street after arriving from New York. God, won't it stop. Those faces. The laughing. What was going on? She had seen people at the hospital behaving in exactly the same manner. Pound, pound, pound, the blood coursing through her veins in frantic pumps. She clenched her teeth hard and could hear herself praying to any God who would ease the indescribable pain, fear and disorientation. Pound, pound, pound.

She was sobbing, but there were no tears. She dug her nails into the bedspread, and her head felt as if there were people on either side of her brain pulling in different directions, and she could hear her mother making those terrible noises as the men took her away, and Pat Sweeney, the man who had given her six children in seven years, was facing the neighbors and he was saying that he didn't know what the hell was happening. He was talking to neighbors and Ma was being taken away and we were all crying.

Her eyes clouded over and the pain became unbearable and she could hear herself scream—and suddenly it was all quiet; very, very quiet.

She got up off the bed, brushed her hair and went downstairs to make herself a cup of strong tea. *My God, what on earth happened to me?*

She sat quietly in the small darkened lounge room in the small frame house on Dorchester Street, sipping the hot tea, deep in thought. She felt quite strong, quite healthy. She dismissed the temporary and painful lapse. *It could happen to anyone,* she told herself. *Nothing to worry about.* She brightened. Next Tuesday she had a date with the very fine Mr. Eddie Wilson.

THERE WERE thirty of the hard-core drinkers left at the bar of the Erin Social Club. The place looked as if it had been the scene of the World Series. The hard core were singing, but they seemed to all be singing different tunes. Nobody cared. Everybody was deliriously drunk after a great blast. As was the practice, their womenfolk had dutifully retreated home.

Frankie Burke had taken off on his honeymoon with Teresa, and he had insisted on driving his brand-new wedding-gift truck to Logan Airport. It had been a fine Southie time.

Sean Keogh sat pleasantly exhausted at the table near the door. Eddie Wilson sat on his left, Father Zeibatski on his right, and old Bernie McLaughlin sat opposite.

Sean sighed with satisfaction. He finally allowed himself a Scotch and water, no ice. He had deserved it. Mr. Mac was well on the way to a glorious drunk, and even Eddie Wilson was looking a little glassy-eyed. It seemed Father Zeibatski had been drinking all afternoon, but he was clear-eyed, cool, coherent and pleasant.

"You did great today, Sean," the priest said, his dark eyes warming.

"Bloody marvelous, son," Mr. Mac chimed in.

Then it was Eddie Wilson's turn: "Remind me, Sean, to tell you well in advance when I'm getting married. Did you see Frankie's face when he saw the writing on the side of the truck? Big old tough Frankie. Thought he was going to burst into tears."

Sean smiled indulgently. He had enjoyed today, and he had enjoyed seeing Frank Burke's face when he realized that he would have a truck of his own to launch his own business and that he would start with a Teamster union card. He would make a lot of money.

Sean looked at Eddie Wilson seriously. Wilson questioned his look with his eyes.

"And then, of course, there is you, Eddie," Sean said.

"Yes, of course there is me," he said with a smile and a gulp of champagne.

"We all have to be settled, Eddie, all of us."

"Couldn't agree with you more."

"Since we were kids at school, what have you always wanted to do?"

"Go insane counting my money," he said with a laugh.

"Seriously."

"Well, it's no secret to you, Sean. I want to be a lawyer, and with a bit of luck I will be a lawyer. Modesty aside, gents, my grades are pretty good, and if ever I do get to the bar, I'll get you guys out of trouble free of charge."

He was still smiling. The smile would soon disappear.

"It appears," Sean said slowly, "that Father Zeibatski's friends are not limited to the Almighty."

Mr. Mac smiled. So did the priest. Eddie wasn't catching the drift.

"It also appears that he has some very influential friends at Harvard, and when he told them about your grades, they weren't the least bit reluctant to accept you for your last year of college."

Eddie Wilson's face fell. He was drunk. He narrowed his eyes.

"Run that by me again, Sean. Slowly."

"Simply that the good Father has arranged for you to enter Harvard. And after that, if you can continue to be the genius we know you to be, ha, ha, you will be accepted at Harvard Law School."

"Sean, what the hell are you saying? Harvard? Harvard Law School? You have to have clout, you have to have strings, you have to have money, lots of it."

"Well, Father Zeibatski has come up with the clout, and we had a bit of loose cash lying around . . . and the rest is history. You start next semester. Case closed, Counselor."

Eddie Wilson was silent for a long minute until it all sank in. He knew Sean was not playing any feeble joke. He ran his fingers through his thick red hair. He sighed deeply and seemed to pale from the shock.

"Harvard . . . I have only dreamed . . . Harvard? I can't quite grasp it, Sean. You guys have done this for me?"

Mr. Mac wheezed with laughter. The priest, as usual, looked inscrutable. Sean gave a warm but economical smile to signal he was serious.

"I just don't know what to say. . . . I . . ."

"I'll tell ye what to say, young 'un," Mr. Mac said as he wiped his beer-moistened mouth with the back of his hand. "Say ye'll get out of

Harvard Law School in under four years so we can put ye to work and not have to pay as much bloody money." They all laughed loudly.

Eddie ran his fingers through his hair for the second time in as many minutes. "Sean . . . Sean . . . now I feel like Frankie Burke. I feel as if I'm going to burst into tears."

"It's not really a gift, Eddie. The Father couldn't have done it if your grades were lousy, and let's face it, as far as the money is concerned it's just good business. The organization will need a top-class lawyer."

"The organization?" Eddie queried.

"Well," said Sean confidently, "I hope all of us and Southie have more to offer the country other than being the first bookie setup to use a tape-recorded betting system."

Eddie laughed. "I'm going to get drunk tonight, God damn it . . . er, sorry, Father."

"Well," said the priest, "He will probably not damn you tonight, but tomorrow when you look in the mirror with a hangover, you'll know His wrath has finally fallen."

They clinked glasses. "To the counselor. To Counselor Wilson."

Sean relaxed, his mind went back to the frail little girl called Rose Sweeney. He was snapped out of his thoughts by the harsh lilt of Bernie McLaughlin:

"Ye did us proud, Sean lad. Best bash I've ever seen in Southie."

"It sure was," a voice said loudly and crudely from the club's entrance. "Best bash I've seen in Southie," the voice mimicked Mr. Mac. It was Paddy Devlin. He was swaying in the entrance. He had Jenny Bryant on his arm.

Mr. Mac looked up. "Well, look what the cat dragged in. Where the hell ye been? Ye missed the whole day. It was a fine time, I'm tellin' ye."

Sean Keogh sized up Devlin's mood in a single glance. He felt his stomach tighten.

Devlin weaved toward the table. He was wearing a nasty sneer. "Oh, I didn't wanna disturb all you boys. Maybe Sean didn't want anyone here takin' the shine off him bein' Santa Claus."

"Steady on, lad," Mr. Mac said with a note of caution in his voice.

"Steady on? Steady on fer what? Who have I got to steady on fer?"

Nobody talked to Bernie McLaughlin like that. "I'd mind yer manners if I was you, son." McLaughlin started to get up.

Sean Keogh, who had remained silent, put a firm hand on McLaughlin's knee.

Eddie Wilson looked nervously at him. The deep, dark eyes of Father Zeibatski smoldered with apprehension.

"C'mon, Paddy, let's leave these squares alone." Jenny Bryant pulled on his arm. He wrestled free of her grip.

"Na, na, Jenny. I've come to my club to have a drink, and no bunch of fairies are gonna run me out."

McLaughlin's eyes were blazing with rage.

Keogh's deep eyes met Devlin's. "Yes, Paddy, why don't you calm down and have a drink?"

"Drink? I'll have a drink, but not with this bunch. I drink with men. Anyway, how long is it since yer mother let ya drink?"

Sean Keogh snapped to his feet. Eddie Wilson looked anxiously across to Father Zeibatski. The eyes appealed for someone to head off a fight. Devlin was a killer. The priest caught the glance. He just gave a reassuring nod. Bernie McLaughlin kept his eyes on Devlin's right hand in case it went inside his jacket.

Devlin smiled as Keogh stood before him. "I've been waitin' fer this."

Devlin shifted his weight and moving off his right foot with his shoulders right behind the punch, threw a lightning left jab at Sean.

Keogh didn't even move his feet. He simply turned his shoulders sideways and pulled his head backward a fraction, and Paddy Devlin went sailing past him as harmless as a child. A lot of people had forgotten but there was a lot of boxer left in the five-foot-eleven-inch frame of young Keogh.

Devlin cursed. "Ya little prick. I'll teach ya." He grabbed a bottle off the table, smashed it at its neck.

McLaughlin yelled, "No Paddy, not that." It was too late. His right hand was slashing the air, and then Devlin charged Keogh, the jagged end out front like a lance.

It was like watching a bullfighter. Keogh stepped quickly aside and threw a table in Devlin's way. He tripped over it. He then rolled with it, and the legs of the table somehow got tangled up with his own. It would have been comical if everyone had not been so tense.

Devlin disengaged himself from the embarrassing heap. His face was crimson, his eyes little slits of boiling liquid. Everybody waited for Keogh to pounce on him. But he just stood there coolly adjusting the vest of his suit. Devlin had had enough of being made a fool of tonight.

Then Sean Keogh spoke in loud, clear, clipped tones, so that the whole club would hear every word. Devlin started to mouth a threat, and Sean simply said, "Shut up, Devlin. Now that you have resigned from this club, I presume I won't see you in South Boston ever again. I do hope you understand me when I say never again. That's all, Devlin. You can go now and take your pathetic tramp with you."

Mr. Mac was breathing hard. Surely now Devlin will go for his gun.

Keogh turned his back on him and walked toward his group's table. Don't do it, Sean lad; Devlin will pull it.

Suddenly Keogh wheeled around on Devlin, who stood there a mountain of rage, and said, "Devlin, if you are thinking of going for that little toy you carry around, think again before I shove it down your throat. Now get out."

The club was stifled into silence. Nobody had heard Sean Keogh talk like that. Nobody had heard anybody talk like that. He made a babbling fool out of the most-feared hoodlum in Southie and then exiled him with the same pronouncement as an ancient king. Even Mr. Mac, Wilson and Father Zeibatski felt the eeriness of it.

Devlin muttered under his breath, "I'll let you go now, Keogh. But I'll be back to teach ya a lesson ya won't fuckin' ferget."

"I said get out . . . now." And Devlin and his whore Jenny Bryant disappeared out the door. Keogh had never raised a fist or his voice. There was something very terrifying about the whole scene. More terrifying than if guns had exploded.

Keogh then suddenly smiled, lifted his Scotch: "Well, here's to Frankie's first night." They all clinked glasses and toasted Frankie, but nobody could get his mind off the scene they had just witnessed.

When Sean Keogh went back to 15 McDonough Street, he lay on his bed thinking, as he had for so many hundreds of nights. But tonight he was thinking about a frail, frightened little girl called Rose Sweeney.

Chapter

4

IT HAD been three weeks since Keogh had bloodlessly but brutally exiled Paddy Devlin from South Boston. It had been the talk of Southie whenever two or more men—or women, for that matter—had got together. Sean had never mentioned the incident, not even when his mother, Molly Keogh, had cryptically said to him over breakfast, "I hope yer keeping yer nose clean, Sean boy." He had only sipped his tea, smiled and said, "You know me, Ma. Always."

Frankie Burke had returned from Martha's Vineyard, his red face made all the redder by an alien element called the sun. He had set up a small storefront office four doors down from the Erin Social Club. On its windows he had proudly embossed in gold lettering: FRANCIS X. BURKE TRUCKING COMPANY.

From the day of his return from his honeymoon, his company did a thriving business. He got all the business a single truck could handle from the docks controlled by Bernie McLaughlin, and already he was talking of buying a second truck. He proved to be an astute businessman.

Eddie Wilson had started his semester at Harvard and seemed to be continuously walking on a cloud. But all three—Burke, McLaughlin and Wilson—lived under a pall, fearing that Devlin's exile would eventually lead to an ugly explosion. Only Keogh himself seemed to have forgotten about the incident. He busied himself with the business at hand of consolidating McLaughlin's small but thriving empire.

Keogh had dropped by at Burke's office on a Monday afternoon before doing the bookie rounds of settling day. He walked smiling through the rough wood doorway of the small storefront. Inside, the office was old but immaculate. Burke was poring over some bills of lading from the docks.

"Ahh, the wheels of industry at work," Keogh said as he sat down in an old swivel chair at the desk opposite Burke.

"How goes it, Sean boy?"

"Fine. Settling day today. Mr. Mac's had a good week. Things are going good. How is it with you, Frank?"

"Couldn't be better. Goin' down to the bank tomorrow. Gonna get the loot for another truck. Can't handle the business. It's pourin' in from everywhere. Movin' stuff twelve hours on the night shift from the docks and doin' short hauls down the coast durin' the day. Hired Dan Mc-Cauley, the bartender, to work part time. Didn't know legitimate business was so easy."

"You see?" Keogh was happy for his friend.

"How goes it with yer ma, Sean?"

"Just the same. She wins at bingo on Monday nights, and that always makes Mrs. Wilson mad because she always loses. And Mrs. Wilson always manages to get to Mass first on Sunday and take the seat on the aisle in the front pew, so she can take up the collection, and that makes Ma mad. But other than that, fifteen McDonough Street struggles through its day-to-day drama." They both chuckled. There was a short silence, and Burke put down his pen. He leaned back in his chair and ran his hand over his tight curly hair. He sighed deeply. The silence over the past two weeks had bothered him.

"Sean, what are we gonna do?"

"About what?"

"Ya know damn well about what. Paddy Devlin."

Keogh shrugged. "It hasn't crossed my mind."

"Bullshit it hasn't. Just because you ain't sayin' doesn't mean you ain't thinkin'."

"Frank, Paddy Devlin doesn't exist in my mind."

"C'mon, boy. Now, don't be a dope. Yer too smart for that."

"I'm telling you, Frank. He doesn't exist."

"Well, he exists in the North End. He exists with all those Italian guys who work for Frank Castellano down in New York. He exists and they have accepted him over there. Have you ever heard of anyone from Southie bein' accepted by those Italians?"

"Whether Devlin is accepted by some Italian gents in the North End has not the slightest consequence to me. So long as that thick-headed bully of an Irishman is not accepted by an Irishman in Southie. That's all that bothers me."

"You know better than that, Sean. Nobody would touch him with a ten-foot pole over here. Everybody was with ya on that move. You handled yerself like a gent, from what I heard."

"So?"

"So it doesn't change the subject, Sean. I'm worried, Mr. Mac is worried; even Eddie Wilson is worried, and what does he know about things outside Harvard?" he said with a grin in reference to Wilson.

"I don't know what you're getting at, Frank. Anyway"—he started to get up—"got to get going on the rounds."

Burke reached across the desk and put his hand on the back of Keogh's hand.

"It's gotta happen, Sean. We gotta do something about Devlin. Because he's gonna do something about you."

"Frank, you are a businessman. One day you are going to be very rich and make Teresa happy. We've got something going here, Frank. It's ours. There are no outsiders like there used to be. Southie is self-sufficient. We're our own bosses. We don't need trouble, don't need the old ways." He smiled.

"I'm with ya there, boy. But I worry about ya. You know that. So do the rest of the crowd. We don't want anything to happen to ya." He opened a drawer and pulled out a tin strongbox. He opened it with a key. Inside was a snub-nosed .38 revolver.

"I would feel better if you carried this, Sean. Please."

"Are you kidding? Ma would belt me across the head if she saw me carrying a piece. No way, Frank. And don't you carry it either. You're a businessman, get it? Businessmen don't carry guns. Understand, you big ugly mug?"

Burke frowned and then gave a smile of resignation as he replaced the gun. "Okay, ya mad bastard. Maybe catch ya fer a drink later on."

"Yeah, Ma will be at bingo. Say about nine o'clock. I'll have finished the rounds. We can watch the Red Sox game on television at the club."

"Okay, gotcha."

Keogh went into the warm July night. Life was good. Everybody was making money who deserved to make money. Life was good. Just about perfect. I wonder what Rose Sweeney does at night. Probably works down at the hospital.

He started on his rounds. She's a pretty girl, that Rose. Frightened, but pretty.

AT 9:15 P.M., Keogh sauntered into the Erin Social Club. Burke was at the bar drinking with a few locals and talking to Dan McCauley, the bartender who was Frank's part-time driver.

Keogh walked up smiling to the bar. "Fine crew here." He put a satchel on the bar. It was the day's takings from the bets. "Dan, lock that up, will you, pal? Mr. Mac will pick it up in the morning. I'll be in town tomorrow."

"Sure thing, Sean." He grabbed the satchel, disappeared to the room behind the bar and locked it in the safe.

Keogh looked up at the darkened television set. Burke frowned. "Damn thing is on the blink. Won't be able to see the game, damn it. Danny, another snap and a gaff here, pal. Sean? Scotch and water?"

"Thanks."

Frank Burke argued baseball with the rest of the drinkers, and Sean Keogh quietly sipped his Scotch and listened with amusement to Burke's animated appraisal of the Boston Red Sox.

"If we don't get rid of that fuckin' pitcher, I'm tellin' ya it's all over. They'll end up playin' in the Canadian League."

Just then the telephone behind the bar rang. Dan McCauley picked it up:

"Erin . . . Yeah, yeah, he's here. . . . What? Jesus. Jesus Christ." McCauley yelled urgently over the heads of the drinkers, "Sean, fer Chrissake, get over to your place. The fire boys are on the phone. Yer place caught fire. They're there now."

Burke slammed down his glass on the bar. "C'mon, I've got my truck outside. Let's go."

Keogh paled with shock. He turned and sprinted toward the door. Then he turned back to McCauley. "Dan, you drive over to the hall at Sacred Heart and tell Ma. I don't want her coming home to the shock of it. You tell her and bring her over. We'll be there."

Burke and Keogh leaped into the cab of the big green truck. Burke threw it furiously into gear and tore out of Quinlan Square and down Dorchester Avenue. He streaked through four sets of red lights, and the tires screeched as he roared through the narrow streets. A hundred yards from McDonough Street, Burke and Keogh could see the glow in the sky.

Keogh tightened his jaw. "This will break Ma's heart. She has lived in that house for forty years. Thank God, I got it insured. Damn it. This will break her heart."

They swerved around the corner into McDonough Street. The street was filled with water from the fire hoses. There were lights flashing, and the conversation from the two-way radios on the fire engines roared through the street. The house was already destroyed, and the fire was only feeding on the embers. Even the frame was just a blackened skeleton. The firemen played their hoses on the walls of the adjacent houses to stop the fire from spreading. The opposite side of the street was filled with neighbors and their kids who had rushed out to watch the sad spectacle of the Keogh household going up in flames.

Burke and Keogh leaped from the truck, which Burke had left in the middle of the street. Both men stopped dead as Detective Jack Crockford and the fire chief approached them. Detective Crockford spoke: "No chance of saving it, Sean. They got here almost immediately." The fire chief nodded his head in agreement. "The timber was dry, Sean," he said. "Went up like matchwood. We couldn't even get any of your furniture out."

Keogh shook his head sadly from side to side. "I know you did everything, fellas. I'm dreading Ma seeing this."

One of the firemen yelled to Detective Crockford and the fire chief. "Excuse me, Sean." The two men left Burke and Keogh.

Keogh looked up as he heard a screech of brakes. It was a late-model Mercury. Keogh narrowed his eyes. It was Dan McCauley. He opened the door and ran toward Keogh without slamming it. His face was ashen.

"Sean, Sean," he started yelling before he reached him. "Yer ma wasn't at the bingo game. She wasn't there, Sean. They said she was goin' to see Mrs. Wilson."

Panic gripped Keogh's stomach. "C'mon, Frank, let's go over to the Wilson house."

He had started to break into a run when he saw a sight that speared through his body like a jagged knife. It was Mrs. Wilson running toward him in a housedress. Her hair was in curlers.

She was shouting. "Sean, Sean, yer ma, where is she? She was comin' over to watch some television. She wanted to watch a show and she didn't go to the bingo game. Where is she, Sean? I had just put the kettle on fer a cup of tea. Where is she, Sean?" She was hysterical and crying. Burke paled. Keogh's teeth had bitten clean through his lower lip, and the blood was running down his chin. He wheeled around to see where Detective Jack Crockford and the fire chief were. Now he knew why they had been called away.

Four firemen were walking down the blackened porch. They were carrying a large canvas bag. It was a body bag.

Keogh ran toward the bag. "No, please, God; no, please, God. I'll do anything, God. Please God, make it not true; please, God, make it not true."

Detective Crockford saw him. He headed him off in full run in almost a stand-up tackle. "No, Sean. God, no. Don't. There is nothing you can do, boy. Please don't look. Please."

Burke had caught up to him. Keogh had no strength to wrestle free of Crockford's grip. Keogh just felt his ankles sag and blood drain from his body. He half-turned and collapsed his head onto Burke's shoulder.

He was numb now. He couldn't feel his legs or his arms. He couldn't hear the cries of grief from Mrs. Wilson. He couldn't feel Bernie Mc-

Laughlin's hand on his shoulder, and he couldn't see Eddie Wilson, who had arrived with McLaughlin. He could not hear the words of Father Zeibatski. He raised his head from Burke's big shoulder, his blue eyes a mist of gray. He focused Burke's face and tried to speak. Nothing came. He tried again and his own voice sounded foreign, as if someone else were talking.

"She . . . she . . . never raised her voice in anger to a single human being. She . . . was a saint, Frankie . . . you know that, Frankie?"

Burke couldn't speak. His eyes were rimmed in tears. He fought to control his emotions. It would make matters worse if he cracked. But he couldn't stand to see Keogh in such pain. He just hugged him to his chest. Teresa was there by now, silent and wiping tears from her eyes. Keogh couldn't feel his legs move as they led him toward McLaughlin's car. He sat in the back seat in a stupor, deaf to the two-way radios and the noise of activity outside. All he could see was the flashing red light of the ambulance as it slid quietly away with the body of Molly Keogh inside. He could hear nothing. He couldn't hear Detective Crockford say to McLaughlin, "We're bringin' in the arson boys on this one. A couple of kids playing down the street said somethin' about a car takin' off from the area in a hurry and the fire happening seconds after the car took off. Don't know what to make of it, Bernie, but I'm gettin' in the arson boys."

Bernie McLaughlin nodded his head. Frank Burke had heard. They didn't need any pictures drawn for them.

THE DOCTOR had given Keogh two shots. The first one had only made him groggy. The second one finally succeeded in knocking him out. He now lay quietly in Frank Burke's big double bed in his new house in Carson Beach. Teresa made tea for McLaughlin, Wilson and her husband. She was silent, and her eyes were red-rimmed.

Burke spoke when his wife left the room: "Well, what do we do?"

McLaughlin sipped his tea quietly. "We have to leave that to Sean, Frankie. Let's wait."

"Wait?" Burke said impatiently. "We waited before, and now look what happened. I say act now, Mr. Mac."

"No, wait. He'll have more protection than Fort Knox right now, lad. Wait, and then you talk to Sean. Wait . . . and be bloody careful, son."

Frank Burke sipped his tea and fell silent as Teresa came into the room.

WITH SEAN Keogh, everything in Southie was the best and the biggest, even when it came to tragedy. So it was with the funeral. There was standing room only for the High Mass at Sacred Heart. Southie came in strength to tell the world how much Molly Kathleen Keogh had been loved as a robust, jolly woman who had the smile of a child and the wisdom of many elders.

The flowers covered O'Connell's Funeral Home, the church and the graveside. The tragedy of the moment was somehow relieved by the upbeat eulogy of Father Zeibatski, who ended it with a simple statement: "Let us not mourn her passing as much as we should celebrate she was with us for such a generous time, given to us by God to show us a life of simplicity, sacrifice and pure old-fashioned joy of sharing. Molly Kathleen Keogh is at last reunited with her beloved Joseph and will wait for us with happiness in her heart in heaven as she did here on earth."

To the priest's right, the beautifully made simple coffin held the charred remains of Molly Keogh. Mrs. Wilson sobbed softly. Detective Jack Crockford fought back tears, as did Bernie McLaughlin, Eddie and Frank Burke. Only Sean Keogh remained dry-eyed, staring straight ahead, oblivious to any emotion. Teresa Burke stood next to him, and she told her husband later, "It was like being next to an unexploded bomb. I could almost hear his heart beating through his chest."

At the graveside at St. Augustine Cemetery, on Dorchester Avenue at Seventh Street, Sean Keogh threw a single red carnation, which fell lightly onto the coffin in the deep grave.

"Bye, Ma," he said almost inaudibly. And he stood there for a long time until Frank Burke gently touched his elbow and shepherded him through the crowd.

As the mourners dispersed, Rose Sweeney, dressed in a simple black dress with a charcoal shawl, approached Sean Keogh. Behind her were her father, Pat Sweeney, and brother, Billy Sweeney.

"Mr. Keogh?"

Absently he turned and looked into her eyes. "Yes?"

"I'm Rose Sweeney."

He looked at her and said softly, "Yes, Rose, I know you. Please call me Sean."

"Sean," she said uncertainly, and held out her hand. "I just wanted to say that my mother knew your mother very well . . ." She looked as if she were about to say something else, but simply shook his hand. She too had lost her mother, Sean thought. She has understanding. Pat Sweeney and Billy shook Sean's hand firmly. Eddie Wilson led the Sweeney family to a waiting car. Sean's eyes followed her until she disappeared inside the car.

"Sean?" Frankie Burke called. "Come on back to the house. Have something to eat and hit the sack. The doctor gave us something so ya can sleep okay."

"Good idea, lad," Bernie McLaughlin said. Father Zeibatski stood silently at McLaughlin's side.

Keogh looked evenly at Frank Burke. "No, thanks, Frank. Think I'll take a drive and clear the cobwebs out of my head. It's a nice day. Think I'll just get a bit of air, if you don't mind."

"As ya wish, Sean boy." Burke looked anxiously at McLaughlin. Christ, I hope he ain't thinkin' anything crazy, Burke thought.

"Mr. Mac," Sean said to Bernie McLaughlin, "mind if I borrow your car?"

"Go ahead, son," McLaughlin replied, fumbling nervously for the car keys. He was thinking almost identical thoughts. Sean took the keys and quietly got into McLaughlin's car and drove off. Burke looked at McLaughlin again. His expression tipped off what he was thinking.

Father Zeibatski caught it. His tone was flat and reassuring. "Don't worry, gentlemen. He's okay." The group broke up and went to Frank Burke's house for tea.

THAT DAY Sean Keogh rode through Boston and all the way down to Narragansett through the warm August day. He parked on the beach and watched the young crowd cavort on the white sands. He had never been that young, and yet the beach parties were made of people his own age. He drove back to Boston and then over to Cambridge, where the tweedy young hung out in bars and talked and made dates and sang songs and drank beer. He had never been that young either.

He went to Kearney's Pub in Cambridge, where a lot of the Harvard crowd hung out. I wonder if Eddie Wilson ever goes to these places, he thought. Probably not. Too busy for fun. Eddie was never young, nor was Frankie Burke. I wonder if Mr. Mac was ever young. Or Father Zeibatski? No, they had eyes that said they had never been young. Do I have eyes like those men? Probably. I wonder if Rose Sweeney was ever young. Probably not.

He ordered a beer. It felt good to be in a place where nobody knew him, where nobody knew of his grief and his cancerous rage.

When a bright young blonde plunked herself down beside him at the bar and unashamedly struck up a conversation, he did nothing to discourage her. He bought her a beer. Then he bought himself another and her another, and then he kept on doing it until one in the morning. And when she showed she was interested in him, he didn't fight that either. They walked to the car and drove across to Boston.

"I have roommates," she said. And Sean Keogh simply drove to the Copley Plaza Hotel on Copley Square and booked in with her.

Sean Keogh was not totally inexperienced with women. But he neither got close to them nor did he use them simply for sex. That night he emptied himself of the blackness inside him, and in the morning when he woke next to the young preppie, he felt good.

When she got up to leave, she scribbled down her name and telephone number. She laughed with a touch of embarrassment as she realized Keogh didn't remember her name. He had been too drunk, although that had made no difference in his lovemaking. She remembered that. She kissed him on the cheek and made him promise to call her. He promised, but he knew he would not. I wonder what it would have been like if Rose Sweeney had been sharing the bed.

He had breakfast and decided to stay in town that day and maybe hit another young bar that night. He didn't have much time. And besides, it was nice being around people whose eyes were young.

The next day the young man, who was growing old before his time, took a small room in a neighbor's house at 27 McDonough Street.

He was lonely, but he was ambitious. The room would be too small for his fortunes.

IN THE rear right-hand booth at the Club 38 on Clinton Street in the North End of Boston, Paddy Devlin sat hunched over a table. Next to him was Jenny Bryant, her arm linked in his. Opposite him sat two burly young men in sport shirts. A third sat nearby at the bar, and a fourth sat with some friends in an adjacent booth. Devlin fidgeted nervously with an empty wineglass.

"Another glass of wine, Paddy," one of the husky men asked.

"Nah, nah, give us a beer and a shot of Jameson's."

"No Jameson's, Paddy. How about a Jack Daniel's?"

"Yeah, yeah, that will do."

He gulped the beer thirstily and threw down the Jack Daniel's in a single gulp. The fire made him feel better.

"Another, thanks, Gino." It was brought to his table. He glanced nervously at his watch. "He should be here by now."

"He's never late," the one called Gino said softly.

As he spoke, a small man, perhaps five feet four inches tall, walked into the bar. He was wearing a dark gray suit and a narrow-brimmed gray hat. The hat was turned up all the way around. He wore a dark maroon tie and he had a white handkerchief in his breast pocket. His shoes were shined to perfection.

There was movement in the bar as several men stood up to greet him, nodding their heads slightly and shaking hands. He smiled, waved to the bartender. He made his way toward Devlin, and the two men sitting with Devlin in the booth stood up to make way for him. He stood for a second at Devlin's booth, took off his hat and handed it to one of the husky young men. As he did, an espresso coffee was delivered at the table with a twist of lemon, and a small shot of Sambuca was set down next to the coffee.

Devlin half-rose and said, "Nice to see ya, Mr. Castellano." Frank Castellano, the don of dons, shook hands sparingly with Devlin. He smiled and nodded. "And you too, Mr. Devlin." He looked inquiringly at Jenny Bryant.

"Oh, this is Jenny, Mr. Castellano."

"Nice to meet you, Miss Jenny," he said, quietly extending his hand. Devlin noticed that his fingernails were manicured. Frank Castellano remained standing.

The man they called Gino caught Devlin's attention and glanced at Jenny. Devlin understood. Frank Castellano never talked business in front of a woman.

"Oh, Jenny, run along, will ya kid? Go upstairs. I'll catch ya later."

She looked curiously at Devlin, but obeyed. Castellano, the man who many said ran Tammany Hall in New York and even perhaps the State Capitol in Albany itself, then sat down.

Castellano came through New England once a month to oversee his interests. He would go to Providence, Rhode Island, to see his old friend Raimondo "Sox" Guccilli, to the Berkshire Downs Race Track and to the North End, where he had many relatives.

He was a quiet man of simple tastes, married happily, with two sons. His quiet life-style did nothing to betray his all-embracing, awesome power. He had been there on 118th Street in East Harlem in New York in "the old days." He had forged ties with the Segal-Lansky mob and bought peace to New York. He talked with well-measured tones in a throaty croak which signaled that like many Italian children of those early years, he had had his tonsils taken out at too early an age.

He sipped quietly on his espresso, waiting for Devlin to speak.

"How goes it with ya, Mr. Castellano?" Devlin started lamely.

"Well, very well," he said with a slight smile in a softly accented voice. "And you, Mr. Devlin?" He looked over the rim of the espresso cup.

"Ahh, you know, can't complain . . . we've got business goin' pretty well here."

"So I hear. You have quite a talent. And I'm very grateful for the way you've brought a measure of prosperity to some of my friends. I'm grateful."

Devlin fidgeted some more and ordered another drink. He guzzled it quickly, as if he were trying to get Castellano to say something first. He did.

"You seemed anxious to see me, Mr. Devlin."

"Well, er, yeah. . . ." He paused, then jumped in with both feet. "Look, Mr. Castellano, ask anyone around here. I've been good for this area. Real good, see."

"I have already said I am grateful." He didn't take his eyes off Devlin's eyes.

"Well, see, I'm askin' a favor."

"If it can be done within reason."

"Well, look, ya heard about the trouble."

"I am aware you have some problems." He emphasized the word "you."

"Look, Mr. Castellano. That guy in Southie. Keogh . . . the little prick."

Castellano frowned at the mouthing of an obscenity. Devlin caught his reaction.

"Well, now, this guy Keogh has hurt me, Mr. Castellano. He took bread from my table, and now he's out to kill me and maybe cause trouble in this area."

"Can you blame him for wanting to kill you, Mr. Devlin?"

"Mr. Castellano, you know that was a mistake. It was all planned. That Molly Keogh was never home on a Monday night. I knew her movements. I mean she was never home, ever. It was an accident. I quite liked the old woman."

"Yet you still firebombed the house."

"It was just to scare Keogh. That's all. My beef was with him and not his old lady. I swear it."

"I believe you, Mr. Devlin." Castellano had hardly raised his voice above a whisper.

"Now I need some help. If I don't hit him, he's gonna hit me. Hit here. I want the help of some of your boys, Mr. Castellano. But they say I have to ask ya first."

"Mr. Devlin, all men have their own minds. I tell nobody what to do. Sometimes, because of my years, I'm asked for advice. Sometimes I give it. But I order no man."

"Well, ya wouldn't mind if I got a few o' yer boys an' got Keogh?"

"If I am asked my advice, I will advise against it."

"But Mr. Castellano, I've been good to your men. Look at the money."

"I am aware, Mr. Devlin. But I and my people have no fight with the Irishers of South Boston. You are an Irisher and you are fighting with these Irishers. If the Irishers don't bother us, why should we bother the

Irishers? There are as many honorable men there as there are here. I would advise against any trouble with the Irishers."

Devlin attempted to speak, but Castellano cut him off by simply raising a finger an inch. He sipped again at his espresso and drank down his Sambuca.

"Mr. Devlin, you have bought money to this area. I am in your debt. You will have the protection of this area. Upstairs, above here, the apartment has steel window flaps. You will have the use of my men for protection as long as you need it. But only as protection. I will advise any of them against going into South Boston for any reason, and unless they are harmed in any way I will advise against any of them going against any Irisher. This is your personal matter, Mr. Devlin. Please accept the offer of protection. But I insist, only protection."

"But this little bum is gonna kill me, gonna hurt your people."

"Not my people, Mr. Devlin; not my people." He smiled, shook hands. Gino handed him his hat.

"The car is outside, Mr. Castellano. See you next month, sir?"

"Hopefully. *Buona fortuna,*" he said.

Frank Castellano slowly walked to the door, waved to the young men inside and slipped away in a large black limousine.

Devlin called for another drink. He was nervous and sweating. Gino sat down next to him. "No good, huh?"

"Na, na. I shoulda shot that prick Keogh when I had the chance."

"Don't worry, Paddy, you're safe here. He's given you six men whenever you move outside of this place. They're six stand-up guys."

"They better be."

He went upstairs to the virtual fortress that served as his apartment. That night he was in no mood for Jenny Bryant and her gunplay. He lay there on the bed and perspired.

SEAN KEOGH stayed at the Copley Plaza for two days, eating well and drinking well. And yet he would soon travel back to Southie, only three miles away, and be in another world. He checked out of the hotel and was soon pulling up outside the Francis X. Burke Trucking Company.

He walked in, and Frank was on the telephone in earnest conversation. Burke looked up. His face spelled relief. "Don't worry, Mr. Mac," he said into the telephone. "he's just walked in. I'll call ya back." He put down the receiver. "Christ almighty, Sean, where in the hell ya been? We've been going' nuts. We've had our cops checkin' the hospitals. Everything. Where ya been?"

"Just took a bit of time off, Frank. That's all."

"Damn it, Sean, you coulda called us and told us where ya was."

"Sorry, Frank. Really. Just needed to be alone for a while. You're right, of course. I should have called."

"Sean, ya know it's dangerous. Ya know Devlin ain't gonna rest now. He ain't gonna rest."

"Neither am I," Sean said quietly. Burke seemed to be relieved to hear that. Good, Sean wants Devlin and we're gonna hand him to him on a platter.

"Our cops over in the North End tell us he's holed up in a goddamn fortress. He's runnin' whores over there, and he's makin' good money over there. He's got six pistoleros whenever he goes out. Like a damned armed guard. It's gonna be tough."

"Well, we'll think about it, won't we?"

"We could send some cowboys over there. He sits in the back booth of the Thirty-eight Club every night. If we couldn't get close enough to him in the street, we could get the cowboys just to go in. One hand grenade. Boom, we'd get him."

"No, no, Frank. Not like that. I only want Devlin. I don't want to harm anyone else. I don't want innocent people hurt. Molly Keogh was innocent. I don't want that."

Burke nodded. "Yeah, an' if we start shootin' up those Guineas they'll come over here in truckloads. I guess yer right. But even if we hit him clean, they still might go to war."

"Don't think so, Frank. We have no fight with them. They mind their own business. Devlin is making money for them, fine. They'll stick to him like glue, but they know this is our beef. They'll keep out."

"Probably right. They ain't bad, some of those Guineas. Met a few of 'em in my time down on the docks. They're not bad people."

"No, Frank, we have to think. That's what we're good at and what Devlin is bad at. And I want the bastard, Frank. Want him bad."

Burke rarely heard Sean use a swearword. He knew his friend was suffering, and he didn't like to see Sean hurt. He would stop all that. He didn't know how, and he didn't want Sean involved. But he would stop it. He promised himself.

"How about a quick drink?"

"Fine. I have a bit of a hangover, as a matter of fact. I'm getting as bad as you are, Frank."

Burke looked at him with amusement. Sean Keogh with a hangover. Well.

Frank Burke locked up the office. He looked hard at Sean Keogh, this young man of twenty-three. Burke, a man of thirty, felt a pang as he looked at the total expression of loss on Sean's face.

"You all right, boy?"

"Guess so, Frank. I just get that terrible feeling deep inside me. I want to put my hands around Devlin's throat and keep squeezing until my fingers meet. I want to *see* him die, Frank."

"Sean, if the positions was reversed I would feel the same way, pal. But you would be tellin' me what I'm tellin' you. Don't get mad; just get even by any way possible. You can't be involved."

"It's just that every second he is living, I feel he is sucking the air out of my lungs. He doesn't have the right to breathe the same air as you and me, Frank. God forgive me, but he doesn't have the right."

"Let's skip it right now. C'mon, let's try and get rid of that damn hangover." He grabbed him around the shoulder with a hug. "Sean Keogh with a hangover. Jesus, ya should be ashamed of yerself. Shame." He chuckled.

They went next door and Sean cheered up. "Better start thinking about work now, Frank. I got to start going over Mr. Mac's books. Don't like to let him down."

Burke seemed distracted.

"Frank, you're not listening."

"Uh? Sorry, pal. No, I wasn't listenin'. Just remembered a half a dozen calls I had to make which I forgot all about. Listen, I better go back and finish off. See ya tomorrow?"

"Well, I thought maybe you, me and Eddie could meet downtown for lunch. Maybe at the Ritz Carlton."

Frank Burke smiled and whistled. "Goin' high class, huh?"

"I just thought for once we might get together and have a lunch that didn't consist of a corned-beef sandwich and a beer. That's all."

"Look, I'll skip it. Give Eddie a call and I'll catch ya later tomorrow."

"As you say, Frank. See you, old pal . . . and thanks for your concern."

"Nothing to it."

Burke left and dashed back to his office. He had some important business to set into motion.

THE NEXT day Sean Keogh arrived at the dining room in the Ritz Carlton Hotel, which is situated on the Boston Common. The Ritz is one of the truly superb hotels left in the Northeast. Its dining room had outlived bistros, specialty restaurants, exotic restaurants. The Ritz had always been just plain good in Boston.

Keogh sat at a corner table. Minutes later Eddie Wilson came through the door. Glancing around, he saw Sean in the corner. He weaved through the tables.

Keogh needed, for the first time in his life, to be among people. Every time he was alone, he could think only of the canvas bag being carried through the smoke into an ambulance. And every time he thought of that, his throat hardened and he could see Devlin's face.

Eddie smiled as he sat down. "We're going up in the world, huh?"

"Then we're going up together," Keogh said with a chuckle, as he noticed that Wilson was wearing an almost identical suit.

Angelo, the maître d', approached. He had seen Keogh dine here only once before, but he gave him a familiar nod. The young man had a certain presence, and Angelo's forte was as much noticing when a man was on his way up as noticing when he had arrived.

Sean ordered a Scotch and water; Wilson ordered a martini.

"How's it going, Sean?"

"Well, Eddie, it's early days, so it's pretty tough. But I'm trying to keep busy and keep from feeling sorry for myself. Not easy."

Wilson looked around the room by way of changing the subject. "There's Sheldon Mathers," he said, indicating a large group of distinguished-looking gentlemen at a round table in the middle of the room.

"Who is Sheldon Mathers when he answers the door?" Sean asked.

Wilson lowered his voice. "Sheldon Mathers of Brookline, Newport and Palm Beach, adviser to Joe Kennedy, friend of Cabot Lodge, blue-blood and publisher of the *Boston Clarion,* the conscience of New England."

"Oh, yes—Mathers. The *Clarion*—didn't that rag give Mr. Mac a hard time a couple of years ago, making all kinds of allegations?"

"Well, it was after the Rooney thing." Wilson talked almost in a whisper.

"Now I know who Sheldon Mathers is. He probably doesn't realize he is dining in the same room as Eddie Wilson and Sean Keogh, but one day he will."

They both chuckled and felt pleased with themselves, dressed to the nines and ordering filet of sole stuffed with crab meat. It was good sometimes to leave Southie for the other world.

Keogh looked over at Mathers. The world at his feet, Keogh thought. Mathers, a man with a shock of white hair, impeccable speaking voice, elegantly tailored, was Sean's idea of how a man should look when he reaches the half-century mark. Young Sean liked him, just by his appearance. He had a warm dignity about him.

The food arrived, and Sean ordered a bottle of wine.

As KEOGH and Wilson enjoyed the luxury of the Ritz, Frankie Burke in his shirt sleeves ate a corned-beef sandwich and drank a bottle of beer between urgent telephone calls.

He was talking to Los Angeles. "Okay, Lou. . . . Look, I don't pay for these telephone calls to talk about old times . . . as much as I think yer a great guy. All I want is to know if ya can get him. If ya can, I can book him two weeks here at top dollar, then two weeks in New York at the Copa and then on down to Miami. Okay? Call me back."

He leaned back in his old swivel chair. He gulped the beer from the bottle and thought, It just might work.

PADDY DEVLIN had not forsaken the idea of killing Sean Keogh. But the word from Old Man Castellano was final. He knew better than to tempt anyone in the North End with money for the hit. If it got back to Castellano, he would lose his sanctuary, maybe his life. However, since the old man had given him the services of the six bodyguards, he felt better. It had been a month since the firebombing of the Keogh household, and with his human shield around him, he felt it safe to venture out.

He strutted down Clinton Avenue with his phalanx of muscle around him. He was a big man again, waving to the whores, most of whom he ran. Castellano wasn't keen on whores, but they brought in the gamblers. Business was business.

He would cruise the bars, buying drinks for his cronies, almost every night. Despite his newfound security, he regularly changed his schedule. He would not fall into a habit. That could prove fatal. He had been assured that no Italian would take a contract on him, not so long as Castellano was the boss of the northeastern seaboard. And no Irishman could move in the North End without a hundred eyes seeing him before he got within a hundred feet of Devlin.

But there were alien eyes watching Devlin, and he knew it. Several of the cops in the North End would be on McLaughlin's payroll. This didn't worry Devlin. They would only report the airtight security in which he operated. This would discourage even the boldest of Mc-Laughlin's men . . . and besides, as time went on Devlin was convinced that Keogh didn't really have the stomach to trigger a hit. Time would drag on and Keogh would get careless and that was when Devlin would make the move, even if he had to do it himself. The odds were all on Devlin's side—that was, if he wasn't accounting for Frank Burke.

Jenny Bryant had put together a formidable work force for her boyfriend—eight girls in all, from out of town. There were three or four others who free-lanced. But without the entrée to the clubs and bars, they soon drifted away.

"Business is good, Jenny. Ya know that, I should have come to the North End years ago. They have a real organization. Old McLaughlin is senile, and Keogh is a fairy. How the girls working out?"

"Two more girls from the South came in today," she said.

"Are they on the level?"

"Sure—they even paid a hundred up front to work the street. I've steered them to the bartenders and the games. They'll turn over thirty percent of their take. They can do well."

"They got old men?" he said, using the euphemism for pimps.

"Not so far. They're okay. We still have the free lancers. They come, they go."

"Don't worry about 'em. They ain't worth the hassle. If they don't want in, we'll starve 'em out. No sense in using muscle. They get the idea after a while that it's best to throw in with us. Makes more sense."

"There's one stuck-up bitch"—she nodded her head out the window of the 38 Club—"she's from New York. She doesn't even talk to the rest of the girls. Stuck-up bitch. But she's starvin.' So she'll move along."

Devlin peered out the window. She was a looker. Long ash-blond hair that hung across her right eye in a Veronica Lake effect. She was tall and had an almost perfect build. She stood propped up against an Eldorado convertible with a sable draped over her shoulder.

Devlin looked at her, then glanced at Jenny. "Hmmm—no wonder ya wanna get rid of her."

"Cut it out, Paddy. You lose me face with chippying around and I'll kill you."

He laughed. She smiled with embarrassment. It covered the jealousy.

"Can't I look?"

"You can look, but keep it that way. You fool around with someone else and these girls who I've recruited will think you're up for grabs. I won't have their respect."

"Don't be crazy. I wouldn't fuck up a good thing. Take it easy."

"All right, then." she snuggled close to Devlin. She could feel the bulge under his left shoulder.

He looked up the bar. The bodyguards responded. "C'mon, Jenny, let's hit a few joints and party."

"Good deal, Mr. Devlin." She was happy when she was near him.

Devlin wheeled into the street surrounded by his muscle. He looked across at the ash-blonde. She gave him a single glance of contempt and looked away. She wasn't impressed no matter who Paddy Devlin thought he was. Devlin hunched his shoulders. Who does that bitch think she is? I'll run her off the streets.

When Devlin returned from his pub crawl, he noticed the long-limbed blonde disappearing into her Eldorado with a prosperous-looking john.

He flashed an angry glance at Jenny Bryant. "So free lancers starve, huh? Make sure ya get her. It's a bad example."

Jenny Bryant felt unsettled by the arrival of the blonde. If she couldn't recruit her she would lose face with Devlin. Then Devlin would get her himself. And if he shacked up with her alone, Jenny would lose face with the rest of the girls. She would be a laughingstock for losing her old man to an out-of-towner. Jenny was relieved the next two nights when the blonde didn't appear.

But on the third night, there she was again, arrogantly slouched against her Eldorado and this time wearing a white mink to show the street she had more than one fur coat. Jenny Bryant seethed. Devlin caught her reaction, and he enjoyed her discomfort.

"Jenny, why don't ya catch a movie? One of the boys will take you."

Before she had time to protest, Gino was at her arm. She knew that Devlin was going to make a fool of her. She boiled inside.

When she left, he smiled at his remaining bodyguards. "Let's go party."

They trooped out the door. He caught the blonde's eye, gave her a smile and a big wave. She turned languorously toward him and gave him a look of contempt, although Devlin's conceit saw it as a mild come-on. He threw her another smile and started off down the road. So this one won't be easy, he thought. She'll come around or I'll bust her melon.

Devlin hit the bars that night with a passion. Castellano's bodyguards were the most efficient he had ever seen. Always three of them surrounding his body, while the rest stood facing in different directions. An army couldn't get through these guys, Devlin thought with some comfort.

"All right, let's head back to the Thirty-eight. What say we have a little party with the girls upstairs tonight? I'll pull the girls in." The bodyguards smiled their approval.

He lurched up Clinton Street toward the 38 Club. He could see the Eldorado a long way off. There she was, the stuck-up bitch. Gave me the cold shoulder.

The group crossed the street to the 38. Devlin looked at the blonde.

"Hey, bluenose, c'mon," he shouted across the road, "yer goin' to a party."

The blonde smiled but didn't move.

"I said yer goin' to a party . . . bitch."

The blonde turned her head away as if she hadn't heard Devlin's words. He lumbered out into the road. The smiles on the faces of the bodyguards turned to frowns as they saw Jenny Bryant pull up in a car from the movies.

"Paddy," she screamed in anger. "Sonofabitch. Yer not goin' to chippy on me." She ran from the car in black anger.

"Fuck off," he snarled over his shoulder as one of the bodyguards restrained her. "C'mon, blondie, do as yer told." He swaggered across the road, and the blonde smiled.

Devlin returned the smile. Suddenly his face froze.

He saw it, but it happened too quickly. He suddenly ground his heels into the roadway and started to backpedal, screaming, "Get her, get her!"

The pump gun came from under the white mink coat. The first blast exploded with a deafening roar. It hit Devlin on the left hip and spun him like a top before smashing him to the ground. "Get her, fer fuck's sake!" He had felt the hot blast hit him, but no pain.

The bodyguards went for their guns. The blonde fired the automatic pump gun over their heads. The concussion of the explosion was frightening, and they sprawled on the ground, tripping over one another and crawling for the cover of the bar.

The orders were simple. Nobody but Devlin. The contract had to be completed.

Quickly the blonde strode within three feet of Devlin and fired point-blank into his face. The coffin would have to be closed. Then another blast over the heads of the bodyguards and the blonde turned swiftly but without panic toward the car. The engine had been running. The pump gun was thrown into the back, and the car took off with a screech of tires. Devlin's demise had taken exactly eight seconds.

As the Eldorado swerved into Wilcox Street, a stunned streetful of people heard a loud animal-like wail as Jenny Bryant pulled herself free of one of the bodyguards. She rushed across the road and threw herself on what was left of Paddy Devlin. As the goon squad pulled her off the mess on the ground, Jenny Bryant reached inside Devlin's coat. She took his .45 revolver from its holster.

FRANK BURKE received the telephone call as he sat at the bar of the club with Sean Keogh. "Fer you, Frank," Dan McCauley yelled out over the noise of the bar.

"Thanks, Danny."

He walked to the end of the bar, reached over for the telephone, which was under the bar.

"Burke here." His face warmed. "Oh, thank you very much for calling. . . . Yes, it is all in order. Thank you once again."

William Thomas put down the receiver in the pay telephone booth at Logan. Ten thousand dollars had been placed in the First National City Bank in New York, where he would play the Copacabana for two weeks at two thousand dollars a week. Then he would go to Miami for another stint.

Willie was always easy to book. The nightclub circuit loved Legs Lolette, the most popular female impersonator in the country.

Burke retured to the bar.

"Sean, let's go downtown. Suddenly I have an appetite. How about Locke-Ober's for a big lobster? And champagne."

"Champagne? Frank Burke drink champagne?"

"Well, you do the ordering of that stuff, but I feel like a night out. Been workin' very hard."

"Okay, let's go. Dinner is on me."

"Since yer offerin', fine." He chuckled.

They jumped into a taxi and went across the bridge from Southie to Locke-Ober, one of Boston's oldest restaurants. Burke ordered the taxi to stop before the street where Locke-Ober was situated. He carelessly picked up a copy of the bulldog edition of the *Clarion*. He rolled it up and walked up the lane with Sean to the restaurant.

Once inside, Sean was surprised to see Bernie McLaughlin sitting at a white-clothed table in the corner, quietly drinking.

"Hey there, fellas." McLaughlin got to his feet, slowly pulling his huge bulk upright.

"Mr. Mac. Good to see you. Surprised to find you here."

Burke chose that moment to unfold the *Boston Clarion*.

"Well, well, it seems that Paddy Devlin lost his head over a girl."

Keogh looked at him questioningly as he sat down, and then his eye caught the second lead story on the front page of the *Clarion*.

HOODLUM BLASTED TO DEATH IN NORTH END

For a split second he could feel the same panic rising in his stomach as the day he had read the headline about Jimmy Rooney. He stared at it hard and his stomach knotted as he forced himself to think of the pathetic canvas bag and the closed coffin at Sacred Heart.

Burke and McLaughlin looked at each other, then at Keogh. Their faces were tense.

Suddenly Keogh smiled, and then he felt the same way as he had when he'd joined up with Bernie McLaughlin's organization. There was no going back. And he felt satisfaction and prayed to God to forgive him for his satisfaction.

"Well," he said slowly, "Devlin never did have much taste in women. . . . Lobster, gentlemen?"

Burke and McLaughlin exchanged relieved glances. "Yeah, I'm starved," McLaughlin rasped, "bloody starved."

Sean looked across at Burke. He gave him a friendly punch on the arm.

"You're solid, Frank. Solid. You too, Mr. Mac. You're both the best."

A huge platter of food arrived, and Sean Keogh wondered whether he would have the stomach to eat after having conspired in the death of another human being.

He took the first bite gingerly. Then he finished every bit of meat from his lobster. He then ordered two more bottles of champagne. He had tested the water and he felt no guilt. And he didn't care.

"Ya know, Sean boy, I been thinkin'!"

"Yes, Mr. Mac. About what?"

"Well, I'm gettin' a bit old, and since you and Frankie have been workin' things out together, I've been makin' good money."

"That's what it's all about," Keogh said with a sip of champagne. He felt good. He felt free. Devlin was no longer sucking the air out of his lungs.

"Well, I've been kinda thinkin' o' takin' a bit of a rest, ye know?"

"You're as healthy as a horse, Mr. Mac. You don't want to rest."

"Na, nah. So I been thinkin' o' handin' things over to you and Frankie. An' soon ye'll all have Eddie Wilson and his million-dollar brains. Ye could do pretty good. Throw me a bone once in a while to keep me busy, but that's what I was thinkin'."

Keogh fell silent. Burke looked a little stunned.

"Well, ain't you bums even gonna say thanks?"

"Mr. Mac . . . I . . . I mean we . . . we ain't even thought of . . ." Burke was stammering. McLaughlin's organization was worth a fortune. Burke looked across to Sean for help.

"Well, say somethin', Sean. . . . What do want him to say? He's gonna make ya President."

They all laughed. Keogh laughed hard, but he was thinking seriously. Maybe not President . . . just yet. But certainly an assemblyman. *I wonder what Rose Sweeney would think of Massachusetts State Assemblyman.*

That night everyone got very drunk, and the next morning Sean Keogh saw Father Zeibatski and gave him a brown envelope.

"For the woman and child," he said.

The priest nodded his head. He looked hard at the young man before him. He had read the papers about Devlin. The priest remained silent a long time. Sean Keogh smiled and said goodbye.

The priest rustled from the church to his private headquarters. Scan Keogh had changed since that day in the confessional after Jimmy Rooney had died.

Chapter

5

SEAN KEOGH had asked for them all to meet at 10 A.M. at Frank Burke's office. Bernie McLaughlin sat in an old swivel chair opposite Burke's desk. It had been one week since McLaughlin in a few words over dinner at Locke-Ober had conferred his entire operation on Keogh and Burke. McLaughlin's "operation" had always made him good money from the very day he'd stepped off the ship from Ireland. But Keogh's expertise, efficiency and creative thinking had turned the operation into a slick and booming corporation.

From the very moment he had handed it over to the two young men, he had felt a massive sense of relief. No longer did he have to play the role of the tough, bluff racketeer. Suddenly he had become an elder statesman, a patriarch to a band of sometimes wild but always ambitious young men. He enjoyed the new role as patriarch, and he even allowed Keogh—under grumbling protest—to talk him into going downtown and replacing his old beer-stained tweed suit with a wardrobe more befitting his role as the wise old man of Boston. Clearly he reveled in the attention the young men lavished on him. They made him feel old, but better, as if he had suddenly enlarged his already formidable family.

He sat there content, smoking a foul-smelling cigar. Next, he thought, as he watched young Keogh walk into the room, they'll be making me buy fifty-cent cigars.

Eddie Wilson leaned against the water cooler, looking as cool as the contents, snappily dressed like an attorney of record. Burke sat in his swivel chair behind his desk, with his big feet resting on an upturned wastepaper basket.

"Ahh, here is the young genius now," McLaughlin said with a grin.

"Gents, how goes it?" Keogh said. He looked around the room like an officer surveying a commando platoon before they went off on a dangerous mission. He liked what he saw.

"I won't beat around the bush," he said, then took a breath. "Frank, it's all your fault."

Burke smiled. "What have I done now?"

"The other night at Locke-Ober's. Frank said the word 'President.' I've been thinking."

"The bloody change will do ye good," McLaughlin said good-naturedly. "Now, whatcha been thinkin'? "

"In a word, men—politics."

"Here we go," Burke said in a voice that suggested he wasn't surprised.

"Yes, politics. Simply that I've decided to run for office . . . assemblyman from the Forty-fourth District. Here in Southie."

"It's been staring us in the face. We have the money, we have the men, we have the ideas. But for crying out loud, the people trust us and like us. Look at you, Mr. Mac—you have given as much money to community and church groups over the last four years as all the charities and government agencies combined. All our faces are known on virtually every street corner, in every candy store, every barbershop, every saloon. There are little kids who tell their dads that big Mr. Mac is the nicest man in Southie."

How could they argue? Keogh was right: the whole opportunity had been staring them in the face for years.

"Look at the Irish political machines here and in New York. Most of them were street guys. Look at Honey Fitz from the old days, became Mayor of Boston out of a saloon. Even the Kennedys knew how to use their street guys."

Bernie McLaughlin nodded thoughtfully.

Keogh went on: "Look at Frank Castellano down in New York. He runs Tammany Hall. All through politics. He had his day when he was a head buster. But he grew up . . . no offense, gents." He smiled.

McLaughlin and Burke chuckled. Eddie Wilson was deep in thought. There was a long silence.

"It costs money, ye know?" McLaughlin said.

"We have money," Keogh countered.

McLaughlin sighed and then said, "But, I gotta hand it to ye—I can't see anything really wrong with the idea . . . that's if ye wanna be a politician.

"It's a bit more than that, Mr. Mac. I really don't know what it is . . . but . . . come on, let's all admit, don't we all want to put Southie on the map? Isn't it about time we had a say in things?"

Frank Burke frowned. "Sean, we do. We run our own lives over here. Always have. No outsiders tell us what to do."

"That's it, Frank. We're a little island outside one of the most powerful cities in the country. What does Southie have to do with the rest of the world? Nothing. Nobody knows we're here. Everybody thinks we're a bunch of wild, boozing Irishmen who are best left alone because we don't understand the outside world."

"I see yer point, lad," McLaughlin said wistuflly. "There was a time in Dublin many years ago when I felt the same way . . . not that it changed a helluva lot of things."

"What do you say, gents? said Keogh. "Shall we give it a try?"

"It wouldn't be too hard, ye know, fellas," McLaughlin said. "Now, we all know old Joe Kane. He's been the Assemblyman for twelve years. Lazy old sod, but a nice old guy. A few bucks in his pocket and a word to the wise, he'd step down and you could step right into the seat. He's got plenty of money, and the Assemblyman's pay means nothing to him —makes a fortune outa his law practice. I've done the old bastard a few favors. I think he'd probably do it for a few bucks."

Sean smiled. "But he's a Democrat."

"Of course he's a bloody Democrat."

"But I'm going to run as a Republican."

McLaughlin's chin visibly dropped a half inch. Frank Burke swung his feet off the upturned wastepaper basket, and there was a giant question mark invisibly drawn across Eddie Wilson's face.

"Yer out yer mind. Ye've gone daft. Stark, raving, fuckin' bonkers." McLaughlin was incredulous. "Son, I've never even seen a Republican in Southie. Not one. There hasn't even been a Republican candidate walk into Southie. Yer a candidate fer nice green rollin' lawns with a pretty nurse wheelin' ye about."

Burke narrowed his eyes in disbelief. "Sean, are ya sober?"

Wilson chimed in: "I must say, it's a bit bizarre."

Keogh reveled in their shock. He chuckled. "All right, all right. Now just hear me out before you throw a straitjacket over me. I'll shut up after this if you just hear me out."

They all nodded without enthusiasm.

"Walking into an Assemblyman's seat vacated by an old, lazy rich guy . . . now, what do you think that will do? The voters will just say to themselves, 'Oh, well, young Keogh has walked into something nice. It's good to have another Southie lad looking after our interests.' But old Joe Kane has done nothing for Southie. And the people don't expect him to. And they wouldn't expect me to do anything for them either. Southie has been used to having nothing done for them, just as long as they are let alone. But damn it, Southie deserves better. They deserve something legit; they deserve somebody legit."

"Now, don't start preachin' about being legit, Sean boy," McLaughlin said.

"I'm serious, Mr. Mac. If the voters think I'm just being rubber-stamped into the job, that's not real support. They won't even know what they're voting for . . . it will be just Young Keogh has been handed the office and we all like him. But what would be accomplished by that?"

"Okay," Burke interrupted as he put his hand up. "No argument there, Sean. But why Republican? Why run as a Republican? That's like running on a Protestant platform in Dublin, ferchrissake."

"Frank, let me tell you. There will be a day, not too far off, when your entire Teamsters' Union will put every man behind a Republican President. Why? I'll tell you why. The days are over when a bunch of fancy-pants snobs put Irishmen into the mines and onto the docks and onto the railroads for starvation wages. The days are over when Irishmen riot against the slave boss. Those days are long gone. We aren't the underdogs anymore. We have as much power in the unions as those bank-president bastards in wood-paneled offices downtown. They know it. The bank and company presidents know it . . . but we don't know it. We haven't realized it yet. We have not realized that organized labor is as big, powerful and rich as the damn Bank of America. Jimmy Hoffa knows it, but not many other people do.

"Here in Southie, we seem to like being underdogs. It gives us a good rebel feeling. But that thinking is fifty years old. The workingman in organized labor is as much out to make a buck as big business. Big business and big labor are the same thing. The party that big business flourishes under is the Republican Party, a party that doesn't set up a whole lot of government guidelines and restrictive laws. They want to make a buck. So do we. Look, the people on Beacon Hill, okay, they've got brains. But we in Southie have acted as if all we're good enough for is to drive trucks, become a cop, haul loads on the docks. We've got brains as much as they do on Beacon Hill, but we have this damned complex. Any man in Southie would bust a guy's head if he said he was better than any man in Southie. They would take your Harvard apart piece by piece if a Harvard man said he was better than a Southie man. But the thing is, deep, deep down, we act as if they are better. And they're not. Is it carved somewhere in stone that my son has to be a dockwalloper? Is it carved somewhere in stone that your son has to be a truck driver? Look at Eddie here. He's a prime example. He's showing those Harvard men what brains and wits are all about. Look at Joe Kennedy—he knew what he wanted."

"Yeah, but he's a Democrat," Burke said glumly.

"Sure, because he was in another time when to get an Irish vote you had to tell the Irish that Beacon Hill was full of Redcoats and we always fought the Redcoats. Those days are over. The Kennedys, they're not Irish Democrats. When did any of the Kennedy boys do a day's work?"

McLaughlin protested. "But we could do all this behind a Democratic ticket with no hassle."

"Yeah, Mr. Mac, but I wouldn't believe it. It's about time Southie and Beacon Hill got a bit closer. It's about time they realized and we realized what we are really worth. Southie deserves better."

Keogh knew he was beating them over the heads with bricks, but appealing to their innate belief in their self-worth was working.

"Now, look at you, Mr. Mac. How would you describe what you do?"

"They don't list our occupations in the yellow pages, son." They all laughed.

Sean Keogh smiled. "Well, Mr. Mac, you're one of the best examples of a Republican businessman I know. You're independent. You've never taken a handout from anybody, never had sick pay, vacation pay, unemployment or welfare. You just built your business and asked nothing from anybody. You're fair, tough and honest—yes, honest. Look, twenty years from now numbers, bookmaking, crap games, that's all going to be legal, and the guys who run these legitimate numbers and bookmaking and crap games will be known as gaming businessmen. They'll come from the big colleges—educated lawyers and accountants. And they'll work for state governments and even the Federal government. You're as much a businessman as the guy who runs a railroad. You're so legit you even pay your taxes to Uncle Sam, even if you might bend the truth about how you get your money."

Keogh caught the thoughtful look in McLaughlin's eyes. There was some pride in those eyes too.

"You, Frank. You get one truck; you go to the bank, get a loan, buy another truck, then another. You run for secretary of Local 109 so you will have a say in how your investment will be run. Business. That's business. You're not rioting anymore against the big bosses. It's the big bosses who need you, and they pay high for your work and your knowledge."

Burke looked a little stunned. He had never thought of himself that way. "And you, Eddie—you best of all. You wanted to learn. You wanted to be a part of the system. So you worked hard, studied hard. And if you had a helping hand, you never let anyone down. You didn't crap out on your investors. You made your investors believe in you more. . . . Look at you all—upwardly mobile parts of the system. There is a thinking here in Southie that we live on the other side of the tracks. But we're no slum. The houses are clean, the kids are clean. The men work and work hard. We just deserve better. Let's get a bit of what the blue-bloods are getting. We don't have to take it."

Sean Keogh's monologue had been slightly unsettling to the gathering. They couldn't argue with him.

Then Mac said quickly, as if to get it over with: "I think I'm goin' soft in the head because of me age. But I'm fer ye, son."

Burke chuckled. "Some of my men will think I've gone nuts, but okay."

Wilson was skeptical: "Hope you know what you're doing, Sean."

"I do."

McLaughlin chuckled. "Well, in fer a shillin', in fer a pound. One is in, that means all of us in. And may God have mercy on our miserable souls. As they say in court, 'Case closed.' "

Sean Keogh gave them all a tight grin.

"Now let's get moving. Frank. You have a back storeroom. Behind is a garage. The storeroom will be the headquarters. I'll rent the garage. That will be for party workers. Frank, use your muscle, old pal. I want you to get some of the Teamsters—make sure they're from Southie—working on the campaign—you know, handing out printed matter and that sort of stuff. Give them the same speech I gave you. But get them. Mr. Mac, if I may presume, I would like you to get some of your dock-wallopers. Good big, strong guys with a good union record. Shows that we aren't turning our backs on our origins. You, Eddie, get some of your preppy friends; we'll need all the bodies we can get, just passing out the message. Make sure they don't wear their Newport clothes into Southie, and school them how to behave when they're here. You know what I'm talking about."

Eddie Wilson looked a little uneasy, but he nodded his head.

Keogh was talking like a machine gun now: "Now I have to see the Republican Committee downtown."

"Why?" said Burke.

"Well, I have to tell them I'm running for them."

Burke looked amazed. "Ya mean yer goin' to a party and ya ain't been invited?"

"Something like that."

"But they may tell ya to go piss in yer shoe."

"Doubt it."

"Ye amaze me, Sean—bloody well amaze me," McLaughlin said with a smile.

"Me too," Wilson said glumly.

"C'mon," Keogh said, almost shouting, "we're on our way."

"To bloody oblivion," McLaughlin countered good-naturedly. "Just one thing, Sean. Yer almost twenty-four now. I could be wrong. But if I know my Keogh, ye haven't even voted before—now, have ye? Out with it. Have ye?"

"Mere detail, Mr. Mac, I'll look after that. Mere detail."

"Jesus be to God, he is runnin' for public office and the young spalpeen hasn't even voted. Sean, you have more fastballs than a World Series."

AT PRECISELY 1 P.M. the next day, Sean Keogh walked through the modest doors of the Boston Republican Club, which was situated on the Boston Common. It had a good address, but it looked as if it had been set up with an eye to economy—not so much for lack of money as for lack of support. There was one large room where there were a stencil copying machine, an attendant, one secretary. At the end of the room, at a larger desk, was a woman in her mid forties who appeared to be in charge. Behind her was a plywood partition. Sean Keogh looked the place over in a single glance. He guessed correctly that behind that partition sat Roger Sharpe, the Secretary of the Boston Republican Club.

He was impeccably dressed in a charcoal-gray worsted suit. His wavy black hair was shining clean, and a faint odor of after-shave lotion followed him around wherever he walked. He smiled to himself.

"Hello there," he said cheerily to the woman behind the big desk. She smiled a perfunctory smile. "What can I do for you, sir?"

"Keogh is my name, Sean Keogh. Here to see Mr. Sharpe."

"Mr. Keogh? Do you have an appointment, sir?"

"Not really, ma'am. But perhaps you could tell Mr. Sharpe that Mr. Keogh, Chairman of the Republican Committee of South Boston, is here to see him."

She wrinkled her forehead.

"Mr. Keogh, Chairman of the South Boston Republican Committee?"

"Correct, ma'am."

If that didn't get him past that partition, nothing would. Sean Keogh felt a little out of character. His title, he thought, *was* a little outrageous.

The middle-aged woman disappeared behind the partition. He could hear her repeating the title he had given her. There was a tone of incredulity in her voice. He heard a mumbled reply.

She emerged a split second later.

"Mr. Sharpe is inside, Mr. . . . er."

"Keogh . . . Sean Keogh." He smiled and walked around her desk. Despite the ambitiousness of his mission, he felt good, and he could almost feel his beloved Southie, with its beautiful memories and black past, slipping behind him. For behind him were the shocking death of Jimmy Rooney, the tragic death of his mother, Molly Keogh, and the bitterly retaliatory death of Paddy Devlin. Shock, tragedy and revenge suddenly seemed to fade as he walked handsome and confident into the office of the Secretary of the Boston Republican Club.

When Sean Keogh walked through that door that late summer day, he couldn't remember feeling so good.

He had always impressed them in Southie. Now this was out of his territory, another league. He was confident that he could handle himself just as well on the Boston Common as he could on Dorchester Avenue. After all, wasn't that his message to his friends?

He turned around the partition and saw Roger Sharpe. He was young —not as young as Sean, maybe thirty. He had young eyes. Roger Sharpe was a handsome man with an open, friendly face, strictly Ivy League from the button collar to the suspenders that held up his suit pants.

"Mr. Sharpe? My pleasure. Keogh. Sean Keogh."

Sharpe looked up and smiled. He shook hands and said, "Hi." He had a nice grip—not the bone-crusher grip that men who have something to prove always give when they shake hands. Keogh liked him immediately.

"Sharpe. Call me Roger."

"Call me Sean," he said with an easy smile.

"Sit down, please. . . . I must say I am curious."

Keogh sat and gave a slight smile which almost signaled he had a twinge of conscience about his title.

"To be honest, Mr. Keogh . . . Sean . . . I wasn't aware the Republican Party had a committee in South Boston."

Sean began quietly, but his voice had a ring of assertiveness to it.

"To be honest, Roger, you do and you don't. Put it this way. You do have a committee if you want. . . . Now, I promise I'm not an insurance salesman. I'm here on very serious business."

"Go ahead," Sharpe encouraged.

"How about some lunch?"

Sharpe looked uncertainly at his watch. What was this all about? He looked at Keogh and he trusted him.

Keogh cut in. "I took the liberty of reserving a table for one fifteen at the Ritz Carlton. I hope you don't think I'm coming on too strong." Then with a laugh: "It's a good Republican hangout."

Sharpe laughed and grabbed his coat. They walked across the Common to the Ritz, through the lobby and left into the elegant dining room, where Keogh greeted Angelo, the maître d', with a cheery but dignified nod. They were seated.

"Well, Sean, now that you have me here, what are you going to do—sell me Faneuil Hall?" He had a very nice, open face, Keogh decided. Keogh laughed and ordered drinks. A martini for Sharpe; Scotch and water, no ice, for himself.

"Well," Keogh started, "you might think what I'm about to say is just as preposterous as selling you Faneuil Hall. Let me jump in with both feet."

"Fine, Sean."

"I am convinced that I could deliver the assembly seat of the Forty-fourth District of South Boston as a Republican seat. Convinced, Roger."

"I'm afraid I would need a lot of convincing."

"My roots, my profile, my contacts and my friends would virtually guarantee it."

"Don't they hang Republicans over there?" Sharpe laughed.

"Seriously, very seriously, I feel that is what a lot of people think about Southie. Southie is a middle-class area. Blue-collar yes, but very middle-class. It is not an Irish slum, as some people might have you believe. It's a clean, viable neighborhood of a kind that is fast disappearing in this country."

Two prime ribs arrived and they ate and they talked, Keogh, in measured tones reciting the average income, ethnic breakdown, occupational breakdown of the residents of the tiny peninsular area.

Sharpe listened with deep but skeptical interest.

As they sipped their coffee, Sharpe finally spoke as if he had stored every fact, every impression about Keogh and his sales pitch.

"Sean . . . look. There is no question in my mind that you genuinely believe what you're telling me. I would be tempted to believe it myself. There is no question about your motives . . . and your instincts. You're right. A seat like Southie would not only have a widespread significance in Boston. It would have a dramatic impact across Massachusetts and the country. The very fact that we could pull off one of the strongest Democratic strongholds in the country would be marvelous."

Keogh stared evenly ahead as he waited for the "but."

"But," Sharpe continued, "my position is very much one of a steersman. I advise the nine-member Executive Committee of the club on what I think is feasible. I'm young. They are old. They don't take that much notice of me. I have some influence, sure, but the operative word is 'some.'

"Now, look hard at what you're asking me. You are asking me to go there and give them a sales job on a twenty-three-year-old man who isn't even a registered Republican, no experience in public life, no real organization, no financial breakdown of how a campaign could be financed, no printed material. Not even a blurb handout. Now, that was not meant to be critical. I'm just giving you the facts."

"Our organization has quite large resources," Keogh said, "as you might find out if you check out some sources. Ask a few newspaper guys . . . Johnny Carpozi on the *Globe,* ask him. It might surprise you a little."

"Sean, I have to be brutally frank. The old boys who are on the committee are as much concerned with maintaining their political face as they are with winning elections. They're all pretty heavy hitters—men who have had Cabinet jobs in Washington; not household names in Southie, perhaps, but big men. They would always be concerned about the prospect of the Republican Party being massacred at the polls. It would be, in their minds, an imprudent, ill-advised adventure that could end in political suicide. Those are the facts."

"Roger. I'm not unaware of what I'm proposing, but these are *my* facts. I could run as a Democrat and win without spending a dime on the campaign. Frankly, to do that I would have to compromise my principles and in so doing eventually compromise the people of Southie— whom I love. But I could do that. I could run as an independent and still win. Win very big. Now, please keep that in mind. What would the committee think after I win as an independent? They would have to believe it could have been theirs. I'm asking you, as a friend of all of ninety minutes, to take the proposition to them."

"Look. I would be lying if I said I would. It's a much slower process than you think. Join our party, get into the mainstream, then try it next time around."

"It's this time around or no time around. Let's strike a bargain."

"I'm willing," Sharpe said.

"Day after tomorrow . . . Saturday. Saturday afternoon. Come to Southie. Erin Social Club about three in the afternoon. It's on Quinlan Square."

"Okay. What's my side of the bargain?"

"Promise me you will make a decision about taking my proposition before the committee after that."

Sharpe smiled warmly and extended his hand. "You've got it. Incidentally, I have a confession to make: I've never been to Southie."

"That's all right," Sean Keogh said as he got up from the table and paid the check. "I have a confession to make: I've never voted in my life before."

Sharpe liked the handsome, serious young man he saw before him.

SEAN KEOGH was thoughtful as he drove across the bridge to Southie. He knew it wasn't going to be easy, and it wasn't. He had confidence in Roger Sharpe. But deep down, did he have confidence in himself? Sean Keogh had never been one to make idle boasts, and he was thinking hard whether he might just have uttered his first one. No. He could deliver what he promised.

When Sean Keogh returned to the offices of the Francis X. Burke Trucking Company, he was pleased with what he saw. He could always rely on Frank. Frank Burke, the big, slow-thinking man, had in the last twenty-four hours moved with the speed of light. The storeroom at the back of his office had been cleared. Inside was a copying machine. Next to it were stencils. An old but reliable-looking typewriter had been requisitioned from the back room of the Erin Social Club. Burke had already arranged a short-term lease on the vacant garage behind his offices. He had opened the back door of his storeroom and the back door of the garage. They were only six feet apart. He had erected a tarpaulin between both back doors in a tent effect, so that the garage and storeroom were joined by a crude canvas tunnel. Rough, but imaginative.

Burke looked up from his desk. "How did it go?"

"Pretty good," Keogh answered.

"Now, really, Sean boy—how did it go?"

"Oh, a lot of stuff about being approved by the Executive Committee, but I met a guy, Roger Sharpe. Nice guy. He'll fix it up. Don't worry. How are we doing about help?"

"As soon as you give the word I can get six guys here for eight hours a day. Mr. Mac has four. The word is already out, of course, mainly because I've been preparing everybody so they don't think you're mad."

"What's the reaction?"

"They think you're mad," Burke said with a smile.

But the smile didn't tell all. Keogh looked at his friend. Whether it was the fact that Keogh's enthusiasm was infectious or whether Burke just liked action, the big curly-haired man was fast becoming a believer.

Keogh pulled up a rickety chair and sat down at the typewriter. He shouted back into the office at Burke: "The slogan is going to be 'Southie Deserves Better.' How do you like that, Frank? Catches the idea, huh?"

"Whatever you say, Sean boy. You're leadin' and we're followin', and I'm fucked if I know where."

Keogh started to tap out his first release, only to realize he had never typed before. He painfully pecked, crossed out words and pecked again at the keys.

Burke looked on with amusement. "Hey Sean, how much does this Assemblyman bullshit pay, anyway?"

"I think it's eleven thousand bucks a year."

Burke laughed. "Do you know that is what we will be makin' each month from now on from Mr. Mac's operations?"

"Well, it's just eleven thousand more to add to the coffers. . . . Damn, I wish I could type."

"Well, Sean boy, I've done enough today for Southie's Messiah. I'm goin' next door for a beer. When you've finished savin' the world on that typewriter, come and join me."

"Okay." He tore out a sheet of paper and started again on the typewriter. "Why would a boy from Southie want to be a Republican?" he typed with the speed of a snail. He ripped out the page with an exasperated curse. He didn't hear the door of the office open and he didn't hear the light footsteps.

"Maybe I could help you do that."

He looked up. His eyes widened with surprise. Then his look turned to embarrassment. Sean Keogh, in a quiet but precise way, was always fully in charge of whatever he undertook. And he felt embarrassed at his awkwardness as his fingers stumbled across his new undertaking of typing—particularly in front of Rose Sweeney.

She stood uncertainly in the doorway between the office and the storeroom. Sean remained silent.

"Mr. Wilson . . . Eddie . . . said that perhaps a few people in the neighborhood could help out. Everybody is talking about what you're doing. It . . . well, it seems very exciting. I have some time off during the day sometimes . . . and . . . well . . . I can type."

Keogh stood up, smiled and said, "Sit down, Rose. . . . Well, you're darn right we need help."

She sat down in the far corner of the room and was surprised to sense that Sean Keogh's quiet confidence was showing a crack of old-fashioned human uncertainty.

He sighed and put his feet up on the desk. It seemed a highly self-revealing gesture for this young man of control.

"To be honest, Rose, I need more than help. I don't know, maybe I've bitten off more than I can chew. I'll be honest with you, since you so nicely offered to help. I could end up with a lot of egg on my face."

She didn't know Sean Keogh at all well. She had admired him from a distance as a decent and honorable young man. But although she didn't know him, she could not help feeling that she was witnessing a rare moment of deep-seated doubt in him.

"I don't believe that, Sean. I don't know anything about politics, but I think what you're doing is exciting. I'm not old enough to vote, but I think I know what you're getting at. We would all love to put South Boston on the map. That's a very decent thought. I believe you can do what you say you can. I really do, Sean. Honest."

She was still wearing her starched nurse's uniform. The half-light coming from the inside office highlighted her tiny, compact frame.

The thin reflection of the sun that peeped into the office shone off her dark brown hair. She looked like a tremendously pretty child.

Sean could feel his throat tighten. He swallowed hard.

"Well, Rose, I just hope the rest of Southie has the same confidence you have in me."

"It might take time, it might take work, but I'm sure they will."

Her tiny pep talk seemed to give him the charge he needed. He swung his feet down and jumped up.

"You're right. Work. Okay, now let me give up on this typewriter. I'm going into the next room and write up a flyer in longhand. I'll give it to you. If you see any stupid spelling mistakes, correct them, please. Okay, let's do it."

Sean went into the next room. He started writing. "It's Time . . . Southie Deserves Better." Then, under a heading of "Why would a Man from Southie Run on a Republican Ticket?" he listed ten short reasons. It was rough, but it was simple and had impact.

Rose had set up the stencil in the typewriter. He handed it to her. She made a few discreet suggestions about spacing and the word count. She typed it onto the stencil in five minutes. Silently but with efficient speed she snapped the stencil onto the duplicating machine, inked it and started to crank the drum like a miniature old-fashioned printing press.

When she had reeled off one thousand copies, she turned to Sean. "One thousand. No, don't pick them up yet. The print is still a little wet. It will smudge."

"How do you know all about this stuff?" Sean asked.

"School newspaper. Nurses' publications at the hospital. It's pretty easy, really."

She had a nice, easy efficiency about her, Sean noticed. No panic, no fuss, just got the job done.

She went inside to wash the ink smudges off her hands. He watched her soap her small, delicate fingers. They were beautiful. When she returned to her work, she passed within a foot of Sean. He could smell her hair.

There was an awkward silence. They could feel each other's presence very keenly.

"Okay. Thank you, Rose. Now I'll get some of these to the good

Father Zeibatski, some to Frank and some to Eddie. It's important that most of the guys who come into the club on Saturday afternoon will have read it."

"Okay," she said with a sigh. "I think I'll get home now. Anything more to do?"

"No, Rose. I just appreciate it all."

"I'm off tomorrow. I'll drop by early—about eight thirty. Too early?"

"No, no. I'm here at seven thirty in the morning. Honestly, I'm embarrassed to ask you, but if you can make it, I would really appreciate the help."

Keogh's conscience pricked him. He didn't know what there was to do the next day. But it would be a good excuse to see her.

She waved a girlish wave and said, "See you at eight thirty in the morning. Bye." Keogh's heart skipped a little.

He shook his head and went next door to the club. He handed Burke a stack of flyers.

"Drink, Sean boy?"

"No thanks, Frank. I want to get these to Father. He can move them around tonight at the bingo game. I hope the Almighty forgives us for involving one of His servants in politics." He smiled and left.

He was thinking about Rose Sweeney as he drove to Sacred Heart Church. He felt a slight tingle. It was a pleasant sensation. God, she gets prettier every time I see her! So fragile. Like a little toy doll.

He dropped the flyers off at the bingo game for Father Zeibatski. Then he drove back to the office to map out his strategy.

Within seconds after he walked through the door, the telephone rang. It was Roger Sharpe.

"Hi," Sean said.

"Hi, yourself," Sharpe said coolly. "Look, we made a bargain, and I was straight with you, but I've just got off the phone with two reporters. They want me to confirm a rumor that we have endorsed you. I had to tell them the truth."

"I can't help rumors. I haven't had any contact with reporters. Roger, you just be here on Saturday . . . and for crying out loud, trust me."

"Okay," came an uncertain reply, "I trust you and I'll be there. Bye."

Keogh put down the receiver and bit his lip. For a split second all the doubts returned. Could he really trust Sharpe? He had met him for only ninety minutes. Was he as sincere as he seemed, or was he just another Beacon Hill Boston Brahmin WASP? All the Southie complexes which Keogh himself had accused his friends of having washed over him. Maybe Sharpe was just being polite and maybe the whole idea of a young Southie racketeer running for office was as bizarre as it sounded and

Sharpe knew it and he was playing me along. He scrubbed his brain clean. No, I can do it and I will do it.

He lay awake in bed that night. One minute he had all the confidence in the world; the next minute the doubts returned. He fell into a fitful sleep and awoke at 6:30 A.M. He felt groggy, and the pall of being made a gigantic fool still hung over him. He brightened. Today he would see Rose Sweeney.

He opened the office at 7:50 A.M. He sat down at Burke's desk deep in thought. He tried his hand at writing some more campaign literature. It was honest, straight talk. That was all Southie wanted.

At 8:30 A.M. there was a gentle knock on the door. It was Rose. She was wearing a feather-light summer dress. Her small breasts strained slightly against the fabric. She was wearing her hair down, abandoning the severe bun. It made her soft face look even softer. She flashed a white, even-toothed smile. "Any typing today?"

Keogh felt strangely adventurous. When he heard himself say: "Typing today? Hell, no—even politicians have to have a day off." It was the first time he had ever referred to himself as a politician. It sounded good.

"Oh, well," Rose Sweeney countered with a hint of disappointment, "just call me at the hospital when you need your next batch of typing done. I'll be only too glad to help out." She half-turned to go.

"Where're you going, Rose?"

"I'll just drop on home."

"Rubbish." He surprised himself by his boldness. He grabbed her by the hand. It was the most intimate gesture he had ever made toward her, and he wondered how many men had grabbed her hand. She flushed, and she could feel the burning all the way to the back of her ears.

"I'm just going to leave a note here for Frank that I have hijacked his car and we're going to take a trip down to the Cape. We'll have lunch at the Lobster Inn in Provincetown. It's indescribable."

He was still clutching her hand as he scribbled a note with his right hand. Rose Sweeney felt her throat thicken, and she was so nervous there was no saliva in her mouth. She felt that her heart must be showing its thumping through the breastline of her dress. But she said nothing and she did nothing to pull her hand from his. She felt ablaze, and she was scared to speak. So say nothing, she told herself. Just go along.

He shoved the note into the typewriter, took the keys from the drawer, looked at her, gave her a reassuring chuckle and walked out the door. It was for Sean Keogh an outrageous act, putting pleasure before business, and Rose Sweeney felt almost as if they were eloping. It had been such a spontaneous gesture. But both felt young, and they felt good. And rarely did either of them feel young.

Sean Keogh looked at the clear mid-August sky. "Too good a day to be a politician. Today we play millionaires." He opened the car door for her. She slid inside and was sorry that he would no longer be able to hold her hand. He got into the driver's seat and started up the car. He felt her eyes on him. He looked toward her, and she blushed. Keogh smiled and she smiled, and then the smile grew into a healthy sweet laugh. "I feel like I'm being kidnapped."

Keogh smiled. "Well, politicians do everything else." The word "politician" rolled off his tongue, and he liked it more and more. But God, what if the committee downtown turns its back on me? What a fool I will be made to look. He again banished the thought, wound down the window and headed toward Provincetown.

It was a weekday, and despite the month, the long sandy beaches were only sprinkled with people. The day was glorious, and he clasped her hand again. She tensed at first and then just relaxed. Holding hands was no big deal. Everyone does it. Both of them suddenly just felt like a young man and young woman, something taken so much for granted by others, but so savored by this couple.

The lunch was exotic, and Keogh ordered with a flourish, even if he felt he was showing off a little. The barriers had now disappeared between them, and they talked with interest to each other and without embarrassment. Several times during lunch they found themselves staring deep into each other's eyes.

They stayed late in Provincetown, and the drive home through the darkness was a long one. Both of them had more fresh air in one day than they had had in a year, and Rose felt herself snuggling up on Sean's shoulder and quietly falling asleep as he drove her back to Dorchester Avenue in South Boston.

She blinked her eyes as the car pulled to a halt outside her home. She smiled. "Oh, I couldn't keep my eyes open. We're home? Yes. You had to drive all by yourself. That was very selfish of me, sleeping on you.

"This has been the best, the very best, Sean, and thank you very much."

She was very close to him now, and her face and skin smelled like freshly cut flowers. He wanted desperately to grab her and hold her. But he simply cupped her chin in his right hand and drew her little frame toward him. He gently kissed her on the lips. Their lips lingered, and he could feel her lips parting ever so slightly, and he felt a burning sensation go all the way from his scrotum to the back of his neck.

After many long seconds their lips drew away. Very little had to be said. Sean Keogh could feel himself tightening all over, and Rose could feel the juices flowing freely through her body into her thighs.

He took a deep breath as he held her face in one hand, and then he smiled. "We've got to do this again," he said, "soon."

"I'd love to . . . soon."

He then jumped out of the car, ran around to open her door, helped her out and said, "I'll call you at the hospital."

"Looking forward to it, Sean. Bye, and thanks for a lovely day." She walked inside to the small two-story frame house where she lived with Pat Sweeney, her father, and her brother Billy. There would be some housework to do now, and tomorrow she would have to get up early to go to the hospital. It was a hard schedule. But she was happy now.

AT TWO thirty on Saturday afternoon, Sean Keogh walked through the doors of the Erin Social Club. There were even more men there today than normal. Maybe a hundred and thirty of them. Most of them had read Sean's flyer.

He was apprehensive about his reception. Sean realized that for a lot of men, voting Republican was a little like quitting the union and taking a hated foreman's job. There was much traditional and inbuilt suspicion. But Sean had gambled on their basic intelligence. They might speak differently from the people across the river, they might even look a little different, but they were intelligent. Keogh was gambling on their intelligence.

He walked to the bar and ordered a beer. McLaughlin, Burke, Wilson and Father Zeibatski were there. Nobody had told them anything, but they had sensed today was important. He was encouraged by the friendly waves and hellos he got from the drinkers. Men of Southie couldn't conceal suspicion. There was no suspicion there that day—just curiosity. And Sean knew that if he didn't satisfy that curiosity, it could turn into suspicion.

Father Zeibatski was sipping a neat vodka. "It's about time the Almighty had some friends in high places," he said. "I'm with you, boy. All the way." God, that priest could make a man feel good with so few words, Keogh thought.

Today he was going to make a speech and he hadn't the slightest idea what he was going to say.

Just before three o'clock, Roger Sharpe walked in the door. Sharpe looked around the unfamiliar surroundings. A few of the regulars checked him out with their eyes. He moved uncomfortably inside until he saw Sean. He gave him a wave. Sean beckoned him over. There were no more inquiring glances.

Young Keogh smiled. Sharpe was dressed in a navy pea jacket, jeans and checked shirt. So he dressed for the occasion, Keogh thought, smiling to himself. That's how he thinks we dress over here. The men in the club were mostly dressed in light, snappily cut summer sportswear. Keogh waved his hand. There were so many misconceptions about Southie. Sharpe caught the look in his eye and peeled off his coat as he ordered a beer. Sean introduced him all around. Sharpe felt at home immediately, and Burke promptly engaged him in a deep discussion about the Red Sox pitching staff. Burke rarely talked about anything else.

It was a good time to begin.

Sean nodded to Dan McCauley. McCauley nodded back.

"I think I'll say a few words," he said to McLaughlin and Wilson.

Burke was still in animated discussion. McCauley banged loudly on a big tin can and yelled, "Quiet, fellas; young Sean has something to say. Quiet, fellas."

Sean Keogh hopped up onto the bar. His heart was thumping. Then he looked out at the sea of faces and he suddenly felt calm. Very calm.

Roger Sharpe was monitoring every movement of muscle in Sean Keogh. This was his test of fire.

Keogh smiled broadly. Suddenly he looked different. So completely in control. His voice was friendly, but it had a firmness, an assertiveness that conveyed to everyone who listened that he knew what he was talking about.

"Well, my friends, I guess you want to know what it's all about. The printed sheets, the talk of my running as assemblyman on the Republican ticket," he said with a smile.

A voice yelled from the back of the room, "Sean boy, when are ye goin' to ask us to join the Masonic Temple?" The room exploded in good-natured laughter. Keogh laughed too. There was no hostility there. Someone yelled, "Give the boy a chance." The room immediately quieted.

"You've known me, most of you, since I was a kid. Old Detective Jack Crockford kicked me in the rear end so many times when he was a cop on the beat I thought my nose would bleed." Crockford laughed indulgently. "And Billy Lonegan—I broke more of his windows with baseballs than any other kid on the block. Freddie Martin, there . . . we fought each other so many times at Sacred Heart we punched ourselves soft." Freddie laughed at the memory.

Sharpe looked up at Keogh on the bar. He knows how to get the crowd on his side immediately. He knows his stuff, he thought.

"Well, now here it is, men. I'm not going to insult you with any political B.S. I wouldn't do that to my friends. I just want to tell you why.

Now, you have read my platform and you all know me well enough that there isn't a word of con in the whole thing.

"My father was a Democrat, my darling mother was a Democrat and there is no reason to believe that I wouldn't have become one. Then one day I just started to think, What have they done for us? The garbage collection comes here twice a week instead of three times a week in Brookline, our wives and mothers and daughters and sisters and girl-friends still shop at the discount stores to get their dresses, we still have to save for a couple of years to buy a car because we can't get bank loans and our fire insurance is the highest in the inner-city area. So I asked myself, What have they done?

"Now, the truth is, I don't think the Democrats who have represented us here are bad guys or dishonest. But I wondered why it was that Southie was always regarded as a second-class citizenry. Was it because the big-money boys in town looked down on us?"

There was a murmur of agreement in the crowd.

Keogh continued: "Or was it because we didn't go up to those guys and say, 'Hey pal, give us a piece of the action'? Did our Democratic representatives ever ask; did they ever cross the river? Did they say, 'Hey, we're Southie and want in'? I don't think they did. From where I see it, nobody gives anyone anything. Ask, tell them you're here, make your case forcefully and things will change. You see, over here we have always been made to think that those big guys in those big offices are our enemies. When we think that way, the big guys get scared of us. Suddenly bank-loan money stays out of here. They're scared. Now, there is nothing to be scared of here. We have one of the lowest street-crime rates in the city. And if you don't listen to Frank Burke talk baseball, your body is safe forever."

More laughter. He was bringing them around slowly.

Someone spoke up. Billy Mathews, an old friends of Sean's. "But Sean, we're let alone. Nobody interferes with us. Isn't that what we want?"

"No, it isn't, Billy. I don't want anyone to interfere with us. But the rest of the world is passing us by. They have completely forgotten about us. The banks, the loan offices, the office construction, housing con-struction. We're standing still and the rest of the world is running past us.

"And fellas, I don't see why we can't get a loan for a car or a house as easy as a guy can in Brookline. And I don't see why our women have to shop at discount stores. Or why Billy Lonegan's son couldn't be a bank president, or Freddie Martin run a supermarket. The Democrats get our votes and they make sure we're let alone. Well, we can be let alone too much and one day wake up and see that the rest of the world is in the twentieth century. Keep our traditions, keep our clubs, keep our strong ties and friendships—but for crying out loud, let's get some money in here and start living a little—if not for ourselves, at least for our families."

They were cheering. McLaughlin and Burke beamed. Wilson looked thoughtful. Sharpe was animated. Keogh knew just the right note.

Keogh held up his hand. "I don't want to bore you any more, but let me end by saying that Willie 'The Actor' Sutton, the bank robber, was asked by a reporter, 'Why do you rob banks, Willie?' Willie answered, 'Because that's where the money is.' And that's as honestly as I can put it. Now I want your support, your honest support—not to have Southie ruined by outsiders, but at least to let a little of their money in here for a better life."

They were cheering again. He jumped down and he was surrounded by groups of men slapping his back. His hand pumped continuously, and over and over the phrase was repeated: "I'm for ye, son . . . ye got my vote." Another friend shoved a beer into Keogh's hand and said, "Not one of the Flanagans has ever voted anything but Democrat. I'm breakin' the mold, boy. Good luck to ya."

Keogh looked over at Sharpe. Sharpe smiled. "I'll speak to them Monday morning and again at the meeting Monday night. No promises, but I'm a convert." Keogh smiled and grabbed Sharpe's hand warmly.

HE WENT to Mass on Sunday, but didn't hear a word Father Zeibatski said. He was on pins and needles waiting for the decision of Monday night.

Monday morning he got to the office early. He called Sharpe at eleven and anxiously asked, "Anything yet? Any reaction?"

"Calm down, Sean. I've spoken to two of them. No promises, remember. I'll see them tonight, and I'll call you first thing tomorrow morning to let you know."

"Call me tonight at the club," Keogh said.

"May not be until after midnight."

"I'll be there."

If Sean Keogh had experienced some painfully long nights, that Monday was the longest day he ever experienced. He ate dinner with Burke that night in the office. He pushed the food away. Then he surprised Burke by asking him for one of his cigars. Sean never smoked.

He puffed furiously as he paced the floor. Burke knew better than to inquire.

At eleven o'clock, Keogh suggested going next door. They ordered drinks and Keogh sipped absently on his Scotch. The telephone rang half a dozen times. Each time Keogh looked apprehensively toward Dan McCauley as he answered. It was always for someone else.

The call came at 12:10 A.M.

"Fer you, Sean," McCauley called. Keogh almost knocked Burke down getting to the telephone.

"Roger?"

"Yes. Sean?"

Keogh was desperately trying to read something into his voice. "What's the verdict?"

"You're in, Sean. You scrambled under the wire."

Keogh wanted to shout, but he retained his composure. "Thanks a lot, Roger. I appreciate what you did."

"It was a bit of a battle."

"Why?"

"Well, one of the old boys here who has a lot of influence was dead against you. Really. Said he had a file an inch thick on all your friends. Nice old guy, really, but he acts like he just came over on the *Mayflower*."

"What's his name?" Sean inquired.

"It's Sheldon Mathers—the owner of the *Clarion*."

Keogh smiled and said quietly, "Sheldon Mathers. Now he knows who I am."

"What was that, Sean?"

"Nothing, Roger; just talking to myself."

Chapter

6

As AUTUMN folded its arms around South Boston, Sean Keogh's headquarters behind the Francis X. Burke Trucking Company had been
transformed into a traditional political boiler room. Eighteen hours a
day the office and the adjoining garage were filled with activity. Keogh's
message had swept Southie. At first there were some who saw it as a
novelty, while others suspected it might be just a gimmick by the
McLaughlin-Keogh mob. A son of Southie running as a Republican
indeed had its novelty value. But as young Keogh's pamphlets clogged
the mailboxes and as he and his band of burly followers took to the
streets and bars with their message, the people of Southie realized this
handsome, ambitious young man was running for office in deadly earnest and nothing was going to hold him back.

Very soon some of the staunchest Democrats showed up at the dusty
headquarters in Quinlan Square, first out of curiosity and soon to find
that they had been won over to the Keogh cause. Both McLaughlin and
Burke had done well in providing a small army of longshoremen and
truckers, their presence underscoring the message that Keogh was not
against the virulently strong union base of Southie. They worked with
the enthusiasm reserved for young political groupies. The campaign was
taking off, and Keogh worked the strings like a puppeteer.

Rose Sweeney had added a touch of glamour by organizing some of
her nurse friends from the hospital. In the weeks since she had first
arrived at the office of Frank Burke, she had proved to be an anchor of
reliability, heading a typing pool and taking care of the mail campaign.

It had been two months since Keogh had first cupped her chin in his
hands in the front seat of Burke's car and kissed her gently on the lips.
That first day on the Cape and that night in the car had led to other
days on the Cape and other nights in the car. Never once, however, had
Sean forgotten his place, and although those nights had left both of
them burning for each other, they had resisted making a full physical

commitment. He was twenty-three and she was nineteen, and even in Southie there were couples of similar ages having affairs; but both seemed to be reserving the final moment for something more meaningful. Marriage, said McLaughlin. And between the boys and in the inner circle of the mob it was generally acknowledged that Sean Keogh and Rose Sweeney saw each other as something very special.

She had felt secure and protected those days and nights in the front seat of Burke's car in Sean's arms. Since her mother had been taken away that day to the institution where she later died, her father, Pat, and her brother Billy had leaned heavily on her for emotional support, which she gave generously.

But it was only in Sean Keogh's arms that she could feel secure. For once *she* had someone to lean on. It was a rare and gloriously comfortable feeling for this pretty, shy and deep girl; one she cherished.

While Keogh worked brutal hours in the campaign, he regularly reserved Friday, Rose's day off from the hospital, for a trip to the country or to the Cape. Keogh's flashing good looks had afforded him his fair share of experience with women, but nobody could remember ever seeing him actually date a girl on a regular basis. It was now assumed that Sean and Rose were going steady, and everyone felt good that he had found a girl from Southie.

If Keogh's romantic life was faring well, he soon learned that politically he was in for the fight of his life. At first, like everyone else, the canny old assemblyman Joe Kane did not take Keogh's candidacy with any real seriousness. But now, one month before the election, Kane saw to his dismay genuine defections in his ranks to the small office on Quinlan Square. He fought back with a blitzkrieg campaign of mail and street-corner rallies. For the first time since anyone could remember, Joe actually took to the streets, and very soon Sean Keogh had second thoughts about whether the election would be a walkover. Southie was swamped with posters proclaiming THIS IS DEMOCRAT COUNTRY, and many who first had been attracted by the handsome young Keogh felt a nagging and genuine twinge of conscience that they had ever been seriously tempted to vote against a Democrat. Keogh recognized this and wondered secretly whether he had made a mistake by starting his campaign too early. Once the novelty of his running had worn off, might they now do some hard thinking and return to the devil they knew rather than the angel they didn't? It made him campaign even harder, pumping hands, buying drinks at the Erin Social Club and even kissing babies. Tirelessly he canvassed door to door.

Sean Keogh had another problem on his hands: Sheldon Mathers and the *Boston Clarion*. The highly respected patrician publisher and veteran Republican had felt that Roger Sharpe and the Republican Club had made a serious error in judgment by endorsing Keogh as a candidate. He had told them they had sold their principles, simply because they were irresistibly attracted by the prospect of a dramatic ego-feeding that a Republican victory would give them across the state—particularly a victory in a traditional blue-collar Democratic stronghold. As a newspaper publisher, he didn't hesitate to remind both his party chiefs and the public.

"Have you seen this?" Burke said, throwing the Metro section of the *Clarion* on the desk in front of Keogh, McLaughlin and Wilson.

On the front page of the Metro section, a large chunk of news space had been devoted to the various political battles being waged in Boston. One column, under the subheading of On the Hustings, asked in the headline: "A New Face in South Boston—Where Do the Campaign Funds Come From?" It was a skillfully written article that posed as a news story but had more of the stamp of an editorial on it. The story revealed that although Sean Keogh had been given an endorsement by the Republican Club, it had promised him no financial support. "He didn't get so much as a typewriter to produce the voluminous mail campaign that has swamped South Boston," the story said. It then went on to report that Keogh's main supporters were Bernie McLaughlin, "a man who has long been tied to gambling operations in South Boston, and Francis Xavier Burke, a man who now heads a trucking concern and who has a record of eleven arrests for gambling and assault."

Keogh read the article with interest. He frowned. "I can't say I didn't expect this."

"Well, something else, Sean," Frank Burke said with an edge of bitterness in his voice. "That old bastard Kane has made sure that this story is in the mailbox of every house in Southie."

McLaughlin grunted, "I can stop that in a minute." He reached for a telephone.

"What are you doing, Mr. Mac?"

"I'm callin' old Joe and quietly advisin' him to knock it off. That is, if he don't want some real trouble on his hands."

"No, no. Don't do that. Let him play his game any way he wants it."

"What are ye talkin' about? Yer mad."

"Mr. Mac, who in Southie doesn't know about all of us? A lot of them have been part of it. That's telling nobody something they don't know. If anything, it will just convince the voters that Kane is on the run and reverting to dirty tactics. They won't go for it."

Bernie McLaughlin scowled. "Yer playin' this game like ye was at Harvard. If we're in this thing, we are in it to win. We can't have newspapers say that we're a bunch of gambling no-hopers."

Keogh smiled. "Forget it." But deep down, he knew those stories could hurt him. One thing was putting a bet on a man you trust in the neighborhood, but another was voting for him. He didn't want any of the old traditional muscle to come into the political battle. That would have made it too easy. But above all—too much like the old Southie. And he didn't want that. He was worried, but he couldn't stir up any bitterness inside himself against Sheldon Mathers. What his paper said was entirely accurate.

Keogh's respect for the white-maned old man had never waned. He relished anyone with principles, even if those principles were aimed at his own throat. One day he would know Sheldon Mathers better, he told himself. He would like to explain to this man who and what Sean Keogh was all about. That was the whole point of this political exercise, after all —to make the rest of Boston understand Southie and its people. However, the story could prove to be a problem. How other people thought about you—particularly a newspaper—was important in Southie. For a moment the dread thought returned to him: What if he was crushed in the political battle? What was left? The rackets.

He swept the gloomy thought from his mind. He stood up in the office. "Okay, how about a beer next door?"

"At last yer makin' sense," McLaughlin said as he wheezed to his feet.

"Yeah," Frank Burke sighed. "Sometimes, Sean, I don't know what yer all about. If we let Joe Kane walk all over us, it won't be good for business in the future."

"Trust me, fellas."

"Famous fuckin' last words," McLaughlin said with a chuckle.

IT WAS Friday morning and eight days before the election. Sean Keogh sat in the small, dark-paneled quarters of Father Zeibatski.

"How do you read it, Father?"

"Close, Sean."

"How close?"

"Very close. Joe Kane has picked up in the last three weeks. A lot of people, the strong union base, are having second thoughts. Joe Kane is no pushover."

"What can win it for me?"

"One thing. If the women get out to vote, you should do it."

"But the women in Southie traditionally don't really vote all that much."

"Right, Sean. You'll have to get them out. They understand better than the men what you are trying to do. The women here at the church, they're strongly behind you. You've seen our handbills at the bingo game. They know I'm behind you. It should help."

"What can I do to get the women to vote?"

"Very little. You make a solid pitch for them and that will annoy the men. You have to tread a fine line."

The priest's eyes were impassive. Nobody could ever quite know what he was thinking. But right now he was thinking for the first time that Sean Keough was having doubts about himself.

"Sean."

"Father?"

"There is something very important for you to remember."

"Yes?"

"And that is that you are right. The platform you have adopted is right. Your moral stand is right. Your concern for South Boston is right. Your fight for public office is right. Joe Kane is not a bad man; he is not necessarily a dishonest man. But he is a selfish man. You are not, Sean. Keep that in mind every second until next Saturday . . . every second."

"I will, Father. I will." He seemed to be buoyed by the quiet confidence of the priest who seemed to have such a strong clutch on reality. He stood up and reached inside the jacket of his tweed suit. He withdrew the familiar-looking brown envelope.

"Here, Father."

"Thank you, Sean. The woman and child are both well, and the money helps."

Keogh flushed slightly at the thought of the Rooney woman now that she had a child. The priest caught the look of concern. The lad had suffered enough over Rooney's death.

"Now," the priest said lightheartedly by way of changing the delicate subject, "isn't today Friday? Isn't there a lady waiting for you somewhere?"

Keogh smiled, slightly embarrassed. "Ah, yes. Well, at least I hope so."

"Going for a drive?"

"No, I think we'll take in a rather well-deserved lunch." He buttoned his jacket, walked down the steps of Sacred Heart and hopped into Frank Burke's borrowed car. He then drove downtown to Tremont Street, where he stopped off at a jewelry store, and then on to the Ritz Carlton Hotel.

He arrived in the elegant dining room a few minutes before one o'clock.

At precisely one, she walked shyly through the large ornate entrance of the dining room. Angelo, the maître d', led her with a well-disciplined flourish to Keogh's table. He stood up, smiled and kissed her lightly on the cheek.

"I'm not late, am I?" Rose said breathlessly.

"Right on time. . . . Like a drink?"

"Just a Coke." He ordered a Coca-Cola for her and a Scotch and water for himself.

"Rose, you amaze me. How are you always so punctual?"

"Habit, I guess. At the hospital, everything works by the clock."

Sean allowed himself a mischievous smile.

"What are you smiling at, Sean?"

"Nothing—nothing really." As he talked he took a black satin case out of his inside pocket.

"Seeing you're so punctual, perhaps you couldn't use something like this."

He handed the case across the table. She looked at it in awe. Nervously she opened it. The subdued lighting inside the dining room caught the tiny clusters of diamonds around the face of the watch. She had never seen anything quite so beautiful.

"Sean, oh my God! I have never . . . I mean it's so . . ."

He took it from the case and fastened it on her delicate wrist. She fell silent and for a moment thought that there might be tears in her eyes. She had never received a real present since her mother had gone away. Occasionally Pat and Billy Sweeney would give her a few dollars to buy some fabric, which she would sew into a dress. But this was a real present. Something of infinite value, and it came from the man who had given her so much. He never stops giving, she thought, and she had an overpowering urge to have him throw his strong arms around her and crush her to his chest.

Her eyes stared at the beauty of the diamond-studded watch, and she heard herself say simply, "Sean . . . I love you . . . I love you, Sean."

"And Rose . . . I love you . . . very much." There was a special meaning in the words they mouthed. They were not in each other's arms, holding each other and yearning for each other's bodies. They were making a clear, cool statement in a restaurant, looking across a table. They meant what they were saying.

"You're so good, Sean, so very good."

"Nothing can be good enough for the woman who is going to be my wife." He gave a little shudder at the shock of hearing himself say those words "my wife." But he didn't regret what he had said.

Her eyes widened. She breathed a little faster, and she allowed herself a tiny smile.

"Is that a Sean Keogh proposal?" She wanted him to say it again. Wanted to make sure what he had said.

"It is, Rose. I want to marry you."

"And I want to marry you."

He gently squeezed her hand, and there was nothing more said. Suddenly he sat back. "I'm starved."

She laughed. It sounded so good. There was no shyness in her laughter anymore.

"So am I, Sean darling. So am I." She had suddenly matured before his eyes.

IT HAD been the priest's idea. At first it had shocked Sean to the marrow. That night Father Velas Zeibatski had come down to the office. Bernie McLaughlin was sitting opposite, and Sean was sitting at Frank Burke's desk.

"I was going to wait until everybody was here, but . . . well, I have something to say," Sean said with a hint of nervousness.

"I hope you say something stupid, Sean lad," McLaughlin said with a chuckle. "Every time you say something serious you push up my blood pressure."

"Well, it's serious, all right. I asked Rose to marry me."

"And she said no?" McLaughlin teased.

"She said yes."

McLaughlin and the priest shook hands with the young man. It came as no surprise to either man, but they were happy for him, very happy. Rose Sweeney was the kind of girl you married; the others one used to keep the scorecard high.

"I hope I'm not presumptuous in believing that you'll be needing my services." The priest was smiling.

"Of course, Father. It has a lot to do with you, of course."

"When are you planning the happy event?" the priest asked.

"Well, we didn't really discuss it, Father. But soon."

"Fine, fine. Is next Tuesday too soon?" the priest asked.

"Next Tuesday?" Sean asked incredulously. "Next Tuesday? With all respect, Father, do you know what day next Tuesday is?"

"Certainly do. It's election day."

"But that would be impossible."

"Why? You can't do any campaigning that day. Why not get married next Tuesday?"

"Impossible, Father. Impossible. Couldn't be done."

Bernie McLaughlin caught the glint in the priest's eyes. Rarely did those eyes give away what was going on behind them. But McLaughlin caught it.

"It's a great day, Sean boy. Ye celebrate yer victory by getting married."

McLaughlin had fallen in too quickly behind the priest. Sean finally got the drift.

"I get it. I get it. Father, you surprise me, really. What you're saying is that if anything would get the women of South Boston out to vote for me it would be me getting married. A woman could never disappoint another on her wedding day. They would vote because I'm getting married?"

"Sean, you are going to be married?"

"Why, yes, Father."

"You are going to be married soon?"

"Yes, we are. But I couldn't use Rose like that to get a few votes. She would never forgive me."

"She might never forgive ye if she knows ye had a man like the good Father here with more sense than ye have hairs on yer head and ye never took any notice of him." McLaughlin was insistent.

Father Zeibatski smiled. "There is nothing in any of our teachings that prohibits letting a beautiful event help a beautiful cause. The Almighty hasn't had a great deal to do with politics lately. It's about time He did."

"Father, I . . . look, I wouldn't feel right unless I ran it past Rose."

"Go ahead . . . call her," the priest said confidently. "If we can get two hundred women out on Tuesday, you win. If we don't, be nice to Assemblyman Joe Kane in the future."

When Sean Keogh called Rose late that night at the hospital he explained the conversation he had had with the priest and McLaughlin.

"I would marry you tomorrow if I could, Sean. Why *not* Tuesday?" she said. He felt himself breathe a sigh of relief.

She replaced the receiver on the hook in the nurses' quarters at the hospital. She smiled to herself. The men of Southie always have to have their way. She smiled again. They're like little boys, she thought as she walked back to the intensive-care unit . . . little boys who always want their own way, just like Dad, Pat Sweeney—big, burly, generous, but had to have his own way, like he did with my mother. My mother. . . . She felt a dark cloud suddenly slide over her happily dancing emotions. She shook her head clear and washed away the thought. She smiled again.

THE NORMALLY cold November wind that swept off the inner Boston Harbor was kind that Tuesday. The temperature had sneaked above fifty-five degrees, and the sun was beaming from a cloudless sky.

The priest and Bernie McLaughlin and Frank Burke and Eddie Wilson had been at Sacred Heart Church from early in the morning. Everyone in Southie knew of the wedding that day. The church fairly exploded with flowers, and the priest had departed from tradition by even having a large, well-printed sign on a trestle on the sidewalk announcing the wedding. It was as much a political statement as if it had been done by a skywriter.

Bernie McLaughlin chuckled. "I hear old Joe Kane is fumin'. How can he ask someone to vote against newlyweds? Sure he's steamin' like the *Queen Mary*. I even sent him an invitation." Old McLaughlin dumped a heavy vase of flowers to the left of the pews. He looked across at the priest.

"Yer a genius, Father."

The dark-eyed Lithuanian allowed himself a small smile. There was much wisdom in that smile.

Outside, it was election day. Inside Sacred Heart it was a wedding day. The quiet behind-the-scenes manipulation of Father Zeibatski had been so skillful that by 2:02 P.M. on November 8 when Rose Margaret Sweeney, petite and beautiful, walked down the aisle awash in white on the arm of her father, Pat Sweeney, preceded by Teresa Burke, Frank Burke's wife, the congregation, which had been jammed shoulder to shoulder and spilling onto the steps of the church, had to stifle a human reaction to cheer. Behind the excitement of politics of the last two months it seemed a perfect climax when most similar events disappoint with an anticlimax. In fact, when Sean Keogh, strikingly handsome in a midnight-blue suit, flanked by his best man, Frank Burke, and ushers McLaughlin, Eddie Wilson and Roger Sharpe, the Republican who had made it all possible, slipped the ring on Rose's finger, the more emotional in the crowd couldn't suppress a yell of encouragement. He kissed her, and every man and wife there that day wanted to kiss too. It was a rare event.

Rose simply looked into Sean's eyes and said, "I love you so very much."

Sean smiled and slipped a strong but gentle arm behind her elbow, and Bernie McLaughlin thought he was going to make a fool of himself as a lump gathered in his throat, and Frank Burke had to look away lest the tears flow. Edward George Wilson—Eddie Wilson, Southie's contribution to Harvard—seemed to be the only one really in control.

Outside, as the crowd surged around the couple as if it had been a wedding of two movie stars, the cameras popped. The timing of this event had not been lost on the Boston newspapers, ever conscious of a good angle. From the church the crowd streamed to the polling booths, and suddenly unions, party loyalties and old Joe Kane were forgotten.

The Erin Social Club had been decked out gloriously for the reception. In the corner a small area had been roped off for the official wedding party. The rest was open house, and anyone in Southie who didn't drop by for a drink either had to be a pathological supporter of the opposition or didn't drink.

When the cake was cut, Sean and Rose toasted each other. It was the first time she had ever tasted champagne. He couldn't keep his eyes off her, despite the fact on this day he should have been preoccupied with votes. But Father Zeibatski had mentioned the election only once. As the crowds surged around the church after the wedding, the priest had simply smiled. "It's your day, Sean, both here and at the polls. Enjoy yourself and forget the election." And it really wasn't until 7 P.M., when the first projections came through, that Sean Keogh had given the returns much of a thought. It was bizarre. This day was what he had worked and worried so hard for, and yet he was more interested in looking at a beautiful, doll-like girl whom he would soon lie in bed with for the first time. The prospect made him feel light-headed.

McCauley, the bartender, who was with the reporter from the *Globe,* handed Bernie McLaughlin the note. He lumbered to his feet and yelled loudly for silence. "Of the 3,651 votes cast today, 1,400 have been counted. Our boy here, Sean"—he hesitated for theatrical effect—"has got 900 of those in his pocket."

Rose turned to hug and kiss him, Roger Sharpe pushed through the crowd to hug him and the party screamed their approval.

By nine o'clock the final results were in, and the pandemonium that could be heard three blocks away told the story by almost a two-to-one margin. The newspaper photographers zeroed in for the victory picture next to the wedding cake, and suddenly a ripple of silence started at the door. The crowd parted to reveal the figure of Joe Kane. There were a few embarrassed glances, but the old boy soon dismissed them.

He smiled and held out his hand. "A helluva campaign, son."

"Thanks, Joe. It was nice of you to come."

"Well, after all, old Mac did send me an invitation. Now how about a drink? And my very best to your beautiful bride." The booze poured; Joe Kane turned to Father Zeibatski. The priest nodded and smiled. "That was a nice gesture, Joe."

"What could I do, Father? Working against the Almighty is a heck of a job."

The priest smiled, and Joe Kane took a long look at handsome Sean Keogh and his lovely bride. "I have the feeling in my bones, Father, there will be no holding that boy."

"Perhaps, perhaps." And the eyes of the priest masked a million thoughts.

AT ELEVEN thirty that night, after a hurried conference with Mc-Laughlin, the priest, Burke, Wilson and Roger Sharpe, State Assemblyman—elect Sean Keogh slipped away from Quinlan Square to Logan Airport, where together with his bride, Rose Margaret Keogh, he boarded a Pan American flight for Bermuda, where they were booked in at the Princess Hotel, one of the most elegant hotels in the world.

Sean and Rose had stopped off to change clothes on their way to the airport. They dashed on board a few minutes before takeoff. Breathless, they were led to the first-class section. The other passengers were older and seemed a lot richer. They eyed the young couple curiously.

They settled in their seats and strapped themselves in. Rose looked wide-eyed.

"Sean, how can we . . . can you afford all this? I mean yesterday I wasn't quite sure where Bermuda was. I had never traveled in a plane before. This is first class."

"Six months ago you didn't know me either," he said in joking boast. She cuddled closer to him, and he felt her breast, her hard, tiny and shapely breast, pressing against his arm. He swallowed and felt himself go hard. She smiled shyly.

"It's all right to want each other now," she whispered, and surprised Sean by kissing him on the ear. He could feel her hot breath burning in his ear.

"I'm sure glad we waited," he said, abandoning any attempt at sophistication. "Won't be long, Rose. This is a two-hour flight. Then straight to the hotel. . . . Now, champagne?"

Rose Margaret Keogh felt herself continually telling herself that it wasn't all a fairy-tale dream. It was all for real. She was sitting in a plane next to a handsome and successful young man who loved her. He had just married her and he had won an election and they were in this plane going to a place called Bermuda which she had only read about in the travel sections of newspapers and magazines. The stewardess was serving champagne. Despite it all, Rose reasoned, she should not be so totally surprised. While not a worldly girl, she was blessed with a rare intelligence and determination. From the very first day she had looked at the handsome, black-haired Sean Keogh, felt his presence, she had felt a tingling conviction that one day they would be together. She snuggled closer to him as he handed her a glass of champagne.

"What do they call the wife of an assemblyman?" she asked lightheartedly.

"Mrs. Keogh," he replied, and felt a warm glow at the mention of the unfamiliar words.

"Well, what do they call the wife of the President of the United States?"

Sean smiled. "The same thing. Mrs. Keogh."

She giggled and sipped her champagne. It tasted superb, and she could feel the heat coursing through her body until she had to make an effort to concentrate on anything other than her desire.

Sean felt the same way. Damn, this plane is going too slow! He sipped his champagne and drew her closer to him. He, like Rose, couldn't help feeling it was all a little unreal. The plane started its descent. In the brilliant moonlight, the ocean below, the pink sand of its bottom reflecting sugar white, looked like a giant emerald-green carpet. The lights of Bermuda came into view.

The harsh streets of South Boston, peopled by its tough men, was far behind now, and so were the rackets. Oh, they would all still need the revenue provided by the numbers, the crap games and the union membership, Keogh mused; but he and Southie were moving into a new era, an era of legitimacy and white-collar respectability. He wanted all of Southie to be as lucky as he in his quest for acceptance. The violent deaths of Rooney and Devlin were slipping far into the past, almost as if they had happened to other people and Sean Keogh had been only a detached spectator. And that made him feel good.

THE TALL, handsome Bermudian room boy opened the door of the suite. He drew back the giant draperies to reveal a sweeping view of the bejeweled harbor.

Rose looked out across the dark sweep of the harbor with the lights from boats dancing on the water. She opened the doors that led onto a curved terrace and breathed in the flower-scented air of Bermuda.

"Sean, it's beautiful. The air. I have never smelled anything like it. I never knew anything like this existed."

Keogh smiled. He gave the room boy a dollar tip and watched as the boy closed the door behind him. At last. Alone. He padded across the thick golden wall-to-wall carpet and onto the veranda. He took her into his arms, and as the cool, clean breeze ruffled their hair he crushed her to his body. She felt as if she had disappeared into his chest, his strong lean arms encircling her. She kissed him and opened her eyes. Above, the stars winked from their remote ceiling. He led her inside, turned the lights to barely a glimmer. Silently but with impatience, he helped her remove her blouse. Then he kicked off his shoes and unzippered his trousers. She hurriedly slipped off her slacks. Her taut, perfectly shaped small body trembled as she unfastened her bra with one hand and slipped out of her panties with the other. Her bold ardor would have surprised Sean if he had not been consumed with a fever of passion.

They stood naked at the side of the bed. He pulled her toward him and could feel her superb breasts almost causing him gentle pain as they prodded deeply into his muscled chest. Her arms circled his body. They had never felt each other naked before, and both had to fight hard to control their breathing as their hands explored each other's bodies. Then Sean eased her back onto the bed. He felt her legs part under him and stretch widely apart. He kissed her, and she sucked hard at his tongue as it thrust into her mouth. He guided himself toward the entrance of her pulsating crevice.

Her body jerked violently upward, hungering for the hardness of Sean. As she sucked in air for breath, her gasp of excitement was almost a sob. Supreme erotic torture.

Sean contained his desire to plunge himself far inside her. It would hurt, and he wanted nothing to endanger their first night. She dug her nails deep into his back as she stifled a scream which begged him to fill her loins. Slowly he allowed the tip of his raging member to slide from her clitoris downward to her moist pinkness. If he wanted to spare her pain, she didn't seem to care. Her fingers frantically felt for his strong buttocks, and she pulled him far into her as her delicate but shapely legs hooked around the back of his legs.

If there was pain, it was the agony of ecstasy as she felt her insides boil like lava. In the dim half-light she could see his beautiful face and his strong, full mouth covering her face with kisses. She twisted and shivered erotically, as if she were being stabbed at from inside with something uncontrollable.

"Sean, Sean . . . I knew . . . I knew it would be like this. . . . I can feel you so far inside me. . . ."

"Rose . . . I knew too. . . . My God . . ."

He buried himself farther and farther into her body and abandoned his earlier gentleness. She responded hungrily until every nerve end in her body screamed out for release at one time. She could feel a throbbing start somewhere far behind her brain and tear up and down her body several times until she could contain it no more.

"Sean . . . darling . . . it's happening . . . it's happening . . . it's . . . oh . . . oh . . . oh . . ."

He thrust himself with one last lunge and his tongue darted far down her throat, and they writhed in a last spasm until both of them felt that every fiber of feeling had been sucked from their bodies.

They lay there silently for a long time, her small body entwined around the well-shaped physique of Sean Keogh. Her face rested on his shoulder, She looked up and smiled. He returned the smile. She sighed, "We're so very lucky, Sean."

"So very lucky . . . darling Rose, so very lucky."

He too sighed with satisfaction, and the blood that had stained his streets washed further into history. He felt good and he felt clean.

When they had exhausted their honeymoon night, the first strong rays of sun filtered lightly through the heavy draperies. They fell into a deep sleep holding each other so close they looked like one.

FOR ELEVEN days Rose and Sean lazed in the sun, toured the lush beauty of Bermuda, dined at fabulous restaurants and made love as if they had invented the act. Neither of them had ever felt so complete.

The next day, both would have to return to the gray coldness of Boston and Southie. Sean had kept in touch on the telephone with Frank Burke, and as he sat on the terrace that Saturday afternoon before making preparations for his return, he had some good news for Rose.

"I've been talking to Frank," he said, as he tinkled the ice in the glass of his white rum and Coke.

"Don't I know it," she replied with a smile from the doorway. "I knew you couldn't be away without talking to your friends. You've spoken to him every day."

"Jealous?" He laughed.

"Very." She smiled. "Well, what's the news?"

"Real estate is the news."

"Real estate?"

"Yes, we're going home to a new house."

Her face lit up. "A new house?"

"In Carson Beach, near where Frank lives. Nothing too grand. A nice two-story wood-frame house. Four bedrooms. Colonial. Think you'll like it. I've had my eye on it for some time. Frank has arranged it. Not furnished, of course. But I've organized it pretty much. It will take about a week."

"Oh, Sean. Sean, I'm so happy. It's great." She walked onto the terrace and kissed him. It was all going so perfectly.

He stood up, pecked her on the cheek and put down his glass.

"Where you going, hon?" she asked.

"Downstairs. Have to organize our tickets on the plane for tomorrow. Just going down to the lobby. Won't be a minute."

"I'll start to organize the packing. I'll be so sorry to leave this place. On Monday it will be back to barking doctors and angry head nurses and bedpans at the hospital. It will be tough."

Sean threw back over his shoulder as he walked toward the door, "Bedpans nothing. I've already told them you've quit. You don't have to work. So don't worry—it's all been fixed. You don't have to go back there."

He kept walking, then turned around, threw her a kiss. "Back in a minute."

She stood there for a long moment. She was silent, and her thoughts were confused. He had already arranged for me to quit. He never said a word. Not a word. I am the best nurse Boston General has. And suddenly I'm not there anymore. Not needed. In one telephone call Sean has suddenly made me redundant.

She bit her lip. She knew he was doing what he thought she wanted. But that was not what she wanted. She had too much to give, too much to contribute. She wasn't just another Southie housewife. She could feel an edge of anger rising in her throat. She flushed and looked at herself in the mirror. The lines of her reflection seemed to fade as the anger built up. The blood pumped at her temples as she looked at her reflection, and when the blurred edges cleared for a split second she could see the face of her mother staring back at her—her poor mother, whose life had been sacrificed because she was treated like an indentured slave by Pat Sweeney. Her mother stared back at her and the fire in her head seemed to burn out of control as a million thoughts speared back and forth through her consciousness. Her mother looked back at her and she looked sad.

Oh, my God, she thought feverishly. That's it. I haven't changed anything. I'm going to be exactly like my mother. God, no. God, no. Her breath quickened and the pain intensified in her head. The image in the mirror suddenly turned black.

Her eyes searched frantically around the room for an object to focus on. No matter where she looked, it was blurred, and no matter how hard she tried, she could not make her surroundings realistic. It was that same terrible feeling, knowing she was conscious but unable to control the flow of conscious thoughts. The images coming in waves. The pounding in the ear, the kaleidoscope of faces and forms, the torture, the visions of a psychotic woman, older than she but who looked so much like her. She could feel the frightening emotion of fear and anger. Fear that it was happening again and anger at what she perceived she had become, just a younger carbon copy of her mother.

When she came to, the hotel doctor was holding a bottle of smelling salts under her nose. Sean was standing by him with a worried frown on his face.

"What . . . what is going on? What happened?"

"It's all right. Mrs. Keogh just had a short fainting spell. How do you feel?"

"A little light-headed," she said as she sipped at a glass of water.

"Baby"—Sean's voice was rigid with concern—"what's wrong?"

"Nothing, really. Tell him, Doctor—it's quite common with some women. I'm a nurse," she said in an aside to the doctor. "I think I've been living it up a little too much. This is our honeymoon. Too many late nights and too much sun."

"You'll be okay, Mrs. Keogh. Call me again if you need me."

"Will do, Doc," Sean answered. The doctor left, and Sean looped a sympathetic arm around his wife.

"You gave me the fright of my life, hon. I walked in and there you were lying across the bed. Don't ever do that again . . . please."

She smiled up at him from the bed. He drew her to him affectionately; his strong hand squeezed her frail arm. It was a loving touch, but although she responded with a smile, she could still feel the resentment in her throat. It scared her to feel this resentment toward the man she loved, but it scared her more to see her life becoming a carbon copy of her mother's, with the ultimate agony of a tortured brain. It would pass, she thought. She was making too much of a tiny gesture that was meant to be a kind thought. They would pass, these terrible feelings, she told herself. But she knew they were growing more frequent. What was wrong with her? She knew she was healthy. All the nurses got regular checkups. What was wrong and when would it happen again? She didn't want Sean to know. She loved Sean Keogh more than life itself.

Chapter

7

THE MEETING was for ten o'clock in the morning. At five minutes to ten, Sean Keogh got out of a taxi at Quinlan Square. He pulled up his overcoat collar around his suntanned face as a vicious wind howled down Dorchester. Twenty-four hours earlier, he and Rose had begun their last day in the sun by the pool in Hamilton, Bermuda. At eight o'clock that morning, Eddie Wilson had summoned him from his hotel room at the Ritz, where Sean had taken a suite while his new house was being furnished in Carson Beach. The call had had a note of urgency. "Sean, sorry to bug you the first day back, but we have to get together today. It's important."

Sean always knew better than to ask questions of an important nature over the telephone. He had simply said, "See you at the office at ten."

He walked quickly across the narrow alley that was misnamed a square to honor John Quinlan, one of Southie's sons, and barged through the door from the cold, his breath coming in short white puffs.

Bernie McLaughlin gave him the traditional, crooked-toothed wheezy grin, Frank Burke made a racy remark about the condition of men's brains after a honeymoon and Wilson signaled his concern right from the start by running his hands through his red hair.

"We've got troubles, Sean," Wilson said without further ado.

Sean threw his coat on a chair, sat on an upturned crate, smiled easily and cracked, "Welcome home, Sean. How did you enjoy your honeymoon?"

Wilson could be too serious sometimes.

"I'm sorry, Sean, but we have some serious business," Wilson said.

"Let's hear it, Eddie."

"Well, one of my friends from Harvard is the son of James Thwaite, the lawyer of Bush, Bush and Thwaite. He leaked to me something we should be concerned about."

"Who is James Thwaite, may I ask?"

"Sheldon Mathers' personal attorney and attorney of record for the *Boston Clarion.*"

Sean nodded with interest.

"Mathers is pushing for a State Legislative Investigative Committee on crime to probe your campaign funds. In other words, where did your money come from?"

"Surely that's no big deal. I got it from personal loans and gifts from Frank and Bernie here."

"Fine. But where do they get that kind of money from? Since when does a dingy office outfit with a couple of trucks give a man the kind of money to finance a campaign out of the goodness of his heart?"

Sean Keogh remained silent.

"And what if the IRS probes a little closer and finds that through you we dumped one and a half million bucks in a Bermuda bank account last week?"

"Eddie, how hot is Mathers for our blood?"

Wilson flicked a copy of the previous Friday's paper across to him. "Read the editorial."

Sean's eyes raced down the column. His face remained impassive. His eyes settled on the last paragraph.

> If the Republican Party can claim a dramatic victory in winning the 44th District of South Boston, its satisfaction might be dampened somewhat if it channeled similar enthusiasm into looking into where Assemblyman-elect Sean Keogh derives his finances. For a man who at twenty-three has no visible earning skills, he amassed a staggering coffer for his assault on the Assembly seat. If the Republican Party in the past has sacrificed common sense for the smell of victory, it should not compound its errors by sacrificing morality too.

Sean flipped the paper back onto the table. He sighed and then said, "Curious that Mr. Mathers should be so passionate about the future of little old Southie at a time when Lyndon Johnson is screwing the country. Ah, well, so much for freedom of the press." He spoke in light, measured tones to conceal the genuine panic broiling inside him. This could dismantle the entire master plan, bringing his friends to their knees, pushing Southie back across the river and torpedoing any ambitions he might have for the Senate—not to mention the presidency.

McLaughlin spoke. "I think Eddie worries too much. We're not worried, Sean boy."

"Well," said Burke, "put it this way. It doesn't worry us, Sean, but it worries us that it might hurt you."

Sean nodded his thanks. He knew Burke meant it. What a wonderful animal the big lug was.

"Well, what do we do, Eddie? You're the brains of the outfit."

"That's it, Sean—I'm not quite sure. We could sue his Brookline ass off because of the tone of the editorial. I mean, it outright accuses you of being a crook."

Sean marveled at that word "crook." He had never thought of himself as anything but a businessman. Crooks lived in Roxbury and mugged old women and held up liquor stores.

"Well, Eddie, would we win in court?"

"Yes, I think we would."

Sean remained silent and then said, "But we might lose more than we win in the ensuing court case."

"Right."

Burke swung his feet off the table and leaned forward in his chair. "There's another way."

Sean knew Frank's "other ways," and much as he loved his friend, he never approved.

McLaughlin and Wilson looked at Burke inquisitively. Burke smiled as he spoke. "We could really hurt him. . . . No, no, I don't mean busting him up. But the Teamsters drive his delivery trucks. I know the local president like a brother. A seven-day strike might teach Mr. damn Mathers a lesson."

Wilson gave it some thought. "It could work."

Sean shook his head. "No, those things don't work on old guys like Mathers. I've never met him, but something tells me he's a pretty decent old boy. No, no. It's too destructive."

"Well," said McLaughlin with a sigh, "you guys remember the early days when I was running around. Now, if a guy had a crap game, we would muscle him out to take it over . . ."

"No, Mr. Mac . . . you don't do that with newspapers," Sean insisted.

"Hey, lad, ye didn't let me finish . . . we would muscle him out, or other times we would just buy him out."

Sean narrowed his eyes as if he didn't understand. "What does that mean, Mr. Mac?"

"Just what I said. We could buy him out. Fancy yerself as a newspaper publisher, Sean boy?"

There was a stunned silence. McLaughlin, the old-timer, had once put little faith in Sean Keogh's ambitions. But the past two months had convinced him otherwise.

"Us? Buy a newspaper? Me a publisher?"

"Sure, Sean. Very appealing. Could you imagine a bunch of us villains running a newspaper? Jesus, could you imagine how far Capone would have gone if he had owned a newspaper?"

Everybody laughed, but Sean laughed less than the others.

"I tell you what, Eddie: give me some time to think about that lawsuit. I agree it could be damaging. I've got to to get downtown now and meet Roger Sharpe. I'll get back here later. Okay?"

The meeting broke up, and Sean buttoned up his coat as a blast of cold air whipped into his face. Perhaps Roger might have a few ideas.

"WHAT DO you think he has against me, Roger?" Sean was sipping his coffee after lunch at the Ritz.

"Simply that the old boy thinks it is quite legitimate for the Democrats to advance the career of young, hustling . . . er . . . businessmen like yourself. But he feels that the Republican conscience is carved in stone. He genuinely thinks you and your friends are using the party." Roger Sharpe could have been blunter in his explanation, but he chose his words.

"Well, there is no question that we are using the party to some degree. Of course we are. Doesn't every politician?"

"It's hard to argue with you, Sean. I'm just telling you how his mind works."

"How stable is his support among stockholders of the *Clarion*?"

"Well, as far as their moral support goes, it's very stable."

"What do you mean by that?"

"Well, frankly, they love his principles, but his principles don't make money. There is strong dissent among those who think they should be making money out of the paper. They're businessmen."

"Does it make any money?"

"Barely breaks even. The old boy has plunged a fortune of his own into it."

Sean suddenly lost interest in the conversation. Quickly, he called for the check.

Roger Sharpe's eyes searched for the reason for the bolt of lightning that had suddenly struck Sean.

"What's the hurry?"

"Thanks, Roger, you have just given me a great idea."

"Idea?"

"Yes. I'll call you later. Bye."

Sean jumped into a taxi and raced back to the office. He tore through the door.

"Frank, where are Mac, Eddie?"

"Mac is down at his office on the docks. Eddie is downtown at the law offices."

Sean dialed Wilson on the telephone. "Hi, Eddie. Sean. Listen: I want you to get me a list of every stockholder in the *Clarion*. I want a detailed rundown on anyone who has a cent in the paper, including every item of information about Mathers' finances. . . . No, Eddie, I'll explain later. And Eddie—line up a meeting with the old boy himself, say in about two weeks' time. . . . Why? Because we're going into the newspaper business, that's why."

Frank Burke gaped as he listened to the conversation. Sean put down the receiver, turned to Burke and gave him a good-natured tap in the ribs. "Don't blame me, Frank. It was all Mr. Mac's idea."

"You definitely have gone nuts."

"Now, Frank, I want you to get a complete rundown on labor costs at the paper, various union contracts, with an idea of which unions we can control and what unions are likely to give us the most trouble. Okay?"

"Okay. . . . Sean?"

"Yes, old pal?"

"You really have your heart set on this, don't you?"

"Damn right."

"Well," Burke said with a sigh of resignation, "here we go again." He smiled good-naturedly.

"Frank, Mac was right. Look what Capone could have done if he'd owned a newspaper. . . . Just joking, Frank. It's guys like us who can make a paper like the *Clarion* make us a fortune. And what's more, think of the faces on Beacon Hill when they hear Southie has a newspaper. Listen—call Mac and tell him I think he's a genius. Now I've got to get down to working some figures." He closed the inner office door behind him. "Oh, if Rose calls tell her I'm caught up. I'll fill her in on the excitement later."

Burke nodded his head obediently. And he smiled at the enthusiasm of his young friend and marveled. Newspapers, Burke thought. There had been a time when he feared newspapers as much as he did cops. And here was Sean Keogh—elected an assemblyman only two weeks before after pulling off an incredible political coup; two weeks married and just back from his honeymoon, and now he wanted to put Southie and its boys into newspapers. He sighed and smiled again. How would Rose ever keep up with him? he wondered.

SHE SAT in front of the television set. She had called all her nurse friends, walked through the Boston Common, had lunch in the coffee shop without even knowing that her new husband was in the dining room and now was passing the time watching television. She felt so useless. She called Frank Burke's office. No, Mr. Keogh wasn't in; tied up, but he would be home early.

He walked through the door at seven o'clock that night. He swept her up in his arms.

"I've got some wild news for you, Rose," he said. "I'm going to try to break into newspaper publishing."

"Newspaper publishing? But Sean, you don't know anything about it."

"What's there to know? I know I can do it. We're making a pass at the *Clarion.* It's going to be tough, but I can do it. Aren't you excited?"

"Why . . . er . . . yes. . . . Of course, darling."

He kissed her again. "Want to go out for dinner? Hope so, because I've booked a table at Mario's. It's a great place."

She nodded obediently and then broached the question. "Sean, do you know I haven't even seen the house you bought?"

"Don't want you to see it yet. Too messy. No furniture. I want it to be a surprise for you, Rose. We'll be in the house in six days. You'll love it."

"I was thinking that maybe I could look at the furniture you bought. Maybe help in the decoration."

"Why? I have the best interior decorator in Boston doing it. I don't want to have you troubled. I want it to be a surprise. I want you to take it easy for a change." He quickly changed the subject. "Spoken to your dad and brother yet?"

Rose masked her disappointment by answering, "Yes, I called them. Going to see them during the week."

"Fine, fine. If they need any help, tell them not to hesitate to ask. They need anything?"

"No," she said wistfully, and realized that none of the men of Southie needed a single thing. But Rose needed something, and every successive day the need became more of an obsession. She needed her identity back. She could feel herself fast disappearing down a huge emotional hole in the ground and heading toward oblivion in very much the same way her mother had disappeared.

SEAN KEOGH had traveled downtown with Eddie Wilson in Sean's new black Buick. Eddie had done a good job of compiling an exhaustive rundown on the stockholders of the *Clarion.* And today was the day. At ten o'clock in the morning Keogh and Wilson walked acoss Hurley Place and trotted up the front steps of the *Boston Clarion,* the proud bastion of a Boston long since gone. It was an ornate, almost Dickensian building, standing as a sort of monument to an era when Boston was regarded a city far ahead of New York as the cultural and political home of America.

Despite his deep roots in the Irish end of town, it was something that Keogh could revere in a way that perhaps his friends and associates from Southie could not. He had never once been inside the building, and he felt a tingle of quiet excitement as he bounced up the steps built 120 years before.

Sean and Wilson approached the reception desk. Despite their young years, they both looked impressive in their snappy three-piece suits.

"Mr. Keogh and Mr. Wilson," Wilson said. "We have a ten-o'clock appointment with Mr. Mathers." The receptionist nodded politely and turned to a large leather-bound appointment book. Quietly and efficiently she checked their names and then picked up a telephone with a direct line to the desk, on the eighth floor, of Mathers' male secretary.

"A Mr. Keogh and a Mr. Wilson to see Mr. Mathers. . . . Yes, right away," the receptionist said into the telephone.

She turned to Keogh and Wilson. "To your right," she said. "Eighth floor."

They walked through a huge marble lobby which was bustling with dignified vitality and into a huge oak-paneled elevator, a relic of another era.

"Eighth floor, please," Wilson said to the elevator operator. The elegant old elevator chugged upward as if it were struggling toward Nirvana. Sean Keogh was intoxicated by the atmosphere. They know how to do it right, these Boston Brahmins, he thought. We could take a page from their book.

They were met on the eighth floor by an impeccably dressed gentleman whose shoes were mirrors. It was the male secretary to Sheldon Mathers. He led them across thick pearl-gray-carpeted corridors to a massive oak-paneled door. He buzzed twice, and a return buzz signaled their permission to enter. Sean took a deep breath.

Inside, the office was cavernous. The walls were adorned with stately oil paintings of past editors and Presidents and mayors. At the end of the giant office was a huge desk, positioned under the largest oil painting in the room, which Sean correctly surmised portrayed an ancestor of Sheldon Mathers. Mathers sat cool and resplendent in a leather chair behind the desk, dressed in a chalk-striped charcoal suit and wearing a high-collared shirt similar to those worn by British diplomats. He was a man of striking looks, with a thick mane of white hair carefully combed, a white mustache and clear steel-gray eyes. A red carnation in his lapel gave him the appearance of a Douglas Fairbanks. In front of him and to his left sat a short, brusque-looking bald-headed man. There was little emotion in either man's face. This was obviously not a meeting they relished.

Sean strode confidently up to the desk.

"Mr. Mathers, Sean Keogh. This is Mr. Wilson, my attorney."

Mathers rose slightly from his seat and gave a crisp, friendless handshake.

"Mr. Keogh, Mr. Wilson, this is Mr. Thwaite, our company counsel and my personal attorney. Be seated." It was almost a command. There was a split second of awkward silence, and Mathers bored his gaze into Keogh as if nobody else existed in the room.

"Mr. Keogh, I think in the interests of my newspaper and the interests of the taxpayers you are to serve, it will be well to get to the point and waste little time. I consented to see you, Mr. Keogh, out of what I hope is a sense of personal fairness. In other words, to see what you have to say."

Keogh nodded coolly. He wasn't going to let this old warrior rattle him, although he did feel slightly weak in the ankles.

Mathers continued: "It may seem curious to you, considering some of the editorial treatment you have been accorded by this newspaper, that I feel as strongly about your individual rights as I do about my own. A newspaper can obviously be a brutal weapon. That is why my newspaper is and has been in the hands of men who have shown rare principles. Now, articles in this newspaper concerning yourself and your political achievements in the past month have not been favorable. In short, Mr. Keogh, they were not meant to be. I can assure you the content of the articles and their thrust does not approach the volume of information we have gathered on you and your associates. I don't believe in mincing my words. I personally was appalled at the situation in South Boston, the Republican endorsement and the caliber of people I believe will be wielding power in a vital section of our city.

"Now, Mr. Thwaite is here to answer any particular complaints or queries that you or Mr. Wilson might have should you be contemplating legal action, which is your absolute right. You, of course, have the recourse of legal action following this meeting. Feel free to speak frankly, and I give you my personal assurance that this conversation is confidential. That is all I can offer you if you are here to ask for a revision of our editorial policy concerning your political career. Gentlemen?"

He had given the signal to talk.

Keogh measured him with his gaze. What a man, he thought with unabashed admiration. However, Sean's face said nothing. He jumped in with both feet lest a silence be misinterpreted to indicate that he was foundering.

"I too wish to get to the point, Mr. Mathers," Sean said calmly. "I can assure you that the presence of your lawyer is totally unnecessary at this moment." The old man's eyes narrowed with curiosity. "I have no genuine complaint personally about the editorial treatment you have accorded me. I argue its accuracy, but let's not dwell on that."

Mathers gave a hint of looking slightly ruffled.

"Again to the point, Mr. Mathers. I am here on business."

"Mr. Keogh, what business could I possibly have with you?"

"Sir, I would like to make an offer . . . an offer to buy your newspaper."

No one could remember when Sheldon Mathers had been left without a sharp, concise, intelligent answer to any contingency that arose in conversation. The old man's face seemed to pale unhealthily. His breathing seemed to be coming in shorter gasps. But he quickly regained his composure.

"Out of respect for your intelligence, Mr. Keogh, I must ask you to elucidate on what appears to be a totally ludicrous notion."

"Certainly, sir. You now own, as the largest single stockholder, twenty-eight percent of the shares, having sold fifteen percent of your stock to personally strengthen your editorial department, to which your directors would not personally commit the paper's budget. It was a rather philanthropic exercise, as most of your financial commitment has been to this newspaper, however fiscally unwise. There are seventeen other shareholders of any substantial measure. Of that number you can count on ten to support you. The other seven, perhaps not as dedicated as you, wish to remove you. Of the ten who support you, you will probably lose five unless you can turn the finances of this paper around.

"Of the nine unions who work here, two of those unions threaten to strike back to back. You might be able to survive a single strike, but not two. Your ability to cope with the unions has frankly been quite poor, although it would be hard to argue with your motives. Our group, quite obviously, offers major shareholders a different kind of future, particularly in the field of profit and peace with the unions, with many of which we are closely allied. Other men might wait until you are finally driven from the paper to pick it up cheaper. I think you're a principled man, and I would like to think likewise of myself. That is why I'm making the offer now, and we are here, to be frank, to talk price."

The attorney Thwaite sat there speechless with his mouth slightly sagging. Sheldon Mathers sat there in his gigantic leather chair like an ancient king whose throne was being challenged by the court jester. Slowly Sheldon Mathers leaned forward as if he were about to give some much-needed advice to an errant youngster.

"Keogh," he started, having now dropped the Mister from his address, "my great-great-grandfather started this newspaper in 1820. My great-grandfather built this building in 1840, when he was not yet thirty. He was the editor until he commanded a regiment in the Union Army and was killed at Fredericksburg. My grandfather then became editor and publisher, and then my father was editor until 1940.

"This newspaper has always been in the hands of honorable and fiercely dedicated men. My father died at this very desk of a heart attack while helping me put out the newspaper the day the atom bomb was dropped on Hiroshima. I give you this short history to let you know exactly where you stand with me.

"This is not a sleazy trucking company, or a front for a bunch of Teamster racketeers; it is not a crap game for money-grubbing lowlifes. This is one of the institutions of this city, of this country, Keogh; an institution of decency and fair play—not a plaything for thugs and self-serving hoodlums who suddenly have got themselves a good tailor."

Sean Keogh felt himself fighting a blush of awe and embarrassment at the old man's broadside. There was very little to reply to.

Sean stood up. Wilson hurriedly followed suit. He was shaken.

Sean smiled. "Thank you for your time, Mr. Mathers, Mr. Thwaite. I think we know our way out. But before I go, Mr. Mathers, I would only like to say that before I came here today I did not know whether I was really determined to become the publisher and save this paper from disgrace. But now I do. I'm very determined. Good day to you, gentlemen."

As Keogh calmly turned on his heel, followed by Wilson, Sheldon Mathers slumped back in his chair as if he had been hit in the chest with something heavy.

He turned to his lawyer. "Thwaite, be so kind as to fetch me a brandy. I have found Mr. Keogh's visit here quite distressing. Quite distressing."

WILSON TURNED to Sean as they trotted down the steps of the venerable newspaper building. "My God, Sean, I would like to bury that old bastard. The filthy arrogance of the man. I would like to bury him."

"Would you, Eddie? I quite like him."

Wilson gave his companion a curious look.

"Eddie," Sean said, turning, "I'll call you tonight."

"Where are you off to?"

"To see some of the major shareholders. I might like the old guy, but I'm going to be publisher of that paper. Give Frank a rundown on what happened. Mr. Mac too. See you."

FRANK BURKE grimaced as Wilson gave him the details of the meeting. "It was a disaster, Frank—a disaster, I tell you," Wilson said. "The old bastard tore Sean to shreds when he came straight out and told him he wanted to make an offer."

"That bad, huh?"

"Yes, that bad. Look, Frank, this whole thing is crazy. Why don't we just forget about the whole crazy thing? It's madness. Sean wanting to go into newspapers. It's just plain crazy. What is this—some kind of ego trip?"

Burke shot Wilson a critical glance. "No, Eddie, it's not. He wants to do something, do something for all of us. You should know that. It's no ego trip."

Wilson should have known better than to criticize Keogh in front of Frank. "Well, I just think it's impossible, Frank."

"I don't believe anything is impossible if Sean sets his mind to it. Let's think of ways to help him, not hurt him."

"I do, Frank; that's why I think we should give the whole thing up. Sheldon Mathers will cool down and forget all about Sean one day."

"Wrong, Eddie. Not if Sean wants to go higher . . . the Senate. Sheldon Mathers will head him off and you know it. Now let's think."

"I've done all the thinking I can, Frank. I give up."

"Eddie, I can't believe this old guy is as clean as everyone says he is. He must have a skeleton somewhere in his closet."

"Not that I know of, Frank. He's as clean as a whistle."

"What about his family . . . any children?"

"Two sons by a previous marriage. She died about eight years ago. He married again. Some society girl. Constance . . . Constance Mathers. She's very social. Old family, all that stuff."

"What about his executives? Same thing?"

"Yes, Frank. He only surrounds himself with the same kind. All blue-bloods."

"There has to be a way to get at him. There just has to be."

At that very moment Sean Keogh was starting to believe there was no way at all. A sweep through the shareholders and board of directors had shown Sean that although there was some concern about falling profits, there was very little enthusiasm to sell out to a man like Sean Keogh.

That night Keogh came back to the hotel a discouraged man. He walked in and kissed his wife.

She had heard from Burke's wife, Teresa, that the meeting with Mathers had not gone well. But Sean remained silent about it. He steadfastly refused to share any of his life with his new wife, and it was something she couldn't grasp.

That night in bed, as he lay staring into the darkness, she decided to ask him about the day.

"How did it go, Sean? Not so well?"

He put his arm around her. "Baby, don't you worry about it. I don't want you concerned with my boring business troubles." And that simply dismissed the whole issue.

Rose Keogh felt her body tauten. Sean Keogh refused to share anything with her. Was he so superior and arrogant as to think she couldn't understand the workings of the male business world? She felt a wave of resentment wash over her. She had not even been consulted about the new house or even the furniture. He had robbed her of her job as a nurse and wouldn't even let her replace it with being a full-time homemaker. More and more the specter of her neglected mother preyed on her mind. Rose Keogh wanted desperately to be a person, not just a simple piece of female furniture.

That night when they made love, she willingly gave him her body. But from that time on, her mind would be her own, and a huge chasm was opening between them—even if Sean Keogh didn't know it. With each act of neglect by Sean, real or imagined, Rose drifted further into her own world, a world filled with her own ambitions and wants, fueled by a horrible memory that frightened her more than the prospect of death. It was the image of her being completely blotted from humanity the same way her mother was.

FROM THE very roots of his origins, Frank Burke was not a fast thinker. He was not a man of ideas but a man of intentions, and his thought processes moved as methodically as an assembly line, starting from a raw thought and slowly refining it. From the moment that Eddie Wilson had told him of Sean's frustration, he slowly set out to accomplish his intention. He knew nothing about newspapers, but he had a rare instinct for people, and he knew that people might come into the world sinless, but they don't live as long as Sheldon Mathers and remain sinless or never have contact with sin. It was this plodding determination which often irked Eddie Wilson, a man whose loyalty had been proved over and over but who had too strong an instinct for survival to tackle unknown odds.

It had been a hard two weeks in which Burke had checked and rechecked the union setup at the *Clarion*. Sean had forbidden any outright attack on Sheldon Mathers' labor organization, although it would have been ridiculously easy to cause a series of strikes through his good offices with the Teamsters. He had pushed and pushed Wilson for a complete rundown on the personnel surrounding the Mathers empire. But they were as Wilson predicted: clean.

It was on the fourteenth day that Wilson came into the office. He looked agitated.

"What's wrong with you?" Burke asked.

"I still have nothing . . . nothing, really . . . nothing we could use."

"What do you mean nothing . . . really? Eddie, I know you're not keen on this caper, but don't hold out."

It was a reluctant Wilson who gave him the news.

Frank Burke's eyes widened with satisfaction. He then set about discussing a plan that made Wilson regret ever imparting the information. He had anticipated what Burke's reaction would be, and he silently cursed himself for not keeping his mouth shut.

Chapter

8

FRANK BURKE pondered the reluctance of Eddie Wilson to go along with his plan. Maybe Harvard Yard had softened him. No, Eddie was a stand-up guy, Frank thought. He shouldn't criticize his friend even in thought. It was just that Eddie had mixed a lot more with the people outside Southie. Eddie was cautious because that's what was best for Sean and the outfit. It had taken Burke two days of verbal arm-twisting before Eddie had finally given in. Then it took another three days for the meeting to be set up.

He sat in a darkened back booth of the Anchor Café on Harbor Street, just east of the South Boston Naval Annex. The customers' drinks and their dress yelled that it was a workingmen's saloon. Burke put a bottle of beer to his lips and gulped thirstily. The contents were as cold as the bleak weather outside. He looked at his watch with impatience. He is due now. How would he handle the guy? He would play it by ear. People didn't worry Frank Burke, no matter where they came from.

As Burke nodded to a plump waitress for another bottle of beer, a tall, good-looking blond man in his early thirties walked through the heavy glass door and looked around the unfamiliar surroundings uncertainly. He wore a starched white shirt and silk tie and an immaculately English-cut checked suit. Clearly he wasn't a regular.

Burke half-stood in the booth and motioned the man toward him. A few of the customers gave curious looks. Probably a lawyer. The blond man walked in an even tall stride toward the booth.

"Mr. Burke?"

"Mr. John Hickey. . . . Beer?" Burke nodded to the waitress. She brought another bottle. The man he called Hickey asked for a glass. The gesture was not lost on Burke. The two men eyed each other with interest and suspicion. Hickey broke the ice.

"Freezing, isn't it?"

"It's healthy for you." Burke took a swig from his bottle.

Hickey poured his beer into the glass and sipped slowly, keeping his sapphire-colored eyes on the bulky curly-haired man in front of him wearing a heavy leather coat.

"I must say, Mr. Burke, I'm not at all sure what this meeting is all about."

"That surprises me."

"Really. Well, I'm not. Mr. Wilson said that it could be advantageous for both of us. A business deal of some sort. Our businesses don't often cross over much. Our type of businesses, that is."

"Well, Mr. Hickey, I could argue with that, but I really don't have the time." Burke had sized up this man. He had researched his background exhaustively, and now he knew he didn't have to play games.

"Well, in that case, Mr. Burke, I'm interested to hear what you have to say."

"Hickey," Burke said, dropping the Mister, "yer here because yer greedy and hungry." Burke saw the muscles moving in Hickey's jaw as he took the insult in studied silence. Burke jumped in with both feet. "Ya were fired from two New York newspapers as a society columnist fer takin' money off rich dames to get their names in the newspaper. Ya've managed to con the ol' man, Sheldon Mathers, because ya've managed to con a lot o' wives o' board members with flattering references to their clothes and their parties. Ya manage all right, but ya live too high for the money ya make. Ya owe yer country club four thousand dollars, not to mention the casino debts ya owe in the Bahamas and London. Ya need a lot of help, Hickey, and guys like you don't get help from nice people."

Hickey managed to contain the tidal wave of anger boiling at the back of his neck. People lined up to hate him, but never had the temerity to throw their contempt in his face like a bucketful of evil-smelling waste. He flushed as he started to speak and found that the smoothness and glib words for which he was well known had suddenly failed him.

Thin-lipped, he said, "You are an uneducated thug, and if you're thinking, Burke, of slugging me, think again. I would have no hesitation in calling some police who are very close and very influential."

Burke's face assumed a look of boredom.

Hickey continued: "You have been arrested twice for murder but never convicted. You spent twenty months in Walpole State Prison for almost beating a man to death who held up a crap game operated by your friend Bernard McLaughlin. Sean Keogh, your Messiah from South Boston, set you up in a trucking business, from which you have infiltrated the Teamsters Union, and you regard this Keogh as a cross between Moses and the Pope. How's that for homework!"

Burke smiled and leaned forward. In a half whisper he said, "I want to give ya some very good advice. Ya ain't built good enough, either yer body or yer heart, to talk that way. So when we meet in the future, remember that . . . just in case I ferget."

Hickey flushed the flush of a coward. He was angry at himself for showing all his cards. It showed that he knew exactly the business at hand. He regained his cool exterior.

"Well, I admire your candor, Mr. Burke. To be perfectly candid myself, I have rarely if ever dealt with, er, people like your good self. Now, if we go into some kid of contract of mutual benefit, what guarantee do I have that you will live up to your end?"

Burke could smell the cologne that seemed to surround Hickey in a cloud. "Mr. Hickey," he said, resuming the 'Mister,' "if you have done so much homework on me, you should know I always keep my end of the bargain. And I expect other people to do the same. Those who don't end up by walking funny." Burke never uttered threats, he just carried them out, and he didn't like talking that way. Words like those were for the likes of Paddy Devlin. But he bent his own rules, he thought, to get the point crystal clear with this fancily dressed fairy.

"Now, Mr. Hickey, let's get to it. How often do you see her?"

"At least once a week. Twice, sometimes three times, depending. Sometimes at my place, sometimes other places. I'm seeing her tonight, and I'll know tonight where I'm seeing her for our next meeting." Hickey had completely caved in.

"Well, Mr. Hickey, then you know how we're going to run this game?"

"I suspect so."

"Then I don't want to waste any more of yer precious hours away from informing the Boston public about the society beat. I'll expect yer call tomorrow, Mr. Hickey. See ya. . . . Don't worry—I'll pay for the beer . . . and the glass."

Uncertainly, John Hickey rose from the booth, put on his heavy overcoat and walked outside. It had all happened so fast. The cold wind felt good in his face. It seemed to clear his head from a meeting that had tangled a hundred thoughts together like a pitful of snakes.

He was visibly worried. Had he gone too far? Bitten off more than he could chew? Conning the society circuit and old dames was one thing, but lying in bed with thugs and murderers was quite a different matter.

He shook his head. Now, think clearly, he told himself. Is there an alternative? No, it's only a matter of time before Sheldon Mathers catches on to my game. The principled old fool would fire me in a second, he thought. Out-of-work columnists with a reputation are out-of-work columnists. No, let's face it, he told himself again, I know what

I'm doing. The rewards would be handsome, very handsome. And anyway, I'm not doing anything criminal . . . really.

He suddenly felt better and walked with a renewed stride toward his Mercedes, parked down the block.

By the time he had parked in the basement garage of the *Clarion,* he was feeling extremely bright about his prospects. John Hickey loved the good life more than anything else because he had to go through so much to get it.

Convinced that his future had taken a dramatic upturn, misgivings notwithstanding, he felt good. He bounded up the three flights of stairs to the third-floor editorial offices. With an athletic bounce to his walk, he swept toward his desk. The secretaries' heads always turned when Hickey walked through the office. He had been with most of them in his elegant apartment on Commercial Avenue in Cambridge, overlooking the Charles River. No question, he was a good-looking man.

In the next two hours he would finish his column. He was sure that her call would come exactly at 6:30 p.m.

She was a minute early.

"Hickey speaking," he said into the telephone.

"Can I talk on this line? Nobody can pick it up?"

"No, no, dear. This is the private line, I told you."

Her voice was girlish, mischievous, as if she were a Vassar girl who was sneaking a boy into her dormitory.

"Great to hear your voice, Johnny."

"Great to hear yours."

"Well, John," she said with forced coyness, "as they say, your place or mine?"

"Since when, Constance, has it bothered you?" he said with a teasing laugh.

"John, you're terrible. It's just that I don't like big hotel suites. It makes me feel cheap." Hickey raised his eyebrows. God, the way women delude themselves.

"Okay, why not drop over to my place, about eight thirty tonight?"

"Wonderful, darling."

"Fine, see you at my place at eight thirty. The champagne will be chilled."

"Bye, Johnny darling, bye."

Hickey replaced the receiver. Dumb bitch. She doesn't like hotel suites, makes her feel cheap. He mimicked her voice in his mind. Stupid bitch, the way she lies to herself. He hated her and her kind. But she was, after all, exquisite in the sack, and it was little enough price to pay for that new Mercedes she'd bought him.

He got up from his desk, slipped into his jacket, threw his coat over his arm and headed for the parking basement. Life was good.

He gunned his Mercedes through the night lights of Boston, crossed over the bridge to Cambridge, turned into Commercial Avenue and pulled up to a modernized three-story brownstone. The front of the building had been completely remodeled with top-to-bottom glass facing. Every room had a clear view of the river. It was the kind of town house he had always dreamed of, and now it was all his. It was the last word in taste, from the imported carpets to the antiques.

He picked up his mail, opening it as he pushed the key into the heavy wood door with brass fittings. He trotted up the thick-carpeted staircase.

Quickly he undressed and hung his custom-made suit on a brass silent valet in the large bedroom. He walked into the bathroom, sprinkled some bath salts into the Jacuzzi and turned on the softly whirring machine. He wanted to be in good shape for tonight. Working as a society columnist might have been his entrée, but it was only a fraction of his work.

The hot-water jets pummeled his muscles as he sat back in luxury. His thoughts turned to Burke. Yes, he did detest the man and his kind. He had never met Keogh, but suspected that his predictably dark Irishness would sicken him also. But he did trust Burke. He knew he would receive his end of the deal if he came through with his. Yes, he could trust Burke, and he *would* come through with his part of the deal—that was, until he could get the upper hand, and then he would dictate the terms to Burke.

He stretched and got out of the Jacuzzi, dried himself with a rough towel and splashed himself with cologne from a big earthen bottle. He slipped on a pair of silk jockey shorts and donned a monogrammed Thai-silk robe that revealed a tanned, lean-muscled chest which was set off by a discreet gold chain around his neck.

When the doorbell chimed at 8:25, the Dom Perignon was already in a bucket of ice, and the caviar and Nova Scotia salmon were laid out on a silver tray. He pressed the buzzer to open the heavy door downstairs and heard the impatient padding of high-heeled feet coming up the stairs.

"Constance . . . honey . . . God, you look ravishing." Hickey rarely told the truth about anything. But his description was close to being accurate.

She had the tall, tight, willowy body of the New York high-fashion model she had once been. A luxurious mane of raven-black hair fell silkily around a perfectly sculptured face, illuminated by eyes the color of the Caribbean and skin the shade of thick cream. She threw off her

Black Diamond mink and stood faultless in an oyster-gray Saint Laurent that was gathered at the waist by a sterling-silver link chain.

She remained silent for a split second, looking hard at the tall, blond presence of Hickey. "I just want to drink you in," she said. And then she flung herself into his arms, her eyes closed and her head tilted upward as Hickey covered her long neck and throat with kisses.

"Oh, Johnny, you've got everything." She kissed him hungrily and dug her nails into his tautly muscled shoulders. Her hands slid under his robe and her fingers found his rounded buttocks. She pressed herself hard against him. She searched his mouth with her tongue and held him a long time.

Gently he eased her away from him: "Constance, my love, you beautiful creature, let's warm ourselves with some cool champagne."

She threw herself down on an overstuffed couch and with a deep sigh tossed off her shoes.

"Johnny, I feel like it's been months since we were last together. Isn't it ridiculous—it's only been a week. I counted every minute. It's very difficult to fill the hours between our meetings, my love. After a while Neiman Marcus and Saks start to feel like jails. It's such a damn bore doing things without you. Parties, hairdressers . . . it's a damn bore, baby. I wish we could run away together. Anywhere. New York, Palm Beach, San Francisco, Acapulco . . . anywhere. It's this crazy job of yours. You could walk out of there tomorrow. You know I have more than enough for the both of us. Who cares who has the money. I wish you wouldn't stand on your stupid pride. It's keeping us apart, you and your pride."

The absurdity of the statement could have made Hickey collapse in a paroxysm of laughter. Oh, he had seriously considered living off her for the rest of his life. But no, once again someone else would be in control of him. He was going to be rich *and* independent. And besides, who could stand sleeping with the same woman every night? Not John Hickey.

He smiled. "Just be patient, honey. Here, drink up." He handed her a cut-glass goblet of champagne.

She sipped at the bubbly. Then she drained her glass quickly. She tried to hold herself back, but it was useless. She slammed down the champagne glass, leaped to her feet and almost in a single move slipped out of her dress and stockings. She was naked in a matter of seconds, to reveal the body of a beautifully developed teen-ager. Hickey knew she was forty-three only because he had sneaked a look at her passport.

He took her by the hand and led her into his giant bedroom. He untied his robe, let it fall to the floor and slipped off his jockey shorts.

She threw herself back on the bed and gazed at the figure standing above her. Hickey had the body of an athlete.

He covered her body with his, running his hands through her beautiful hair and covering every inch of her with burning kisses. With each touch of his lips she could feel herself losing control as her head swam in a pool of lust. Everywhere he touched her seemed to experience its own separate orgasm. She bit her lower lip to stop herself from shouting her ecstasy as she could feel his rigid penis rubbing all over her body.

Gently and in a single perfect stroke, without so much as losing a split second of his sexual ballet, he slid himself inside her. Slowly and gently at first, as if taunting and promising at the same time that there was much more violence in his loins. She had now lost total control as she wrapped her legs around his buttocks, her ankles striking violently against him as if to drive him farther inside. Her tongue thrust deeply inside his mouth, and her nails drew deep welts across his shoulders.

His movements accelerated now, and he seemed to go on and on, throwing himself into her body like a glorious piston. Orgasm after orgasm shuddered through her body, and still he pumped, his hands covering her face, running through her hair, and his lips and tongue covering her with caresses. As each climax shafted through her, she would grind her teeth as if to keep from screaming to the world at the top of her lungs that she was in the most personal of heavens, inhabited by nobody else. Hickey was an expert when it came to handling other people's bodies, women's or men's.

As she felt a final explosion inside her, she could no longer stifle a signal that she could take no more. She covered his mouth with hers, and yet the scream could not be muffled.

Her body went completely limp as her eyes glazed over in a semiconscious act of exhaustion and ultimate satisfaction. She whimpered now. She felt his hot stream inside her. His timing was perfect.

"Johnny, Johnny," she whispered, "promise me, promise me, you would never do this with anyone else. I would die if I thought you gave this pleasure to another woman. I couldn't take it. No, I couldn't."

He calmed her with soft, even-toned words: "Impossible, baby; you know it, and I know you know it." She curled under him with a light smile of reassurance on her face. Like a well-stroked cat after a meal.

She left just before 11:30 P.M., as gorgeous, as fashion-perfect and as elegant as she had walked into the apartment. She lingered and felt the temptation to do it all over again. But Hickey coaxed her to go with a word of caution.

"Of course, you're right," she answered. "You're always right." He kissed her hand lightly, signaling that anything more ambitious might disturb her new light layer of makeup.

"When, Johnny—when?"

"Can you make it Friday? Friday okay with you?"

She smiled and rolled her eyes upward. "My God, three more days
. . . I'll be counting the seconds." She threw him a kiss as she draped her
fur coat over her shoulders and disappeared quietly down the stairs into
the street and into her Jaguar XK custom-made sports car.

Hickey could hear the engine disappearing in the quietness of the
street. He smiled to himself, poured himself a cognac, lit a Cuban cigar
which he always ordered from Montreal and sat in a huge armchair
overlooking the city.   .

Within twenty minutes she had crossed over to Boston and was already among the austere mansions of Brookline. She stopped at No. 20
Tewksbury Crescent. The lights were still on. She pulled into the driveway of the huge, gleaming white Colonial. As she fumbled with the key,
the butler opened the door. He gave her a warm smile. She returned
the smile and said, "Frederick, is everyone still up? It has to be midnight."

"Mr. Mathers just beat you home, madam."

She walked into the huge foyer. Off to the left was the red-carpeted
library.

"Ho, ho, we are a pair of night birds. If I had known where that
confounded art-gallery opening was, I would have come and picked you
up for a nightcap, darling." Sheldon Mathers walked across the room
and embraced his wife. He pecked her on the cheek. "How was it, anyway? A lot of New England talent, I hope."

"Oh, Sheldon, it was deadly dull. Really, I don't know why I keep on
going to them. It really is a waste of time."

"Nonsense, my dear—gets you out of the house."

"Sometimes, Sheldon, I think I would just as soon curl up in bed with
a good book."

"Ah, how about a sherry before bed?"

"You have one, darling; not for me. I'll wait up. How are things at the
office?"

"Same old story—the board screaming for obscene profits. They
should be in shoe manufacturing. Ahh, but at least I give them something to make them legitimate at their interminable dinner parties.
Come over and sit down, Connie. I'll just have a short nip and I'll call it
a day."

"You work too hard for that paper, Sheldon. You do look tired."

He smiled at her as he poured himself three inches of vintage Spanish
sherry. "And may I be so bold as to say you look beautiful." He held up
the thin-stemmed glass in a toast. He stood there silent, his thick mane
of snow-white hair glistening under the chandelier.

"I'm a lucky man, Constance."

"We're both lucky, Sheldon."

JOHN HICKEY could just see the tip of the *Clarion* building across the river as he sat in the chair overlooking the city—a reminder of the time when it had been the tallest building in Boston. He luxuriated in these silent moments by himself, surrounded by his apartment, his custom-made clothes, his antiques, his art collection and his satisfaction that the onetime male prostitute who had solicited "chicken hawks" at Third Avenue and Fifty-first Street in New York, was getting his own back for all the filth and indignities he had suffered at the hands of others. He allowed himself a thin smile as he thought of Constance Mathers in bed right now with that self-righteous, pompous old fool who made a profession of ethics, honesty and good taste. Fuck him. What would he do with his ethics if he knew that that slut of his had just crawled from my bed? He chuckled and poured himself another cognac. As he sipped, he took the telephone in his lap and dialed the number of the Erin Social Club.

Frank Burke came to the telephone. "Burke."

"All set for Friday night, my fine South Boston friend."

"Right. Don't screw up."

"That, sir, you can count on." Burke returned to the bar and felt filthy.

On Friday night at eight thirty, one hour after Constance Mathers had kissed her husband goodbye, John Hickey repeated his perfect act of lovemaking. But this perhaps was even a better performance than ever before, and it was all caught by an automatically set infrared-ray camera and a tape recorder.

On Saturday morning, ten eight-by-ten-inch prints and a duplicate tape were delivered into the hands of Frank Burke at the office of his trucking company. Burke tipped the messenger lavishly.

Eddie Wilson looked uneasy. "Frank, this is madness. The old boy won't budge for this. He is just as likely to go to the cops and point the finger at Sean."

Burke looked pale at the suggestion. "No, Eddie—it might not work, but he won't go to the cops. He won't. As Brahmin and blue-blood as he is. He has his weakness, and his weakness is that cock-happy whore he married." Then he added glumly, "Poor old bastard."

"Well, don't say I didn't tell you so," Wilson warned.

"Eddie, whatever happens, be careful in even the way you react to Sean, if the whole scam works. He must never know about this. Not while I'm alive, anyway. He would hate my guts for it . . . even though we're doin' it for him."

"You got it, Frank. But I think you can take loyalty a bit too far."
Burke was thoughtful for a moment, then said quietly, "No, we can't."

Burke discreetly acquired another copy of the tape and set of photographs. His stomach turned as he realized what he was doing. Burke had killed men, but he had always rationalized that they had it coming. He had robbed men, but the men he had robbed were robbers. This, to Burke, was indeed a sin.

He carefully repacked the original set, making sure there were no fingerprints on the thick, shiny brown envelope. He marked it URGENT AND CONFIDENTIAL. Later that night he personally dropped the package into the *Clarion*'s mail chute, eliminating the need for a postmark. The package contained no message, no demands, no threats. Its content would communicate all: Sell the *Clarion,* or else.

After dropping off the package, Burke drove back to Southie and to the Sacred Heart Church, where he sought out Father Zeibatski to take his confession.

THE NEXT day, Sunday, found Sheldon Mathers at 3 P.M. in the huge, imposing old office on the eighth floor of the Clarion Building. It was the one day when he never wore a suit. Even so, he was immaculately turned out, in gray flannels, a double-breasted blazer and a rep tie. As board members and stockholders began to rankle at the paper-thin profits, he had decided to recapitalize his out-of-town printing plant with money diverted from his own trust fund. Two more printing presses and he would be able to expand the print run and the circulation to the outlying areas around Boston. With a bigger circulation, perhaps as much as an additional hundred thousand, the newspaper could boast just under a million copies. It would take a year, perhaps eighteen months, but if he could just get the circulation over the magic million mark, he could then in good faith increase the advertising rates. And that, he muttered softly to himself, would "stall those carpet salesmen in their demands for increased profits."

He had run the plan by the board. They were delighted. He had run it by his personal accountant and he was horrified. It just wasn't sound business practice to dip into personal capital to finance what was on one hand a personal dream and on the other the greed of others. Sheldon Mathers had smiled at his accountant and with a flourish of a handful of papers had told him, "Rubbish; how much money can one person spend?"

He pored over the purchasing plans of the new printing presses; then carefully he examined the floor plan of the printing plant. He would of course have to come to terms with the delivery union, because its members would be called upon to deliver more papers . . . that meant more money. But it would be worth it. He was determined to make the *Boston Clarion* not only the most respected paper in the country, but also one of the most fiscally viable.

From the far end of the giant office he heard a discreet knock. It was his male secretary and man Friday.

"Come in, Phil."

The secretary had a stack of mail in his arms.

"I've gone through most of it, sir. Usual stuff. Invitations—luncheons, dinners. One invitation perhaps you might look at, from Governor Rockefeller of New York—a state dinner in Albany. There are a few letters and packages marked for your eyes only, which I have not opened.

"Good God, man, what are you doing here on a Sunday?"

"I knew you were coming in, sir."

"Now go. I said go, go out to dinner, get drunk somewhere—but for God's sake, out of the office. Out, out." His tone was a good-natured scold. He warmly appreciated loyalty around him. Oh, if he only had another dozen men like Phil. They just didn't make them anymore.

"Thank you, sir. See you tomorrow. Don't work too late." Despite the years in Boston, his Scottish accent was noticeable.

Sheldon Mathers waved him away. Then he went back to his plans. After half an hour, he sat back in the big leather chair and sighed with satisfaction. "I think the whole crazy plan will work," he said quietly to himself.

He started to get up to leave. Damn it, the confidential mail. There were three letters and a brown paper package. The first letter was no more confidential than a press release, an editor pleading for a raise. He got four letters like that a week. He put it aside in the file for Phil.

His fingers wrestled with the brown package. I should put these things in water first, he thought, smiling. Could be a bomb.

The pictures were face down. He noticed the tape. Probably a free-lance journalist offering his wares to the top of the organization. The ploy often worked.

He flipped over the eight-by-ten glossy prints. He caught his breath in a short gasp. Quickly he fumbled for his glasses to confirm what a pounding head and a thumping heart had told him. He wasn't breathing for several seconds. He just sat there mummified in horror. One, two, three—all of them. Those pictures. My God, oh, my God. Constance . . . and Hickey . . . John Hickey . . . in the most grotesque poses. My God, no. Then he shouted out aloud, "No, no. Filthy, filthy vermin . . . no, no!"

He was standing and shouting to nobody. He felt the blood drain from his body, and involuntarily he collapsed like a rag into his chair. He stared straight ahead, his eyes blazing, his glasses now drooping off his nose. His shoulders were slumped forward like an invalid's. His back was bent.

He sat there for long, long minutes, or was it half an hour? He didn't know. He couldn't quite grasp if he was totally conscious. His body would go rigid, then limp as it experienced overwhelming shock, then grief . . . and at last anger, terrible anger.

Despite his age, and his position, and his morals, and his principles, he was, above all, a man—an old man, but a man. The rage seemed to flood his body again with blood. His deathly pale face turned light crimson. Hickey, the manicured guttersnipe, and Constance, a pampered slut.

Slowly he could feel himself gaining control. He crossed the room and lit the huge log fire. It blazed ferociously. Good. He crushed the pictures in his hands, picked up the tape, which he spared himself from hearing, and hurled them into the fire. They crackled, and the odor of burning tape and print paper seemed to give him a moment of satisfaction. It was as if Hickey and Constance Mathers were being incinerated for their monstrous treachery. Then he walked back to his desk and sat calmly in his chair.

"Those filthy South Boston pigs," he said in a conversational tone. He had got the message. "Those lowlifes." And Hickey, an ameba; Constance Mathers, ugh. The future will look after them all—every one of them. He was not a religious man, but his overwhelming sense of fairness told him they would suffer for this act.

"No, they won't," he said as if arguing with his own instincts. "No, they won't suffer; they will prosper, they will prosper." He could feel the rage grabbing again at his chest.

He looked at the time: 4:30 P.M. Hickey would be working downstairs right now, at this moment. Now that rage had replaced shock, he looked down at his bottom drawer. It was always locked. Inside was a .44 Colt Special. It had been his father's. He had fought under Dewey in the Philippines. A vicious weapon. He smiled as he grimly entertained the thought of shooting the elegant Mr. Hickey as he sat at his desk downstairs, a desk which he didn't deserve. He chuckled perversely. Oh, if it could only happen!

He shook his head as if to clear away the thoughts of a madman. Slowly he stood up and walked from the office.

He walked all over Boston that night: Beacon Hill, the Back Bay, through Chinatown, the markets. He strolled deep in thought. He didn't feel sorry for himself; the Mathers family didn't dwell on self-pity. He just felt shame, deep shame that he had blotted the honor of his impeccable antecedents: his proud father, and grandfather and great-grandfather before him. All decent, hardworking men of principle who knew of vices only in others, who tolerated kindly the weaknesses of others but never subscribed to weaknesses in themselves.

What a fool you were, Mathers, he said to himself. Did you really think that the tall, slinky New York model had committed her life to you through love? And Hickey? What a fool, Mathers. You knew his record. Why did you go along with his employment? Of course, you know why: the wives of the board members simply adored him, darling. It was one way to get them off your back when they started waving annual reports in front of your face. Your father would have thrown them out; your grandfather would have horsewhipped them all. But no, you gave in. And Keogh, Sean Keogh. That was the one person who didn't jell. He was an Irishman, and what could you expect? You knew eventually he would dip his fingers in the gutter. Brooks Brothers doesn't change that, now, does it? No, you were wrong about Keogh. You were right all the time about the model, you were right all the time about Hickey, but you were wrong about Keogh. You didn't like Keogh, but you respected him. If he had been thirty years older or if I had been thirty years younger, we could have been friends despite the fact that he was an Irishman. I was wrong about him; I wouldn't have thought he would do something like that. It shows my father was right all along. An Irishman's fidelity starts with the bottle and stops just short of the priest until he feels the cold winds. Keogh, you surprised me. I didn't think you would do that.

He walked steadily through the thin Sunday-night traffic. He had been walking for four hours. Sheldon Mathers no longer felt bitter, betrayed or angry. He trotted up the steps of the *Boston Clarion* and caught the elevator to the eighth floor. He strode with a new step from the elevator into the office. He felt much better. He sat at his chair and looked at the paintings of his forefathers. All of them proud, all of them decent; and now *he* felt decent.

He had nothing to be ashamed of. He might have been a bad businessman, but he was a superb newspaperman and a generous employer. He had been a wonderful husband to his first wife and father to two strapping sons, even though an old man's ego had finally caught up with him when he snared a wife young enough to be his daughter. He had never cheated in business. Never. Nor had he cheated at cards or golf. Wouldn't it be strange if a biographer ever asked him to sum up his life and he answered, "I never cheated in business, cards or golf"? They would love that quote at the Palm Beach Club. He chuckled a good-natured chuckle.

He twisted the key in the lock, withdrew his father's .44 Colt that had fought under Dewey, put it to his temple and blew his brains out.

WHEN PHILIP McKENZIE, Sheldon Mather's Scottish male secretary, walked in at eight thirty the next morning, the smell of stale cordite and an old log fire still hung in the air. He wasn't horrified by the sight of the body. He and Mathers had seen many of them—Mathers as a member of America's OSS and McKenzie as a member of Britain's MI-5. They had met on Omaha Beach. They had traveled back to Dover on the same hospital ship. He looked at the embers in the fireplace. The tape frame was still there, and there were charred segments of a glossy print—two of them. He shoveled them all into a briefcase. He looked across at the body slumped in the chair, face turned upward toward the ceiling. The .44-caliber had been invented to stop charging Moro tribesmen in the Philippines. When fired at close range it made a frightening wound.

When the police offered to break the tragic news to the wife of Sheldon Mathers, Philip McKenzie insisted on taking the responsibility. His voice was flat, correct and without emotion: "Mrs. Mathers . . . I'm afraid I have some very tragic news . . . very bad."

"My God, it's Sheldon, isn't it? There's been an accident. He didn't come home last night." Her words fitted the bill of grief, but her delivery didn't. She would be a very rich woman.

"Yes, madam, Mr. Mathers is dead. He blew his brains out in his office." He delivered the words without euphemism or solace. She gasped, half in shock and half because she knew Philip McKenzie, the ever-watchful McKenzie, must have known about her string of infidelities.

McKenzie delivered the last slash: "There was no note." He was telling her that Sheldon Mathers had spared her to the end.

With those few words Philip McKenzie picked up his briefcase, walked two blocks to Keenan's Ale House, where they served warm Whitbread's ale, and got very drunk. Later that night he got on a plane to New York. As the plane flew over Boston and he imagined roughly where the *Clarion* would be in the darkness below, Philip McKenzie could have sworn he felt a tear trickle down his cheek.

EDDIE WILSON was the first to hear. The news came from a reporter on the *Boston Record*. He had filed the story for his first afternoon edition and met Wilson soon after having breakfast at the Copley Plaza. Wilson reacted with called-for shock. But as soon as the reporter was out of eyesight, he paid the check on his unfinished eggs and dashed to the pay phone. Burke had just got into the office.

"Frank, Eddie here. Have you heard?"

"Heard?"

"Yeah—old man Mathers knocked himself off. Blew his brains out. The way is open."

Burke didn't answer. He was trying not to throw up.

"Frank, Frankie . . . you there?"

When he was confident he was not about to spray his insides all over the office, Burke replied, "Eddie, what have I done, boy?"

"Nothing at all Frank, nothing. People kill themselves in Boston every day. Every day, Frank. Now, look . . ."

"No . . . fuck it . . . You look, Eddie . . . You listenin'? That's not the way it was gonna be. You hear me?" He was now shouting.

"Frank, Frank, cool it, calm down. You never even knew the man."

"You know what I mean, Eddie."

"Don't know what you're talking about, Frank. . . . Look, I'll call you later."

"Eddie . . . Eddie . . . Sean . . . he must never know."

"Don't know what you're talking about. Call you later. Don't bother yourself."

Burke slumped in his chair. He wanted to tell the world to get the guilt off his back. A confessional was no good anymore.

Wilson quickly called Sean Keogh.

"Rose? Eddie here, Rose. Sean there?"

Rose and Sean were at breakfast in the lovely, sunny breakfast room at the house in Carson Beach.

"Yes, Ed, what you got?"

"Sean, some bad news and some good news."

"Give me the bad news first," Sean said with half a laugh. He was becoming accustomed to disappointments ever since the board members of the *Clarion* had given him the thumbs-down sign.

"Mathers—old Sheldon Mathers. He blew his brains out sometime last night." He let it sit there for reaction.

"He *what*?" Keogh shouted louder than he could ever remember himself shouting.

"That's right. Helluva shock."

"Are you sure, Eddie—sure?"

"I just ran into a reporter friend of mine from the *Record*. He saw the body. In his office. You know the office."

"Jesus Christ . . . Jesus . . . I . . . I mean he was the last person in the world . . . Jesus . . . him; him, of all people. He had everything. Such a straight-up old guy. God, I'm sorry."

"Sean, now, steady on. You didn't grow up with him, he wasn't a relative of yours. You owe him nothing."

"I don't get it, Eddie."

"The *Clarion*. Now. Now. It could be done."

"Eddie, how can you think like that? It's like jumping into another man's bed with his wife. No, not that way—no."

"Sean, you don't have to lift a finger, old friend. I could canvass the board members through a third party. He's a big timer there on the paper. John Hickey. You just give me the go-ahead and the paper will be yours. Everybody is worried—the staff, the board, the stockholders. They don't have a publisher. It's time, Sean. Say the word.

"Sean, listen. You are not taking over a gold mine, you know. Nobody wants the damn paper. If you take it over, you will be saving it from extinction."

"I can't believe there wouldn't be other bidders. And what about his wife, his kids? I wouldn't get into one of those hassles."

"Are you kidding? Sheldon Mathers was the only one who wanted it. The kids are fat. The wife has been left a fortune. Give me the word."

There was silence.

"Eddie, if you can convince me that nobody else has rightful ownership, I'll give the word. And we'll buy at the price we first offered the board. Then nobody can talk . . . You got it, Eddie? Now, it must be right. It must be right. I'm not a grave robber."

"Okay, Sean, I'll make it right. Your name won't come up until the very last. I'll do it all through this John Hickey."

"Who is this Hickey?"

"You know—the society editor."

"Yeah, sure—I see the name all the time. Can he be trusted?"

"Sure can . . . for a consideration?"

"How much?"

"Not money, really—just the job and a salary and few get-well expenses."

"Eddie," Sean said cautiously, "what job?"

"Oh, something like Executive Editor in Chief."

"What do Executive Editors in Chief do?"

"Nothing, Sean, nothing. It's just a gentlemanly payoff."

"Well, okay. Go ahead. But make it right." And then he muttered to himself, "And may God forgive me."

"What was that, Sean?"

"Nothing, Eddie . . . I just said okay . . . okay." The telephone went dead.

Rose Keogh looked up. "Well, darling, what was all that about?"

"Nothing, Rose, nothing." He looked down at the tablecloth and gulped some coffee. "Sorry, baby—nothing really. You know, business, business . . . Look, sorry, I have to take off. Sorry, dear. I've got to get dressed. Call you later."

He dashed into the bedroom, showered, shaved and hurriedly dressed. He kissed her and dashed out to the garage.

As the car revved out of the driveway, Rose Keogh sat outwardly calm as she sipped her coffee. Then she surprised herself by talking aloud and by saying what she said.

"The fucking, all-important, fucking Mr. Sean Keogh. Our Savior. Huh."

Sean Keogh burst into Frank Burke's office. His face was tense.

"Suppose you've heard, Frank boy?"

"Yeah . . . fuckin' amazin'. Never met the old fella, but it seems a bit strange, don't it?"

Keogh caught an unfamiliar look in Burke's eyes. Burke sensed it. He looked away and shuffled some papers. The moment was gone. Keogh was preoccupied.

"I don't know, Frank. You talk to Eddie?"

"Yeah, he thinks you can get it. He knows some big shot down there who he thinks can swing the whole deal."

"What do you think?"

"Sean lad, what the fuck do I know about newspapers? The *Clarion* newspaper, of all things. My name has appeared there a few times, you know."

Keogh gave a wry smile. That fact alone suddenly fueled him with a new enthusiasm about the whole deal. What a complete assault it would be on Beacon Hill.

"The only thing is that the move, as the Jews would say, isn't really kosher."

"Sean, like I said, I dunno. But if the paper is in real trouble and if you ain't stealin' it from somebody, well, I dunno. You'd be some kind of savior, or something. But like I said, don't listen to me. Eddie is the brains. I just dunno. I don't wanna have a say in this."

Keogh smiled. "You thickheaded Mick, you have to have a say in this. It's your money, Mr. Mac's money, Eddie's money too. Get Mr. Mac . . . Eddie is off talking to this guy Hickey, whoever he is."

Bernie McLaughlin arrived ten minutes later.

"Ah there, lads. I've heard all about it."

"Mr. Mac, as I was telling Frank here, Eddie is making the moves and I'm all fired up about it, even if I do feel like a bit of a grave robber. But how do you feel about it? Newspaper money doesn't turn over as quickly as numbers or sports betting—or even pension funds . . . You've got a helluva stake, old fella."

McLaughlin defused the seriousness of the conversation immediately. He feigned insult.

"Listen, ye little bastard, ye call me 'old fella' again and I'll kick ye so far ye'll wear yer shoes out walkin' back."

Frank and Sean laughed.

"Seriously, Mr. Mac. Say something." Sean was worried about committing the mutual fortune they had won from the streets of Southie.

"Look, Sean boy, there was a time when I thought ye was stark, ravin' mad. Now I know different. Ye *are* stark, ravin' mad. No point in arguin' with a madman. Look, ye ungrateful young spalpeen, remember it was my bloody idea in the first place . . . ye got a kettle on fer some tea, Frank?"

Burke scurried away to make some tea for the elder statesman.

"Sean boy, seriously. I know what yer saying and I know we're all thinkin' with our stupid hearts instead of our heads. Truly, lad, we want that newspaper as much as you do . . . and for all the same stupid reasons. In for a penny, in for a pound. Go after it, son."

"What do think Father Zeibatski thinks?"

"I know what he thinks."

"And?"

"And, ye great lump, have ye ever heard of a priest who didn't want to have his heavenly fingers in a newspaper? Grace be to God, the Pope hisself would buy *The New York Times* with the ring on his pinkie finger if he had a chance. Father, forgive me fer sayin' that. Sure, the good priest is with you all the way . . . like he has always been with us. Go to it, lad, an' ferget about us . . . fer the time bein', that is, lad. Do it, an' if we fall flat on our face, well, we'll go back to what we know."

Burke served Mr. Mac a steaming mug of tea, black with three sugars. The old man took a noisy sip and looked silently first at Frank Burke and then at Sean.

"But let me tell ye somethin'. Listen hard, because this is the only time I'm gonna say it. Sean boy, you made this operation what it is today. You did it, boy. Me an' Frank would still be ticklin' Guineas under the arm and plottin' how to drop an atom bomb on the North End if 'tweren't fer you, boy. So don't get scared about the money. There is plenty here in Boston, plenty in Bermuda. Plenty . . . an' if 'tweren't fer you, what would Eddie be today? He could never have been a villain, an' he would never have been goin' to Harvard nayther. Ye've all probably fergot, but in ten days' time young Eddie boy gets his law degree . . . He can hang out his shingle, lads, an' you did it."

Sean warmed to the compliment, the recognition. He felt what would pass for a blush filling his head from the neck upwards. For a moment the atmosphere was very emotional.

"Now," McLaughlin roared, "get the bloomin' hell to it, lad, or it's the back o' me hand ye'll be havin' fer breakfast." His roar was like that of a quarterback slapping his hands together after the conference in the huddle.

The timing was perfect.

The telephone shrilled.

"Burke Trucking," Frank Burke answered formally. "Yes, Eddie, all present . . . Sean . . . Eddie, he's all fired up."

Wilson's sudden enthusiasm wasn't lost on Frank Burke, but as Burke had said to himself, Eddie Wilson was cautious . . . *Was* . . . but now he was gung ho.

Sean grabbed the phone. "Yes, Eddie . . . Good . . . how many people does Hickey have to see? . . . Great. I'll be back of Frank's place for the next hour . . . got to put a bayonet up the ass of the sanitation department. After that I'm going down to see Roger Sharpe on the Common. I don't want to meet Hickey yet. Only when we know we have it in the bag. . . . Yeah, that's a great idea. See you, Eddie." Keogh replaced the receiver and turned to Mac and Burke.

"Eddie says this Hickey guy has three board members in the bag already. They almost kissed his heinie. He's working on the others. Of course, there'll have to be a secret shareholders' meeting to swing it. Eddie says don't worry.

"And hear this: Poor old Mathers hadn't even been carried out of the Clarion building before his loyal staff and top board members went to Hearst offering him the paper for nothing. The Hearst boys told them to jump in the Charles, go down three times and come up twice. They wouldn't take it for nothing."

"So?" Burke queried.

"So our son of Harvard, on hearing this, said there was a man willing to take it over as a contingency publisher . . . pay the losses for the first year and after the second year assume fifty-one percent ownership. Damn genius, that boy."

Burke and McLaughlin both shook their heads silently in mute tribute to the fledgling legal genius they had hatched in Eddie Wilson. They were not only impressed but proud that he was their product. In Southie everybody took a little of the blame and a little of the credit for any act just by virtue of living on that curious peninsula.

WHILE THE financial pages of Boston's newspapers pondered the fate of the proud *Clarion,* Wilson and Hickey were working like two commando battalions with the precision of an eight-day clock.

It was to take a total of eleven days. First the board fell into Hickey's arms; then Wilson charmed the secret shareholders' meeting. Yes, there were a few nervous coughs when Wilson hinted at the consortium whom he represented. The WASPs would never be comfortable with the Irish, particularly the Irish from South Boston, but at least there was a compatibility of color in the interests—Southie and a buck were the same color.

The final signing came one day after Eddie Wilson's name appeared on the Dean's List at Harvard Law School, a day celebrated with much pomp at Harvard over tea and lemonade and much beer and Jameson's at the Erin Social Club soon after.

The man who signed the *Clarion* contract was, of course, Eddie Wilson.

Sean Keogh had said it with an economy of words and a definition of leadership when the clan gathered at Frank Burke's office. "Eddie will be the publisher. No need to elaborate on reasons. Obvious. The holding company will be SACBUR." He chuckled. "I think you call it an acronym, don't you, Eddie?—a contraction of Sean, Mac and Burke. You missed out there, Eddie . . . small price to pay for the job of publisher."

They all laughed. Eddie was beaming. Attorney Edward George Wilson, Publisher of the *Boston Clarion.* He turned to the men.

"Right now, gents, all I can really say is thanks . . . I mean really thanks . . . Sean, Mr. Mac, Frankie. What can I say?"

"Oh, shut your redheaded, flame-brained mouth," McLaughlin roared.

Keogh spoke: "Eddie, quite obviously I'll be there a lot of the time. I want to learn the business . . . It's perhaps a little presumptuous, but I fancy myself a bit as a newspaperman. But I am the Assemblyman-elect here, and we mustn't forget that. We all have to keep our own parts of the machine working—Frank with the Teamsters, Mr. Mac with the other unions, me here and you, Eddie, as the front man. Don't let's get tempted to use the newspaper for our own ends. It has to be politically right down the middle or we'll have Beacon Hill kicking our asses till our noses bleed. No matter how much we might be tempted, it's independent of what else we may be doing. That way it will make money

... and ... and besides ... er ... I think that's the way the old boy Mathers would have done it."

The three other men contained their surprise in silence at Keogh's reference to Mathers.

The next day when the four of them walked unobtrusively through the lobby of the *Clarion,* they were accorded proper but subdued respect by the old-timers.

On the executive floor, Wilson got out of the elevator first. He had an ebullient spring to his step. They clacked down the wide, polished wood corridors. There was Sheldon Mathers' office. The throne room.

Eddie Wilson walked toward the door and started to push it open.

"Walk in, Sean. It's yours."

Sean stopped short. "No, Eddie. No. That office stays empty. That office doesn't belong to any of us. . . . Get someone to fix me up a little hideaway in the back."

Wilson eased the heavy door closed again. They all nodded. They all learned a little more about Sean Keogh every day. McLaughlin mentally shrugged his shoulders and thought, Christ, is he a Mick.

That afternoon, after the initial landing on the beaches of the *Clarion,* they all had a big lunch at the Ritz and got a little self-indulgently drunk.

At four in the afternoon, Sean Keogh realized he had not said a single word to his wife, Rose, in thirty-six hours. A twinge of guilt twisted at his gut, a gut that was worn thin by guilt. He bade them all goodbye. In another hour none of them would be able to walk. He raced back to Carson Beach and burst into the house.

"Rose, Rose," he shouted. "It's all over, darling. We established the beachhead this morning."

She was in the front room overlooking the water. She turned to him and smiled.

He swept her up in his arms. She put her arms around him and hugged him. But her body was stiff all over.

"We did it, darling. We did it. Let me tell you."

"Sean, I've heard all about it on television, and it's in the afternoon newspapers—all of Eddie's words to the press. Everything." Her tone was mild, but her mind was black with rage. Once again she had been excluded to the point of embarrassment.

He kissed her cheek.

"Like a drink, Sean?"

"God, no. Cup of tea, perhaps. Mr. Mac, Eddie and Frank have tried to drown me in booze. . . . Hey." He suddenly grew serious. "Hey, I just noticed, you look terrible. I don't mean ugly, baby—I mean you don't look well. God, you're as white as a milk bottle."

"True, I haven't felt well at all. Been a little sick all day. Too much French food at your fancy restaurants, I suppose." She said it without rebuke. But she did look sick.

"Stay put, little darling. Don't move—sit where you are." He leaped to his feet.

"What are you doing, Sean?"

"Calling the damn doctor is what I'm doing. That's what I'm doing. I'll get Dr. Dixon Hughes over right away."

Nobody called Dr. Dixon Hughes on a house call right away, particularly calling him into Southie, but even Boston's best doctors realized that their summer homes and European vacations came from men like Sean Keogh.

The doctor stepped quietly through the front door one hour later.

"Don't know what it is, Doc. She's lying down, but God, she looks like death. Take a look, will you? She's a healthy girl. Never seen her like this. She looks like death."

The doctor slipped into the bedroom. Forty-five minutes later he emerged. Sean looked up apprehensively. Dr. Dixon Hughes seemed completely unperturbed.

"She's far from deathly ill, Sean. I can't be certain. No, damn it, I *am* certain. She is just quite pregnant."

Sean Keogh's face registered relief, surprise and exhilaration in an incredibly short space of time. He wanted to shout, laugh and roll on the floor like a childish madman.

"Doc, Doc. You can't be sure." He was holding back his celebration lest his euphoria be dashed.

"No doctor can be without a medical test, you silly young man. I'm not a gambling man, but I would stake my practice on it."

"Have you told her?"

"Certainly not . . . I presumed the honor should be yours. I am reporting to you. You're the person who'll get my outrageous bill for making a house call in a day when Dixon Hughes doesn't make house calls."

Keogh slapped him hard on the back, and he laughed.

"Let yourself out, Doc." He raced into the bedroom. He was guffawing like a loon.

"Rose Keogh, you immoral lady. Didn't your parents tell you that sleeping with men could get you into trouble? Well, you're in big trouble, and I fess up. You're pregnant."

Her face lit up, and she hugged him as he threw his arms around her.

But her inner self swore: Even this I couldn't have. *He* had to tell *me* I was pregnant. It won't always be like this, Sean.

For the next hour Keogh pampered her as if she were a Dresden doll.

"Mary, Mother of God . . . I forgot, darling." He hurried outside the bedroom and made at least twenty telephone calls before he could track down Bernie McLaughlin, Frank Burke and Eddie Wilson. The news only added to their drunkenness that night.

Sean Keogh couldn't remember when he had felt so good. Everything was going so perfectly. First it was being elected assemblyman; then it was the *Clarion;* now it was the beautiful, dainty little Rose with child. He heard himself muttering his thanks a dozen times over: "Thank you God, thank you God . . . I won't forget You for this." It was the kind of sincere if slightly childish contract that so many have with the Almighty.

And then, as if by the same contract, which decrees that nothing can be received without return payment, he felt a touch of the Gaelic gloom that is a part of so many Irishmen's psychic makeup. He walked into his study and moved the desk away from the wall safe, which was six inches off the floor. He opened it and scooped out five thousand dollars in cash that lay inside. He roughly stuffed the bills into his pocket.

He ran back into the bedroom. "Madam Keogh, I have to leave this house of ill repute where ladies get in trouble. I'll be gone about twenty minutes. I'll be straight back, and don't move. Don't move—you hear?"

She smiled at him and blew him a kiss.

He drove far too fast to Sacred Heart. He walked through the entrance and carelessly dipped his fingers too far into the holy water and he crossed himself, spilling the water down the front of his shirt. He didn't bother about the Stations of the Cross, he strode across the sanctuary into the sacristy. He knocked impatiently on the door and exploded inside without waiting for the priest to bid him enter.

The broad, handsome face of Father Zeibatski broke into a smile as Sean stood framed in the doorway.

"Father . . . Father . . . Rose is pregnant."

The priest responded with a congratulatory laugh that resounded in the confines of the walls. He hugged Keogh, and the young man felt safe, happy and clean.

"Father, so much good fortune . . ."

"Good fortune falls upon the deserving and the Irish—the latter being totally undeserving but for the pity of the Almighty," he teased.

The priest was very happy.

"Father, I have to go, and pardon this rudeness, but I was in such a hurry . . . He scooped the crumpled bills out of his pocket.

"For the woman Rooney, Father. For the Rooney woman and hers."

The priest nodded as the bills spilled on the table.

"I have to get back, Father. I have to get back."

He sped back to Carson Beach at breakneck speed. Other men would have killed themselves. But Sean Keogh that night would have survived the wrath of Thor.

As Rose Keogh heard his car pull into the driveway, she closed her eyes. Darkness is the absence of light, but blackness is the product of rage.

Dr. Dixon Hughes had diagnosed her pregnancy correctly—but not her sickness.

Chapter

9

CONSIDERING THE implications of the takeover of the *Clarion*—a consortium of South Boston "businessmen" invading the heartland of the New England media establishment—it was reasonably painless. Yes, Boston was changing. Within the first six months at the helm, Sean Keogh proved that he was just as adept at the business of newspapers as he was as a young racketeer in South Boston or as a politician. It wasn't easy. His hours were crushing. Religiously he would spend the hours from nine in the morning until noon in the converted garage behind Frank Burke's trucking company wrestling with the real problems of South Boston as the district's state assemblyman. In that capacity he had to walk on eggshells, dismantling ever so carefully the machinery set up by his predecessor. The primary problems were education, sanitation and jobs.

The board that presided over the public schools were all cronies of the defeated Joe Kane. To come down with a fist on the ineptitude of this body would invite an open revolution. Kane's machinery had to be taken apart very slowly—first the nuts, then the bolts.

Sanitation was just as sensitive. The city Department of Sanitation had treated Southie like a poor cousin and had reduced its pickups from three to two times a week. Kane had used this as an excuse to augment the sanitation pickups with a private carting contract, which, in the setup of organized crime that often runs Boston more efficiently than City Hall, was given to an Italian firm operating out of the North End. Keogh did not dare throw the Italians out of the private carting business in Southie. There had been a long peace between Southie and the North End, and Keogh was not going to jeopardize the peace. When Sally Guarino, the don of the North End, approached him about this apprehensively, Keogh assured him that there would be no change in contracts—in fact, that he might even expand the contract when finances permitted, in return for a small provision that Guarino take onto his payroll a few Irishmen here and there who were without work. Guarino readily agreed, and there was a strengthening of bonds.

When it came to other jobs, Keogh leaned heavily on Burke, whose expanding trucking empire and Teamsters contacts gradually managed to absorb more and more of the unemployed of Southie.

He would regularly meet with his political mentor Roger Sharpe—at least three times a week—for lunch at the Ritz. It was here that Sharpe skillfully engineered Keogh's acceptance into the stifling Establishment club of the local and state Republicans—a group who, though few in numbers, were tenacious in their standards of class and caste.

Keogh's brilliant, if unofficial, position as boss man of the *Clarion* made Sharpe's task easier. Keogh's well-known past and connections, his religion and the geography of his home seemed to lose their consequence. With the gradual arrival of invitations to cocktail parties, luncheons and dinners, Sean Keogh began to feel more and more a part of the Establishment which he secretly loathed. There were other times when he would marvel at how little difference there was between him and the much-hated Protestant barons. It never failed to amuse him just how much ado there had been about relatively nothing.

His attendance record at the State House was impeccable, a fact not lost on the Republicans, the Democrats or the press corps. Although his outward demeanor was a trifle stiff and colorless, he was very quickly getting an enviable reputation as a political "comer" and a somewhat dashing figure for a politician.

He accepted the small shafts of the limelight graciously. Although it belied his basic nature, he managed to hold himself back from accelerating into a gallop.

Despite what many might have thought of his past as a Southie racketeer, it was only Keogh who realized how crushingly tedious his burden had been in his early days. He had been more of a creative accountant than a glamorous, gun-toting thug. There had been the occasional disciplinary actions he had reluctantly had to order, but they were rare. Keogh had come up "the hard way"—none of the devilish strut that the people of Southie had seen in their past racketeers. It had been, as so many hoodlums euphemistically describe their past, "just business."

His political career had differed very little. It seemed only an extension of his life on the street—listening to people, handling problems and finding new ways to widen an economic base. It was, in short, very hard work.

But with his involvement in the *Clarion,* it was totally different. He knew absolutely nothing about a business which often takes the toll of thirty years before one starts to see the light at the end of the tunnel.

Keogh had to compress that time into months, and he accepted the challenge with an almost boyish, if intelligent, enthusiasm. Making it even more difficult was the fact that although he was fooling nobody, he had to minimize his visibility at the *Clarion*. For reasons of political ethics, Edward Wilson was the publisher. Keogh closeted himself in a tiny office, more than a hundred feet from what had once been the seat of power of Sheldon Mathers. It was there, together with Wilson, that he would pore over the running of the newspaper, hungrily picking up newspaper jargon and the mechanics of producing a great metropolitan daily morning newspaper. His ignorance of journalism was only slightly outpaced by his agile mind, his retentive memory and his enthusiasm to learn.

He had to do it fast. When he had first walked into the building he didn't even know that "copy" was what a reporter wrote on his typewriter. He knew nothing about what a compositor did, what a pressman did, how advertising suddenly appeared on pages and how the deliverymen got the finished product to the stands. He was mystified by the art of photoengraving, and felt a bewildered, prickly sensation at the roar of the mighty presses as the newsprint raced through the rollers. He relied heavily on Wilson, just as ignorant, to transmit his learning process to him as quickly as possible.

When the newspaper had "gone to bed" and when most of the staff had gone home, he would wander for hours through the big building like a schoolboy on an outing. At first he would slowly stroll at seven in the morning through the newsroom, noting where the reporters sat, which desk belonged to which reporter. He then would trace the imaginary copy to the copy desk, where copy editors put the stories into shape. He followed the route of the copy to the Linotype machines. He would play on the keyboards and see how the letters were punched into oblong lead chunks the width of columns and then see how the compositors locked those lead chunks into "forms," or pages, then see how those heavy forms were impressed on the stereotype machines to be fitted around the big drums on the presses, how they were inked and then rolled at tremendous speed across the newsprint. Like a child with a model airplane, he mentally dismantled and reassembled the operation in his mind a thousand times. It was exhilarating to him, and nothing short of amazing to the people who saw the learning process gallop at breakneck speed. Between his political career and his learning process, he regularly put in six eighteen-hour days a week, jumping from one challenge to another with infinite glee.

While it was physicaly devastating, it was emotionally addictive, like a never-ending high, and the more he got involved, the further names like Paddy Devlin and Jack Rooney receded into a dim past. It was only then that he felt the pangs of regret that his mother, Molly Keogh, had not been alive to see it all. She would have been so proud. And what of the father he had never known? God, he would have loved it!

It had been a month after the surprisingly tranquil takeover that Keogh had met John Hickey. Eddie Wilson had prearranged a casual, informal meeting. Wilson and Hickey had been walking past Keogh's tiny office when Wilson had casually asked, "Have you met Mr. Keogh?"

"No, Edward—matter of fact, I haven't."

"Let's see if he's in. He wanders by occasionally." It was a bad lie, but who cared?

He had knocked on the door. "Come in," came the voice. Keogh sat at his desk looking happily exhausted. His tie was pulled down, and his pin-collar shirt was open at the neck.

"Sean, got a moment?"

"Sure. Come on in."

"Mr. Keogh, this is John Hickey. As you know, he is our Executive Editor in Chief."

Keogh stood up and gave him a warm smile, and they firmly shook hands.

"John, heard a lot about you."

Hickey's face showed no sign of register at the remark. He gave a healthy smile, showing well-kept teeth, and replied, "May I be so presumptuous as to say the same. It's a pleasure to meet you."

It was a warm friendly exchange.

"How's the paper going, John—anything that Mr. Wilson should know?"

"Well, as you know, we work fairly closely together, and I hope I've been able to keep Eddie up on things as far as the editorial floor goes. Frankly, there doesn't seem to be any major crisis there. We have a pretty good staff. Of course, we have our weaknesses, but overall they're a pretty dedicated bunch."

"How do we get a million circulation? What do you think we should be doing that we aren't right now?"

"As you know probably better than I, a man would be foolish to pretend he had an instant recipe for that goal. There would be some who would argue with me, but I find little fault with our editorial department. Of course, I'm somewhat biased. But back to the question of the magic million. I think it all has to do with distribution. We're still treating Boston like a small hick town. The middle class is moving farther and farther away from the Common. Many of those people grew up on the *Clarion,* but when they move out of town, we're not there."

Keogh studied him. Hickey was good-looking, had an engaging personality and talked with a simple, intelligent manner. He didn't confuse.

That impressed Keogh. But Keogh also knew he was self-indulgent, dedicated to a life-style on which Keogh frowned, and he didn't trust him. He felt there was an edge of treachery in Hickey's having been so helpful in swinging the deal. Keogh wanted someone else to share the guilt he felt for taking over Sheldon Mathers' newspaper, even though there had been no other bidders. But for all of it, Hickey was at the very least a good front man—perhaps a great front man.

Hickey continued: "As you probably know, at the time of his death Mr. Mathers was working on plans for expanding his plants outside the city."

Keogh nodded.

Hickey referred to Sheldon Mathers in just the correct tone of respect. Hickey, of course, would never had done otherwise. He knew Irishmen. Knew them—and hated them.

Keogh nodded. "Mr. Wilson," he said, careful not to informalize his friend's position by calling him Eddie, "has seen those plans. Frankly, Mr. Mathers' plans were basically sound; a little too ambitious considering our financial basis at the present time, but sound—very sound."

Hickey looked pleased with himself without showing it too much.

He recognized the moment when Keogh called the meeting to a halt. Hickey stood up, shook hands again. "Mr. Keogh, Mr. Mathers was a great man," he said, inwardly laughing at the preposterousness of his own lie, "and I think a lot of us are genuinely grateful for the way things have worked out. It's a great paper, and there are a lot of great people working for you."

There, that should do it. Keogh is smart, but not so smart that he can't be greased with a veiled compliment about his place in destiny. Hickey, you handled him well, very well. He's smarter than most Irishmen—but just a little bit.

"Thanks a lot, John. I look forward to talking a bit more in depth about the newspaper with you very soon."

Sean sank back into his chair as Hickey and Wilson disappeared through the door. He's a cool customer, Keogh thought; cool and a trifle too slick; but he's smart, and God, do I need smarts around me! He had just better be smart. That's why I pay him ninety thousand bucks a year —almost four times what the Mayor gets paid.

"Helluva guy," Wilson said as he and Hickey walked toward the elevator.

"Intelligent, too," Hickey threw in, "and a genuinely nice kind of fellow."

Their eyes met as they stepped into the elevator. They didn't say a word until they reached the editorial floor.

Keogh rested his head on the back of his chair. He exhaled deeply and felt himself dropping off to sleep. He shook his head. No sleep, old fella; there is work to be done.

There was always work to be done. Education, sanitation, jobs, newspapers, learning, helping, making Southie men feel real, looking after Mr. Mac, making sure Frankie didn't overstep with the Teamsters, hoping that Eddie was as good as he thought he was.

And then there was himself. Sean Keogh, what have you done for me lately? Nothing. Have you lain in the sun on the the Cape? Have you skied in the Berkshires?

Ever been to Europe? Never even been to County Wexford, Ireland, where the old man came from. When was the last time you were in New York? Damn it, you don't even get drunk with Mr. Mac and Frankie anymore. You're pushing yourself, boy.

He suddenly felt a rare moment of feeling sorry for himself. You ain't Moses, Sean, and anyway, things are changing. The Irishmen don't need to be held by the hand anymore. They can do things outside a bar. What's driving you, boy? Hey, laddo? You're twenty-five; it's 1967. There's a war on in Vietnam, and there are men five years older than you with younger eyes leaving parts of their bodies in places like Da Nang, and Lyndon Johnson is telling us we're winning the war and he's a liar, and I'm here saying nothing except worrying about how many times the Guineas come around to pick up the garbage in Southie because I don't want a Vietnam in Southie. Are you out of your fucking tree?

A newspaper, Sean laddo. What are you talking about? By October you are going to have to fork out close to half a million bucks of your money, Mac's money, Frankie's money, Eddie's money to pay some fucking stupid deficit left you by a white-haired Protestant who hated your guts. You're going nuts, laddo. Nuts, I say.

He took a deep breath and exhaled loudly. It was a little like going to the john the morning after a ridiculously huge Chinese meal. Out of you, Sean boy? Have you given yourself enough pity? There's a woman named Rooney with a kid somewhere in this world who is probably starving to death because you set her husband up. Your ma, Molly, she's dead because you had to be a tough guy with Paddy Devlin. Devlin is rotting in a grave somewhere and he had a good mother and good father who probably look at his Korean war medals sometimes and cry, and ferchrissake Sheldon Mathers, a man you didn't know from a turkey's toenail, is in a grave without his brain. Okay, you don't know why he did it, but somehow everything you touch turns black, and here you are trying to be the Bishop of Southie. That's Father Zeibatski's job, not yours. It's just not worth it. Not worth it. But it is. Christ, it is. Damn it, it is.

There is a little lady in Carson Beach. Her face is beautifully pale, and she gets embarrassed because she has to urinate a lot, and her belly is out to here, and she has pains, and the pains are because of you because she wants to give an Irishman a son, and she's beautiful.

A son? Why does an Irishman have to have a son? Don't Irishmen sire daughters too? Of course they do, you blatherskiting idiot. No man has a right to pray to God for a boy. You only have a right to pray that he or she has ten toes and ten fingers. You pray hard enough, Sean laddo, and you'll get a boy. St. Theresa will answer your prayers and you'll get a boy, but you don't know what kind of a boy. Prayers are always answered, so shut your gob and pray that you have a child with ten fingers and ten toes.

Having thus purged his thoughts, he drifted off into an exhausted sleep with his feet on the desk and his mouth open. He was on a beach and there was his ma, Molly. She sat under a big umbrella and she sipped lemonade. Big Joe Keogh was pitching a baseball to him on the beach, his big, broad back arching every time he threw the ball. He could see his father now, the broad, flushed face with the young eyes. His beer belly quivering a bit every time he threw the ball. He could see that face; he knew what his father looked like. Big and beer-bellied, of an indeterminate age—but he had young eyes, very young eyes. The little kid of twelve, skinny but handsome with his black curls cascading around the alabaster face, was laughing, laughing loudly because his father had had young eyes, and anyone who looked at the twelve-year-old kid could tell that those eyes were those of an old man. The scene was suddenly splashed with madness and blood, and he could see Rose there looking on in bewilderment, and Molly was crying and big Joe was crying, but the twelve-year-old boy just stood there amazed that people could be so young.

He slept fitfully in the chair for half an hour, tormented by his subconscious.

He was jerked from his dreams by the ringing of the telephone. He picked it up feeling slightly groggy.

"Sean, Mac here."

"Yes, Mr. Mac. What's going on?"

"I think I've got trouble, Sean boy."

"Trouble?"

"Yeah. Down here on Number Twelve pier today, there was a whole bunch of guys—Guineas, Jews and a coupla Micks."

"What were they doing?"

"Well, that's it. I couldn't pin anyone down, but I got the drift they're formin' a breakaway union."

"Do you know the guys?"

"Never seen 'em. Figure they're from Providence an' New York—an' if they are, you thinkin' what I'm thinkin'?"

"That could be right, Mr. Mac, but don't let's jump to conclusions."

"How about let's sit down and talk, Sean lad?"

"Okay, Mr. Mac. Why don't you come over to the house tonight for dinner? Rose will love to see you. That's a good idea; how about dinner? We can talk. There will be nobody else around. No booze; just let's talk and straighten this thing out."

"I'd like that, Sean. Be over about, say, seven."

"Fine, seven it is. See you then, Mr. Mac." He put the receiver down and stared into space. Trouble, more trouble. Always trouble and problems. He sighed. Well, that's the price you pay in a high-stakes game, whether on the street or in the boardroom. There would always be trouble.

He walked into the tiny washroom adjoing the office. He turned on the cold-water tap and sluiced his face. The cold water felt good. He blinked his eyes and wiped his face with a towel.

He walked back into the office and called his wife. "Rose? Darling, hope you don't mind, but I've invited Mr. Mac over for dinner."

"That's fine, Sean. Haven't seen much of him."

"Nothing fancy; just throw on a couple of steaks. It's really just to talk business. I'll cook, if you aren't feeling well."

"Sean, I feel wonderful. Pregnant women don't lie in bed for nine months, you know. I'll manage fine."

"Okay, darling. It's just that I want you to take it a little easy."

"I do take it easy, Sean. Don't worry about me, dear. I'm fine."

"Well, it's only two more months."

"I'll be fine—fine, I tell you. Now, what time will Mr. McLaughlin be over?"

"About seven."

"Okay. Will you be home before that?"

"Yes, I'll make it about it six. See you then. Bye, darling."

"Bye, dear."

As the telephone clicked, his mood brightened. Rose, God, she's a gem. The only one with any real sanity around us bunch of mad Irishmen. I'm damn lucky.

A little after seven, the big, bluff figure of Bernard McLaughlin strode through the doorway of the house in Carson Beach.

"Darlin' Rose, now, how ye be?" He pushed a huge bunch of white roses into her hands.

"They're beautiful, Mr. McLaughlin."

"I wish ye'd stop callin' me Mister. Ye make me feel as if I'm bein' measured fer the undertaker."

"You'll always be Mister to me." She smiled warmly, and Sean Keogh chuckled as he led him through to the living room.

"Jaysus, Rose, I haven't been here in months. Ye've fixed the place up beautiful. Ye have a great touch."

"Not me, Mr. McLaughlin. It's the touch of a decorator. Sean took care of it all."

Sean grinned. "No sense in worrying Rose about it. She would have been in stores for six months picking the color of the drapes. I didn't want to worry her. I just wanted to throw open the door and say, Here, girl, here's your house. Live in it."

McLaughlin sat down. "Ah, yer a lucky one, Rose. Sean looks after everythin'. Ye got a good catch here, girl."

"I like to think so, Mr. McLaughlin. A drink?"

"A dash o' Jameson's would do fine."

She disappeared into the kitchen. "Yer a lucky man, too, Sean. What a little lady." They were both sitting down.

"Damn right, Mr. Mac. I lucked out with that one. She's a gem."

Rose returned with the drink. She sipped a lemonade. "Dinner will be in half an hour. Medium-rare steak, just as you like it."

Sean beamed with pride. She was everything a Southie boy could wish for.

Promptly at seven thirty, Rose piled the dining table with a feast. The three of them indulged in small talk and banter until Rose brought the coffee. That was the signal for her to excuse herself. She slipped into the next room with her needlepoint.

McLaughlin cleared his throat and lowered his voice.

"It's real trouble, laddo. They was there goin' from man to man. Almost in front o' me own bloody eyes. I couldn't ask any of 'em about it. 'Twould have shown I was worried. I just tried to pretend I wasn't interested. Guineas, three of 'em; two Jew kids, and some Micks too. Musta been on the pier on an' off fer eighteen hours and then in the saloons. Guineas, Jews an' Micks together."

"Didn't recognize any of them?"

"No, just faces. But they was hard kids. Could tell that. It's trouble. They're tryin' to take my local away from me. I've seen it before, boy. Did it meself in the old days. First one local, then the next, and the next thing ye know I've got my prick in my hand."

"Well, what do you think?"

"Gotta be Castellano, the Calabrese son of a bitch."

"Why Castellano? Not Guarino?"

"No. Guarino is Sicilian. He don't fool with Jews and Micks. He nearly shit a brick when ye asked him to get some Southie boys jobs in his outfit. He wouldn't touch us or the Jews with a barge pole. No, this is New York—Castellano. Raymond, down in Rhose Island, he's in it too. He answers to Castellano. Him an' Raymond, both Calabrese. They got a thing goin' with Genovese down there in New York. Genovese is pushin' 'em. Castellano an' Raymond ain't gonna take it, but they can't afford a war with Genovese. Genovese would wipe 'em all out over a plate o' pasta, but the membership down there is sittin' on the fence to see if Castellano is as strong as he always was. He's got the politicians down there in his fist. Genovese is just an animal, an' the boys know it. They're seein' how strong Castellano is, and the bastard is choosin' to take the Boston docks first. If he can move Southie out o' the docks, 'twill be a signal, and the boys will push Genovese aside. Genovese has got a big bit comin' anyway in the Federal Pen in Atlanta. Castellano has to show he's still got it, and the one fuckin' place he has picked to make the stand is our backyard."

Sean furrowed his brow. Mac was never a worrier. He took care of business in his own way and never burdened anyone else with problems unless there was real trouble.

"What are you saying, Mr. Mac?"

"Simply this, sunshine. First the docks, then the numbers, then sports bettin'. Then we ain't got that money rollin'. All that money, Sean— we're rich, very rich. Castellano knows how much we make. He knows it's good territory. Ain't been no wars. We leave the Guineas alone an' they leave us alone. It's safe territory with big rewards and no trouble. We're the only real Irish mob left on the whole Eastern Seaboard apart from a couple o' cowboy outfits on the West Side o' New York."

"Mr. Mac, as I said—what are you saying?"

"Now, come down, boy. I'm not talkin' war or trouble. That would be crazy. They would squash us like grapes. They're tough bastards. No. That's not what I'm sayin'. What I'm sayin' is, boy, it's up to you. Yer the only one who can talk from any position of respect, power, clout. Yer a politician; Frank Castellano will respect that. Yer goin' places. A newspaper, ferchrissake. Castellano doesn't wanna fuck around with that."

"You say I should go to New York and threaten him with newspapers and politics?"

"No, no way, son. Ye don't threaten Castellano. No, ye talk to 'im. Talk to 'im man to man. Be straight."

"And then what?"

"Ask 'im, boy—just ask 'im. Ask 'im very respectful to lay off. He's not an animal like Genovese or Tough Tony. Ye can talk to 'im. Christ, ye can even lay out the prospect that ye could do him some favors. Tell him about Guarino, the contracts. It's no big deal, but it shows you ain't pushin' Guineas around. Ask 'im. Talk to 'im. Ye gotta, Sean, or we could all go up in smoke. It's that serious, boy-o."

"If you say so, Mr. Mac, I'll do it. I'll organize a meeting. I'll ask him. I'll ask him. But Mr. Mac, let's avoid trouble. No more blood on our hands. Okay?"

"Yer preachin' to the converted, Sean. I seen enough o' that shit to last two lifetimes. I wanna die in bed with a nice pair o' flannel pajamas on an' me hair combed."

"Mr. Mac, I'll pull it off, I promise. I would never let you down. Never."

"I know, son. God bless ye." He drained his coffee and straightened his big, broad frame as he threw his arms around Keogh in a giant bear hug.

Rose had expertly finished her needlepoint in the next room and just as expertly heard every word of their hushed conversation.

AT LUNCH the next day at the Ritz, Sean Keogh passed the menu to Roger Sharpe, the ramrod of the Republican Club in Boston.

"Rog . . . you know you've done wonders with the introductions."

"You've done wonders on your own, Sean. I think we both recognize that."

"I like the way it's going. But I would like more of it. I want to be known outside Massachussetts too."

"I agree. But why so suddenly?"

"Well, I'm glad you're seated. But eventually I want to run for the U.S. Senate. I think I can do it."

Sharpe whistled and rolled his eyes upward. "You don't want the treetops—you want the stars too."

"Something like that." Sean Keogh smiled. "Now, what's happening down in New York?"

"Well, we have a glamour boy called John Lindsay who is Mayor, and he's knocking them dead. Old Rockefeller is screwing his ass off as Governor, but doing a pretty good job. Lindsay is the glamour boy, however. Some of the old hard-liners are a bit worried he's too liberal, but he's getting a great press."

"I'd like to meet him."

"No trouble."

"How?"

"Next Monday night. They're having a big bash at the El Morocco in

New York. Every man and his dog will be there. Fund-raising affair. Lots of pols, models, movie stars. You know—the usual bullshit."

"I'd like to get an invite."

"You've got it, old boy. Taking your wife?"

"Hell, no, she's seven months pregnant."

"Oh, yeah. Tend to forget about that. I don't know how you keep all the balls in the air with politics, your newspaper, your friends and contacts, the Teamsters and a pregnant wife."

"It's all designed to keep me out of trouble," he said with a smile, "but I'm very lucky in Rose; she's a very special lady. The average wife just wouldn't put up with it."

"Sean, are you serious about the Senate?"

"Of course."

"It's a different ball game, Sean. You have to be a little more than the neighborhood hero, you know."

"I'm fully aware of that."

"It's a lot different. There are multimillionaires with impeccable contacts in every sector of society—even yours—who just don't stand a hope in hell."

"What sort of friends do they have?"

"The best and the richest."

"Real friends?"

"No politician has any real friends."

"Then I have the advantage, now, don't I?" He grabbed for the menu. "Now how about a bottle of Mouton Cadet?"

"Fine." Roger Sharpe looked at him hard. He liked Keogh, admired and respected him. And even though Sharpe was not from the inner circle of Southie, he knew Keogh liked him. But more than his personal feelings toward Keogh was the overwhelming curiosity he had about the man. Keogh's background was about the worst-kept secret in Boston, and yet Keogh never made any move to put distance between himself and his old friends, never denied them and had no compunction about rolling into the finest restaurants and bars surrounded by McLaughlin, Burke and Wilson.

If he was serious about the U.S. Senate, his admirable trait of loyalty might hurt him. Tolerance in Boston was one thing. It was a completely different thing in Lowell and Pittsfield. But Sharpe felt good about knowing this man, whether he made it big politically or not. There was an intangible decency about the man. And he saw it in the others from Southie. Many of them drank too much and fought too much and hadn't been to school enough. But there was a decency there, a decency that Sharpe remembered in his old neighborhood which had dissipated when all his friends had fled to the suburbs. It was as if Keogh had given Roger Sharpe a neighborhood, some drinking friends, and Sharpe had given him a political career. It was a fair exchange.

Keogh snapped him out of his skull searching.

"Roger, how is the Executive Committee receiving me . . . really?"

"Frankly, the same way as your board at the *Clarion* receives you. You would be a shanty-Irish idiot if you made a botch of things. But while you're a winner, you're a charming, ambitious young man who, through the American dream, has become successful despite the fact that he's Irish."

Sean chuckled. "Funny. Everyone calls me an Irishman; same with us all in Southie, I've never been to Ireland. Some of our fathers in Southie weren't even born there. But we're still Irish."

"Never thought of it, really. My parents were born in England, but they never call me an Englishman," Sharpe observed.

"I'm Irish, a guy called Cohen is Jewish and a guy called Mario is Italian . . . but you're never called English."

"You're right. We're like Negroes. They don't call them Africans, they call them niggers, and they call us WASPs. It can work against you, y'know."

"Never thought of it. . . . Come to think of it now"—he laughed— "I'm glad they call me Irish."

Keogh enjoyed these long lunches with Sharpe. He listened carefully to Sharpe's observations. They were lean and with a minimum of emotion or personal coloring. He talked straight, worked hard, and Keogh thought he was decent. Secretly he wished Sharpe had been a Mick. Then he could have let down the cool exterior, grabbed him in a bear hug and kissed him, the way he did Mac, Burke and Eddie. He reproached himself for bringing religion into it. Well, it wasn't religion, really. Guarino, the hood from the North End, was Catholic, but he wouldn't have hugged him.

"Roger . . . about Sheldon Mathers."

"Yes?"

"You know, the *Clarion* board, the directors, the editorial staff—they hardly talk of him. It's as if he'd never been there."

"That's right."

"What about the Republican Executive Committee?"

"Same thing."

Keogh sipped his wine and then picked up a fork as his Dover sole was set in front of him.

"Not right, is it, Rog? Man works all his life, building, being kind, working for an ideal. Then poof! he goes, and nobody ever thinks of him. I think of him."

Sharpe cut a slice of prime rib. "You do?"

"Damn right."

"But you tried to squeeze him out."

Keogh looked hurt. "Buy him out, Roger, buy him out. Jesus, if it had gone smoothly and the sale had come off as I wanted it, he still would have been the Chairman of the Board. I liked the old guy—really liked him."

"I guess you did. So did I. But that's what it's all about."

"What's all about?"

"The board, the committee. They liked him too. But he was a loser and you're a winner."

"Is that all that counts, Roger? Really?"

"Not with me it doesn't, pal, but with the rest of the barracudas, that's all that counts."

"I'm pretty lucky, then."

"You are, Sean; you are."

Keogh changed the subject quickly. "Now, about next Monday at the El Morocco. You say everybody will be there."

"Everybody . . . Republicans and Democrats too. Anyone who counts will be there."

Keogh cleared his throat. He lowered his voice slightly. "Do you know of a man called Frank Castellano?"

"Sure do."

"Would he be there?"

"Certainly will. Sean, pardon me for asking this; it's not my business. But I hope you're not going to get involved with him. First of all, he's a Democrat, pulls all the strings of the Tammany Hall crowd, and secondly—"

"Yes . . . I know."

"Well, why?"

"Roger, it is your business to know, but I can't tell you. All I can say is, and you have my word, the only reason I want to meet him has nothing to do with any business dealings I have, nor has it to do with politics. I give you my word. I would never embarrass you or the GOP. I give you my word."

"Enough said. . . . Let's eat. This is sensational."

When Keogh returned to the small office garage behind the Burke Trucking Company, he called Bernie McLaughlin.

"Mr. Mac, Sean."

"Hey, laddo."

"I'm meeting with that gentleman in New York on Monday."

"Bless you, boy. Bless you. I dunno what's goin' on fer the life o' me. If it ain't him that's doin' all this stuff on the docks, then I can deal with it—if they're just young punks. But if it's him, we'd be crazy. See what ye can find out, Sean, m'boy. It's fer you as well as me. It's fer all of us."

"I know, Mr. Mac. I know. I'll be back on Tuesday. See you."

"See ye, son, an' be careful down there."

"I will. Bye."

On Monday afternoon at three o'clock, Sean Keogh kissed Rose good-bye, promised to be back in twenty-four hours, drove to Logan Airport and caught the four-o'clock shuttle to New York. He took a taxi to the Carlyle Hotel at Seventy-sixth Street and Madison Avenue, checked in and dressed in his best Brooks Brothers. He then called Jim Anderson, the man whom Roger Sharpe had called to look after him.

Anderson was an affable man in his forties who seemed to marvel at Keogh's good looks, quiet manner and youth. They had a quick drink in the bar of the hotel, and Keogh was quietly surprised that his name was so well known among the GOP veterans in New York.

"You did something sensational up there in South Boston, Sean. I'm not bullshitting you. It's a pleasure to meet you, really."

Keogh took the compliment in stride. They knew about South Boston in New York.

"Yeah, you really showed them. Wish there were a few like you down here."

Keogh looked genuinely surprised. "Aren't there?"

"Are you kidding?"

"But you have the Mayor—a Republican mayor. What more could you ask for?"

"Well, for a start we could ask for a Republican. It won't be long before he becomes a Democrat." Anderson was genuinely disgusted.

"I don't understand."

"Neither do I, Sean. Just let's say that John Lindsay behaves more like a Democrat than most Democrats I know. If he had his way, he would give Park Avenue to Harlem."

Keogh sipped his Scotch and water. He was beginning to realize what big-city politics was all about. South Boston was a pimple on the ass of an elephant. And he wanted to run for the Senate?

"I don't understand New York, to be frank."

"You're missing nothing. In five years' time this city is going to be on its knees. Right now one person in seven here is on welfare. Our Mayor would give it all to them."

Keogh was aghast at such disloyalty. He had met the man only half an hour ago, and already he was bad-mouthing his boss. But it wasn't his place to criticize. No, Sean Keogh would just listen. This wasn't South Boston. Already he felt a little homesick for the people he knew and the people he could trust. This was a can of worms down here.

Anderson was a marginally attractive guy. Fifteen years ago, he had probably been handsome. If the booze had taken its toll on his body and the bitterness of politics had made him cynical, he was a master front man.

The limousine was waiting outside, and there were some hangers-on awaiting its arrival at El Morocco. They opened the doors. The lights dazzled Sean's eyes. Cameras were popping, television klieg lights turned on at full strength. This was New York. Anderson swept him through the door, and as Keogh adjusted his eyes to the darkness he began to understand what people meant when they said the beautiful people. Well, at least, beautiful girls. The men were all slightly puffed and red-faced and prosperously decadent.

Politics made strange drinking partners. It seemed that every Democrat's best friend was a Republican and vice versa. George Wirth, the Republican Majority Leader, grabbed his hand warmly and put a drink in his hand. Governor Nelson Rockefeller made a line for him and called him by his first name without being introduced. "Sean fella," the Governor gushed. Jesus, Roger Sharpe has done a good P.R. job on me. The Governor grabbed him tightly by the arm and guided him toward John Linsday, tanned and exquisitely handsome. Still, Keogh stood out almost as if he had been a movie star. Was it his looks, his youth or the face of an honest man?

Keogh immediately felt at home. Even if they were a bunch of sharks, at least they knew how to throw a party. Keogh's eyes scanned the room after half an hour of invitations and introductions. Where is he? Where is Castellano? He couldn't risk asking outright to meet the man. Not Castellano. People would want to know why. Another half hour passed. He was beginning to enjoy himself. Where was Castellano? He had seen newspaper pictures of him, but in this light he wouldn't have recognized the Almighty Himself.

Keogh felt a gentle tap at the back of his elbow. Nobody tapped you politely in this gathering. Everyone threw his arm around your shoulder and pumped your hand as if he'd grown up with you. Keogh turned.

Before him stood a short, thin, balding man, dressed in a neat gray suit, maroon tie and highly polished shoes. A white handkerchief that peeped from his breast pocket made him look like a mildly successful insurance salesman. It was only when he spoke with that gravelly voice born of 116th Street in East Harlem that Keogh knew.

"Mr. Keogh," the man said in a slightly accented voice. "Castellano, Frank Castellano." They shook hands.

"Pleased to meet you, sir," Keogh said evenly. "A drink?"

"No, no. Doctor's orders." Castellano inclined his head and a waiter was at Keogh's side with a Scotch and water.

"No—no, thank you. I've had enough tonight. Thanks all the same."
Castellano nodded and the waiter disappeared.

"Then let's get some fresh air, Mr. Keogh." Sean Keogh looked at the
man warily. How did he know his name? Why had he made the introduction so blatantly, and where the hell was he going if he left with him?
After all, this was the guy the tabloid newspapers said was head of
Murder Incorporated. Now, that might be just journalistic expediency,
but one thing he felt sure of and that was Frank Castellano didn't screw
around.

It was as if Castellano had caught the reaction.

"I would like to talk to you, Mr. Keogh, because I know you came
here to talk to me. So I am going to disobey my doctor's orders and have
some very excellent espresso coffee and maybe one small glass of Sambuca. Please come."

Quietly but confidently Castellano slipped through the crowd, allowing Keogh to follow at the discreet distance that Castellano knew would
be appreciated.

Keogh managed to get to the door without too many lengthy farewells. He picked up his coat from the checkroom and walked outside.

Castellano was in the back of an undistinguished-looking compact
Ford. As he explained later, the days of the big limousines were long
gone for his kind. Too much attention, too much showing of wealth.
The Ford hopped past the double-parked limousines and pulled to a
stop farther up Fifty-fourth Street. Keogh followed the car. Fifty feet
from the entrance of El Morocco, Castellano leaned over in the back
seat and opened the door for him. The driver simply sat there in front
and made no extravagant moves to open doors.

Keogh got into the car.

"Let's go uptown, Jimmy," Castellano said to the driver.

"Sure thing." The driver turned around. "Hello, Mr. Keogh. Jimmy
Gallagher. I went to Sacred Heart five years after you. How are ya?"

Keogh smiled and recognized his face. He relaxed. "Well, what's a boy
from Southie doing down here?"

"Money." The driver laughed.

Castellano was enjoying the exchange. He wanted to put Keogh at his
ease. "You see, Mr. Keogh, I also hire Irishers."

Keogh looked at him with interest, wanted to know what he meant by
the comment, but kept quiet.

"I have seven dress factories. All Jews. I have three restaurants—some
Italians, some Irishers. One trucking company, the same. Two dry-
cleaning places. The same. I am an equal-opportunity employer," he
said with a smile.

Keogh nodded and smiled. He remained silent.

Castellano looked out the window as the car traveled uptown. Past Ninety-sixth Street on Manhattan's Upper East Side, the buildings became seedy. There were people on stoops drinking out of bottles.

Keogh looked apprehensively at Castellano.

"Here they're Puerto Ricans. New Yorkers call them Spics—same way you do in Boston. Do you know, Mr. Keogh, the first people to be called Spics in this country were Italians? Do you know where the word came from?"

"Frankly, no," Keogh answered directly.

"It simply comes from "I no spica da English.' Yes, Mr. Keogh, I was once a Spic."

"Mr. Castellano, I'm not sure what either of us is getting at."

Castellano held up his hand as if to ask for temporary silence and smiled.

The car pulled into 116th Street on the corner of Pleasant Avenue, the very heart of East Harlem. The street was like a little oasis. It was clean. There were subdued lights behind the windows. It was very quiet.

"On this street, Mr. Keogh, I have fifty-two immediate relatives and a hundred very close friends. Over there"—he pointed to a newly painted four-story walk-up—"is where I was born. My father, he was a barber. Today my two sisters and their husbands and their families live there. It's very beautiful inside. The husbands of my sisters work in the First National City Bank. They worked first as tellers. Now they are managers. When they first came to this country, they wanted to come in with me into the numbers. I said no. I found them jobs. First as cleaners, then I got them bank jobs. Those people have never seen a gun."

Keogh forgot his feeling of trepidation. He was suddenly interested in the excursion, for whatever it accomplished.

"Now, over there"—Castellano pointed opposite his sisters' house—"there are some wise guys who work for me. They know if they ever speak to my sisters or their husbands, I would be very angry. Jimmy, let's go downtown."

The car swiftly drove out of the neighborhood and zipped to Seventy-second Street, where it pulled onto the East River Drive. What seemed like only minutes later, the car had swerved off the Grand Street exit and into the Lower East Side.

Castellano waved his hand around the area. "Once there were many Irishers living here. Many. It was a good neighborhood. Much the same as where you live today. Now they have left."

The car approached Cherry and Monroe streets.

"Over there"—he pointed to a bar on Monroe Street—"my brother goes every day. His friends, his wife, they go there. They stayed in the neighborhood. They are surrounded by much street crime, but they stayed. The Irishers, they leave, but we stay. I think the Irishers never liked us, maybe we never liked them, but we stayed. Over there, my cousin, he has a meat store. Over there the Italo-American Club. My other cousin owns that place."

"Mr. Castellano, I appreciate this tour, but I don't understand."

The car pulled into Mulberry Street and double-parked outside Ferrara's, one of the best pastry-and-coffee shops in New York. Castellano led Keogh inside.

The place was crowded. He nodded discreetly at some of the customers as they half-lifted themselves off their seats in a respectful gesture of greeting. Nobody approached him. There was no overt sign of recognition. Just a smile here, a nod there. The waiter led them to the back of the café and sat them down at a small table.

"Espresso, Mr. Keogh?"

"I'd love some."

"It's very good here." He held up his fingers for two. Two small cups arrived, accompanied by a half-empty bottle of Sambuca.

Castellano poured himself a drink. "I allow myself one . . . and maybe a cigar for later."

"Mr. Castellano . . . I did come here to New York to talk to you."

Castellano again held up his hand, as if to signal that now was not the time to speak of the problem at hand.

"In this neighborhood, I have relatives and friends. Maybe two hundred of them. Some bars, some restaurants and, yes, some bookmaking places. I will show you these places."

"I don't want to see them, Mr. Castellano."

Costellano smiled and sipped on the thick, excellent espresso.

"But I have shown you where my family lives, where I go, where I frequent. Why do I show you this?"

"I have no idea."

"Mr. Keogh, I am a very rich man."

"So am I, Mr. Castellano." He said it only for the record. Sean Keogh never boasted.

"But I live very simply." Castellano took another sip of his espresso.

Keogh followed suit and countered, "My office is a converted garage."

"Then you are as smart as I heard you were."

Keogh looked at the old man. He felt that the preparation was over. He was going to talk turkey.

"I am seventy years old. I have a son older than you. The old Italians call me Don. The newspapers call me a Godfather. I was not born in

Italy, so the word Don means nothing. I don't know where this word Godfather comes from. People say I am the head of the Mafia. I am Calabrian. Calabrese can't be in the Unione Sicilone. What have I done in my life? Much that I regret. I am not a man without sin, as is true of yourself. Perhaps I discovered politics too late in my life. You are lucky there. You discovered it early. And a newspaper. Ah, to have had that in the old days! There was too much blood then. Some of it was necessary—the same way if a man rapes a woman, he should go to the electric chair. Yes, I am a law-and-order man."

Both men saw the humor in it and favored each other with indulgent smiles.

"I go to Belmont, Aqueduct and down to Miami. I like the horses. Sometimes I cheat at pinochle when I go to Mutchie's, which is a bar on South Street. But then I give the money back. I'm an old man who wants to show how smart he is. That's all."

Keogh poured Castellano a second drink and one for himself. He was warming to this old man, although he was mystified as to why he was laying an autobiography on him.

"I have one son who is a lawyer, another who is at West Point. I have a daughter who is a teacher. Not only am I rich, but I'm very contented. Tonight, I will go home—stop off and buy some apples and tomatoes and walk a few blocks and then go home. My wife, a good woman, will be waiting up for me, as she has done for forty years, and some of those years there were times when the telephone rang and she didn't know whether somebody was going to tell her I'd had an accident."

"You sound very happy, very content."

"You see, there can be no accidents happening to me anymore because whatever happens, I haven't been involved in the business for twenty years. Sometimes, Vito wants to know about a judge, I tell him. Angelo DeCarlo in New Jersey, he gets in a jam, so I help him out. Lilo Galante needs a little help so we sit down at Tre Amici and eat. There can be no accidents happening. Why am I telling you this?"

"I would be interested."

"Because you tell your Irisher friend Mr. McLaughlin that if he has any trouble on the docks it does not come from me. It doesn't come from Raymond in Providence. I would know. I can speak for Raymond.

"Oh, if we wanted to, we could, and we would win—I could take his docks. But why? Maybe then we would win, but in winning I could be a casualty. I don't want any accidents to happen to me. I want to die cheating at pinochle.

"So you, young Mr. Keogh, you tell your friend Frank and Raymond don't know what this thing is that's going on up there. We don't care.

"Once before, there was this man Devlin. I gave him my protection in the North End, but when he wanted to hurt you and other Irishers, I said no. He had an accident. There have been too many accidents."

Sean Keogh smiled. He put a hand on the old man's arm. Keogh appreciated two things. One, old Castellano made it easy for him by carrying the subject to him. He had spared him the embarrassment of broaching a sensitive and potentially explosive situation. And two, he believed and trusted Castellano.

"And Mr. Keogh . . . you stay with that newspaper. It's much better than this wise-guy stuff. You know what I mean. Newspapers and politics. That's good business for a young Irisher. Shall we go?"

They stood up without paying, and the old man led him back to the modest Ford. Without a word they headed toward the Carlyle.

Keogh had not told him where he was staying. Castellano chuckled. "You Irishers. All of you stay at the Carlyle. The old man Kennedy, I knew him very well. He always stayed there. You know, if I had fooled around like him, I would never have had to worry about trouble from the outside. My wife would have had me hit. You Irishers. Very funny."

The car pulled up and Castellano opened the door. As Keogh got out, the old man grabbed him by the arm. "Mr. Keogh, it's not my business. But if you're having trouble up there and you know it isn't us, then maybe you should look closer in Boston."

Keogh remained thoughtful a moment, nodded his head and said, "Good-bye, sir. One day I hope you will be my guest in Boston."

"I would like that, young man. Remember, you stay in newspapers and politics. You can never lose. *Ciao*."

Keogh had a nightcap at the downstairs bar. He remained deep in thought as he slowly sipped his Scotch. The old man oozed wisdom. He was like a statesman in his measured tones and reasoning. The only throwback to the old days was his expression "Irisher." Sean smiled. He trusted him. Trusted him the way he trusted his own boys in Southie. He felt good that he had kept his promise to Mr. McLaughlin and the news he would have would be good news.

He finished his drink, went upstairs and fell into a contented sleep. It was one o'clock Tuesday morning. He had left his house in Carson Beach at three. He had accomplished his mission.

On Monday, as the four-o'clock shuttle took Sean Keogh to New York, Rose Keogh had made a telephone call.

Chapter

10

THE TELEPHONE shrilled on the private line of Edward Wilson. He picked it up before the second ring.

"Wilson."

"Hello, Edward."

"Rose, what—"

"I presume you can talk."

"Yes, but—"

"Just listen, Edward. . . . I want to see you. Could you be at the house at six o'clock? The maid will be gone by then."

"Don't be silly, Rose, I will do no such thing. Are you crazy?"

"Don't ever say that, Edward. Just be here at six o'clock."

"For God's sake, Rose, I can't walk into your house when Sean is away. What would I tell him if he found out? Why would I be there?"

"Stop babbling like a frightened child. Just be here, Edward, I mean it. At six o'clock. Be here."

He started to say something, but the phone went dead. Slowly he replaced the receiver. She had spoken with that cold command in her voice which Wilson recognized . . . recognized as the other Rose Keogh. Gone was the charming quiet way she mouthed her words. It was the other Rose now, giving commands like a cool-headed field marshal.

He ran his fingers through his carefully combed shock of red hair. His jaw muscles tensed. He had known things were going too smoothly. Damn it. He looked at his watch. Four ten P.M. He had an important meeting with some editors in twenty minutes. It would be a long conference, discussing the future direction of the newspaper.

He had purposely scheduled the meeting for when Keogh was out of town. He desperately needed to consolidate his position as Chairman and Executive Director. What Sean Keogh knew about the business and publishing world could be put on a thumbnail, Wilson thought in silence. He was sick and tired of the man's shadow falling over him wherever he walked. Let him stay with his cronies in Southie. The *Clarion* was uptown.

He bit his lip. Rose Keogh's call had thrown his ice-smooth thinking totally into confusion. He cursed her silently. He knew she would haunt him. But nobody was going to stand in Edward Wilson's way. Not Rose Keogh, not Sean Keogh, not any of the roughnecks he had grown up with and silently hated through all his years struggling to be someone.

He would cancel the meeting. He just couldn't concentrate until he got Rose Keogh off his back with whatever she was going to propose to him—and he knew she wanted something; otherwise she would never have called him. Never. If she'd had her way, Edward Wilson would have died the night he told her Sean Keogh, his confounded master, had taken an interest in her and maybe it might be a good idea if they ended their brief but tempestuous liaison. Of course he would be there at six o'clock. He would do as she said.

He called John Hickey downstairs in his editorial office.

"John, Ed here."

"Yes, Ed?"

"I'm sorry, old man," he said, affecting his best Harvard delivery, "I'm going to have to cancel that four-thirty meeting."

"Oh, okay. Pity. I think we were all looking forward to thrashing things out. The editors were very much interested to hear your comments." Hickey knew how to flatter Wilson.

"Well, something has come up. I'll call you tomorrow to re-sked it. Okay?"

"No problem. Bye, Ed."

Wilson leaned back in his chair, his eyes searching the ceiling. He was a smooth operator, that Hickey. Very smooth. I like him. He knows what he wants and goes after it. A good ally. I'll need him one day.

He went into his executive bathroom. On one side was a wardrobe full of finely cut custom-made Brooks Brothers suits. A half dozen freshly laundered shirts lay neatly stacked on a shelf. Three pairs of highly polished shoes lay on the floor. Wilson's attention to appearance and dress bordered on the fanatical. He always changed his clothes in the evening. He stripped and showered and dressed.

It was four thirty. He left the office and walked across to the Ritz Carlton bar and slowly sipped his way through three Scotch and waters. The barman knew exactly how he liked his Scotch, because Sean Keogh always liked his Scotch with water, no ice.

He was deeply worried about the meeting with Rose. She was not a well woman, and her problems had nothing to do with her pregnancy.

He walked back to the office garage and called for his Mercedes. It was five thirty. He would drive slowly and be there at the Carson Beach house at exactly six o'clock. He hoped no one would see him walking inside. It would be just his luck to have one of Keogh's cronies see him going inside the house of his pregnant wife. In Southie you didn't visit a man's wife when he wasn't in the house.

Wilson pulled into Carson Beach. Keogh's big but unpretentious white house was barely distinguishable from the others on the street—every Southie Irishman's idea of luxury. Wilson looked at the house with a mixture of contempt and curiosity. With all his money, Keogh has to live in this ugly shack just so he won't be far from his beloved children of Southie. He can't leave Southie. He would be a midget anywhere else. But deep down, Wilson knew he was lying to himself.

He parked the car four houses down from the Keogh residence. Briskly he walked to the front door. He rang the bell impatiently. Answer the door, damn it. He was standing there for everyone to see.

Rose opened the door. She smiled slightly mockingly. "Why, Edward, you look nervous."

He hurried inside. Despite her being almost eight months pregnant, she still retained her petite beauty. Her dark hair hung loosely around her shoulders, setting off her pale but pretty face, which sported not a touch of makeup. Despite her protruding belly, she walked with delicacy and grace as she led Wilson into the sitting room. A bottle of champagne sparkled in an ice bucket next to the sofa where Rose sat herself.

Wilson was fidgety. He looked questioningly at the champagne. "I didn't know you imbibed."

"Always on special occasions, Edward darling. Now do the honors and open the bottle."

"Look, Rose, I don't know your game, but I didn't come here for a champagne celebration. You know I'm not comfortable here."

"Not comfortable? You're terrified."

"Now, listen—"

She cut him off sharply: "Now, do the honors, Edward. Pour us both a glass and sit down."

Testily he obliged. He handed her a glass. She sipped and looked him in the eyes over the rim of the goblet.

"Well, what is it, Rose?"

She laughed. "Edward, you know you don't fool me."

Wilson exhaled with exasperation. For Christ's sake, woman, out with it, he thought angrily.

She continued: "I'm amazed you manage to fool anybody with your little act."

"I don't know what you're talking about."

"Oh, yes, you do. Your little act of undying loyalty to the male version of Joan of Arc, my dear husband."

"What's this all about?"

"Edward, I know as well as you do that you hate every tissue of Sean's body. You detest every split second of his existence. You loathe every moment you have to be with him and his cross-bearing cronies."

Wilson's eyes widened in shock. "Rose, that is palpable rubbish. You know that's stupid, vicious nonsense."

She smiled and took another sip of her champagne. "Drink up, Edward."

"Damn it, Rose, let's stop this stupidity. I'm going."

"Sit down and shut up."

He didn't move.

"You see, I know, Edward, as you do, you didn't break up our affair because you sacrificed your love for the man to whom you have everything to be grateful for. Oh, no, you shunted me off onto him because you didn't have enough guts to tell him about us. You thought you might fall into disfavor and not reap all the handsome rewards he has heaped on you. No, Edward, you are a conniving rat."

Edward George Wilson had seen it before anyone else. It was near impossible for him to believe that the shy, sexy, frail-boned child-woman whom he had taken out before Sean Keogh decided to marry her, was the same woman sitting in front of him now. The face, the body, pregnancy notwithstanding, were the same. But it was the sophisticated harshness that had changed her so dramatically. The curl of the mouth. The way she spat out the name Sean Keogh. The way her lids dropped in conspiracy, hiding the beautiful deep brown eyes that had so attracted him.

Edward Wilson was no doctor, but he had known from early days that the delicate Rose Keogh, the sweet, subservient, pretty South Boston housewife, very definitely had a second side. And the second side was frightening.

"I didn't come here for a treatise on my ethics, Rose," he said limply.

"You're just biding your time until you can take it all over, Edward. You think you're sharp enough, cunning enough, bright enough to outsmart Sean Keogh."

"I do all right," he said, half-conceding her assessment of his motives.

"But I will tell you something, Edward. You are not sharp enough, cunning enough or bright enough to outsmart my dear husband."

Wilson reddened slightly in anger at the implication of his inferiority.

"But," she continued, "you could be. You could have it all. But you couldn't do it alone. You just don't have it."

"Explain yourself, Rose. . . . After all, why shouldn't you believe your husband to be a genius? You're the one who fell madly in love with him —with him and his power." He hit back with even, measured tones.

Rose bristled. "Yes, I fell in love with him because I thought he was so different from you. He had gumption, vision and humility."

"Oh? What happened?" he said sarcastically.

"I found that he was as much a chauvinistic egomaniac as you are. A sniveling, backstabbing coward."

"I didn't come here for this." He was angry.

"No, but you are listening because I'm the only one who can guide you in your ambition to put Sean Keogh in his rightful place."

"Why this? Why so suddenly?"

"Because I hate him as much as you do. He is a pompous ass who thinks he has a hot line to God, who thinks he is the arbiter of good and bad."

It was Wilson's turn. "You know, Rose, you are not well. You are not well at all."

For a moment Wilson thought she was going to throw the glass of champagne in his face.

She composed herself. "What do you mean by that, Edward?"

He saw the danger sign and adjusted his manner. He looked at her with genuine concern and sympathy.

Her bizarre schizophrenia could turn her from a loving, obsequious and dutiful wife to a coldly scheming virago with a stunning if sometimes frightening intelligence.

Solicitously, he refilled her glass and sat next to her.

"What are you really thinking of, Rose?" His voice was quiet.

"I'm thinking exactly the same way as you, Edward. I want to bring Sean Keogh to his knees. Not right now, mind you. He is going places fast, and let's face it, we are going with him. I don't want to pull down his castle. I want the castle to stay, but with him out of it. Confess Edward—that's what you are planning."

"You have got me wrong. It's only obvious, Rose, that when it comes to the newspaper and business I think I'm more suited to run things, and let's face it, he must think the same. He was the one who put me in charge."

"Come on, Edward. Everything from the clothes you wear to the drinks you drink to the way you talk. It's all in his shadow. You are just a well-educated convenient tool. He can pull in the reins anytime he wants to. He is in charge . . . in charge of everything."

He could feel himself getting angry again. She was speaking the truth, and he hated being Sean Keogh's puppet.

He spoke cautiously. "Rose, just for argument's sake, suppose some-body wanted to make sure that his position was guaranteed with Sean. What would you propose."

"So many, many things. But we have to start slowly." She spoke now as if she were assured of Wilson's cooperation.

"You see, Edward, you can't do a thing without me. But I need you too. Now, for instance, you have no idea why Sean is in New York."

Wilson shook his head.

"Well, Sean is down there to make peace for Bernard McLaughlin."

"I don't understand."

"McLaughlin thinks Frank Castellano, the mobster in New York, is moving on his docks."

"Why would Sean get mixed up in that?"

"Typical. He thinks he owes McLaughlin. But also, an attack on the money base of Sean's empire—the numbers, the docks, Burke's trucking business and his Teamsters—would hurt him severely. The newspaper is not making much money, as you know."

He nodded. "But it will. It will make a fortune."

"I agree. But when it's making a fortune, do you think Sean will let you run it? No, that will be his big, respectable front to launch him into big-time politics. He is going to be a very powerful man. But we must be sure that when he is about to be his most powerful, he will have no allies, no power base, no strength."

Wilson remained silent.

"And who is his strength? It's McLaughlin, Burke, yourself and a handful of dim-witted Micks."

"I'm surprised to hear you talk like this, Rose."

"You wouldn't be if you knew what he's done to me."

He looked at her questioningly.

"He has tried to bury me, strip me of who I am. He treats me like a brainless child, all in the name of his sickening paternalism. He is quite dangerous and quite mad." She talked with an edge of sharp anger. When she mentioned his name she seemed to spit it out. Wilson had seen the change come over her since he'd walked into the house. There was something quite frightening about the tension locked inside her. She stood up and walked across to a table, opened the drawer and took out some pills. She took two and washed them down with champagne.

"Are those for your headaches?"

She nodded silently.

Wilson took a deep breath. "I'm just interested in hearing you talk."

"Well, we can capitalize on Sean's problems right now. We can capital-ize handsomely."

"Go on."

For the next half hour Wilson listened in awe and finally horror as she laid out her plan. He had not said a word, but by the time she had finished he felt quite sick. He had stood up and walked to the liquor cabinet to pour himself a Scotch. He noticed that his hand was shaking. He was terrified.

"I won't have anything to do with it, Rose. Nothing. I wish we had never talked. Please don't count on me."

"Ah, but I must, because you're the only one who knows those thugs in Charlestown. I must."

"Damn it, Rose, God damn it. No. Count me out. Forget we spoke. Forget it. I'm leaving. I won't help."

"You'll help, Edward. What do you think Sean would do if I told him about this?" She ran her hand over her rounded belly.

Wilson paled. "That's a damn lie."

"No, it's not, Edward. What do you think would happen to your empire if I told Sean everything?"

"You wouldn't, Rose, because he would kill you."

"No, Edward. He, McLaughlin and Burke would kill *you*. You, Edward . . . *you*."

Wilson could feel panic running through his veins like electricity. His head swam and he felt as if he were going to throw up. God, what had he got himself into?

"Rose," he said, trying to steady his voice, "why mess up everything? Why don't we forget the whole conversation and go on the way we are? Everybody is doing well. Everybody is making money. Everybody is happy."

"Everybody," she spat, "except me, and Sean Keogh is standing in my way. Now, you will help, Edward. Otherwise I'll pull you down with me, and it could be very ugly for you."

He left that night at nine o'clock, and despite a pleasant breeze that whipped off the bay, he was in a cold sweat.

The next day he made some calls to Charlestown, and one week later he met some men.

"IT'S STRICTLY small potatoes, Mr. Mac," Sean Keogh said with confidence. Keogh had been happy to report in the office the next day to McLaughlin and Burke that the meeting with Castellano had gone well.

"Yer sure, lad?" said McLaughlin.

"Mac, Castellano doesn't even know what it's about."

"How about Raymond, in Providence?" Burke asked.

"Frank, you know the Italians. Castellano is Raymond's boss. He spoke for himself and Raymond. This trouble down there on your docks is nothing more than a bunch of local young cowboys from across the river."

"If 'tis just that, Sean boy, 'twill be easy to handle. Just so long as we know we ain't goin' up against some war machine."

"Castellano and Raymond are old men, Mac. Castellano wants to die in bed. You know, I was quite impressed with him."

"Well, ye shoulda seen him twenty years ago. He is one tough sonofabitch."

Frank Burke remained silent.

"What's wrong, Frank?" Sean asked.

"Don't know. There's something about this whole thing I can't understand. We haven't had anyone trying to move on Southie in ten years. Why now?"

"Frank, people know we have the best outfit in New England. They have some idea of the money we make. They know we have peace here, and they know the neighborhood supports us. If someone has enough guts to take it away from us, they would have a very good operation. But this thing now is strictly punk stuff. Castellano gave me his personal assurance. I believe him. He is a man of his word, whatever else he might be."

"I trust yer judgment, Sean. What's more, I talked to Father Zeibatski and his brother Vinnie. They seem to agree with you. Well, I'll go down there tomorrow and have a sit-down with these lads who are tryin' to muscle in down there. I think I can make them see to reason. An' if not, well, maybe we'll have to crack a few ribs here and there."

"Try to keep it peaceful, Mr. Mac. Peace has been very good for business. We cleared sixty-two thousand after expenses last month. We're doing very well."

"Yer right, laddo. I'll keep it peaceful."

"Okay, I've got to be leaving. Got to be taking Rose to the doctor's."

"How is it goin', son?"

"Everything is fine. She's a bit big, but the doctor says it's going fine. About six weeks, maybe seven, and we'll have another Keogh in the brood." He slapped McLaughlin on the back as he bade him and Burke good-bye. Then he disappeared through the glass-paned door of the office, and McLaughlin sighed.

"He's a gem of a lad, that boy."

"Damn right, Mac," Burke agreed. "Where would we all have been without him? Damn genius."

"We'd prob'ly all be planted six feet under now. The Guineas woulda wiped us out. Who woulda believed we'd be at peace with the Guineas? Well, it's better that way. This way we all live to be dirty ol' men."

That afternoon Sean Keogh took Rose to Dixon Hughes for a checkup. After the checkup, he drove her to the Ritz for afternoon tea.

"I think I'll skip the tea," he said with a smile to the waiter. "I'll take a Scotch. And how about tea with cheesecake for you, Rose?"

She smiled. "That sounds fine, Sean."

"You're looking beautiful, darling."

"With this belly?" She smiled self-consciously.

"Yes, with that belly . . . Well, what'll we call him if it's a boy, and what'll we call her if it's a girl? Tell you what: Daniel if it's a boy, Katherine if it's a girl. How about that?"

"They're good names, dear. Which do you want—a boy or a girl? Don't answer. I know you want a boy. Every Irishman does."

"No, I don't think you have the right to demand of God what child he'll give you. All you can pray is that the child will be healthy. That's all —and a healthy mother, so we can have some more."

She smiled, and her smile was a genuine smile as she looked at the handsome black-haired man who sat across the table from her. There was a look of warmth and affection in her face that always made Sean feel secure and comfortable with his luck in choosing such an ideal wife.

"I feel so guilty, Rose . . . all the hours I spend away from you; I really do."

She put her hand over his. "It won't be forever, Sean. I know you're doing it for me and the baby. But Sean, you're pushing yourself."

His Scotch and her tea arrived. She sipped on the steaming tea and continued: "I worry about you, Sean. You've been looking very tired lately."

"Sometimes I just dream of having three days straight in bed and doing nothing but sleep. But I can't. There is so much to do. Business, newspaper, politics. Getting the neighborhood on its feet. But it's paying off. We've cut unemployment to the lowest in years. And, at least the garbage gets picked up regularly. The schools are running smoothly, and there are chances that some big companies may want to build their plants in Southie. God, think of the jobs there would be, and all here in Southie. The money would be made here and spent here."

"You've done some wonderful things, Sean. Men like my father and my brother would do anything for you."

"They're fine men. But I couldn't do it without men like Mr. Mac and Frank . . . they're like rocks."

"You're very lucky, Sean, to have the loyalty of those men. Very lucky. But you earn it, darling."

He squeezed her hand. "And I'm very lucky to have you ... very lucky."

She squeezed his hand back and smiled.

IT WAS as the doctors had told Edward Wilson when he had gone to the clinic in Lowell, Massachusetts, posing as her husband, in the early days of their courtship. It was a classic case of the worst type of schizophrenia, a complete duality in personality, transforming her into a totally different human being. It had been the same way with her mother, and the doctors had speculated that there had been a genetic defect on the mother's side of the family.

Their diagnosis had enraged Rose as she speculated on the prospect of ending her days like her mother. It was at that time that she simply blocked her illness from her mind, and in so doing produced the tragedy of being totally unable to control her other self by both ignoring the black side of her nature and outright not knowing it existed. The healthy Rose Keogh loved and honored her husband. The sick one plotted cruelly for his downfall and that of his friends with a rare and vitriolic intelligence that Wilson could hardly believe had been nurtured in the once simple and beautiful child-woman, the daughter of Pat Sweeney, the rough-and-ready Southie longshoreman. It was an intelligence that terrified Wilson. His prosperity depended on this woman, and while he was aware of her brilliance, he was frightened as to where it would lead —or where it had already led.

KELLY'S CAFÉ was, as usual for a Friday night, full of payday longshoremen. In decor it was indistinguishable from many of the other bars in Southie. Formica-covered bar, a few tables serving hot cheap stews and hero sandwiches, the flags of Ireland and the United States hanging limply where they had hung for thirty years. There were a few dog-eared photographs of local baseball teams of many years ago, when the customers had had thinner middles and thicker heads of hair. It was a brightly lit place near the corner of Old Colony Road and Dorchester. It had a jukebox full of Irish rebel songs, and the noise and singing on a Friday night crept well into Saturday morning. It was a favorite of the men because it had no telephone, thereby robbing the wives of a chance to call up and disturb their revelry.

At the end of the bar, Bernie McLaughlin was buying drinks for Pat Sweeney, the father of Rose Keogh, and her brother, Billy. Bernie was in an expansive mood.

"I think we did it, Pat, old son," McLaughlin said as he threw down a shot of Jameson's and put out the fire with a glass of cold beer. "Those smart-ass little fucks didn't know where they was comin' from. They was shittin' in their pants when we told them what we would do to them if they came around the pier again. Sassy little fucks."

"We shoulda cracked a few heads to teach 'em a lesson, Mac," Sweeney said. "We woulda in the old days."

"No need, Pat. Ye can't blame 'em fer tryin'. That's how *we* started up."

Billy Sweeney listened enraptured as the two old wharf rats talked. He looked up to both men as idols—hard men with their fists, generous with a buck and cast-iron bellies for the enormous amount of booze they drank.

McLaughlin ordered another round. They clinked glasses, and Mac gave his traditional toast: "May yer soul be in heaven a minute before the devil knows yer dead."

It was going to be a heavy night. The three of them downed drink after drink and then joined in a raucous rendition of "Dublin in the Green."

At one o'clock in the morning, young Billy Sweeney was green, and with excuses and apologies, he weaved his way out of the bar toward his home.

"Yer gonna have to train 'im if he's gonna be like you," McLaughlin chuckled.

"He can throw 'em back, but ye can't expect these young uns to keep up with the likes of us—now, can you?"

McLaughlin slapped him on the back. "Yer a lucky man. He's a fine boy, an' yer daughter, Rose, had made young Sean a very happy man."

"I don't mind sayin' it: I'm proud, Mac, very proud."

They called for another round.

"Pat, what's the time?"

"One thirty."

"Well, if we're gonna make a party of it, let's see who's up at the club. Maybe Frankie and Eddie are up there."

"Don't know about Eddie, but Frankie should be there. It's Friday. He always buys his boys a few pints on Friday."

"Let's call him and tie one on."

The two men walked happily from the bar, red-faced and jolly, with a slight roll to their gait. They walked down to the corner, turned left on Damrell Street and headed toward the pay telephone.

"Ye know, Pat, we've been a lucky pair o' bastards. Here we are as drunk as monkeys. Yer about to be a grandfather. I'm gonna be a Dutch uncle. We're hooked up with one of the smartest guys in Boston. We're just lads from Southie, but bejaysus, we're lucky . . . we're lucky."

"Yer right, Mac. Damn right ye are."

They put their arms around each other and started to sing in appalling tones:

> "Oh, we belong to Southie,
> Good ole Southie town.
> Now, there's somethin' about old Southie
> That is goin' round and round . . ."

Mac stumbled into the telephone booth and called the Erin Social Club. "Mac here. Is Frankie Burke there?"

Seconds later Burke answered.

"Frankie Burke . . . I'm down at Kelly's with Pat Sweeney . . . we're tyin' one on. How long ye gonna be there? . . . Come on, now . . . hang around. We'll be up there in ten minutes."

Sweeney crowded into the booth. "Let me talk to Frankie, Mac."

"Pat, the bastard wants to go home . . . Jaysus, Pat, get outa the booth! Yer squashin' the bejaysus outa me."

Burke, on the other end, was protesting his need to get home when McLaughlin saw them. Two men with ski masks. They had appeared from nowhere. They had shotguns leveled from their shoulders.

McLaughlin roared, and Burke could hear it all on his end: "Pat get the fuck outa here! Quick . . . Jaysus, no, ye bastards, no!"

Pat Sweeney looked at him with curiosity for a moment and then he saw what McLaughlin saw. They burst from the telephone booth. The two men in ski masks stepped back and closer together so they wouldn't be shooting into each other.

Burke was screaming into the telephone, "Run Mac, run! We're comin'."

The telephone receiver dangled in the booth and recorded the first blast, which hit Sweeney on the left side, hurling him three feet and smashing him back into the telephone booth. He rolled over and tried to crawl to the gutter. Seconds later the second gun barked and caught McLaughlin in the left shoulder, spinning him like a top and crashing him into the side of the booth.

The old man bounced back from the booth, and before the masked gunmen could position themselves he had charged into one of the attackers and knocked the gun to one side and in the same motion grabbed the man by the throat.

McLaughlin gave a triumphant roar: "Got ye, ye bastard . . . got ye." It was a roar that came from deep inside his stomach.

The second gunman couldn't get a clean shot without hitting his partner. The nails of the old man dug deeper into the throat, and the gunman started to gurgle.

The lights of Damrell Street were flashing on, and already the voices from Kelly's Café could be heard coming down the street.

The second gunman finally managed to get behind his partner. Swiftly he thrust the barrel over his partner's shoulder and flush onto the left cheek of McLaughlin's face. There was a resounding boom, and the old man somersaulted backward—headless.

"Tough old bastards," the mortally wounded Sweeney heard them say as they disappeared into a car and roared off down Damrell Street.

Burke arrived on the scene five minutes later and was joined seconds afterward by a pale-faced Sean Keogh, who had been summoned from his bed by the barman of the club, who simply said, "Somebody's shot Mr. Mac and Sweeney real bad down at Kelly's."

McLaughlin's body was covered. The pools of blood covered a ten-foot-square area.

Burke and Keogh elbowed their way through the crowd. Sweeney was clinging to the last seconds of life. The ambulance attendants were preparing to move him.

He looked up at Burke and Keogh. "The fuckers did us in, boys . . . did us in." His body shuddered, and his eyes glazed over. One of the ambulance men looked up. "He didn't have a chance."

Slowly Burke and Keogh turned to the covered body of McLaughlin. Tears streamed down Burke's face, and he heard himself choking back sobs. His chin dropped onto his chest. There was no life left in him.

Keogh looked blankly at the sprawled form under the sheet and clamped his jaws until his teeth hurt. There was no blood in his face, and he stood like a mechanical man. It was if his soul and his feelings were outside his body. The body just obeyed vague orders as if it weren't part of his being.

Detective Jack Crockford burst through the crowd. "Jesus Christ . . . Sean . . ."

"It was Mr. Mac and Pat Sweeney."

"Jesus Christ," Crockford repeated as he surveyed the carnage, "who woulda done this?"

Burke lifted his tear-stained face from his chest and looked at Keogh. "Maybe some of their friends from New York."

The comment shot through Keogh's body like a whaling pike and seemed to bring him back into consciousness. He bit his lip until it bled at the realization that Burke might be right.

"Jack, I'll tell Mr. Mac's wife—leave it to me. I don't want any cops going there now. I'll tell her."

"And you'll look after Rose too, Sean?"

"Of course. I'll break the news to her and her brother."

Silently Keogh and Burke got into the same car. Neither could hear the other breathing, and they didn't exchange a word as they drove first to McLaughlin's house, then to Billy Sweeney and then to tell Rose Keogh that she no longer had a father.

On the way, Sean roused Dr. Dixon Hughes from his bed. He was equipped with sedatives. By the time they reached Keogh's house, after informing the McLaughlin family and young Billy Sweeney, they were drained of any emotion.

The lights switched on frantically as the car cruised into the driveway. As they walked to the door it opened, and Rose was standing there.

"What's wrong? . . . Something has happened. . . . What's the doctor doing here? Sean, tell me."

"Come inside, baby."

"Sean, tell me."

He guided her onto the sofa.

"Some very tragic news—very bad. Darling, prepare yourself. Your father died tonight . . . there was a very bad accident."

She sat dry-eyed, looking into space, as he told her what had happened. She called her brother Billy and talked to him in mechanical tones.

"Billy is coming over to stay the night, Sean," she said blankly.

"Fine. . . . And you, Frank . . . you better stay too."

"No, I have to get back to Teresa. She'll have heard by now. I don't want anyone pounding on my door tonight with a shotgun, especially if they're from New York."

The comment hurt Sean. "We don't know that, Frank."

"You could be right," Burke said blankly. "What does it matter now? We'll take care of that afterwards."

"Don't make it worse, Frank."

Burke simply shrugged and walked dazedly from the house as the first streaks of dawn came through the windows.

Long after both Billy and Rose had been sedated, Sean Keogh sat on the sofa, the tears now coming freely and coursing down his cheeks in blood-warm rivers. He had loved old Mr. Mac . . . and Sweeney too. But Mr. Mac was like the father Sean had been robbed of at such an early age, and now Mr. Mac had been taken away from him.

Unshaven and crumpled, he got into his car at eight thirty while Billy and Rose were far from consciousness and drove to Father Zeibatski. He knelt in church for an hour praying fervently. He needed to get clean —quickly.

He wandered from Sacred Heart after hardly exchanging a word with the wise priest. It was all said in his eyes.

The double funeral, three days later, was a bad affair. A cold, heavy wind lashed the mourners and tore at the flower petals on the hundreds of wreaths that were carried from the Donlan Funeral Home in South Boston. It was all that Keogh could do to keep from cracking. He stood erect with his pregnant wife, virtually emotionless, beside him. He held back his tears by closing his ears to the words of Father Zeibatski and sucking in lungfuls of damp air while trying to think of everything except the two shattered bodies that lay bloodless in the caskets.

Eddie Wilson and Frank Burke stood on one side of Keogh, and Billy Sweeney stood next to his sister, Rose. Sweeney and Burke let the tears fall without shame. But Keogh knew that the tears showed not only sorrow, but deep and black anger.

At the farewell drink later in the Erin Social Club, Sean Keogh recognized the look in Frank Burke's eyes. Sean tugged him by the elbow and led Burke from the main room of muffled mourners.

"Frank, level with me."

"What's there to level?"

"Promise me you won't do anything until we know who did it."

"But we know who did it, Sean. You know better than anyone."

"Please . . . old fella, please, just hold off until we know for sure."

"And go to half a dozen more funerals?"

"Frank, I'm telling you, I don't believe it's Castellano, or Raymond, in Providence, or any of the Italians. If you hit, they're going to hit back twice as hard."

Frank Burke looked at Keogh. "Sean, I'll wait, but I'm relyin' on you to set it all straight. An' I'm not gonna wait forever. It's Mr. Mac we just buried, you know. He's fuckin' cold, Sean."

Keogh caught his breath. "Don't I know it, fella."

They returned to the packed room of maudlin drinkers. There was a scuffle at the door as some of the local lads threw out some press photographers trying to get shots of the mobland gathering. Keogh looked on with detachment. One of those newspapermen probably worked for him. What was he—a publisher, a politician or just a hoodlum mourning a departed friend who had died in full hoodlum style with full hoodlum honors? Who might have died because Sean Keogh was not a good enough hoodlum to have seen that Frank Castellano was lying.

Sean could feel the hot and silent vibration of anger and revenge in the room. It was in Vinnie Zeibatski's eyes. It was in Billy Sweeney's eyes. They say old men start wars for the young ones to fight. In Southie it was the young and careless who had started the wars, leaving the old to mourn.

Sean bought a round of drinks. He handed a beer to young Billy Sweeney. His eyes were red-rimmed, and his face was puffy with grief. He was a handsome young man with the strong, broad features of his father. He had been back for only a year from South Vietnam, where he had been trained as a demolition expert.

"It's hard to grasp, Sean," he said absently. "Dad and Southie was all I really ever had." He looked self-consciously at his sister. ". . . And you too, Sis." Her face was strangely vacant. "I just can't think of going home and Dad not being there to have a beer with. I can't think of going down to the docks not to see his big smiling face. You understand, Sean, don't you?"

"Very much, Bill, very much." He put a reassuring hand on the young man's shoulder. He didn't know why he allowed himself the gesture. It never helps.

As the booze flowed across the bar, the crowd became noisier and more self-indulgent in its public mourning. Toast after toast was hoisted to the two departed men of Southie.

Rose looked tired and pale. She had been on her feet now for almost two hours. Sean Keogh couldn't leave. If Father Zeibatski was the spiritual head of Southie, he was the temporal head. He kissed his wife's cheek, and turning to Eddie Wilson, said, "Ed, would you mind taking Rose home in your car?"

Wilson seemed to be surprised. "Yes, of course, Sean . . . of course. . . . Rose, would you like me to drive you home?"

"I think so . . . yes, that would be fine." She looked at her husband.

"I better hang on here for a little longer."

"Okay. I understand, darling." She elbowed her way through the mourners who shook her hand, kissed it and even hugged her to signify their common loss.

They were always the same faces. They were the same faces who'd come over to the house after her mother had been taken away, a raving lunatic. Those faces swarming around her with pity were always the spark to touch off her rage.

As Wilson led her into the street, she sucked in the cold air for relief. Her temples were pounding. He opened the car door. She backed into the front seat, her protruding belly making it almost impossible to get into a car normally. He gunned the motor of the Mercedes. He was pale and seemed frightened of speech.

She spoke first. "Your friends from Charlestown really did a job, didn't they, Edward?"

"Rose . . . I . . . I don't know how your father got mixed up in it. It was a shocking mistake. They were told only McLaughlin."

Rose Keogh's eyes observed the passing traffic with mild interest.

"Probably settling an old score and got two for the price of one. . . . Turn left here, Edward. Have you forgotten your way?"

Her nonchalance sent a shudder through Edward Wilson. It was a shudder of disbelief . . . and fear.

Finally she spoke again. "Well, now let's sit back and see what happens."

Beads of cold sweat formed on Wilson's upper lip.

THE NEXT seven days seemed to pass like one single time period for Sean Keogh. There were no nights and no days. The week seemed like an ever-stretching elastic band. He felt guilty, but he had virtually ignored his work in his garage office, spending hour after hour sitting with Burke in his office, drinking tea and occasionally going next door to the club for a quiet whiskey. He hadn't been to the *Clarion*. Wilson seemed to have a good handle on affairs there. He had canceled his lunches with Roger Sharpe.

The Boston newspapers had played the assassination of McLaughlin and Sweeney for three days straight. The *Clarion* had been no exception. It was hard for Keogh to rationalize, selling papers off his beloved friend. But he had been insistent that nobody tamper with the editors handling the story. The veteran newspapermen who had some inkling of Keogh's friendship with McLaughlin applauded the move as professional. Keogh hated himself for it. But deep down, he quieted his conscience with the thought that McLaughlin would have wanted it no other way. In the end the newspaper would be very valuable to the Southie organization, even if the picture of his sheet-covered body was splashed all over page one.

Keogh worried desperately about Rose. The emotion seemed to be drained from her body. Dr. Dixon Hughes had prescribed total rest, aware that the trauma of the past week could prove dangerous to a pregnant woman. To Sean, however, she seemed fine physically. It was her blank, mechanical movements that bothered him—almost as if he were living with a stranger. There was a set to her mouth that occasionally made her look hard. It was a pretty mouth—delicately shaped lips covering a beautiful set of flashing teeth that lit up a room when she smiled. But she rarely smiled. It was if she were always fighting the urge to snarl. It was never anything she said. Despite her pregnancy, she insisted on cooking for Sean and was never less than totally attentive. It was just the look that masked her very pretty face, somehow shadowing its natural beauty with a mysterious darkness of mood.

He dismissed his misgivings. What could he expect? She had just lost her father.

From Burke's office Keogh had made several calls to Castellano in New York and Raymond in Providence. They had gone to Puerto Rico together, Keogh was told. This had made Keogh uneasy about the charge that Castellano had been behind the hit after all. It reinforced Burke's belief that the Italians were moving on Southie and McLaughlin had been only the first victim. Keogh was aware that the majority of assassinations were carried out while the real executioners were out of town or out of the country.

On the eighth day after the murders, Keogh again called Castellano on his private line.

"Hello." It was the gravelly voice of the New York don.

Keogh's tone was quiet and distant. "Mr. Castellano?"

Burke watched him closely as he spoke to the Italian. Keogh could see the jagged lines of revenge in Burke's face.

"Yes. Who is speaking, please?"

"This is Keogh. Sean Keogh."

"Ah, Mr. Keogh. I suppose I could have expected this call. I heard all about it."

"Yes?" Keogh said coldly. "What did you hear?"

Castellano noticed the barely concealed suspicion in his voice.

"Mr. Keogh, please. I know how you feel about this man."

"Mr. Castellano, I don't wish to be rude, but what did you hear?"

"I hear many things, Mr. Keogh, many things."

Keogh grew impatient with Castellano's circumlocution. "Mr. Castellano, when we had a talk, I believed everything you told me."

"As you should now believe." His tone never varied. No trace of emotion, fear or guilt.

"I think I and my friends want a restatement of that promise."

"Mr. Keogh, you are young, but I will still tell you that as old as I am, I do not break my word. And"—he let the words hang in the air—"I do not take threats."

Keogh felt the words fall like an axe.

"One could hardly blame me, Mr. Castellano, for feeling a little suspicious."

"Perhaps not. You are young. I can tell you what I'm going to do."

"I'm listening with great interest."

"A telephone is not for these discussions."

"I agree."

FRANK BURKE looked confused. He had faith in his friend's judgment. He had *always* been right. Right for him, right for the organization —always right. And he wanted Castellano not to be involved. If Castellano had hit Mr. Mac, then Burke was duty-bound to get Castellano, bound by centuries of dark and sometimes twisted Irish codes that he himself could never understand. And even though the statesman in Keogh always opted for moderation, Burke knew too that his friend would act likewise, Assemblyman and newspaper publisher notwithstanding. And they both knew that to openly go against Castellano would most certainly mean the signing of their own death warrants and the end to a Southie that belonged to the Irish. Both desperately wanted to believe in Castellano; but if they didn't believe, they could not let their most pressing fear stand in the way of what the code demanded.

"Maybe you're right, Sean. I hope to Christ you are."

"So do I, Frank. So do I."

And then Burke knew they were both playing on the same side . . . a losing side, but the same side.

"C'mon, you stuffed-shirt bastard," Frank said, slapping Keogh on the back. "Let's get a drink."

"I think I need one," Keogh said with a smile.

Keogh called Father Zeibatski from the club. He would want the priest to be there at the meeting on Tuesday night. Keogh knew of no one else who could read a man's mind like the dark-eyed priest whose face held so many secrets. It would be good for the priest to be there.

Keogh lifted his glass and clinked it against Burke's. They said nothing, but both realized the message in the toast. They could well be toasting their own demise. Burke smiled as he gulped his Jameson's. Keogh laughed and ruffled Burke's unruly hair. The moment held much love.

THE NEXT day, Monday, Keogh found it impossible to work. He felt like a kid on the eve of an important school examination. He used his inability to work as an excuse to be with Rose that day. The birth was less than a month away, and Keogh marveled at her physical toughness—fussing over lunch, insisting on cleaning the kitchen floor by herself, making afternoon tea for Frank Burke and Teresa, who came over to visit, and busying herself preparing dinner.

Keogh had called Wilson at six o'clock that night. The ever-confident

Wilson had some good news. Two major cigarette companies had just signed long time advertising contracts.

"The contracts alone will put us in the black next year, and we expect some real action from GM and Chrysler in Detroit. It looks good, Sean."

"I'd tell you that you're a genius," Keogh said good-naturedly, "but you know that already. Thanks, Ed. I won't be in until Wednesday. Sorry to put the load on you, but I have things to look after around here, what with Rose and everything."

"Sure thing. Don't worry. I think I've got it all under control."

"Incidentally, how is that guy Hickey working out?"

"He knows his stuff, Sean. He was a good move."

"Fine, fine. Okay, then, I'll see you. Bye."

Keogh picked up that morning's *Clarion*. There was no question that the paper looked superb. He felt a little uneasy as he found himself looking at the newspaper with detachment. Somehow he couldn't think of the newspaper as something he owned a lion's share of. It was good, tasteful, entertaining and responsible, all the things that Keogh had aimed for in the paper, but somehow he couldn't bring himself to believe it to be his, despite all the backbreaking hours and days of the learning process he had put into it.

Strange—it felt as if the paper belonged to someone else. Not Sheldon Mathers nor his ghost; just someone else.

Despite the fact it was early, he could feel himself drifting off to sleep on the sofa. He was not physically tired, but his body felt as if it had gone through a car crusher.

He was slipping cautiously into sleep when the clanging sound of the telephone jolted him abruptly to his senses. He grabbed for the phone.

"Sean." It was the voice of Father Zeibatski. There was an alien trace of panic in his voice.

"Yes, father."

"Vinnie has disappeared."

"My God, you don't think . . ." Oh, no—had his trust in Castellano cost him another life?

"No, I don't. . . . Billy Sweeney has gone too. The two of them were seen getting into a taxi."

"What, then?"

"New York," the priest said grimly.

"Good Christ, no. Please, no."

The priest cursed. It sounded strange coming from him. "Yes, God-damn New York."

"Father, stay where you are. I've got to call Frank. I'll call you straight back."

He frantically dialed Burke at home.

"Frank. Vinnie the Chin and Billy Sweeney have taken off. Father Velas thinks they're headed for New York."

"Oh, shit."

"Frank, I've got to call Castellano. I've got to. This could trigger a massacre."

"Sean, you call him and Vinnie and Billy are as good as dead."

"No . . . I'll guarantee them."

"With what, ferchrissake?"

"My own life." He slammed down the receiver. He could make Castellano understand. He just had to get to him and tell him to hole up until they could find Vinnie and Billy. Keogh would go alone to New York after that and he would patch it all up. He would make Castellano understand. If he couldn't, then Rose was going to be a widow.

He dialed Castellano's private number. No answer. He tried the Tre Amici Restaurant. He wasn't there. He tried Angelo's Clam House. Hadn't seen him since last night. He called his house in Hampton Bays. No answer. Good Christ, where is the sonofabitch? He called the home again. Nothing.

For three hours he dialed the haunts of Little Italy and the Upper East Side and Castellano's apartment on Central Park West thirty times. Nothing.

It was now ten thirty. He tried Ferrara's in Little Italy. He asked for the boss and identified himself. Otherwise no one would ever concede he knew who Castellano was.

"Yes, he left about fifteen minutes ago."

Thank God. He would be heading home now. Keogh kept dialing his home. His finger was sore.

FRANK CASTELLANO's Irish chauffeur cruised slowly up Broadway. The old man didn't like fast cars. The car turned onto Amsterdam Avenue and slowed when it came to Seventy-second Street.

"Okay . . . right here. I'll get my tomatoes." Next to pinochle, Frank Castellano loved tomatoes. He grew them in his house at Hampton Bays; he inspected them in grocery stores to see if anyone grew bigger tomatoes than he. He ate them and loved them.

The car pulled up to Sepino's, an old Italian store where he would often stop to buy prized tomatoes. He would spend fifteen minutes browsing through the store before finally choosing two choice specimens. He would eat the tomatoes, sliced on toast, for breakfast the next morning. After leaving the grocery store he would walk slowly up Seventy-second Street, with the car protectively cruising alongside. He would then walk to his apartment hotel on Central Park West, where he lived with his wife, two poodles and window boxes full of tomato seeds.

He walked into the store.

"Hey there," he said, calling around the store. "Angelo?"

A young man appeared.

"Angelo off tonight?" Castellano asked.

"He's out eating dinner," the young man said.

"Angelo? He's getting lazy, huh?"

He browsed around the crates of apples and oranges.

"Come for your tomatoes, sir?"

"Yes, yes. But don't rush me, young man. You new here?"

"I work sometimes during the weekends, and now I'm working a few nights."

Castellano was never in town on the weekends.

The young man picked up a fat ripe tomato. "How about this one?"

"Oho. You have a good eye, young man. A good eye." He reached for the tomato, softly squeezed its plush firmness. "Yes, yes."

He took a five-dollar bill from his pocket, received two tomatoes in a brown paper bag and waved good night to the young man without waiting for his change. He turned right and then started to walk up Seventy-second street, the old Ford following closely by the curb.

The young chauffeur couldn't quite grasp what happened. There was a blinding flash and then a loud bang. Castellano seemed jolted backward, and his body seemed to burst outward before sagging in pieces to the ground. The rim of his felt hat had flown off his head and flew through the car window, striking the chauffeur in the face.

The sensation didn't last long. Vinnie Zeibatski, whose brother was so close to God, had his Smith & Wesson aimed about six inches from the chauffeur's left ear. He had run across the street and pointed the gun through the window.

"This is for you," he said quietly, and as the chauffeur began to turn in panic, he was suddenly very dead from a single blast.

Vinnie walked from the scene, being careful not to run lest he attract attention. He turned right on Columbus and met Billy Sweeney two blocks down. He shook his right hand, the same hand that had activated the bomb inside Castellano's rigged tomato. They caught a taxi to LaGuardia and went into the airport lounge. They ordered beers from the bartender, who was glued to the television set. He was watching the eleven-o'clock news.

The bartender served the beer. "Jesus, you hear what happened? The hood Castellano got whacked out!"

"Yeah," Billy said, feigning mild interest.

The bartender topped the foam on the beer. "Brother, when a guy like him gets it, you know there are gonna be bodies lying around in the gutters like confetti after a wedding."

"It's a tough town, New York," Vinnie said.

"The toughest," the bartender said with chauvinistic pride, "the toughest."

"Glad we're leaving on the next plane."

The two men touched their glasses in a toast.

Chapter

11

"WHAT DID you expect, Mr. Keogh? What do you expect for the future?

"We didn't start anything. We left your people in peace. You did not leave our people in peace."

The thin-faced man, dressed in shabby work pants and shirt, looked slightly comical as Keogh observed he was wearing milk-white socks. They were Don Raimondo's trademark. His friends called him Sox. His enemies rarely had time to call him anything because he moved too fast. He sat there in the back of his coin laundry on Federal Hill, the headquarters of his operation in Providence, Rhode Island.

Keogh felt unsure of himself. Rarely did he feel this way. He was bidding in a game in which he held no cards. The bizarre and brutal assassination of Frank Castellano had brought the expected response of which Keogh had so grimly warned. Billy Sweeney, his young brother-in-law, had been dead within eight days, found beaten to death on a golf course in Asbury, New Jersey, where he had been hiding. His pockets had been stuffed with Monopoly money by his killers, a sign that he had made the mistake of killing for the wrong mob. Vinnie "the Chin" was in hiding, nobody knew where, but Keogh knew it was only a matter of time before Don Raimondo's boys found him.

The nerves in Keogh's body were screaming in unison. In one black month of early summer 1967 he had seen the bodies of Bernie Mc-Laughlin, his surrogate father, lying headless on Damrell Street, the expiring and bloody body of his father-in-law, Pat Sweeney, lying not ten feet away. He had identified the body of young Billy Sweeney, and any moment he expected to get a call to hear that the priest's brother Vinnie was also a casualty. His wife was only weeks away from delivering her first child, and Keogh was barely hanging on by his fingernails as he saw everything he had built collapse before his eyes. He was aware, too, that his own life was not without hazard. He had risked this meeting with "Sox" Raymond knowing that Raymond and Castellano had been as close as two men could get without sharing the same blood.

Keogh spoke in a low voice, trying to quell the feeling of uneasiness that flowed through his body. "Don Raimondo," he started with respect, "as you know, I had met with Mr. Castellano. I sought him out. I sought him out believing him to be an honest man."

"Believing?" the old man interrupted. The voice was a whisper. The anger was loud.

"Knowing him to be an honorable man. Many of my people in South Boston have had little contact with your people over the years. They were suspicious."

"Frank gave his word. You passed that word on. That was enough. Frank was going to see you in Boston on your own terms. How much do the Irishers have to have as a guarantee?"

He did little to hide his contempt. He smoked on a tiny butt of a cigarette. There was none of the veneer of respectability on this man that Castellano had had. He had led his men always from the front. Castellano had left his hoodlum days behind. Raymond at seventy-two was as tough as the day he had stepped off the ship.

He continued. "You come to me, Mr. Keogh, pleading for the life of a priest's brother. *My* brother is a priest. You come here angry and stupid because you think the deaths of the two Irishers in Damrell Street were the work of our people. Frank had told you to look in your own backyard. You stupidly didn't believe him. Stupid, Mr. Keogh. Then I lose Frank. His father and my father grew up less than thirty feet away from each other. You Irishers have made all the mistakes; now you come here and plead. What kind of man would my people think I am if I listened to you. You are pleading for the lives of people who killed Frank." The old man threw the cigarette butt onto the dusty floor and ground it out with his shoe.

Keogh knew it was a losing proposition. In his present mood, Keogh surmised, it would take very little for the old man to have him killed on the spot.

"What gesture could we make, Don Raimondo?"

"What gesture can a wolf make when he is looking up the barrel of a hunter's Lupara?" He wasn't giving an inch.

"Don Raimondo, none of my friends doubt your strength."

"Then they are getting wise, but wise too late."

"But Don Raimondo, do you think they will sit back and do nothing? No matter who wins eventually, everybody will lose."

Raymond knew it was so. He had been in wars with the Irish before. He remembered Big Hugh Denny in 1930. Many Italians had died in the street.

The old man lit another one of his cigarettes and drew the smoke deep into his lungs. "You would like to buy peace. Buy these men's lives. It is so?"

"I could do it easily."

"So you give money for my brother's blood and then get strong and rich in South Boston, and one day a drunken Irisher will make another stupid mistake and will move against me or maybe Guarino. You give me money, how do I tell my people that I won this battle? You give me fifty thousand dollars, do I give one hundred of my people five hundred dollars each? Do I give Frank's widow fifty thousand dollars to look at pictures of her dead husband? No, Mr. Keogh. The answer is no."

Keogh was getting nowhere.

"This stupid thing happened because you made a stupid mistake about Frank moving into South Boston. Why would we want South Boston?"

"With respect, we make ten times the amount of money you make here. We have a political structure. We even have contacts with a newspaper, a respected newspaper. It is lucrative." He was throwing out a hint. The old man fell silent, never taking his eyes from Keogh's face, searching for the slightest indication that he might be bluffing his hand. He suddenly stood up. His tiny frame didn't come to Keogh's shoulder. He moved his right hand in a vertical slashing movement. "Basta, basta," he said signaling that the conversation was over.

Keogh looked questioningly at him.

"I must talk to my people. Perhaps there is a way. Perhaps. But I promise you nothing. Go in peace and tell your stupid friends we will talk in three days' time. Tell them to stay at home." He needed to give no other warning.

Keogh was driven silently to a modest motel that had been provided by Don Raimondo. Normally, Keogh would have been put up in the most lavish of quarters. It was a measure of the old man's anger that Keogh found himself in a single room of a motor lodge. Keogh understood perfectly. He walked into the small room and called Frank Burke.

"Frank," he spoke as the telephone was picked up on the second ring.

"Sean, how did it go?"

"Not well. . . . Castellano had nothing to do with Mr. Mac's death. But he sure as hell had everything to do with Billy's."

"What do we do?"

"We can do nothing. Billy and Vinnie made the wrong move. The old man wants us to pay, and maybe not only with Vinnie. He hasn't given an inch. There is nothing to bargain with. We were wrong."

"Yeah. We all shoulda listened to ya, Sean."

"It's too late for that, pal."

"What next?"

"Tell everybody to stay off the streets. He won't make a move for three days and then he'll get back to me. But there are a lot of his cowboys roaming everywhere, and if they see any of the boys around they might act and ask questions later. Just stay inside, and for God's sake make sure everybody else does too. The old man thinks we're stupid. Don't convince him he's right."

"Gotcha."

"I'll call you tomorrow, Frank. Be careful."

"Same to you, boy."

Keogh then called his wife, Rose.

"How's it going, my love?"

"Fine, Sean. I feel well. What are you doing down in Providence?"

"Just some tiny business. Boring as usual. Did you go to the doctor today?"

"Yes. He said I was coming on fine."

"Sure?" he said, marveling at the strength of a woman who has just had a father and brother slaughtered. "Sure?"

"Sure, Sean. Don't worry about me. Please."

"I love you."

"I love you too, Sean."

"Call you tomorrow. Bye for now."

Sean Keogh fell into a fitful sleep. He wasn't used to being totally at the mercy of another man. The call came at seven thirty in the morning, jolting him out of a thin slumber.

"Mr. Keogh."

"Don Raimondo?"

"Yes. I will see you in half an hour in your room. We will have coffee."

"Fine."

The telephone clicked. Keogh's heart pounded. What sort of meeting takes place at eight o'clock in the morning? He hurriedly showered and dressed and bought coffee in the coffee shop, which he carried personally to the room in lieu of the nonexistent room service.

At precisely eight o'clock there was a single knock on the door. Keogh opened it. Don Raimondo stood there alone. He didn't need bodyguards to impress anyone with the measure of how lethal he could be. He hadn't shaved. His eyes were bleary. He hadn't slept. He walked in without a word of greeting.

He sat down, emptied three packets of sugar into the thick black coffee and stirred vigorously. He took a loud sip. He then looked up at Keogh, who was still standing. The old man gestured for him to sit. Keogh sat on the edge of the narrow bed.

The old man lighted one of those foul-smelling cigarettes.

"I have talked much during the night," he said, and let the statement hang in midair. He continued: "You have much bravery, Mr. Keogh. Some of my friends wanted to kill you here. It won't happen. My friend and brother Frank liked you very much. He was a sentimental and good man, Frank. Me, maybe not so much. But I'm a businessman and I care for my people as you care for your people. We share that."

Keogh remained silent and apprehensive. The rub was about to come.

"My people do not kill for pleasure. We don't kill by mistake." The accusation was clear. "You want the priest's brother spared?"

Keogh nodded once.

"You want no trouble from my people?"

Keogh nodded again.

"Then we will strike a business deal."

"Which is?"

"You were right—your organization is a very good one. Congratulations. Now, you mistakenly thought that Frank was moving into South Boston. That mistake has caused much blood. So if blood was spilled on a mistake, it should not have been spilled in vain. You agree?"

"I'm not sure."

"There will be a lasting peace, Mr. Keogh, in exchange that you turn over a portion of your business interests to my representatives. Simple, no?"

"Simple, yes. But there are other people I would have to sell it to, not only me."

The old man shrugged as if to signal that that was Keogh's problem.

"Exactly what portion of the business are you talking about?"

"Fifty-one percent of the pier unions and the numbers and a complete contract between you and Guarino giving him all the garbage-collecting routes."

Keogh's face struggled not to show emotion. He would have gladly given the old man a hundred-thousand-dollar gift for Vinnie's life. He would have given it personally. But he would have to go to many men in Southie and tell them he was giving away more than half of their business take. Difficult? It would be damn near impossible.

"It might be very difficult to accomplish such a deal."

The old man shrugged again. He finished his coffee and pulled his tiny frame upright.

"Then you must talk to them. Call me within forty-eight hours. Good-bye, Mr. Keogh." He walked from the room, his pants cuffs riding high and showing his milk-white socks. He disappeared without closing the door behind him.

Keogh watched the strange little figure bob down the hallway. Inside, he knew that the old man was harboring a blood feud for his friend Frank. But Keogh also knew the aged mobster would honor a deal. But what a deal.

Keogh exhaled with exhaustion and sat down on the bed. He then threw himself backward and lay there for long minutes, his eyes on the ceiling. Caving in to his demands would bring peace, but it would also spell the end to Sean Keogh's political career in Southie. What man would vote for another man who had sold out Southie to the Italians? Suddenly he felt like a kid whose card castle had been toppled over by a careless breath of wind. He would never sacrifice Father Zeibatski's brother, but how could he sacrifice the financial welfare of so many men and women?

He stirred from the bed and paced up and down the small confines of the room. He peered out the window as if the wet, gray streets of Providence might provide a simple solution to the most frightening dilemma he had ever faced. Then he lifted the remainder of his coffee, which had now gone cold. Any distraction to divert him from the overwhelming conclusion that there was no real answer which would satisfy everyone.

He jumped as the telephone clanged. He grabbed for it quickly. "Hello."

"Sean, Frank." His voice had the edge of urgency to it. "Sean, now, take it easy. You're gonna have to get up here right away. Rose is in labor."

"Oh, my God."

"Now, don't worry, it's just a few weeks premature. Teresa is with her right now, and they're waiting for an ambulance this second. Doc Hughes will be with her. There's nothing to worry about. Premature babies are born all the time."

Keogh bit his lip. Jesus Christ, what is God doing to me?

"Okay, I'll be there. Which hospital—Boston General?"

"That's it."

"I'll get the next flight out." He slammed down the receiver. He could feel panic seizing his body. It was as if Rose hadn't suffered enough. Now this. Please, God, make her strong for this. Please, God.

He had to get out of Providence quickly. Damn it, what were the airline schedules? In his fluster he had completely forgotten all about it. He dialed Information for the airport number. There wouldn't be a flight out for two hours. Then he would charter a small plane for the short flight. There were no planes available . . . at any price he offered. He swore at the woman on the other end of the telephone. He could not remember ever doing that. He ran his hands through his hair a dozen times. He felt like a trapped animal.

Desperately he reached for the telephone again, and dialed a number. A voice answered. Sean didn't waste time on protocol. "Tell Mr. Patriola that Keogh is on the line."

Seconds later a voice from the coin-laundry telephone booth whispered across the wire, "Speak."

"Don Raimondo, I'm in a fix."

"Tell me."

"My wife. I just got a call. My wife is having our first baby. It's premature. I'm worried stiff."

"What can I do?"

"The damn airport doesn't have a flight out for two hours. There are no damn charter planes available. It will take too long to drive. I have to get there. I have to. Can you help?"

"I can help. Stay where you are. A car will pick you up within ten minutes. It's a short ride to the airport. There will be a small plane that will be waiting. The flight is a short one. You will be there in less than an hour. Satisfactory?"

"Christ. God bless you."

"It is well that a man should be with his wife at this time. Perhaps you could call me tomorrow."

"I will. I will. Thank you again. Thank you."

"Not necessary," the voice whispered, and the conversation was over.

In the minutes he spent waiting for the car, Keogh mused about this man Don Raimondo, this curious little man with white socks, who always seemed to have a day's growth of beard on his tiny, thin face. A man who at all times had the power of life and death in his hands as he did at this very moment. A man who would happily order his execution and yet could provide a plane within minutes for a mission of mercy to a man he distrusted and probably hated. Keogh could never figure Italians. Few Irishmen could.

He bit his knuckles as he anguished at the thought of Rose. Please, God, make her well, he silently prayed, please God. And as humans often do, he found himself in a one-way conversation with whoever it was who was The Almighty. You have punished me severely recently; maybe it's because of the life I have led. But just give me this one time to get out of this mess and make Rose well and I promise, I will live a better life. I promise.

The car honked outside. Keogh dashed out. Don Raimondo himself was sitting in the back. The old man put a hand on his shoulder. "I have been through this seven times myself," he said reassuringly. Keogh managed a thin smile of acknowledgment for the old man's care.

The car streaked off with screeching tires and ran three stoplights in succession. At the airport it pulled straight onto the tarmac, ignoring any gates or guards, and nobody took any notice.

The Cessna was waiting, and its engines were roaring.

The old man held out his hand and shook Keogh's. "Be well, Mr. Keogh. My regards to your wife."

"I'll never forget you for this. Thanks again." He then raced into the plane and slammed the door shut behind him. Momentarily the small plane began to move and within forty-five seconds lifted into the air.

Keogh looked back through the small window. Raymond Patriola was standing outside his car on the tarmac watching as the plane disappeared into the clouds.

The plane had taxied to the closest point of the terminal, and Keogh had jumped out of the craft even it before it had come to a dead stop. He charged through the terminal and pushed past three people waiting in line for a taxi.

"Boston General as fast as you can . . . double the meter."

The driver nodded, and the taxi took off like a bullet.

As it pulled into Boston General, Keogh flung the man a twenty-dollar bill and ran through the big glass doors of the downstairs lobby. Breathlessly he inquired for the delivery room.

The girl behind the desk recognized him. "Oh, Mr. Keogh, your wife is on the fourth floor."

"Thanks very much."

The elevator seemed to take an eternity as it groaned and rattled upward. The doors parted slowly on the fourth floor, and Keogh darted through the space before they were fully opened.

As he wheeled left, he could see them standing in a group. The doctor, Dixon Hughes; Father Zeibatski; Eddie Wilson and Frank Burke. Their heads turned. Their faces were masks.

The priest was the first to move toward Sean, but Dr. Dixon Hughes gently touched his elbow and walked away from the group to get to Sean first.

Sean stopped dead in his tracks, and he felt his body contract, each muscle as taut as a piano string.

"It's Rose, isn't Doctor?" He wasn't speaking. He was gasping.

"No, Sean, Rose is fine," the kindly-faced doctor said soberly.

"The baby. The baby didn't survive," Sean heard himself say.

"The baby survived, but there is a problem—a serious problem."

"Tell me, for God's sake."

"The little boy," he said, and that was the first time Sean knew he had a son, "has been born blind."

He could feel the pain of a dozen knives thrusting through him.

"Blind? The little boy is blind? But . . ."

The priest, Burke and Wilson had joined Sean and the doctor. Eddie Wilson was white. Burke led Sean to a leather couch in the hospital hallway.

Keogh sank onto the couch, and as he did he could feel his entire insides sagging. There was nothing left in the man. He put his head in his hands, closed his eyes tight and opened them again quickly, the way a boxer does when he receives a sharp blow and wants to quickly see where the next one is coming from.

Nobody spoke for a long while.

"You can see your wife now, if you wish, Sean," the doctor said. "She is in good health."

"Is the little boy with her?"

The doctor nodded. "Other than the problem, he is quite healthy. He was about two weeks premature, but fully formed."

Sean stood up numbly and gestured with his head along the hallway. He and the doctor walked side by side, leaving the group behind. Keogh felt guilt through his numbness. Here he was stricken with shame that he had sired an imperfect human being. He felt dirty for the shame, for at this moment Rose was with the child after the ordeal and pain of pregnancy and giving birth. He found it hard to speak. His tongue had thickened, and there was no saliva in his mouth. The lump at the back of his throat told him he wanted to cry, but he tensed himself to ward off the tears that would have come so easily.

"Doc, I still don't understand. . . . How?"

"Sean, I have been delivering babies for many years. In cases like this parents go through many agonies. The agony of shame, the agony of guilt that something imperfect in them might have caused it . . . even anger at the wife, or even the doctor. Please, I know it's hard, but try to dismiss that feeling."

"But how do you know he is blind? Totally blind?"

"After the umbilical cord is cut, the senior attending nurse cleans the infant's eyes with a mild fluid. It was then that she noticed the opacity of the pupils. All babies are born with poor eyesight, but their eyes track and they react to strong light. I'm afraid, Sean, we are quite positive about the situation."

"Is there any hope for an operation in the future? Any hope? Money is not a problem."

"Frankly, not at this stage. I'm being as honest as I can with you. But there are breakthroughs in the treatment of blindness every year, and if it happens, it will happen right here in Boston at the Retina Foundation, which is the best in the world."

Sean tried to recharge his body with inner will as he felt every atom of strength drain from his body.

Dr. Hughes indicated the door of Rose's room. As Sean started in, the doctor touched his arm. Sean turned to face the man who had just delivered him a blind child.

"Sean, at this time I know you are in too much pain to be burdened with rationalizations. But you should understand that while blindness is a huge handicap, it's a handicap that thousands of people overcome every day . . . and Sean, most unsighted people develop senses that the sighted never develop. Now be brave and see Rose and your little boy."

The doctor turned away, to leave Sean standing alone outside the door. God give me strength. He strode through the door.

Her face was a little pale, but her long hair around her shoulders made her look angelic. Sean Keogh was awed by her serenity.

She looked up and gave a little smile. "Darling." She cradled the pink little child in her arms as gently as one holds a feather. He was sleeping quietly and snuggled against her breast. Rose talked in a gentle, controlled whisper.

"He is beautiful, Sean. He is beautiful."

For a frightening second, Sean Keogh was struck with the shock wave that Rose had not been told about the child's blindness.

"He will overcome all the problems," she said as if she sensed Sean's apprehension. "He will have more love than any other child in the world."

He bent over and kissed her with warmth on the forehead. She tilted her head backward and returned his kiss, touching him on the lips. Keogh found it hard to grasp the absence of anguish and anxiety that he found in her.

"How are you feeling, my love?" he said tenderly.

"Quite fine, really. It's just like a dream. He is so beautiful. . . . Do you wish to hold him?"

"I don't want to wake him up," Sean said awkwardly, and again he was ashamed because he felt this great distance between him and his newly born.

She snuggled him closer to her breast and sighed contentedly. She closed her eyes for a few brief seconds, then looked at Sean Keogh and said, "I love you, Sean."

It was the Rose Keogh who had loved and married her handsome young man from Southie—so different from the other Rose, the Rose who could change with a movement of an eye, a single word, a frightening classic example of the worst case of dual personality and a dual life.

Sean sat there for an hour until Rose drifted into a contented sleep, with a nurse in attendance. She had taken the tiny pink baby from her limp arms and put him in a crib behind the huge glass wall.

"We gave her a sedative, Mr. Keogh," the nurse said. "Why don't you come back tomorrow? Here, don't be afraid—you can hold your son."

"I . . . I don't want to wake him."

"Perhaps that's a good idea. He'll be awake soon enough, and screaming for his supper. I'll see you tomorrow." Then she walked out, holding the tiny, sleeping little thing with a band attached to his ankle bearing the name KEOGH.

Slowly Sean Keogh trudged outside. Father Zeibatski and Frank Burke were sitting down the hallway sipping coffee from paper cups.

"There was no need for you to wait," Keogh said abstractedly, "but thanks anyway. Has Eddie gone?"

"Hickey picked 'im up about five minutes ago," Burke said. "He told me to tell ya he's in the office fer the rest o' the night if ya need anything. He knew we were waitin'. How are ya feelin', boy?"

"You look as if you've been through it, Sean," the priest said.

"How goes it with you, Father. Vinnie?"

The priest shook his head.

"Well, don't worry, Father. He's going to be okay."

The priest and Burke looked anxiously at Sean's face.

"There's not going to be any more killing, Father."

"Raymond?" Burke said.

"Well, yes, we had some talks. I'll tell you about it tonight, Frank. Could you drop me home? Father, need a lift?"

"Appreciate it. Sean, I feel guilty asking you about my problems when you have your own pain, but what about Vinnie?"

"I give you my word, Father, he will not be touched. We'll talk more tomorrow."

The three men got into Burke's car and drove in silence first to the church to drop off the priest and then to Sean's home in Carson Beach.

Wearily Sean put the key into the door and opened it.

Burke could see that his friend was close to dropping. "Can I get ya a brandy, pal?"

"No, thanks, Frank. Wouldn't mind a cup of tea if you can find your way around the kitchen. Damned if I can."

"Sure thing, pal."

Keogh slowly walked into the living room and collapsed onto the sofa, his eyes staring upward as if searching for some sign from the heavens.

Burke came in with two cups of steaming tea.

"Black and sweet, huh? Just the way old Mr. Mac liked it," Sean said as he sipped slowly on the brew.

He put down the cup. Burke's face mirrored concern as he looked at Keogh, his head slumped down, his chin resting on his chest. His shoulders convulsed as the sobs tore through his body.

"Sean."

"Frank, I've got to get out of it all . . . the killings . . . Rooney, my mother, Devlin, Mr. Mac, Pat, Castellano, Billy . . . How many more, Frank? . . . And now a little boy born blind." The tears streamed down his face, which was the color of ash.

"Sean . . . ya can't blame yerself. Ya can't. He'll be all right."

"Yes, Frank, how long before it's you or me? . . . We're not fighting against gangs, Frank . . . No . . . no . . . it's nature . . . it's God, Frank, and by Christ, He is paying us back. . . . Damn it, it's God . . . and He isn't going to give up. . . . For crying out loud, Frank, how many more signals do we have to get . . . how many more?"

Frank Burke remained silent. He was content to let his closest friend cry it out of himself. There was nothing he could say that would help now.

"Sean, how about hittin' the sack?"

"Yeah, yeah . . . if I could only sleep it all away."

"Try, old buddy."

Keogh got to his feet. "Maybe you're right . . . maybe you're right."

"Hey, I'll sleep here on the couch, Sean."

"No, no, no. You go home to Teresa and the kids. They need you. I'll be all right." He wandered, like a man lost, out of his living room and toward his bedroom.

"I'll see you in the office early tomorrow, Frank. We'll talk. We'll talk."

"See you at eight thirty, Sean."

"Oh, yeah—and will you tell Father Zeibatski to be there if he can make it?"

"Sure thing. . . . Take it easy . . . call if you need me. Tomorrow, Sean."

"Tomorrow, old pal. Bye, Frank."

He walked into the bedroom, set the alarm for 7:30 A.M., kicked off his shoes and collapsed fully clothed on the bed, where his body, his mind and his soul allowed him the respite of an exhausted sleep.

The priest and Frank Burke were waiting for him at eight thirty. Both were amazed at his appearance. In just one short night he had pulled back from the edge of emotional collapse. He walked in freshly shaved and immaculately tailored. He was determined to bounce back no matter what the adversity.

"Father . . . Frank . . . thanks for yesterday. Thanks a lot. Now to the problem of Vinnie."

"Raymond is going to give up?" the priest asked incredulously.

"At a price."

"We'll pay, then," Burke said.

"Well, Patriola believes that the mistake was not so much a personal mistake as a mistake of statesmanship."

"I don't understand," Burke said.

"Nor do I," the priest said uncertainly.

"Simply that when such a mistake is made, states lose territory."

"Oh, oh." Burke knew what was coming.

"No, he doesn't want everything. Just fifty-one per cent. That two percent means he can save face in front of his people for not waging a war against us."

"What are we going to do, Sean? Not every guy on the street in the organization will stand still for it. There'll be more trouble."

"Well, we all agree that Mr. Mac's widow and family continue to get their take. So we have to do a little bit of making up."

"There is no other way? Like a direct payment?" Burke asked.

"No way. It's not only a money thing. It's mainly a pride thing. But my mind is made up. I'm getting out. I get a small salary as an Assemblyman, and I like it. The newspaper is eventually going to make money. I'm walking away from the street. My money goes into the pot."

Burke handed Sean a hot cup of tea, and the trio fell silent for a minute.

Burke spoke: "Ya know, Sean, I'm makin' so much money outa that truckin' business and the money I get from being secretary of the local Teamsters, what the hell—pardon me, Father—do I need with the docks, the numbers and the crap games?"

Sean Keogh looked quietly at the pudgy, smashed-in face of Frank Burke with the love that can be experienced only between two men. He knew exactly what Burke was doing.

Their combined total of shares in the organization would add up to exactly fifty percent. They could get the other one percent from somewhere else. They would walk out of the rackets without Patriola's ever having to touch any of the lower-echelon workers in the outfit.

Keogh never said a word but just grabbed Burke on the forearm and squeezed hard. There was no more said. The priest understood, and he knew they were sacrificing to save the lives of his brother and perhaps many others.

"Sean, Frank . . ." he began.

"Forget it, Father. I have to get downtown, go to the hospital, and after they throw me out I'm going to look up Roger Sharpe, our old Republican blue-blood friend. Then I have to get to the office at the

Clarion and start the wheels rolling again. The voters will be forgetting who I am. Father, I'll contact you later about Vinnie. He'll be okay. See you." He dashed out the door, and the spring had come back into his step.

The priest looked at Burke as they saw him leave. The priest shook his head in wonderment as if he were witnessing the birth of a man who was a mixture of saint and genius, although he knew neither to be true.

The nine-thirty Eastern Airlines plane plunked Sean Keogh down on the apron of the Providence Airport in Rhode Island at 10:05 A.M. He had not told Burke and the priest where he was going. Twenty minutes later a taxi had deposited him in front of the coin laundry on Federal Hill. He walked through the unwashed glass door.

He chuckled to himself as he viewed the surroundings. One of the most powerful mob minds in America and this was his headquarters. But then again, he mused, his own garage office was hardly the Chrysler Building either.

The old man was sitting in a tiny office at the rear sipping coffee and smoking. He opened the office door and the room reeked of stale tobacco. Two men with the old man shuffled off their stools and disappeared.

The old man poured Keogh a mug of coffee. "This is better than the stuff at the motel," he said with a playful smile.

"I've come to talk."

"I'm here to listen."

"You'll get your fifty-one percent. No argument."

"I can't believe it will be as simple as that."

"You'll get the piers and the pier unions, the numbers and the crap games. You're free to inspect our books now, so you'll have an idea what days, weeks and months we have our highs and lows. The pattern is fairly consistent."

"I'm still listening, Mr. Keogh."

"For you, sir, to tell me that I should stick to politics, it has to be made clear that the appearance of your people in my neighborhood would certainly mean the end of my political career."

The old man sucked the cigarette down to the butt, squashed it out and lit another one. He was still listening hard, and Sean continued.

"That means your people must stay out of the neighborhood. No appearances whatsoever. The transfer of cash money need not be difficult. Guarino is guaranteed the private carting contracts. But nobody—none of my people—must know of any new partners."

The old man smiled. "You did not get the fifty-one percent from thin air, Mr. Keogh."

Keogh smiled wanly. "No, but sometimes resignations can make a company payroll much lighter."

The old man bent down and reached into a lower drawer to take out a stained half-empty bottle of Sambuca. He poured some into a water tumbler, passed it across to Sean and poured one for himself.

"But you say none of my people in the neighborhood. No pickups, no physical partnerships."

"None. The Irish have pride also, Don Raimondo; they have to save face just like the Italians."

The old man chuckled and clinked his glass to Keogh's.

"It is done. My word. It is done. Maybe sometimes my people will vote for you."

"I would like that. Now, Vinnie Zeibatski."

"Oh, we have been holding him for some time, Mr. Keogh. He has not been ill treated. He will be with his brother at Sacred Heart before you return to Boston. You have my word."

Keogh finished his drink. He stood up and shook hands with the curious little man with white socks. The old man made no attempt to detain him with conversation. He walked outside with him and saw him into a taxi. The taxi arrived in time for Sean Keogh to catch the eleven-fifteen plane back to Boston.

As soon as the plane touched down in Boston, Keogh dialed the priest's private line in the rectory.

The priest said only, "He is here, Sean. God bless you."

"He is safe, Father. He is safe. You have my guarantee. It's all over now. Much has happened. It's all over."

He put down the receiver and headed for the hospital to see Rose, and as he got into the elevator to go to the fourth floor he silently prayed he would be able to hold the boy in his arms.

Book
Two

Chapter
12

RoseKeogh loved the majestic old mansion outside McLean, Virginia. The gently, rolling green hills provided a security blanket of comfort against the recollection of the years spent in the harsh, gray streets of Southie, where the tough population seemed to spend their lives dedicated only to survival against an outside world they always felt had rejected them. Perhaps nowhere else in the country had one single area so quarantined itself against a society it considered alien.

The years had been very kind to Rose, even generous. Her hair was still a warm brown, with a minute strand here and there of gray. Her face, at thirty-nine, radiated health, and her body was as shapely and petite as the day she had met Sean Keogh. If anything, the years had given her appearance a touch of exciting maturity—the certain way she smiled when an attractive man was introduced to her, the way her head would tilt slightly, allowing her long hair to hang over one side of her face. The wide-eyed innocence had been replaced by the knowing look of experience.

On Senator Sean Keogh, the years had left their mark. His dashing good looks had never left him, but there were strong reminders that he was a man of forty. His coal-black hair was prematurely sprayed with white, and the creases around his eyes and across his forehead were deep trenches. On the Hill and at the endless round of cocktail parties, however, Rose still looked on with amusement at the way the young secretaries and the legion of faithless wives threw themselves at him. He was a very attractive man still, physically, in a town where a man's attraction was measured rarely in the way he looked but rather in how much power he had.

It had always amazed the South Boston contingent that a man like Henry Kissinger had once been regarded as something of a Casanova. Senator Keogh was both physically and politically attractive, and few noticed his prematurely graying hair or the deep creases around his strong face. Not since John Kennedy had quit the Senate had there been such a presence on the Hill.

Keogh had swept into the Senate in 1980, riding a mounting wave of conservatism that had romanced a giant middle class, angered by taxes for welfare and disgusted by a school system force-fed by integration that had left their children without learning.

Keogh had won the hearts of the country as the wire-service pictures showed him standing at the doors of South Boston schools defying state troopers who had been ordered to integrate the schools—by force if necessary—in South Boston. It had almost been a carbon copy of Governor George Wallace's act so many years before in Montgomery, Alabama. But where the once-liberal Northeast had reacted with outrage to what it perceived to be a typically ignorant, racist, red-necked performance, the Northeast had changed. With their cities pockmarked with charred ruins and plagued by crime, the liberals had now done a complete about-face, and suddenly they had chosen to forget the teachings of their fathers.

In one fell swoop, Sean Keogh, the Irish Catholic from South Boston, had become the Great White Hope—not only to the men in the bars of Southie and New York's Brooklyn and Queens, but to the heads of industry and banking who saw him as their only savior against bumbling, mindless Washington bureaucrats bogged down with ideals formed in universities that had long since been closed because of campus disruption or burned down. If he had ever been resented on Beacon Hill in the 1960s, in the '80s he was greeted as a messiah, the same way he had been embraced by his own in Southie.

Rose Keogh smiled inwardly as she sat in the warm morning sun of the Virginian fall of 1982. The great Sean Keogh had finally become the messiah that she believed he so lusted to be.

He had been greeted by the people from the right side of the tracks. He had become respectable, shunning the money of the gamblers that had made him so fabulously wealthy as a young man of twenty-four, throwing himself into building the *Boston Clarion* into one of the most widely read and respected newspapers in the country. Expanding his empire into radio and television stations across New England. Building a huge political machine with the help of his newspaper empire and his good friend Roger Sharpe. But all the time keeping his finger on the pulse of the voters with the help of Frankie Burke's gigantic network of Teamsters.

Even Rose had been incredulous at the way he had sucked in support. The Italians had voted for him to the man and to the woman. She had been told the support had come from a feeble, wheelchair-confined old man in Providence, Rhode Island, who with a single weak nod of his frail head had put the entire Italian population of Massachusetts behind the dashing Irishman. She had heard that the old man, well into his eighties, was called "Sox," and he had been a frequent visitor to the mysterious priest Father Velas Zeibatski.

She was annoyed she did not know more about that liaison. She always got annoyed when Sean Keogh did something or acquired another huge chunk of power from sources which she did not know about. Edward Wilson had told her that it had something to do with the war of reprisal triggered by the murder of Frank Castellano, which in turn had been prompted by the assassination of her father, Pat Sweeney, and Keogh's mentor Bernard McLaughlin. That had made her laugh hysterically, seeing it had been Wilson who on her instructions had hired the gunmen from Charlestown to kill McLaughlin. Hitting Pat Sweeney had been an error, but not one mourned by Rose, who had always blamed Pat Sweeney for having her mother taken away from her.

And Sean Keogh was not very different from her father or any of the other men in Southie who seemed to believe they had some mystical power over women. Oh, Sean Keogh was smoother, but deep down he was the same—perhaps worse, because he hid behind a tailor's dummy and forced manners of the civilized. Sean Keogh was worse. And that was why he had to be destroyed and eventually would be destroyed. No matter how many years it might take—and already it had taken many years. But the bigger he got, she reasoned, the more impressively his destruction would be felt.

She had miscalculated Keogh's resilience, miscalculated his basic intelligence, his tremendous resourcefulness and—yes—even his courage. The loss of his beloved Bernard McLaughlin had been a giant one. Not a week would go by, even now after all these years, that somewhere the old man would not creep into the conversation of Keogh and Burke. The gang war that had followed McLaughlin's death should by rights have claimed their lives, or at least decimated their empire. Instead, Keogh and Burke had abandoned the empire and in so doing put their resources into building two more empires, one in the media and the other in organized labor, a frighteningly powerful combination.

She had miscalculated, she admitted—that was, in the beginning. But as it had worked out, it would be much better in the long run. Keogh had become one of the few giant power brokers in the country, holding positions on at least a half-dozen top Senate committees. He was feted by presidential candidates, anxious to align themselves with his huge appeal. Even in the West and particularly in the South, Keogh's name was a household word. He had even passed into the common usage of conversation. It was not rare to hear someone in a bar, no matter in what part of the country, say, "I'm a Keogh man." It was the buzz word for conservatism. He accepted his accolades with what she saw to be a phony humility.

Of course, it never angered her to the point where it would show. Her control was as good as, if not better than, it had been in the years when she found herself inexplicably slipping into another person. Physically she was in good shape. But the destiny of her personality had not changed. The doctor Wilson had secretly contacted explained it all to him. In classic cases of severe schizophrenia, eventually one personality would completely dominate, with the second personality providing a convenient curtain to mask the secret self.

Wilson had more to fear from Rose Keogh than anyone else. She terrified him. She held a secret which endangered his very life. And she used that secret to push Wilson into the most dangerous waters, waters which he feared to tread. Wilson was as brilliant as he was weak and cunning. He could handle himself like a street fighter in a boardroom. But that was where he liked to keep his street instincts.

He was no Burke, and he was no Keogh. Rose Keogh, that day back in Carson Beach, had forced him into the street when he contacted the Charlestown mob. The brutality of the act had had little effect on his conscience, but the magnitude of the treachery and the fact that other people knew of the treachery hammered at his instincts of self-preservation. Rose Keogh was the most perfectly tuned mechanism of intelligence he had ever seen, but her ambitions and secret, festering hatred of Sean Keogh provided no rudder for self-restraint, and Wilson often wondered silently, in a bed which he shared with no one, how far it would go. Deep down, he knew one day it would go to the limit.

She luxuriated in the memories of how well she had covered her tracks as the black servant brought her a chilled glass of gin and tonic.

Sean Keogh used the house infrequently, spending long hours in his suite in the Senate Office Building on Constitution Avenue or long days with Frank Burke and Roger Sharpe and their political cronies in South Boston. He had bought the rambling mansion in McLean, Virginia, mainly for Rose and the son who had been baptized Terrence Patrick Keogh. But he had never sold the house in Carson Beach or left his roots in Southie. Sean was an elegant figure whether in the boardroom, as an observer at the *Clarion* or in the round of cocktail parties that seemed to oil the machinery of Washington. If he had contempt for the phoniness of Washington, he realized it was the only game in town, and it was through this network of weaklings and sycophants that he could get things done for his constituency. And apart from his national profile, Massachusetts had much to thank Keogh for.

As a member of the Senate Foreign Relations Committee he had used his contacts, with the help of the old Italian they called "Sox," to forge lasting friendships with some Italian industrialists. And when he heard that an Italian shoe manufacturer was anxious to open a plant in America, he was quick to point out the advantages of constructing the plant in Brockton, Massachusetts, a heavily Italian town which had once been the shoe capital of the country. The plant had revitalized the entire economy of the once-rich town of Brockton, which had fallen on hard times, and the town—and the Italian community—were forever indebted.

The Jewish community in Boston, long a foreign force to the men in Southie, were encouraged to open their garment factories in South Boston. He had arranged generous credits with the two banks that had opened their doors in Southie for the Jewish merchants. He had pointed to the advantages of having a work force where the workers lived near their employment, and the garment factories prospered and the Jewish community knew they had a friend in Sean Keogh. He had woven a fabric of ethnic support—except among the blacks—that covered his political aspirations like a blanket, a fact that was not overlooked when he was campaigning for a seat in the U.S. Senate, which he had won by a landslide.

That had been a time when Rose Keogh showed her husband a completely different side of herself, campaigning with a low-keyed intelligence and enthusiasm that surprised everyone who remembered the quiet, pretty child who had once worked as a nurse in a hospital and been a surrogate mother to a father and brother, both of whom had met their deaths violently.

If her past and Sean's past were one of the worst-kept secrets in Boston, they were rarely mentioned or written about. Sean Keogh was now "one of them," and the Brahmin-owned media had little reason to embarrass someone who was valuable to their conservative ideals. It was of little interest to them to regurgitate what some had once considered a seamy background. It was of little interest to them that he was perilously close to the giant network of organized labor. The 1980s showed that organized labor was as capitalistically oriented as the capitalists it had once sought to destroy.

Sean Keogh had it all covered, and Rose always secretly resented his all-encompassing success, feeling deep down that Keogh was really no match for her when it came to intelligence or perception. And she might have been right. If she had the opportunities that a man had, she would be constricted by no horizons, she often thought. She was not bound by the mystical bond that held Keogh to his church or the curious priest. She was not burdened by the crucifix which she wore in superficial service to her husband's deep involvement in his religion. She was not bound by any real loyalty to her fellow man—with the exception of her son and one other. Yes, there was another.

Terrence Patrick Keogh was no man's son, she would often repeat to herself silently. He was *her* son. And if she had never said it to the handsome, slightly built boy with the sensitive features of his mother, there was a bond of understanding that bound them as one. It was a bond that neither Terrence nor Sean Keogh recognized openly, but one that nonetheless they acknowledged to themselves.

Sean Keogh had been a loving father and a generous one, and often a very proud one when he recognized that despite the handicap of blindness, Terrence had prospered, winning marks at school that established him in the minds of his teachers as approaching genius. At fifteen, he was both a stunning student and a popular one. His quiet but intelligent demeanor held a rare attraction for his fellow students, and it was obvious that his blindness was no barrier when it came to dates.

He had so completely overcome his handicap that the cane he carried was held more as a walking stick than as an aid to help light the blackness that had been with him since the day he was born. It was as Dr. Dixon Hughes had said the day Sean had first learned of the child's incapacity —that he would develop senses that sighted people would not. He had learned to ride a specially trained horse that Sean had bought for him, and he even played racquetball with a specially equipped ball that contained a tiny bell inside.

But while he was admired by people he came in contact with, he rarely developed claustrophobic friendships, keeping people at a polite distance bridged only by the closeness he felt toward his mother. That was not lost on Sean, who had tried on countless occasions to get closer to the lad. It was as if their veins carried a different blood. And by the time he had reached fifteen, Sean had long since given up any real hope of crossing the wide river that separated them. Their relationship was of respect, generosity, politeness, but never a real father-and-son warmth. If this was not seen by Keogh's friends, who shared his pride in the lad's accomplishments, it was seen by Sean, who always felt it as a mild but constant pain in his heart. No matter what he did, he could not warm the inexplicable chill that came between them. Money didn't buy the warmth, nor did Sean expect it would; attention didn't help either, and gradually he felt a hopelessness that seemed to make both Rose and Terrence drift farther from the mainstream of his life.

Even while in Washington, Senator Sean Keogh found it easier, after long hours in the office followed by dinner parties, to stay in the Watergate apartment complex, rather than make the drive to McLean. He felt some measure of comfort in that he had provided Rose and his son with a house that she had always wanted, a house that she decorated and painted, but it would never be home to him. No matter how many times he slept there, he would always feel like a visiting relative, rather than the master of the house.

Rose secretly did little to alter the impression, although in front of Sean and his friends she was never anything but the devoted and caring spouse from Southie that she had always been, even though some friends had noticed a pleasant and stylish change in the way she dressed and carried herself. If some thought it a natural progression, Rose reveled in the secret that it had a lot to do with the other person, other than Terrence, whom she cared for.

She would often recall their first meeting alone. It had happened in the *Clarion* office. She had gone to meet Sean before going out to dinner. She had met John Hickey many times in a group, or at a dinner party. Their contact was distant and respectful. That night, however, after most of the staff had gone home, she had wandered into the office of John Hickey, the Executive Editor in Chief of the *Clarion*. He had looks that no woman could totally ignore. Some women went out of their way to attract him; others simply felt his looks and charm too far beyond their reach to believe that anything serious would develop.

Up until that night, Rose Keogh had felt nothing either way. Looks in a man never particularly mattered to her. It was a man's command of others that made him attractive—the same command which she knew was one of her own innermost attributes.

"Excuse me, Mr. Hickey," she had said with a polite knock on the half-open door of his office. "Is my husband in the building?"

He had looked up quickly, as if caught in an illicit act, and shut the volume he had been studying at his desk.

"Mrs. Keogh," he had said, standing up and straightening the handmade tie that had been hanging loosely open at his neck. "Pleasure to see you. No, Mrs. Keogh, Mr. Keogh will be back a little late—perhaps about another ten minutes," he had said, flashing a quick look at his watch. "Please sit down. Can I get you something? Cup of coffee, perhaps?"

"She had walked demurely into his office and sat down on the office chair.

"Tea if you have it, Mr. Hickey."

"Certainly." He went outside and dispatched a copyboy to get a cup of tea for Rose and a cup of coffee for himself in double-quick time. Seconds later he returned to his desk. The tea and coffee were brought in. He settled back in his chair, and his normally self-confident manner had an edge of uncertainty to it. She recognized it immediately and helped out with some small talk.

"Well, how are my husband and Mr. Wilson treating you?"

"They're both quite amazing. Their capacity for work and for energizing ideas is quite phenomenal, as you probably know better than I."

"Oh, yes—don't I know it!"

She saw it for a fleeting second. The look. She recognized it immediately. She had seen it in Edward Wilson's eyes so long ago.

If she was right—and she prided herself in rarely being wrong—John Hickey brimmed with resentment of Sean Keogh. Did he resent Wilson too? She didn't know, but she would find out.

"It is quite a fascinating experience working with your husband, Mrs. Keogh. And I think most of the staff feel the same way I do. He inspires quite incredible loyalty."

There it was again. Just a tiny movement of the eyes as he avoided hers as he talked about her husband.

Just then the door opened and they were joined by her husband and Wilson.

"Ha, John, thank you for looking after my wife in my lateness," Keogh said cheerily. It was quite obvious from his attitude that Hickey had completely charmed her husband. That in itself, if Hickey really did resent Sean Keogh, was enough to endear him to her. She admired the perceptiveness of anyone who saw through her husband's impervious front.

"Well, now we're going out to dinner. Care to join us, John?"

"Thank you, but no, sir. I have a few hours of pressing work that I would like to finish tonight. But thank you anyway."

"Okay—don't say I didn't ask. Coming along, Ed? Where will it be? Locke-Ober?"

"Fine by me. How about you, Rose?"

"She loves the place," Keogh answered for her.

"Then Locke-Ober it will be."

Hickey was standing. He had one hand over the huge volume. Rose noticed it. It was a volume of back copies. As he moved quickly from behind his desk to escort them from his office, she caught a glimpse of the gold-stamped title. BOSTON CLARION, VOLUME 137, 1957. It had piqued her curiosity. Both the volume and John Hickey.

One week later, while in the office, she wandered into the *Clarion* library. Although she was not a familiar sight in the office, everybody knew who Rose Keogh was. And it wasn't long before the word went across the editorial floor that Keogh's wife was in the building and in the library.

With the help of the librarian, she had pulled down the volume of back issues from the dusty shelves. She pulled out Volume 137, the year of 1957. She had gone to a rear alcove away from the office staff and opened the stiff black leather cover. The front page of the paper told exactly what she had somehow suspected. The headline screamed HOODLUM MURDERED IN SOUTH BOSTON. The subhead went on in clear black type: "Limbless Body Found Floating in Bay."

After their first meeting, John Hickey had been impressed with this woman's easy manner toward him. His basic ambitions had told him that it didn't hurt to be well received by Sean Keogh's wife. He had heard that she was in the library and had left his office with the express purpose of accidentally encountering her there. It was highly politic to his survival to be liked by the wife of one of the most powerful men in Boston, a man whom he hoped he would one day have enough on to make sure he would live in the way he was accustomed for the rest of his life.

He turned left at the entrance of the library and spied her in the rear.

He came over with a cheery, lighthearted greeting: "Hi there, Mrs. Keogh. Doing some research?" His manner was now confident, after their first meeting alone the previous week. Confident until he saw the volume she was reading. He battled to conceal the jab of panic that seized him as he recognized the volume she was scanning as the same volume he had been absorbed with.

"Oh, hello, Mr. Hickey," she said airily. "I love going through old newspapers when I have nothing else to do. Although it sometimes makes me remember my age.

"I really love these old volumes . . . don't you?" She had thrown out the line. She was certain now of Hickey's motive. If he was half as smart as she thought he was, he just might get the hint and pick up on it.

He seemed to regain his confidence.

"Oh, yes, yes. Even just to convince myself how far we've all come."

It was an extremely clever reply. It could have been taken as a signal —or if she was the loving, adoring wife everybody said she was, it was purely an innocent remark.

She let her gaze fall directly on his face for a short second.

"Well, I have to be getting upstairs to my husband. Nice seeing you, Mr. Hickey. Nice seeing you," she repeated.

"Same here, Mrs. Keogh. Always a pleasure."

They both left the brief meeting with their senses filled with question marks. Had he gone too far? Was he leaving himself open to be informed on by Rose Keogh? Then Rose thought, had she miscalculated? What if he was loyal to Sean Keogh after all? After a brief debate, both believed they knew the real answer, and both felt secure in the notion that each had a potential ally.

The next time they met was at a City Hall cocktail party where most of the senior executives of the *Clarion* were gathered. She had been standing with her husband and Edward Wilson. Hickey had swept into the party a few minutes late. The heads of many of the women turned. Hickey, ever elegant, greeted Rose, Sean and Wilson.

When her husband briefly excused himself to talk to the city's Comptroller, Rose took the opportunity.

"Mrs. Keogh," Hickey greeted her politely.

"Mr. Hickey, nice to see you."

"I didn't know you were a cocktail-party goer."

"There are some one can't avoid, Mr. Hickey. But you appear to have a taste for them."

"It's simply good business."

And then she gave the signal.

"It will be so nice to get a break from Boston, actually."

"Oh—taking a vacation?"

"Not really . . . just a shopping trip. Down to New York."

"When are you off?"

"Oh, just a four-day weekend next week."

"You stay at the Carlyle?"

She smiled. "No, that's my husband's hotel. Sort of an Irish tradition for people from Boston. I prefer the Pierre."

He was about to reply when Keogh was at his side. "Well, John, spy any curious partnerships here tonight?"

"Ah, Mr. Keogh. Well, the Comptroller and the Mayor are looking unusually friendly tonight. Maybe their feud is over."

"Over?" Keogh smiled. "Over some poor soul's dead body. Not a very wholesome crew, are they?"

"You're so right," Wilson chimed in.

When Hickey left early that night, his handshake with Rose had lingered for a telling second longer than would be customary. He was still cautiously testing the water. But his years manipulating minds and bodies told him what he wanted to know. Either she wanted him physically or she wanted help in a conspiracy. Hopefully, she wanted both.

He had packed his two best suits for the shuttle flight to LaGuardia that Friday night when he left his apartment in Cambridge. He would stay at the Carlyle in case anyone needed him urgently in Boston. It was not uncommon for him to travel to New York; he went there often on newspaper business. And during this weekend he would probably not be missed. Before Constance Mathers had taken off with a young tennis instructor, Hickey had wheedled out of her enough money to buy himself a handsome retreat in Southampton, and if anyone asked, he could be at his summer home. He was safe.

He arrived in New York at 7 P.M., and by seven forty-five he was walking through the door of a comfortable suite at the famous hotel.

He felt his heart quicken as he walked to the telephone. This would be one of the most hazardous leaps he had taken in his life since he had set up the blackmail plot that had landed the *Clarion* in the hands of a bewildered Sean Keogh.

"Hotel Pierre," the operator intoned. He took a deep breath. God, what if he was wrong? He could lose it all.

"Mrs. Rose Keogh, please. She is a guest there." What had made him think she would be in her hotel room waiting for this call?

"One moment, please. Putting you through."

Christ, have I gone too far?

He wet his upper lip as the voice at the other end spoke softly into the telephone.

"Hello?"

"Mrs. Keogh?"

"Yes. Who is this, please?"

"John Hickey, Mrs. Keogh. Just happen to be in town, and I recalled your saying last week that you would be at the Pierre. I hope I'm not disturbing you."

"Not in the least, Mr. Hickey. Just watching a little television."

"Ah, ah, say, have you eaten yet?"

"I was about to order from Room Service, as a matter of fact."

"Oh, well, then, I'll leave you to it. Call me if I can be of any service." He was waiting for an opening.

"Well, why don't we have dinner before you return."

"Love to. How about tonight?"

"That's fine with me, Mr. Hickey. I don't particularly relish eating by myself. Why don't we meet down in the Café Pierre?"

"Fine. In about an hour. Say nine o'clock?"

"Wonderful," she said with a hint of warmth in her voice. "Until then."

The Café Pierre was ideal. It was patronized only by out-of-towners or the very rich and very discreet who lived in the hotel on a full-time basis.

Rose Keogh looked out across the clean, green hills surrounding her estate in Virginia and recalled that very first night. She had set it up exquisitely, she allowed herself no small measure of pride that she had read John Hickey with perfection. She had walked into the darkened café in an expensive but extremely sensible dark blue two-piece suit, a costume she had thought quite elegant. In the months to come, Hickey would emend her tastes and show her the luxuries of Halston and Saint Laurent. He would direct her to Kenneth for her hair and teach her to read a French menu, a part of her education that had not been catered to by the Irishmen who were lost on anything outside of lobster or steak. Hickey had certainly given her her money's worth.

He had been sitting at the bar that night, impeccable in a Ralph Lauren two-piece pin-striped suit and a starched white shirt with a silk tie and pocket handkerchief. He beamed as she walked daintily across to the bar. There was no hint of nervousness in her, and it put him at ease.

He swiveled on his bar stool and stood up, flashing his movie-star-perfect smile.

"Mrs. Keogh, how nice to see you."

Touching her lightly on the elbow in a gentlemanly gesture, he guided her small frame onto the bar stool next to his.

She returned his smile demurely. "What a pleasant coincidence."

"Yes, it is, Mrs. Keogh. What would you like to drink?"

"What are you having, Mr. Hickey?"

"John. Please call me John. I had an editor once who called me Mr. Hickey whenever he was angry at me. . . . I'm drinking Scotch."

"Well, John, I don't want you to think *I'm* angry. . . . I'll have a Scotch too. And while we're at it, please call me Rose. We're not in Boston now."

His mind raced. Her message was clear. She was telling him, he thought, that outside Boston she was a different woman.

After two drinks they sat in the corner of the restaurant farthest from the bar. He ordered a superb dinner of canard à l'orange and crêpes for dessert, washed down with an excellent light Mouton Cadet. They talked casually, and as the night grew older, she said simply, "John, this is one of the finest nights of my life." The statement was like an outright invitation.

"Mine too, Rose."

"I'm telling you nothing you don't know, but you're a very attractive man."

"And you're a very charming lady."

She smiled unselfconsciously. "Is that what a man says to a woman when he can't honestly say she's beautiful?"

"But you are beautiful . . . very."

Hickey's mind reeled. The outrageousness of it all. His sitting over candlelight exchanging compliments with the wife of the almighty Sean Keogh. He tingled with excitement as he realized the preposterousness of it all.

And then Hickey felt something that was totally unfamiliar to him. For a short moment he stopped thinking of his prospects of turning this imminent conquest into an advantage. He felt a genuine attraction to the petite beauty staring into his eyes across the flickering candlelight. He blinked, as if surprised by the feeling.

Rose Keogh knew Hickey's reputation, but she never underestimated her own attractiveness. Surprisingly, given the fact that for so many nights she had lain in bed hating every tissue in Sean Keogh's body, she had never once been unfaithful to him, although their lovemaking was both irregular and an increasing strain on both of them.

Both recognized that pretense in lovemaking made it one of the most exhausting of pastimes. This was an admission both would make only to themselves. For Sean Keogh it was a source of guilt. The woman he loved was still Rose Keogh. At least, if supreme respect was any fraction of love, then he still loved her.

For Rose, of course, love had died within a few short months of their marriage, poisoned by what she perceived as an intolerable arrogance that she believed was born of ambition that Sean held only for himself, to the exclusion of all others, particularly women and more particularly her. An obsession she had nurtured since her tragic childhood grew from obsession to sickness.

That very moment at the Café Pierre when she looked John Hickey directly in the eyes and he returned her gaze, life had changed dramatically for Rose Keogh, although the only outward sign to friends had been a change for the better in her appearance. Now she was living not only for a mission, but also—for the first time in years—for a man.

As Hickey ordered the espresso and cognac, there was not a single hint of awkwardness between them. It was as if they had dined like this dozens of times. Neither of them seemed capable of putting into context the fact that only two hours earlier Rose had been calling him Mr. Hickey and he had been calling her Mrs. Keogh. The thought was too remote to entertain.

When they had finished their first snifters of cognac, Hickey put his right hand over the palm of her left hand, caressed it gently and said quite naturally, "How about one more—a nightcap?"

"I've never had more than one cognac in my life. Champagne yes, but never cognac."

Hickey chuckled. "It stokes the fire."

"I don't think I need that particular helping hand," she said girlishly, and she could feel the inside of her loins dampen. "But I would love one."

At a silent command the waiter arrived with two more snifters of twenty-year-old Napoleon cognac. Rose inhaled the gently pungent aroma as she took a tiny sip. She breathed deeply as if trying to control the urges boiling inside her. Hickey was experiencing the same emotion. And again it all seemed foreign. This was the first woman he had felt it with. He was not plotting the coming hours as he normally did. Gone were the campaign plans normally attendant to a tryst such as this. John Hickey had abandoned his normal but highly skillful game of playing a rich and powerful woman the same way a big-game fisherman would play a blue marlin. He was simply being John Hickey, a man who had been incredibly struck by this delicate and intelligent lady with the tiny, tight body and doll-like face.

Hickey sighed as the cognac wafted through his nostrils. "It takes twenty years to mature a cognac like this. God, when I think of the number of years of other men's works in the vineyards that I have sluiced down my throat! Quite immoral, really, don't you think?"

"If you like something, what difference is there in the cost?"

"I couldn't agree with you more, Rose. . . . Do you mind if I smoke?"

"Not at all. . . . Could I have one?"

"You smoke?"

"Sometimes. Particularly when I'm relaxed and enjoying myself."

"I'm flattered."

"Frankly, John, so am I."

Hickey could feel the hardness pressing against the narrow trouser leg of his custom-made suit.

For long minutes they sat back and smoked John Hickey's Dunhills. They looked at each other silently, knowing that small talk would only destroy the idyllic moments they were savoring. If there is such a thing as telepathy, then surely they were experiencing it in those moments in the tiny darkened table in the Café Pierre. Eventually Hickey called for the check and paid with his American Express card. The irony was noted silently by both. The American Express charges, of course, would be paid by Sean Keogh's company.

"There is some champagne in my suite, generously provided by the management," Rose said quietly, the candlelight dancing off her eyes. "Care for another nightcap?"

"Most certainly . . . but perhaps I should join you in a few minutes."

She threw him a questioning glance and then at once understood. Leaving together, no matter how discreet the surroundings, would indeed be foolish. They both stood up. Hickey shook her hand formally. She smiled through the semidarkness.

She walked out of the restaurant into the baroque, marbled lobby, turned left and caught the elevator to her eighth-floor suite, which was positioned directly underneath the suite still maintained by the Onassis family and directly above the suite owned by the family of Italian banker Michele Sindona.

Hickey returned to the bar, ordered another cognac. It was unlike him to gulp his cognac, but he was anxious. He couldn't remember when he had last felt so youthful. He always looked youthful, but he always had the feeling that his insides were jaded and gray.

It had been ten minutes since she left. He drained his snifter, paid the bartender in cash and left a two-dollar tip. He nodded politely to the bartender and headed for the door, turning right instead of left. He then circled the lobby, walked out the Fifth Avenue exit and turned down Sixty-first Street, where he entered the side entrance of the Pierre. He then retraced his steps and caught the elevator to the eighth floor. He turned right at the elevator and walked to suite 801.

As he loosely clenched his knuckles to knock on the door, he noticed a slight quiver in his fingers. He marveled at his nervousness, and again he could not remember when he had felt like this. The knock was hardly audible.

The door opened, and she stood there in the softened light of the elegant suite. Silently he entered, and she gently closed the door. Without a word she handed Hickey the chilled bottle of Dom Perignon. Expertly he popped the cork. The vapor gushed out of the throat of the bottle, and they looked at each other through the smoky luxury.

He poured the champagne into two long stemmed, European-style goblets.

He clinked his glass to hers and said, "To us, Rose?" It was a question. "To us, John."

Almost simultaneously they put down their glasses. He grabbed her by the wrist and hurriedly led her to the bedroom. He threw her down on the bedspread. They were fully clothed. Hungrily he kissed her wide-open mouth. Just as ravenously she kissed him back, at the same time spreading her legs as far as the tight skirt would allow. Savagely he fumbled with her suit jacket.

He stood up, threw off his coat. This was not the smooth John Hickey who would caress the clothes off a woman. His coat and his tie were flung on the floor.

She managed only to get her jacket off before he had plunged on her again. Her skirt had inched up to above her thighs, and her legs enveloped him. Their mouths didn't part as he removed her panties, half-tearing them in the effort. She grabbed for his stiffness, and he felt as if he were going to explode. He unzipped his fly, and his trousers fell to his knees.

If he had learned the finesse of the lover par excellence in his life as a boudoir politician, then in one short moment he had forgotten it all. No longer was this work. It was pleasure, and if he was capable of a cool thought he might have surmised that this was the careless, hungry, insanely passionate way it would have been when he was sixteen in the back of a car instead of stalking Third Avenue near Fifty-first Street looking for aged, pink-faced businessmen. And if Rose had been capable, she might have believed that this was what sex and love were really about. Unconstructed, and without shyness or propriety.

He thrust himself into her tight wetness, her nails dug deep into his buttocks, and with each thrust came yet another release inside her, and for Hickey each thrust was a statement of wanting instead of what it had always been—a statement of using and manipulating. For long, ecstatic minutes they ravaged each other in their state of semidress until they both burst upon each other.

They lay there drained and silent for ten or fifteen minutes. This time Hickey undressed, and she stripped naked as the intense heat returned to her body. They made love again, just as violently but with more understanding of each other's bodies.

They made love four times that night. Certainly no record for John Hickey. And the last time was even better than the first—for both of them.

It was now 5:20 A.M. John Hickey was sweating after the last climax. John Hickey had never sweated. He had always been too much in control. For once he had been out of control. And the same was true with Rose.

He lit a Dunhill.

Rose Keogh's small breasts crushed across the lean body. And she giggled.

"Why do they always smoke after making love when you see movies?"

"I guess art follows nature."

"Do all men smoke after making love?"

"Darling"—he said the word. "Darling . . . I really don't know."

"You've smoked many times like this, haven't you?"

"Truth time?"

"Yes, truth time."

"Well, the answer is yes . . . yes, I have. I have made love to many women. . . . Pardon the boast. Damn it, what a silly thing to say."

"Is it silly?"

"Well, it is. I mean it's just damn silly."

He pushed the Dunhill into the ashtray.

"I feel . . . Jesus . . . I feel like I just got laid for the first time."

Rose was silent.

"I don't know what to say. . . . What do you say when it's been . . . well, it's been perfect for me. . . . I don't know about you."

John Hickey had never said anything so corny in his life. But he wasn't lying. The wet stain on every corner of the bed told her he wasn't lying.

Her voice was very small.

"Do you expect me to believe this?"

"Not really."

His arm could have encircled her almost twice. And she snuggled smaller.

Sean Keogh could kill him with guns. And he was sleeping with his wife. And that was a good excuse to get killed with guns. The thought made him light another Dunhill. And she snuggled closer.

"Do we know what we're doing?"

Rose put a hand between his legs and felt a spent penis. She wasn't aggressive about it. She just felt it. And he got hard again. They made love and it was as beautiful physically as it was emotionally.

"Do you really want to smoke again?"

Her voice was cool and sensible.

Hickey couldn't quite grasp it all. In one fell swoop she had been transformed from a lady giant to a female kitten. She was his. But he didn't want to take advantage of the obvious. She had money. He had some. But it struck him like an axe. He had never enjoyed getting laid. He was an athlete when it came to sex. He gave and never received. That night he had received—and then some. He had even kissed her full on the mouth, knowing what the breath of a lady who has been drinking Scotch, cognac and champagne would taste like. He kissed her again, and he loved it.

Between lovemaking she was silent. She was testing his nerves. Anyone who went against the great Sean Keogh had to be *someone*.

There was no question that John Hickey was scared. But he just didn't want to admit that to himself or the lady in his arms. Men don't like to admit they have fear when they are conquering. And John Hickey was like anyone else. And he said to himself silently, "I'm no different."

She threw a wet thigh across his firm belly.

"I know your reputation."

"That's a bore."

"Not really . . . you're better than the gossip."

"What gossip?" he said half defensively.

"Does it matter?"

"Rose, I'm telling you, no matter how badly I'm putting it: tonight was . . . well, it was special, Rose."

"If you believe that, then you will call me Rose in the office on Monday morning."

They both chuckled. And they hugged. And they kissed. He pecked her on the eyebrows, without passion but with affection.

Hickey had been perfect once again. But this time for himself. And perfection for him had coincided with perfection for someone else.

Hickey's hungry body was still taut. She felt it. She grabbed under his rib cage. His muscles were like wire.

"You're frightened, aren't you?"

"Well, I'm frightened, yes," he said frankly, "but who can make love to a lady like you and not be? But if I were really frightened I wouldn't have made the move in the first place."

"I know it." And she sighed. And she kissed his handsome neck.

"But Rose, I . . . I . . . oh, Jesus."

"What? Say it."

And he said it all. The whole story. The men when he was a boy, the rich women, the perfect confidence machine. He told all.

She was silent throughout. Then she looked up. There was a silver streak running down his right cheek. Do men cry out of one eye?

She adored that moment. She adored Hickey. In that moment, as he recounted the torture of his childhood, John Hickey was impressing nobody. She never even drew a deep breath when he told her about Constance Mathers and the blackmail and the *Clarion*. She just moved closer to him. John Hickey was being honest. Totally honest.

"A personal question." She breathed slightly more heavily.

"Yes . . . how much more personal could I be?"

"Are you a Catholic?"

"Christ, no," he said. "Am I condemned forever?" He smiled.

"No, you are not, but let me be telling you, as they used to say, about it all." And with her lush brown hair spreading across his chest she told it all. She was as frank as he had been. And while what he had told her had surprised her, what she told him shocked him to the molars. But he never showed it.

"You are shocked, aren't you? You don't think I'm very nice, do you?"

"You can only prove it by my not making love to you again." He was sincere as he felt her gush from her loins. They were very close now. And he introduced anal sex. Her screams were of pain but not of protest. And when it was over they collapsed in a lather of perspiration. She asked him to do it again.

"I'm not sixteen, you know," Hickey said to her. She quietly caressed his member.

"Maybe you are." And she giggled. Four minutes later she wanted to scream. And then she kissed him again.

It was just before seven o'clock when each of them had convinced the other there was nothing else to do with each other's bodies.

Semen had cascaded all over the bedspread. She suddenly felt self-conscious as the light stabbed in. Hickey was near sleep. She ran her hands through his generous blond hair.

"John," she said with more of an edge of seriousness, "you know, if you don't love me, I could have you killed."

He gave a thin-lipped smile. And he crushed the tiny body to his chest. "Go ahead—have me killed. I've seen Naples; why shouldn't I die?"

"I'm serious," she said with some intensity. "Love me, John—love me."

"I love you. I love you . . . I love you. . . ." And he laughed. It was a genuine laugh.

"Just love me, John. No jokes. Just love me."

He grew very tender. "I love you, Rose. I really do. In many ways, before I came here tonight I was a virgin."

"Love me, John"—and she gripped his slim, muscled shoulders.

He pulled her close.

"Do you hate him?" Hickey caressed her closed eyes. She was waiting for the answer in expectant silence.

"Do I hate him? No. Eddie Wilson hates him. I don't hate Sean Keogh."

Her eyes wrinkled with anxiety.

"I detest him and all that he stands for. A self-righteous punk who believes he had the corner on the trade of having it tough. He sickens me, as does his sanctimonious lot."

She wrapped herself around John Hickey that morning and fell into a deep, contented sleep. She had found a lover—and an ally.

As Rose sat there on the porch inhaling the air of McLean, Virginia, she looked back with satisfaction. Her affair with Hickey had grown and grown. Wilson, of course, knew about it, and deep down she suspected that her son, Terrence Patrick Keogh, sensed it. If he did, he would celebrate for her. She sighed and sipped her gin and tonic.

The time was drawing closer. She was going to have John Hickey alone for herself. She deserved that, she mused. Sean Keogh owed her that—and a lot more. She would have it all.

Chapter

13

THE OLD white-haired priest puffed his way up the stoop of No. 220 West Twelfth Street. At the top of the stoop he paused to get his breath, and standing outside the handsomely polished wood door, he pressed the buzzer for the first-floor apartment.

Momentarily a voice came scratchily through the intercom: "Who is it?"

"It's me, dear—Father Comerford," the old priest said, regaining his breath.

"Coming."

He opened the door with a click as the buzzer sounded, and within seconds he was greeted by a fresh-faced honey-blond woman in her late thirties.

"Hello, Jane darlin'. How are you this morning?"

She smiled and ushered him inside the tastefully furnished first-floor apartment of the brownstone, which stood on one of the nicer streets of Greenwich Village.

"Good to see you, Father. How have you been keeping?"

"Battlin' on, darling. The good Lord doesn't want my company just now."

"Can I get you a little something?"

"Oh, maybe a little drop of somethin' to thicken the old blood," he said with a smile.

Jane Rooney, as she had done from the very first day she had met the kindly-faced old priest, went to the liquor cabinet and pulled out a bottle of fine sherry. She poured him a small glass, and he sipped it with satisfaction.

From the bedroom the sound of a record player could be heard. The old priest turned his attention to it.

"I have to live with that sound just about twenty-four hours a day when Mary is home from college. Some new group that seems to make a lot of money playing tunes that all sound the same," she said with a laugh.

"And I suppose you didn't drive your parents mad with Elvis Presley when you were young," he said with a chuckle.

She laughed at the reference, but there was an emptiness in her mirth. It was always the same when anyone referred to "when you were young." She had much to want to forget about when it came to her youth. But it often came back to her with a sharp jab whenever the old priest visited.

The door to the bedroom opened. It was Jane Rooney's daughter, Mary. She was a tall, thin, gawky young lady with long blond hair carelessly combed like matted rope.

"Hi, Father," the young girl gushed as the old priest stood to kiss her lightly on the forehead.

"Look at you," he said with an indulgent smile. "I can't believe how you've grown. In your last year of college—look at you. Seems only the other day you made your First Communion. . . . Ah, I'm gettin' too old."

"You look wonderful. Why, you could have been a movie star, you're so handsome."

He chuckled. "And I hear that's what you're studyin' in your spare time. That right, girl?"

"Well, I'm taking acting classes. Which reminds me, Mom. I'm going uptown now, and I'll be at Actors Studio until about six tonight."

"Will you be home for dinner?"

"I'll grab a pizza with the gang. . . . See you. Bye, Father; good seeing you." She bounced merrily out the door.

She had a fresh, unselfconscious manner which, although she had not fully developed into a beauty, gave her an attractively vulnerable quality. It was a way in which she would toss her head, splaying the untidy mop of gold hair around her face.

As she disappeared into the Greenwich Village street, both mother and priest looked after her with pride.

"You've done a fine job with that one," the old man said. Jane Rooney sighed. "She's a very good girl . . . a little wild, but a good girl."

"You've been lucky, Jane."

Jane struggled hard to mask the bitterness that welled in her eyes.

"No, Jane, no matter what happened many years ago, you've been lucky. You have a fine job, you've worked hard and you have given young Mary the very best. You have a lot to be proud of."

"I suppose so," she said with resignation.

"I know it's been hard, darlin'. You know, Jane, you're a beautiful woman; the men must be lined up in your office to take you out. Why don't you go out a little more? Mary is a grown girl. You've done your duty and then some. The Lord has nothing against love, you know. A good woman should be with a good man. There are exceptions like myself, of course," He chuckled. "No, seriously, Jane, you have so much to offer. I would love to be the priest who could marry you and the man of your choice."

"It's so hard, Father. I'm not young anymore."

"Oh, that's a lot of bilge. You're a beautiful woman. Now, I'm not in the business of being a social secretary, but I would love to hear that you were going out and having a little fun."

"I will, Father. I really will. Now that Mary is in her last year of college, it will be so much easier. It's just that I have so many dreams for Mary, so many things I want her to do that I just didn't get the chance to do."

"It's a fine thought, Jane, a fine thought; but there is no law that says you can't think of yourself occasionally. Now, look at me. I'll confess. I get tickets from a newspaper friend of mine for the baseball; I would never miss it. I don't think the good Lord begrudges me that. So I want to hear about you and some relaxation the next time I see you."

He sighed and drained his sherry. Then he got to his feet and hesitated, silent. This was always the part he dreaded. He reached inside his shiny black suit and produced the heavy brown envelope. He discreetly put it on the table, leaned over and kissed her forehead. "I better be goin' now. Look after yourself, my dear."

Jane Rooney's eyes avoided the envelope. They always did. She remained thin-lipped. "Thank you, Father. Please drop around more often. It's wonderful to see you."

"Same here, same here." The old man left more quickly than he had arrived, almost as if he were anxious to leave before his completed mission stirred in the tall, handsome blond woman the heartache that always attended his delivery of the brown envelope. She waved him good-bye.

She slowly closed the door behind her and went into the living room. The envelope was on the table.

The ritual rarely varied. She would look at the envelope of heavy brown stock for a long time. Then slowly she would prise it open with her nails. She would reach inside, and a feeling of revulsion would run through her body as her fingers felt the wad of crisp bills.

She withdrew the money. Five thousand dollars in hundred-dollar bills. It was the money. It had come every month: at first five hundred dollars, then a thousand, and now it was up to five thousand dollars a month. It had bought the brownstone where she lived and had put Mary through the best private Catholic girls' school that New York had to offer. It had paid for Mary's liberal-arts course at Columbia. It had come for twenty-five years. How much was a man's life worth?

At first, when a younger Father Comerford had knocked politely at the door and wordlessly slipped the envelope into her hands, she had needed the money desperately. She had come to New York a month after Mary was born and three months after they buried what was left of Jimmy Rooney. At first she'd used the extra money to put herself through secretarial school at night, while she worked as a waitress during the day and had Mary looked after by a legion of baby-sitters. Then the money had increased. She could get herself a decent job with International News Service as an executive secretary. She was attractive, bright and extremely well trained as a secretary.

She had used the money wisely. After the brownstone had been bought, she had rented out the two top floors. She had given Mary the best of everything. Everything that she had never had herself. Mary had turned out to be a good product of fine schooling, and she was very proud of her. But the money couldn't buy a human being. It could never replace the man who had shared a hand-me-down bed in a tiny frame bungalow in Southie.

Jimmy Rooney should have stayed a taxi driver. He wasn't much. He tried too hard to be a big shot. He was impressed by the racket guys. He lusted to be one of "the boys." But the track was too fast. He wasn't much, wasn't much to look at. Wasn't even much to talk to. But Jimmy Rooney was hers. And nobody had been hers before Jimmy Rooney or after him.

She threw the wad of bills onto the table and choked back a sob. He was a lovely old man, Father Comerford. But his visits never took more than five minutes. From the first day he had come to deliver the heavy brown envelope, he had approached his visit as one would approach a visit to the dentist. He wanted to get it over and done with.

In the beginning he had resisted with such steadfast grace any questions as to where the envelopes actually came from that Jane Rooney had long since given up asking.

It was as if the priest felt guilty over holding back anything from this decent woman but was duty bound to keep his counsel. He never enjoyed it. There was always an element of deceit in it for him, but he recognized that it was better that she have the envelope than go without. On other occasions when he would visit, he would sit and talk for hours. But when he had to deliver the envelope, it was always the same. A polite sherry, the envelope on the table and hasty withdrawal. If he had only stayed, then perhaps the crashing depression wouldn't set in as it always did. But it never failed.

She looked hard at the money. What was it now?—over twenty-five years, and more than three hundred thousand dollars had arrived. There was little mystery to her. Someone was paying for her husband's half-hacked-away body. Was that what Jimmy Rooney's body was worth? How much for an arm? Two arms? A leg? Two legs? And she felt it coming on as it always did. The tears.

She had long since stopped mourning for Jimmy Rooney's skinny little frame. She mourned for herself. She had led a scrupulous life because she knew of no other way. She was neither a square nor a prude, just a very serious adult. She also was not sexually frustrated, despite the interminable nights alone in a three-quarter bed. She had long since overcome that. Sex was not part of her life. But she feared she had gone too long denying herself the love of a man—denying herself the pleasure of being loved. It wasn't sex, she told herself. And she didn't lie.

So now they had given her three hundred thousand dollars for the privilege of living in a chasm of loneliness. God, how she hated them, and God how she hated herself for ever taking a cent. That in itself was a betrayal of her husband's memory, no matter what the circumstances.

All that money. For what? To erase the memory of that August Sunday when she had awakened at 8 A.M. to find that Jimmy Rooney had not come home. Of course, there were many nights that Jimmy Rooney never came home. There were the nights he was driving his taxi and there were the nights he had been boozing with the likes of Paddy Devlin. Jane knew Devlin was a womanizer, but she trusted her Jimmy, and her trust was not misplaced.

She knew why Jimmy hung out with Devlin. He liked to hang around the wise guys. He would come in after one of those nights with Devlin smelling of stale booze, give her what dollars he had in his pocket and tell her, "Listen, babe, I'm gettin' into the big time. They like me. And they know the score." It was bad James Cagney at the very best. At its worst, it would lead to his death.

And then there was that muggy summer morning when a big cop had arrived, a Portuguese cop called Pete Delgado, who told her he was new in Boston, just moved from New Bedford. And outside there were kids from the neighborhood hovering around in front of the small house, electrified with curiosity. And there were a whole lot of men who looked like cops whom she later found to be reporters and photographers. And she remembered through the daze of half-sleep and half-shock big Pete Delgado lowering his voice with consummate kindness. He was saying, "Mrs. Rooney. It is Mrs. Rooney? I'm terribly sorry to bother you. I really am."

"Yes, Officer, yes. What's happened? Something has happened. What is it, Officer?" She felt her lower lip quiver because she knew that Pete Delgado, the cop, was there about her lovable, weak big-shot husband.

"Mrs. Rooney, do you know the whereabouts of your husband? Look, I'm sorry to ask all this." Delgado was pretty new at the job.'

"It's Jimmy. It's Jimmy, isn't it? He's in trouble. I know he's in trouble." And she prayed to every saint the nuns had taught her about that he was only in trouble. But the saints and the nuns failed her that day, because she knew in her heart that Jimmy was beyond trouble.

Pete Delgado took a deep breath. He was doing it all wrong, he knew. "Well, Mrs. Rooney, there appears to have been an accident, a very bad accident. . . . May I come in?"

She realized then that she had been carrying on the conversation through a screen door. She opened it quickly and grabbed his arm, almost pulling him through the entrance, no longer self-conscious about her pregnant belly which pushed through her pajamas. Jimmy Rooney couldn't afford maternity wear.

"Mrs. Rooney, I can see you're expecting. You have to be calm, Mrs. Rooney. You have to think of the little one."

She didn't have to be told. She let out a terrible howl—not a scream, but a howl—and the reporters outside who heard it noted the howl in fifteen different ways.

"It's Jimmy . . . he's dead . . . I know he's dead. . . . Where's my Jimmy? Take me to my Jimmy. . . . I want my Jimmy. . . . You're a policeman; take me to him—take me to my Jimmy."

Pete Delgado suddenly wished he had stayed home in New Bedford.

"It could be a mistake, Mrs. Rooney," he lied, "but you must prepare yourself for the worst."

She didn't hear what he had said. Her body was shaking uncontrollably, and her sobs came in short little coughs.

"I'm . . . er, I'm afraid I will have to take you to the morgue. Please understand."

He knew he had somehow said the wrong thing. It was one thing to tell a person that someone was dead, but the very word "morgue" had a coldly macabre ring to it.

She nodded her head repeatedly between her sobs. She couldn't raise her head. Her chin was dug into her chest as if she didn't want to look the world in the eye.

Mechanically she slipped on a winter coat on that hot August morning. She didn't even own a housecoat. She recalled how terribly shabby she looked that day with the heavy coat hiding her pregnancy, being led to the morgue by a big cop.

When they had arrived in the police car at the morgue, the motorcade of newspapermen that had followed them had arrived a couple of car lengths in front of them. The flashbulbs from the Speed Graphics on that day in 1957 were popping like hand grenades. Just one more shot to make sure they did not miss any detail of the dramatic squalor of this fantastic gangland-execution story.

They all seemed to be shouting "Mrs. Rooney" at the same time. "When was the last time you saw Jimmy?" one shouted. "Mrs. Rooney, did you give him a farewell kiss?" "Mrs. Rooney, if the baby is a boy will you call him Jimmy?" "What was your last memory of Jimmy, Mrs. Rooney?"

She was such a naive girl she thought that she was obliged by law to speak to the press. Through her grief, she timidly stopped, and for a second she was about to say something.

Pete Delgado pushed through the newshounds with a heavy hand. "Take no notice of these vultures, Mrs. Rooney." It was all he said as howls of protest came from the gentlemen of the press.

Even when she went to the squeaky-clean front desk of the morgue, the attendant in charge, a fat, pink-faced man with soft hands, pushed a note into her hand. It read: *The* Boston Record *will pay you $1000 for your exclusive story. Call me, George North. I'm a reporter.*

Delgado glanced at the note and scowled at the morgue attendant in a way that told him he was nothing but a morgue attendant.

Quickly, as some of the newspapermen started to force their way inside, Delgado escorted her down the long green-painted hallway. He turned left through a frosted-glass door. He was holding her elbow firmly at all times. Standing in front of a huge set of big cabinets were the plainclothes detectives. She had seen enough movies to know what those cabinets contained. There was a terrible smell of cleanliness in the big, cool room. She would remember that smell every day of her life.

The plainclothesmen made a space for her in front of one of the cabinets. She nodded politely, and two of them who were wearing hats took them off.

Delgado wasn't wasting time now. "Steady yourself, Mrs. Rooney." He approached the cabinet that had the card number 486600. Jane Rooney remembered that number in the same way she could recall Jimmy Rooney's prison number when he was in Walpole: T-R-6-3890.

Delgado pulled the cabinet open. It seemed to slip open ever so easily for such a big cabinet. It revealed a crisp white sheet, the color of a milk bottle. Pete Delgado moved closer to her side. He was gripping her elbow so tightly that he thought later that he must have bruised her elbow.

"Easy, Mrs. Rooney. It will be over in a second." Delgado took a small, quick breath as he pulled back the sheet cover.

"Yesssss . . . oh, yes. Yes. That's my Jimmy. Oh, God. Oh, God. Yes. Oh, God."

The attendants had worked on the face for the past two hours to take the bloat out of it after the long hours in the harbor. He looked like a pale little boy—not a man, but a little boy.

Delgado moved quickly to replace the sheet. But as he pulled it over the still face, she grabbed at the edge of it to kiss the marble-cold forehead. As she did, the sheet slipped over the corpse's chest and revealed the horror of Paddy Devlin's handiwork with the buzz saw.

"Oh, my God," she screamed, "what have they done to you? Jimmy. No. No. No." And that was all she could remember until the curious odor of smelling salts brought her back into the nightmare as she lay in the hospital bed.

The doctors marveled that she hadn't lost the child. Her body was incredibly strong, she heard the doctor say to the cops as she came out of her faint. Jane Rooney had often wondered what was the use of a strong body if the body's heart had been almost surgically removed by loss and grief.

Jane Rooney walked across and picked up the five thousand dollars from the table with her fingertips the same way someone would pick up a dead rodent. She looked at it hard and then let it drop, the money in big bills falling on the floor. She felt the overwhelming urge to strike out at something, someone. She felt like screaming at the top of her lungs to tell the world about the vengeance rotting inside her. The tears trickled cleanly down her high cheekbones. "Bastards, bastards, bastards." She repeated it over and over until she was yelling at the top of her voice.

Jane Rooney couldn't remember the last time she had actually used a swearword. She stopped herself suddenly as she ground her teeth in anger. If only she could get a just vengeance. If only she had not been bought off for her husband's mutilated body with money.

She breathed deeply, as if hyperventilating, to regain control. She repressed her emotions to a simmer and poured herself a glass of sherry from the still-open bottle. She never drank alone, but she felt better. It was almost as if by her indiscretion of drinking alone she felt a little more like part of the human race. She allowed herself another. And then she just had an old-fashioned cry. It made her feel better, although she knew that next month, when Father Comerford returned, she would experience the same feeling of emptiness—of being cheated out of the man she loved, no matter who he was or what he was like.

"CONGRATULATIONS, YOUNG Terrence. I think this calls for a little toast," John Hickey said. He reached for the bottle of champagne. "I daresay he is old enough to have a little drink?" he added, looking at Rose Keogh.

"Certainly, John." She smiled.

Terrence gave a good-natured laugh. "In high school these days, you get plenty of practice at celebrating with booze." He had an easy charm.

Hickey popped the cork and poured champagne into Terrence's goblet. The three of them were alone in the house in McLean, Virginia. If Terrence ever wondered about Hickey's regular visits, he never mentioned them. Terrence reached for the glass without hesitation. It was very easy to forget the boy was blind. The three of them clinked their glasses. "Good luck, Terrence. It's quite an accomplishment to be accepted in that preparatory school."

Terrence sipped his champagne and smiled. "You mean it's an accomplishment to be accepted at Exeter considering I'm blind. . . . Don't be embarrassed. I agree, I'm quite lucky." He said it without any self-consciousness, and it caused no embarrassment.

"Your father must be very proud, Terrence," Hickey added.

"As a matter of fact, I haven't gotten around to telling him. I must, of course."

Hickey flashed a questioning look at Rose.

She smiled. "You know how busy Sean is." And that seemed to tell the whole story.

To Hickey, the rift between the son and father was monstrous. He found it difficult to understand—but then, he had yet to learn all the facts.

"Are you staying another night with us, Mr. Hickey?"

"No, Terrence . . . off to New York in a little while on business, and then back to Boston."

Hickey was amazed how much at ease Terrence's presence put him. He must have known he was having an affair with his mother. The constant visits. The intimate way they spoke. The way Hickey disappeared whenever Sean was around. The way his name or his presence was never discussed in front of Sean when he made one of his rare visits to McLean.

But then, Hickey didn't realize how close Rose and her son were. She told him everything. John Hickey was the one true romance in her life, but with Terrence it was different. She idolized the boy and he idolized her. It was as if each made the other complete.

Terrence finished his champagne and stood up. "Mother, I think I'll go upstairs now. I have a little reading to catch up on."

"Fine, Terrence."

He leaned over and kissed her on the forehead. He then held out his hand to Hickey. "Nice to talk to you again, sir."

"Always a pleasure, Terrence."

Terrence slipped away quietly upstairs.

"He amazes me, that boy," Hickey said after a long pause. "It seems there is nothing he can't do. Of course, he is one hundred percent you, Rose."

"I agree." She smiled proudly.

"Do you think he knows?"

"About what?"

"Us, of course."

"John, I tell Terrence everything. If he is told everything, then he will understand everything. I have great ambitions for that boy. Greater ambitions than I have for myself."

Hickey smiled. "You're quite something."

They finished their bottle of champagne. They would not make love that night. That would have been foolish. Although Sean Keogh never arrived unannounced, it would just be a stupid move, one that could destroy everything they were working toward.

They lingered on the huge porch before Hickey left to drive to Washington. He kissed her gently. Both of them looked out across the huge expanse that rolled in front of the house.

"It's beautiful here, Rose."

"One day, it will be ours to enjoy alone."

"Do you really believe that, Rose?"

"I know it."

"There will always be Sean and his crowd standing between us."

"I doubt it. Incidentally, what do you honestly think of his chances?"

"Of running? I certainly think he will run. What are his chances of winning? Well, there is no question, he is the most visible, has the highest profile. He is very well respected in the Senate. But then, one has to wonder how far the traditional party hacks would get behind him. There's still a lot of resentment toward him in the party. They think he gives the impression that his platform was made up solely by himself. In fact, it embodies the most traditionally Republican ideals of all. Still, Keogh acts as if they were exclusively his."

"Typical," she said, with no attempt to hide her disgust. "But from where you stand, he has a better-than-even chance?"

"Absolutely."

"Then that is when, my love, we will move on the great Sean Keogh."

Hickey knew better than to ask what she was thinking. He kissed her lightly on the lips and bade her farewell. "Next weekend, make sure you come up to the house in Southampton."

"I will, John. I'll have no trouble getting away. Bye, my love."

"Bye."

He got into his rented car and headed toward Washington National Airport, where he would get the nine-thirty shuttle to New York. There he had some business to attend to for the *Clarion*.

John Hickey did little to extend himself for the paper. But given the circumstances of how it had changed hands, he correctly surmised that his work effort was not too closely scrutinized, particularly by the likes of Wilson and Burke. And Keogh, who knew nothing of the treachery he had triggered, was too much involved in politics to know anything substantial of the real workings of the newspaper. But one day, Hickey promised himself, Keogh would know a lot more about him. And with Rose's help, it would hopefully come sooner rather than later.

As he drove through the darkening Virginia countryside, he marveled at the similarity he found between himself and Rose. How it had come about, he didn't know. There was a very strong physical attraction. Was that it? Or was it that they were joined by a common ambition to bring Sean Keogh to his knees?

To him, Keogh represented everything that was morally phony. Hickey did not believe in basic morality. People were good, or moral, or hardworking only because they were frightened to be anything else. Basic goodness did not exist for Hickey, and he believed that Rose felt the same way. The only thing that kept people on the straight-and-narrow was fear. Fear of losing a job, fear of going broke, fear of getting caught. Anyone would take whatever he could lay his hands on, if he thought he would get away with it.

Hickey was convinced he was right—particularly about the likes of Edward Wilson. With Rose, it was different: she feared nothing. And given the right odds, Hickey too feared nothing. Wilson? Well, he would have to see about Wilson. He was a handy ally, but how far would he go? He would find out.

The flight to New York, as usual, was boring, and he was glad to sink into a hot bath at the Carlyle before slipping between the crisp sheets of the great old hotel. It was early—still a respectable enough time to call Hugh Morris, the warm, gregarious Editor in Chief of International News Service. Morris, like most people, was thoroughly captivated by Hickey's charm.

"I'd love to, John," the patriarch of the news service boomed over the telephone. "Yes, tomorrow would be just fine. I have an uptown meeting with some magazine people, but I'll come back to the office at one P.M. and we'll have lunch. Look forward to seeing you."

"Okay, Hugh. One P.M. in your office. Fine."

Hickey replaced the receiver and slid under the covers of the bed. He was asleep in seconds.

He rose late the next day, missing breakfast. He took his time dressing in an impeccable dark blue suit and left the hotel at 11:45 A.M.

He loved to walk through Manhattan. It gave him a feeling of accomplishment. This was the city that had abused him, rejected him, hurt him beyond all concept of physical pain. He loved to stroll the streets where he had once hustled. Now he was a somebody. The streets were just older and hadn't gone anywhere. He had aged, but aged like a perfect wine. He was a somebody.

He wandered down Fifth Avenue. He was always amazed how people stared at you when you walked down the famous street. Everybody immediately assumed that just because you were there you must be someone. Even if you were an attractive secretary.

The men always looked hard to see if the face was familiar: was it a face of a model, or a movie star? Women looked hard at John Hickey. He was always pleasantly surprised by Fifth Avenue.

He wandered into Saks and to kill time bought a sport coat. Charged it, and ordered that it be delivered to his town house in Boston. He loved that kind of service.

He was feeling satisfied with himself when he took a left down Forty-second Street and to the Daily News Building between Second and Third Avenues, where the International News Service had its offices. He took the elevator to the fifteenth floor and walked through the big open wooden doors and into the main editorial office.

He waved to some old familiar faces and smiled at some young women who weren't so familiar. He then took a right through the executive offices and to the main office of Hugh Morris.

A striking green-eyed blonde was sitting at the huge desk of the executive secretary. Hickey eyed her with little concealment of his admiration.

"Hi. I'm John Hickey."

The blonde flashed an even, businesslike smile. "Yes, from the *Boston Clarion*. Mr. Morris just called to say he would be a little late. He was very apologetic. Would you like to take a seat? Perhaps I could get you coffee?"

"Fine—black with sugar. Thank you."

She returned with the coffee and walked back to her desk. She had a perfect figure, Hickey noted. Perhaps a model, maybe ten years earlier. "Tell, me," he said, "where is Miss Frost? She's still working here?"

"Oh, yes, Mr. Hickey. Miss Frost is on vacation. Normally I'm Mr. Phillips' secretary, but he's out of the country, so I'm just filling in for Miss Frost. I'm Miss Rooney—Jane Rooney."

The name hit him like a brick. Jane Rooney. Was it possible? Could it be?

Hickey's mind raced. No, he told himself, there must be thousands of Jane Rooneys in New York City. Nonetheless, he would find out.

"I don't think we've met before, Miss Rooney. I often have lunch with Hugh, but this is the first time I've seen you. Are you from out of town?"

"No, not really. Not for a long time, anyway. It's just that Mr. Phillips' office is at the other end."

"Yes, of course. You said 'Not really.' Aren't you from New York?"

"Well, originally, Mr. Hickey, I'm from your part of the country. Boston. South Boston, as a matter of fact."

Hickey could feel his pulse quicken. This was she. This was the widow. He didn't know how or when or where, but finding Jane Rooney would pay off in the scheme to bring down Sean Keogh. This could be a stroke of luck.

"Er, Miss Rooney, is there somewhere I could make a telephone call?" There was a telephone on her desk. But she knew what Hickey meant.

"Certainly. Right over there in the alcove there's a private booth . . . or you could use Mr. Morris' office if you wish."

"No—no, thanks," he said, and walked toward the private booth.

He flashed for the switchboard. "Er, yes, this is John Hickey. I'm calling from Mr. Morris' office. Could you get me a number in McLean, Virginia? . . . Yes, thank you." He gave the operator Rose's number.

The servant answered.

"Is Mrs. Keogh in?"

"Who's calling, please?"

"Just tell her Boston is calling." He dared not give his name, just in case Sean Keogh was in the house.

"Hello. Mrs. Keogh speaking."

"Are you alone? Can you talk?"

"Yes, John. You sound excited."

"I think I've found Jane Rooney. That's right—*the* Jane Rooney from South Boston. She's a secretary at International News Service. I'm calling only fifteen feet from her desk."

She was silent for a long moment. "I don't know what we can do with her. But I can't help feeling we should get to know more about her. She could be very helpful."

"That's the way I figured it. What do you want me to do, Rose?"

"Do what you are very good at, John . . . get close to her."

"How close, Rose?"

She gave a throaty laugh. "That's not like you, John—to ask a silly question like that. Get as close as you have to. Nothing can come between us."

"John Hickey grew serious. "Well, just as long as you understand."

"I understand, my darling. I understand." Her tone was almost maternal.

His voice had a trace of hurt in it. "Okay—whatever you say." He couldn't believe she would take such a step so lightly—virtually telling him to go to bed with another woman. She was very hard to understand.

"Bye, Rose."

"Bye, my darling, and keep yourself in good shape for next weekend at Southampton."

"I will."

He walked out of the booth. Jane Rooney was holding up the telephone on her desk.

"Mr. Hickey. Mr. Morris on the line. It seems he's been delayed."

He picked up the phone. "Yes, Hugh . . . No, don't be silly. . . . Not at all. . . . Then let's make it tomorrow. . . . Fine. I have all the time in the world. . . . No, tomorrow will be just fine."

He handed the instrument back to Jane Rooney. "It looks as if your boss has just stood me up," he said, smiling.

"I'm sure it couldn't be avoided, Mr. Hickey. Mr. Morris is an extremely punctual man."

"Of course. But there is only one problem. I have an aversion to eating by myself. Now, young lady, how about joining me?"

"That's very kind of you, Mr. Hickey, but I really can't leave here. Thank you all the same."

"I admire your dedication. But you do eat, don't you?"

She smiled shyly.

Hickey was not going to be put off. "All right, then, how about dinner? Unless you're married to the boss of this organization or you're going to work here for twenty-four hours straight, I won't take no for an answer."

"Well, I'm not married, Mr. Hickey," she said, warming to him, "And I'm not going to be here twenty-four hours. But honestly, it's just a case that we don't know each other."

"Now, look, Miss Rooney. Do you know we are one of the biggest clients International News Service has? You wouldn't want to lose the contract for them just because you wouldn't have dinner. I'm a bad loser."

His smile was captivating Jane Rooney.

She returned the smile. "I'm sure International News Service will survive without my having dinner with you."

"Then *I* won't survive. Look, have you a date tonight? Now, be honest."

"No, I haven't, Mr. Hickey," she said. She was quite amused by this tall, charming gentleman.

"Then I won't take no for answer."

"I don't know you, Mr. Hickey."

"Yes, you do. My name is John; your name is Jane, Now, every John has to have a Jane."

She was laughing.

"Now, the 'Twenty-one' Club has imported a new chef from Paris. I'll meet you at the Sherry Netherland for cocktails at seven thirty. Then we'll go on for a gourmet adventure at 'Twenty-one.' "

"Mr. Hickey . . . I . . ."

"Please call me John."

"John . . . I . . ."

"Very good, then. I'll see you tonight at seven thirty." He turned on his heel and started for the door.

Then Jane Rooney heard herself say the impossible. She laughed. "Well, if you think the future of this company depends on it, all right at seven thirty."

Jane Rooney could feel her cheeks burning. For many seconds she seemed to forget all about work—in fact, all about everything. Her pulse had quickened, and she suddenly felt very girlish. She had a grown daughter, and yet she felt like a teen-ager just for those few fleeting moments.

She had been on dates before. There were always the office parties, and one of the single men would always ask to take her home. Of course, nothing ever happened, and she promised herself nothing would happen on this date either, but there was certainly something about him—a boyish cockiness and yet a profound sophistication. She decided that John Hickey was an extremely attractive gentleman.

That night Jane Rooney did something she could not remember ever doing before. She took off a half hour early to make sure she could get to a beauty parlor. After the beauty parlor she took a long time preparing herself. Her daughter, Mary, was away with her college friends. There was nobody home.

It all felt a little strange. She was doing something indulgent for herself. It felt very strange suddenly, but she liked the feeling. She put the finishing touches to her makeup and slipped into a pearl-gray dress. It had a modest neckline and shortish hemline and was just tight enough to show off an hourglass figure. It had been an expensive designer dress she had bought at a sale in Bloomingdales. She slipped on her best blue sandals and dabbed herself with some Diorissimo from Christian Dior. She was pleased with what she saw in the mirror.

She looked at her simple but expensive watch. It was 7 P.M. exactly. She called for a taxi. It arrived at seven ten, and at seven thirty on the dot, she was walking through the revolving door at the entrance of the Sherry Netherland.

She was nervous. She walked uncertainly into the lobby, almost as if she were doing something wrong. She turned right and went through the door to the bar. What if he were late? She couldn't wait at a bar alone.

Only two steps inside the door, the cultured voice of Hickey put her at ease: "Jane." He had taken a stool near the entrance.

He took her lightly by the elbow and led her to a table behind the piano. As he moved through the bar, he nodded to some people who called out his name, stopping here and there for a quick handshake. John Hickey was very well known in New York.

He looked impeccable, his blond good looks set off by a charcoal-gray suit, starched white shirt and club rep tie.

He sat her down at the table. His eyes settled on her face. She was even better, he thought, than he'd first believed. Not in the least sophisticated, but with an attractive ladylike charm.

"It's good to see you," he said as she settled behind the table. "Waiter," he called with quiet command. The waiter appeared from nowhere.

"What would you like, Jane?"

She hesitated. "Perhaps a light gin and tonic."

"Fine. A gin and tonic for the lady, and for me Chivas on the rocks, please. . . . So what have you been doing of world-shattering importance since I last saw you?"

"Oh, breaking world records answering the telephone," she said lightly. Their drinks arrived. "And you?"

"Trying to find things to do, frankly. Apart from business lunches, I confess I haven't been very busy. But that will all change when I get back to Boston."

"You're originally from New York," she said, "but Boston is your home now."

"Yes, and I love it. New York can get on your nerves after awhile. And you?"

"I found it the other way around."

"Oh? Why did you leave?"

She lowered her eyes momentarily and then said, "I'm a widow. My husband died in an auto accident many years ago. I just wanted to start all over."

Hickey knew now she was lying, and not very well. This was *the* Jane Rooney, all right, the Jane Rooney who had been widowed by Sean Keogh and his hoods. A lot depended on this conquest, and this would not, he sensed, be an easy one.

An hour after ordering the first drink, Hickey called for the check. He stood up and guided her outside. A limousine was waiting. Hickey could see that she was impressed.

"It beats taxis," he said with a grin as he nodded to the doorman of the hotel. He helped her inside, and minutes later they were pulling up to the famous jockey-lined entrance of the "21" Club on Fifty-second Street.

Once again Hickey went through the routine, nodding and waving to friends and acquaintances. This was one of the reasons he and Rose could never go out in New York. It always had to be out-of-the-way, unchic restaurants or hotel suites. He so much wanted to be seen with Rose, but it was not meant to be.

Hickey and Jane were ushered to a corner table in the downstairs section by the bar of the restaurant. Upstairs was for the less-valued customers. Their table was the one where Onassis had once sat when he used "21" almost as an office.

Hickey glanced at the menu. Correctly he guessed she was not an exotic eater. He ordered vichyssoise, prime rib medium rare and a modest claret.

Jane Rooney tried to hide just how much she was impressed by her surroundings, but she found the evening delightful. Hickey's company was perfect, and conversation came easily with the occasional visitor who stopped by to shake his hand.

It was twelve midnight, and she wished the clock would stop. There was no real pull of romance—just a gentle fascination with the man.

"It's been a wonderful evening, John," she told him as he helped her into the waiting limousine.

"For me too, Jane. Now where can I drop you off?"

She gave him her address in the Village.

"Charming area. Lived there long?"

"About ten years. Yes, I like it there. Don't get much of a chance to enjoy it, with a growing daughter and a job, but it's nice."

He leaned forward. "After we drop off Miss Rooney, in the Village," he said to the chauffeur, "would you run me back to the Carlyle."

She was pleasantly suprised. At least the evening would not end in an unpleasant wrestling match. She was pleased that she had assessed John Hickey correctly. He was a gentleman.

The limousine pulled up to her brownstone.

"What a charming place, Jane."

"I love it."

"You're very lucky."

Jane let the comment turn over in her mind. Was she really?

He slid from his seat and opened the door on her side. "Jane, it has been so pleasant. Promise we'll do this again. Soon."

"John, I would really love to."

In easy, natural movement, he held her hand, drew her slightly toward him and kissed her lightly on the cheek.

"I'll be in your office tomorrow. Good night, Jane."

"Night, John."

She trotted up the steps to the brownstone, feeling ever so slightly giddy. She had consumed more liquor than she was used to. Was that it? She felt a warm glow.

At the top of the steps, she turned. He looked up from inside the limousine, smiled and waved. She waved back.

Once inside, she undressed slowly. Her mind was not so much on what she was doing as on John Hickey. What would she have done if he had made a pass at her? She would have been disappointed, she told herself. She looked in the mirror as she stood there naked, and for a fleeting moment she wondered what it would be like to be naked in bed with John Hickey. She felt her cheeks burn. She put on her nightgown and slipped into bed feeling pleasantly tired and even a little fulfilled.

And for the first time in a long while she slid into a careless sleep unaware that she was sleeping in a bed alone.

When Jane Rooney arrived at her office at five minutes past nine the next morning, she was mystified by a dozen red roses, sitting in a vase on her desk. There was a sealed envelope discreetly pasted to the vase. It was addressed to her. Excitedly she opened it. It contained a simple message: *Every John has a Jane.*

She was thrilled. Suddenly Jane Rooney felt very young, very fresh, even desired. And she had to admit, she even felt a little sexy.

When her boss, Hugh Morris, left the office at twelve thirty that afternoon to meet Hickey, she felt suddenly disappointed. She had hoped Hickey would come to the office. Instead, her boss was to meet Hickey at the Palm Restaurant.

The feeling of disappointment stayed with her all afternoon. Would she see him again that day? Would she ever see him again? The thought of not seeing him made her prickle with anxiety. She might have even confessed that it put her in a slightly sharp mood.

John Hickey knew the game plan well. He knew he could not sweep Jane Rooney off her feet in a matter of minutes. It might be a bit corny, but there wasn't anything wrong with playing a little hard to get.

The next day, Jane Rooney was having second thoughts about ever seeing the tall blond man again when at three o'clock in the afternoon she heard his voice on the telephone.

"Hey, it's a guy called John looking for a girl called Jane."

She laughed girlishly. "Looks like you found the lady without much of a problem."

"Sorry I couldn't call yesterday. Got simply loaded down. I have to get back to Boston tomorrow. Any plans for tonight?"

"Well, there is an oil tycoon who asked me out, and then there was the movie star, and the other man who asked me out was a bank president." She was laughing at her own nonsense. Jane Rooney never spoke like this. "However, I have put them all off," she said.

"Well, if you hadn't, I would have *bought* them off. How about tonight? Around eight?"

"Love to, John."

"Okay, then eight o'clock it will be. I'll pick you up at your place. No fancy clothes tonight. Let's just relax a little."

"Wonderful. . . . See you then."

He arrived in jeans and a sweater. Jane offered him a drink as she finished dressing. He sat alone in the living room quietly surveying the elegant apartment. This was not the living quarters of a secretary. Even an executive secretary. The brownstone itself would have cost a small fortune. On the mantelpiece were several pictures of a tall girl with slightly stringy-looking hair.

Jane emerged looking delectably fresh in neatly cut slacks and a polo-necked sweater.

"The girl. Your daughter?" Hickey said with mild interest.

"I'm afraid she's no longer a girl. A few more months of college and I fear I will lose her to the wilds of Hollywood."

"Hollywood?"

"Oh, she has a wild idea of becoming an actress."

Hickey laughed. "Spend a fortune on them to go to college and they want to do some crazy thing like going to Hollywood."

She smiled. "Don't I know it!"

He held out his hand. "Shall we?"

That night they went to Elaine's. Jane welcomed the switch from the elegant formality of their earlier date.

Suddenly, as she sipped a glass of wine, she felt very comfortable with John Hickey. There was no awkwardness. She marveled at how well she got on with the man. It was as if she had dated him for months.

The wine made her feel mellow, and John Hickey sensed it. He locked his fingers in hers in the dimly lit restaurant. She made no move to resist the intimacy. He then simply picked up her hand and kissed the back of it.

Jane Rooney could feel every nerve in her body tighten. Then she suddenly relaxed. Slowly her mind examined the situation. She was a grown woman with a grown daughter who had given everything of herself for others. She wasn't being a martyr. That was just the way it had happened. She had led an impeccable life and denied herself most of what other women would have readily accepted as part of being a widow.

In the moment she made her decision. She had become sickened with the loneliness of her bed, sickened by the feeling of barrenness inside her. It was as the priest had said—God had nothing against people loving each other; and although she had to admit to herself that at this stage she could not say she loved Hickey, she could not remember meeting a more perfect, handsome and sophisticated gentleman.

When he leaned over and kissed her on the lips, they parted in moist invitation. She knew exactly what the gesture meant. They were not kids in the back row of a movie house. But did it matter? Was she going to spend the rest of her life being only half a woman? At that moment, Jane Rooney made one of the biggest and most frightening decisions of her life.

As THE light filtered through the draperies, her eyes opened. John Hickey was already awake. He was looking down at her. She was snuggled close to his chest, and the odor of lovemaking mingled with the slightly scented and pefectly muscled body of the man she had surrendered to the night before. She allowed herself a smile. But where Jane Rooney's smiles had always had a hint of shyness, the shyness had gone. Hours in bed with this man had swept her shyness away.

Hickey had given yet again one of his premiere performances. He crushed her closer to him and covered her with kisses. She felt the flame dance through her again as his mouth covered her nipples. They made love again. Jane Rooney felt no guilt. Just pleasure and satisfaction.

Hickey had felt no pleasure. That was reserved for Rose. But he felt great satisfaction. He and Rose were getting closer to Sean Keogh.

Chapter

14

THE LABOR DAY weekend of 1983, Senator Sean Keogh had decided, would be for a gathering of the clan. He had called Rose Keogh the week before. "Darling, how would you like to have our house crawling with people on the holiday weekend?"

"If that's what you want, Sean, I think it would be delightful. We don't have all that many chances to show off the house, you know."

"Fine. I'll drive down tonight and we can work it out. We'll have Frank, his wife, Teresa, Roger Sharpe, Eddie, Father Zeibatski, Terrence—and why not invite John along, John Hickey? A good weekend in the country with you supervising a great kitchen and we'll sit around and work a few things out."

"Anything in particular, dear?"

"I'll fill you in tonight."

The weekend was blessed with perfect Virginia sunshine. On Saturday and Sunday, the group went riding through the lush countryside and returned to the house to swim in the pool. Sean was in an expansive mood, and the party had been skillfully planned to the minutest detail by Rose. The Sunday dinner had been a huge affair, with the best food McLean, Virginia, could boast.

It was over coffee, during a fractional break in the busy conversation, that Sean Keogh said it.

"Well, at this table are the only people I love or trust," he said in a tone serious enough to stop all conversation. He paused for effect, and all present felt an edge of apprehension.

He took a breath and continued: "Now, then, what do you think my chances are?"

"Yer chances of us understandin' ya are a bit remote," Frank Burke said with a smile.

Sean returned the smile good-naturedly. "I'm talking about my chances of running for the presidency."

The room fell silent. It was a curious reaction. All those present had mentioned it, at one time or another, among themselves. There had been several references to the possibility in newspaper columns, and an occasional bold reporter had even asked the question, only to be waved away by Sean Keogh with a smile. What gave the question drama was that Sean Keogh had never actually spoken the words.

"Well, now. What have I said that was so terrible?"

Frank Burke jumped in: "I think yer chances are fantastic. Fantastic, Sean boy, and that's no blarney, Mr. Senator. You know it, we know it."

The others remained silent. They were thinking, and thinking hard.

"Now, then, let's take a poll. Rose, what do you think, my dear?"

Rose was quietly surprised that he would ever consult her on anything as momentous. But she knew Sean Keogh, and secretly she had not been fooled by his silence on the subject.

"Sean, I can't think of a better man for the job."

"But my chances?"

"You could do it, dear; you could do it."

"Roger?"

"One thing is wanting it; another thing is having the machinery, the cash to do it."

"Eddie?"

"I agree with Roger. Sure it could be done, but we would have to work out how."

John?"

"I study the polls closely; I study the social trends. A man like you could do it." Like Rose, John Hickey knew the presidency was foremost in the mind of Sean Keogh.

"How about you, Teresa?"

"If my Frank says you can do it, I say you can do it."

"And you, Terrence. You're in touch with the younger generation."

Terrence Keogh gave a warm smile. "Well, Father," he said, clinging to the formal manner of address, never once having called Sean Keogh Dad, "when I was accepted into the club at Exeter my key ring was inscribed, 'Terrence Keogh, son of the next President of the United States.' So somebody up there likes you."

They all chuckled.

"Father? What do you think?"

"I like the idea of being priest to the President."

Sean cleared his throat. "Roger, now to realism. What do you believe a winning campaign would cost? A winning campaign."

"Well, President Lionel Rawlins in the 1980 campaign spent a hundred million dollars. A campaign for 1984, realistically, would cost a hundred and thirty, a hundred and forty million dollars. And that means announcing in two months' time and rolling the machinery at breakneck speed for the New Hampshire primaries. It also means wooing from now on, in Manchester, New Hampshire, James Tolbin, the owner of the *Manchester Express*. Get him on your side and you have New Hampshire. To date, Tolbin is enamored of Ron Harris from California. Tolbin is stubborn, tough but honest. He's the first key after you get your financing."

"A pretty clear assessment, Roger. What about the National Committee? How much would they be behind me? There are still many who aren't too happy with my presence in the Senate."

Roger Sharpe paused before answering. "They wouldn't have much of a choice. Get the money, get Tolbin, get New Hampshire and lock up two other primaries. The train runs itself then."

"Frank, modesty aside. What are your chances of winning the presidency of the Teamsters in November during the convention in Las Vegas?"

"Better than even, Sean, better than even. I have the young guys on my side. All the old tough guys from Union City, New Jersey, and Detroit are still strong, but they've lost their support to some degree. I gotta good shot, Sean."

"Roger, what would happen come November at the Teamsters election in Vegas if I announced my candidacy and immediately swung my support behind Frank for the Teamsters presidency?"

"It would obviously help Frank immeasurably," Sharpe answered.

Rose Keogh and John Hickey exchanged subtle looks. Keogh was no modest adversary. If they were going to rob Keogh, they would have to be careful not to let him become so strong that he would be invulnerable.

Roger Sharpe was thoughtful for a moment. "It's a highly attractive game plan. Given your grass-roots support among the middle class, given your own media machine, it's a highly attractive game plan whichever way you look at it."

Sean Keogh chuckled. He was feeling mellow with a few too many drinks inside him. "Well, Rose, my darling, how would you like to be the First Lady?"

"I've never really thought of it," she lied. "Let's get you elected first."

"And you, Terrence lad—how would you like to be the son of a President?"

He smiled. "Do you think it would get me into M.I.T.?"

Everyone laughed loudly. It was Roger who spoke again as the laughter subsided.

"But Sean. A hundred and forty million dollars."

Frank Burke burst in enthusiastically. "I could get the union behind you, Sean. We could get the money."

"No, Frank, that would show our hand, and we would miss the advantage of us both endorsing each other. No, that wouldn't work."

Terrance spoke quietly. "Father, there are, of course, the vast resources of the *Clarion* company."

"That couldn't be done either, son. A man can't rape a company's resources for his own ambitions."

Roger Sharpe was relieved to hear him talk that way. Keogh picked up his glass of beer. "Well, I was just thinking out loud, ladies and gentlemen, just thinking out loud. My God, Frank, your glass has been empty for fifteen minutes. You must be getting old."

It was a subtle signal that the conversation was now over. The party would now continue. But it was Frank Burke who grew silent. He quaffed his beer with the rest of the party, but that night, when he went to bed with Teresa in one of the guest rooms, he was still silent and thinking.

The next day, various hangovers notwithstanding, the party, led by Terrence Keogh, assembled at the stables to go horseback riding. Even his closest friends had to keep on reminding themselves he was sightless. It was uncanny to see the boy on his horse cantering across the hills of the Virginia property.

As Sean Keogh stepped down off the porch to join the group, Frank Burke motioned to him.

"Can we sit this one out, Sean?"

Sean looked with interest at his friend.

"There's something I want to talk to you about, old pal."

"I was thinking of riding with Terrence. I spend so little time with him."

"Ride with that kid and he'll only make a fool of you. He's amazin', that boy."

"You're right. Okay, Frank, if it's important." He waved for the others to go on, and the two old friends took seats in the pleasant sunlight on the porch.

"What's on your mind, Frank?"

"What you said last night."

"About running? I think I had a few too many to drink."

"Not about runnin', Sean. I know in my heart you'll run. I can feel it in my bones. Always could since that day when Mr. Mac handed things over to you. You said it then. You want to be President."

"You've got a memory like an elephant. But what's going on in that mind of yours?"

"You were talking about money."

"Yes, well, we all live pretty well. We're rich, in fact, but we just don't have a hundred and forty million bucks lying around handy right now."

"You need the money. I have an idea where to get it."

"I'm all ears."

"In a word—Del Vecchio."

"Del Vecchio? Robert Del Vecchio? We're speaking about the same Del Vecchio, Frank?"

"Yes, we are."

"Frank, he's a fugitive. Ever since he ripped off the International Mutual Funds for that five hundred million bucks, he hasn't set foot in the country."

"I know he's livin' in luxury down in Costa Real, in Central America. He wasn't a bad guy, Sean. You remember him from the old days when he ran the trucks out of Detroit."

"Not a bad guy in a funny sort of way, Frank—you're right. But he's not a philanthropist. And he hasn't set foot inside this country since Nixon."

"Right, Sean, and despite all his millions, he'd do anything to get back here. Above all else, he's an American. He's very bitter."

"With five hundred million dollars he's bitter?"

"Sean, you remember the score. He got the money okay, but he didn't start screwin' anyone until the other crowd started screwin' him. And then they made him the patsy. Jesus, Sean, there's a half a dozen senators still on the floor who had him railroaded when the trail led back to them."

"Frank, I knew Del and liked him—but where do we get off getting a hundred and forty million bucks from a guy who can't put his toe inside the country?"

"He wants to come back. Maybe he wants to even pay a few bucks back. None of the investors were American, remember. He wants to come back."

"And you figure he might give a handsome loan for the privilege if we could arrange it?"

"Put it this way: if you gave him your word that you could get him back once you were in office, he's the kinda guy who would give out the loot."

"Frank, haven't we left that kind of guy behind?"

"Sean, he would have to come up with the proof, sure. But all he would need is your word."

"God bless you, Frank, it's good thinking, but there are too many ifs involved."

The heavy-lidded eyes of the pudgy-faced Burke looked out into the blue-green grass that sprawled before him, and they registered disappointment. "So then I ferget all about it, eh, old pal?"

"Hell, no, I want you to get to Costa Real as soon as you can and talk to him."

Burke laughed. "You got it, pal."

The next day Burke took the shuttle to New York on the pretext of business. Sean went to Washington; Wilson, Hickey, the priest, Teresa Burke and Sharpe returned to Boston and Terrence stayed with his mother in McLean preparing for his return to school. Hickey and Rose sensed that something was going on. They couldn't pinpoint it, but before the others went their separate ways it was Terrence who put it all into focus from behind his blackness. He simply said to his mother and Hickey, "Father is no doubt ready to run for the presidency." Neither Rose nor Hickey underestimated the depth of the boy.

From his hotel room in New York, Burke contacted Costa Real. He had a telephone number few people in the country had.

The telephone answered on the second ring, and a man with a faint accent announced himself in English: "Alberto Morales speaking." Morales, a Dominican exile, was Del Vecchio's right-hand—and left-hand —man.

"My name is Burke, Frank Burke. I'm calling Mr. Del Vecchio."

"Can I be of any assistance?"

"Hopefully, sir. Could you tell Mr. Del Vecchio that Frank Burke from South Boston is calling?"

"Are you a personal friend of Mr. Del Vecchio's?"

"As a matter of fact, I am."

"Give me your number, please. You will be called back in forty-five minutes. I do not know if I can contact Mr. Del Vecchio, but you will be called in forty-five minutes. Good-bye."

Burke lit a cigarette, picked up a newspaper and waited patiently. An eyelash away from forty-five minutes, his hotel telephone shrilled.

"Mr. Burke? Alberto Morales speaking. Mr. Del Vecchio is coming on the line. One moment, please."

Many years had passed since their last meeting, but Burke recognized the flat Midwestern accent immediately.

"Frankie? You old shanty-Irish sonofabitch, how the hell are you?"

"Hey, Del, what's happenin', old pal?"

"Oh, it's tough down here. Weather is about seventy-five degrees. The food is far too good for an old truck driver like me, and the girls? Well, the girls, their faces are too pretty, their bodies are too tight and their morals are too loose. It's pretty tough."

"Yeah, it's tough all over, Del."

"Things a little hot up there? You planning a vacation? You're welcome anytime, old friend."

"Not exactly a vacation."

"Hell, the last time I heard of you is when that partner of yours, Paddy Devlin, got into a bad accident."

"Long time ago. No, I would like to talk business. And I don't want to waste your telephone money."

"I think I can pay the bill."

"Del, I'd like to see you as soon as I can."

"Be my guest, old-timer. When?"

"Yesterday."

"No more said. My old partner here, Alberto Morales, can leave in two hours. We have a little plane that gets us around. You're in New York. Why don't you be at the Butler Marine Terminal, near LaGuardia, at midnight—just so long as you have your passport in order and all that stuff."

"I got it all."

"Then my friend Alberto will pick you up about midnight. You can get a little sleep on the plane and we'll have breakfast together. Depending on your business, you can stay awhile or head straight back."

"See ya for breakfast, Del."

"Until breakfast."

Burke called Sean in Washington. "Sean. I'm havin' breakfast with Del tomorrow."

Keogh whistled in appreciation at how fast his friend had moved. "Hell, Frank, what took you so long making the arrangements?"

"He was takin' a piss when I first called, so I couldn't get through right away."

They both laughed.

"Now, Sean, I go down there, eat his eggs and bacon, then ask him for a hundred and forty million bucks. What do we tell him?"

"The truth. Only the truth. He was always straight with us in the old days. Just tell him if we get elected—*if*, mind you—we guarantee him a clean bill of health if at least he can come up with some proof he was railroaded. That's all we can do."

"I gotcha."

"And Frank, look after your ugly mug."

"You too."

At precisely midnight, the giant DC-8 glided from the sky and purred to a stop in front of the Marine Terminal. As the rolling stairs were wheeled to the plane's exit, the door was opened. Two men, who obviously hadn't gone to prestigious prep schools, trotted down the steps and stood on either side. They both sported bulges under their armpits. Seconds later, a well-built man wearing an immaculately tailored silver-gray suit came down the steps. He walked across the apron and into the immigration section, where he chatted with two immigration officers. He was tall for a Latin, perhaps six feet two, and he walked with a slight limp, which Burke was later to learn was a memento of a fusillade of bullets fired by Castro goons when he and his father were seeking asylum in the Brazilian embassy in Havana in 1959. His father had died. This was Alberto Morales, a man educated at Northwestern University, an accomplished lawyer. Burke was later to observe that he was the only man he had ever met who could instill fear whether in a courtroom or in a back alley.

Burke was hurried through security. Alberto Morales was waiting for him at the exit.

"Mr. Morales," Burke said, extending his hand.

"Please call me Al."

"They call me Frankie to my face, but a lot of people call me other things," he said with a laugh.

"Mr. Del Vecchio has told me a lot about you."

"I hope you didn't believe it."

"I did believe. We all have a lot in common." They chuckled and walked toward the giant plane. They hurried up the steps and were ushered inside by two beautiful stewardesses. There Burke's eyes popped. He had never seen such opulence. And this thing flies, too, he thought. It was difficult for him to conceal his bewilderment.

Morales smiled. "Mr. Del Vecchio likes to do things right."

"You know, the first time I met Del, Al, he was living above a store in Detroit. At one time we thought he was going to come to work for us. I remember asking what he wanted to be. He just said, 'A somebody.' Well, he sure as hell is a somebody."

The engines roared, and within minutes they were high above the lights of New York.

A stewardess appeared with a silver tray. The tray held two giant goblets filled with Dom Perignon. Morales toasted Burke and sipped the ice-cold liquid. Burke gulped it thirstily.

Morales smiled. "I forgot. I'm being a poor host." He called in English to the stewardess: "A cold bottle of Heineken for Mr. Burke . . . and a shot of Jameson's, please." They both smiled.

Burke eased off his shoes, loosened his tie and sank back into the plush richness of the airplane seat. Morales was impressed by Burke's healthy disregard for sophistication. But he knew too much about him to underestimate the rough-hewn, pug-faced man from Southie.

Morales flicked a switch. A video screen slid down about ten feet in front of them. It showed a videotape of the Boston Bruins–Chicago Blackhawks hockey game. "Now, this is what I call flying in style."

It was for Frank Burke a perfect flight.

As the big bird glided over the pre-dawn darkness of the exotic city of Santa Maria, the capital of Costa Real, Burke was clutched by a feeling, a warm feeling, that he might just be on the verge of electing his friend Sean Keogh to be President of the United States. The plane set down, and Burke marveled at the sight of the beauty of the countryside surrounding the airport.

Morales led him outside the plane and without a hint of customs ushered him into a giant six-door custom-made white Mercedes. In front and back of the limousine were two red Jeeps carrying four armed guards apiece.

The armed motorcade slipped from the airport and into the cool, scented air of the countryside. Burke drew a deep breath. This smelled a lot different from Southie.

Fifteen kilometers from the airport, the motorcade started uphill. On top of the hill Burke could see what appeared to be a tall, very long, brightly lit prison wall. As he got closer he observed that no prison wall was kept in such exquisite condition. Nevertheless, the top of the wall was electronically wired, and in the dim light he could make out armed-guard posts.

The limousine approached the main gate. It was huge and made of steel. Morales pressed a button on a hand console. The console buzzed three times. He pressed it twice again. The giant grid opened.

Morales turned to Burke. "It's a coded electronic security system . . . necessary, unfortunately."

Burke nodded.

Inside the forbidding exterior, the scene changed dramatically. "Jesus," Burke gasped, "it's like a Garden of Eden."

"Yes, it is quite nice," Morales agreed. Giant willows hovered over the roadways like green rainbows. Huge lighted fountains sprang up every fifty yards. Two hundred yards inside the compound a huge manmade lake glistened in the dying moonlight. Around the shoreline stood small cabanas painted in Mediterranean pink. Exotic flora hung everywhere. Deer drank at the water's edge.

"It's just hard to believe," Burke gasped.

The limousine pulled up to a big white Moroccan mansion. Morales led Burke inside. He then took him to a large balconied guest room which provided the last word in comfort.

Morales shook hands: "Frank, seeing this is a business trip, I know you'll be anxious to see Mr. Del Vecchio. Get a good couple of hours'

sleep. I'll have you awakened at ten fifteen for an eleven-o'clock breakfast. If you need any company here, that can be arranged."

Burke smiled but shook his head. "No thanks, Al."

"Okay. See you later, Frank."

Despite the excitement of the wonderful surroundings, Burke collapsed naked into bed and slept like a giant oak. At ten fifteen the gentle
tingling of a telephone awakened him. A pair of shorts that fitted him
perfectly and a fresh linen sport shirt were laid on an armchair for him.
He showered and dressed, and at 10:55 A.M., an aide silently slipped
into the room. He didn't speak any English, but he motioned for him to
follow.

Burke walked through the thick carpet of the hallway and was breathless at the setup. He knew Del Vecchio was rich, but how rich could one
man get?

He was led into the sunlight. The sky was cloudless; a gentle breeze
carried the scent across the estate from a million flowers. A hundred
feet from the mansion, Del Vecchio sat at a table overlooking a crystal
lake. The table had a crisp cloth on it and boasted a fortune in silver.
Close on his left was Morales.

As Burke approached, Del Vecchio jumped to his feet and ran toward
him.

"Frankie, you old sonofabitch . . . Jesus . . . you old sonofabitch."

They hugged. Burke stood back and looked at him. The Clark Gable
mustache which had been his trademark had grayed, as had the straight
dark hair. But he still had the tall, lanky look that Burke remembered
when Del Vecchio, son of poor immigrant parents, had said that he
"wanted to be a somebody." Del Vecchio had, from the ranks of labor,
become a labor lawyer and amassed an enormous wealth without
ever making it in the social columns or Dun and Bradstreet. He had
suddenly emerged during the Nixon years as an international financier, then as one of Nixon's biggest contributors. When the empire
started to fold, the dossier of names who were rumored to have been
involved in the world's greatest swindle read like a Who's Who of
Washington.

He sat there in his opulence in a white terry-cloth robe, monogrammed.

"Jesus, Del, what are you taking? Monkey glands?"

"The worry keeps me young. It's the suntan."

"Yeah, you Guineas sure tan."

Del Vecchio chuckled. "Listen, you bog-Irish bastard, you mean we
Detroit gentlemen of Italian descent. How've you been? Come on, have
some breakfast."

Morales discreetly excused himself. He knew this was not exactly a social visit.

Del Vecchio pushed a mango across to Burke and said, "I heard about Bernie. It must have hit you guys hard."

"Yeah, well, it did. But there is no more of that with us. I'm doing well, very well—er, not like this, Del, but good enough. With a bit of luck I could be president of the Teamsters come November. Sean, well, he's become a real wheel in Washington."

"I get all the papers delivered every morning, Frank. I know. Sean is big business."

"And with some more luck, he could be bigger, Del. The biggest."

Del Vecchio waved an impatient hand. "I know, Frank. I know everything. Which brings us to the business part of it. I know why you're here."

"We don't bullshit each other, Del." Burke swallowed some mango.

"I'll make it easy, Frank. I wish to Christ you could stay awhile and soak up the sun, but I know you want to get back as fast as you can . . . hopefully with an answer."

Burke nodded.

"But let me level with you first. The money? Sure I ripped it off. But I have emerged as a nice scapegoat for all those lying bastards in Washington and Switzerland. They have proved to everyone's satisfaction that I ripped off the investors . . . the little guys . . . the little old ladies' savings.

"Not true. I ripped off the gnomes in Switzerland and those bunch of pricks in Washington who saw a chance to make overnight fortunes. I ripped them off when I found out how they were going to use my system of running the fund. They owned half the financial writers in the country. They were going to use them, with generous payoffs, to hype the fund. Then they were going to vote me out of my own company, sucker the investors dry, send me broke, and put the entire blame on me. But I got them first.

"It's very convenient for them to have me in exile. They're terrified. I have so much on them, in black-and-white, that when it was rumored that I might get back into the States and get a hearing, the Goddamn SEC even sent a hood down here to blow me away. Yes, the SEC and a half dozen senators who the public thinks don't go to the bathroom. That's for openers—and I'm telling the truth. I have four warehouses of documents."

"Del, I don't doubt you. You have put the record straight. But now the deal."

"Well, I know Sean could get the presidency . . . maybe if he had a hundred and thirty to a hundred and forty million bucks."

"You have pretty good intelligence."

"And I know that I could provide it. Not lend it . . . give it. And if he were in the White House I know he would give his word to get me back into the States, which I want.

"Why? Yes, you look at this and you think it's beautiful. It is. But my kids don't know how to play American football. Their first language is Spanish. My wife used to be in the PTA. Corny? Not so corny. That's why the fuck I fought in Korea."

"Keep talking, Del."

"But Sean would need more than money, if he were going to do it right. He would have to destroy the whole goddamn machinery and rebuild it. And only I can do it. To prove the whole Watergate deal was a setup. To prove that *The Washington Dispatch,* that pillar of journalism, had the proof but their half-fag boss, James Fulton-Scott, didn't have the guts. He didn't want his invitation card pulled in Washington. If the *Times* or the *Post* had the information, the damn jails would be full.

"Oh, yeah, I've been a crook. So have you, Frank—no offense. But those pompous bastards, just the fact that they're walking around full of respect and honor—damn it, every time I see their pictures in the newspaper I want to slit their throats."

"Heavy artillery, Del . . . but what's the deal?"

"Simple Frank . . . I want to be Sean's running mate. I want to be his Vice President."

Frank Burke was too good a poker player to let his face register the shock wave that pounded his brain. Del Vecchio looked at him and smiled. "I wish you could stay, Frank, but I know you want to get that message back."

"Only that message, Del?"

"Just one other thing. Before he makes up his mind either way. Tell him to trust me as I trust him and tell him to give me a little time . . . give me some time. I promise he won't have egg on his face."

"Okay, Del." Burke shook his hand warmly.

"Morales has the car waiting. The DC-8 is already refueled. Seems a pity you couldn't have hung out here longer. But there will be other times."

"Hope so, Del. Look after yourself."

Seven hours after he'd set foot in Costa Real, Frank Burke was heading back to New York. When he arrived in New York he caught the shuttle to Washington. He had arranged to meet Sean Keogh at the Sans Souci Restaurant. He looked tired as the headwaiter escorted him to the table.

He was surprised to see Rose Keogh sitting there. He threw a quick look at Sean. He never talked business in front of his wife.

"Go ahead, Frank. I want Rose to hear this. If we're going to play this game, we're going to play it together. Rose has to be involved."

Frank Burke didn't touch his drink. He just said quietly, "Two messages, Sean. The money is yours—as a gift in exchange for some pretty heavy weight."

"And that is?" Sean asked with an edge of anxiety.

"To be your running mate."

The muscles in Sean's jaw tightened. "And the second message?"

"Trust him as he trusts you and give him some time to show you that you won't get egg on your face."

Sean Keogh lifted his Scotch and took a long drink.

"Well, now, he is a high roller. What are you having to eat, Frank?"

He didn't mention the subject again during that dinner. But that night, on one of his rare visits to McLean and sharing a bed with Rose, he lay awake taut with apprehension. Somehow he knew Del Vecchio could come through, and the thought of it shot excitement through his body. Because if he did, he was certain, he could be the next President of the United States.

And Rose felt it too. She too was tense. Was she letting the whole thing run away from her? Was there a point of no return at which Sean Keogh's fortress would be impenetrable? She could feel a searing headache coming on. It was like the headaches she had gotten so long ago. The headaches that were so unbearable.

Sean Keogh rolled over and put his hand on her shoulder, and he drew her to him. God, she wished the man next to her were John Hickey.

She lay awake for two hours battling the pain of the headache until she lapsed into a fitful sleep. She was starting to feel very insecure. Maybe if she just ran away, disappeared with Terrence, her son, and John Hickey? That would be ridiculous. Hang on, she told herself, the break will come. It had to come or her whole life would have meant nothing.

When she awoke in the morning she had to take a handful of aspirins before the headache relented.

"I THINK it's madness, Sean. Total madness," Edward Wilson said with conviction. "It's just too crazy to imagine."

In Sean Keogh's small office in the Clarion Building sat Wilson, Burke, the priest, Roger Sharpe and John Hickey.

Burke shifted uncomfortably in his chair. It wasn't Wilson's comments that caused the reaction. He was always uneasy when his friend Senator

Sean Keogh took a man like Hickey into his confidence. He was equally uneasy that over the years Keogh had regarded Hickey as one of the inner circle. The dilemma, of course, was that he, Burke, could never expose Hickey as a liar and a cheat without confessing to the man he loved above all that he had been involved, however, unwittingly, in a treachery that led to the suicide of Sheldon Mathers.

Sean Keogh nodded his head. "I know, Ed, how crazy it sounds. But let's give Del Vecchio a chance to prove his claim. You wouldn't deny him that?"

"Of course not, Sean, but even if he does have some proof, his name is synonymous with 'world's most accomplished crook.' "

Burke smiled. "Ed, what does synonomous mean?"

The conversation was getting too heavy for Frank. His friend Wilson had never known Del Vecchio. Wilson had been at Harvard when Del Vecchio was hustling trucks out of Detroit. He knew Wilson as a close friend, respected him, loved him as only Burke could love a friend, but Eddie was too closed-minded.

Roger Sharpe interrupted. "Sean, his proof would have to be so dramatic as to leave not the slightest doubt in the minds of voters that he was as innocent as the driven snow. Look, even the fact that Frank, on your behalf, has talked to him makes it politically explosive. That could knock you out of the running just for openers."

John Hickey noted the importance of Roger Sharpe's observation. It could be something that he and Rose could use at a later date.

"Father?" Keogh asked.

"Let's wait for the man's proof before we look a gift horse of a hundred and forty million dollars in the mouth."

"He's right," Hickey said. "Del Vecchio is no fool, and he knows you're no fool. He won't give you half-assed proof, Sean. If he wants to be your running mate, he must know what he must come up with."

John Hickey would never discourage Sean Keogh from making a cataclysmic mistake. Frank Burke eyed Hickey suspiciously.

Wilson was different from Hickey. Wilson secretly resented Sean Keogh every time he walked into the Clarion Building. He believed the place belonged to him. He believed that the success of Keogh's legitimate enterprise over the past seventeen years was entirely due to his own financial wizardry. And to a large extent he was right. To him Keogh was a giant on the streets of South Boston, but a midget when it came to business. If he wanted to play street games as a Senator in Washington, then he was well suited for it as far as Wilson was concerned, but the *Clarion* and all of establishment Boston was his.

However, Wilson was in a difficult situation. While he fully recognized the expertise of Rose Keogh, he was terrified of an insane act on her part, born of pathological bitterness, that would bring down the whole empire, thus bringing him down. No matter what his resentment against Sean Keogh and his suspicion that Rose and Hickey were having an affair, he didn't want his lucrative apple cart upset. If Rose emerged a winner, he would throw in with her. But if she didn't, then he could swallow his secret hatred for Sean Keogh, stay rich, stay away from Rose and her blackmail—and stay alive.

"Well, gents, I know the whole thing sounds a bit bizarre," said Sean. "But I like to keep you up to date. On the face of it, of course, Eddie is right. But Del Vecchio is an extremely resourceful man—and I might add, in his own curious way, rather honest. Let it rest for now; let's see what Del comes up with. Frank, we'll leave it to you to keep in contact with Del."

"I don't think he'll call, Sean, until he's ready to present his proof, if he does. But I know Del—he'll come up with something. Just let's hope it's a hundred and forty million bucks' worth of something."

"All right," Sean said, standing up, "let's keep our lips closed."

They all stood up to leave. Then Sean said as an afterthought, "Oh, Father, could I see you for a second?"

The meeting's participants trooped out of the room. Sean Keogh opened his desk and pulled out a brown envelope.

"I didn't get a chance, Father, last week," he said as he handed the envelope to the priest. "How are the woman and the child?"

"I am told both are well and very, very happy, not to mention comfortable."

Sean nodded. Wordlessly, the priest walked out of the office with the envelope containing five thousand dollars.

Alone in his office, Senator Sean Keogh sat motionless for a long while as he thought. Is it all possible? Can I pull it off? Or am I letting my ambition cloud my intelligence? No, damn it, I'm not. I can do it. I did it in Southie, I did it with the *Clarion* and I did it in the Senate.

United States Senator Sean Keogh. He had to keep on reminding himself he *was* a Senator. He never really regarded himself as a member of the Senate. It was all too hard to grasp. Senator Sean Keogh, former numbers racketeer from Southie. A Senator. But he was, and the nation knew he was, even if he didn't. He got things done for Massachusetts and he could get things done for the country. He scolded himself. Keogh, don't be so consumed with your Gaelic sense of doom.

SECONDS AFTER the meeting, John Hickey was on the telephone to Mc-Lean, Virginia.

Terrence Keogh answered the telephone.

"Terrence, John here. Is your mother there?"

"Certainly, John. One second." His voice was warm and friendly. Hickey was amazed at how well the bright young man with no sight took to him.

Rose picked up the call.

"Rose, he is hell-bent on giving this Del Vecchio plan a try. It's insanity, of course. But it can't hurt us."

"Sean isn't stupid. He must have faith in Del Vecchio; otherwise he would never consider the proposition. For now, it's in our interest to see that Sean climbs as far as he can go. That way he'll fall much farther, and that way we'll have much more to gain. But don't let's break his pot of gold just yet."

Hickey's voice softened. "Of course, you're right, my darling. God, how I miss you!"

"Me too, John; me too."

"How have you been?"

"Oh, bored without seeing you and driven crazy by headaches."

"Have you seen a doctor?"

"I'll get around to it, baby. Probably just tension. There is so much happening. So much is tied up in this. I have waited so long."

"Me too. Call you tomorrow. Have to go now."

"John?"

"Yes?"

"How about the Rooney woman? Anything more from her?"

"Not right now. But I feel it all in my bones."

"I trust you. Bye, darling."

"Bye."

John Hickey put down the telephone. He felt a tingling. God, how he wanted Rose Keogh to be his and only his!

MIKE McGAVIN's tall frame was hunched painfully over a typewriter in the New York office of the *Boston Clarion* at the New York Post Building on the Lower East Side. The night before had been not unlike so many nights before. He could have written a documentary on his hangover, rather than at this moment be writing a feature for his newspaper. His dark, handsome looks were marred from the night before. The circles under his eyes were underscored by the puffiness under his right eye. While in a brawl at Costello's, his local saloon, he had zigged instead of zagging. He felt like death. Despite his pursuit of the good life, he was the best reporter who had ever come out of Chicago, and he continually proved himself in the newspaper fraternity with scoop upon scoop. He was as fast with the ladies as he was with his fists or typing fingers. But right now, he just wanted to roll over and die.

He had gulped down his third cup of black coffee when the adrenaline suddenly fired his body. From the wire room, all the wire-service machines seemed to be ringing their bells at once to signal that a bulletin story was upcoming. He leaped to his feet, knocking over what remained in his coffee mug, and raced to the wire room. He looked down at the copy that spurted from the news-agency wires.

"Holy shit," he rasped out as the bulletin came across.

Bulletin

SAN LUIS, PUERTO BRAVO—A RAIDING GANG OF LEFT-WING TERRORISTS STORMED THE AMERICAN EMBASSY COMPOUND EARLY TODAY AND ARE HOLDING 300 U.S. CITIZENS AND DEPENDENTS HOSTAGE.

RAID—1ST ADD.

THE TERRORISTS HAVE THREATENED TO SLAUGHTER ALL AMERICANS LIVING IN THE COMPOUND UNLESS 30 MEMBERS OF THE OUTLAWED F.A.L.N. ARE FREED FROM U.S. JAILS.

LEADER OF THE TERRORISTS IS A MAN WHO IDENTIFIES HIMSELF AS ENRICO SOARES, WHO SAID IN A TELEPHONE INTERVIEW FROM THE COMPOUND: "UNLESS OUR COMPATRIOTS ARE RELEASED FROM AMERICAN IMPERIALIST JAILS, THE AMERICANS WILL BE TREATED AS WAR CRIMINALS."

SOARES WARNED THAT ANY MOVE BY THE U.S. TO SEND IN MARINES WOULD SPELL CERTAIN DEATH FOR THE AMERICANS.

HE SAID: "WE HAVE BROUGHT SEVERAL POUNDS OF PLASTIQUE INTO THE COMPOUND. ANY MOVE OF ATTACK BY THE AMERICANS AND THE EXPLOSIVES WILL BE ACTIVATED."

McGavin gasped, and his body shook off the hangover. He yelled to the copyboy; "Ferchrissake, get the City Desk in Boston . . . quick!"

McGavin ripped the wire copy off the machine. His mind was racing. He hit the telephone. The only flights into San Luis, Puerto Bravo, in Central America were five hours away.

The copyboy yelled out, "City Desk in Boston on the line, Mr. McGavin." Barry Nathanson, the veteran City Editor, was on the phone.

"Barry, Mike here. You've seen the wires. Helluva story down there in Puerto Bravo. There are no goddamn flights out of here for another five hours."

Nathanson was silent for only a moment. "What the hell, charter a fucking plane. We'll worry about the cost later. Get going, Mike. We have a stringer down there. A good guy, Juan Villas. He works for the local paper, speaks good English. Get going, guy."

McGavin snapped his passport out of a folder in the filing cabinet, grabbed a tape recorder and a camera. Then the bells in the wire room started clanging again. He raced inside.

"Jesus, what a story," he said as he looked at wire copy. "Holy Christ." He tore off the copy and got on the telephone to arrange a charter flight.

The wire-service copy in Mike McGavin's hand had made his eyes bulge.

Bulletin

SANTA MARIA, COSTA REAL—FUGITIVE FINANCIER ROBERT DEL VECCHIO HAS VOLUNTEERED TO BE A NEGOTIATOR WITH THE TERRORISTS WHO HAVE SEIZED U.S. HOSTAGES IN NEIGHBORING PUERTO BRAVO.

DEL VECCHIO COMMUNICATED THE OFFER TO THE U.S. EMBASSY IN SANTA MARIA, WHERE OFFICIALS ARE REPORTED TO BE NOW DISCUSSING THE OFFER.

DEL VECCHIO SAID: "THE TERRORISTS ARE FROM COSTA REAL. MANY OF THEM ARE KNOWN TO ME. IF ANYONE HAS A CHANCE TO TALK SENSE INTO THEM, I CAN."

IF HIS OFFER IS ACCEPTED, DEL VECCHIO COULD CONCEIVABLY EXPOSE HIM-SELF TO EXTRADITION. WHILE COSTA REAL, WHERE HE HAS BEEN LIVING IN LUXURY EXILE, HAS NO EXTRADITION TREATY WITH THE UNITED STATES, NEIGHBORING PUERTO BRAVO DOES.

WHEN ASKED ABOUT THIS, DEL VECCHIO REPLIED: "BEFORE ANYTHING ELSE I AM AN AMERICAN, AND IF I CAN SAVE AMERICAN LIVES I WILL. I KNOW SEVERAL MEMBERS OF ENRIQUE SOARES' FAMILY. I HAVE A CHANCE."

"Sir, with respect," McGavin barked into the telephone, "I don't give a fuck how much it costs; I want a jet plane to get to San Luis, Puerto Bravo . . . Yes, check with Barry Nathanson, our City Editor in Boston. I will be at the Marine Terminal in forty-five minutes . . . no later . . . and I expect a plane . . . All right . . . Yes, my passport is in order. You get the plane and we'll do the paying. Fine . . . okay."

McGavin reread the wire-service copy. "Jesus, this is the story of the damn decade," he said to anyone who was listening.

Then the next bulletin came through:

U.S. STATE DEPARTMENT OFFICIALS IN COSTA REAL SAID THEY WOULD WAIVE EXTRADITION RIGHTS FOR 48 HOURS, DURING WHICH TIME FUGITIVE FINAN-CIER ROBERT DEL VECCHIO WOULD BE FREE TO NEGOTIATE WITH LEFT-WING TERRORISTS WHO HAVE TAKEN OVER THE U.S. COMPOUND IN NEIGHBORING PUERTO BRAVO.

THEY SAID THEY WOULD MAKE NO ATTEMPT TO TAKE ADVANTAGE OF THE EXTRADITION TREATY THAT EXISTS BETWEEN THE U.S. AND PUERTO BRAVO WHILE DEL VECCHIO IS IN THE COUNTRY FOR A SPACE OF 48 HOURS. A STATE

DEPARTMENT SPOKESMAN SAID: "THE SAFETY OF U.S. MEN, WOMEN AND CHIL-
DREN TRANSCENDS LEGAL RAMIFICATIONS OF MR. DEL VECCHIO'S DIFFERENCES
WITH OUR GOVERNMENT.

McGavin raced to Costello's bar and confronted Freddie the bartender. There was no time to get a bank transfer.

"Give me every cent you have," McGavin demanded.

Freddie looked up. "You fag fuck, whadaya think I am—Rockefeller?"

"I'm serious. I need at least twelve hundred in cash. I've got to get out
of town on a big one," he whispered.

The other journalists in the bar looked suspiciously toward him. Freddie knew he was serious. Dutifully he peeled off the bills. McGavin raced
outside to a waiting taxi and ordered it to get to the terminal. He could
feel the pores on his scalp prickle with excitement. He would get there
before anyone else.

The plane was waiting with jets roaring. He leaped aboard, flashed his
identification and within ten minutes was headed for Puerto Bravo and
the story of the decade. It would take six and a half hours to get there,
and McGavin's stomach was in turmoil all the way. Damn, couldn't this
thing go faster? Like any reporter worth his salt, McGavin was having a
bad case of nerves. It was the only way to win. Be scared.

McGavin felt the jolt of excitement hit his body as the countryside
changed its face. He could see palm trees. He was getting closer.

The chartered jet with its solitary passenger put down like a big eagle.
When McGavin walked down the rolling stairs, the tropical air hit him
like a blast from an oven. He threw off his heavy, worn tweed coat. He
had not had time to change in New York, and if he had, all he would
have done was leave the tweed coat behind. He threw the coat over his
shoulder and jogged to the immigration booth. The airport was bristling
with National Guardsmen laden with every conceivable automatic
weapon. Armored personnel carriers circled the airport. San Luis was
on a war footing.

He flashed his passport. The immigration man, who looked more like
a colonel than an immigration officer, beckoned him closer. In broken
English he stuttered, "A man . . . he wait for you . . . Señor Villas . . .
over there." It was Juan Villas, the *Clarion*'s local stringer. He was a
short, good-looking man.

McGavin didn't waste time on niceties. "Villas? McGavin. What's the
situation?"

"A standoff. The whole compound is secured by the terrorists. Ambassador Cabot Trumbull, your former Senator, he is under house ar-

rest. We have had some communication on the telephone with him. He is speaking at gunpoint. These terrorists mean business."

"Is anyone else here? Any other newsmen, anyone from Boston? New York?"

"Yes, Danny Cahill from the *Daily News* arrived half an hour ago."

"Fuck it. . . . He got anything?"

"Nothing. He's just hanging around."

"What do you think we should do?"

"Hang around too until something happens. You'll get good color pieces from outside the compound. It's very tense."

"Fuck that. Can we get into the compound any way? Any way possible?"

"Impossible unless you want to commit suicide."

"That tough?"

"Tougher."

"Well, Juan, if you're with me, I have an idea."

McGavin told him his plan. Juan Villas went pale.

"Are you with me?"

"Blessed Mother, I have never seen you before in my life and you are going to get me killed. Yes. I'm with you."

"Good man, Johnny."

IN FARAWAY Boston, Sean Keogh was on the City Room floor. He was huddled with Edward Wilson, John Hickey and the City Editor, Barry Nathanson. It was one of the rare times that Keogh had been seen on the City Room floor when it was not almost deserted.

Keogh was looking serious. "Who have we got covering the story for us?"

Edward Wilson looked to Hickey; Hickey looked to Nathanson.

Nathanson answered. Wilson and Hickey couldn't. Wilson and Hickey were remote from the reporters.

"Our man in New York," Nathanson answered.

"Name?" Keogh asked.

"Mike McGavin."

"What's he like?"

"The craziest Irishman that ever came out of Chicago," Nathanson said. He didn't mince words.

"Is he good?"

"The best, Senator."

Keogh liked Nathanson's delivery. It had told him what he wanted to know. He nodded to Nathanson. Nathanson went back to the City Desk.

Keogh went into Hickey's office with Hickey and Wilson in pursuit.

"How do you gents read it?" Keogh asked.

"It could be a grandstand play," Wilson answered.

"What do you mean?" Keogh asked sharply.

Hickey interrupted: "I think Ed means that this may be a way of getting national sympathy on his side."

"It will," answered Keogh, "but what are his chances of pulling it off?"

"There is every chance he will get his head blown off."

"You think so?" he asked Hickey.

"Well, for starters, Ambassador Trumbull is the man, if you remember, when he was Senator, who was responsible for Del Vecchio having to take off. There were rumors that Trumbull was mixed up in the whole scandal, but Trumbull turned the tables and proved that Del Vecchio was a villain. If Del Vecchio survives the whole thing, Trumbull will have him locked up if he gets out of this alive. It's hard to understand what Del Vecchio is doing. He can't win either way."

"Anyway, we're going to get good coverage?" Keogh wanted reassurance. "You say McGavin is the best?"

"I didn't say so, the City Editor said so. I don't know the man," Wilson said.

"Well, you should," Keogh said curtly. He turned on his heel and left for his house in Carson Beach. John Hickey watched Edward Wilson's eyes blaze silently with anger at the way Keogh had cut him dead.

Late that night, Hickey called Rose Keogh at her home in Virginia.

"You know, Rose, I think we're about to get an ally."

"Really, darling? Who?"

"Mr. Edward Wilson."

"You silly darling, you shouldn't underestimate your Rose. He's been with us all along."

Hickey never ceased to be amazed at the frail, beautiful lady whose body he so cherished.

Chapter

15

AMBASSADOR CABOT TRUMBULL sat drained. He was at his big oak desk in his office in the majestic U.S. Embassy inside the beleaguered compound. His normally crisp linen suit was crumpled and sweat-stained. He had removed his silk tie. His thick thatch of white hair lay in an unruly mop. He hadn't slept. He had been in constant contact with the State Department and President Rawlins on the telephone, a privilege allowed by Comandante Soares and his men for the sake of negotiating.

The responses from President Rawlins had infuriated the Ambassador. He had committed himself totally to getting Rawlins elected twice, and the only response he could get from the President sounded as if it were being read from a press handout.

The siege was now seven hours old. The terrorists had set a forty-eight-hour deadline on their demands. And all he could get from President Rawlins was "We are pursuing every conceivable course to ensure that you, your family and the three hundred other American hostages will not be harmed." At one stage Trumbull had felt like screaming when the President said in a monotone, "Just one hour ago on network television I led the nation in prayer for a solution." Trumbull at first had been formal, but in the last conversation he had cursed the President for his lack of gratitude for all he had done for him.

From then on President Rawlins had referred Ambassador Cabot Trumbull's calls to his chief aide, Benson George. Trumbull felt that he had been deserted. He looked with horror at the clock on his desk which ticked away the minutes of his life.

Two armed guards stepped aside as the big white doors to the office snapped open. The visitor was Comandante Enrique Soares. He was a short man with massive shoulders, an almost hairless crew cut and a formal, clipped manner. He looked more like a product of West Point, which he once had been, than a product of the hills of neighboring Costa Real. His manner was calm and polite.

Trumbull was desperate as he spoke. Soares had not yet sat down at the desk when Trumbull, speaking in formal Spanish said, "Señor Comandante, you must know that this action of yours is one of suicide. If you kill us all, do you really believe you will escape unharmed? Your families will be hunted and you will be shot down like dogs. This will accomplish nothing. Surely you have made your point."

Soares lit a thin cigar and waved his hand. "We undertake no action, Señor Ambassador, without knowing the consequences . . . but you are wasting your breath. I believe Señor Benson George, your President's spokesman, is on the line. He wishes to speak to you again. If you pick up the telephone, my man on the switchboard will put you through. If you wish, I will leave you in private."

Trumbull shook his head in a frantic signal to show respect and motioned him to stay as he grabbed for the telephone.

"Hello . . . hello . . . hello . . . Benson? For God's sake, man, what's happening? There are women and children here whose lives depend on you bunch of bastards up there. . . . No . . . no . . . nobody's been hurt. But these men will carry out their threats, damn it. Doesn't anyone realize this?"

He fell silent for thirty seconds. Then an incredulous look crossed his face.

"What? Are you mad? Is that the best you can do? Send in a gangster we all ran out of the country to negotiate for our lives?"

He fell silent for a long minute. Then he spoke. "They won't listen. . . . You're condemning us to death. You know that . . . you know that."

The phone went dead. Ambassador Trumbull slammed down the telephone with vicious force.

The face of Comandante Soares remained impassive.

"Del Vecchio," Trumbull gasped. "They're sending Robert Del Vecchio here. Madness. Have you agreed to this?"

"I have agreed to nothing. Señor Del Vecchio will be allowed into the compound. I will speak to him. I know much of him. He is a capitalistic hoodlum. But I will speak."

Trumbull appeared to be on the verge of breaking. "They're wasting time. Can't you see we are all being used? You and I. Del Vecchio can't speak for a country that disowns him."

"I fear I agree with you. I am sorry. Can I do anything to make you more comfortable? Your family are well. They are in their house. Coffee?" Without waiting for a reply, he poured the thick black coffee.

Trumbull had a sudden thought. "Is he here to offer you money? If it's money, I know I can get money from our government. Is it money?"

Soares shook his head slowly. "Not money, but freedom for our compatriots."

Soares drank his coffee, snapped to his feet and marched out the door without another word.

Trumbull's head slumped on his folded arms. President Rawlins had deserted him. He had sent in his single worst enemy to bargain for his life. He was as good as dead. Damn you, Rawlins—after what I have done for you, you pompous, God-boxing bastard!

Outside the Embassy building, the compound was deserted, save for the ominous presence of the heavily armed terrorists. All families had been confined to their houses. Food supplies to the families were carried from the supermarkets into the homes. Apart from the terrorists, the compound looked like a sumptuous ghost town.

Overhead and outside the compound, the contrast was dramatic. The skies around the perimeter were filled with U.S. helicopter gunships and gunships of the Puerto Bravan National Guard. They circled like scavengers, careful not to get too close to the siege below lest they trigger an overt act, but close enough to observe every single movement inside.

The United States and the world were taking the threat very seriously. Headlines screamed the bold siege across six continents. There had never been a standoff like this one since the Cuban missile crisis.

Senator Sean Keogh and the staff of the *Boston Clarion* read every single word that spurted over the wires. John Hickey, mystified but suspicious of Del Vecchio's move, relayed every development by telephone to Rose and her son, Terrence, who were closeted in McLean, Virginia.

Outside the compound, the road leading to the Embassy gates looked like a movie location for a war film. Armored personnel carriers, tanks, ambulances, fire trucks and paramedic units crowded in a chaotic jam that could have been produced only by a Central American republic unused to any form of organization.

Wandering through the armada was a massive battalion of the world press. Barricades had been set up by the National Guard one hundred yards from the Embassy gates. The newsmen, hundreds of them, had interviewed everyone in sight and taken thousands of feet of film. Most of them were now driven to interviewing peddlers who had set up makeshift beer and rum stands to cater to the listless but tense crowd. All civilians except the peddlers had been kept out by another barrier farther down the road. Danny Cahill of the *News* had just about written himself out. There was nothing more to say or do but wait for the balloon to go up. It was nerve-racking. Mike McGavin had made a quick reconnaissance of the area, gathered a color story and headed back to town to a telephone to file his story.

Suddenly the press corps turned their heads as one as the tense boredom was broken by the stream of police sirens. Coming up the road fast

were two uniformed motorcycle cops, looking sinister in their black outfits and sunglasses. They weaved through the crowd of newsmen who
automatically took pictures without knowing what significance the presence of the cops held. The cops zoomed up to the barrier set up by the
National Guard. Newsmen were held at bay while the cops handed some
communication to the colonel in charge. The cops then got on their
bikes and disappeared down the paved road. Seconds later they returned, this time flanking a four-wheel-drive vehicle.

As the newsmen converged to block their way, the guardsmen pushed
them aside with batons and rifles to make a path. The four-by-four
swept toward them. The photographers positioned themselves. It was a
Soviet-made Volga, one newsman noted. Then two tiny flags of Cuba
could be seen fluttering on either side of the vehicle. A small notation ·
on the side read DELEGACION DE CUBA.

Before the newsmen could burst through the human barricade of
National Guardsmen, the Cuban vehicle had pulled to a halt inside the
barrier. It was hard to see, but it looked as if the bearded driver wearing
Castro fatigues had handed over his side arm and taken back what
appeared to be an envelope or a telegram.

Ten minutes passed, and then the guardsmen searched the driver and
a man riding in the rear. They were then waved toward the Embassy
gate. Once there, the occupants of the jeep were subjected to the same
search routine by the terrorists. Then they disappeared inside. The
four-by-four, moving at a walking pace, was then escorted on foot by the
terrorists to the Embassy building itself. Those outside with binoculars
could see the two men from the Cuban vehicle moving inside.

Inside the large vestibule, Comandante Soares appeared from an office. His heels clicked on the cool marble floor with military precision.
An aide handed him a telegram as the two bearded Cubans stood to
attention. Soares ripped open the telegram. He barked a command in
Spanish. The smaller Cuban replied.

Then the taller one pulled off his cap. Mike McGavin's hand shook as
he peeled off a false beard.

"*No hablo español,*" he said, his voice quivering. As he talked, Juan
Villas also removed his cap and beard. Villas tried to stop his teeth from
chattering.

Soares spoke, his tone belying the rage in his eyes: "I speak English,
whoever you are, and you had better speak English pretty fast before
you are shot where you stand."

Mike McGavin, looking ridiculous with parts of the beard still pasted
to his face, battled to control his speech and his bowels.

"Your Honor . . . I mean . . . sir . . . señor," McGavin stammered, "I am a newspaperman. Mike McGavin, *Boston Clarion.* This is Juan Villas; he is also a newspaperman."

Soares seemed to be having a difficult job controlling his temper.

"Well, Mr. whatever-your-name-is . . . how do I know this? . . . Where are your credentials? How do I know who you are? How do I know you are not a CIA man?"

"Sir, señor, obviously I couldn't have credentials on me. I was searched by both National Guardsmen and the terro—I mean your men."

"And you gained entrance with this feeble trick." Soares held the telegram bearing a Cuban seal. He crushed it in his hand. "Mr. Newspaperman, you and your friend have landed yourselves in serious trouble."

"It is just that as Mr. Del Vecchio is arriving . . . surely you would require an accurate account of what happens here. So that there will be no lies told by the Western press."

"You are making a feeble attempt at rationalizing this outrage." Just then the clatter of a helicopter could be heard overhead. Soares barked an order. A guard looked outside the door. It was a huge silver helicopter which had just set down in a storm of dust right outside the Embassy. Soares barked a question, and the answer in Spanish told McGavin that Del Vecchio had arrived. Soares snapped his fingers and four guards moved closer to McGavin and Villas, their automatic weapons pressed against their throats. McGavin tried to remember the prayers he had been taught at Our Lady of Angels. His memory failed him.

Minutes later Soares reappeared leading a phalanx of armed men. In the middle was the tall, calm presence of Robert Del Vecchio. Behind him was a big man, a handsome man: Alberto Morales. Del Vecchio looked curiously at the pair standing with guns at their throats. Soares turned to Del Vecchio, surveying the scene.

"Two of your resourceful newsmen from the capitalistic press, Señor Del Vecchio. Their resourcefulness could cost them their brains."

Del Vecchio looked at them with slow eyes. He said nothing. Soares barked another command, and McGavin and Villas were dragged off to the side. A door to what looked like a library opened. They were hurled inside. The door clicked behind them just as McGavin saw Del Vecchio disappearing into the office of Ambassador Trumbull.

The windows of the library were shut; the telephone wires had been ripped from the walls. There was no air conditioning, and the atmosphere was stifling. Guards peered through the windows at their catch like keepers in a zoo. The furniture had been removed. The two men sat on the floor. They were silent for a long time.

McGavin spoke. "I'm sorry, Juan—sorry, pal. It was a fucking crazy idea." He put a reassuring hand on Villas' outstretched leg as they sat on the floor. Villas felt McGavin's hand shaking. He managed a weak smile. Then he bit his lip. McGavin silently cursed himself. Crazy fool. This sort of bullshit worked in Chicago, but not with this insane bunch of animals. He had often been faced with problems and risks, but not the risk of losing his life. Now there would be no story . . . and maybe no nothing.

They waited silently and waited some more. Two hours, three hours, McGavin guessed. Then he lost track of time. Darkness fell, and the lights had been disconnected. It made them feel worse. Every tiny noise outside made their hearts leap. How would it come? An explosion and rattle of crazed gunfire? A fire? God, please, don't let it be a fire, McGavin thought.

Suddenly the subdued conversational tones they heard from time to time outside grew to a loud chatter. McGavin wanted to move his bowels and vomit at the same time. This wasn't like fighting in Vietnam. This was the death of a thousand cuts. This could be it. He prayed silently, then aloud. Villas prayed alongside him.

The door swung open and the light blinded them. A command in Spanish got Villas to his feet. McGavin obeyed in panic. They were motioned through the door. McGavin couldn't quite feel himself walking. He was, but he couldn't feel it. The scowls on the terrorists' faces didn't help.

They were ushered into an office next to that of Ambassador Trumbull. Inside, the air conditioning was working. It was beautiful. Sitting around a large desk were Soares and six of his men. On the other side sat Del Vecchio and Morales. They seemed realxed. Had Del Vecchio sold them out?

"Gentlemen, I'm sorry for this inconvenience," drawled Del Vecchio, "but Mr. Soares can be excused if he felt your intrusion was arrogant. There are two sides to every story. We have talked now for eight hours. We have reached an agreement of sorts which guarantees your safety and that of the staff and their dependents. As you are the only representatives here at this moment, you are free to ask questions within the limitations imposed on you by Comandante Soares. There are some things I can say, some things I can't."

McGavin looked at the clock. It was six in the morning. Eight in the morning Boston time. He was alive. He found words difficult. He was still frightened it might be a terrible hoax.

"Is it over, Señor . . . Comandante Soares?"

Soares chose his words carefully. "The people's struggle . . ." he began.

Suddenly McGavin found he was without paper or pencil. Morales picked up a legal note pad and extracted a gold ball-point pen from the top of his shirt pocket. Soares waited and started again.

"The people's struggle will never be over, Mr., er . . ."

"McGavin," Mike answered. "Sir, are you letting us all go?"

"In time, in time."

"Will you surrender yourselves to the authorities?"

"No, we will not, but I don't wish to talk about that. I do not surrender my men . . . Shall we say the following. While the freedom of our patriots in imperialistic jails will always be our main concern, other concerns have arisen, points raised by Señor Del Vecchio."

"Which were?" McGavin was regaining his confidence.

"Señor Del Vecchio employs twelve thousand of my people, mostly campesinos. Señor Del Vecchio has made a case that if we were to take action, he would withdraw from Costa Real, thus leaving them to starve, as has happened to many under the brutal regime of Costa Real. If we were to execute him here, roughly the same thing would happen."

"I might add," drawled Del Vecchio in a voice so lazy it sounded as if he had just gotten out of bed, "I have guaranteed to employ on my coffee plantation and in my cornfields an additional two thousand peasants to be nominated by an emissary of Comandante Soares."

McGavin interrupted and looked at Soares. "Sir, what guarantees have you that Mr. Del Vecchio will keep his word?"

"He has little choice. You saw how easily we took a United States armed compound without shedding a drop of blood. To take the life of Mr. Del Vecchio would be a simple matter. The lives of him and his family."

"Sir . . ."

"Enough questions, Mr. . . . er . . . enough questions. There are still some details to work out."

"One last thing, sir. Could I get a picture of this group?"

Del Vecchio looked at Soares. Soares donned sunglasses as did his cohort, and then a combat helmet.

"I have no wish to advertise my face. Make it quick," he said curtly.

McGavin suddenly remembered: "Damn, the camera is still in our four-by-four." There was a flurry of commands, and the camera, in full working order, was provided. McGavin started to take the picture, but his hand was shaking too much with the excitement of the moment. He handed the camera to Villas and stepped into the picture himself to prove to his editors he was really there and hadn't been taking LSD.

Seconds later, Soares stood up.

"Now, gentlemen, goodbye. No, no thank you, no handshakes. I'm not of your kind. You will all be taken with Mr. Del Vecchio to another office. There the telephone is connected, but only for incoming calls. You will wait in the office one hour. You will receive a call. You will wait another five minutes and then leave the office. I will leave it up to you, Mr. Del Vecchio, to inform the Ambassador. Should you venture outside the room before the call comes, I give you my solemn word, you will be shot dead. That's all."

The guards hustled Del Vecchio, Morales, McGavin and Villas into a nearby office. It was air-conditioned. McGavin could feel himself gasping for breath with the prospect of the exclusive.

The door slammed behind them. Del Vecchio and Morales offered them both cigarettes. Neither man could hold a light, they were so keyed up.

McGavin now peppered Del Vecchio with questions. He drawled his answers.

"What happens now?"

"I would presume, Mr. McGavin, that they are making their escape."

"Do you think we're safe?"

"As long as we don't step outside that door until we get the telephone call."

"Do you think the authorities will try to extradite you from here?"

"I doubt it—but they won't have the chance."

McGavin pumped Del Vecchio mercilessly about his exile, the swindle, everything he could think of. Del Vecchio waved the questions aside. "Just let's concentrate on staying alive. That will come later." Juan Villas took more pictures.

Del Vecchio had never been interviewed before. McGavin had interviewed him with an exclusivity that would be hard for his City Editor to believe.

At 7:30 A.M. exactly, the telephone rang in the office. Del Vecchio picked it up. "Yes, okay. Five more minutes. Certainly."

Del Vecchio turned to the others. "Not a move yet. Five more minutes. Let's make it ten for sure," he said back into the mouthpiece. "Okay."

"Mr. Del Vecchio, after the ten minutes are up, will this telephone be operable to the outside world?"

"Presumably, I don't know."

"Well, I want you to do me a favor. I want to dictate my story to Boston, then together with you interview some of the people who are still inside their houses. You will be like the liberating army of General MacArthur—that sort of thing."

"What do you mean?" Del Vecchio said with a smile.

"Well I want to get you with them before the rest of the press know about Soares' departure."

"You mean a scoop," Del Vecchio said with a smile. "Shoot!"

"Thanks."

Ten minutes later McGavin picked up the telephone and got through to Boston without hardly a minute's wait.

"City Desk, please," McGavin looked anxiously at Del Vecchio and Morales. They still had the keys to Ambassador Trumbull's office. He was not aware of what had taken place outside his confines; his telephone line had been disconnected.

"Barry Nathanson, please. McGavin. Urgent."

Nathanson's voice barked down the telephone: "McGavin. Where the fuck you been? What about the Cubans going in there? We had to run a wire story and pix. You were nowhere."

"Barry, now listen. I'm not drunk. Just listen. I don't want anyone else to take this copy, just you. I don't want it to leak out. How long before the next edition?"

"Twenty minutes, you fucking idiot."

"All right, Barry. The siege is over. I am in the compound with Del Vecchio. He has made a deal with Soares. Soares is gone. The picture of the Cubans was a picture of me and Villas driving a Russian Jeep; that's how we got in. I have the story of the century. And nobody even knows it's over. Now don't talk. I'm dictating now. . . .

"Fugitive financier Robert Del Vecchio today successfully negotiated the end of the siege of Puerto Bravo, freeing three hundred Americans from the hands of a gang of left-wing terrorists.

"Freedom for the three hundred hostages, including U.S. Ambassador Cabot Trumbull, came at eleven thirty A.M. after Del Vecchio made a deal with the terrorist leader, Comandante Enrique Soares.

"It climaxed a tense twenty-four-hour cliff-hanger in which I and colleague Juan Villas were held captive inside the compound for eight hours. . . ."

At the revelations in each paragraph, the veteran City Editor gasped. And so far not a word to the outside world.

After taking down the story, Nathanson was drained. "Holy hell, man, you'll get a Pulitzer for this . . . I can't believe it."

"Also, we have pictures of the whole crew. Juan will be sending them up to you by satellite. I will refile in one hour."

McGavin felt like screaming for joy.

Del Vecchio smiled. "Well, have you stopped holding us hostage?"

"Yeah. Now let's get the Ambassador free. Ready with the camera, Juan?

They opened the door with their key. Ashen-faced, Trumbull sat silently in the chair. Hurriedly McGavin explained his presence; then he dashed out with Del Vecchio for some freedom pictures.

Del Vecchio looked apprehensively at McGavin. "Let's make this quick. Morales and I have to get on that big bird soon, just in case Ambassador Trumbull changes his mind."

"He didn't say a word when you told him the news."

"He knew already. He's a beaten man and he knows it."

In the next five minutes Del Vecchio broke the news to the Marine guard, who had still been in ignorance behind closed doors. No one had noticed that the rebels had left as silently and as efficiently as they had arrived, leaving their arms and uniforms behind and melting into the surrounding mountains which they knew so well.

The Marine sergeant found it hard to believe Del Vecchio's words. He stood to attention and saluted and said something that made Del Vecchio feel like bursting out laughing: "Sir, your country is indebted. You are a brave, brave man. As a representative of the United States I thank you from the bottom of my heart for your self-sacrificing courage."

Del Vecchio turned away to smile. It was the same government that was trying to put him in jail for life. The Marine then said something about securing the gate and "effecting an orderly transmission to normality."

McGavin was pleased. He would keep out the other newspapers for at least another hour.

They walked outside into the eerily silent compound. The others had not been informed.

Del Vecchio looked anxious. He motioned to Morales, who was waiting in the street, and said, "Let's get going." Without a word, Morales took the controls of the 'copter, and Del Vecchio jumped aboard. Villas took pictures of the helicopter that had brought mercy flying into the open skies.

"C'mon, Juan," McGavin said. "Back to the Ambassador before the rest of them get here. Sergeant, may we go with you to the Ambassador's office?"

"Sure, sir. Er, who are you people?"

"We came from Costa Real with Mr. Del Vecchio."

Villas took McGavin aside and asked, "Why did he take off? What happened to the big victory celebration?"

"Trumbull, the Ambassador. He was the one who got him indicted and got Rawlins in for two terms when he was in the Senate. This was a helluva blow—the old man's ego being saved by the guy he'd called a thieving sonofabitch. Didn't trust him. Maybe I don't blame him."

The reporters outside the compound trained klieg lights on the helicopter and got their last shots. McGavin relished their defeat.

They trotted up to the Ambassador's office. He knew what would happen. Trumbull would have them thrown out. He didn't want anyone

to rub it in, particularly the press. It was going to be bad enough as it
was. The *Boston Clarion* was only minutes away from putting on the
street in huge headlines, FUGITIVE FINANCIER SAVES 300 YANKS.

"Get your camera ready before this asshole Marine throws us in the
street."

The Marine strode through the door.

"Sonofabitch. Jesus."

Ambassador Trumbull was sprawled backward in his chair, his head
grotesquely to one side. A small bullet hole could just be seen on his
right temple. It was worse on the other side of his head, where the
.22-caliber bullet had come out.

"My God, he's been murdered! Those bastards killed him!" the Marine gasped. He walked closer. The circumstances proved sadder. The
tiny pistol hung by its trigger guard from a crooked index finger.

McGavin flashed a look at Villas. Villas clicked off several shots of the
macabre scene. The Marine sergeant hadn't noticed yet. But McGavin
did notice the immaculately handwritten note that lay neatly on the dead
man's desk. It was a suicide note of the most mammoth proportions.

> Since by the time this note reaches the Congress of the United States,
> Robert Del Vecchio will have gained admittance back into the country, I
> find there is no other way. I have served my country the best way I knew,
> although my zeal sometimes interfered with my judgment. . . .

It was a chapter-and-verse admission of his part in the entire mutual-
funds fraud and how he had sought to frame Del Vecchio. It revealed
account numbers and the names of five current Senators who were
involved in the fraud, including a member of the Senate Banking
Committee. McGavin couldn't read all of the single-spaced, elegantly
written note on the legal pad, but he knew what it was and knew it was
explosive.

Villas needed no prompting. As the Marine sergeant knelt down beside the desk, careful to touch nothing, Villas leaned over and clicked
off a close frame of the sheet.

This time the sergeant heard the camera. He looked up with black
rage. "You sonsofbitches . . . you're fucking newsmen. . . ."

He lunged at the camera, but Villas was too quick for him. He swung
at McGavin, catching him flush on the cheek. Never had such a blow felt
so good. This was one Marine who wouldn't let another newsman within
a bull's roar of this scene.

McGavin scrambled to his feet and raced after Villas. He could hear
the sergeant yelling "Guard!" but there were no guards. If the sergeant

hadn't been disarmed in the takeover, McGavin was sure he would have shot at them.

They bounded into the street, where some of the dependents had now cautiously dribbled out of their homes, not quite sure what was happening. Then the National Guardsmen outside the barrier noticed the activity. They cautiously ventured inside. When there was no gunfire, they approached the Embassy building.

McGavin and Villas made it to the four-by-four. They quickly ripped off the Cuban flags and pulled down the canopy of the vehicle to expose themselves lest a trigger-happy guardsman wanted to be a hero. But as the seconds fled, the entire compound had burst into the street.

There were still good pictures to be had, but McGavin decided to let the wire services handle them. He had an exclusive beyond his dreams. The terrorists. Del Vecchio with them. Del Vecchio announcing to the sergeant that the siege was over, and the suicide of the Ambassador.

Villas gunned the vehicle as the horde of newsman swarmed into the compound. Those who recognized it looked on with curiosity; those who recognized McGavin looked on as if they had very bad pains under their hearts. They had been taken—conned and beaten in the world's worst way.

As the Volga slid through the gates, McGavin saw some faces he remembered from his days as a copyreader on the wire desk of *The New York Times.* He just allowed himself one indulgence: "Yahoooo!"

Within fifteen minutes he filed the second sensational scoop, and within half an hour Juan Villas had transmitted the exclusive pictures.

Back in Boston, the old City Editor, Barry Nathanson, just looked at what lay in front of him. "Sonofabitch . . . sonofabitch . . . we won fucking big, man!" He was talking to no one in particular.

That night after McGavin had mopped up some minor angles, he got monumentally drunk with Juan Villas. When he boarded the plane to New York, he wanted to wrap Villas up and take him along.

At the airport, McGavin was spare with his words. "Wish we could do it again, you prick."

"Next time, Gringo. Next time."

McGavin stayed drunk on the plane. When it arrived at Kennedy, he caught a taxi to Costello's. When he staggered in, Freddie, as was his custom, honked an old taxi horn. McGavin was still drunk. The other journalists greeted him with smiles and slaps on the back. As drunk as he was, he knew they would all have liked to see him fall down a manhole. Never had anyone so completely scooped the world on such a story.

WHILE THE *Boston Clarion* hit record sales through Boston and while other newspapers were forced to buy or steal the thunderbolt exclusive, Senator Sean Keogh was heading toward Washington. Roger Sharpe sat silently in the plane next to him. Sharpe was uneasy. He knew exactly what the Senator was about to do. Sharpe had said only one thing: "Not now, Sean; don't do it just now. Wait, please. You will turn the Senate against you. It's a gentlemen's club. Don't do it."

Sean Keogh looked at him and smiled. "I consider myself a gentleman, Roger. I consider you a gentleman, so we could always be in the same club. But the Senate are not the kind of gentlemen I like."

The Senator indulged himself only as far as to say how proud he was of the reporter who had pulled off the scoop of the century. This made Woodward and Bernstein look like small beer. President Rawlins didn't know which way to turn; half the financial community was in an uproar; the Justice Department was already prepared for a long list of resignations and some members of the Securities and Exchange Commission simply prepared to leave the country.

Senator Keogh and Roger Sharpe spent what was left of that night at Keogh's Watergate apartment. As he sipped a single Scotch and water with Sharpe before going to bed, Keogh said, "Tomorrow you will see something that may shock your sensitivities, Roger . . . but that old sonofabitch Del Vecchio showed them, showed the lot of them—the bunch of well-dressed, suspender-wearing crooks. Let nobody ever look down their noses at my past again, Roger—never."

"I understand, Sean, but it's a bad tactical move. I've said it twice—that's all."

"That's right, Roger, you said it twice. Good night."

In the morning, Keogh waited until the last minute before going onto the Senate floor. The breakfast hangouts, the lobbies and the hallways that morning were electric. There was only one conversation. Puerto Bravo and Del Vecchio. Everybody had read the copies of the *Clarion* that had been flown to Washington. But the club decided to push on as if nothing had happened. The Senate was five minutes into its procedural routine when Senator Keogh, a man noted for his low profile on the floor, swept in. Nobody could remember anything like what followed in the history of the Senate.

"Gentlemen, before I apologize for this departure from my customary behavior, I think we should all be ashamed of ourselves."

There was a hushed silence. In the Visitors' Gallery, Roger Sharpe cringed.

"Gentlemen, in the past twenty-four hours, this country, this world . . ."

The Senate Majority Leader had risen to his feet in a feeble attempt to wave Senator Keogh down. The President pro tem banged his gavel, but Keogh roared on with a resonance and fervor that brought the Senate to silence.

". . . this world, and particularly this country, have been consumed with concern for the safety of three hundred American men, women and children. One man delivered them to safety. One man who present and tragic events have shown was severely wronged by the Justice Department and this very body in which we so proudly sit; one man was responsible for all that. While this body, Republicans and Democrats alike, wrung their hands in unison with the President, one man made it possible for those Americans to be alive today. And right now we are more concerned with the business of procedure than with the real business at hand."

There were a few brave "Hear, hear's" from some of the younger members, but mostly the Senate sat there, as a man, in a collective fume. How dare this thug from South Boston grandstand on this play; how dare this political clown seize the limelight for this one; how dare he put the well-being and livelihood of other Senators in jeopardy? Oh, they would have addressed themselves to the subject. The veteran members would have worked it out among themselves who would propose the bill. They would have worked it out over drinks, like gentlemen. Ronald Harris, the Republican Senator from California and former nighttime talk-show host, glowered silently in rage. He gritted his teeth as he watched the crude masterstroke and cursed his aides for not advising him to get in first. There was still silence, and Senator Keogh refused to let them get their breath.

"Robert Del Vecchio is a man who has been cruelly cast into exile by hearsay, in much the same way people were burned in Salem, and this august body had much to do with that. History will show for what end."

Dozens of temples pounded with rage.

"I, from the floor here now would expect that a bill be expeditiously passed by both houses allowing Mr. Del Vecchio to return here without any further threat to himself or his freedom. While this body is not empowered to administer the law, I would also hope that the Justice Department would very quickly review its case against Mr. Del Vecchio and promptly take a closer look at allegations that have been made through a signed document by the late and respected Ambassador Trumbull. That's all I have to say. Gentlemen, I only ask your indulgence for the rather unusual way I have presented what every fair-minded American man and woman is thinking today. It is Robert Del Vecchio whose name is on their lips . . . not the Senate."

He strode from the chamber.

The hallways were a cavalry charge as a phalanx of reporters from radio, print and television mobbed him like a gaggle of geese. Senator Keogh didn't miss a beat as the klieg lights blazed on him. "Here we have a genuine homegrown hero; a hero whom the man in the street, the woman in the house would want to personally thank; a man who has been greatly wronged. Not only he, but his family also.

"We gave a hero's welcome to MacArthur. . . . Well, I want to go on the record as saying I'm planning a hero's welcome for Robert Del Vecchio, a man who risked his life to save others."

The questions rose to a roar. Other Senators, of both parties, who had dribbled into the hallway, stood pathetically alone and watched with rage. The questions rained eternally, with Keogh skillfully turning each answer into a brisk campaign speech.

Squashed against the wall, Roger Sharpe stood and watched quietly. He smiled in wonderment and thought, The very first time I met him, he proved to me I was wrong. This is the next President of the United States and I'm proud to be a part of his career.

When Keogh and Sharpe finally struggled back to the Watergate Apartments and took the telephone off the hook, Senator Keogh smiled. "I hadn't shown my old Southie style for a coupla decades . . . it was long overdue."

Roger returned the smile. "The party is going to hate your guts. But then, you know, Mr. President . . . nobody likes a loser . . . but then again, everyone hates a winner."

Senator Sean Keogh took a long look at Roger Sharpe. He had liked Sharpe since the day he met him, Boston Common and all. Sharpe was not like Bernie McLaughlin, or Frankie Burke, or Eddie Wilson. They were . . . well, he *loved* them; they were his. But he liked Roger Sharpe, and he took the compliment with silent respect and humility. He would have liked to have been on the street with Sharpe; he was, as they said in Southie, stand-up. It was a wordless emotional moment.

Senator Keogh cleared his throat. He changed the subject.

"I think I'd better invite this young man Mike McGavin down to see me."

"He's got to be some sort of genius."

"Have you ever met him?"

"Not in person; know him by sight. Pretty wild boy."

"What do you know about him?"

"Used to drive a taxi in Chicago . . . that's all."

Keogh sighed. "Mary Mother of God, don't you get tired of being surrounded by Irish Catholics?"

"In the Democratic Party, the Jews used to say it was an occupational hazard. The face of the Republican Party has changed. It's an occupational hazard for Republican Jews and Republican WASPs. One of these days it might even be an occupational hazard for blacks too."

"Blacks?"

"Yes, blacks."

"You know, Roger, I never thought of that. We're pretty damn insular in Southie, aren't we?"

"Sometimes."

"Now, about this madman taxi-driver–reporter called McGavin. Would you mind tracking him down for me, Roger? Something tells me I owe him a few bucks or a favor or a promotion or some damn thing. I'm going into the bedroom and watch the television news. Damn it, what a lie! I'm going to watch how I just got twenty million dollars' worth of free air time. I must be becoming a politician; I'm lying to my friends."

They smiled.

Ten minutes later, Roger Sharpe called from the living room. "I think I've got him . . . but Sean . . . to be fair . . . he's celebrating. I think it's a bar. Costello's in New York."

"Damn it, I'd be celebrating too."

Sharpe handed the telephone to Keogh.

"Senator Keogh here. Is this Mr. McGavin?"

"Yeah, it's McGavin. Don't bother calling; I just fired Keogh." His words were slurry.

"Mike, this is Senator Sean Keogh. Are you conscious?"

McGavin laughed and turned to the audience at the bar. "That fucking Brian Wood from *London Express* is doing it again," he shouted. "This time he's Senator Sean Keogh."

He turned back to the telephone. "Listen, Brian, come on have a drink. I'm buying. That mean bastard up in Boston has to give me a few bucks on my expense account. Come on down."

Keogh smiled as he spoke. "Listen, young man, if you don't come to your senses very quickly you will have a few bucks in your severance pay. This is Sean Keogh."

McGavin broke out in a cold sweat. Oh, my God, how could I be so close to the top and fuck it up by abusing the boss . . . and drunk?

"Mr. Keogh . . . Senator . . . my profound apologies. You know there's always someone playing practical jokes. I apologize. I really apologize."

"Accepted, young man. I think you did a fine job for us. Now why don't you sober up? Catch a shuttle down to Washington, see me in my office in two hours—about six P.M.—and I would like to have dinner with you. In other words, the mean bastard up in Boston is going to buy you dinner. Got it straight?"

"Yes, sir. Yes, sir, Senator."

Keogh chuckled as he replaced the receiver. "You told me he was a wild sonofagun."

McGavin was panicked. He hadn't shaved or showered in two days. He had nothing to wear, and what's more, he had no money apart from his signing privileges in Costello's.

He went to Mick the photographer and borrowed two hundred dollars. He bought himself the first dark suit he saw that fitted him, showered at Mick's place, then caught the shuttle on his American Express card down to Washington. When he arrived at the Senate Office Building in a taxi, he had a dollar fifty left in his pocket.

The secretary ushered him into Senator Keogh's wood-paneled office. McGavin had seen Keogh many times but never spoken to him. He was clearly nervous. This was his week for nerves.

Senator Keogh stood up with a genuinely friendly smile. So did Roger Sharpe. McGavin towered over both of them, both tall men.

"So you're the mad Irish taxi-driving reporter from Chicago. God, I can smell the booze from here. Good to see you, Mike. Celebrating? Who wouldn't?"

McGavin smiled sheepishly. He was not always so reticent.

"Well, you've covered yourself with glory. This is Roger Sharpe. Did you really disguise yourselves as Cubans to get in? You were captured?"

"Yes, sir," McGavin said evenly, "as I said in the story and as the photographs bore out." McGavin thought he was being tested. Don't fuck with my profession, he thought.

"Well, look: as you know, today has been busy for me. Keep a low profile; otherwise it will be busy for you, and you will have people like yourself hounding you if they know you're in town—particularly this town. They're such a bunch of second-rate failures, they think success is being close to someone who is successful."

"Maybe I got lucky, Senator," he said respectfully and with humility.

"Yes, and so did I," Keogh said. "Now, look: see my secretary. She'll fix you up with a hotel and some expenses from the mean bastard in Boston. Now go to your hotel and take another shower, brush your teeth, wash your hair and see us at the Sans Souci at eight thirty P.M. Roger, why don't you help out? Come to dinner, Roger? Good. My wife and son will be there tonight too."

McGavin shook hands politely and walked outside with Roger Sharpe.

Above all sensibilities, Mike McGavin, drunk or sober, had instincts.

He liked this man Senator Keogh. He liked him a lot. He didn't know Roger Sharpe, but he liked him too. He felt relaxed. Hell, he didn't feel relaxed; he felt on top of the world.

"The Senator . . ." Mike began.

"Yes—the Senator?"

"Well, he's a regular guy, isn't he?"

"He's human, you know, and what's more, he's only ten years older than you. What did you expect—some old guy with a cane? No, Sean Keogh is one of the all-time regular guys. Hey, listen, let's get you to a hotel, clean up and we'll have a drink before going to dinner."

McGavin chuckled candidly. "You know, this is the second time today I've cleaned up."

"You probably need it. Seriously, you did a heck of a job."

"Thanks, Mr. Sharpe."

"Roger."

"Thanks, Roger."

Sharpe took him to a generous-sized room in the Mayflower Hotel. At seven fifteen they met for a drink in the lobby bar. They watched a segment of the news together. It was all Sean Keogh.

When they walked in, five minutes early, at the Sans Souci, they were surprised to see Senator Keogh, his wife, and their son, Terrence, already at their table. McGavin was feeling more confident now. Now he was himself. His charming self.

"My wife, Mrs. Keogh, and my son, Terrence—Mike McGavin," Keogh said. McGavin had heard about his blind son. He held out his hand and was amazed that Terrence found it as if he had eyes. Terrence had a very pleasant, breezy manner.

"Ah, the Hildy Johnson of my father's paper," Terrence quipped.

"At least until tomorrow, Terrence," Mike said. "I was good yesterday, but they're not selling yesterday's newspapers today . . . unfortunately."

McGavin noticed Rose Keogh above everyone else. He was smart enough not to show it. She had a quiet intensity that intrigued him. She was extremely attractive even for a politician's wife. Not pretty, but attractive and very feminine. She had an easy way of talking and seemed genuinely interested in his exploits. As McGavin retold the story of Puerto Bravo, everyone fell silent. Those at the table were fascinated, and nobody wanted to take a second away from McGavin's storytelling.

When their dinner orders had been taken, Rose Keogh asked simply, "What kind of a man is Del Vecchio, Mike?"

"Nerves of steel, Mrs. Keogh. There we were in a crisis. Frankly, I thought we were going to die. Mr. Del Vecchio and a man named Alberto Morales, they looked like they were on vacation. Both men have a

quiet air of confidence. They don't ram it down your throat. They're
. . . well, they're just there."

Terrence's dark glasses looked straight into McGavin's eyes. McGavin
had forgotten this boy was blind.

"Mike, is he an intelligent type of person?"

"I really can't say. It just seems that he's in charge. He's a very in-
charge-type guy without having to shout or pound the desk."

"He seems very interesting," Rose offered.

"He saved my life, Mrs. Keogh," McGavin said sincerely.

Neither Keogh nor Sharpe had said a word during the conversation.

"Well, Mike, you heard about today in the Senate. I'm making no
bones about it. I think he should be a national hero."

"You'd get my vote, Senator."

"Mine too," Terrence said. "He saved Hildy Johnson's life, and Father
has to have men around like Hildy to make money for the paper; otherwise I have bad news. Do you know tuition at Exeter is going up again
next semester?"

Rose seemed to laugh too much at Terrence's small quips. He was a
great guy, Mike thought, but he was no Henny Youngman. McGavin's
natural reporter's instinct observed that all those at the table had talked
to each other that night except Sean Keogh and Terrence Keogh.
And yet there was not the slightest animosity between them—just
distance.

At 1:30 A.M. McGavin finished a cognac and said unself-consciously,
"Senator, I believe I'm drunk all over again." All the others laughed
heartily. They had their share of booze too—except, of course, for Terrence, who was drinking Perrier and lime.

The party broke up as Rose Keogh went to the ladies' room and the
men stood outside waiting for their respective limousines. When Rose
emerged into the fresh air, she looked as dainty as the moment McGavin
had first seen her. He warmly thanked her. He then shook Terrence's
hand, which found his at once. McGavin had formed an undying respect
for the lad. This sixteen-year-old boy had never once made anyone
aware that he was without seeing eyes. This impressed McGavin.

"See you soon, Terrence, I hope."

"Me too. Do you ride?"

"Horses?" Well, no."

"Then I'll teach you."

Senator Keogh said his first words in reference to his son since their
introduction. "He'll embarrass you, Mike; stay clear of him. . . . Oh,
Rose, would you mind going on home with Terrence? I've got an early
day tomorrow. I'll drive back to the Mayflower with Roger and Mike,

and I'll see you for dinner tomorrow night. Is that okay with you, dear? Terrence?"

"Certainly, Father."

"Of course, dear. We have a chauffeur. God, remember the times in Boston when you used to steal Frank Burke's car?"

Senator Keogh looked at her tenderly. It had been so long ago. He looked as if he were about to say something special, but he just said, "I'd sooner forget, my darling, but it will look good for the autobiography. People think we were born rich. Now get along. I'll call you in the morning. Bye, my love." He kissed her. "Bye, Terrence." He slapped him hard on the shoulder. Rose and Terrence Keogh got into the chauffeur-driven limousine.

Once inside the car Rose put thumb and forefinger to her temple and winced in pain. Terrence immediately sensed that something was wrong.

"Headache, Ma?"

"The confounded things never stop. . . . What do you think, Terrence darling?"

"About McGavin? Oh, bright, brash, energetic, highly popular . . . and I think he will become very close to Father. Very close."

Sean Keogh's limousine pulled up in front of the Mayflower. "I think I'll buy you a nightcap," Keogh said warmly.

Sharpe and McGavin got out first, Keogh following. They went into the bar. Keogh and Sharpe ordered Scotch. McGavin smiled. "I'm dying for a beer," he said defenselessly.

It struck Keogh then. He knew why he liked him. God, he reminded him of Frankie Burke! The same kind of shyness to begin with, the same kind of cockiness once he knew his ground. Yes, when he ordered that beer he was trying to impress no one—not me, not Roger, not anyone. He wanted a cold beer. Yes, Frank Burke all over again.

Senator Sean Keogh felt good when his instincts were right.

McGavin gulped lustily at the beer. Keogh tapped his elbow. "Now it's time for business, young Mike."

"Yes, Senator."

"This will take a very short time. A very short time. Within the next two days, Congress will pave the way for Robert Del Vecchio to come back to this country, as they damn well should. What you are about to hear has not been heard by many, so listen closely."

McGavin got serious. "Yes, sir."

"I plan to run for the presidency, and Robert Del Vecchio will run with me."

McGavin gulped. He couldn't believe things like this were said so casually over a bar. Jesus, he was just a reporter, not a Senator's diary.

"Now, Mike, I want you to work for me."

"I do now, sir, in a manner of speaking."

"Now just listen. I want you to work for *me*. Don't ask me why you're so lucky. I want someone with guts, imagination, drive and a touch of the street."

"How would I work for you, Senator?"

"First by saying Yes, I'll work for you; second by not calling me Senator and third by being my press spokesman. Now, all this in liaison with Roger Sharpe. Roger is smarter, wiser, older and not as handsome as you, so he won't get in as much trouble. You work for me. I want to be President, and I want you to want me to be President. Now, I have had too much to drink tonight. But I like your style, and the offer will stand in the morning. Right, Roger?"

"I'd say so."

Senator Keogh and Sharpe left before Mike could even finish his beer.

Jesus, he thought, am I dreaming? Two years ago I was in hock to a bookie for four thousand bucks. Now the guy who has the best shot at being President of the United States imparts a secret that he is going to run with a onetime fugitive for office and he wants me to be his press aide. It's a little too much all at one time.

Mike gulped down his drink and went to Fourteenth Street, where he got well laid. But before he went to bed, the words of the night rang in his ears. It was all true. It was all true. Just because he'd pulled off an exclusive? Yes, that was the reason. Shit, he had been doing that all his life and nobody had taken any notice at all. He liked Sean Keogh for taking notice.

Early the next morning Rose Keogh called John Hickey. She made the call from the breakfast table in front of Terrence. Nobody knew when everyone had stopped pretending. Nobody knew the exact day or time. Rose had never even spoken to Terrence about the affair. But as she spoke, Terrence quietly continued to eat his scrambled eggs. They were very close, and his mother could do nothing wrong.

"John, darling. McGavin. Mike McGavin, boy hero. He has joined the parade, I think. And Del Vecchio will be here soon. It's building, John. It's building."

"It's building too fast," he said.

"The woman. The Rooney woman. Surely there is something. There must be something."

"I'll get to it, darling; give me a little time. Just a little time. I miss you."

"Me too. Bye."

She smiled at Terrence as if he could see her smile. "How's breakfast, young Terrence?"

"As always, great, Ma. You're better than a French chef."

She leaned over and pecked him on the cheek.

Then Terrence spoke again: "Ma, you've still got that headache."

"Oh, it will go away. Don't you worry, my darling."

ON A HIGH mountaintop called Buena Vista in Costa Real, overlooking the Atlantic side of the isthmus country, Robert Del Vecchio smoked an excellent cigar. Alberto Morales sipped thoughtfully on a brandy.

"What do you think Sean Keogh will do, boss?"

"Keep his word, as I'll keep mine. He's a good man, Al, a very good man. He never understood our ways, but he's a good man and I don't know anyone who can legitimately serve better than I."

Morales understood perfectly. Robert Del Vecchio could be the political genius of all time back in the United States. In Costa Real, he had to be a crook. But in the States he could be someone, and so could he—Alberto Morales—be someone. He wouldn't need bodyguards or to carry a gun or have an electrified fence. things would be much different in America, as they had been when he first went to school at Northwestern. He wanted it badly for his boss, and wanted it badly for himself.

They were high up in a beautiful chalet and were feeling very mellow. The last forty-eight hours had gone very smoothly. The third man with them sipped at a glass of Moët et Chandon.

Del Vecchio puffed on his cigar and said in that slow, noncommittal way of speaking, "Now, Henry, what do you figure we agreed on?"

"Two hundred thousand American dollars exactly."

Del Vecchio smiled over teeth that clenched a cigar.

"You old sonofabitch, here," he said as he pulled a stack of bills out of a satchel. "That's two hundred fifty. A fifty-grand bonus, old buddy, because you did it right."

"Thank you. Thank you, señor."

"Shit, Henry, you even had me convinced when you were strutting around doing all that communist-guerrilla shit. I think you have a bit of the ham in you. You liked playing Enrique Soares, fervent left-wing terrorist."

"The role came easy, señor."

"Shit, I like you better as Henry Da Silva, head of the right-wing secret police. That left-wing shit has to go—but it was one helluva scam. How did you manage to do all that shit without firing a shot?"

"Well, your instructions were clear. No American was to be harmed. We harmed nobody. We just took them by surprise. But frankly, while I respect that you are American, the security, the Marines? *Madre!* Terrible."

"Well, you did it, Henry, old boy . . . without a shot."

"Well, there was one shot. I hear there is much surprise about Ambassador Trumbull's suicide."

Del Vecchio took a sip from the glass of champagne of Colonel Henry Da Silva, head of the Costa Real Secret Police, and said, "Well, it was a surprise to everyone. Certainly was. Even to that lying, cheating prick Trumbull—right up until the time Al put the gun to his head, after forcing him to sign that shit, and blew his brains out."

Chapter

16

THE INTERNATIONAL ARRIVALS BUILDING at John F. Kennedy Airport was a sea of bodies. It was one thirty in the afternoon, October 23, 1983. It had taken Senator Sean Keogh just two weeks to have all charges withdrawn against Robert Del Vecchio and a vote of confidence carried in both houses. He had promised Del Vecchio a hero's welcome, and this was it. The Pan Am plane was due in ten minutes. Senator Keogh, Roger Sharpe, Frank Burke and the new young press aide Mike Mc-Gavin had worked it all out to the last detail.

McGavin was learning fast and giving good advice. It was McGavin who had pointed out the advantage of an early-afternoon arrival, thus getting coverage in the first editions of all the morning papers plus the perpetually news-starved network television news programs.

Frank Burke had performed well. The huge crowd was mostly his doing. He had arranged that members of seven locals would be paid time and a half for their turnout, and turn out they had, holding placards aloft which read HOME IS THE HERO, WE LOVE YOU DEL, GOD BLESS A GOOD AMERICAN. Burke had also made sure that there had been a respectable turnout from the Veterans of Foreign Wars. There were also many people who arrived simply because they wanted to get a glimpse of a real-life hero whose name had been resurrected from the Wanted list.

But there had been other members of the Senate, members who had been outraged by the way Senator Keogh had made them all look like a bunch of ingrates, who were aware of the press mileage the event would attract.

The front running Republican presidential candidate, Senator Ronald Harris, was highly conspicuous with a large delegation of aides and cronies. He wasn't going to let his fast-approaching rival, the Senator from Massachusetts, steal the thunder from him on this one. He was duly surrounded by friends and supporters like Senator Julian Jarvis from New York and Senator Burt Barker from Maryland. This, he was determined, was not going to be a one-man show on the part of Senator Keogh. He stood in a large circle of newspapermen and television crews.

He quipped good-naturedly with the newsmen, most of whom he knew on first-name terms. Harris had rocketed to the forefront of conservative politics in the last eight years, since leaving his million-dollar job as a television host on a popular nighttime talk show. His politics appealed to roughly the same kind of people who followed the Keogh line, but his one great advantage had been with women supporters, who felt he was almost one of the family since he had been in their living rooms as a guest every night on television.

He had gotten a steam-roller start on other presidential hopefuls by announcing his candidacy early and making his imprint on the minds of his potential voters like a television commercial to the point at which literally millions could think of no other candidates—perhaps with the exception of Senator Sean Keogh.

Senator Harris and his aides seemed pleased with the circle of newsmen surrounding them. But the plane was due in only five minutes, and he looked with concern at his watch.

"Where the hell do you suppose Keogh is?" he asked Senator Jarvis.

"He'll probably try to make a grand last-minute entrance. But the press are here. He'll never get through that crowd. Looks as if his big entrance has backfired."

The big jet had now pulled into the terminal gates. Some of the passengers began to deplane. It was McGavin who had advised Senator Keogh to tell Del Vecchio to leave his own flying toy back in Costa Real.

Del Vecchio waited in his first-class seat, with Alberto Morales sitting quietly by his side. He waited until all the other passengers had left. He would be given the VIP treatment through customs, so he would not have to wait.

As the arrival of the plane was announced, the crowd started changing, "We want Del . . . we want Del." It was a rousing welcoming party.

Outside, in a limousine, sat Senator Keogh; his wife, Rose; their son, Terrence, Frank Burke; Roger Sharpe and Mike McGavin. Burke looked at his watch. "Come on, let's go . . . now."

They quickly filed out of the limousine to confront the gigantic crowd. Burke nodded his head as a signal and just seconds before Del Vecchio came through the big double doors of customs, a narrow pathway suddenly opened in the crowd. As Senator Harris strained on tiptoe to see what was going on, he and his colleagues missed something very important. It was just one man at first, then two, then three, then a whole human wall that had neatly knifed between the main press corps, which was slightly in front and to the left of Senator Harris and his large group. As the press corps was cut off from the Senator Harris group, the crowd seemed to melt in front of them. There was a clear pathway straight to where Del Vecchio and Morales emerged, a clear pathway that adjoined at right angles the pathway taken by Senator Keogh and his party.

By the time Del Vecchio had emerged into the terminal lounge proper, he, Keogh and the press seemed to meet all at the same time, with a solid wall of humanity surrounding them. Senator Harris was twenty yards behind, separated by a mass of tall heads and broad shoulders. The crowd had done exactly as they were told.

Del Vecchio played it well. He smiled with humility as he waved to the chanting crowd. He warmly shook hands with Keogh and said, "Bless you, Senator. Thank you for your faith."

There were no first-name terms here. Nobody knew that Del Vecchio and Keogh knew each other from the old days.

Rose Keogh stepped forward. He took her hand and gently kissed it. The crowd roared its approval. He grabbed young Terrence Keogh almost in a hug. The boy behind the thick glasses smiled, then shook his hand. The crowd roared itself hoarse. The cameras were popping like an electrical storm, and the klieg lights made the scene look as if it were under a desert sun.

Reporters pushed around the scene, and the pictures were of Del Vecchio and Sean Keogh's family. He even posed once kissing Rose Keogh on the cheek. Everyone went wild. Then he made his statement:

"I will make this brief, mainly because I am overwhelmed by this showing and also because it's an emotional moment for me and I don't want to make a fool of myself. I wish my wife and my family were here at this moment, but they will be joining me at a later time as there are many domestic issues that still remain to be taken care of in Costa Real.

"I want to thank the American people for their faith in me, and members of the Senate who had the fair-mindedness to back me once there was sufficient proof of my innocence. I particularly want to thank Senator Keogh, who took a particular interest in my predicament. It won't be forgotten. Other than that, I want to thank just about everyone."

The questions came all at once: "Are you bitter?" "Do you intend any legal action against your accusers?" "Any ambitions for political office?"

Del Vecchio smiled and held up his hand. "I have no bitterness. What has been done is done. I only have gratitude that my exile from my country is over. I plan to do nothing but return to my law practice as soon as I clear the matter with the bar association."

The reporters held on like barracudas. The questions and pictures were ceaseless. It was a giant media event.

Senator Ronald Harris' face burned crimson through his even California tan, and his perfectly capped teeth gritted in anger as he and his claque stood impotent, trapped by the huge crowd and deprived of the priceless publicity that Senator Keogh was scooping up with both hands. He turned to the New York Senator.

"So, Jarvis, his grand entrance was going to flop, eh? Look at us."

Senator Jarvis bit his lower lip and looked at the other embarrassed men, all dressed elegantly in their best television suits.

"Don't worry, Ron. We'll show him what it's all about when we get to the primary in New Hampshire. He can't use this ex-hood as a prop right up to the election. It's a seven-day wonder."

"You'd better be right, Julian, or all that financial support you get from our Golden State might suddenly get very wet and rainy."

Senator Jarvis bit his lower lip.

Keogh was now leading his wife, Rose; son, Terrence; Del Vecchio and Morales to a waiting limousine. The cameras were still popping as they got into the car. Sharpe, McGavin and Burke followed in a second car. They would meet at the Carlyle Hotel, where John Hickey had arranged an elegant champagne reception which would be attended by civic leaders including the Mayor of New York, Edward Wenner. Keogh had scored well. There would be more pictures, more interviews.

It was at the reception, as the Mayor was chatting animatedly to her, Keogh and Del Vecchio, that she took an appraising look at the situation. Her face was concerned. Hickey caught the look, and his eyes asked her what was wrong.

Rose Keogh saw the impeccable organization, the well-oiled springs and wheels in the machinery of Senator Sean Keogh, her husband. She had been surprised at the way he had pushed her to the fore for the cameras. She was clearly worried. Sean Keogh had thrown off so much of his naive, self-sacrificing seriousness. He had become a politician. He knew how to play to the gallery as never before. No longer was he driven by a mission. Now he was driven by the ambition of a man who knew he could touch the stars, not only the treetops. He had the gut instinct to go for the jugular of his enemies. He no longer waited for someone to strike him first before he struck back. Sean Keogh struck first with the might of a cool-headed winner, and it worried her. This was very formidable opposition—Frank Burke, the new young man Mike McGavin, the quiet but forceful Roger Sharpe and now the multimillionaire Robert Del Vecchio. She directed her look again at John Hickey, and Hickey started to move toward her.

Father Velas Zeibatski was suddenly at her side. "Anything wrong, Rose? My dear, you look unwell."

She panicked at his touch. Had the dark-eyed priest deciphered the look she had given Hickey! Damn the man, she never knew what to make of him.

"Er, no, Father, not really. It's just all been a little much. Haven't had much air with all these people. But I'm fine."

The priest gave her a gentle smile. "Fine, fine." He then joined John Hickey and Edward Wilson, who were absorbed in a conversation with the Mayor.

Rose edged to her husband's side as if to put to rest any suspicions that might have attended the look in the priest's eyes. She could feel the burning in her temples, proceeding from the right rear side of her skull. The pain in her head seemed to force its way right to the center of her brain. The pain was unbearable. Then it passed. She mixed amiably with the hand-picked party. Sean would soon be away. She would have to be with John. We have so much to plan. So much. She edged closer to her son, Terrence. He reassuringly squeezed her arm. "This comedy can't go on much longer, Ma." She looked at his face. He gave her that special all-knowing smile of his.

Sean Keogh came up from behind them and hugged them both. "It's quite a crew, wouldn't you say, you two? One way and another, it's been quite a triumphant day."

"I think you've done great today, Father."

"Wonderful, Sean. Simply wonderful."

"I loved the way you played it for the cameras. You quite surprise me sometimes. You handled those newsmen like putty," Keogh said.

Terrence smiled. "I would think she's getting used to it. But it's good practice."

"Practice for what, Terrence?"

"When she becomes the First Lady," he chuckled.

"You don't say much, young fellow, but when you say it you make it count." Sean Keogh put his hand affectionately on Terrence's shoulder.

"It was fairly obvious, Father, I thought. From what I gathered of what was going on, Senator Harris felt very lonely tonight. It was like Moses opening up the sea the way that crowd parted. Quite masterly."

Sean Keogh laughed proudly at Terrence's keen sense of observation. This boy had better eyesight than a team of marksmen with 20/20 vision. Terrence Keogh had the stuff bravery was made of, Sean Keogh thought.

Suddenly the Senator from Massachusetts cut his laugh short.

"Well, speak of the Devil. That takes some nerve."

The Senator was looking at the entrance of the crowded room of revelers. There stood Senator Ronald Harris with New York's Senator Julian Jarvis, both of them making their entry with confidence although neither of them had been invited.

"Excuse me, dear," Keogh said, and he strode toward them with a big smile.

"Senator Harris, good to see you. Julian, how have you been? Come in, come in. Waiter, would you look after the drinks for these gentlemen? Thank you. Well, let me introduce you around. Where have you been?"

"Oh," Senator Harris said with a mirthless smile, "we were at the airport, but there seemed to be such a crowd."

"Heck of a crowd, wasn't it?" Senator Keogh agreed with an equally mirthless smile.

Keogh saw that Senator Jarvis was not as skillful as Harris at containing his obvious rage. Keogh didn't underestimate Harris. It wasn't for nothing that twice he had almost had the presidency in the palm of his hand. No, the movie-star-looking Senator from California was no pushover. Senator Keogh with a surprising flourish introduced Harris and Jarvis to the party, most of whom the two men already knew. Keogh felt more triumphant than ever. He had scored a telling wound against Senator Harris for him to be so desperate that he would virtually admit defeat by coming to a party like a petty gate-crasher.

The wire services clicked off a few pictures of Harris shaking hands with Del Vecchio. So what? The pictures might make a late edition in some California newspapers. The national press coverage and the network news screamed Keogh.

The party lasted into the night, with the press corps, led by Danny Cahill of the *News,* being the last to leave. Keogh warmly shook the hands of Harris and Jarvis. Rose Keogh was particularly charming. Sean looked on with admiration. She certainly knew how to fall in with the program. Her low-key sophistication was dazzling without being obvious. She would make a fine First Lady, Keogh thought. Then he gave himself a sharp reprimand: Stop dreaming. It would be hard enough to get the nomination from the cunning and handsome Harris, let alone the presidency, although deep down Harris would be a harder man to beat for the nomination than the listless, politically impotent President Rawlins, the incumbent. Senator Keogh ran his hands through his handsome head of black-gray hair. He would have to be devastating in the primaries to court his fellow Republican delegates, who probably hated him more for his style than they did President Rawlins for being in power right now.

He walked over to Mike McGavin, who was bidding farewell to his friend Cahill. He took the big, handsome man discreetly to one side.

"Mike. You know New Hampshire?"

"Very well, Senator."

"Really?"

"I used to work on the *Manchester Express* after leaving Chicago and before going to work on the *Times* in New York. Yes, I know it well."

"I knew I had gambled well when I asked you to come to work for me."

McGavin's face was all questions.

"Then you know the old war-horse Tolbin? James Tolbin?"

"Personally gave me a raise, Senator. Personally."

"Then you know what I want you to do, and you're the perfect man for the task. He is the most powerful man in New Hampshire. I know him, respect him, like him. But he's come out for Senator Harris in the last two campaigns. For us to lose New Hampshire would wipe us off the map. From where I sit now, Harris has the old boy in his pocket. I want you to sound him out—sound him out very deeply."

"He's a very strong-minded old boy. Very strong-minded. He's not known to change in midstream, Senator, and he needs nothing from anybody. Nothing. As you know well. But certainly I'll see him. Any special instructions? And when do I go?"

"No special instructions: just a deep sounding. And you go tomorrow."

"You got it, Senator."

"I'm counting on you, Mike. In three weeks we go to Vegas for the Teamster election. That will be D-Day for us. But I have to know where I stand; otherwise I might have to miss New Hampshire, and that would be disastrous—for all of us."

Setting up an appointment with the colorful old James Tolbin was no problem for Mike McGavin. Tolbin's office had an open door, despite his reputation for back-room politicking. He was a hard-line conservative who ran New Hampshire from an energetic newspaper empire, a no-nonsense commitment to conservatism and a history of sticking to his guns no matter how much hot water he landed in. But come election year before the New Hampshire primaries, he was the best-liked man in the nation—even by those who hated his insides.

It was already bitterly cold in Manchester, New Hampshire, and Mike wished he had bought an overcoat as he trotted up the stairs of the old gray bilding. He gave his name to Tolbin's secretary at precisely ten o'clock in the morning. The old man hated tardiness; it was a human weakness he couldn't tolerate. Before the secretary could emerge to ask

Mike to enter, the old man dashed from the door. He was as Mike always remembered him: the same thin-muscled body despite his age, a well-kept crew cut that had gone white since he had first served in the U.S. Marines and the same staccato delivery of his words that Mike imagined was much the way Hemingway had talked. It was a sort of journalistic cable-ese, only in conversation.

"Ha, Mike. Mike McGavin. Yes, I remember you. . . . Come in. . . . Remember you well. Wondered how long it would be before you came up."

McGavin was ushered into an office as spare as the old man himself. Tolbin sat down. A cat with handsome black fur jumped onto his lap, and the old man stroked it affectionately. Mike remembered the old man's love for cats.

"Drink, boy? Drink?"

"No, thanks, sir."

"Don't No thanks me, young Mike. You were always a juicer. Have a drink. Drink." Tolbin grabbed a half-filled bottle of Scotch from his drawer and produced a tumbler. He poured a generous drink. You just didn't say no to James Tolbin.

"Well, yes . . . heard all about you. . . . Done well . . . yes, you've done well. Wondered when you would come. You're the first. Good to see you. Won't be good to see some of the others. Won't be good. At least, I like you. Like Keogh. Like him, yes. Got guts."

Mike felt comfortable. James Tolbin wouldn't say he liked Keogh if he didn't mean it.

"Well, sir, it would be unnatural if I hadn't taken advantage of the fact that I knew you and had worked for you."

"Damn right. Unnatural. Keogh, young Keogh—when is he going to throw his hat in the ring?"

"Well, sir, as you know, that hasn't been decided. About his running, that is."

"Rubbish. Running, all right. Running like a thoroughbred. Good thing, too. Got guts. Like guts."

"Well, sir," Mike said, and took a hefty gulp of Scotch to shore him up for being so direct so early in the conversation, "the question is obvious."

"Certainly is. Would I support him, this tough Irishman who has taken the country by the gonads? No. I wouldn't. No, Mike."

Mike took another drink to mask his disappointment in the bombshell which had come as early in the conversation as his own proposition.

"Why, you ask? Well, now, if Harris and Keogh had a head-to-head contest tomorrow, it would be a helluva battle. Helluva battle. Now, Keogh would get most of the blue-collar with the exception of what there is of them in the West. New York, Jersey, Connecticut might be split. Keogh would run away with Massachusetts. Harris would get the Wall Street boys, no question. Midwest would go to Keogh with the exception of Illinois. Illinois. Important. Keogh would get the South. Oh, easy, particularly after his anti-busing stand. So it would be a helluva fight."

"There is something missing, sir—with respect."

"Yes, there is . . . blacks. The black vote."

"Because of Senator Keogh's stand on busing?"

"No, no rubbish. Harris has the blacks. And in 1984 they will vote as they've never voted before."

"Republican?"

"Of course. Open your eyes, boy. The liberals made fools of the blacks. The black radicals don't sit well with the blacks today who want an education. In 1984, the blacks are thinking about money. Money buys education. Who promises money? Republicans do. Sure, that's oversimplified. But look at black business today. Look at your commercials on television. If they want the black consumer, you have to have black businessmen, black advertising men. Stupid politicians. They've forgotten that. They always thought the black vote could be won with a few verses of 'We Shall Overcome.' Rubbish, boy. Rubbish."

Mike sat there waiting for Tolbin to get his breath. He didn't interrupt. Tolbin asked all the questions and answered them. "Now you see, boy, I said there would be a helluva battle if they had a face-off tomorrow, but we don't run things that way. Primaries. That's what gets the fence-sitting delegates looking at the racing form. And where does the racing form start? New Hampshire."

Mike felt Tolbin had given him a whole spiel only to come back to the original point, the New Hampshire primary.

"I've supported Ron twice. I won't desert him now. He's stronger than ever. Look at what he's done in California. Look who is on his team. Black Mayor of Los Angeles, Black Congressmen in the north as well as that black police chief in San Francisco. They're law-and-order men. They're for money for the blacks. Tough men. As conservative as any I know. No, I wouldn't dump Ron now. Not now that he's poised. Like Keogh, like him a lot. In another time I would put everything I have behind him—everything; but Ron has it this time."

"Personal question, Mr. Tolbin, and you must excuse me. Is it friendship with Senator Harris?"

"No. Doesn't come into it. I respect him. Respect his strength. Respect his tight-fisted attitude toward government spending. Respect the way he's made me change my feeling about blacks. Yes, I admit it. Twenty years ago I wouldn't talk like this. Never. I respect him."

Mike mentally took a deep breath. What he was about to say could alienate the old man who had been straight, pleasant and very flattering toward Senator Sean Keogh.

"You know, talking about Los Angeles, where Senator Ron Harris is from . . ."

"Yes, Mike. Yes?"

"I was always a frustrated jock. Loved football. I used to bet on it a lot with money I really couldn't afford. Now, I respected the Los Angeles Rams. I respected them for their offense, their defense, their team-work, their camaraderie, their coaching. Everything. And I liked the way they won . . . right up until Super Bowl . . . which they never won. I wonder how much of the Rams is in Senator Harris, whom I too respect."

The short and slightly corny analogy hit James Tolbin like a line-backer. His machine-gun delivery came to a dead stop as he thought of the two bitter elections in which Harris had run out of the money.

Tolbin slowly stroked the cat curled on his lap, oblivious to the sparks that were flying around it. Then he said thoughtfully, "Maybe he was in the right place at the wrong time."

"Not if he wasn't the right man, Mr. Tolbin. Senator Sean Keogh has two rather attractive habits. He is the right man in the right place at the right time. And one other thing. He's a winner."

Tolbin was silent. He smiled, then stood up as the cat scuttled onto his desk. He held out his hand and gave Mike a vigorous and genuinely warm handshake.

"Should never have let you quit here. Shouldn't have let you go. Bye, Mike . . . and call me. . . . That's all, call me."

Mike walked into the cold Manchester air and caught a taxi to the airport. He would have to think hard before talking to Keogh, because he was mystified as to whether he had come away from the meeting winning or losing.

In Sean Keogh's Senate office he went over the conversation ten times, giving every word of the exchange to Senator Keogh, Frank Burke, Roger Sharpe and Robert Del Vecchio. Every word; and each time he repeated, "Senator, he started off with a virulent flat no, then said noth-ing and then told me twice to call him."

"But he seemed high, very high on the black vote. He believes that in a close election, it will be the black vote that wins the race," McGavin said.

Keogh, Burke and Del Vecchio seemed distressed. They wrestled with the subject for an hour.

Finally Burke spoke. "Sean, there just ain't a hope in hell we could get the niggers. We're a white blue-collar party—a very white, blue-collar party. They would go with Rawlins rather than us. Nobody's forgotten you standin' there at the school in Southie barring integration."

Del Vecchio nodded his head. "We're just going to have to make sure we clean up with our own."

Keogh was thoughtful. Sharpe looked at him closely. He knew that expression on the Senator's face. He had seen it many times. It was a look he had when he was about to do the unpredictable.

"Roger, I've spent years completely ignoring blacks. I can honestly say I have no prejudice. My stand in Southie was even supported by the blacks in Roxbury. Everyone recognized that forced integration just never worked. It still doesn't work. The blacks recognize that. Damn it, you know that old sonofagun Tolbin is right, and he's right about Harris. He has that California black caucus strongly in his pocket. We can't take that away from him, and the nation's blacks will follow that caucus."

"Right," Sharpe agreed, "and there's nobody big enough, of enough stature, in the black community who isn't committed to someone else. If we don't woo Tolbin in New Hampshire, maybe we should pass on it and go into the primary in Florida, where we would be better assured of victory."

Del Vecchio shook his head. "Roger, if Tolbin gets behind Harris, as he says he will, he'll win so big in New Hampshire it will start a steamroller effect that will make Harris unbeatable. I don't honestly believe Sean can afford to shy away from the first battle."

"You're right. No question of it," Sharpe said glumly.

McGavin was thoughtful. He found it hard to grasp that these sophisticated power brokers were so disastrously ignorant about the black community.

"What do you think, Mike?" Keogh queried.

"I think, Senator, that we all better get off our butts and get a black of some standing and make sure Tolbin takes us into the fold."

"Do you know one?" Keogh asked.

"Could be . . . could be. . . . The Reverend Leroy Jefferson."

Burke groaned. "Oh, that mad Bible-thumping nigger." Burke had no deep racial hatreds. His attitude toward blacks was very typically Southie. Let them prosper, but not next door to you.

"Frank, I know how you think, friend. But isn't it about time all of us got a little realistic? Blacks aren't going back to Africa. They're not going to be bellhops and busboys forever, and if we force them to, we'll all end up fighting them in the streets. Now, Mike, the Reverend Leroy Jefferson. He's a moderate, has always preached against revolution—right?"

"Right, and what makes him attractive is that he is totally color-blind. He preaches to the kids in school that the only color that has power is green power . . . money for jobs, homes, education. Now, traditionally he is obviously a Democrat, but . . . you never know."

"Okay, Mike, line up a meeting with him—fast. I want you at the meeting, Frank. You might be the ace in the hole."

"Me? I never thought it would be me helping you to get the nigger vote. Me, of all people."

The meeting broke up with Burke and Del Vecchio going to lunch together and Roger Sharpe returning to Boston. Keogh asked McGavin to stay behind.

When they were alone, Keogh spoke. "Mike, what would bring a man like Jefferson to our side?"

"It would be damn hard, Senator. As everybody said, your fight against integration in South Boston doesn't make you a prime candidate for a black."

"Could he see it? Could he be made to believe that I acted only out of concern for the kids, white and black?"

"Difficult."

"Okay, then, Mike. You line up the meeting. His headquarters are in Atlanta. We'll go down to see him." McGavin nodded, stood up and went to his office outside.

Half an hour later he returned to Keogh. He was smiling.

"I spoke to his aide at first, who thought it was some kind of practical joke. Then I spoke personally to the Reverend, who said he would be very happy to meet with you but warned that he thought there was little chance that the meeting would produce any commitment from him."

"When do we see him?"

"Tomorrow, four o'clock, in his office in Atlanta."

"Good man, Mike. That's action. Tell Frank, will you? I'll need him with me."

Senator Keogh seemed pleased. McGavin was mystified. The chances of a black civil rights leader putting his weight behind Keogh were about as good as the Ku Klux Klan donating money to the NAACP.

That night Keogh talked to Burke on the telephone. The conversation clearly worried Burke, but as always he agreed to do what Senator Keogh asked of him.

The next day, the plane carrying Keogh, McGavin and Burke set down in clean sunshine in Atlanta. They caught a taxi to the Peachtree Plaza Hotel, where two spacious suites served as headquarters to the Reverend Leroy Jefferson's Southern Christian Leadership Conference offices. The Senator was surprised to be greeted by a white male aide, who ushered them into the inner office. A tall, broad-shouldered man with lean hips and dressed casually in a white bush jacket appeared at the entrance of an office. He held out his hand and flashed a big smile, showing a perfect set of even teeth. He gripped Keogh's hand.

"Senator, very pleased to meet you," he said, then gripped Burke's and McGavin's hand in turn. Then, as he led them into his office, he added cheerily, "I must confess you were the last politician I thought would be walking into this office."

Keogh returned the smile. "Politics makes strange bedfellows."

"Indeed," countered the minister as they all sat down.

He clasped his hands on the desk in front of him. Keogh was clearly impressed with his appearance. He had a healthy shine to his face, and the body of an athlete which hadn't changed since he had played tight end for Georgia Tech.

Jefferson spoke first. "Well, I assume this meeting is of some importance."

Burke and McGavin remained silent as Keogh answered: "Well, yes it is. I trust this meeting will be held in confidence, because quite obviously I'm going to tell you something that I have not told the rest of the world."

The clergyman smiled. "That you're going to run for President? With respect, Senator, I don't think that will come as a surprise to anyone who knows you. I would like to say I personally believe you have a very good chance."

"Thank you, Reverend. Now to the point."

"Yes, exactly." Jefferson leaned forward as if to show his keen interest.

"Reverend, there is a little misapprehension that I stand on the conservative wing of the Republican Party."

"Quite."

"We don't have any black support, Reverend, because to be brutally frank, we haven't courted it."

"I've noticed."

"It's obviously a very serious error. An error for which I take full responsibility."

"It's gratifying to hear that, Senator."

"But it's something we have to rectify very quickly."

"And you have come to me for my support?"

"In a nutshell."

Jefferson leaned back in his chair and was thoughtful for a few seconds. Burke shifted uneasily in his chair.

"Senator, I have a great deal of respect for you as a politician and even for some of your principles and what you stand for. But clearly, Senator, your voting record in the Senate would make it impossible for me to support you, and I don't think that comes as any surprise to you.

I urge you not to take that as an insult. We have come a long way into understanding that your principles are not necessarily racist, but they are contrary to the interests of minorities."

"Can't argue with that, Reverend, but my voting has been against forced integration and against the escalation of welfare costs. I have heard you personally speak out against both. I hazard a guess that as an educator you are as concerned as I am about the effects forced integration has on kids of any color. And on welfare—who can argue for the escalation of welfare? Your continual call for employment as opposed to welfare puts us on the same side."

"Perhaps more than you think," Jefferson said, shifting his gaze now to Frank Burke. He continued: "But gentlemen, it's what you represent, the gigantic blue-collar unions, that has presented us with the biggest problem . . . jobs. While you wield such strength in those unions, the door is closed permanently to minorities."

Burke coughed and spoke: "Reverend, the situation is quite clear. There is just an economic climate that has held the job market down."

The handsome black churchman smiled. "I would like to believe that is the only reason why we have so few blacks in your Teamsters' union."

"Well," said Keogh, "if, as you say, you are in accord with much of my platform, the major stumbling block between us is jobs for minorities."

"That would be the major concern."

"What would be your attitude if I were responsible for opening part of that job market up?"

"I would be in a position to give considerable thought to supporting you and thus helping you with the black vote. But I would have to have many guarantees. We delivered for Carter in 1976, but what did it get us? Very little."

"Reverend, Frank here, as you probably know, stands a very fair chance of becoming the president of the Teamsters' union at the election next week in Las Vegas. I will also be present. During the convention I will announce my candidacy and support Frank's election."

McGavin interrupted. "Mr. Burke, of course, will swing the Teamster vote behind Senator Keogh. Something that no other candidate can expect. So it is, Reverend, a very strong package."

"And of course," said Jefferson, "black support would make you unbeatable."

All three men in front of him nodded their agreement. Jefferson continued: "Senator, you might very well be unbeatable without my support. But there are other candidates whose records would make my support of you highly questionable. I don't think I can sell you to other black leadership."

"What, Reverend, would be the situation if we could show you in the coming weeks a genuine effort to make your support of me highly attractive?"

"Such as?"

"Opening the ranks of some job categories that in the past have been closed to blacks and other minorities."

"You feel Mr. Burke could deliver on that promise?"

"I could," Burke said without enthusiasm.

"Then let's see what happens in the coming weeks. Senator Keogh, I trust you."

After the meeting broke up, Keogh, Burke and McGavin had a drink in the lobby bar of the Peachtree Plaza Hotel.

Burke was looking mildly surprised. "You know, he was a helluva nice guy for a nigger."

Keogh winced. "For God's sake, Frank, please—black. He's black."

"They started off being darkies, then they wanted to be called colored, then they wanted to be called Negroes and now they want to be called black. How do I know what to call them?"

"You're incorrigible, Frank. But I love you."

Burke and McGavin exchanged smiles, clinked their glasses. "Well, here's to you. The next President of the United States," Burke toasted, "with the help of a . . . er . . . black man."

Burke headed for Las Vegas, to be there in preparation for the election. Keogh and McGavin went back to Washington, where over dinner in McLean Keogh told his wife, Rose, and Del Vecchio, Wilson and Father Zeibatski, who all had come down from Boston for the conference, of what had taken place in Atlanta.

"I feel confident that if we can guarantee loosening up the job market in just the Teamsters alone, Jefferson just might have the excuse he needs to throw in with us. He's a very impressive guy. You would like him, Father."

The priest seemed enthusiastic about Keogh's strategy. "Once you have Jefferson behind you, Tolbin can't help supporting you in New Hampshire, and then you'll be rolling."

"Father, will you be able to come to Vegas with Del and me next week? I think a little spiritual support would be welcome."

"A churchman going to Sodom and Gomorrah . . . I'd love to."

"How about you, Rose, dear? Coming?"

"No, I think I'll stay at home, Sean."

"There could be an advantage, exposurewise," McGavin offered. "When you announce your candidacy in Vegas, if Mrs. Keogh is here we should get double exposure. Stories on you from out there and a story on the candidate's wife from Washington."

"That's sound thinking, Mike," Keogh said. "How about you, Rose? Ready for the hordes of press?"

"I'm getting very used to it, Sean."

"And very good at it, too, if I might say so," Del Vecchio commented.

It was true: in recent months Rose had completely emerged from her shy shell, had spoken to women's groups and shown she had a rare charm with the press.

That night after dinner Rose slipped away from the company and called John Hickey in Boston. She relayed the latest news to him. "He's building up quite an election force, John," she said in a voice tinged with bitterness. "He just might not be able to lose."

"Well, it can hardly hurt us, Rose."

She pursed her lips and was silent. Then she said thoughtfully, "I guess not . . . I guess not."

"Next week when he's away, will I have a chance to see you?"

"Of course, my darling. Come down here and we can stay in a house I can rent. It's in the mountains. Nobody to see us."

"You've got a date, my love. Bye for now."

Rose returned to the men talking in the sitting room. She felt strangely uneasy. Sean Keogh was getting everything he wanted. As he always did.

That night she excused herself early as she felt a headache, which continually plagued her, coming on. She lay awake in pain until Keogh came up to bed. She then pretended she was asleep.

The next day, on the floor of the Senate, Senator Keogh surprised some of his conservative colleagues by reporting statistics from the Department of Labor on the percentage of minorities working in craft unions. His speech pleased the liberal wing of the Republicans and mystified some of Keogh's right-wing friends.

Senator Keogh's grandstand play got good linage on the wire services, made Frank Burke in Las Vegas wince and had the desired effect on the Reverend Leroy Jefferson, who called him in his Senate office. "You seem to be making up for lost time, Senator," Jefferson told him with obvious gratification.

"Well, I told you I keep my word."

"I appreciate that. We'll all be watching you closely."

CAESAR'S PALACE Hotel in Las Vegas was bursting at the seams. The lobby was filled with Teamster delegates from every part of the country for the election of the most powerful union leader in the country. Hospitality suites set up by various delegations were on every floor. The biggest was that of Frank Burke. His local had flown in a bevy of girls from Los Angeles to serve the delegates drinks and food on a twenty-four-hour basis. One-armed bandits lined the walls of the suites, and the scene resembled one giant New Year's Eve party rather than the gathering of the single most powerful voting bloc in the country.

Sean Keogh stood in the center of a large group flanked by Father Velas Zeibatski and Robert Del Vecchio. Mike McGavin and Frank Burke stood off in the corner. He was surrounded by a large group of newsmen whose interest was piqued by the appearance of Del Vecchio.

Keogh surveyed the newsmen. There were representatives from both major wire services, the *Los Angeles Times* and *The Washington Post*. This would be the moment.

The questions were directed at Del Vecchio. What was the significance of his presence? one reporter asked.

"Simply here as a gesture of support for Frank Burke. That's all." Del Vecchio's former status in the union would help Burke's candidacy dramatically.

"And what about Senator Keogh?" one of the reporters asked.

"Exactly the same reason, gentlemen. I'm keenly interested in the outcome of this election, having had long contacts with the union and obviously a long personal friendship for many years with Frank Burke, who I believe is the best man for the job."

The *Los Angeles Times* reporter interrupted: "Isn't it a little unusual for a member of the Senate to campaign and lobby so openly for a union official, Senator?"

"Well, how would you like me to lobby, young man—secretly?" His tone was good-natured, but it reminded the reporters that Senator Keogh had a record for straight talk.

"Quite so, Senator, but if you'll pardon my bringing up the old question, it is as if you're courting Teamster support for other reasons."

Senator Keogh gave a big smile and gestured to a long-limbed, sun-tanned hostess. "Another round of drinks, boys?" He politely ordered the drinks from the shapely blonde, who smiled warmly toward him. The drinks arrived. Then, almost absent-mindedly Keogh asked, "I'm sorry—what was that last question?" The reporter repeated it.

"Other reasons? Well, you could be quite right, young man. Quite right."

It was like a bolt of lightning among the group of reporters. This was it.

They all started to babble at once. "Then you're running for the presidency? Is that right? That's been the continual word."

Keogh smiled again expansively and looked at the priest and Del Vecchio. "Really, the way these guys manage to wheedle words out of you that you want to keep secret."

The reporters went wild again, shouting questions over one another. Keogh held up his hands for a silence he didn't get. He was chuckling as suddenly the group of newsmen expanded. The odor of a story was in the air. They pressed the question. He would play with them for a little while.

"Well, the presidency is an attractive proposition for any politician, wouldn't you say, gentlemen?"

"But are you denying that you're running?

"I would deny nothing."

"Senator, without mincing words, are you a candidate for office?"

Keogh looked at Father Zeibatski, smiled again and winked. "Do you think I should tell them, Father?" He turned back to the reporters: "I can't tell a lie in front of a priest. . . . Yes, gentlemen, I am."

The two agency reporters dashed for the telephones in the hospitality suite, almost knocking over the long-legged blond hostess. They dictated bulletins and dashed back to Keogh to press him for more details. Burke had joined the group. Suddenly the suite was full of reporters as the news spread like wildfire to the other delegates throughout the huge hotel. Keogh had announced his candidacy, and he was supporting Burke for office. Any of the delegates who hadn't made up their minds on how to vote quickly did. Burke was traveling in heavy company: a presidential candidate. Frank Burke beamed at his friend.

That night at a huge banquet the various candidates made their final bids for support in a series of speeches. The news broken in the afternoon had hit the television networks, and the banquet was all abuzz with two names—Burke and Keogh. The announcement had taken the edge off the efforts of the other candidates, and with the exception of Tommy Pruitt from Union City, New Jersey, most had resigned themselves to a Burke victory.

Senator Keogh cut a dashing figure that night in his dinner jacket, strolling among the delegates accompanied by the priest, Del Vecchio, McGavin and Burke. His hand ached, it had been shaken so many times.

As the leading delegates filtered out of the huge banquet hall, Burke cornered five of them and led them to the lobby, where they sat down at a big table for a nightcap. They were quickly joined by some of the hospitality hostesses whom Burke had had flown in specially from Hollywood.

Burke was in an expansive mood, picking up tabs everywhere he went, smoking the obligatory cigar and glad-handing everyone in sight.

Sitting at the big table surrounded by cigar smoke and young women, he waved to Keogh as he emerged from the banquet room. "Here he is, gents—the next President of the United States," Burke yelled to the assembled company as he pulled back a seat for him at the drink-filled table.

Keogh shook hands all around and sat down. He turned to see that he was sitting next to the long-legged blonde whom he had noticed at the hospitality suite that afternoon. He smiled politely.

Burke cut in: "Sorry, young lady—I was introduced to you this afternoon, but I forget your name. This is Senator Sean Keogh."

"Hello," she said in cultivated tones. "I'm Anne Williams-Fraser. How do you do, Senator? I've read a lot about you."

She had a full mouth and large green eyes. Keogh couldn't remember seeing anyone so fresh in several years.

"Hello there. Aren't you the young lady who was almost knocked over in that rush of reporters?"

"Yes," she said, "I was there when apparently you dropped your bombshell. I wish you all the very best." She looked him straight in the eye as they talked. She was beautiful.

Keogh was curious about her. "Do I detect an accent? British?"

"Yes. I was born in England. Been here for about five years. The accent is wearing off a little now, I think."

"What do you do, Anne? You're not a hostess all the time, are you?"

"No—none of us. The usual: struggling models and struggling actresses."

"You're an actress?"

"Well, I belong to the Screen Actors Guild, but to be honest, I've only had a few walk-on parts in some television shows. It's very tough in Hollywood if you don't fall in with the casting-couch set or know somebody extremely well."

"That's a pity. I'm sure you're a very good actress. If I may say so, you certainly have the looks for it."

Her eyes flashed, and she smiled a full-mouthed smile and continued to look straight at him. Keogh felt himself growing a little uncomfortable until he realized his discomfort was just old-fashioned shyness.

She continued to look at him over the rim of her glass as she delicately sipped from it. Keogh turned away to order a drink and involve himself in political gossip, but every time he turned back to her she always seemed to be looking at him. Keogh studied her. Maybe this was a come-on. So many part-time actresses were full-time hookers. In this cathedral of garishness, looks could be so deceiving. But there was an innocence deep behind the grcen eyes. Sure, it was tinged with worldliness—the way she tossed her head and the cool, even look that she so constantly leveled at him.

Clumsily the Senator with the handsome face and gray-tinged hair indulged in small talk.

"A lot different here than in England, I suspect?"

"Very," she said as a smile crossed her lips.

"How about Los Angeles?"

"It can get boring, frankly. I often wonder if there's anyone there who doesn't have capped teeth."

Sean chuckled. He was warming to her. "Maybe you should have chosen a career as a dentist."

"It would have made a change in my bank balance," she said as she drained her glass.

The noise at the table grew in proportion to the drinks accumulating on the table. She sighed. "I'm afraid my early-to-bed, early-to-rise regimen in Hollywood doesn't prepare me for this sort of life. I'm very tired. If you would excuse me, Senator, I think I will try for some beauty sleep."

"You're staying here in the hotel?" Senator Keogh found himself blurting out.

"Eighth floor. Very generous, really. Every girl has her own room."

Keogh couldn't believe what he heard himself say.

"I think I'll turn in too. I'm on the tenth floor."

She eyed him suspiciously. He caught the look. Boldly he took her by the elbow.

Burke looked at him hard through the cigar-smoke haze. The men at the table voiced noisy farewells, and a few of them winked at Burke. There were no cameras allowed in the casino lobby, and this was where half of Washington did their cheating. Anonymity among so many.

"Tomorrow, Frank: early breakfast by the pool?"

"Fine, boy-o." The others repeated their farewells. Keogh turned and calmly guided Anne Williams-Fraser through the gaudiness that Keogh observed was almost a culture unto itself.

She smiled an honest smile. The suspiciousness was gone. "Senator, really, I don't think I'm going to get mugged, but it is very gracious of you to escort me to the elevator."

There was a hint of teasing in her voice. She knew what their departure looked like. But it mattered little to a girl who fought in a town like Hollywood where flesh was like money. She could not have cared less. She was very secure in the thought that her body was her own. She knew how her girlfriends operated. She never condemned them, just pitied them. They were paying too high a price.

The long-limbed blonde was no virgin. She had had her big affair with a young screenwriter until she found that all the physical attributes that had attracted her to him were also shared with a homosexual producer who bought two of his screenplays. It broke her heart. No so much for her lost love but for the fact that he had lost himself forever to the drug of Hollywood. What a waste.

Keogh stood there smiling gently as the elevator door opened. The elevator Muzak was playing "Brazil 66." God, this place looks upon peace and tranquillity the way a cobra looks at a mongoose, he thought. He stepped aside and she entered. The elevator, apart from the Muzak, was empty.

He pressed the eighth-floor button, then the tenth. She seemed relieved. He gestured around the elevator, with his gaze noting its emptiness. "Seems the quietest place in the hotel," he said with a smile.

"I wonder what people do who live here in Vegas," she said.

"Go stark, raving mad or join a church group," he answered lightly.

He found it difficult to keep his eyes from her. *This* was stark madness, he thought. She is young enough to be your daughter, and you're carrying on like a school kid.

The elevator slithered to a halt at the eighth floor. He felt his heart pump a little.

"Well," he said.

"Well, Senator, it was a pleasure to meet you."

"Same here, Miss Fraser—I mean Miss Williams-Fraser. I forgot about that hyphen."

"So do I. Call me Anne, please." She held out her hand. He shot his hand out quickly. He had always been told as a young man that you never shake hands with a woman, only with a man.

Her touch was light, feminine but assertive.

"Er . . . oh . . . Fine. Yes, good night. Perhaps we'll see you tomorrow."

"Oh, I'll be there. Tomorrow will be a big day."

"For us both," he said.

"Good night."

"Good night." She moved out the door, and it closed a split second behind her. She was gone, and in seconds he was putting the key in the door of his tenth-floor suite. He gave a deep sigh as he hung up his dinner jacket. He was weary, worried about the outcome of the morrow. But it was all washed away with his own thoughts, very personal thoughts.

God, she was beautiful, he thought for the twentieth time as he slipped naked into the sheets, his tautly muscled shoulders rubbing against the cool stiffness of the bed. Were they the thoughts of a middle-aged fool going through some kind of male menopause? It happened all the time, he thought. That's how twenty-year marriages go on the rocks. Some potbellied idiot tries to grab a fleeting last fling at a youth he never had.

He smiled to himself in the darkness. Brother, am I a prime target for it! Youth. Youth? What youth had he had? West Broadway; Dorchester, Damrell, McDonough streets. A man without legs and arms being thrown alive into the bay off the point. A smoldering house and the small body bag containing what was left of his beloved mother, Molly. The grotesqueness of Paddy Devlin and his body polluting the pavement of Clinton Street in the North End. Poor, dear, proud old Castellano, who like his mother was not whole when he was buried. Not whole, like Sweeney and his son; not whole, like the beautiful, beer-bellied Mr. Mac. And Sheldon Mathers. Mathers way back. A man whom he would have loved to have as a friend and tutor. Proud, decent; without vice except his commitment to the rules of being a gentleman. Yes, some youth.

Could it have been different? No, it could not have been different—he leveled with himself. Never. Not while behind that quiet, strong, handsome exterior, an inferno of ambition burned. While that fire blazed, no, it could never be different.

He found himself saying a childish prayer in his mind. Please, God, can't I have the ambition without the indelible stain of blood and violence on my hands?

He slipped gently into sleep, confident that somehow God would answer his prayers.

In the morning he awoke to the Las Vegas brilliance feeling hung over. Not from the booze, but from the guilt. He had indulged himself in wild, childish dreams while his wife, Rose, held the fort at home, clinging bravely to a loneliness that his ambition had imposed on her.

He showered and dressed hurriedly. He felt his old cool self again, having banished juvenile notions from a now clear head. He went downstairs for breakfast by the pool to meet Burke, Del Vecchio, McGavin and the priest.

The priest was wearing sports clothes. Keogh was incredulous, and he said so as he sipped a glass of orange juice. "Father, really," he said with a smile.

"He's been corrupted," Del Vecchio said with a good-natured laugh. "What next?"

"Booze, broads and then the tables, After that, ruin," Burke taunted sacrilegiously. Everybody laughed, and the priest said through a wide smile, "Remember, boys, Jesus walked in the cloth of his fellow man."

"My God," Sean said, "next you'll be walking across that pool, Father."

"No, Sean," Father Zeibatski said slowly, "I leave the walking on water to you." The mysterious priest looked deep into the eyes of the Massachusetts Senator, and Keogh wondered if he could have read his thoughts of the previous night. Sean looked back hard at him, and the priest caught his look. Father Zeibatski smiled. He knows so much about so many things, Keogh thought. He's probably a genius.

The way that had been worked out for the Teamster election on that crisp Las Vegas day was for the two thousand delegates to cast their votes in twenty curtained booths set up at the entrance of the huge convention hall. Pinkerton guards stood outside the booths. Inside were big steel cans, electronically locked and timed for an hour and a half.

By that time all two thousand delegates would have voted for the president of their choice. The ballot boxes would then be taken to the stage of the convention hall and counted. All the ballot slips were actually computer cards. The cards, once extracted, would be fed into a computer standing on the stage. The result would be known within fifteen minutes. It was a foolproof system which precluded any of the skullduggery that had marked so many Teamster elections.

The lobby was abuzz with quiet excitement. The boisterousness of the previous day was absent. The atmosphere was typical for a situation in which men of the street find themselves in roles of establishment importance. Right now, these former truck drivers, assembly-line workers, factory hands were confronted with the prospect of their own significance. While they relished it, they didn't take it lightly.

The group led by Senator Keogh were at the booths first, showing a quiet but high profile. Now it was serious, and the backslapping was over.

All of Keogh's group marked the perceptible change in Burke now. He was downright nervous. Confident, but not overconfident. He could not rely on every vote promised him, and the New Jersey delegation was almost openly hostile to Burke and his friends. Burke kept on taking deep breaths.

Mike McGavin sidled up to him. "It will be a breeze, Mr. Burke. Don't worry."

Burke smiled. "Who's worried? Huh? Who's worried? Well, I am, for a start."

The group shuffled in with the rest of the delegates with a minimum of fanfare.

Father Zeibatski stood between Sean and Frank Burke. They looked around the huge convention hall where they had been the day before. A giant bar and buffet had been set up at the rear of the hall and to the left as they entered. The hostesses, most of them provided by the public-relations-conscious Burke, were busy behind the bar making setups and preparing the food for the banquet that would follow the announcement of the elected winner.

Sean caught Anne Williams-Fraser out of the side of his eye. Compulsively he looked. She was even more gorgeous, despite the revealing mesh tights and Playboy Bunny–type costume. He wanted to look away as he felt his stomach jump like a schoolboy's on his first date. But he didn't. Was it middle-aged puppy love that made him engage her eyes? No, he decided in a split second. Was it fading vanity? No. He had ambition, but it was ambition without vanity. He turned his head and gave her an almost paternal wave.

The other girls giggled. My, how she had scored! Almost in defiance of their giggles, she flashed a voluptuous smile and, placing her fingers to her lips, blew him a rather outrageous kiss. She threw her head back and laughed.

Burke was too nervous to notice a thing. The wily priest turned his head away from Sean's gaze so as not to make him aware that the redness around his shirt collar was showing. Senator Sean Keogh was blushing, and the priest smiled inwardly at the deep reservoir of stored information that Velas Zeibatski never gave a hint of possessing.

Keogh recognized the gesture. My God, there is so much to this man, he thought. Then he looked away, not quite aware of where he was walking. He wanted desperately to get closer to Anne Williams-Fraser, the semisophisticated, semivamping beauty from the other side of the Atlantic.

He sat down, his gaze fixed on the stage. Robert Del Vecchio was now at his side. Del Vecchio nudged him with his elbow.

"Are you sick or just nervous?" Del Vecchio asked, observing Sean's curious behavior.

Keogh smiled. "Both. But at least in terminal stages."

"Relax, Sean. It's in the bag."

"Tell Frank that."

Del Vecchio looked at Frank Burke. He was a basket case. The big, rough, tough guy from Southie looked as if he were making his First Communion and had forgotten how to read.

The convention hall was now filled. There was a nervous hush over the group of men, some of them very tough, not used to being quiet or nervous. A loud voice in conversation brought looks of reprimand from the audience. The gathering grew quieter as the first ballot box was bought onto the stage. The boxes would soon be opened by the automatic timer. Soon they were all there on stage. Burke gulped.

McGavin drummed his fingers on his knee. He was not of this ilk. He was a newspaperman. But he felt at home. He liked, perhaps even loved these men whom he worked for. The always paternal Senator; the attractively slick Del Vecchio; the disarming, semiliterate Burke and the deep, mysterious priest. They seemed to be a composite of everything he had ever been at various times of his life.

It had been ordained that the agony would be prolonged. The secretary of the Teamsters, Hugh McEvoy, flushed from a night of drinking the evening before, got up to make his speech.

McEvoy used all the buzz words that Keogh had heard—and even said—a thousand times before. It was always the same. The piety of men who worked with their hands to build a stronger, better country; the decency of the work ethic. Work ethic, Keogh noted mentally. That sonofabitch had caused more strikes, put more men at odds with their mortgages than anyone before in the history of labor, yet McEvoy owned half of the Florida Keys.

The words of McEvoy drew sporadic rounds of applause, and Keogh found himself clapping but never actually feeling his hands hitting together. It was so much fucking bullshit. They were all hoodlums.

We are all hoodlums. The bankers, the politicians were all hoodlums.

Why was he thinking of so much blackness? he asked himself. Simply because on this day into which he had put so much energy and emotion, he was suddenly lost in childishness. He was thinking of the green-eyed lady with the cultivated accent and the long legs who he knew was somewhere behind him, behind a huge bar. And the sooner this goddamn speech and this goddamn vote were over, the sooner he would have an excuse to order a drink from her and perhaps even touch her accidentally.

He no longer reproached himself for his apparent foolishness. He suddenly felt alive. Not cool, not quietly in charge, as he always was. He just felt alive, and if being alive was foolish, well, so be it.

McEvoy wouldn't stop. He was squeezing this moment for every ounce. The reporters were there. But more important, the men were there, and they had to be made to feel important. This was an election, perhaps marginally as important as the presidential election itself.

Keogh stared straight ahead, outwardly emotionless, as did Burke, like two stars at Oscar time, fearful of showing a trace of feeling, lest it be mistaken for hope. McGavin was nervous. The priest never showed a sign of anything. Del Vecchio was the only one who seemed at peace. He never backed losers.

Finally, as McEvoy droned to a close, the ballot cards were slipped into the computer. There were only three real contenders: Burke; Tommy Pruitt from New Jersey, the leader of the so-called "Joisey Boids" gang; and Nathan Clarke, a man from Louisiana.

The computer began to flash the numbers. There were only two thousand men voting. Ten for Pruitt, twenty for Pruitt, thirty for Pruitt.

Burke's knuckles whitened. Jesus, what's happened to the other ballot boxes? he demanded silently. Ah, there it is. Burke, fifty—eighty. Clarke, thirty. Pruitt, forty. Burke twenty—eighty. With each big jump in the numbers, some of the more demonstrative among the delegates allowed themselves a cheer.

Nathan Clarke was obviously well out of the running. He had positioned himself near the exit to save embarrassment. He turned and walked out. It was Pruitt and Burke, obviously.

Sean Keogh looked across at his old pal, sitting one seat away. Burke gave him a small smile. Keogh wanted to hug him. Burke for once looked vulnerable. Keogh wanted to hold him. He loved him so much.

The numbers kept flashing. Out of 1800 votes counted, Clarke had received a dismal 150. Pruitt had notched 800 and Burke 850. Another flash. Pruitt 75. He was ahead of Burke, and Sean Keogh felt a little sick. Even Del Vecchio seemed to move closer to the edge of his seat. McGavin gritted his teeth. Jesus, no. The priest seemed to be taking little interest in the electricity.

Then, very much like a prizefight, it was over. The computer just flashed the name. For a moment there was no cheering. The name just registered, flashing at split-second intervals.

BURKE . . . BURKE . . . BURKE . . . BURKE.

Pandemonium.

Frank Burke sat there drained. Del Vecchio turned, smiled and gave him a gentle pat on the back. "Knew you could do it, you Mick sonofabitch."

Burke looked at him limply. He leaned over Del Vecchio and grabbed his friend Sean. Keogh could feel the bristles of his beard rubbing into his face. They hugged.

Then the swarms descended—well-wishers, hangers-on, reporters. Pruitt walked stiffly up to him for the cameras and gave him a perfunctory handshake. He then strode without elegance from the big room with Chickie O'Toole and Polack Joe. Pruitt was very angry. Then again, no one had thought Pruitt would get that close.

Burke seemed to be a cork on a wild, thrashing ocean. He was backslapped, embraced. But all he did was cling to Sean Keogh's arm. Both were without speech. They nodded, they smiled, they laughed, they shook hands, both of them. But neither seemed to remember saying anything.

Somehow Keogh managed to find a break in the crowd. He wanted to run, but he edged through handshakes and congratulations toward the end of the room seemingly oblivious to it all. Frank Burke clung to his arm. They waded through the sea of bodies and yells and felt a hundred hands pounding their shoulders and backs.

They made it to the bar, with Del Vecchio, McGavin and the priest close behind them.

Keogh breathed hard, looked at Frank Burke. "You made it, pal."

"*We* made it, pal."

"How about a drink?"

"How about a thousand?"

Anne Williams-Fraser had also done a little of wading through bodies. She was exactly where the Keogh group had come to rest, surrounded by the legion of well-wishers and reporters.

Keogh turned quickly to look over the bar. It was almost as if he had known she would be there.

"Drinks, Senator?"

Keogh flushed. "In Mr. Burke's words—a thousand of them."

He looked hard into her eyes. She returned the look. It was one of mischievousness. Was she playing with him? The thought erased the moment of celebration.

Then, above the roars of laughter and congratulation, amid the chaos of pushing bodies, she said in a quiet voice, "For you, Senator—anything."

Her brashness was gone, and there was seriousness in her voice.

She then busied herself getting a thousand drinks—if that was possible.

Senator Sean Keogh suddenly felt very young, and he didn't even say to himself that he was a middle-aged fool. And if he could have looked in a mirror, he would have seen the change in his eyes which had been too old too long.

Chapter

17

THE HOURS following Frank Burke's triumph seemed to be a blur to the Keogh party. A continuous procession of newspapermen, radio reporters, and television interviewers trekked to Burke's side, which was well protected by the media-wise McGavin. Once over the initial trauma of his victory, Burke, with the subtle guidance of McGavin, found that while not sounding too profound, he could ably field even the most difficult questions from the newshawks. He had to handle the inevitable tough ones. His background. His arrest record as a young man.

"I was too wild and not very smart," he said philosophically, "but twenty-five years of hard work managed to straighten me out. I wish some of the hophead kids today could have the opportunity of workin' as hard and we wouldn't need to spend so much on fightin' crime."

Did he think he could swing the labor movement behind Senator Sean Keogh's bid for the presidency?

"I don't think I have to. Senator Keogh seems to be the only candidate to recognize that business and the labor movement can't survive without each other. Who needs convincin'?"

Then came the toughest question of all. Would the Teamsters, one smartly dressed female reporter asked, show more sensitivity to opening up the ranks of the union to minorities?

"When I was a kid, *I* was a minority of a sort. I know what it's like. But to answer your question, as long as a man knows how to do a good day's work for a good day's pay, nobody is gonna keep him or her outa a job even if he or she is green with pink spots."

Did his presidency signal a new era?

He laughed. "You betcha ass."

The reporters walked away satisfied. He talked from the shoulder. What he said wasn't wishy-washy liberal rhetoric. It was the talk of a man who regarded the street as his college. And even if deep down Frank Burke was both personally and professionally apprehensive about how some of his membership might receive his opinions on minority hiring, it seemed to satisfy for the moment.

Before the long celebration which would mark that night, Senator Keogh gathered Burke, Del Vecchio, McGavin and the priest in his suite.

"Now, Frank, we'll get this over quickly, as I don't want to cut into your drinking time." Everybody smiled. Keogh continued: "Who in your crowd is a Jewish guy you could give an important role to?"

"Oh, yeah," Burke answered with little thought. "You know him. Tough Izzy. You know, Izzy Cohen, used to be a fourth-ranked middleweight in the fifties. Tough sonofabitch. You know him."

"Izzy Cohen . . . can he think with his head as well as his fists?"

"Real smart bastard."

"Okay. Now, we haven't heard from the Reverend Leroy Jefferson yet. He's waiting to hear from us. We made a promise. Your stuff you gave to the newspapers is a start, but he's been conned before. He wants that commitment to employment solid. Right?"

Everybody nodded.

"Okay. Now, we don't want to win the black vote only to lose the Jewish vote in the Northeast. Right?"

Everybody nodded again.

"Well, the rift between Jews and blacks has been serious. No candidate could get both. So you get Izzy to make the offer to Jefferson about opening up the jobs. Would he go for it?"

"Yeah, Izzy is solid people."

"Okay, get moving on it. Tonight. Leave it to Jefferson to make it public to the media. We don't want to make it look as if we're being a bunch of rich paternal Micks dabbling in race relations. Sound good?"

"Sounds brilliant," McGavin said. He never ceased to marvel at the seemingly easy elegance with which the Senator moved through the most hazardous political minefields.

Del Vecchio nodded. The priest smiled and said, "How do you intend to win the election, Sean? By a ninety-nine percent margin?"

"It would be nice," he answered quietly. "Now, Frank, go out and get yourself stiff . . . after you talk to Izzy. I'll join you in the lobby for drinks after dinner. I have to make some calls. I'll have to call Eddie in Boston—and I've totally neglected to call Rose all day," he added with a touch of guilt that only the priest picked up on.

The four men filed from the room in high spirits, and Sean darted straight to the telephone to call Rose in Virginia. She answered the phone and told him in warm terms of the avalanche of press who had besieged the mansion.

"This is the first time the telephone has been free, darling. You certainly have made a splash, you and Frank. It sounds as if you handled yourself very well."

"No, my lovely Rose, it's you who handled it well. It seems you charmed the press off a tree. You are becoming quite a stateswoman."

"I try, darling. But then, I have a wonderful teacher."

Her words made him wince slightly. He felt the burden of guilt bearing down. He thought of the sacrifices that Rose had made for him throughout their married life, and yet how he felt captivated by a shapely young woman named Anne Williams-Fraser. He was becoming a stupid, boring middle-aged fool, he told himself.

"How's Terrence?"

"He'll be here for another three days. He's having a wonderful healthy time, riding, jogging, studying. He's fine. Want to speak to him?"

"Give him my love, darling. I have to dash now. I have a lot of hand-shaking to do."

"All right. When will you be back?"

"Don't know exactly. Maybe a couple more days. Call you tomorrow."

He put the receiver down and flushed. Why had he lied? He could be on the first plane back tomorrow.

Rose Keogh put down the telephone in the dining room of the marvelous mansion.

The table was elegantly set for four people. Seated on her left was Terrence Keogh, on her right John Hickey, and opposite was Edward Wilson. She picked up a delicately cut Waterford goblet. Hickey filled it with Dom Perignon. She was silent for a long moment as she gazed into its foaming contents.

She then said—at first to no one in particular, "Well, it seems my husband, the Senator, is in an incredibly strong position. His right arm, Mr. Frank Burke, has come through for him once again. Frank is very strong, isn't he, Edward?" She looked straight into Wilson's eyes. The sightless look of Terrence Keogh turned toward Wilson, as did the piercing and unremitting coolness of John Hickey's stare.

"Of course he is, Rose. Of course; you know that as well as I do," he said with much discomfort, "But what can I do about it? Why address the question to me?"

"You're quite right, Edward, quite right. Champagne?"

"Thank you, Rose."

SEAN KEOGH showered and shaved for the second time that day and put on a fresh suit. He caught the elevator to the lobby, where he would again be surrounded by boozy Teamsters, his own claque of boozers and the inevitable stream of newspapermen who were committed to squeeze yet another telling quote from him. He emerged from the Muzak-filled elevator and started toward the far corner of the lobby, where he knew Burke, Del Vecchio, the priest and McGavin would be holding court and starting their night of celebration. As he turned left and walked in a straight line toward his friends, he heard her.

"Senator. Senator. Over here."

It was Anne Williams-Fraser. She was sitting at a table with two other girls who had also worked the convention floor that day. She looked breathless in a biscuit-colored dress, simply designed but obviously to the educated eye a product from Georgio's. Her flaxen hair was tied in a careless ponytail, and she looked much fresher after abandoning her working tights and Bunny-type costume. He looked across at her. She gave a warm, almost girlish wave with a big smile.

He crossed over to her. She introduced her two friends, who offered congratulations and good wishes.

"Care to join us for a celebration drink, Senator?" Anne asked lightly.

"Certainly," he said without certainty.

"Girls, this is the next President of the United States." Both her friends gave him admiring glances. Keogh felt as if he had suddenly been plunged into a pool full of alligators. He managed to summon up a polite command for a round of drinks from a waitress.

Anne appraised the waitress. "I sympathize with the poor girl, trussed up in all that tight-fitting gear. It nearly killed us." The other girls laughed in agreement, and Sean Keogh somehow hung on bravely through ten minutes of small talk. Then, politely and all too conveniently, the two girls remembered a date they had and cheerfully said their goodbyes. Keogh felt a little better now. He hoisted his glass in toast to Anne: "To you, young lady."

"To you, Senator."

"I told you my name was Sean."

"And I told you my name was Anne," she scolded unself-consciously.

Keogh marveled at the ease of the girl's personality. At first it came across as slightly brash. But then Keogh recognized she was simply a very warm and friendly girl who seemed to say what she thought when she thought it. It was an asset that all too long, in Keogh's business, had been foreign to him.

As if reading his thoughts, she smiled: "I hope you don't think I'm too forward. It's just that you're the first important man I've ever met whom I liked immediately." There it was again—saying the first thing she thought of. "I meet important men in Hollywood all the time. But it's always the same. Whoever said the casting-couch days of Hollywood were over must be living in the Mojave Desert. I guess that's why I haven't had many parts."

"Well," Keogh said sincerely, "I wouldn't call that a failure. Rather a triumph."

"I hope you're right," she said with a resigned sigh.

Keogh felt a sudden surge of boldness. She had put him totally at ease with her matter-of-fact attitude. Totally.

"Have you eaten yet, Anne?"

"No, I haven't, and I'm starved," she answered with the candor of a grade-school child.

Keogh smiled, drained his glass. "Well, how about it? I have no idea where to go in this town, but I would like to get the heck out of these four glistening walls, as beautiful as they may be . . . and . . . er . . . well, I don't take someone to dinner every night of the week."

He looked around and could see his friends in the far corner at the lobby bar. They hadn't noticed him.

"Oh, great. The first night we came here, we went to a great little French restaurant down the street on the Strip. Let's go."

She stood up and boldly took him by the hand, leading him through the myriad of housewives and insurance salesmen from the Midwest playing the slot machines.

As they disappeared through the lobby, the eagle eye of Father Zeibatski caught them. His face remained impassive, but he smiled inwardly.

They lingered for three hours over dinner, and Sean Keogh could not quite remember when he had been so totally relaxed with a person of the opposite sex. Somehow the age difference seemed to matter very little. If anything, he found himself asking her about Hollywood with the interest of the unsophisticated.

She was quick to dispel any illusion of glamour that Keogh might have harbored about the town. She spoke, in her cultivated accent, in animated bursts, asking Keogh in turn about political life in Washington. He too dispelled some commonly held notions.

He had lost all his initial shyness and projected the Sean Keogh for which he was so well known on the Hill—measuring his words, amusing in a low-keyed way but driven by his beliefs in what the country should have in political leadership.

Soon the beautiful child-woman found herself almost totally silent, listening intently rather than talking. There was a rare tone of conviction in Senator Sean Keogh's voice, particularly when he talked about Southie and his friends, friends like Frank Burke.

Her lighthearted flirting seemed to have come to an abrupt end. In its place was a sudden, growing infatuation—not of a younger girl seeing in an older man sensual worldliness, but of a woman discovering a basic superiority, not of wealth or power, just of old-fashioned, well-honed decency and loyalty. When he laughed, she liked to look close at the deep wrinkles around his eyes; when he listened, she liked to look at the intensity of his eyes; and she liked the way, when he was trying to explain a point, he would run his fingers through his gray-black hair, almost in deep concern that he was not making the point clear enough.

When Sean Keogh called for the check and they walked outside onto the glistening Strip, where everybody drove and nobody walked, it felt totally natural for her to cling to his arm.

After her running battle with a continual stream of Hollywood hucksters, she felt suddenly irresistibly attracted to the only true man she had met in years. It was now she who felt a twinge of conscience, because she felt she had not been totally honest in the way she had come on to him.

Sean Keogh felt the gentle grip of her hand on his elbow, and while he tensed under the weight of its intimacy, he did nothing to discourage it.

They walked silently through the brisk desert air along the sidewalk fronting the blaring beat of the casino hotels. For all the noise and lights, they could have been walking in the desert itself.

The bright illumination of Caesar's Palace snapped Keogh back to reality, and as they walked past the fountain into the entrance, they mutually disengaged, although both wanted the intimacy, no matter how slight, to linger. At a respectable distance apart, they both approached the desk for their keys. The lobby bar—now, at midnight—was almost bursting with people and noise. Somewhere in the human jungle in the lobby he could hear the strains of Southie.

As they separately received their keys, the desk clerk handed Senator Sean Keogh a telegram. He opened it with a slice of his thumb. Keogh never liked to get telegrams. They usually meant that someone didn't want to confront him directly with the message on the telephone. He felt an edge of apprehension as he stood silently in front of the hotel desk clerk with the beautiful Anne quietly by his side. Then he smiled.

TRIED TO CALL YOU BUT NO DOUBT IN THROES OF CELEBRATION. WARMLY RECEIVED NEWS REPORTS OF MR. BURKE'S STATEMENT. MORE WARMLY RECEIVED COMMUNICATION AND COMMITMENT OF MR. ISADORE COHEN. FEEL YOU ARE A MAN OF YOUR WORD. LIKEWISE MYSELF. TOMORROW WILL ANNOUNCE THROUGH WIRE SERVICES AND ATLANTA CONSTITUTION INTERVIEW MY WHOLEHEARTED SUPPORT FOR YOUR CANDIDACY. INCIDENTALLY VERY SMART GETTING MR. COHEN TO MAKE THE GESTURE. I THINK BOTH SIDES NEED THE PEACE OFFERING. REVEREND LEROY JEFFERSON.

Keogh smiled again and folded the telegram neatly into his top pocket. The silent beauty beside him smiled too. "Looks like good news. I'm glad."

"Yes. Good news. How about a nightcap?"

"I'd love one," she said chirpily. "I have a bottle of thirty-year-old Napoleon Champagne Cognac in my room. I'd love a nightcap."

Sean Keogh endeavored to hide the deep breath of fear and panic that made his chest heave. Somehow he fought back the terror, smiled and led her to the elevator. Once alone inside the car, she snuggled close to him. It all seemed so natural. Maybe it was the French wine playing tricks, or maybe it was just that he was a middle-aged fool, or just maybe he felt a rare and strong attraction toward this child-woman. Because Sean Keogh, the Senator from Massachusetts, felt like a very young man. And somehow, despite the fact that he had banished the thought of Rose Keogh from his mind lest he be clasped by the powerful grip of guilt, he knew now why he had told his wife it would be "a couple more days" before he returned to Washington.

When he awoke in the morning he could still taste the cognac in his mouth, but somehow the taste was overcome by the memory of the real taste of the beautiful, young and lithe body that was sleeping soundly and almost wrapped around him. She had gone to sleep with her head buried deep in the hollow of his neck, and the sun-gold hair fell carelessly and almost comically across the matted black and gray hair of his chest. He lay on his back, and her breasts pushed hard into his side; her legs were somehow tangled up in his, as if she had tried everything to get just that little bit closer to him.

He sighed with deep satisfaction as he thought back to the hours before they had collapsed almost simultaneously into sleep. How he had been so awkward to begin with. How he had been unsure of his ability to make love to a much younger girl; how the panic had blocked his brain to the point where he felt it impossible to get an erection, and how his incapacity had panicked him more and more; and then he recalled how she had laughed with genuine amusement and said, "Why do men worry so much about being great lovers? Just be a lover. There are no such things as good lovers or bad lovers if two people are in love." And then it had all happened as if someone had waved the proverbial wand, and Sean Keogh had no longer had to wonder or be terrified about his virility. He felt so satisfied, even a little proud of his performance, although he knew he was indulging himself in a sense of male triumph that should never enter pure enjoyment.

Her eyes flickered open. She looked up at him for a long moment. Her finger rubbed across the graying stubble in his one-day-old growth. She sighed and snuggled closer. He turned to kiss her lightly on the lips, and they made love again. By now they were experts with each other.

Afterward they lay silently in each other's arms for a long while.

Sean Keogh sighed deeply and looked at the clock. It was ten fifteen in the morning.

"Oh, my God," he moaned with resignation. "The time."

"Forget it, Sean."

"I wish I could. . . . Just a second." Keogh tossed off the bedclothes on his side of the bed, threw his legs to the floor and sat there naked as he reached for the telephone. He reflected for a moment on the boldness of his nakedness in front of a girl whom he had hardly gotten to call by her first name. But everything seemed so in place. The shyness was long gone.

He called the front desk and asked for his messages. He listened and breathed with relief. Burke, the priest, McGavin, Del Vecchio all had called. They were at breakfast by the pool. There had been no important media calls, and Washington and Boston were silent. He leaned back on a propped-up pillow. He felt good.

She bounced out of bed naked, and he could see the exquisite lines of her body.

"I'm starving. Starving," she giggled as she walked around the bed and reached for the telephone with one hand while caressing Keogh's chest with the other.

"You like eating, young lady," Keogh chuckled.

"Almost as much as I like making love to you."

Keogh was flattered.

She ordered eggs, bacon, orange juice, coffee. Keogh declined breakfast other than coffee.

"Don't think I'm being too square, but I think when Room Service comes, I might choose to be in the shower."

She laughed loudly. "It doesn't look good, does it?"

"What doesn't?" he asked.

"For the next President of the United States."

"Er, well, you might have a point there. I don't think a room boy is ready for that quite yet."

The breakfast arrived, and the room boy left. Keogh emerged glistening with water from the shower, a towel wrapped around his lean but powerful body.

She looked hard at him. "Do you know you're gorgeous?" she vamped.

She returned to her eggs.

Over coffee they both lit cigarettes, and she suddenly became noticeably thoughtful.

"What's wrong, young Anne?"

"Nothing, really. It's pretty corny, really. I mean, I can't expect you to believe that a woman spends one night with a man and falls in love."

It was an awkward statement for Keogh to field. He remained silent.

"And it's because of that—I mean, I know I'm coming out with it pretty strong, but that's the way I am; I don't tell lies—that I feel a little funny."

"I don't understand," Keogh answered, his thoughts turning. He could feel something in his bones.

"Oh, it's just that I haven't been totally truthful to you, and I want to be."

"Well, don't let me push you. . . . Are you going to tell me you have a secret life as a call girl and shock me?" He chuckled.

"No, nothing like that . . . it's just that I've been a little phony. Not very much, but just a little, and I have an explanation."

"I'm not twisting your arm."

"Well, it was all my silly damn agent's idea. He said I have to have a gimmick. So I became Anne Williams-Fraser, the blue-blood English girl." She laughed. "Actually I was born in South Boston and my name is Mary Rooney . . . that's right—just where you come from. My father was dead, and my mother and I left there soon after I was born, and I picked up the fancy accent in schools in New York. So I'm just plain Mary Rooney from Southie. Maybe that's why I was so attracted to you in the first place. Never been to England." She giggled; then she laughed loudly. "That's Hollywood for you. Nobody has her real name. Everybody pretends to be somebody else. So, Sean, let me introduce myself all over again . . . Mary Rooney from South Boston via New York and Los Angeles. You're not mad at me, are you? It's only a very little white lie."

A poker face had been too much a part of Keogh's life for the stab of pain to show. As she good-naturedly held out her hand to shake on the new introduction, Sean Keogh silently and viciously cursed his God for the obscene trick.

"You hand is shaking," she said as she grabbed it.

"Your champagne cognac, I suspect," he said, with amazing outward control that hid the revolution in his stomach, brain and heart. If he could have thrown up on the spot, he would have. His temples pumped, and he felt his knees tremble. She noticed nothing and continued to talk.

"Damn, having to go back to Los Angeles today. Sean . . . Sean, are you listening?"

"Sure. Sure—every word."

"Have you got any time? Couldn't you spend a few days with me in

Los Angeles? Just a few days? I'm not putting my claws into you. It's just . . . oh, I get so lonely there, and I can't stand all those beach boys and men who look prettier than I do when I go out. Could you? Please?"

Sean Keogh felt like a man drowning. He could see the surface and the sky above, but he couldn't suck in the life-giving oxygen. Mary Rooney. My God—Mary Rooney. I have just slept with the girl whom I helped leave fatherless. What have I done to anyone to deserve this? My God.

Somehow he managed to bluff his way through his coffee and her breakfast without making any commitment and yet without making her feel it had been just a one-night stand.

She was quick to pick up on his mood. "Maybe all the girls tell you this. But I don't do one-night stands. I wasn't a virgin, but I don't sleep around."

Keogh felt like bursting into tears. "All the girls? There are no other girls, little one. And I believe everything you say. Look, let me go to my room, fix up some business, and I'll call you in an hour. Okay?"

When the door closed behind him on the eighth-floor room of Mary Rooney, Sean Keogh felt sudden relief. He had feared that at any moment he might crack in front of her. No man was made to withstand that shock.

As he reached his tenth-floor suite, he burst out in lathering sweat. The pleasure of the night before had suddenly made him feel dirty. He ripped off his clothes and threw them on the floor, and again he showered, in a futile attempt to wash something out of his system that had been imprinted there indelibly. He found it hard to breathe.

He lay dripping on the bed, trying to clear the cauldron that his mind had become. Like a mechanical man he got to his feet and pulled on his shorts, then his trousers. Then he stopped in mid movement. He reached for the telephone and ordered Father Velas Zeibatski paged.

The priest entered within ten minutes.

Sean Keogh bit the top of the first knuckle of his left hand.

"Father, I don't know whether this counts as a confession, but if it's humanly possible I have to share something very painful."

"We always have, Sean."

"The girl . . . I stayed last night with a girl."

"I know," he said impassively.

Keogh did not stop to question his knowledge. He knew better than that.

"The girl. Her name is Mary Rooney. Mary Rooney, Father! Did you hear that?" Keogh was now shouting and close to snapping.

The priest's face was without emotion. He stood there for almost a minute looking at the agony his beloved friend was suffering. This priest of many years but of indeterminate age looked hard with his large slanted Slavic eyes. This was no confession.

Keogh moved forward and hugged the priest, and both remembered another year when a black-haired, pale-skinned teen-ager had done exactly the same at Sacred Heart Church while the dismembered body of Jimmy Rooney lay in Boston City Morgue. God gives and takes away—and with Sean Keogh he did both in such large measure.

It was as the jet plane settled after its thirty-five-minute hop from Las Vegas to Los Angeles that Sean Keogh had ceased to agonize. Mary Rooney had left on an earlier flight. He had decided to join her in Los Angeles. He had made up his mind. If his driving ambition had been the cause of so much pain and heartache, it was not because he had sacrificed others for his own selfish ends. It was his quiet, simple but unshakable conviction that it was only through his ambition that he could show a better way, a way of joining and not splitting, a way of enriching and not impoverishing.

He smiled to himself as he thought a psychiatrist would have a field day with that rationalization. But it did not worry him. If this was so—if he harbored no selfish desires for personal gain, then wasn't he allowed any personal indulgence? He had not been selfish with his friends, with his family, with Southie or even with the political hacks in Washington. Why was he not allowed the selfishness of having the love of Mary Rooney?

He had rationalized and rationalized until the cool, analytical mind of Sean Keogh simply took over. Let's face it, Keogh, she is a young and beautiful girl and you are just like any middle-aged man terrified of the climacteric and waking up one day to find that a penis is only for urinating.

Don't kid yourself, boy-o. No matter how gross the circumstances of sleeping with this child, you are showing simple, old-fashioned weakness. Enough of this bullshit about love and tenderness: you have just found your penis. Face it and tough it out. Face it like the damn man you pretend so much to be. The excuses and the self-crucifying had to stop, he told himself, and as the plane touched down he ordered himself to forget the burden of a nation resting on pained shoulders—Go out and enjoy yourself, boy-o. Live a little, boy-o. Live a little.

And for the next five days he did. Through the many contacts of Roger Sharpe's, the daytime hours were filled with useful meetings of local Republicans, leading businessmen, various ethnic groups and the media. Sharpe had mapped out his itinerary with genius and flair. At night he returned secretly to Mary Rooney's small but neat apartment off Sunset Boulevard, leaving his room at the Beverly Hills Hotel empty. There, away from the cigar smoke of the wheelers and dealers, the glad-handing of the hangers-on and the ever-searching questions of the hysterical media, the Senator was simply Sean Keogh, whom Mary cooked for, played records for and made love to. The monstrosity of the secret he held deep inside him was relentlessly vanquished by the sheer pleasure that he enjoyed by her side or in her bed. Live a little, boy-o.

The affair grew through his many trips to the West Coast—some necessary, many totally unnecessary—and her occasional trips to the East, which were discreetly arranged by Sean. Frank Burke knew about it—and he understood. The priest knew about it and said nothing. Del Vecchio knew about it and cared nothing about the morality of it, only the potential danger of it politically. Perhaps even McGavin knew about it.

Keogh cared little. He was riding a very fast roller coaster both personally and politically. Virtually every voting bloc in the country was behind him. He was unstoppable. He worked long hours, and his political acumen had never been sharper. He thrived on work and seemed to have the energy of six Sean Keoghs, and he often wondered if it had anything to do with the lithe, blond body in a small apartment off Sunset Boulevard.

Sean Keogh was not oblivious to the darker side of his feelings. The sight of Rose Keogh filled him with a special pain. She never ceased to be an adoring wife, and a vital political asset, stumping at his side in crowds and meetings, traveling to speak to women's groups and exhorting their members to vote for her husband—so much so, in fact, that in a poll by a national magazine, which was putting together a mock "kitchen cabinet" of the women whose husbands its readers wanted to see run the country, Rose Keogh was voted "First Lady" by an overpowering margin. But she never complained, spending her free time at home in Virginia and whenever possible visiting Terrence at school or entertaining his friends at their mansion.

Even Roger Sharpe commented regularly that she appeared to be the most able wife on Capitol Hill—"and," he added, "probably one with the best potential as a politician." Keogh was proud for his wife. He had given her so little else apart from the material gifts in life.

THE FIRST months of 1984 were a deliriously happy time for Sean Keogh. As the New Hampshire primary approached, the media—even the cynical New York newspapers and television—were content to re-flect the love affair the nation was having with Sean Keogh. Never since the days of the Kennedys had the hackneyed "charisma" been so over-used.

Frank Burke's Teamsters Union was running like clockwork, and the appearance of black and Hispanic faces in blue-collar jobs held tradition-ally by whites caused only a minimum of dislocation. The country was at last, Keogh felt, growing up. A vigorous emergence of a black and His-panic middle class had fueled the process, and the working minority seemed as bitterly opposed to the cancer of welfare as their Irish, Italian, Polish and WASP counterparts had been a decade earlier.

The Reverend Leroy Jefferson had proved to be a riveting force in getting minority support behind Keogh, and Keogh's home state felt that its favorite son had overcome a racial disaffection that would have lingered with the nation for all foreseeable time.

Big business felt very comfortable with the Senator's bond with the labor movement, and in press conferences and rallies he was continually referred to as President Keogh—even ten months before the election.

Robert Del Vecchio gradually began to assume a higher profile, hav-ing been strategically placed on a dozen service committees in Washing-ton, while his corporate law practice flourished. He and his right-hand man, Alberto Morales, were never far from Senator Keogh's side, either at public functions or at private dinners.

And Mike McGavin, with a skillful hand, never let Del Vecchio's hero status stray far from the media's scrutiny. With the New Hampshire primary scheduled for February 28, McGavin had planted the first germ of Del Vecchio as a Keogh running mate in a syndicated Washington column. Other columnists and commentators were quick to pick up on the item, and the notion gained a nicely paced snowball momentum.

Still, Senator Keogh was worried. While he had everything running perfectly at a high pitch, New Hampshire would be no pushover. Sena-tor Ronald Harris, the television darling of an entire female generation, had not been letting grass grow under his feet. Despite Kcogh's bottom-less coffers, courtesy of the string of fat bank accounts provided by Del Vecchio, Harris showed dramatic strength in the polls, only a shade behind Keogh. And a victory for Harris in New Hampshire would have the party hacks, who almost to the man detested Keogh and his clique, rushing to his support. Any excuse would have them at his side, and a loss there would have a debilitating effect on Keogh's steamroller.

Keogh had been careful even with his own newspaper, the *Clarion*, which was blooming under the deft hand of Wilson, to see that it did not push his own barrow too hard. It was, as Keogh explained, in case the all-powerful James Tolbin, the press baron from Manchester, New Hampshire, saw it as a way to bulldoze him, or even pressure him into support.

Tolbin liked Keogh. He had said as much to McGavin. He was worried that Keogh couldn't carry the black vote and still keep the other voters united. Keogh had indicated that. The Senator had been also careful not to make any further contact with Tolbin. He knew that the tough crew-cut power broker was too much his own man to wither under pressure. He had just left him alone. Although the temptation had never been far away to pick up the telephone and make a personal plea, Senator Keogh had resisted.

But Sean Keogh's life was basking under a special sun. Nothing would be denied him.

The clan had gathered in Keogh's office in the Senate Office Building overlooking the windswept February sidewalks of Delaware Avenue in Washington. Senator Keogh had the latest polls in front of him. They showed him leading Senator Harris of California for the Republican nomination by a single, solitary point. Del Vecchio, his man Morales, Burke, Wilson and McGavin examined the polls. Father Zeibatski was back in Boston.

Del Vecchio looked concerned. "Sean, you're going to need an extra push for New Hampshire."

"Don't I know it!"

"It could get sticky," Wilson offered.

Burke furrowed his brow. "Harris could get New Hampshire . . . easily. If that happened, we might as well fold our tent."

Mike McGavin remained silent and then allowed himself a tiny smile. "Gentlemen, Senator, I think I'll ask a small measure of forgiveness before I say anything more." The men in the office all looked to the darkly handsome McGavin. He had what could pass for a smirk on his face. McGavin spoke.

"Well," he said, his face lighting with a sunny smile, "you see, technically I wasn't holding back on you gentlemen."

"What the fuck are you talkin' about, Mike? Out with it, boy-o." Burke was always impatient with the young men.

McGavin reached inside his custom-made suit and pulled out a folded piece of paper.

"Well, it was addressed to me, you see."

"Mike," Keogh snapped, "get on with it."

McGavin seemed to be savoring the moment.

"It's a telegram."

He pushed it across to Keogh. The Senator read the words at least three times, and then he smiled. "I should get Frank here to give you a swift kick in the backside for holding out. When did you get it?"

"It was here when I came in this morning. I knew you would all be together this afternoon, so I thought I would let everyone know at the same time."

Del Vecchio spoke. "Sean, let us in on the damn secret."

Keogh read aloud from the telegram. "It's addressed to our young star here—Mike. It says, 'Mike, tell your boss Keogh that he's my man. Also congratulations to Burke on the way he pulled everything off with the Reverend Leroy Jefferson. I like to be on the winning side. Editorial announcing my support will appear in upcoming Sunday editions. Would like lunch. Regards, James Tolbin."

The room was electrified, with chuckling, joy and congratulations all round. Senator Keogh slid back in his leather chair behind the big oak desk. He seemed very pleased with life.

Del Vecchio grabbed the knee of the seated Morales. "That's it, Alberto. That's it for us. We're there. We're there."

Burke spoke. "I think it's all over but the shouting, Sean."

"Looks good, Sean," Wilson said. "Roger Sharpe will be very relieved to hear this in Boston."

"Yes, it looks good," Keogh repeated. "You did a fine job with the old war-horse, Mike."

There was nothing more to be said. The meeting broke up in high spirits. What was needed now was for Roger Sharpe to work on the party hacks after the editorial appeared and the New Hampshire Republican delegates to make New Hampshire Keogh territory.

It was two weeks later, at a similar meeting, that the room was again filled with joy. This time it came from a telephone call from Boston. Father Zeibatski was on the phone. His message, like most of his communications, was brief.

"Sean, I have met with the old man, Raymond. He simply told me to tell you that there wouldn't be an Italian in the country who has not got his message.

"And what is Don Raimondo's message, Father?" Keogh asked.

"Simply that a vote for Sean Keogh is a vote for Italian dignity. That's it. He has been very loyal to us, Sean, despite the past."

"A wonderful old man," Keogh said before telling his clan. The smell of victory was in all their nostrils. After New Hampshire, his Jewish vote, combined with his strong conservative appeal to the Southerners, would easily carry him through the all-important Florida primary. The door of the White House was beckoning.

After that meeting, Keogh called Mary Rooney in Los Angeles. He

called her several times a week, and would often confide in her the latest
in his conquests as he trekked toward the biggest job in the country. It
was something that a man did with a wife. But while Rose Keogh was
involved dramatically in the everyday politicking, it was Mary to whom
Sean confided his innermost thoughts and triumphs. There was, Keogh
admitted, a subdued element of boast to his recounting of his successes.
It was natural enough in any man who wasn't beyond trying to impress
a woman with whom he was infatuated.

And that same afternoon, Edward George Wilson caught his plane
back to Boston and from Logan Airport a taxi to Cambridge, to Commercial Avenue, where John Hickey's elegant town house stood. He
rang the chimes.

Hickey's voice inquired, "Yes?"

"Eddie, John." The buzzer sounded and the thick door opened. Wilson hurriedly jogged up the stairs. Hickey appeared in a silk robe. In a
corner of the sumptuous living room sat Terrence Keogh, his unseeing
eyes turned toward the picture window that overlooked the Charles
River. He was listening to Mozart.

"Hi, Terrence. How goes it?" Wilson said nervously.

Young Terrence waved without turning his head toward the sound of
Wilson's voice. No matter what blood flowed through their veins, Terrence Keogh regarded Eddie Wilson with contempt. Sean Keogh Terrence despised, but respected. John Hickey Terrence both respected
and liked. Any choice of his mother's was perfect for him.

Rose Keogh walked into the room. She had hurriedly combed her
hair. She too was wearing a silk robe. "Afternoon, Rose," Wilson said in
a tone dripping with obsequiousness.

"Edward," she said with a hint of dismissal. She crossed to the coffee
table and picked up a wafer. She spread sour cream and caviar on it.
"Terrence, a little afternoon snack?" she asked her son.

Young Terrence swiveled in the leather chair in which he was sitting.
His hand went unerringly to where his mother was holding out the
wafer.

Hickey brought in some espresso and a snifter of cognac. He set them
down in front of Rose.

"Well, Edward. I assume you are here this afternoon with some kind
of news development?

"Well, er, yes. First he gets Tolbin to back him. Now that crazy old
Italian hood has put his word behind him. That old bastard Raymond
may be half crazy, but the Guineas listen to every word he says. Sean has
it all. Tolbin is even doing an editorial praising Burke's handling of the
Teamsters. I don't think Harris has a chance, no matter how many
women have fallen in love with him."

"You're telling us things we don't know, Edward?" Rose said quietly as she sipped at her espresso.

"Of course not, Rose. Just telling you. You asked to be told everything, so I'm telling you everything, damn it." His voice was sharp. He was tiring of being a messenger boy. Rose threw him a sharp glance, and Wilson quieted his temper.

"A drink, Edward?" she asked.

"Sounds as if you need one," Terrence Keogh said with measured contempt. "Kitchen getting a little hot?"

Wilson looked across at Terrence Keogh. Wilson's face looked sad, very sad.

Hickey sipped quietly on a cognac and said finally, "Well, Rose, when do we move?"

"Move? John, we haven't stopped moving. Now, Edward, isn't it time you called your friends?"

Wilson looked ill.

Rose seemed impatient with the way the conversation was going.

"Damn it, Edward, what do you want? You want to be Sean Keogh's servant for the rest of your life?"

"I've never been a servant, Rose," he said evenly.

"The jury is out on that, now, isn't it?" Terrence asked. His voice had a mocking edge.

Wilson reddened. "Shut your smart overeducated mouth, Terrence. Remember whom you're speaking to."

Terrence smiled.

Rose lifted her eyes to meet Wilson's and said evenly, "Remember, Edward, whom *you're* speaking to."

Wilson reached for a glass of cognac. He cleared his throat and in tones of the *Clarion* boardroom said with a new hint of authority, "Has it occurred to the assembled intelligence quotient that it might be a good and profitable idea to go along with the program? There's no stopping Sean now, and for Christ's sake, why should any of us try? We're prospering—damn well prospering. Have we all gone a little nuts? What's wrong with life the way it is now? Nobody suspects anything in the past that any of us have done. We're safe. Christ, we're rich. How rich can anyone want to be? We're powerful. John, let's be honest: where the hell would you be now if it weren't for the *Clarion?* Third Avenue in New York?"

Hickey curled his lip. "Shut the fuck up, you coward. You little rat."

Wilson had taken his step toward independence too far. He felt the coldness of the room. Whatever resentment he had toward Keogh, he had never felt so belittled as he did now in the company of Rose, his former lover; Terrence, his estranged flesh and blood, and John Hickey, the cold-hearted stud who was completely subjugated both physically and emotionally by the petite lady known as Mrs. Rose Keogh. It was an unpleasant encounter, and Wilson was glad to get out of there and head for his office at the *Clarion,* where he buried himself in the work that he had welcomed so much, that had both made the newspaper such a success and made him forget parts of his life that he so desperately wanted to blot from his mind.

It was ten days later, when the last frantic days of planning were honing the campaign to a fine edge for the New Hampshire primary, that Wilson was again called to a summit meeting. As he looked around the room that day, he stared hard at Frankie Burke. The tightly curly blond hair had grown dirty brown with age and thinned at the temples and crown. The belly was larger now, and his shirtfront always seemed to peek out under the bottom button of his vest.

Wilson smiled to himself. It had been such a battle, so many years earlier, to get Burke to wear a three-piece suit instead of the light blue or chocolate-brown gabardine suits he had so favored. But so much of Burke hadn't changed. The way his whole chest and stomach jiggled even when he chuckled; the look of softness that crossed the scarred cheeks and broken-nosed face whenever he was looking at Sean Keogh and Keogh didn't realize he was being observed by his hulking friend. Burke still dropped his G's, and it was always goin' and comin' and drinkin'.

Wilson couldn't help admiring Burke's staunch love and loyalty, even though they had long since been sacrificed in his own life. And yet for all of Wilson's double-dealing, he was no better off than Burke. Both men were rich, rich beyond their dreams, and yet Burke, with his tiny wife, Teresa, who bossed him and their three kids around, was infinitely happier. Wilson couldn't quite grasp that, but he recognized Burke for the tough, lovable, once-wild friend that he had been throughout the years.

The Washington air was cold and cloudy. It was noon, and Wilson followed Burke, McGavin and Del Vecchio out of the Senator's office.

"What are you doing for lunch, Frank?"

"Think I'll skip it. Teresa never stops about my weight. Drivin' a man mad, she is."

"Cheat a little, Frank. Come on, let me buy you lunch. Del, Mike— how about a little lunch for you guys? There's a great new French Provincial restaurant out beyond Bethesda. How about it? Lunch on the *Clarion.*"

"Sorry, Ed, can't. Alberto and I have to go over some stuff that's going on in Costa Real. And we have to prepare for the wife and kids coming up. Take a rain check on it." Del Vecchio waved cheerily and disappeared down the hallway with Morales.

"Me too, Mr. Wilson. The Senator has a committee meeting this afternoon," McGavin said.

"Well, Frank. You and me. I don't have a plane until tonight. How about it?"

Burke patted his belly. "Ah, what the hell—so long as nobody goes rattin' on me to Teresa. Do they sell beer in this fancy joint?"

"Sure do. Got your car here?"

"Yeah. New one. It's the gold-colored Cadillac. See over there?"

"Okay, Frank, follow my car. We'll be there in twenty minutes. Twenty-five tops."

Wilson took off in his Mercedes and Burke followed in the rather garish Caddy. They drove out Wisconsin Avenue and were quickly in the lush countryside that is so speedily available to those who live in Washington. At a fork in the road Wilson waved to Burke to take a left turn, and soon both cars pulled up outside a neat farmhouse-style restaurant called Le Coq Rouge.

They entered together. The maître d' led them to a wooden corner table with a green-and-white-check cloth. Burke sat down and looked around the place. His back was to the door.

"Fancy joint, Eddie." He turned around, appraising the clientele. Then he laughed.

"Tell me the joke?"

"Ya know, look at us. Both drivin' big fancy cars. All the money in the world, and eatin' in places like this. Yeah, and me—me sittin' with my back to a door." He chuckled again.

Eddie Wilson smiled. "We've all come a long way."

"Ya know, remember in the old days, whenever we'd go to the Erin Club, when we'd sit down, we'd all scramble for the wall seats at the table, and then we'd end up sittin' in a line, all with our backs to the wall? Maybe you don't remember. You were at Harvard then a lot of the time," he said without any rancor over the fact that Wilson had been spared the street.

"Oh, yes, I remember. Particularly after Joey Connors got it. He got it with his back to the door."

Burke grabbed Wilson's arm affectionately. "Yeah, yeah, that's right —ya remember. Jesus, those days!"

Wilson returned Burke's affectionate touch with a genuinely warm look that came as close as Wilson ever could get to love. "They were good days," Wilson said nostalgically.

"Yeah—and rough days too. Sean was so right. Ya know, we shoulda got outa the rackets even sooner. So many good men. Ol' Mr. Mac; ol' Man Sweeney and his boy Billy. Even ol' Castellano. Shit, that was a mistake. Fuckin' lousy mistake." Burke looked off into the distance.

The waiter arrived with menus. Wilson gave his careful scrutiny, ordered a carafe of Chablis, consommé and canard à l' orange.

Burke waved away the menu.

"Ya got a big sirloin?—medium rare. Yeah, an' some tomato soup . . . an' say, have ya got a cold Heineken's? With some Jameson's on the side."

The waiter's face looked pained. "We don't serve Irish whiskey, sir."

"Sure, sure. Then Jack Daniel's will do."

Wilson smiled and looked tenderly at the mashed-in face. "You never change, do you, Frank?"

"Don't get insulted. It's just that the fancy food . . . well, I like steak."

Wilson chuckled.

The drinks arrived. Burke gulped thirstily at his beer.

"Ya know, Eddie, I thought Sean was crazy when he got us outa the rackets. But look how it's worked out. Look at Sean. He's dead to rights gonna be the next President. Look at you, a big newspaperman, and me? Me, boss of the Teamsters. I walk in joints where I never been and people come up and shake my han'. It's like bein' a celebrity. Ya know, we have a lot to thank Sean for. Jesus, that guy never quits."

Wilson looked down into the consommé that had just arrived.

Burke attacked his soup and kept talking. "An' then I remember Sean tells me, 'No more guns, Frank.' That's what he tells me—no more guns. So I ain't never carried a gun in all these years. Still have it in Southie. Thirty-eight revolver. Never used automatics like they do in the movies. Automatics always jammed. But never carried it ever since them days, and ya know, sometimes I feel naked without it. Even after all these years."

"Well, we don't need that anymore, Frank. Our guns are the biggest in the country."

"Right. Ol' Sean. He's some sonofagun. Ya know, I hate to say things like this in case somebody thinks I'm a flamin' faggot, but sometimes I think I love the guy. Know what I mean?—really love him. Ya know?"

Wilson's face grew soft and his eyes narrowed. "Yes, Frank, I do. I know what you mean."

Frank Burke waded heartily through his steak, and Wilson played with his food as the two talked about Southie in the old days. Why, Wilson wondered deeply and regretfully, could he not be like this wonderful lump of a man who sat before him? Why had Edward Wilson chosen the wrong side?

After Wilson paid the check, he drew a deep breath.

"Well, now, Frank, I have a confession to make."

Burke smiled. "Where's the priest?"

Wilson returned the smile and said, "Now, you don't think I brought you all the way out here just for a steak, do you?"

"Seemed a bit funny."

"Now listen, and I don't want any protests because I'm under very strict instructions. You and Teresa will be moving to Washington seeing this is the Teamster headquarters—right?"

"Right."

"And you have to have a place to live. Right?"

"Right."

"Well, Sean has been looking around for you.'

"Whattaya mean?" Burke said with an edge of suspicion in his voice.

"Well, Frank, your anniversary is coming up, and . . . well . . . Well, here goes. Sean wants to make a present to you . . . a house."

"No, no, no, no, Eddie. Sean's done enough fer me. Enough fer all of us. I just won't stand still for it."

"Well, I knew that would be your reaction, and so did Sean. But he'll skin me alive if I don't talk you into it."

"Then stay skinned," he chuckled.

"Look. He's seen a place about three miles from here. It's beautiful. Really beautiful. A white Colonial. Teresa will go nuts about it."

"Don't want to know."

"Well, at least come out and look at it. If you won't go along with Sean's plan, you might want to buy it yourself."

"Might."

"Then let's get out of here and I'll be the real estate agent and guide."

They walked out. Wilson got into the Mercedes. "Might as well drive with me. I'll drop you back here."

Burke shook his head. "That Sean. He really is a pisser. Sonofagun, he's always thinkin' of somebody else."

The Mercedes pulled out of the parking lot, down a fork in the road and onto the Rockville Pike. Wilson drove for a mile and half and took a right down a beautifully wooded country lane.

Burke's eyes were popping. "Jesus. It sure is beautiful. Sean has taste."

The car slowly drove past a shimmering pond sheltered by willows. Wilson turned onto a gravel driveway, and Burke could see the top of an elegant white mansion over the treetops.

"Get ready, Frank. This is some house."

They pulled through a wooded area, and a huge white Colonial stood atop a gentle rise.

"Christ. It's better than the White House."

They drove up the sloping driveway. Wilson fumbled in his pocket and pulled out a console as they approached the garage. He pressed the button.

"Damn—doesn't work."

Burke leaped out, yelling behind him, "Is it open? I'll open it for you."

"Thanks, Frank," Wilson called from the driver's side.

Burke leaned down for the handle and heaved the door up. He turned to Wilson. "Okay—drive in."

Suddenly Burke felt his lungs explode, and the air hissed from him as he doubled over, stumbling backward into the garage. The shovel had him clean in the solar plexus, and he lay gasping for air, not knowing what had happened.

Burke shook his head a dozen times to orient himself. He heard the garage door close. He was in the garage now. A light switched on. Then he heard the screeching of the Mercedes' tires as it reversed down the drive.

His head cleared now. His eyes focused on the men around him. Christ, this is a setup!

He rolled to his feet and jumped backward, with his back to the door. He was recovered now. Wilson . . . Eddie Wilson . . . Eddie Wilson . . . Jesus, no—not Eddie. He had set him up.

"C'mon, Frankie, don't fight it. You know the score." It was the voice of Joe the Polack. They were all there in a big semicircle. The Big Swede, Fitzie Jones, Red Bianco, Chuckie Connell. All of them Tommy Pruitt's boys from Union City, New Jersey, otherwise known as the "Joisey Boids."

Fitzie held a gun on Burke. The others were armed with baseball bats and shovels. They circled close to him, edged closer.

Burke's head was clear now. He felt for his waistband. Jesus, don't be crazy, he told himself. There hadn't been a gun in that waistband for twenty years.

The men from New Jersey were being careful. The Big Swede lunged first with the shovel. A vicious swipe caught Burke full across the shoulders. He grunted as the blow struck him, but then he got inside the shovel and let out a lightning kick that caught the Swede in the testicles.

The big man fell to the ground, and his shovel clattered on the concrete. Burke dived for it. As he did, Red Bianco caught him on the left arm with the baseball bat. The arm dangled useless, the elbow shattered to splinters.

Burke grabbed the shovel with his free right hand and swung it like a sword over his head. The blade caught Bianco full in the throat, slicing his jugular vein and causing blood to spurt four feet in a thin stream.

The blow had thrown Burke off balance. The Swede stumbled to his feet.

"Shoot the fucker. Shoot him. Shoot him."

Fitzie, who was holding the gun, backed up. "No, no. You know the orders. Get him. Get him."

"Yeah," Burke spat. "Come on—get me, you fag fucks." His eyes were blazing as he charged in again with the shovel. His swiped again, missed, and his footing slipped.

That was all they needed. They descended on him like sharks on the carcass of a whale. First Bianco with the bat. Then the shovel, wielded by Big Swede, came crushing into the side of Burke's head. He was still conscious and rolling over on the concrete, trying to dodge the blows. It was useless. Joe the Polack hammered the side of Burke's ribs with another bat, and Burke felt the fire in his lungs. The blood came up from the burst lung, and it choked in his throat as he tried vainly to cough it out.

He could still see them, but he couldn't move. He coughed up the blood, and it splashed on the boots of his attackers. He felt more blows as the Swede, Joe the Polack and Chuckie Connell thudded the blows to his head and body.

Burke heard a crack. It was his skull, but he felt nothing. He saw the light blazing above him, but then the light became peppered with black rings, and then the rings filtered out the white until there was just blackness.

He coughed again, and as his throat cleared he managed a deep half-gurgling, half-growling sound. The men said they couldn't make it out, but they thought he said, "Wilson . . . you Rat . . ." And then as the last breath hissed out of his body they clearly heard him say twice, "Sean . . . Sean."

The killers stood around, their shoulders heaving for breath.

"Why the fuck didn't you shoot him?" the Big Swede asked of Jones.

"Ya prick, ya knew the orders. No bullets. The whole plan would have been fucked. How's Red?"

"Long gone. Got him clean across the throat. Poor Red."

Fitzie Jones seemed to take charge.

"Chuckie, you run down the road to where Wilson is. He'll take you back to Burke's car. Get the keys outa his pocket. Bring the car back here. We'll load him in the car, then back onto the service road. We gotta make the crash look good. We've busted every bone in his fuckin' body, I bet, so when the car crashes into the tree Burke's gotta be banged up so bad nobody will know the difference. He's got a bit o' booze in him now. It'll just look like a bad accident. He always was a crazy driver, old Frankie."

"What'll we do with Red?" the Swede wanted to know.

"We'll have to dump him closer to home," Fitzie said absently. "Now, Chuckie, go on—split. See Wilson. In the meantime, we better clean the joint up."

Connell nodded and ran down the road and jogged toward Wilson's Mercedes. He looked into the driver's seat and asked politely, "Mr. Wilson?"

"Yes," Eddie Wilson answered. He had been vomiting.

"Would you like me to drive, sir?" he said, again with almost painful politeness.

"Yes." Wilson said limply. They would have to drive back to the restaurant to get the gold Cadillac.

The man they called Chuckie drove back at a moderate, cool pace. Wilson felt as if there were no blood in his veins.

At last, as the car pulled to within a hundred yards of the restaurant, where Connell was to alight, Wilson managed to half-whisper, "Tell me —did he go quick?"

Connell looked at him quizzically. "Oh, Christ, no, sir. Your friend was a real tough guy. Went out like a man, too. Frank Burke was a helluva man. Went out like a man . . . sir."

Chuckie Connell then jogged down the road. Wilson sat drained in the driver's seat now. As he started up, the gold Cadillac slowly drove past. Chuckie Connell gave him a wave and tooted the horn of Frank Burke's car. The car that had been owned by someone who "went out like a man . . . sir."

Chapter

18

In ANOTHER era, many years before, Velas Zeibatski once could have done the examination much more easily. That was before the Nazis came, when he was a first-year medical student in Lithuania. The priest now stood over the stainless-steel table in the morgue of the Bethesda Naval Hospital and battled with his emotions to look dispassionately at the naked body of Frank Burke. It had taken state troopers an hour to untangle his broken body from the wreckage when a motorist early that morning had sighted the ghastly crash off the service road of the Rockville Pike. Burke had been half-hurled through the windshield, and the medical examiner had hardly given the body a second look. "Middle-aged Caucasian identified as Francis Xavier Burke. Death caused by massive internal injuries, fractured skull and internal hemorrhage. Multiple fractures, ruptured spleen and punctured lungs."

The priest, no stranger to death on any level, had taken the news from Mike McGavin earlier that morning with a frightening stoicism. He had flown to Washington to be by the side of Senator Sean Keogh.

Keogh, when told the news, had only gasped a single phrase: "I knew it had to happen. God had to take him from me." Then he had lapsed into what McGavin saw as an almost frightening catatonic state.

McGavin had reacted with speed. He had quickly checked the Senator into a suite in the Mayflower Hotel under an assumed name to spare him the scrutiny of his colleagues in the media. There a hastily summoned doctor had knocked Keogh unconscious with a powerful shot. McGavin was worried that the shock of his beloved friend's death might prove too much of a blow. It was essential to keep the gravity of Keogh's reaction totally secret.

Del Vecchio, Morales, Sharpe and Wilson had gathered in the suite that afternoon. Rose Keogh had stayed in Boston at the side of Burke's widow, Teresa Burke. All were silent. Edward Wilson was gray. But it was the priest who had quckly put to Mike McGavin a simple request.

"I want to see the body, Michael. Arrange it—and please, this is just between you and me."

As the priest stood in front of the stainless-steel table, his inner self revolted against the antiseptic cleanliness of the surroundings. It was almost as if the priest would have preferred to be leaning over Frank on a sidewalk, administering the last rites surrounded by a circle of policemen and gawkers. There was an obscenity about Frank Burke's going out in a driving accident . . . and Father Velas Zeibatski didn't believe in obscenities and he didn't believe Frank Burke had died in a driving accident.

The priest had exactly half an hour alone in the morgue. McGavin had pulled strings. Father Zeibatski slipped on surgical gloves and switched on the powerful light above the table. He fought back the waves of grief that swept over his old but taut body. The Medical Examiner, had, as required, gone through the motions. But by any standards it had been a rough, perfunctory autopsy.

The priest remembered well what he had been taught. Quickly he detached himself from the fact that the body of Burke was the same body that had sat in his confessional at Sacred Heart. He blotted out the memory of the beaming, fleshy face on the day he had married Teresa, and he refused to linger on the picture of the same face as he recalled for a split second the moments of baptizing his three children. He was now working, probing, investigating.

The grotesqueness of it all was well behind him now, and he started at the very tips of the corpse's toes, ticking off the injuries listed in the Medical Examiner's report, squinting his eyes as he examined the cruel fractures.

It was the fracture on the instep, just above the toes, that first absorbed him. According to the state troopers, Frank had been thrown almost clear of the engine block, which had crushed in the driver's seat. Had he been pinned behind the wheel, the fracture would have been consistent with his other injuries; nonetheless, the impact had been massive when the Cadillac wrapped itself around the tree.

He wiped the perspiration from his brow as concentration absorbed every fiber of his body. He quickly looked at his watch and continued the examination. Carefully he rolled the body onto its front. Again he went from the feet upward. His eyes narrowed, and he adjusted the light above him to a more intense beam. There appeared to be bruises on the backs of the leg, backs of the thighs, buttocks and shoulders. This was the exasperating part. When a body is laid out, the remaining blood settles in the lower portion, giving it a bluish, purple effect. He pressed hard with his fingers. No, they were contusions—definite contusions.

Quickly he examined the rest of the body. There it was. At the rear of the skull, base of the neck, was a clean wound. It was more like a slice. The edges of the flesh were not jagged, nor was the bone shattered. It was a clear, clean incision, as if had been inflicted by a scalpel, or a large knife, or an axe, or an instrument like a shovel.

There. There was another one. He was certain. There was simply no doubt.

Hurriedly the priest restored the cadaver to the position in which he had found it. He asked for forgiveness for violating Burke's body with the touch of his hand, stuffed the surgical gloves into his pocket and quickly moved out a side entrance. He caught a taxi to the Mayflower Hotel and hurried to the suite where Sean Keogh was under sedation.

The door opened, and McGavin's eyes questioned his. The priest's eyes said nothing, but behind those dark pools fierce fires of revenge blazed, and Father Zeibatski did not rebuke himself for very foul thoughts. The secret smoldered inside him. No one would know that Frank Burke had been murdered . . . not yet.

"How's the Senator, Mike?"

Del Vecchio stood up and answered for him: "Doctors have hit him with a bomb. He'll be out for three more hours. What should we do, Father?"

"Stay put, Del. Mike, you go back to the office and handle life there. Eddie, you would be more useful in Boston. See Father Daly at the church. Make the arrangements; then go to Teresa and Rose. Hickey can look after the office. I'll be here until tonight. We'll fly the body back tomorrow morning. I'll call Teresa myself soon. In the meantime, I'll stay here and wait to see how Sean is."

Mike McGavin looked at him incredulously. It seemed quite natural to be taking orders from the quiet-spoken priest, whose mind never ceased to amaze.

Father Zeibatski looked at Roger Sharpe. "Roger, Mike will man the office, but it might do well if you worked the lobbies and made sure that everyone thinks Sean is in seclusion for a couple of hours. Avoid the obvious political ramifications of what this means to the succession of the Teamster leadership. That goes for you, too, Mike. And Mike, by the way, contact Izzy Cohen; make sure he knows he's stepping up in the union. Nothing changes. Right?"

They all nodded their heads and obeyed like wound-up toy soldiers.

As they filed out the door, the priest went into the bedroom and sat down by the still form of Sean Keogh, his chest rising in even, shallow breaths.

It was 3:30 P.M. when Keogh's eyes flickered open. At first they seemed not to recognize the priest, and for a brief moment Father Zeibatski held his breath. Then Keogh's eyes focused, and they softened with recognition.

The priest smiled. "How goes it, fella?"

The pain returned to Keogh's face. "They knocked me out, huh? Scared I was going to do something crazy?"

"No," the priest said evenly, "just an old-fashioned way of pushing away the pain, Sean."

"He is gone, isn't he?"

"Yes, Sean. We all have to come to terms with that." The priest attempted no religious or intellectual rationalizations. His voice was flat, factual.

"Teresa?"

"Bearing up well, Sean. Tough. Rose is with her. Terrence is flying to Boston now from school. He'll be there now. Del is outside, very concerned. Mike and Roger are working things over on the Hill. I sent Eddie back to Boston to hold the fort there. Izzy Cohen is on standby."

Keogh nodded his head. The priest had fixed everything.

"I think I'll get up and face life, Father."

"Good idea, Sean. Good idea. Tough it out, son."

They went outside. Del Vecchio handed Keogh a stiff Scotch and water.

"Thanks, Del."

Alberto Morales looked silently at the priest, and he reached for the bottle. "I think I'll have one of those," the priest said.

And as he sipped, the rage of his secret bubbled inside him. McLaughlin, the two Sweeneys and now Frank. Who was behind this? This isn't gang warfare, he thought as he rolled the Scotch around his mouth, this is a fifth column.

"The funeral, Father?" Del Vecchio asked.

"Day after tomorrow . . . same place . . . the same place." It was always the same place in South Boston.

THE EYES of Senator Sean Keogh scanned the faces at the graveside. They were the same faces, the same faces always—fleshier now than in earlier years, but still the same, who came out to bury their dead with the black solemnity that was so much a part of Southie.

Keogh silently cursed the brilliant early-spring sunshine and the pleasant breeze. He would have liked it to rain, or at least be gray and overcast. His mood could not justify the sunlight.

Beside him Teresa Burke clung to his arm, a proud, tough little woman who had done her crying in private and looked straight ahead, determined to stay dry-eyed. The children, two boys and a girl, stood likewise, knowing that their father would have chastised them if they showed their emotions.

Keogh's wife, Rose, stood on the other side of Sean, and her son Terrence held her arm, his sightless eyes trained toward where Father Velas Zeibatski stood over the coffin intoning the last words of the medieval rites that the people of Southie embraced as much as they did prayers of joy. The gentle wind waffled through the priest's chasuble, and he seemed to shudder slightly.

Sean Keogh could not remember when the priest had shown any real overt sign of emotion. But Keogh detected a tremble and slight crack in the priest's voice.

"Absolve, we beseech Thee, O Lord, the soul of Thy servant Francis Burke that he who is dead unto the world may live unto Thee . . . and wipe away by Thy most merciful forgiveness whatever sins he may have committed in life through human frailty. Through Christ our Lord."

Sean Keogh's lips mouthed the words automatically. He was not thinking now of a God who had failed him so brutally.

"Eternal rest grant unto him, O Lord, and let perpetual light shine upon him."

Keogh stared at the coffin. It was so difficult to grasp that Frank Burke was lying so cold and stiff inside.

"May he rest in peace."

Sean heard himself again say "Amen."

"May his soul and the souls of all the faithful departed, through the mercy of God, rest in peace."

The dark faces and pink lips of Southie uttered the final Amen, and the priest stood there motionless in front of the coffin for a long moment and nobody moved.

In almost half a whisper, Father Zeibatski simply said, "Bye, Frank. We love you."

Keogh's body shuddered all over, and he cared not that he could feel the warm, sticky tears rolling down his cheeks into the corners of his mouth. He looked across at Edward Wilson and silently wondered whom he summoned for his control. He stood like a marble statue.

Father Zeibatski crossed to the Keogh and Burke families and with his arms wide apart seemed to clasp them to himself.

Nobody spoke until they were in their cars heading back to Teresa Burke's house in Carson Beach. There drinks were served, and the women stayed close to Teresa sipping their tea.

Del Vecchio, Morales and McGavin stayed glued to Sean Keogh. They feared he might crack; but the Scotches helped ease the pain, and gradually Keogh could feel the blood again circulating through his body. It was as if he had been dead himself since he had first heard the news.

He wished Mary Rooney had been here. He could have shared his feelings with her. With Rose, it was different. She was a model of caring propriety, but Keogh never felt he could share anything with her. This made him feel bad, very bad. He couldn't remember a woman he respected more; but he knew one could not base love on respect.

As Sean Keogh looked around the room—the men in their dark suits which didn't quite fit them anymore, the women in their discount clothes —he wondered what the past twenty-five years had been about—his work, his dreams, his hopes. And yet nothing in Southie had really changed. They still died in the streets, they still felt alienated, and the few—like him, Frank, Eddie, McLaughlin and all the rest—who had the chance to make big money, they still clung to it and built on it and kept it.

Could it have been different? Could McLaughlin still be alive? Sweeney? Castellano? Frank? . . . Molly Keogh? Even Jimmy Rooney and Paddy Devlin. Could they have lived? It was as if the dark origins of Southie had written the script, and nobody dared change the scenes or the dialogue.

Senator Sean Keogh felt tired, very tired, and he asked himself how long before his part would be written in and he would be the object of mourning; how long before the same faces would gather to nod sympathetically at his passing. In Southie, he thought, men seemed to die so differently from the rest of the world. The dark suits always hung neatly pressed in the closets, the owners knowing that there would always be an occasion for them.

"How goes it, Sean?" The priest was at his side.

"I feel as if I'm losing my strength, Father."

"You're being very egocentric, Sean."

"Egocentric?"

"Yes—you think you have a corner on the grief market."

"Haven't I?"

"It's arrogant, Sean. Goddamn arrogant."

Keogh's face visibly registered the curse that he had never heard before from the priest's lips.

There was an edge of anger to Father Zeibatski's voice. He went on: "Do you think the loss of so many of our close friends hurts you more than it hurts me? Hurts you more than it hurts Teresa Burke, or more than the McLaughlins? You're losing your toughness, Sean, and you're losing it at a time when we need you to be even tougher. We have a stake in you, Sean. Don't let us down. You have to go to New Hampshire and swallow your grief, as the hundreds of men from Southie have done for decades. You have to go and win, win for us. Not you . . . us."

It was as if someone had given Sean Keogh a tiny electric shock. His eyes seemed to widen, the sleepiness of grief vanished. He yearned to get on a plane and go to the arms of Mary Rooney; he yearned to be able to walk out of Southie and never see it again. But he had fed off the men and women of Southie, and now it was pay-back time. New Hampshire and the White House could no longer be held as an ambition. They were now an obligation. He had to serve no mystic dynasty like the Kennedys. He had to pay back the people of Southie as surely as if he had received a personal loan from their pockets.

"I think I needed that, Father. . . . Now, how about another drink?"

"Sure. Why not? But Sean, don't think you have seen the end of tragedy with the passing of Frank. Tragedy will never be far from people like you and me."

Keogh looked hard at Father Zeibatski. It wasn't a philosophy, these words from the mysterious priest. It was a prediction; and somehow Sean Keogh knew he would pay dearly for whatever God gave him. God gave and took away, and with Sean Keogh, he did so in large measure.

Rose Keogh, from the other side of the room, sensed the rearmament in Sean. She fidgeted nervously as she held the arm of her son, Terrence. She looked around at the faces, which seemed to close in on her. The faces, always the same faces. Her head was burning. The terrible pain in her brain jabbed with tormenting barbs. Rose Keogh was not far from losing her entire grasp on reality.

It would get worse. She desperately needed help. And that night, when Teresa Burke had been sedated and Sean Keogh left to return to Washington, she kissed her husband on the cheek.

"I'll be back in Washington the day after tomorrow, Sean. See you, darling. I think I'll keep an eye on Teresa."

"Good idea, Rose. Keep strong. I'm going to need you. New Hampshire is only three weeks away."

"You're going to win. *We're* going to win. We're all behind you."

THAT NIGHT, Rose, Terrence and Wilson dined with John Hickey in his apartment.

Wilson had hardly uttered a word all day. Rose Keogh seemed to derive some pleasure from Wilson's discomfort. Terrence Keogh smiled inwardly as he heard his mother speak.

"You don't seem happy, Edward."

"Really? Should I? Do any of you know what this has been like for me?"

"I didn't realize you were so sentimental toward our departed Francis Xavier Burke."

Wilson remained silent. He was convinced of the truth. Rose Keogh was completely unhinged. Never before had he felt himself so terrified in the presence of danger.

"John, Terrence, for Christ's sake, will you tell this woman we can't go on like this? We've been lucky, very lucky, so far. It's not going to work. Can't we leave Keogh alone? Damn it, so what if he becomes President? It doesn't hurt us. We will all prosper. Let him alone. Frank Burke was no threat."

"There you go again, Edward." Rose's voice was like crackling ice. "Your stomach always fails you. Frank Burke was Sean Keogh's greatest strength. He was the danger . . . the danger to us. I think you have forgotten our resolve. Does the supreme power belong to Sean Keogh, a power-crazed maniac who wants to dominate everything he touches? Or does it belong to us? Are you telling me, Edward, that he is superior to us? Tell me, Edward—tell me."

Her voice had risen, and it had an irrational ring to it that terrified Edward Wilson. John Hickey and Terrence remained silent as Wilson squirmed.

Wilson remained silent and picked at his food.

Hickey spoke. "Well, Keogh will certainly win New Hampshire. The polls have him eight points ahead of Harris. With his across-the-board support from the black coalition, the ethnic groups and organized labor, his road to the presidency should be a relatively smooth one."

Terrence Keogh sipped quietly at a glass of champagne. "Is that how we want it, Ma?"

"Not quite, Terrence. But don't let's rush things. I think, however, from now on, all our profiles should be higher. Rallies, meetings and the National Committee meetings, and particularly with the delegates to the convention in New York. That's important. Keep that in mind. The delegates."

"Well, I'm sure your plan will be perfect, Rose." Hickey offered.

"I can assure you, John, it is."

Terrence Keogh was thinking aloud: "We do everything we can up until the convention to make sure the good Senator gets every possible help from us. Right?"

"Correct, Terrence dear."

"And then?"

"Well, we'll cross that bridge when we come to it. . . . But in the meantime, John, how is the lovely Jane Rooney doing?"

"Rather well," he said with a thin smile.

"And her starlet daughter, Mary Rooney?"

"Hopelessly infatuated with the front-runner in the presidential race, the august Senator Sean Keogh."

"Perhaps it's time Jane Rooney knew where her generous gifts of cash come from, and perhaps it's time that Jane Rooney knew why someone would pay such conscience money to her. Then it might be an auspicious time for Jane Rooney to realize that her daughter is sleeping with a man who left her fatherless."

"When would be a good time for this to happen, Rose?"

"Perhaps sometime after New Hampshire, when Senator Keogh is at his most euphoric. Agreed?

"Fine."

Hickey picked up his glass and smiled at the silent Wilson. "Come on, Eddie, drink up. We're on the last leg of a breathtaking triumph."

Wilson lifted his glass, but there was no celebration in his face. If only he could put a million miles between him and the three obsessed people at that table. It was hard for him to grasp that such an insane, unbridled lust for power and revenge could exist in the hearts of three human beings. How he wished he had not been so possessed by selfishness so many years earlier when all this had begun.

He was now living with terror. The magnitude of the treachery was difficult to comprehend, even though he had been a vital tentacle in the black conspiracy.

There was no question of Rose Keogh's brilliance, even though it was born out of a horrible sickness. What terrified Wilson most was wondering how long before Rose Keogh's sickness and her insanity could remain a secret. Sean Keogh would always be too blind. His mindless faith in other people's faith in him made it so. But Father Zeibatski. He was different, Wilson thought, and it chilled him to recognize that there were vibrations of suspicion emanating from this strange man. The priest was a man to contend with.

And what if Rose's scheme came to the final and horrible solution? What then? What of Eddie Wilson? How long would Rose Keogh tolerate his having the key to such treachery? How long before someone arranged a convenient accident for him? No, whichever way it worked, Edward Wilson believed he was doomed. They all were.

He felt sick as he walked out of the apartment, leaving Rose and Hickey to fall into bed with each other and Terrence sleeping in the spare room. It was all filthy and sick, and he was in the center of the sewer.

THE KEOGH forces had hit New Hampshire like a cloudburst. They swept through Manchester and Concord and blitzed the rural areas of the beautiful state for a full eight days before the primary. Ronald Harris had been bitterly stunned when publisher James Tolbin had told him with a frank but brittle delivery, "Ronnie, I'm sorry. Very sorry. We want to elect a Republican to the White House. Can't support you this time around. Don't want to drive a wedge in the party. Keogh's my man. I like you, honor you and admire you . . . but Keogh is my man. Must get a Republican elected."

It was not that Ronald Harris rolled over and died. He still had a superb machine, and some of the party faithfuls stayed with him right to the wire. But it was those with ambitions in the party, the untrustworthy who needed a winner, who flocked to Keogh's side—not, obviously, out of affection but simply out of survival.

Senator Keogh had split his forces. Rose, Terrence and Del Vecchio would storm through one town while he, McGavin and Father Zeibatski, with the help of the newly emerging power of Izzy Cohen in the Teamsters, would hit somewhere else. Then they would interchange.

Rose Keogh proved to be a stunning success, campaigning with a rarely seen fervor for a woman, speaking from backs of trucks to big crowds, rubbing shoulders at church meetings and standing outside schools talking to mothers. Terrence Keogh was always at her side and provided an able and cool-headed buffer against the press, fielding questions with an expertise and maturity far beyond his years. Del Vecchio capitalized on his image as a hero, waltzing through workingmen's bars and shaking hands and downing boilermakers with the men, with Morales always a step behind him.

The nation's eyes were now all on New Hampshire, and Senator Sean Keogh squeezed every ounce out of the massive exposure. He seemed to dominate the television screen, guided by the expert hand of McGavin, who seemed to have a sixth sense of what would grab air time and headlines. The priest had abandoned his pastoral duties and called on the various religious and ethnic groups to solidify support. Izzy Cohen was never far from his side, a reminder to the black population that he had opened up the Teamster job market to minorities. And while the minority vote was not essential in New Hampshire, it was vital in the big cities, where every move in the primary was closely watched.

Sean Keogh campaigned with a fervor, fueled by the priest, putting personal tragedies behind him, mindful of his debt to those who had put their lives in his hands.

On the day before primary day, Roger Sharpe flopped exhausted in a chair in Sean Keogh's hotel suite in Manchester.

"Tomorrow there will be a turnout of a hundred and seventy-five thousand. We've got sixty-five percent of them. It's as simple as that. Your wife, Rose, seems to have stolen the female vote from Harris completely. I was amazed at the way she handled herself. I had no idea she knew so much about the issues."

"A smart girl, Roger. Really smart," Keogh said as he sat, drained, on the bed, too tired even to undress. "I should have let her have her head in politics a long time ago. But I guess I'm just an old male-chauvinist pig from Southie."

"Well, she was great, And Terrence too. It must be in his blood."

Keogh mused on that statement. He had somehow never accepted such a contingency as possible. Terrence, he thought; brave, tough Terrence—he seemed so many miles away from him, and yet he worked and sacrificed all the time in campaigning.

"He's a fine lad . . . a great brain. I have high hopes for that boy. Everything seems so effortless with him. It's amazing: nobody ever seems to recognize his handicap. I'm very proud . . . very proud."

"You're a lucky man, Sean."

The Senator fell silent. A lucky man.

"Well, I'm bushed. I've had it. I'll call you at six in the morning, Sean. We'll have an early breakfast. Then we'll get down to City Hall about eight forty-five for the usual pictures and television coverage of you greeting the voters. We'll make it a family affair. Always looks good for the cameras."

Roger Sharpe got up from his chair and wearily headed for the door.

"Thanks for everything, Roger. You've worked very hard. Thanks."

Sharpe smiled and gave a silent wave good night.

Keogh lay on the bed exhausted. Rose, Terrence, Del Vecchio and Morales would arrive in Manchester the next day for the voting. He suddenly felt so alone. Confident of the morrow's outcome, but so alone. He picked up the telephone and called Mary Rooney. Her voice on the telephone was flat. Suddenly, at the sound of his voice, it brightened.

"I'm feeling awful, darling. Awful."

"What's wrong, Mary?"

"I've been watching you on television all night. The news, specials, everywhere."

Keogh chuckled. "Well, I certainly hope I have a different effect on the voters tomorrow. What's so bad?"

"You're going to win, aren't you?"

"Hope to."

"You'll win, Sean, and after that the news commentators say you'll definitely get the nomination and probably the presidency."

"Could be."

"Then what about us? . . . Am I to be a President's mistress for the rest of my life and be written about in somebody's book in a hundred years' time?"

"Don't talk like that, Mary."

"But it's true, and you know it. You have a wife, a family. I'll always be a secret person, never able to introduce you to my friends. . . . Oh, God, Sean, you'll have to forgive me, but it's almost as if I didn't want you to win. I wish you were a salesman or something."

"Mary . . . please . . . I . . . There will be a way. I promise you."

"I love you so much, Sean, it hurts. It hurts, Sean."

"I love you too, Mary. We both just have to be patient."

They talked for half an hour, and when he replaced the receiver, the exhilaration of the anticipated victory seemed so terribly empty. Everything Mary Rooney had said was true. And not only that: how long would his dark secret be safe from her? If she found out, she would hate him—and he would deserve her hatred.

He undressed wearily and slipped into bed, limp. But he must not cave in, he told himself. He remembered the words of the priest.

The next morning, Rose had arrived for breakfast. Manchester was alive with activity. James Tolbin had called him earlier to wish him luck. He felt a little apprehensive. The butterflies were there, but above all he was confident.

The entire clan sat down for breakfast.

Keogh looked across the table at his wife. "Roger tells me that you're the real politician in the family, Rose, my dear."

Terrence Keogh, sitting on her right, smiled.

"Really, he tells me that you positively swamped them."

She flashed an exuberant smile. "I must confess I surprised myself."

She lied. Rose Keogh was very much aware of her ability to manipulate people, whether it was a single person like Eddie Wilson or whether it was a mass of people. Rose Keogh was a master politician and probably every bit better than Sean Keogh, as she and Terrence supposed. Her grasp of people—their strengths, their weaknesses, their vanity, their ambitions—was nothing short of awesome. And Terrence, in the same quiet way as his mother, was almost identical in his skills.

"Well, shall we?" Keogh announced as the group finished their coffee.

"This is it, Sean," Del Vecchio said, standing up. Morales pulled his chair back for him. "This is the first round. As an old fight fan, I think you're going to win by a knockout."

"No, Del. *We're* going to win by a knockout. . . . What do you say, Roger? When do we announce Del as a running mate?"

"Hmmm. Maybe after the Massachusetts primary. I don't know—maybe we should hold off until the convention. We can chew that one over later. Now let's get down to the polling booths and put on our best smiles for the camera."

The newsmen rushed them in the lobby of the hotel. All the top national reporters from Washington were there. The New York press and its columnists were also there by the planeload. Keogh was the story. Not only that, so was Rose Keogh, who over the past six months had shown herself in such an uncanny light. It was an attractive double for the newsmen—not to mention Del, the hero of Puerto Bravo: Robert Del Vecchio.

Mike McGavin played his colleagues like a violin. He knew what they wanted, and he laid it on for them in massive doses.

Outside the polling place, Keogh and his group were mobbed. The crowd around him chanted "Ke-ogh, Ke-ogh, Ke-ogh." Everywhere in the sea of people he saw the big round badges they were wearing. They all read I'M A KEOGH MAN or I'M A KEOGH WOMAN.

For a Republican primary it was surprising. Gone was the quiet and sometimes dour understatement of New Hampshire. The people somehow felt they were showing the rest of the nation the direction to go in for a savior.

Keogh smiled, waved, gave the victory salute and posed with his arms around his wife and son. The media lapped it up. The reporters descended on Rose, and after one interview, the television reporter faced the cameras and said, "There is a quiet and dignified confidence about Mrs. Rose Keogh that says she is already looking through the decorating books as to how the interior of the White House should look in 1985."

Outwardly, Keogh bathed in the adulation; but as they posed for photographers, he said in an aside to Father Zeibatski, "Wouldn't Frank have loved all this?"

"Don't think about it, Sean," the priest answered. His voice was full of sadness, but it was tinged with anger. He had loved Frank Burke as much as anyone, and he didn't want Sean Keogh to fold at the point of victory.

That day was an arduous one, with the Keogh family and clan being ferried around by helicopter to make appearances throughout the state. At 9 P.M., they returned to the Manchester City Hall, where the press had set up their cameras and the first returns, supplied by computers, were announced on television.

City Hall was shoulder to shoulder with Keogh supporters and the press. Ronald Harris was nowhere to be seen. The first returns began to trickle in at 9:30 P.M. and showed an early lead for Keogh. By 10 P.M.

the lead had increased, and already the newscasters were predicting a landslide for Keogh.

At 11 P.M., Walter Cronkite broke into the coverage.

"The CBS computer has chosen Senator Sean Keogh as the victor in the New Hampshire primary. First computerized figures show that the Senator from Massachusetts gained in excess of sixty percent of the vote in a heavy turnout today."

At the Keogh party headquarters, the crowd erupted in loud cheers, and again Sean Keogh and Rose found themselves in the eye of a hurricane.

As Senator Keogh battled his way to a makeshift podium, backed by huge color posters of himself, Terrence Keogh edged close to his mother. "Well," he said, "it looks as if the Senator is well on his way."

"I think I could correct that a little. *We're* on our way." She smiled at her sightless son, and although he could not see her smile, he returned it.

The Senator stood on the podium.

"I wish I could shake everyone's hand in New Hampshire . . ." An approving roar drowned out his words. He held up his hand for silence, grinning broadly.

"Friends, I thank you for your support, I thank you for your faith and I thank you for your choice." More cheers.

"Today, we have shown a state in this great country a way to the future, a way for a unified nation, a nation that deserves the fruits of prosperity from the labor of men—and women—who work with their hands, men and women who work in offices, men and women who work for the betterment of our educational system—all men and women. We have shown that the old wounds and old divisions are only for the history books, that no job, no amount of money, no religion, no color, no geography can ever divide us again. We have shown that suspicions and prejudices are also antiques, relics of an immature past. We are all, you and I, experiencing a gratifying growing-up period. We have shown that today. And next month we will show it in Massachusetts, and after that Vermont, and after that Florida and Georgia, where I'll be participating in primaries. And then we will show it at the Republican convention and later in the presidential elections. New Hampshire has shown the way. Let's go down that road together. God bless every one of you."

City Hall reverberated with thunder. The newsmen swarmed in again. Rose had her arm around him now, and she planted a kiss on his cheek and made a victory sign with her fingers. The nation was in love.

Sean Keogh was as good as his promise in Vermont and Massachusetts and then in the Florida and Georgia primaries. He was as much adored in the South as he was in the North. California and Oregon would tie up the count. The love affair the nation was deep into had no restraints. When Senator Ronald Harris dropped out of the Florida primary, he announced his unconditional support for Keogh. The party hacks could now muster little opposition as the California primaries approached. The nation as one was solidly behind the Senator and his petite and brilliant wife, Rose.

When the Harris Poll came out, it showed that if an election were held immediately, Senator Sean Keogh would defeat the incumbent President Rawlins by an overwhelming 63 percent to 37 percent, the biggest edge a challenger had ever had over an incumbent in United States history. The Keogh machinery worked like a Swiss watch, capable of covering every contingency on issues from inflation to unemployment, race relations to foreign policy. He had welded a voting public into an uncanny and optimistic single-mindedness.

It was over dinner that Sharpe made the next move. He looked across at Keogh and Del Vecchio. "I think the time is ripe. We have started the rumors in the press. Now it is time to confirm them that Del will be your running mate."

Keogh smiled, and Del Vecchio shook his hand.

The news was greeted enthusiastically, partly because Del Vecchio, as the savior in Puerto Bravo, was held high in the minds of the average American and partly because the public couldn't comprehend Senator Keogh's making anything but a wise choice.

But if the political action fed a tiger inside Sean Keogh, he realized it. His clandestine meetings with Mary Rooney were becoming more difficult to effect. For one thing, his physical appearance anywhere was far too noticeable, and for another, his backbreaking schedule allowed him almost no free time. The telephone conversations got longer and more frequent, but the visits rarer. He was now a slave to his mission, and once again Sean Keogh felt duty-bound to put his personal wishes far behind those of the people who relied on him.

Politically, either on the Hill or on the hustings, he worked more perfectly with each new appearance. "But Father," he confided in a private meeting in the Sacred Heart Church, "I feel like a programmed robot. I love the girl, Father. I love her."

"I told you, Sean, on the day we buried Frank Burke, pain, suffering and tragedy would not end with the passing of Frank. There is no alternative, Sean. You are a married man. You are going to be the next President of the United States. You owe it to yourself, to Southie, to the country and to us to go through with it."

"Isn't it strange: my greatest ambition within my grasp—an ambition to put us on the map that consumed me through the years on the streets of Southie, through the building of the *Clarion,* through the Assembly, through the Senate; always the burning, burning . . . but suddenly the light has gone out. The burning has ceased."

"What do you think Bernard McLaughlin or Frank would say if they heard you say that?"

Sean Keogh gave a mirthless chuckle. "They would probably say something that shouldn't be repeated within these walls."

"That's right, Sean. Remember that. Remember their love, and remember what they did for you in their blind fidelity . . . the organization that was handed to you on a platter . . . and yes, remember I was here when Paddy Devlin died. Mac and Frank—that's how much they loved you."

It was always the same. Whenever he felt he was running out of gas, he knew the priest could be relied upon to snap him back into line. Father Zeibatski didn't relish making the burden of obligation rest so heavily on Sean's shoulders. But a job had been started, and it could not be aborted now through mere human frailty. Too many had suffered and died on the upward climb.

Sean Keogh reached into his pocket and withdrew the familiar brown envelope. The priest looked hard at it.

"Is this necessary anymore, Sean? The child is grown up. You are looking after the Rooney girl directly. Is this necessary?"

"Who knows? Guilt doesn't evaporate because an obligation becomes less urgent."

"Perhaps."

After leaving Sacred Heart that night, Keogh drove to the empty house in Carson Beach. Sleep had become very difficult over the months. His political future was so certain, and yet his personal future was so shot through with question marks.

That night he had been observed.

"I THINK it's time, John," Rose Keogh said into the telephone from the house in McLean, Virginia. "First Jane Rooney. She must know."

"I have the serial numbers of the money sent to her. We intercepted the registered package. That will be concrete proof. Then she will tell her daughter. The balloon will go up."

"But she must be counted on to say nothing to the authorities or police. That would ruin everything for us."

"I can count on it, Rose. She will take my advice. I have her exactly where I want her."

"I bet you do, John. Bye for now, darling, Be careful."

"I will. It's all coming together. I think you are a genius, Rose."

Rose Keogh put down the telephone and turned to her son. "I think we're getting close, Terrence. Very close. It's time."

"When do you want me to move?"

"A week or ten days."

"Fine, Mother. Then what?"

"The master touch, Terrence. Open a bottle of champagne for me, will you dear? I think you'll like it."

The next day, John Hickey boarded the afternoon Eastern shuttle from Boston to New York. He had called Jane Rooney at work earlier that day. In the evening they would eat in at Jane's Greenwich Village apartment. She liked to cook for him. It gave her the feeling she wasn't being just a good-time girl, going to the elegant restaurants where Hickey was such a well-known and sometimes popular figure. It gave her a feeling of permanence with Hickey, although his time in New York had dwindled in the last months. She understood the pressures. She wanted no more than to be with Hickey—in his company; in her bed—whenever he could spare the time. She was content. She made no demands on him, and she scrupulously dated nobody else. Anyway, who could compare to the dashing and charming Hickey?

He arrived at her apartment from the Pierre promptly at seven. He was suitably garbed for an at-home dinner in a crisp sports jacket and slacks. He was always so appropriately dressed. His elegance had its effect on Jane in much the same way it was pervasive with Rose Keogh. Jane was simply but stylishly clad in tailor-made slacks and a cashmere sweater. She was wearing a Cartier watch that he had given her.

When he walked through the door, she had to suppress what would have passed for an almost girlish squeal of delight. It had been three weeks.

She threw her arms around and kissed him full on the mouth. When she disengaged, she sighed his name.

"Jane," he said, "you make me feel so guilty, leaving you here alone in this apartment for weeks on end." He was very convincing.

"It's worth every second of it when I know I'm going to see you."

He walked into the living room. His face was serious.

She felt the difference in him. "John. What's the matter?" Her face was only inches from his. He could smell the discreet perfume that drifted from her. His brow furrowed.

"John, will you tell me what's the matter? Have I done something wrong?" The thought panicked her.

Hickey gave her a sympathetic smile and drew her close to him. She trembled with relief.

"No, my darling. How could you do anything wrong?"

"Thank God for that. Tell me, please."

He stalled. His timing was perfect. "Could I fix us a drink?"

She nodded, mystified at his behavior. He was always so charmingly jocular.

He poured two Scotch and sodas. He handed one to her. He sipped silently, then sat on the couch. With deliberate and serious motions he pulled out a cigarette case, took out a Dunhill and lit it. He drew heavily on the cigarette and slowly exhaled. She had not said a word.

"Jane, I think I have some important information. I have had the information now for over a month. Frankly I haven't had the gumption to tell you. For that I'm ashamed."

"John, I can't imagine you could do anything that would cause any shame . . . to anyone."

"Well I have, and I am ashamed."

"Tell me . . . please. Let me be the judge."

"Jane, did you receive your usual parcel this month?"

"You mean money? Yes. Yes, as always. Father Comerford simply brought it here. It's no use my telling him I don't want it. He simply shakes his head and leaves it. I don't need it anymore, John. Not with Mary now working out in Los Angeles. What do I need?"

He took a theatrically deep breath. "Well, it just so happens that I know you got a package. I know how much you got."

"But how? I haven't mentioned anything. How?"

"Because of the seriousness of this situation, there are some things I can't tell you. It's very serious. For instance . . ." He paused and withdrew a slip of paper. There were neatly penciled numbers on it. "I even know the serial numbers of the hundred-dollar bills. Here—compare them with the money you received."

She looked hard at the numbers. Her face registered complete bewilderment.

"Please, John, I don't understand this, Please explain."

"I have found out who has been sending you all this money over the years."

Her face went ashen. She never questioned anything Hickey said.

Her voice came in a half-whisper, half-gasp. "You know? You know? But . . . oh, for God's sake, tell me."

"Please, Jane, steady yourself. I've debated about telling you. I didn't want to. But it's a duty for any man who loves a woman to keep no dark secrets."

She was silent.

"God forgive me," he said, "it has been Senator Sean Keogh. Keogh —that's right: my boss, my benefactor, your benefactor, the man who will be the next President of the United States."

Her voice was small. "You are sure, John? Positive? It couldn't be a mistake?"

He shook his head grimly. "Check those serial numbers. How else would I know? He has always given the parcels to his priest. Zeibatski. He transfers the money to you through Father Comerford."

"What did he have to do with Jimmy Rooney's murder?"

She no longer called Jimmy Rooney her husband. At least, not in front of John Hickey. She wanted to make sure that he knew he was the only man in her life now. The cancerous bitterness had dissolved since she had known John Hickey.

"What did he have to do with the murder?" He repeated the question. "Probably very little. He was too young. As best as the authorities can work out, he probably set your husband up. Maybe even unwittingly."

"And this is his black conscience? How sorry I feel for the vermin."

"Jane, there is more."

"Oh, God."

"This is the most painful of all . . . he is having an affair with your daughter, Mary. She wasn't to know—and to be fair, he wasn't to know. They met in Vegas, and she was using a phony screen name."

It was too much for the sensitivities of this serious, loving and caring lady. She collapsed to her knees in front of Hickey, who was sitting on the couch. Her head fell heavily in his lap, and he could feel her sobs soaking into his slacks. He ran his fingers in a soothing motion through her hair.

"Tell me, Jane . . . tell me I was right in letting you know."

Many seconds passed before she lifted her tear-stained face.

"Oh, John. Yes, yes, yes, yes. You were." She sobbed some more.

"You are certain of that, Jane?"

"Yes, my darling. I have lived with it for so long. Mary—poor Mary. Does she know?"

"No. I leave that judgment up to you."

"The poor child. The poor, beautiful child. Do you think she really loves him?"

"I just don't know. They have spent a lot of time together, according to independent investigations. I had to know, darling, for your sake. How could it go on? If she found out farther on down the line, it would kill her."

"You're right. Yes."

"But Jane, if you tell her. This must only be between the three of us at this time. There is not enough evidence. Not nearly enough evidence. Much is at stake. Right now it would shatter the country. You must understand the responsibility I have imposed on you. For openers, he may not have had anything to do with the actual murder. Maybe he knew who did it and this was his way of assuaging his conscience."

"I understand, John. In a way I understand. But . . . Oh, my God. I don't know what to do."

He held her close for a long time. She clung to him like a frightened animal. So much of the past came hurtling back into the present. She lay folded in his arms for half an hour.

Finally, she raised her head and attempted a smile.

"I don't feel very hungry. Do you?"

"Not really, Jane."

"Will you stay with me tonight, John . . . please?"

"Of course I will—you know that."

"No, not that way. Not the way we usually do. I just have to hold on to something I love and can trust. I just want to hold you. That's all."

They went to bed, and Jane Rooney cried herself to sleep. For the first time that they had shared a bed, they did not make love.

Long after she plunged into a fitful but deep sleep, Hickey lay there awake thinking. I believe I've pulled it off to the letter, he reflected.

She awoke late that morning, called the office with an excuse of sickness. Her face was pale and her pretty eyes were puffed. She managed a wan smile. "I'm okay now, John, darling. I'm okay. Don't worry."

"That's the girl." Hickey smiled and pulled her to him.

"Breakfast, darling?"

"Yes, I think I could manage it."

"Me too," she said cheerily. She went into the kitchen and prepared breakfast. They allowed themselves only small talk.

"Could we stay together today?"

"I'll cancel everything."

"You're wonderful. I've been doing a little thinking."

"I guessed as much."

"I think I'll call Mary. She's a strong and intelligent girl. She must stop seeing Sean Keogh. I'm determined."

"Could she handle it? Could she handle knowing that she must keep this an absolute secret until we know more?"

"Yes, yes, I believe she can. She is a rare girl, my Mary."

"I believe it."

THE SPRING sunshine of Washington blazed through the window of Senator Keogh's office in the Senate Office Building. He sat at his desk. Before him were McGavin and Del Vecchio, poring over scheduling sheets.

"Five weeks and I think we'll have California in the bag, Senator," McGavin said confidently as he scribbled on a clipboard he was holding.

"It gets better every day, Sean," Del Vecchio offered. "Your announcement of me as your running mate before the convention hasn't hurt the polls a bit."

Keogh laughed loudly. "You're fishing for a compliment, you sly old dog. It's helped them, and you know it. Listen, it's not every day we get a savior, a hero, a messiah. It's helped enormously."

"Do you know, we could skip California if we really wanted to," Del Vecchio said.

"Don't think so," Sean answered. "It just might give our pretty boyfriend Senator Ronald Harris new ideas." He looked out the window. "God, what a beautiful day."

"Why don't you take the rest of the afternoon off, Senator?"

"I might do that later. But I think I'll go down for my workout in the gym. It's really become a habit. I feel great. Lost eight pounds since I started."

"Sounds like hard work to me," Del Vecchio chuckled. "You swim; you punch the bag; then you bake yourself in that confounded steam room. Not for me."

The light banter was interrupted by the shrill sound of Keogh's private line. He picked up the telephone.

"Keogh."

"Sean?" Mary Rooney's voice sounded strained.

"Just one second." He put his hand over the mouthpiece. "Is that all, gents? Do you need me for anything else?"

"No, no," Del Vecchio said. "Certainly not," McGavin chimed in. They took the hint and hurried from the inner office.

Keogh's voice softened. "This is a pleasant surprise, darling."

"Is it?" Her voice was weary. She had spent many hours in agony, the kind of agony that comes with heartbreak.

"Mary, what's wrong? Are you okay? You sound terrible. You sick?"

"No, Sean. It's just that I have just lost something very precious, very dear to me."

"My God, what's wrong, baby? What have you lost?"

"You," she said flatly, and he could hear her choking back tears.

Keogh's voice grew frantic. "Christ, Mary, what the hell are you talking about? Tell me, for God's sake. Is there someone else?"

She laughed irrationally, and her tone terrified Keogh.

"Sean. I know. I know all about you. The money to my mother. My father, who I thought was killed in a car accident. What a joke. I could forgive you for the money . . . I somehow understand it. I didn't know about my father, but you knew."

"Mary—Mary, for God's sake, listen. Stay where you are. Let me fly out tonight. I swear I can tell you everything. It's not what you think."

"It never is, Sean. It never was the way I thought. How could you lead me on like that? . . . particularly after my father. Oh, my God, it's so sick. Is that who you really are, Sean Keogh? You must own everything you see? You must control everything?"

"Mary, I pray . . . I beg, please . . ."

"No, Sean. No need to beg. I'm not going to make a fuss. I'm not going to the newspapers. I'm not going to blow your secret. Your ambitions are safe. Don't worry, my darling Sean."

"Believe me, I don't give a damn about ambitions. I—"

He felt a stab in his lower stomach as he heard her sobs trailing off and suddenly a click. The phone went dead.

He called her number, but there was no answer. He dashed outside, panic, an emotion rarely seen on his face, painted all over him.

"Mike . . . Mike," he yelled. "Mike, get me on the first plane to Los Angeles, will you?"

"But Senator, we weren't going to—"

"Damn it, McGavin, can you do as you're told?"

Mike McGavin had never heard Sean Keogh address him like that—or for that matter, anyone.

"Yes, sir," he said quietly. McGavin and Del Vecchio exchanged worried glances.

One hour later Sean Keogh was on a plane bound for Los Angeles. He twisted in his seat in the first-class compartment, refusing any refreshments except coffee. He chain-smoked all the way, agonizing at what he might find when he arrived.

When he reached the apartment later that day, the pain increased. The apartment was exactly as it always was. Clean, neat, tastefully furnished in a cute and economical way. He swept through the apartment looking in the bathroom, in the closets, behind the draperies, under the bed, even under the sofas. There was nothing. Not even makeup.

Mary Rooney had disappeared completely. There was not a single trace of her ever having stayed there. Gone.

Chapter

19

IT HAD been five days since Senator Sean Keogh had returned from Los Angeles. He rationalized his misery. The agony had come so quickly on the heels of the loss of Frank Burke, Keogh told himself there was no fiber left inside him to hurt anymore. He walked into his offices in the Senate Office Building. He was calm. He smiled at Mike McGavin. It was the first time he had come face to face with his press aide since he had stormed from the building in a panic.

"Hi, Mike. You still talking to me?"

McGavin was flattered by the Senator's manner. "Don't be crazy, Senator." He knew all now. McGavin knew better than to embarrass Keogh. He handed him a folio. "California . . . That's the schedule."

"Fine." No matter how much pain Sean Keogh had endured, the toughness of Southie was never far from the surface of this man, and it amazed his associates just how quickly he could bounce back from the wells of darkness. He walked into the inner office, sat down and started poring over the details for the California primary.

Del Vecchio and Sean's wife, Rose, were in Baltimore, speaking at a luncheon for the Greater Baltimore Businessmen's Association. Rose had made appearances at luncheons and rallies for fifteen straight days. Her recognition factor on television and in newspaper photographs had stunned even the most astute media watchers. Her command of audiences and crowds, in direct contrast to her private demeanor, was in much the same style as her husband's. She would make the perfect First Lady, Sean Keogh thought as he glanced over the exhaustive schedule for California.

It was always in these moments that he felt the pain. How he wished it were going to be Mary Rooney instead.

What a preposterous thought! How preposterous all his thoughts had been lately. He felt as if he were caught in the vicious undertow of a booming surf. He never allowed himself arrogance, but he knew the presidency was his. Such a prize—but such an empty prize considering the state of his emotions. God, if the voters could only read his mind and emotions. They would stay away in droves. What a perfect act.

McGavin popped his head through the door. "Want to go out to lunch or order in, Senator?"

"Neither, Mike. Think I'll skip it and go down to the gym."

"You're really on a kick, Senator."

"At my age, those pounds around the middle count."

McGavin smiled and disappeared.

Senator Sean Keogh had embraced the physical therapy of his daily visits to the Senate gymnasium with a rare passion. Keogh had led such a narrow life. His fellow Senators were forever inviting him to come sailing or skiing. Sean Keogh, born in the sailing town of Boston, had never been on a boat until he was thirty-five. One didn't go sailing in Southie, and he had never had time to learn how to ski. Even his horses in McLean held little interest for him. One had to learn early in life to like horses. He had never even owned a dog.

People were Keogh's passion, and sailing and skiing and horseback riding didn't have a lot to do with people. But in the gymnasium he could call on his very reliable physical skills. He would swim in the pool, and he was a good swimmer from his days as a child at Carson Beach, where he had later bought a home. He would furiously punch the heavy bag. He had been an exquisite boxer as a kid, although from the day he saw Paddy Devlin's handiwork on Jimmy Rooney, he had never lifted a fist in anger or aggression—even though Devlin died through the most aggressive instinct of revenge that Sean Keogh had ever harbored. He would go into the steam bath and sweat the impurities out of himself, impurities both real and imagined—not an unusual act for a man whose life was haunted with guilt and self-doubt, no matter how he outwardly appeared.

A quiet had settled over the Senate Office Building. It was always the same. Between the hours of noon and three in the afternoon, Keogh mused, a bomb could be exploded in the Senate and not a single Senator would be killed. They would all be at the Sans Souci or one of the smart restaurants in Georgetown—or not in Washington at all. It was indeed a very special club, the Senate.

He walked into the gymnasium at 2 P.M. There were two old codgers in the pool. They were regulars. Amazing, he thought: the Senate had voted a hundred and eighty million dollars for a new Senate building complete with a new gym, and nobody, perhaps with the exception of Senator Bill Proxmire, ever used the old gymnasium. He gave a friendly wave to the old attendant, who spent most of his time in the equipment room watching television and drinking coffee.

The old man waved back. "Hi there, Senator. You're lookin' fit, sir."

He dived into the pool and felt the cleanliness of the chloride streaking through his hair. He stroked slowly and strongly until he felt his muscles grow taut. He wanted his body to ache, in the desperate hope that it would distract him from the hurt in his mind and heart. Dripping, he emerged. He dried himself roughly. The old codgers had left the pool. The entire place was empty. Such a waste, he said with a mental scowl.

He changed into his sweat suit, and went into the weight room, slipped on a pair of boxing gloves and approached the heavy bag. He assumed a classic boxer's pose, slightly crouched, his chin tucked close to his left collarbone, his stance slightly bowlegged in its wide spread, his fists like two snug hand grenades.

He pounded the bag with a straight jab, ripped with his right, hooked twice with his left, moved closer to the bag and let a right cross wallop the leather. The resounding slap gave him a satisfaction. He pounded with both fists, and his face grew sweaty with intensity. He could feel his actions letting loose the demons in him. Bam, thud. Damn it, Frank, that's for you, you sonofabitch; how dare you die on me? Whomp. Frank, how could you leave me? Bam, bam. You too, Mr. Mac, I loved you, and you too, Sweeney, you ignorant, thick-headed oaf. Whomp. Young Sweeney, you young fool. Thud, whomp. Frank, Mr. Mac, Sweeney . . . you too, Old Man Castellano; how could that happen to you? How strong he could have been with them; how secure he could have been.

Then he was punching in a frenzy and the bag had no face on it. He was punishing himself, for Mary, for Mr. Mac, for Sweeney, for Castellano and for Frank. If they had never met him, they might be alive today. His arms were like lead, but still he pounded, teeth gritted, with a madman's fury until he had to lean his dripping forehead against the sweat-stained leather of the punching bag, too exhausted now to care about the pain that stabbed at his inner self.

Weary with the pleasant pain of physical exhaustion, he trudged into the steam room. He stripped off his sweat suit and took off from his neck the gold chain and crucifix that always got hot first and burned his chest whenever he took the steam. He put a towel on the tile bench and sat down, slowly inhaling the pine-scented steam. It gave his lungs a pleasant sting. He exhaled heavily.

He looked down at his belly with satisfaction. It was much flatter and tighter than it had been a year ago. Then he looked at his penis and scrotum dangling over the towel-covered tile bench. He gave a grim chuckle. If it weren't for that ridiculous appendage and the clapped-out male ego of middle age, he would not be thinking of Mary Rooney right now.

He drew in another deep breath as if to shock himself out of thoughts that he would bring him pain. It worked, at least for the moment. He had confidence. He would be able to expunge Mary from his mind. It would just take time. Then he could return to being a loving husband and father.

Father? In all these years he had never grasped the thought that he was a father. Not a real father. He was a father, big brother and uncle to so many people, but he couldn't bring himself to be a father to a brave, brilliant boy named Terrence. Brave and brilliant—things that Sean Keogh could not think of himself as being. Energetic, pathologically hardworking, charming and in a strange way very honest, maybe even resourceful and tough. But not brave and brilliant like Terrence Keogh. Good boy.

He looked up at the thermometer on the wall: 180 degrees. God, this is good! The sweat was streaming now from every pore in his body. He would leave now and take a cold shower. No, not a cold shower, he thought; that's how old fools get heart attacks. A lukewarm shower.

Enough; he had been there ten minutes. He picked up his towel, grabbed his chain and crucifix and his soggy sweat suit. He wrapped the towel around his middle and walked through the steam to the door. He pulled at the large wooden handle of the big door with the small plastic window set in it.

Damn. Damn thing is jammed. No goddamn maintenance.

He gave it another jerk. Damn it. It's stuck. He flexed his muscles hard and pulled with everything he had. My God! He braced one foot against the tile wall and pulled with both hands. Holy Jesus! Again. Nothing.

"Hey . . . anyone there? The damn door is stuck . . . You there? Superintendent! Hey . . . hey . . . help! . . . hello out there!" Damn it. No bastard there.

He looked around the steam-filled room for something heavy to heave through the small plastic windowpane. Christ, nothing.

The panic started to rise in his stomach. He ripped off his towel from around his waist. The steam swirled about him. His body was bright pink now. He swathed his fist in the towel. He drew back his right fist and slammed it with a mighty punch into the middle of the pane. It just thudded hard, and he could feel the jar from the impact all the way to his liver. Oh, my God, no. No.

"Help . . . help . . . help!" he was screaming frantically now. Sean Keogh had never screamed for help.

Oh, God, please, God, not this way. Not this way. Not in a stupid steam room. God, hear me, hear me. Please for Chrissake, God, hear me, please. I'm pleading.

"Anyone, help, help!" He was screaming at the top of his lungs, and the more he screamed the more his throat burned and his lungs blazed. He hit the pane again with his wrapped fist. It just bounced again, and the pain shot through his arm all the way to his shoulder. He then hit it with his bare fist. Once, twice. The steam scorched his body. He pounded desperately with both hands on the door. The dull sound of his hand slapping against the heavy door must be heard. He punched the pane again. Useless. It was triple thickness.

His body was puffed now and deep red. His temples were bursting. He could actually feel the blood boiling in his veins. Oh, no, God. His throat was closing, and when he screamed his voice came out in a grotesque strangled squeak.

He was losing his vision. Now he couldn't see. Only white and steam. Then the white started to darken. Gray, then blackness.

He was still clinging to consciousness. His hands were weakly slapping the door as he sank to his knees. He could feel no pain now. Just nothing. Nothing. Just nothing and blackness as he sprawled half-leaning against the door. There was silence apart from the hissing of the steam. Silence. Long, deathly silence for several minutes.

Then there was a scraping sound from outside.

Terrence Keogh slid the broom handle from between the outside door handle and the other side of the wall. He grabbed the broom in one hand, using his other hand to hold his cane, which he lightly tapped on the ground as he walked with confidence through the empty gymnasium. He strode to the end of the gym, placed the broom against a wall where the super always kept it. It was 2:45 P.M. The super would return, as he always did, at exactly 3:05 P.M.

Terrence took a left-hand turn, opened the entrance to the fire escape, descended to the ground floor, trotted out a side entrance onto the street, where he got into a waiting car.

"Done?" John Hickey asked from behind the wheel of the Mercedes.

"Done," Terrence Keogh said, quietly and without a trace of emotion. The Mercedes pulled off slowly.

MIKE MCGAVIN was halfway through his sandwich in the outer office when the telephone rang.

"McGavin, Senator Keogh's office."

"Mr. McGavin?" The voice had an edge of panic to it.

"Yes, McGavin."

"It's Willie, Mr. McGavin, the gym super. I've just called the ambulance; there's been an accident. It's . . . it's Senator Keogh . . ."

"Yes, man, out with it."

"He's had an accident . . . in the steam room . . . I pulled him out."

"What? Senator Keogh—is he all right? . . . An accident?"

"The ambulance men have just come in. . . . I think he's dead, sir."

McGavin slammed the phone down hard. The half-eaten sandwich rebelled in his stomach as he pelted out of the office to the gymnasium.

He arrived as the ambulance attendants were putting the naked form of Senator Keogh onto a stretcher.

"McGavin . . . I'm with the Senator," he yelled, still running, before he arrived at the stretcher. "Is he . . . Is . . . ?"

The ambulance attendant ignored him.

A small group of cleaners had gathered around the stretcher. "Get the fuck away," the attendant said with angry authority.

"McGavin . . . I'm—"

"I know who you are. . . . Jim?" He was talking to his assistant. "No, he's not dead . . . not yet. . . . Faint pulse . . . no guarantees." He roughly slammed a portable oxygen mask over the bloated face of the Senator. It was ugly, and the veins had swollen and there were tiny blisters all over the naked body.

The ambulance attendant roughly pushed McGavin aside. He held the oxygen mask tight with one hand and covered the naked Keogh with a sheet with the other.

"Christ, McGavin, make yourself useful. Grab the other end of the stretcher. And don't fuck around. We're fighting with seconds."

McGavin leaped into action. Seconds.

McGavin's face was ashen. He shuffled, holding the end of the stretcher, through the small group of open-mouthed cleaners who crowded around.

"You heard what the man said—fuck off!" McGavin screamed.

By the time they got the stretcher into the street and into the ambulance, the press in the gallery had gotten wind of the accident. The cameras clicked as McGavin got into the rear of the ambulance.

There, the attendant quickly changed oxygen masks. Senator Keogh's chest was still. McGavin could not see any movement. He was sure there was no sign of breathing. Hurriedly the attendant, without any ceremony, frantically drove an adrenalin needle into Keogh's limp arm.

McGavin couldn't clear his head. It was flooded with emotion and panic. He found it hard to talk.

"Please . . . just one word. Is he going to make it?"

The siren screamed through the afternoon Washington traffic. When he could feel the ambulance slowing, McGavin found himself irrationally cursing the cars around him. "Fucking bastards, can't they see an ambulance? . . . You tell me—is he going to make it?"

"Shut up."

At the hospital, McGavin leaped out first. He went to grab the end of the stretcher. Flashbulbs went off in his face. The press was there in legion. Word had spread very fast.

Two medics roughly pushed him out of the way. Senator Keogh was now on a hospital trolley, and the doctors and nurses sliced through the crowd like a circular saw. McGavin jogged after them as reporters plagued him with questions. He couldn't hear what they were saying. The Senator was rushed into Emergency, and a door slammed shut in the faces of McGavin and the hordes of press and television newsmen.

McGavin stood there in his shirt sleeves, his tie askew. Ringed by the newsmen, he shuffled in a daze to a bench.

"What happened?" "Was it a heart attack?" "Did he have any history of heart trouble?" "What do you know about his health?" "Could it be a cerebral hemorrhage?"

McGavin lifted his face from his hands as he sat on the bench with his elbows on his knees. He looked up as the cameras popped again.

"I don't know . . . I don't know. I got a call—three o'clock, maybe a little after . . . it was the gymnasium super . . . forget his name. He just said there had been an accident. He had called the ambulance, and they were there when I arrived . . . I came in the ambulance. . . . I don't know . . . I don't know."

McGavin's eyes were glassy. As more newsmen arrived, he answered the same questions over and over. He bit his knuckles.

"Jesus." He leaped to the pay telephone and called the office. He spoke to the secretary.

"Where's Mrs. Keogh? Mr. Del Vecchio?" He was oblivious to the eavesdropping ears around him.

"Okay," he answered. He was slowly getting a grip on himself. "And also get Father Zeibatski in Boston. Tell Mr. Wilson too. And try to find young Terrence. Is Mr. Morales around? . . . Oh, he's with Del . . . okay. . . . Yes, I'm okay. There's no news. None. Oh, yes . . . and find Roger Sharpe."

Minutes later, the hospital administrator arrived in the emergency room accompanied by uniformed security guards. To a chorus of virulent protests, they cleared the emergency room of the press.

McGavin recognized their anger. "Fellas, I promise you all. As soon as I know anything, I'll come outside and give you a bulletin. I promise. I've always been straight with you guys. Promise." He wasn't being altogether frank, despite the fact that he understood the way they felt.

At 4:30 P.M., Rose Keogh burst through the door. She was battling back genuine tears. Behind her was Terrence Keogh. He seemed calm. Del Vecchio and Morales followed minutes later. Del Vecchio hadn't believed it when he was first hit with the news. He remained silent, content to let the family do the talking. Father Zeibatski, Edward Wilson and Roger Sharpe arrived soon after, having chartered a plane from Boston.

McGavin shook his head. "It's been an hour and a half. They're still inside. . . . Nothing yet. . . . He looked very bad."

Rose Keogh burst into tears and buried her face in McGavin's shoulder. He could feel the wetness of her tears.

"Mike . . . Mike . . . I can't believe it all . . . I can't. . . . Sean is so healthy. There was nothing wrong with him. How, Mike? How?"

"He went down to the gym, same time as he's gone every day for the past few weeks. There was nobody there. Not even the damned superintendent."

The priest spoke slowly and deliberately. "Mike, he was breathing when they brought him in?"

"Father, you know as much as I do," Mike said with mild exasperation. "They had oxygen masks and gave him needles and stuff like that and he's been there for an hour and a half."

Rose Keogh leaned heavily on Terrence's arm. Young Keogh remained stone-silent. His lips were drawn in a single line.

The priest turned away and began to pace like a panther. He buried his fist in the palm of his hand several times in a punching motion. The rest sat down on the benches and chairs. The priest kept pacing. He remained silent, and for a moment McGavin thought that even the priest would not be able to withstand this blow, not so soon after Frank Burke.

Rose Keogh seemed like a limp little rag doll, half leaning against her son's shoulder. Terrence's lower lip was trembling, and McGavin thought he might burst into tears. Roger Sharpe and Del Vecchio chain-smoked, and Morales stood like a stone near the entrance as if on guard. Nurses hurried back and forth from the emergency room and every time the door swung open, they all half-leaped to their feet. The waiting was agony.

At 5:10 P.M., Dr. Eberhard West and the hospital administrator walked through the door. Their faces were grim.

Rose Keogh's teeth tore at a handkerchief she was holding to her mouth. She was the first to speak.

"Doctor, will he live?"

All those in the anteroom held their breath for the answer. The doctor spoke.

"To answer your question, Mrs. Keogh, your husband is alive . . . alive physically."

"What do you mean—physically?" she snapped at him.

"Just what I said. He's breathing, and the oxygen is feeding his body. He has responded to the drugs we have given him. We opened his chest and repaired many damaged vital vessels around the heart. The heart is beating, but weakly. The problem is that a clot has lodged at the back of his brain . . . near the motor section of his brain. It's a tiny clot, from what we can gather, and not a hemorrhage. But the problem is that there is a total absence of peripheral function."

"Please, Doctor, we are not physicians," she said tartly.

The priest cut in softly. "I think what the doctor is telling us that Sean is in a very deep coma."

"Correct, Father. Precisely. Only it's more than a deep coma. He is paralyzed. Every fiber and nerve tissue in his body. We have connected him to a life-support system, and he is now in Intensive Care. The operation was a risk, but we took that risk and he survived the trauma. It's just that while Sean Keogh is clinically alive . . . and I apologize for saying it . . . he is almost as close to not being here as if he were dead. I'm sorry. I really am sorry."

"Well . . . well . . ." Rose was jabbering now. "Well, can't you do anything to remove the clot?

"Removal of the clot . . . or should I say an attempt to remove the clot . . . would almost certainly be fatal."

"What are you saying, Doctor? Please. Please."

"In crude terms, but best understood by the average person . . . your husband . . . ah, the Senator . . . is . . . er . . . well, he is virtually a vegetable."

Her knees sagged, and Terrence Keogh helped her to a sofa.

Tears streamed down McGavin's face, and everyone else either bit his lip or winced. Roger Sharpe threw his head back against the wall and closed his eyes. Damn—such a man; such brilliance; such a leader.

Del Vecchio wiped his eyes.

Father Zeibatski quizzed the doctor further: "Are you suggesting we take him off that life-support system, Doctor?"

"That is a matter of personal and family conscience. Not for me to decide."

"Well, if you were a betting man, Doctor . . . let's be straight: what are the odds of the clot dissipating, restoring a normal flow of blood and oxygen to the brain?"

"Frankly, Father, so remote as to not even present odds."

Rose sobbed softly.

The priest persisted: "Doctor, there have been many cases, many similar cases . . . look, I'm not trying to tell you your job, but in the Soviet Union they have brought people back from comas after five years. They have techniques . . . new drugs."

The doctor nodded patiently.

"I understand what you're saying, and it's understandable to have hope, but it's my job to be totally frank with you. Even if the news is brutal. I'm giving you a qualified opinion. By all means invite second, third, fourth opinions. I'm afraid it's hopeless."

The priest seemed to be jutting his jaw out as if tempting someone to punch it. "You can be sure we will, Doctor . . . no disrespect."

"Of course not."

"Can we see him, Doctor?"

"Not tonight. He's in Intensive Care. In three days' time he will be removed to a private room linked to a life-support system. Call me at any time. There is nothing we can do right now—I swear it." He turned slowly and together with the administrator disappeared through the door through which he had entered. Everybody just stood or sat silently for long minutes.

"I feel so useless," Terrence Keogh said quietly. He meant it.

"Father." Rose Keogh spoke weakly.

"Rose?"

"Why don't we all go back to McLean tonight? There is plenty of room for everybody."

"Good idea," Wilson said.

The others all looked at each other and nodded.

"I'm afraid I'll have to stay in town, Mrs. Keogh. The press."

"I understand, Michael," she said quietly.

"I think I'd better stay close by too, Rose. Maybe I can help out in the office early tomorrow with Mike," the priest said.

"All right, then the rest of us will go back to the house."

"Mike." Roger Sharpe spoke. "I think it would be a good idea to keep the press stuff low-profile. Just say heart problem. Talk with the doctor and make sure your stories check out. Heart problem, critical but stable condition. We can amend it later. We don't want to throw the people into panic immediately. Let the seriousness creep up on them."

"Sure."

The Keogh clan wedged through the battalion of newsmen. Rose Keogh and Terrence gave brief interviews, deferring to Mike McGavin to give the medical report and take the brunt of questions—which, in view of Sean Keogh's condition, centered around the possibility of whether he would still run for the presidency.

"As I said, gentlemen," Mike said patiently, "the Senator's condition is critical but stable. Clarification of his heart condition would have to be arrived at before an assessment is made in the future of the Senator's physical eligibility. It is now completely in the hands of the doctors . . . and God. I'll be in the office at eight o'clock tomorrow. That's all I can say."

Mike McGavin and Father Zeibatski got into a taxi, with a trail of reporters asking forgotten questions. Mike stonewalled them and repeated he would see them all again tomorrow morning. Exhausted, he flopped into the back seat of the taxi with the priest.

"You might as well stay at my place tonight, Father."

"Sure. Sure, Mike. Fine," he said distractedly. His intensity seemed to overtake his grief. Mike looked at him, wondering but never daring to ask what was going on the dark mind of the man whose life held so many secrets.

The priest was deep in thought. He would have to talk to Jane Rooney. Why had she abruptly refused the money from Father Comerford that Keogh had sent so regularly for so many years? What had it to do with Mary Rooney, Jane's daughter? Where was the link?

The taxi arrived at Mike's small Georgetown apartment. They went upstairs, and Mike offered the priest a drink.

"No, thanks, Mike."

"Father, I know it's been a terrible shock to us all," McGavin said, "but there is something else, Father. What is it, if I may ask?"

"Well, you're right, Mike—there is something else. But the trouble is I don't know what it is."

"Hard to follow."

"Mike, Frank Burke was murdered. Now, Frank had a lot of enemies. He was no saint, and maybe someone from the old days had a grudge. But he was murdered. . . . Now this . . . now this . . . Sean. My God, I can't believe it. I can't believe it. I don't know whether to cry or get mad at someone or something that is taking these people away from me. I just can't grasp it, Mike." He looked straight ahead, his smoky eyes gazing into nowhere.

"Father, what are you saying? That someone made an attempt on the Senator's life?"

"I don't know what I'm saying."

"But who? Another politician? I know they're a bunch of rats, but not trying to kill an opponent."

"Right."

"Not anyone from Southie. He's revered there like a saint."

"I guess so. But Sean came up the hard way, you know."

"Like Frank Burke?"

"Something like that. But I agree. I just don't think there would be any grudges. Sean cleaned all that stuff up."

"Then what?"

"Something I can't put my finger on."

They sat there for long hours, alternately talking, then lapsing into morose silence.

At four in the morning, a weary McGavin pulled himself to his feet, stripped off his shirt and said, "I'm drained, Father. Today was the worst day of my life."

"Me too. Why don't you hit the sack?"

"Yeah."

"Oh, Mike, I need to use the telephone for calls. You go to bed."

"Sure." The tall, handsome man disappeared into the bedroom, set the alarm for seven o'clock and collapsed onto the bed.

The priest sat silent for several minutes. Then, when convinced that Mike McGavin was sound asleep, he reached for the telephone. He dialed the international operator. He fumbled for a number in a small black book.

"Operator?" He paused. "I want Moscow. In the Soviet Union."

An hour later, the call came in. In flawless Russian he spoke into the telephone.

IT WAS six o'clock the next morning. Rose and the guests had risen early at the Keogh mansion in McLean, Virginia. Rose had already called Dr. Eberhard West at the hospital. She joined her guests at the breakfast table and took a seat next to Terrence.

"I just spoke to the doctor."

Everyone looked up, anxious for the news.

"There is no change, although the doctor said his body physically seems to be gaining strength. But he is still completely paralyzed, with no recognition factor. Not a muscle. Not a fiber." Her eyes welled with tears.

Terrence Keogh squeezed her hand.

"But they are removing him to a private room earlier than expected. We can see him later today."

Robert Del Vecchio shrugged. "But there is no change. My God, I still can't grasp it. He was so damn healthy. Fitter than a bull."

"Who knows?" Wilson countered. "I've known him since we were kids; can't remember him having a sick day. But his work schedule, the pressure. It was enormous for so many years, so many years—since he was only a teen-ager."

Wilson sounded almost sincere. And maybe in his own way he was. Wilson was sickened with himself.

"Well, we have just kissed the White House good-bye," Del Vecchio said. "No matter what the polls say, I might as well pack it in and go back to law." Del Vecchio looked philosophically at Morales, who remained silent.

Roger Sharpe looked up. "I was talking to Hickey last week. He and Mike together have the most fantastic breakdown of the polls throughout the country. Sean was so incredibly strong everywhere. A lot had to do with him personally. His personal charisma, his character, his directness and the way he kept his word. But a lot of it had to with his principles, his platform. There are a lot of Americans out there who are madder than hell."

"It's a pity to see them all go over to Senator Harris, our California pretty boy," Del Vecchio mused, "but I guess it's better than the idiot we have now."

"Maybe." Roger Sharpe was reflective and sipped quietly at his coffee.

"What do you mean, maybe?" Young Terrence spoke with quiet interest.

"Just thinking. The Keogh name means something in this country."

He said no more until after breakfast, when he turned to Wilson. "Eddie, could you get John Hickey down here? Maybe the whole bunch of us with Mike and Father Zeibatski should get together."

"Sure thing."

HE COULD feel a sense of movement. When his eyes opened, the white ceiling above him seemed to be flashing past him. Sean Keogh could not orient himself. He heard the voices but couldn't distinguish what they were saying. The voices at first came in waves, like an old-fashioned radio broadcast. Then, as his ears became attuned, he could put the words together, but did not understand.

"In here," the nurse said. "It's the most remote and private. It's the biggest room, too."

Sean Keogh was wheeled inside. The life-support machine to which he was connected was wheeled alongside him.

His eyes flickered. The light was bright. He tried to turn his head away from its glare. Nothing happened.

"There's eye movement there, Doctor," she said.

"There always is in these cases. It's a nerve reaction. But they don't track. If ever I'm not here and the family sees it, make sure you tell them it means nothing. Poor devils, I don't want them getting their hopes up. This man is dead, and it's a waste of time, money and emotion to keep up the technical pretense of life. But the Keoghs seem to have plenty of all that."

Dead? Dead. Keough's mind boiled with confusion. What is this dead? Or am I dead? Is this what death is really like? Where the hell am I? Dead?

The nurse leaned over him to adjust the pillow under his head. A nurse. It's a nurse. It's a hospital. Damn it, a hospital.

I'm not dead. He wanted to scream it all out in joy. I've had an operation of some sort and I'm just coming out of the anesthetic. I'll snap out of it in a while.

The nurse and the doctor left the big room with the heavy door. He lay there motionless, his eyes moving fractionally. He could see a window. A machine of some sort. The bright white ceiling. I'll be okay soon. I'll snap out of it. It seemed like hours, but it was minutes. The anesthetic should be wearing off now. What was I operated on for? There's the nurse again. What on earth is wrong?

She switched off the light as the early-morning sun streamed through the window.

The window . . . the windowpane. He could remember it now: the windowpane, the steam, the burning sensation in his lungs. Jesus Christ, the steam bath. The steam bath. The door jammed. Yeah, and I tried to punch my way out. I hurt my hand. I just remember the blackness. Now this.

Let's get the hell out of here. The mind commanded movement, but his eyes were the only things that moved—not all the way up or down, and not all the way to the right and left. He could see a window on one side, but he couldn't turn his eyes all the way. What the fuck is going on? I can't move. Can't move a damn muscle. That's right, now. The steam room.

The realization came slowly at first, and then his senses picked up speed with a panic that produced no pain in his limp body but fear that he had never experienced in his mind. My God, I'm paralyzed. I'm paralyzed. I can't move. What did that doctor say? I'm dead. Dead. Oh, Holy Father, what have you done to me?

He lay in panic for two hours, screaming in silence.

When the Keogh clan finally edged their way through the reporters, answering questions politely as they moved inside the hospital, every major newspaper and television network in the world had a newsman on hand. Rose Keogh put on a very brave face, smiling with restraint and dignity for the cameras, expressing ignorance of the exact details of her husband's ailment, deferring to McGavin, who never left her side.

"Gentlemen," she said firmly, "at this stage I can only say that it has slowed down the campaign of Senator Keogh. I don't think anything really stops my husband."

The reporters smiled and nodded with sympathetic approval.

When they were inside Senator Keogh's room, her mood changed. The tears streamed down her face as she stood among Wilson, Del Vecchio, Sharpe, Terrence, McGavin and the stone-faced priest.

"My God, Father, he looks terrible. Oh, my God, Sean. Oh, my God."

"Don't give up hope, Rose."

She leaned against Terrence. Mike felt his throat closing with emotion. Only three days ago, this man had been the only hope of leadership this country had had in the past ten years. Now, a vegetable, lying like a slab of pale plastic connected to what looked like a twenty-first-century machine. It was a grim gathering.

Sean Keogh's eyes flickered as each face passed in front of him. He could not see who was standing on his extreme right or left, only those within the tiny radius in which his reluctant eyes moved.

His heart seemed to strain at its muscles with emotion as he saw and heard Rose talk. What have I done to this woman? I have neglected her, imposed upon her, cheated on her—and finally this. A goddamn steam room. How cruel.

The clan stayed there in the room long after the prescribed visiting hours, standing around uncomfortably, sipping coffee and struggling for even the smallest of small talk.

Rose Keogh sat by her husband, occasionally stroking his hair or touching his face.

Terrence Keogh, behind the dark glasses, felt tiny. He had been so good at everything he touched, and he had made his mother so proud. She had never asked anything of him. But the only time he had done something for her, he had botched up the whole job. God, how he wanted Sean Keogh to die—if only so as not to mar his record of perfection in every pursuit.

His mother had said nothing about it. When Terrence had expressed shock and anger that Sean Keogh was still alive, Rose had soothed him: "It wasn't your fault, my darling."

"Mother, I just feel I've let you down."

She had kissed the lids of his sightless eyes and told him, "You have never let me down, my Terrence." Terrence could do no wrong. If Edward Wilson had committed the same act of imprecision, she would have sacrificed him.

When the group left the hospital room that night, Sean Keogh felt pathetic. The urge inside him was overpowering. He wanted to leap out of the bed and walk out the door with them. Instead he was trapped in a prison of torture he was sure few other human beings had ever endured. If he couldn't walk out with them, he wished he could be with Frank Burke. But when Dr. Eberhard West punctuated the unbearable with his arrival with a nurse, he realized that being with Frank Burke, wherever he was, was not what he wanted. Dr. West monitored the machines. He shook his head as if puzzled by the circumstances.

"Why don't they let this poor creature die? Why won't they pull the plug? This man is dead."

A noiseless scream cried out in Senator Keogh's silent and motionless body: "No, no, damn you, I'm alive! Sean Keogh is alive, you fool, you fool. I'm alive. Don't dare pull that plug. *I'm alive.*"

The nurse looked up at the doctor. "Doctor, you realize they are very strict Catholics, the Keogh clan?"

"Of course I know that. But Nurse, you'll learn in this profession that in matters of living, dying and medicine, Catholicism has very little do with the shape of things."

Keogh's body screamed again: "You damn fool."

JOHN HICKEY arrived at the Keogh mansion in Virginia just after everyone had finished dinner. He shook hands all around, looking somber enough to warrant the moment of sadness.

"Scotch, John?" Rose asked formally.

"Thank you, yes."

"John," Roger Sharpe started, "I asked you down here for a special reason—both you and Mike."

"I'm listening."

Everyone in the room fell silent.

Roger Sharpe continued. "I have to apologize for a certain insensitivity here. That being said, with Sean in a most critical and tragic state, I think we owe it to our support across the country, and the country itself, to decide what we are going to do politically."

Del Vecchio spoke. "Roger, I don't think anyone considers you insensitive to talk this way. We all know you feel about Sean the same way we do. But the question is: Is there any question? What can we do politically? I'm disappointed that given the situation, the vice presidency for me has just gone out the window. Without Sean, I don't think there is any alternative but to fold the tent."

"Perhaps," Sharpe said, toying with his snifter of cognac, "but the polls that John here and Mike have compiled have shown such a stunning swing toward Sean, one must ask whether we're going to throw it away."

Del Vecchio spoke again. "But without Sean . . . nothing."

"This morning at breakfast, before we went to the hospital, I pointed out that what you're saying is basically right. The overwhelming appeal was for Sean Keogh . . . Sean the person. But in swinging to Sean, the country has embraced and been educated to his platform."

"But," Del Vecchio countered, "those ideals could just as well be embraced by their swinging behind Senator Harris, given the fact that Rawlins hasn't got a chance. The Republican Party hacks always felt more comfortable with Harris anyway."

"Correct. But he's been around the track twice before . . . as a loser. Americans don't like losers."

"They took Nixon after Jack Kennedy beat him."

"Sure, and when he made one slip the country cannibalized him. No, the country still wants Keogh."

"I don't quite grasp it," Del Vecchio said.

"Well," John Hickey started slowly, "perhaps what Roger is saying is maybe we have some alternatives. For instance, should we look for another candidate to head the Keogh machinery? We have huge financial resources, and we have the support of the people."

Roger Sharpe looked enthusiastic. "Exactly. Now, do we go for a guy like Paul Castle, the New York Republican Congressman? He's a Keogh man through and through."

"I think perhaps too young," said Hickey. Father Zeibatski remained silent, his eyes hardly moving but rarely off Hickey's face.

"Could be right," said Sharpe. "Or what do we think of you, Del, carrying the load yourself, with Castle as a running mate?

Del Vecchio made a face. "I'm flattered, but we all know it's one thing to run for Vice President on a hero's reputation—pardon the immodesty—but it's totally another thing to run for the presidency. The last hero we had in the White House was Eisenhower, and look at the mess he made."

Rose smiled benignly. "I think you are underestimating your potential, Del."

"Thank you, Rose," he said with a smile.

"Well," Sharpe began again, "we could get behind Harris with the provison of a big trade and have Del as his running mate. He would have to make big concessions to us. But we would have to make the bigger ones." Most of those in the group nodded their heads in approval. It was better than nothing. There was silence. Drinks were poured all around by Mike McGavin.

Then McGavin spoke: "It just seems a pity that we have to compromise. We have it all so much in the bag. Damn."

"Maybe it's the only way out, Mike," Father Zeibatski said quietly.

A think-tank silence settled over the group again. Wilson stole a look at John Hickey. Father Zeibatski's eyes snared the glance in midair. John Hickey took a deep breath and then said almost in a whisper, "If you are prepared not to have me certified, I would like to throw in an idea from left field."

"Go ahead, John," Wilson encouraged.

"Well, I'll jump in with both feet. How about Mrs. Keogh?"

It was as if everyone in the room had suffered a mild electric shock. Nobody said a word lest it be interpreted as disrespect to Rose.

Terrence Keogh broke the silence. "It sounds crazy, but—"

Roger Sharpe cut him off: "It does sound crazy, but—but it's right . . . it could just work. Damn it. It could just come off."

Rose jumped in: "Gentlemen; gentlemen, please! Aren't we forgetting I'm a woman?

"Not at all," said Sharpe, speaking more quickly, as if the more he thought of it, the more he liked the idea. "Look, Rose, I've seen you campaigning. I have seen you work groups—large groups; men and women. I have seen you handle the press. I have heard you on policy, both foreign and domestic, in question-and-answer periods. You have been stunning over the past months."

"But Roger, there has never been a woman President in history."

"Nor was there ever a woman justice on the Supreme Court. No, Rose, it could be brilliant. People would be voting for a Keogh; they would be voting for a woman who has had tremendous media exposure, a woman who is devoted to a man they love . . . and a woman. Rose, in 1980 there were thirty-nine million women in the nation's work force. Today there are forty-five million working women—more than a third of the work force of the country. The women's movement has grown from the bra-burning stage to the point where it is a genuinely respected, mature voting bloc. We would catch that solid bloc—not to mention the ones we already have."

"We might have to sacrifice the rural South and Southwest vote," Mike said intelligently, "but we would pick up more than we would lose. Imagine a First Lady who really was a First Lady. What do you think, Father?"

The priest lifted his dark eyes. "All along I have never pretended to be an expert on these things, and I don't intend to start now. But how could I talk against it?"

Sharpe looked across at McGavin. "You know, Mike, we might even have a crack at the South. There is a precedent of sorts. Governor George Wallace, whose wife was elected Governor of Alabama when he couldn't run again. Alabama loved her. . . . Look, the more I think of it, the more I think it's a fantastic idea. Rose . . . Rose, think of it. Would you do it? I know the sacrifice, I know the anguish and the work . . . but . . . but somehow I think this is what Sean would want. He wouldn't want to see all those years go up in smoke. Think of it, Rose."

"I must admit the prospect is terrifying," she said.

"No more terrifying than what you already have been doing. You have shown yourself to be a marvelous politician."

"Speaking engagements and rallies, Roger, are one thing. But cold, hard politics is something else."

"I think now you are being too modest," Del Vecchio said. "The potential is staggering, and I can't help feeling that as Roger said, Sean would want it this way. He wants that name Keogh in the White House."

"I agree, Mother," Terrence said.

"An attractive idea," Wilson threw in.

Only the priest was politely silent.

Rose carefully surveyed the room. "If I genuinely thought Sean would want it, I would not hesitate. If I thought this was our only way of salvaging what we have all striven for, I would do it. But this is something I must think about. If you'll forgive me. I'll have to think about it."

"I understand, Rose. But please, for all our sakes, make it quick." The gathering broke up late that night. The next day, it was agreed, they would all go to the hospital and keep the lid on Sean Keogh's real condition at least until Rose Keogh made her decision. Rose and Terrence shook hands with each guest as he left the room. When John Hickey, the last one out the door, stopped to formally bid Rose good night, he too shook her hand. Then he squeezed it and gave her a reassuring smile.

Her smile was just as reassuring. They had pulled it off. Perfectly.

Even Edward Wilson snapped out of his perpetual low mood. He had backed the winning side after all.

When Mike McGavin offered Father Zeibatski a bed again that night, the priest was deep in thought. "Father . . . Father . . . will you be staying with me tonight?"

"Oh . . . oh . . . sorry, Mike, I was a million miles away. No. No, thanks. I have to go back to Boston, but I'll return day after tomorrow."

Mike knew better than to ask questions. He dropped the priest at Washington National Airport.

The priest did not go to Boston that night, but to New York's Greenwich Village. In the next weeks he would return many times to Greenwich Village, watching from the shadows.

AFTER TWO days of consciousness, Sean Keogh had learned to brighten the prison cell that was his body. The sun streaming through the windows was an indescribable pleasure. Funny, he had never really gotten any pleasure out of something one would take for granted. He longed for the visits of the doctors or the nurses, even though he thought Dr. Eberhard West to be a faithless congenital fool. He liked one particular nurse who would fuss around the bed and pay attention to him, as if he really were alive. At night he would listen to the faint strains of the transistor radio playing quietly at the head nurse's desk. That was a great pleasure. Fresh flowers decked his room, and their scent filled his nostrils with a sweetness he could not remember ever experiencing before. Such were the simple pleasures of a man condemned to solitary confinement.

But his black thoughts dwelt long and heavy. How he cursed a steam-room door! The black humor of it. This because he had been trying to get fit. But why? Why him? Why Frank Burke? The stupid senselessness of accidents. But maybe it was God's way. No man had a hand in another man's murder without retribution. Paddy Devlin was getting his revenge, as vengeance had been wreaked on Devlin.

At eleven o'clock that morning, he could hear the muted tones of his people's conversation. He could hear Roger Sharpe's voice, he picked out Mike's voice and he could hear Rose saying, "I just have to see him first." Moments later, everyone but Father Zeibatski was there. Ah, there was John Hickey too, who had joined them.

She bent over him and kissed him tenderly on the cheek. He could smell the clean and simple beauty of her shampoo as she leaned close. How he longed to hug her. But all he could do was trigger a fractional movement of his eyes, no matter how much he strained inwardly. And everyone had been told to not take it as a signal that inside the useless body was Sean Keogh, grotesquely trapped like a genie in a bottle.

"My darling Sean," she said in almost a whisper, "how I pray that you could hear what I am about to say. How I pray that I could get your approval." She talked as if no one else were in the room. The others stood in a somber semicircle.

"Today, Sean, I am telling the world that I am going to step into your place, that your ideals, your work, your name are going to be carried on."

Roger Sharpe smiled. "Rose, thank God. I know he would want this of you. I know it, Rose."

Mike McGavin was happy too, although there was a nagging discomfort at the slightly maudlin way in which she had chosen to make her decision known to the clan. But hell, he thought, she is his wife and she loves him.

But then, so do I love him. McGavin concealed his feelings with a smile.

Chapter

20

LATER THAT day, Mike McGavin reproached himself for his thoughts about Rose Keogh's words in the hospital room. He had thought she was playing too much to the gallery, and it wasn't like her. Yet here he was being swept away with the same emotion. He was working on the draft of the announcement to the press. And he was playing to the gallery too. He would first, together with the hospital administrator, give a lengthy and factual medical bulletin on Senator Keogh's true condition. The questions would come in frenzied bursts from the reporters. He would answer them all. They would ask many questions to expand their stories. Then they would play themselves out. Just then he would pause for effect and say, "There is another announcement that I would like to make." Their ears would prickle. Then he would drop the bombshell.

"In view of the tragic indisposition of the Senator, the Keogh organization feels that the vacuum left in the hopes of many millions should be filled. It is with this in mind that I can announce that the Senator's wife, Mrs. Rose Keogh, will run in her husband's place as a presidential candidate."

There would be some reporters so stunned that they would ask him to slowly repeat his words. Then there would be pandemonium. They would be rubbing shoulders with history.

He tingled with excitement, and then his solar plexus hurt. Damn, here I am rubbing my hands with glee about the world reaction, basking in the word called history, and not one mile away, lying motionless in another world, is Senator Keogh, the man I love and respect, the man who has made everything possible. He had enjoyed politics. It was a game, much easier than newspapering—if you didn't have a part of your anatomy called a heart. With the Senator, he had wheeled and dealt the way anyone would have, but Keogh had made it possible for it to be done with a heart. Now Mike wasn't so sure. He was in the big league, and he wasn't sure he liked it. Maybe he should have stuck to being a newspaperman. Too fucking late now.

He sighed and typed out with bulletlike precision the rest of the announcement. When he finished, he went inside to the inner office. Rose Keogh was sitting behind the Senator's desk, looking tinier than ever in the huge chair. But despite her size, she seemed to fill it. There was an unquestionable air of control in her that seemed to have grown since the Senator's accident. Good. No, damn it—bad. The twinge of resentment was still there. That's *his* desk, madam.

Roger Sharpe sat in front of the desk. Del Vecchio to one side. Del Vecchio had carried off his role as running mate perfectly. Solid, dignified, supportive. The ball fitted the socket without a hint of his rowdy past. The world recognized him as a wronged man, a man who had withstood inflicted disgrace and still emerged as a reticent hero. Stuff movies are made of.

McGavin handed everyone a copy. They all read it carefully and in silence.

Roger looked up and flashed his warm, patrician smile. "Perfect, Mike. No wonder Sean thinks so highly of you. You are some team." He flushed slightly at his use of the present tense out of deference to Rose, but he didn't bother to correct himself. Roger Sharpe was a good man.

"What do you think, Rose?" Roger asked.

"Fine. Very good, Michael. Very good. It has a nice dignified ring to it. I appreciate your stress in the announcement that nothing has changed. Very good."

"Yes," Del Vecchio said, "it could almost be our catchphrase—nothing has changed. Good, Mike."

"Mike," Roger queried, "when do you think is the best time for this announcement?"

"Oh, I would say eleven A.M. Soon enough for the news-starved midday television news and enough time for the morning-paper boys to develop the main story with half a dozen sidebar stories. Mrs. Keogh, I am afraid you will have to undergo some grilling. There will be political reporters asking you about inflation, budgets, defense, and then you will have the others writing about you as a little girl, and then the fashion girls will come along and want to know what designers you favor and what your recipe is for corned beef and cabbage. It can be a terrible bore, but it's very important."

"I realize that, Michael, and I am completely prepared." She said it with a slight chill. As if she were putting Mike in his place for even suggesting that she would not be able to handle questions of inflation, budgets and defense. She was right, of course; she perhaps knew more than any man in that room, and it angered her to think that men would doubt it.

Roger Sharpe sighed. "Well, now we talk. The good news, of course, Rose, is that you have consented to run. Now the tough news. Realistically, we're going to have a battle on our hands at the convention in New York. First, I have to get the party hacks back on our side; then, most important, the delegates. Many of the delegates we swept up for Sean may not be as enthusiastic in the new situation. I say that with respect. But we're talking realism."

"Of course, Roger, of course." She wanted him to get on with the business. She knew exactly what kind of fight was ahead, and it didn't scare her for a split second. Rose Keogh always won in the end.

"Well, the first thing that will happen after our announcement tomorrow will be that Senator Harris out there in California will throw himself back into the race. He's cranking up already, suspecting that Sean's condition is a lot worse than has been made public.

"Now he will lock up the delegates from California for certain. When some of the other state delegates realize this, it will influence them considerably.

"Now, Del, we still have a king's ransom in our campaign chest. We're going to have to risk spending a lot of it just to get the image established."

Mike smiled. "I've already locked up twice as much television time as any two other candidates put together. Harris will come on strong, but we will outspend him and image him to death."

"Good," Roger said. "Rose, we are going to have to throw ourselves in right away. I fear you're going to have to spend a lot of time away from Sean."

"Yes, I realize that, Roger. That's one of the prices we all will have to pay."

"Now, today, Mike, organize a shooting team. We're going to have to make several spots of Rose and Sean together on the hustings, showing their togetherness, emphasizing that Rose stands one hundred percent for what Sean stands for."

Rose Keogh allowed herself a secret inward chuckle. She nodded in agreement.

"Then stuff with Rose and Del together, and some separates of Del, with his message keyed to Rose to get it across that the same team that made Sean successful is behind Rose. Now we have to get plenty of the man-in-the-street stuff—you know: a banker in a three-piece suit, a black, a Hispanic, a young woman and an old woman, all in tight rapid-fire frames, all saying just 'I'm a Keogh man.' or 'I'm a Keogh woman.'

You know—stuff like that. Repeating the message over and over until it is in people's consciousness.

"You got it," Mike said.

Rose and Del listened. They were impressed. There was no campaign man in the country like Roger Sharpe.

"Now, Rose, it's important that we dodge the Equal Rights Amendment issue. The ERA thing is dangerous. Most people equate the ERA with stubborn feminism. No good. Your stand will be that how much more equal could a woman be in 1984 than to run for the land's highest office? On that issue you just revert to the position that whatever the states vote, you'll support it. Frankly, ERA hasn't got a chance."

"I think you're right, Roger." She sat back in the chair content to listen.

"Now, Rose, through your very considerable experience in the campaign with Sean, you're solid on the issues of defense, race relations, education and foreign policy. You are weak on the economy. We're going to have a crash course on that. I'll get in a few Wall Street friends to help out there. We have to draw up an inflation-fighting machine and hammer away at the message. That's important.

"Now, that's just a very general briefing. Very general. Tomorrow night we'll burn the midnight oil. Mike, get a stenotypist we can trust to get notes of our meeting tomorrow, have the points typed up for the morning and then we'll go over them until we almost have it by heart. We must all be consistent in our answers as to what we stand for. People have to be impressed with the solidarity of our machine.

"Okay—until tomorrow, let's bust it."

The meeting broke up, and Rose sat alone at the big desk. She was exhausted, and her head was splitting. It was the same terrible, searing pain that almost blinded her. She reached for her handbag and took out three pills and swallowed them quickly without water.

It was long minutes before the pain subsided. The pressure was causing momentary blackouts. She would attend to that problem after the election. She couldn't risk it now, when everything was almost in her grasp. She had pulled off a masterstroke.

Perhaps it would have been better if the shadow of Sean Keogh were not still around, but there were some advantages imagewise in having him still physically on earth—although she would gladly have seen him go. Terrence couldn't be blamed. The poor child; it was amazing that with his blindness he was so incredibly talented.

Rose Keogh vanquished the pain at the rear of her brain. She looked around the big oak desk that belonged to her husband. The neat fourteen-karat penholder with Keogh's initial inscribed. He must have had that penholder for twenty years. She remembered when Frank Burke had given it to him. It had been chosen by Burke's wife, Teresa. Burke would never have had the taste.

She stared long and hard at the little wooden notice on the front of his desk that proclaimed I BELONG TO SOUTHIE. And she remembered the songs they had sung in Kelly's Café, around the corner from Damrell Street in Southie, where a shotgun blast had ended the lives of Bernie McLaughlin and Pat Sweeney, her father.

Then there were the pictures on the wall: Keogh as a young man with a once-young Nixon and a fit-looking Eisenhower; one with Reagan, and one there with a handsome Teddy Kennedy. Although in all the pictures Sean was by far the handsomest of anyone. There was something about him—the way he always looked as if he were in charge, with that big Irish smile that hinted he knew something that nobody else had access to.

Suddenly the tears streaked down her cheeks, and she could hear herself sobbing. Such a handsome, strong man. But just as suddenly as the tears had flowed down her cheeks, they dried, and the pain of grief in her face was replaced by a tight-lipped anger. Damn Sean Keogh and all his cross-bearing arrogance. He had imprisoned her long enough, and now she was free—free to be her own woman and show the world what Rose could do. Do far better than any shanty Irishman who thought what hung between his legs gave him license to be in charge. Nobody was in charge of Rose.

The violent changes of mood would become more and more frequent in the months ahead. If Rose Keogh had been hovering over the line of insanity, she had crossed it very quickly now.

SEAN KEOGH had learned now to fight the urge to scream. It was only frustrated by a sickening silence. But he couldn't fight it as over the rim of his fixed vision he could see the priest.

It was ten forty-five the next morning. McGavin would lead the Keogh clan into the lobby of the hospital in fifteen minutes' time. The priest had arrived there early, and he was on his knees at the foot of the bed. Senator Keogh recalled that he had never seen the priest pray in private, although he had seen him celebrate Mass many hundreds of times. Even when his brother Vinnie was in grave danger of his life, he had never seen him pray personally. But now he was praying fervently. The words sounded strange, as if the priest held a dark secret. Sean always believed there were many secrets locked inside the priest, but there was a fervor in his words that indicated a deep depression in this wonderfully strong man. And as he prayed, Sean wanted so much to kneel beside him and share this most intimate of moments. But it was a strange prayer, as if Father Zeibatski had seen the face of real evil.

The priest believed he had. He had spent many days in Greenwich Village, and in the dark hours he had watched the house of Jane Rooney, the stylishly neat brownstone. And while he didn't know what he was looking for, he received confirmation of the dark thoughts that danced in his mind. It came when he saw the elegant John Hickey trotting up the stairs to Jane Rooney's living room. It proved nothing for certain, but the wildly disjointed jigsaw puzzle hinted at a sinister conclusion. And now the priest felt the presence of evil, and for the first time since his youth in Nazi-occupied Lithuania, he felt confused—and yes, even frightened. And now, outside, the reporters were babbling like a symphony of machine guns.

The questions hadn't stopped for thirty minutes. McGavin noted the excitement in their voices. It was very hard for them to digest the magnitude of the announcement.

Some of the questions bordered on the hysterical, and some were rough.

"Mrs. Keogh, with all respect, what on earth qualifies you, do you think, to run for the highest office in the land?"

Despite the aggressiveness, Rose Keogh smiled politely and answered with aplomb and economy: "Simply having the advantage over you gentlemen by living with the greatest political mentor of our time."

"Does that extend to the complicated issues such as the economy, double-digit inflation, balance of trade?"

"I would welcome now or in the future any questions in those areas where the intelligent press might think I am wanting."

When she delivered a slightly stinging reply, she was extremely careful to accompany it with a generous and feminine smile to extract the sting. She would get her message across forcefully and intelligently, but without rancor.

Clearly, after the reporters had exhausted themselves of questions in the madhouse of that hospital lobby, they were impressed. It had been McGavin's idea to hold the press conference at the hospital, instead of more formally at the Senate Office Building, and when the television anchormen flashed the bulletin and later gave exhaustive reports, and when the headlines fairly screamed the news, the sympathetic twist was not missed. Again McGavin felt it slightly tawdry, but he was in this thing to win—for the Keogh family, for Sean and maybe even a little for himself. Sean Keogh would have had it no other way.

The news hit the nation like a nuclear missile. In terms of free publicity, it could be computed only in the tens of millions of dollars. But it was quickly accompanied by an announcement that Senator Harris was now confidently back in the race, together with Brett Townsend, a straightlaced but politically canny former director of the CIA.

The Democrats and the incumbent President Rawlins sat by and simply gaped at the way the Republican wave had swamped the country. There was no question that Rawlins would soon be surrendering his key to the White House, and he would be surrendering it to a Republican. The only question remaining was Which Republican? As one commentator put it in *The Washington Post:* "There is an increasing belief in Washington that the presidential election looms as one of the great anticlimaxes in political history. That belief is dramatically reinforced by the notion that the President of this country will be elected in New York's Madison Square Garden at the Republican National Convention in August."

The observation was right on the money—an observation that Roger Sharpe, as campaign manager, well knew.

That night, in a strategy meeting, Sharpe was doing most of the talking. He looked at Del Vecchio, Rose and McGavin.

"We have to make the decision now. Okay, we've had a fantastic free ride with the publicity, but the party chiefs are as incredulous as the public is ecstatic. Now no matter what the euphoria is out there, if the party bosses don't sit with your running, and many of them are outright hostile to it, their feelings will drift down to the delegates. Now, the gamble is this. We have to flood television, radio and the newspapers with advertising in the six weeks before the convention. The party bosses and the delegates to the convention must be blitzed even more than the public. Sorry, Rose, but there are some in the GOP who think this whole thing is opportunistic, frivolous and downright undignified."

He felt Rose Keogh bristle in the atmosphere. But she knew he was right.

"Look, *I'm* not saying it. That's just the facts."

"I'm not in the least offended," she said with a smile. She was lying.

"Now, Mike, I don't care how you manage it, but we have to buy up a lot of local time right now in California. With a hundred and sixty-seven delegates—the largest delegation—and with their ruling at the convention that the majority winner in the convention ballot takes all, it is essential we beat Harris on his own turf. Also, his nominating speech will probably come from California."

Mike nodded. "I've already done it, Roger."

"Great. Well, now we're cooking with gas. Next, make sure we have plenty of local time slots in New York State, Pennsylvania and Illinois.

They have the next-biggest delegations. Go to it, Mike—right now. I won't go near any of the delegates until next week. By that time they will have been soaked. Now, the cost. Just that exercise alone, Del, will cost one and a half million bucks. Do we go for it?"

"Damn right we go for it. You're the guru when it comes to these things."

"Okay." He was slightly breathless from the speed of his delivery. He was normally a quiet, reserved man, but politics and campaigns ran thick in his veins, and the adrenaline was pumping through him. His excitement was contagious, and everyone in the room—even Alberto Morales, who stood quietly in the corner behind Del Vecchio—could feel the electricity.

Rose Keogh smiled. "You're a changed man, Roger."

"It always happens like this. It's my heroin."

They all smiled, and everyone scuttled out of the office with a purpose in his stride.

Because of the sudden turn of events, it would be two weeks before Harris and Gallup could put out responsible polls. It was vital that Rose Keogh figure dramatically in those polls. It was not necessary for her to be in front, but she had to be close enough to Harris for the delegates to take the woman-led Keogh platform seriously. To vote for Sean Keogh was one thing; something else was to vote for another Keogh who might be the first woman in American history to be nominated by a major party for President. Many millions of males in the country found it hard to accept—and just as many females had their doubts too when it came to the highest office in the land.

This fact was foremost in all their minds, and the next day, Sharpe and McGavin confronted Rose and Del Vecchio with an overpowering itinerary.

"Well, there it is, Rose, Del. Eighteen hours a day, six days a week."

Del Vecchio looked at Morales and smiled. "Well, I didn't say it was going to be a rose garden."

"What do you think, Rose?" Sharpe asked.

"Exhaustive, but obviously very necessary. Now, Roger, if a poll were taken today, how would it split between me and Harris?"

"Well, you would have to figure that since Townsend has entered the race, he will get the Keogh vote that is reluctant to go for a woman. Frankly, Harris would get almost half, with us and Townsend splitting the rest."

"I see. So this is very necessary."

"No question."

Rose Keogh wasted no time. She immediately summoned her son,

Terrence, to the Senate Office Building. They would leave that afternoon, crisscrossing the country for thousands of miles. Sharpe would
accompany her and Terrence. McGavin would spend some of the time
on the road with Del Vecchio and Morales. While they were traveling,
the airwaves and newspapers would be blitzed with a carefully planned
advertising campaign. Wilson and Hickey would join Rose and Del Vecchio at various stages of the campaign.

Conspicuous by his low profile was Father Zeibatski. He was concerned with a more troubling campaign: finding out the truth. And
between his investigations, he was busy on the telephone to Moscow
tracking down an old friend of his.

The two weeks were as exhausting for all concerned as Sharpe had
predicted, sometimes both candidates hitting as many as three towns in
a single day and attending as many as nine and ten rallies and meetings.
As the ad campaign blasted across America, Sharpe could gradually feel
the feedback on the hustings, both from the response of the crowds and
from the attitude of the press.

Sharpe and McGavin stayed in constant contact on the telephone during the next two weeks. And as the Keogh steamroller got back into high
gear once again, both men worked feverishly on the delegates and the
alternates to the convention.

"What's your news, Mike?" Roger asked as the two-week campaign
neared a close.

"The appointed delegates seemed to be leaning toward Harris. But
the elected delegates are solidly on our side. Of course, there is a huge
bloc of uncommitted. How about you?"

"Pretty much the same. But at this stage California is definitely locked
into Harris. He's got a clear majority, and that means we could lose the
whole hundred and sixty-seven delegates on the first ballot. Good news
from New York. Likewise Pennsylvania. How about your end?"

"Townsend makes a strong showing among the committed delegates
in Illinois. I fear many of them were once with us. Of course, he is from
Iowa, and the Midwesterners like him. Texas, surprisingly, was very
encouraging. I think it was the energy speech that Sean had made so
many times and the way Mrs. Keogh followed it up strongly. We're not
in bad shape."

"It's not good enough. We have to make a breakthrough. I'm letting
go with another half-million dollars of television time. I know I'm burning up the loot, but it's a gamble we'll have to take. I'll check it this end
with Rose. You get an okay from Del."

"You got it."

It was one week later, when they were again together in Washington, that Sharpe learned that the ABC-Harris poll would release the results of an exhaustive survey within three days. The news made them all feel a little nervous. A bad showing in the polls would swing the uncommitted delegates clearly behind Harris or Townsend. A sound showing would give the Keogh people a solid chance with the uncommitted delegates and even a better-than-even chance with the committed delegates on the second ballot. It was a curious game, this convention.

It was the day before the official release of the ABC-Harris poll that Sharpe burst into the office. He had gotten hold of an early release. He was beaming. "Great news . . . great news," he said, flinging down the wire-service copy on the desk that had once been Senator Keogh's. He spoke with a ring of triumph.

"Look, don't worry about the breakdown on the issues; we'll talk about that later. But there it is: Harris has thirty-seven percent; we have thirty-three percent, with Townsend picking up twenty and an uncommitted ten. It's three weeks to the convention. With luck, we can do it; we can do it. Now let's hit them again with another television and newspaper campaign. Meanwhile, the Teamsters this week are rolling across the country with the most massive handbill distribution this country has ever seen. I just have that feeling.

"Now Rose, Del, out you go again. Mike, hand me the sked. It's as bad as the last one. This time, Del, you hit California hard. We have a couple of tame television interviewers who are going to ask you to recap on the Puerto Bravo siege. Play it for all you're worth. We have you in just about every American Legion and Veterans of Foreign Wars hall headquarters in the West. Invaluable. The Reverend Leroy Jefferson has swung a massive rally behind you, Rose, in Atlanta day after tomorrow. Then both of you hit Chicago together and hit Townsend where he's strongest. We need more Illinois support. After Chicago, New York and New England. We're safe there, but we want to make sure of the uncommitted delegates. Good statewide polls will help us.

"Let's go."

When the others had all left, Rose turned to her son, who now rarely left her side. "How do you read it, Terrence?"

"Tough, very tough. But I know you'll make it, Mother. I know you will."

"Only with your help, darling." She kissed him lightly on the cheek. Then she led him through the door. "Come on back on the road."

"What is the news of Senator Keogh?" he said dispassionately.

"No change," she said with indifference, "but Zeibatski is trying every doctor in the country. It's hopeless. He should stick to saving souls instead of lives. He would find it easier."

Terrence smiled and walked out the door with her to go back on the campaign trail.

In the next weeks, the Keogh machinery, orchestrated by the wise Roger Sharpe and fanatically energetic McGavin, picked up even more steam. From a dubious start, it had become the dignified alternative to Senator Harris, the onetime television glamour boy. With each day on the road, with each speech, with each press conference, the nation watched goggle-eyed at the petite, commanding figure of Rose Keogh exhorting farmers, blue-collar workers, bankers and homemakers. Even the most cynical observed with awe an uncanny grasp of the most complicated fiscal issues, which she could break down into simple man-in-the-street terms for everyone to comprehend.

Four days away from the convention in Madison Square Garden, the contest was a horse race between Rose Keogh and Senator Harris.

Roger Sharpe looked around the Keogh clan in the Plaza Suite of the elegant Plaza Hotel, overlooking the lush greenery of Central Park. He studied a sheaf of papers in front of him. Rose sipped at a cup of tea. She was sitting between John Hickey and her son, Terrence, on a large overstuffed sofa.

"The latest, Roger," she commanded softly.

"The best way I can see it is that on the first ballot, Harris will get thirty-nine percent of the two thousand three hundred delegates. We should pick up thirty percent, with Townsend snipping away twenty percent."

"What does that tell us, Roger? The obvious?"

"Exactly," interrupted Mike. "Harris will not be able to get a clear fifty percent on the first ballot. In the interim between the end of the first ballot and the beginning of the second, we have to bird-dog the delegate caucuses overnight. We have to get Townsend to throw in the towel and virtually push his entire twenty percent to our side. Not all of them will go for it, of course, so we have to make sure the delegates who are now uncommitted but go with Harris on the first ballot swing over to us on the second. It could even go to three ballots, but if it does we're in trouble. We must make it a great showing on the first ballot and scoop up and overtake Harris on the second to wrap it up."

"Do you think it can be done?" Father Zeibatski asked quietly.

"It's a cliff-hanger," Roger Sharpe commented. "In the last two weeks we've made huge strides. Both Rose and Del made up tremendous ground. The television and the newspaper campaign had the old party hacks sitting up taking notice, and they kept their mouths shut. The delegates we won over, committed to us, made up their own minds. That was the key—their making up their own minds and not waiting for a message from the National Committee. That was a blessing. But I think we could make it, Father, with a little bit of help from you and the Man you represent here."

The priest smiled.

Roger Sharpe frowned. "Father, I haven't seen Sean for the past week, for which I feel very guilty. How's it going?"

Before the priest could answer, Rose cut in quickly, as if she were indignant that anyone but she should have that question addressed to him. "He's still the same, Roger. Not an ounce of change. I have seen him these past two mornings. When all this is over, we'll all be able to spend more time with him . . . although"—her eyes grew moist—"I don't know what good it's going to do him."

The priest's eyes avoided Rose's. He feared if he looked at her she might be able to detect his secret thoughts.

It was at the Oak Bar, over a light lunch, that the priest, alone with McGavin, talked gravely.

"Mike, have you seen any change in Mrs. Keogh?"

Mike flushed and paused before he answered. What the hell—one couldn't lie to Father Zeibatski.

"She is much more assertive since . . . since she began to run for office. Much more assertive. Why do you ask?"

"Oh, health reasons mainly. I worry about her health. The strain of Sean was enough to break any woman, but add to it the campaign. It was brutal. I worry about her health."

"Well, she has given no real indication of fading. Apart from an occasional headache, she is a very strong woman, despite her small frame. Very strong. Both she and Terrence have thrown themselves into this campaign like people possessed. I have never seen such energy. She is quite an amazing woman."

"Quite."

McGavin's eyes searched the priest's face. McGavin sensed that something was very wrong. He had felt it ever since that first day when he saw Rose Keogh at the Senator's desk.

He quickly changed the subject. "Father, do you think there is any real hope for Sean? You have consulted every doctor there is."

"Not every doctor, Mike. But there is always hope. Isn't that our belief?"

"I guess so. It's just that it all looks so terribly hopeless."

"Perhaps. Perhaps not."

SEAN KEOGH knew what it would be like. New York was a brassy lady, and a convention in New York would be what the lady could be best at. No city in the world likes a parade better than New York, and the convention would be the biggest parade for many years to come. The hotels would be brimming, the bars packed and the action at the gambling tables, which had been legalized only six months before, would be staggering. The hustlers, pimps and hookers would be working around the clock, as would the cops, firemen, newspapermen and television crews. It would be a glorious, bawdy party, with a frightening undertone of the raw ambition of power-hungry men and women.

If a body without life could cry, then Sean Keogh felt like crying then. All his life had been shaped, sculptured for this moment, and now he lay alone, trapped in an antiseptic hospital bed, looking forward to the pleasures regarded by others as the ultimate in boredom: sunlight coming through a window, the sound of a radio, the sound of a laughing voice, the restricted glimpse of a face that smiled.

The first night of the convention would be ritual. Rose Keogh arrived at seven thirty that night in a silver limousine, accompanied by Terrence, Mike McGavin and Roger Sharpe. In the following limousine were John Hickey, Edward Wilson and Father Zeibatski. Robert Del Vecchio, her running mate, cruised up to the glittering entrance of Madison Square Garden in a third limousine, accompanied by the smiling but silent Alberto Morales.

Seventh Avenue on that warm August night was the closest to Mardi Gras that New York had seen. The cops had closed off Seventh and Eighth avenues from Twenty-Third Street to Forty-second, and the pavements were jammed with people carrying placards, singing songs and chanting slogans. Searchlight beams stabbed through the half-light of the still-illuminated early evening. Everywhere there was noise and people's voices in the air.

Rose Keogh had decided to break with tradition by attending the convention. As she stepped from the limousine, surrounded by a solid wall of Secret Service men, klieg lights lit up her tiny frame. The few bystanders who could get close enough for a glimpse of her were amazed at how tiny, fragile and pretty she looked. Dressed in a simple white linen summer dress with biscuit colored shoes, she looked like a tiny little angel. She gripped the arm of Terrence on one side, while Roger Sharpe on the other side held her by the elbow. She smiled demurely and stopped for a few courteous seconds in front of the battery of press and television.

Terrence smiled from behind his thick dark glasses. "That's as much love as I have ever heard in my life." She squeezed his arm. She was not nervous, however. She was breathless with excitement, although it did not show in her pert features. Walking through the entrance, she was confronted by the "cheerleaders" of the delegation. Some of the states' delegates had brought bands with them, and inside, the banners of states and towns and slogans poked toward the ceiling like a sea of lances held by an occupying army.

As she walked into the cavernous lobby of Madison Square Garden, the chant started: "Ke-ogh, Ke-ogh, Ke-ogh." The chant traveled down the tunnels and through the gates and into the main arena. By the time she appeared on the floor amid an explosion of red, white and blue, the chant had grown deafening. "Ke-ogh, Ke-ogh."

The Keogh clan assembled on the floor and edged their way through solid walls of delegates and designated alternates to get to their box. Harris and Townsend had arrived twenty minutes earlier and had received a similarly enthusiastic welcome, but at Rose Keogh's appearance there was an edge of glorious hysteria in the crowd. The newspapermen could feel their skin prickle as a sensation of mounting excitement swept through the giant arena which was like an echo chamber of human voices and blasting tubas, trumpets and trombones. The convention band played "Rose, Rose I Love You" and "Rose of Tralee," and when several other bands joined in, the convention band started up with "God Bless America" to restore some semblance of order.

It was a full hour before the reverberating sound waves ebbed to a respectable roar. When they did, the Chairman of the Republican National Committee jumped onto the podium, rapped with his gavel and in a monstrous voice magnified many times by a perfect public-address system simply said, "I declare the 1984 Republican National Convention open."

Again there were cheers. All in the Keogh party smiled like a class of movie stars as the searchlights settled on them, and Mike McGavin was rendered totally breathless by the pure high-fidelity madness in the air.

He looked out among the twenty thousand people in the giant Garden and audibly laughed. There was something about all conventions, political or otherwise, that brought out the child in the man. There they were, wearing preposterous hats and with giant carnations in their lapels, waving enthusiastic banners and rekindling political friendships that had been dormant for years. There was something definitely primal, as if they all lusted for a touch of the Roman Empire. But beneath the hysteria, most knew that the nomination assured the recipient of the most awesome job in the world. The election would be redundant.

By eleven that night there had been more than a dozen speeches, some heard, some not heard as the cheering and chanting drowned everything sensible and political out of earshot.

The next day would be different. When Roger Sharpe noticed groups of leading delegates edging out of the Garden, he knew it was time for him and McGavin and a handful of the more trusted campaign workers to get cracking. He leaned over to Rose Keogh. "Rose, now is the time. We will go over to the boxes of Harris and Townsend, shake, wish them luck and then slip out. The delegates will soon be in caucuses all over town. Mike and I have to get moving."

Without breaking her smile, which had been under almost constant television scrutiny, she said, "Fine, Roger."

They passed by the main press box, where the network heavyweights like Cronkite, Mudd, Mike Wallace, Roger Grimsby and David Brinkley were positioned in their places of honor.

She crossed to Harris first, flashed a sparkling smile for the cameras and over the deafening roars simply said, "All the best, Senator. Some turnout." Harris flashed a similar smile and kissed her hand.

She then crossed to Townsend and repeated the gesture. It was not lost on the delegates that she approached the men first. Roger Sharpe had beaten them to it again.

She walked through the crowds followed by a beaming Hickey and Wilson and flanked by Terrence, Sharpe and McGavin. Father Zeibatski followed in the rear with Morales and Del Vecchio, who was swamped by similar idolatry by men who normally wore three-piece suits and did nothing more adventurous than run a bank and drink an occasional cocktail. Tonight it was their Christmas, New Year's Eve and birthday all rolled into one, and their traditional GOP conservatism had flown out the window for the event.

"Del," Sharpe screamed over the noise, "I want you and Rose and Terrence to go back to the hotel. Mike and I and the others will hang around the caucus meetings of the delegates. We will have to buttonhole them and do some last-minute hustling. I have the Secret Service guys already waiting. I'll call you and Rose for a late breakfast. I won't be in until about five in the morning. Let's meet in Rose's suite at nine. Then she has some last-minute television and newspaper interviews which Mike has lined up. . . . See you."

He was screaming now, and he and Mike had dashed off after the leader of the Illinois delegation, who was heading back to the Hilton Hotel to caucus with his top delegates. He was important.

Mike glanced quickly behind to see where the priest was. The priest had lost himself in the crowd.

That night he walked the streets of New York for many hours. Father Zeibatski was very troubled. Again he was on the telephone for much of the night.

Sharpe and McGavin split up the hotels and delegations, buttonholing the delegates in lobbies, bars, restaurants and hotel rooms, dealing, promising trade-offs and giving handshakes of faith in exchange for promised support. By the time the two men met back at the hotel a little after 5 A.M., both believed they had won over a handy chunk of the uncommitted delegates. Of course, a handshake was one thing; actually getting up on the floor and delivering the vote was another.

That night Rose Keogh had returned euphoric to her hotel suite. At one in the morning, John Hickey passed the security guards for a final meeting with Rose in her suite. When he left two hours later, Rose Keogh lay smiling, exhausted and dripping with perspiration and semen from the glorious ravages of Hickey. It was a perfect way to end a night.

It was a haggard-looking Sharpe and McGavin who the next day over breakfast sounded cautious optimism.

"I think we can rely on Illinois if it goes to a second ballot," Sharpe offered. "Texas is definitely ours for sure. The Midwestern states that were flying Townsend's banner should go with us. I had a long talk with Townsend. It would mean the Health and Human Services job for Townsend. It's a good deal. He's a tough and talented man. There were some other trade-offs, but too minor to cause any problems. Mike?"

"I think Texas might cost us a few jobs in promises. Also Iowa, Wyoming and Utah. They're all good bets. Pennsylvania is ours anyway; likewise New England. California we have to figure is all his, so that will give him a good leg up."

That night the ritual at the Garden was repeated. But where the hysteria the previous night had been triggered by the sheer youthful joy of being in on a very important occasion, the second night was different. The hysteria was fueled by a massive reserve of nervous energy. Tonight the country could be picking a President.

At 8:30 P.M., after the convention band had played the National Anthem, followed by "God Bless America," the delegates began to feel the weight of importance bearing down heavily on their shoulders. A massive layer of cigar and cigarette smoke wafted above the 2,300 delegates on the floor like a bright blue cloud. Nerves began to scream out. The chairman, on the rostrum, pounded with his gavel. His announcement was almost overly simplistic:

"We shall now proceed with the selection of a presidential candidate for the Republican Party. The chair recognizes the secretary."

The secretary of the convention, a large, buxom woman, stood up and read a roll call of the states in alphabetical order. She then called on the first state, Alabama, to make a nominating speech.

"Mr. Chairman," the head of the Alabama delegation intoned, "Alabama, the Yellowhammer State, yields to the great State of California" —giving the Governor of California, a man who owed his job to Harris, the opportunity to make the first nominating speech. The band struck up "California, Here I Come," and Governor Jason Stevens made a brilliant nominating speech, impressing on the delegates Senator Harris' record as an earlier governor of the state. From Alaska, the next state in alphabetical order, came a seconding speech for Harris, and by the enthusiasm of two delegations, Sharpe knew that California and Alaska were a lost cause on the first ballot.

Arizona, the next state to be called on, had been universally expected to yield to Massachusetts for a Keogh nomination. But Senator Townsend, the favorite-son candidate of Iowa, had made a generous political gesture. Late the night before, he had asked the chairman of the Arizona delegation to yield to his own state instead, so that he would be nominated next and Rose Keogh would have the advantage of the last and perhaps longest nominating speech.

The nomination of Senator Townsend was preceded by the band's playing the Marine Hymn, in acknowledgment of his being a decorated Marine hero.

After each speech, the various bands and delegations marched around in a loose snake dance for the allotted forty-five minutes.

Colorado yielded to Massachusetts; and when the chairman of the Bay State's delegation rose to deliver the nominating speech for Rose Keogh, the band started out with the first few bars of "The Battle Hymn of the Republic," quickly followed by "Dixie." It was supposed to signal the unifying spirit represented by the Keogh platform. There was another forty-five minutes of marching and tooting of horns and klaxons.

Then the business at hand started in deadly seriousness. The secretary called on Alabama.

"The State of Alabama's 37 delegates nominate Mrs. Rose Keogh by a margin of 25 to 12." Thunderous applause. Rose smiled and did not change her expression. It was too early in the battle. Alaska followed— Harris. Then Arizona. "The State of Arizona's 30 delegates nominate Mrs. Rose Keogh by a margin of 28 to 2." Then Arkansas.

Sharpe held his breath. Now it was California. There was a deathly hush.

"The State of California unanimously nominates Senator Ronald Harris."

Her first early lead was wiped out in one fell swoop. Roger Sharpe made discreet mathematical notes.

It was neck and neck right up to the last two roll calls. The Secretary seemed to drag out the process to a painful degree in calling the states. Outside the Garden, even those who hadn't written down the delegate count knew it was too close to call.

Roger Sharpe bit his lower lip until it turned blue. Del Vecchio shifted uncomfortably in his seat, but managed to keep up a glossy smile. McGavin could feel himself breathing more heavily. God, with luck we could do it on the first ballot. Hickey and Wilson were pale, and Terrence Keogh gripped his mother's arm. Father Zeibatski looked inscrutably out onto the blue layer of smoke. Wisconsin, damn. Harris by a margin of three to one. "Jesus Christ," Roger Sharpe muttered. Wyoming? Come on, Wyoming. Damn it, don't fuck around. Oh, no. Another three to one. The chairman stood up to announce what Roger Sharpe already knew.

"Of the 2,300 delegates and designated alternates, 966 have cast their votes for Senator Harris of California, 876 for Mrs. Keogh of Massachusetts and 460 for Senator Townsend of Iowa." He went on talking, but nobody in the Keogh clan seemed to be listening. A searing pain shot through Rose Keogh's brain. Terrence gripped her arm until his hand left a blue mark. Forty-two percent of the delegates had voted for Harris, thirty-eight per cent for Rose Keogh and twenty percent for Senator Townsend of Iowa.

Roger Sharpe sprang to his feet. "Come on, Mike—tonight we work as we have never worked before in our lives. Don't let Townsend get out of our sight. After I tackle Townsend, you work on swinging the rest of Illinois behind us. Let's go."

They hurried from the Garden as the Chairman of the Republican National Committee moved to adjourn the convention until the following day. That night the second balloting would be held, and the winner had to get more than fifty percent of the votes. The outcome all rested now on Sharpe and McGavin to swing the needed extra 13 percent of 299 delegates.

Senator Townsend looked across the coffee table of his suite at the Hilton Hotel and sipped on a soda. "Roger, it's as simple as this. Sure the deal is on. But I think I can only guarantee ten percent of my delegates' votes. I'm willing to play ball, but I'm being honest with you. You need at least another thirteen percent."

"Okay—shake on it. Guarantee it now and the Administration job is yours. You have never known me to go back on my word. I don't have time for niceties, so I'll shake and go."

Senator Townsend smiled, shook hands and saw Roger Sharpe race from his room. Somewhere they needed that extra three percent.

McGavin had hit the easy ones first. Alabama and Arizona welcomed him in their suites. Harris had been there before him. They were polite, friendly, but very independent-minded. They would meet in caucus again tomorrow morning and up until then would make no promises.

At six that morning, Sharpe and McGavin dropped exhausted into adjoining twin beds in their suite. Sharpe spoke as he looked wearily to the ceiling: "What do you think?"

"Don't know . . . don't fucking well know. Damn it."

"Get some sleep. I can't do any more."

"Me neither. . . . Jesus, we're so close, but I have a terrible feeling we might just miss it by a whisker."

"You know what? I have the same feeling."

That night in the Garden, McGavin and Sharpe's mood had seemed to filter down to Rose and Del Vecchio.

Terrence sidled up to his mother. "Mother, relax; you are going to win. You are going to win. You will win. . . . Smile, Mother."

She smiled at her unseeing son. Her smile had genuine warmth. Then she turned to the camera, and although nobody had noticed, it had turned plastic. The agony was about to begin.

Sharpe had started to develop an intense dislike for the buxom secretary of the convention, who seemed to drag out the roll call with a special relish. It started.

Alabama. Rose looked down at her hands. They were bloodless. Alabama. Great. She picked up three delegates. Alaska. Still for Harris. Arizona. Good: another two. Arkansas. She had it. California stood faithful. . . . New York. God, she needed New York.

"The New York delegation votes unanimously for Mrs. Rose Keogh." Sharpe wanted to jump through the roof. Rose controlled herself. New York with 154 votes, all in the pocket. But she needed an additional 299. Painfully the voting followed almost identical lines. The Keogh campaign had picked up exactly 159 extra votes. They needed an extra hundred. She looked across at Senator Harris. He seemed frighteningly confident. Is he, she asked herself, or is he in as much agony as I am? There was a deafening cheer from the Keogh supporters as Illinois gave her an extra 52 votes.

McGavin felt sick. Terrence held his mother's hand. Hickey remained stern-faced, while Wilson saw all his plotting evaporating before him. Wisconsin and Wyoming were left, and the previous night they had abandoned Keogh. First came Wisconsin. The secretary stood again to call on the delegation. Sharpe wanted to throw something at her. Sharpe had trouble controlling his bladder with the painful excitement. Bang. Right on the money, Wisconsin had turned. All went to Rose.

McGavin looked up at the cavernous ceiling of Madison Square Garden. A bizarre thought crossed his mind. What would happen if the ceiling collapsed now? He was trying not to hear the vote from Wyoming. He mentally blocked his hearing. His stomach physically couldn't take it. That stupid secretary was at it again.

Suddenly McGavin felt the pain. Roger Sharpe had crushed him in a bear hug so tight that the air rushed from his lungs.

"Mike, Mike, Mike, Mike, that's it . . . ha-ha-ha." Sharpe couldn't contain himself. "We did it. Fifty-one percent, fifty-one percent, thirteen lousy percent, two hundred and ninety-nine lousy votes. We did it. Rose, Rose, we did it."

Rose Keogh felt her whole body stiffen as the balloons floated down in a rainbow shower from the ceiling. Her body was afire with excitement. Terrence leaned over and kissed her cheek. "I knew you could do it, Mother. I knew."

A momentary tear glistened in her eye. Hickey reached across and gave her a gentlemanly handshake. God, how she would ravage him tonight, she thought in the mixture of emotions. Wilson's face had suddenly regained color. Del Vecchio had stood up with a victory salute, and Morales was beaming. The priest smiled broadly for the camera. But his heart mourned. The bands marched around for half an hour, and then the chant went up. "Ke-ogh."

Daintily Rose Keogh walked down the steps from her box, past the main press enclosure and onto the madness of the floor, her son, Terrence, on one side with Del Vecchio on the other. Morales looked eagle-eyed from behind. They inched their way through the crowd with the help of the Secret Service, and Rose Keogh walked up to the rostrum. The cheers and music simply refused to stop. She held up her hand many times, only to laugh demurely when the pandemonium continued. Forty-five minutes later, she got the break she needed to make her short speech.

"Mr. Chairman, ladies and gentlemen, delegates, friends, my gracious rivals, fellow Republicans and Americans." The cheers started again.

It was a short speech, but one with punch, emotion and clarity. The night belonged to her. Both Townsend and Harris went to the rostrum for short congratulatory speeches pledging their unflagging support for her in the coming election. Senator Harris raised an uproar when he said, "However, I think the support for this wonderful lady is so complete, the whole of California could stay in bed on election day and she would still be elected."

Rose Keogh was swept out of the Garden in a circle of idolatrous humanity. First would come the press, then she would attend several delegate parties. After that she would host a small and handpicked reception in her suite.

As the people milled around her and the television crews lit up her small features, she looked across at John Hickey. After that she knew what they would do. Crawl inside and outside of each other like voracious animals.

SEAN KEOGH had been awake all that night. He was so terribly alone. But he knew it would be different tomorrow, or perhaps the day after, when the convention was over. He understood they all had to be in New York. He understood it all. But he felt so terribly lonely in that pitch-black room whose emptiness was filled only with the faint humming of the series of grotesque-looking machines he was attached to.

He heard the night nurses coming on duty. He knew all their voices now, and his hearing could pick up a voice from far away. It was the plump, jolly one who was talking. The nurses always talked in whispers when they changed shifts. Very well trained. But the plump, jolly one was talking with the breathlessness of excitement: "Well, how about that? What do you think of it? Rose Keogh, and I've met her, held her hand. She will be the next President. You can bet on that. Can you imagine— the next President. Imagine."

Sean Keogh smiled to himself, closed his eyes and fell asleep contented. God bless her. She did it.

Chapter
21

IT HAD gone exactly as predicted. The Republican Convention had sealed the election. Rawlins had been renominated by a limp Democratic Party, and he had gone into the election with an even limper campaign, with the odds hopelessly stacked against him. The results had been as one-sided as the 1964 triumph of Lyndon Johnson over Barry Goldwater. The rout was complete.

Madam President Rose Keogh now held the country in the palm of her hand. All promises made by Roger Sharpe at the convention were being strictly honored, and the Congress was already shaping up as the most cooperative since the early days of President Johnson.

The majesty of office seemed to enhance Rose Keogh's vast intellect and understanding of the people around her, and the country was responding with warmth. The hysteria and the novelty attendant on the installation of the first woman President in U.S. history had now worn off, and people found themselves asking why it had taken so long for a country to elect a woman in the first place. A year earlier, the thought had been preposterous; now it seemed perfectly natural.

Within hours of moving into the White House, President Rose Keogh had ordered that Sean Keogh be taken from the hospital and his bed and equipment set up in a big sunny room on the mansion's third floor. For this he was eternally grateful. In a bizarre way, Senator Sean Keogh seemed to experience a small sense of accomplishment—he had made the White House after all. In the third-floor sickroom a constant stream of familiar faces stopped by to visit. At first there were three nurses, attending the patient around the clock, and the doctor would come twice a day. As it became more apparent that his condition was hopeless, the shift was cut to two nurses, and the doctor, Dr. Eberhard West, had cut his visits to twice a week.

Sean Keogh instinctively disliked Dr. West. He was one of the world's losers, the type that gave up. And it was a constant source of annoyance that he seemed to upset Rose when there was a gathering around the bed. On one occasion he actually heard him advising Rose that it would be better to pull the plug and let Keogh "die with dignity." What a congenital moron!

There was also, the still Senator got the distinct impression, a serious rift between Rose, his wife, and his beloved friend Father Zeibatski. The priest had brought in at least five specialists from all over the country to examine Sean Keogh. They had all concurred in the opinion of Dr. West.

"Father," President Keogh said with ice in her voice, "while I realize you are doing what you think best, I must remind you that he is my husband. This constant stream of doctors coming and going produces not only a false hope in our hearts but one in the hearts of the public when their visits leak out in the press. I must ask you to discontinue your humanitarian efforts. It's painful enough."

"Rose, are we to be the judges of life and death?" the priest had asked with equal chilliness.

It was then that Father Zeibatski, in the presence of Dr. West, extracted one last promise.

"Doctor, you have heard of Dr. Gerdnar Butya?"

"Yes, I have."

"He is a Soviet doctor, living in Moscow. Actually, he came from my home town in Lithuania. I knew him very well many years ago."

"He is certainly the best in the world."

"You agree with that, Doctor?"

"Certainly. Of course I do."

"Well, I have arranged for him to be here in three weeks' time. He has been working with a new formula which is only in the testing stage, but he has had some limited successes with animals."

President Keogh seemed infuriated. "You are now making my husband a guinea pig, Father. Really, I have to question that."

"What is there to lose?"

Dr. West shrugged his shoulders. "If it will convince you, Father, by all means. Perhaps it is best that you be totally convinced. I have no objection. It can't do any harm, Madam President, and it might serve to convince the good Father that when it comes to life and death, my profession is a little more clinical in its observations than yours, Father."

"I understand. Well, Rose, surely just this one last time."

"If it will convince you, Father."

"Then three weeks from now, perhaps you would like to meet him, Doctor?"

"I have already met him at a medical conference. Thank you, Father."

Sean Keogh's heart filled with hope. If the priest believed, he too would believe. But it was filled only with hope. Not expectation.

In a small way life had improved for Keogh, if it was just from simply seeing friendly faces. The tragedy of his condition seemed no longer to shock his visitors. Del Vecchio, Sharpe, Morales, Terrence and Rose would drop in several times a day. They would sit for as long as half an hour. Sometimes they would talk to him, as if he were more than an inanimate object, but more and more they would just sit there, eagle-eyed for any trace of movement. Occasionally one of them would tell a nurse that he could swear he had seen a finger move. Often the finger did move, but the visitor would be assured that unfortunately it was only a single nerve reaction. The eyes themselves, although seeing, could move only a little.

It was the visits of Mike McGavin and Father Zeibatski that saddened Sean most because it seemed to sadden them the most. Often the priest would kneel and pray, and on one occasion both the priest and Mike knelt at his bedside in front of a nurse and prayed. God bless them, those brave hearts. And now Father Zeibatski had arranged to bring in this Dr. Gerdnar Butya in three weeks' time. Dared he to pray also? Yes. He prayed and prayed and prayed. It would be only another three weeks.

But Sean Keogh was wrong. The very next day Father Zeibatski, who had taken a short leave of absence from his parish in South Boston, got on the shuttle to New York. He then took a taxi to John F. Kennedy Airport and waited for an hour.

"Aeroflot Flight 2000 arriving from Moscow," the loudspeaker announced. The priest tingled with apprehension. Would he recognize him? It didn't matter—he would find him. He stationed himself behind the glass partition overlooking the arrival area. It would take an hour to clear the passengers of a Soviet plane through Immigration and Customs.

Half the plane had disgorged when the priest saw him. A portly little man in a heavy, bulky suit and a funny little small-brimmed hat. No mistake—that was he. His hurried short-step walk. That was he. The priest smiled. He would never forget him. He raced down to the arrival area.

At last Dr. Butya, looking slightly bewildered, emerged into the arrival lounge. The priest hurried toward him.

"Gerdnar . . . Gerdnar"—and he yelled out something in a strange language.

The little man dropped his suitcase, and his face lit up in a beautiful smile. He waddled toward the priest, and they threw their arms around each other, covering each other with the embraces so accepted in Eastern Europe but frowned on by the Western world.

They babbled excitedly in their native tongue for many minutes. And the portly little man wiped some tears from his eyes.

"So long, Velas—or should I call you Padre now?"

"Velas. Velas, my dear friend."

"It has been so long since that day. So long. So many painful memories. So many."

The priest refused to dwell on the tragic past. "You look well, very well."

The doctor took off his hat to reveal a bald pate, and he ran his hands through the thick straight hair of the priest. They both laughed. They linked arms and walked together toward the exit. Suddenly they were silent, content to be in each other's company. They got into a taxi and sped toward the Carlyle Hotel. The chubby doctor stared wide-eyed as the yellow cab raced, screeched and jerked crazily through the packed concrete canyons of Manhattan. He smiled and shook his head in wonderment.

"Velas . . . it's amazing. So different."

After the priest installed him in his room, the two returned to the ground floor and ordered a bottle of ice-cold vodka. In the corner of the bar they gazed at each other for a long time before breaking into speech. There was much mystery to the visit.

They spoke in the comfort of their native tongue as they sipped their vodka.

"I have told them three weeks," the priest said.

"That is good."

"But Gerdnar, we must start now." And then he related a story that the little doctor found hard to believe.

After twenty minutes the doctor was goggle-eyed with astonishment. "You are sure?"

"No, I am not. I am sure only that much evil exists surrounding my friend."

"But Velas, I am a foreigner. To do such a thing in secret . . . I mean. . ."

"I know. To be caught would mean an end to your life's work. You work in Russia. Much trouble. International trouble. Much trouble."

"But you asked, and I will do it. I have never forgotten that border. The way you took me and your brother, after we returned home from the woods that day. I will never forget. Of course. I will do as you say. But the White House itself. Won't it be difficult?"

"No. I have a complete security clearance. I have arranged similar documents for you. I know the place we call the White House as well as our forest. But it will have to be done at night. And in total secrecy. Total."

"Whatever you say, my good friend."

"Then it is done. More vodka?"

"Most certainly. We will drink today."

PRESIDENT ROSE Keogh stood in front of the bed with her son, Terrence, by her side. Although Sean Keogh could not see her at first, he had even learned to smell her perfume at the door. She was now standing in sight with Terrence. The day nurse had slipped out.

"This doctor, Terrence. Have you checked him out?"

"Yes, I have. I've had someone read me newspaper files. Dozens of them."

"What do you think?"

"No question he is a genius in all forms of medicine, but he is the master brain surgeon in the world, and he has perfected methods that make surgery itself almost a thing of the past."

"Any particular successes?"

"One outstanding one. A young soccer star. Totally paralyzed . . . like this."

The words "like this" hurt Sean. Terrence's voice was very cold. And equally cold, he noted curiously, was the voice of Rose, his wife. He had never heard her use this tone before.

"Do you think there's a chance that meddling priest knows what he's talking about?"

My God, what are they discussing? What are these words?

Terrence remained quiet for a moment. "There is always the chance with an unknown quantity. Personally, I believe we're safe. Very safe. But why leave the door open to chance? Particularly now. Now of all times, when it is all yours."

She smiled. "Ours, darling. Ours."

Keogh's head swam in a whirlpool of confusion. That is Rose. That is Terrence. My God! What fresh torture, God, do you have in store for me? What are they talking about?

The conversation that followed certainly answered all his questions.

"Well, let it go for a time," she said. "The doctor arrives in three weeks. No, eighteen days. Don't arouse Zeibatski's suspicions. Pretend enthusiasm. But before he arrives, I think it should be done."

"It will be relatively simple. At night there are no nurses. Just disconnect the machine . . . perhaps for only a few hours . . . then reconnect it before morning. There will not be a single trace. The body will just give up. I don't think it's necessary, but why take the risk that this confounded doctor might be some genius?"

"You're right, Terrence. And Terrence?"

"Yes?"

"I don't think Hickey and Wilson need to know."

"Of course not. This time it will be done. It will be different from the gymnasium."

A nurse's footsteps came tapping down the hall. She walked in. "I'm sorry I took so long, Madam President," the nurse gushed in apology.

"Not at all, Nurse. Thank you for your vigilance," she said warmly. "We'll be going now. See you tomororw."

Both she and Terrence leaned over the still form and warmly kissed its forehead. Sean Keogh felt nausea gripping his body.

It would get worse. He would hear more in later conversations. Conversations that sent such a flame of hurt dancing through his inanimate body that he thought it impossible to bear. McLaughlin, Sweeney, Burke and now him. Wilson, Hickey. They all played hideous, filthy roles in the insanely macabre act. What had his life been to come to this? Did he want the Soviet doctor to succeed, or would he be just as happy if the infamy of their plans worked? He would change his mind many times.

It was four o'clock in the morning, four days after he had learned the truth. His fitful sleep was interrupted. He felt a presence in the room. My God, is this it? Is this the time?

A covered blue light went on in the room, the type that would not be seen from outside. He heard the gentle voice of the priest.

"Over here, Gerdnar."

The funny-looking, portly man bent over the body. He fetched a series of small electrodes from a case and fitted them to a console. He then placed the electrodes on the Senator's head, heart and neck pulse and in his armpits. Long minutes ticked away.

"It is but a small blockage. A clot that started elsewhere and lodged in the motor section at the entrance to the top and left of the brain. The clot is congealed. Probably as hard as the top of a matchstick." Keogh could not understand their language.

"There is a hope. It is the same way I treated our young soccer player. The clot cannot be surgically removed without causing a massive hemorrhage. It has to be dissipated . . . gradually, from the center of the clot. As the clot is opened, a tiny amount of blood slips in and feeds the brain. The tissue then regains its health and heals the wound caused by the clot. Then gradually the rest of the clot is dissipated."

"It sounds very simple."

"No—almost impossible. One has to control that passage of blood. Too much and the weakened tissue will cause a flood. Not enough and his condition would never change."

"Is there a chance? If you can't do it surgically, how?"

"My formula. It is not thoroughly tested. Many successes on animals. One success with our soccer player. Impossible to promise."

"Is there an alternative?"

"None. I inject a formula of provocaine and a new form of decoagulant. These are very bad conditions.

Are you sure?"

"It's all I can provide."

"Then so be it."

He withdrew a needle and filled it. "Now we have to very temporarily stop the blood flow so I can inject this formula in the base of the neck behind the ear. You take this needle and when I say so inject one cubic centimeter. You still can use a hypodermic, no doubt?"

"Yes."

"Okay, now. Just one c.c. Now." The doctor then plunged the needle in the other side.

Sean Keogh felt a sudden tightening of his chest, and the light before his eyes turned black. It was only momentary. The discomfort then suddenly vanished.

"Let us wait for fifteen minutes. Then we try again."

They waited in silence, and the priest could hear the faint noise of light traffic outside in the distance past the entrance to the White House.

The procedure was repeated. Then little Dr. Butya sighed as he packed his equipment away.

"What now?" the priest asked.

"We repeat that until until the scanner tells me there is blood movement in the brain."

The two men slipped out the door, and the priest smuggled the doctor out of the White House.

That morning Sean Keogh could have sworn he felt a slight headache. It was the first physical pain he could remember feeling since the accident. He grimly corrected himself . . . since the attempt on his life by a person he had once mistakenly believed was his son. But it was there, a slight headache—and he welcomed it.

The priest and the doctor stole into the room every night for the next five nights. After the second night the little doctor smiled, and that morning Sean Keogh could have sworn he felt his right toe itch. After the third morning he managed to make a fist when the treatment caused pain.

The doctor nodded his head and chuckled. Tears glistened in the priest's eyes.

"It just might work, my friend," the doctor said from behind the eerie blue light; "it just might work. You see the scanner. There is a flow of blood. Small, but it is there. The body is very weak and atrophied from disuse. It will be some time before normal function returns. But his heart, his lungs, his kidneys and his liver are in good shape. There has been no uremic poisoning. That is good."

After the next-to-last treatment the little doctor saw the fist clench. He lifted the arm, bending it at the elbow, and allowed it to drop. Instead of flopping uselessly by the patient's side, the arm fell slowly as the impoverished muscles fought the weight of the arm.

"See, see." The little man was beaming.

Father Zeibatski became excited, and instead of whispering he said in a loud voice, "Sean, Sean. Sean, if you can hear us, blink your eyes."

Just then they heard the steps of a security guard in the corridor. The priest and the doctor froze. Hurriedly they scrambled to the side of the room as the door opened. A single flashlight beam sliced through the dark. Then it switched off. And the footsteps were heard drifting down the corridor.

When the little doctor returned to the bedside and switched on his blue light, Sean Keogh was blinking his eyes at a rapid rate. The priest could not speak. His throat was too constricted.

The next day Sean Keogh felt the agony of his muscles that had been useless for so long. He could now move his head from side to side, and when the nurses disappeared he practiced frantically and painfully.

Three days later, Father Zeibatski bade the little doctor farewell. Tears streamed down the priest's face. "How could I ever thank you? If only you could stay."

"It is done. He will mend. Stay? How I wish it. But the work. It must go on. I must work. I know so little about America."

"Gerdnar, my great and wonderful friend . . . bless you."

"Bless you, Velas. Bless you."

And then he boarded a plane and was gone, this funny, portly little man who knew the priest from another era of tragedy.

PRESIDENT ROSE Keogh looked out one of the beautiful big windows of the third-floor Georgian parlor which faced Pennsylvania Avenue. There was a light snow on the February streets of Washington. The sky was clear. The lawn in front of the White House was a blanket of powdery white. The President of the United States opened the window and inhaled deeply the clean, cold, crisp air of Washington. Her Washington, the capital of her nation. She closed the window.

"Well, gentlemen—she turned to John Hickey, Edward Wilson and Terrence Keogh—"shall we break out the bottle of champagne?"

Wilson obliged: "What are we celebrating?"

"Nothing in particular. Perhaps a celebration of some new appointments."

"Appointments?" Wilson asked.

"Yes. I have decided to make John here a roving ambassador, and frankly, I'm now looking around for a job for Terrence."

"Rose, do you think that's wise? I mean the press will be all over you for making such nepotistic appointments. He's only a boy—a brilliant boy, but only a boy."

She flashed Wilson a murderous look. Terrence tightened his jaw. "Press? press? They don't run this country, Edward. Press? Congress? Senate? I'm sick of hearing what I have to do for them. *They* have to serve *me*. I'll do what I like. I run this country. I will save this country."

Wilson paled as he noted the edge of hysteria in her voice. He dutifully opened the bottle of champagne and poured. His heart began to pump with fear.

ROBERT DEL VECCHIO received the call at his mansion. It was Alberto Morales. The message was clear. Enrique Soares, the Secret Police chief from Costa Real who had organized the "siege" of the American Embassy, thus elevating Del Vecchio to hero status, had been captured by real left-wing guerrillas. Under torture, he was in the process of telling all.

Del Vecchio remained cool. "How long before the jet can be fueled?"

"Being done now, señor," Morales answered in Spanish.

"Good. One hour?"

"Two hours, señor, if I may. We have much time."

"Why two hours?"

"Very important."

"All right. Two hours. Dulles," Del Vecchio said calmly. He then packed a small bag.

WHEN TERRENCE slipped away for a few minutes from the get-together with the President, Hickey and Wilson, he was hardly missed. The nurse had gone home early that night. He walked confidently through the long corridors of the White House, unhurried and without fear in his step. He slipped into the big room, walked across to the machine. He picked up a towel that he felt for with the sight that was in his hands and moved toward the machine. Unerringly in his own darkness, his hand went to the switch. He used the towel for fear of fingerprints. He simply turned the switch, replaced the towel and returned to the Georgian parlor on the third floor. He sipped the champagne. It tasted superb.

MIKE MCGAVIN was weary. All days in the capital were weary. He felt strangely inhibited working under the President, although he was the envy of all his old colleagues and although she was generous with her time and compensations. There was just something terribly alien about working for this woman whom he still found hard to call "Madam President." He picked up a sheaf of papers. There was much to be done with Congress, much to be done. One thing was winning an election; another thing was to make sure Congress didn't take the victory away from you.

He called the President's personal secretary. "Sorry, Elizabeth. I wonder if I could manage a half-hour tonight with the President."

"The President is engaged right now, but she said she expected you later. Perhaps nine o'clock."

"Fine. I'll drop across now. I'll go to the library, and then you can call me and tell me where the President would like to see me."

"That will be fine, Mr. McGavin."

The taxi dropped him off at the gate. He flashed his clearance to the guard and walked into the breathtaking mansion that dictated so much of the future of our lives. He took the small elevator to the third floor. He hadn't seen Sean for three days. It pricked his conscience. Not that it helped. He would just sit there and gaze and end up feeling rotten.

He walked into the semidarkened room and switched on a small light.

"Jesus Christ," he said aloud as he saw the machine above Keogh's head devoid of any light of configurations.

"Jesus," he repeated as he moved closer to the blank screen.

What happened next almost stopped his heart.

"Don't panic, Mike . . . I'm not dead."

McGavin's eyes widened, he gasped. A bolt of terror seized his heart.

"Don't panic, and shut your mouth." It was Keogh speaking. The voice was strained, painfully strained, and the body moved to one side. Keogh lifted his head.

"There is a great deal to tell you, Mike. This won't be the last shock of the night."

McGavin fell across Keogh and hugged him.

"WELL, GENTLEMEN, we should have more of these quiet little get-togethers," the President said as Hickey, Wilson and Terrence stood up to go. "They are very pleasant. I have a meeting now with the ever-faithful Michael McGavin. I'll see you tomorrow, John. Terrence is returning to school. Edward, you call me from Boston."

"Fine, Rose."

"I'll wait for your call."

The three left silently. Outside was Hickey's Mercedes.

"Are you staying in town, Eddie, or do you want me to drive you to the airport with Terrence?"

"I'll get an early flight tomorrow. I'll book in at the Mayflower for tonight." Wilson felt sick. Rose Keogh was in the throes of the blackest insanity. Soon it would arrive at his doorstep.

"Hop in, Terrence. I'll drive." Terrence sat in the back, and Wilson slid in the front next to Hickey.

Hickey's highly polished Guccis gunned the accelerator and the car purred through the gates, left on Pennsylvania Avenue. It stopped at the Seventeenth Street intersection.

Wilson spoke quietly: "I'm sorry to bring this up . . . but do you think Rose would like to have a vacation now? I mean the strain of the last months."

Terrence Keogh knew exactly what his sniveling father—his real father—meant. He blistered with anger and started to talk.

But the words never came out.

The reverberating explosion drowned the words and anger. The yellow ball of flame took care of the rest. It shot upward from under the accelerator, with searing fragments tearing into Hickey's groin and hurling the steering wheel into the chiseled features, pushing what was left of his head through the roof. The plate in the back seat was blown diagonally upward, slicing into Terrence's neck and neatly tearing off his head.

Wilson, who caught the corner of the blast, was hurled sideways through the door and onto the pavement, one arm missing, both legs mangled. As the flames licked around the car, which resembled a badly opened tin can, Wilson tried to drag himself clear with his remaining arm. He tried to scream, but only a terrible croak issued from the blackened throat. He slithered along the roadway like a shockingly wounded animal, making terrible sounds as he did. The traffic had screeched to a halt, and Wilson could hear everybody yelling.

"Hold on, fella, we're getting help. Hold on." Wilson lay there propped up on his one elbow, his bloodshot eyes staring from his smoke-blackened face. He wore that curious bewildered expression that is seen when a person knows he has only seconds to live. There was no pain.

Everywhere there were legs around him. He peered between the legs. He was intrigued now.

He saw him. He summoned all his strength. He wanted to cry out a name. "Ha, she'll get you . . . she'll get you . . . she'll . . ." His eyes rolled upward and he slumped on the roadway, his head making a loud crack as it met the concrete.

The man on the corner turned and walked slowly to a waiting car.

"It is done?" Alberto Morales asked.

"Done," the priest said quietly. They drove to the airport.

The two men casually boarded the DC-8. The jets were already screaming. The priest walked inside. Del Vecchio was sitting calmly in a plush seat.

"Father."

"Del."

"Traveling with us?"

"I believe so. . . . Where are we going?"

"I would say Uruguay. . . . Great climate, Uruguay."

The plane circled low over Washington, and Father Zeibatski could see the White House. He waved his hand. He would never see Sean Keogh again.

It had taken only seconds. The Marine guard had tried desperately to keep her from going to the scene, but she had fought him off. Hysterically she tore at the smoldering car and clawed at Terrence's headless body.

"Wake up, Terrence. Come, Terrence. Let's go home. Come, Terrence. We have to leave now."

The next day a stunned nation learned that the President of the United States would be admitted to a mental institution. But it had not learned the whole truth.

"There is no other way," Sean Keogh said as he sat propped up against a stack of pillows.

"But Senator, it would mean the end of everything for you."

"What is everything for me? What have I?"

"No, I couldn't to it, Senator. First of all, for your knowledge of the murder of Paddy Devlin, you would go to prison."

"I don't care. I want the whole story told. Every word, every breath. I want it told, Mike, and you will be the man to write it. And I can assure you it will get printed because it will be printed in the *Clarion*, no matter what happens to me. I still own the *Clarion*."

"No."

"If you respect me as you pretend to, Mike, you must do this one last thing. I've been trapped by death, I've been trapped in my own body. I don't want to live the rest of my life trapped in my conscience. No. It must be done."

And Mike McGavin did exactly as he was told. Everything that had happened; everything. How Sean Keogh had seized the streets of Southie. The deaths of Rooney, his mother, Devlin, McLaughlin, Sweeney, Castellano. And now the most recent massacre.

It was frightening reading, and it tore the innards out of a public who believed that after Watergate they could no longer be manipulated. It was the ultimate horror of absolute power corrupting absolutely.

McGavin had no illusions. It would most certainly bring a prosecution. And the prosecution would have been triggered by McGavin's own hand.

WHEN SENATOR Sean Keogh pleaded guilty to complicity in the murder of Paddy Devlin, McGavin and Keogh were certain of the outcome. He was sentenced to from one to ten years in Walpole State Prison.

Before leaving the courtroom, McGavin wiped the tears from his eyes and shook hands with the man he loved.

"It was the only way, Mike. The only way."

McGavin left Boston.

LONG AFTER Sean Keogh was sentenced for his knowledge of the Paddy Devlin murder which had taken place so many years before, the country devoured every word of Mike McGavin's exposé of the Keogh clan and marveled in fear and shock that it was possible for a family so entwined in violence and criminality to come so close to being the stewards of a people's destiny.

The conspiracy was chillingly complete. The President, the Vice President, the Senator's wife who had shot America into the international limelight by becoming the first woman President of the United States. Keogh's aides—Burke, Wilson, Hickey; and even the twisted Terrence.

What, then, of the priest? Somebody said he was somewhere in South America. Somebody said he was with the master con man Del Vecchio and Morales. Nobody really knew.

McGavin's newspaper series read like horrifying fiction. But it was grim fact.

The ever-mounting scandal decimated the Republican Party. When Roger Sharpe was drummed out of the party, Keogh felt he had ruined an honest man's life. Still the owner of the *Clarion,* he installed Sharpe as its Managing Director.

It would be a miracle if the *Clarion* survived it all. Somehow it did. After all, it was the *Clarion* that had first run McGavin's sensational series.

McGavin, shattered, had simply left town. Some of his colleagues had heard he had been seen living in Baja California. He was. He worked on a fishing boat, consuming his daytime hours in backbreaking physical labor. The work helped him forget, and during the night there were always the tequila and the whores. That made him forget too.

Rose Keogh had never uttered a single lucid word to another person since being admitted to the institution. She was totally psychotic, spending ceaseless hours in front of a mirror addressing herself in conversations as Madam President.

As for Keogh himself, he welcomed the punishment of prison. Somehow it lightened the burden. There were no more secrets now. No dark recesses hidden from the public, or even himself. Curious how he regarded prison as therapy.

He had no trouble at Walpole State Prison, the grim top-security facility where the worse male offenders of Massachusetts make up the population of seven hundred. He kept to himself in the dark gray stone walls. He was not a snob. He just kept to himself.

And there was no trouble from his fellow inmates, some of them the most violent and unhinged in the country. Little old Raymond, whom the Italians called Don Raimondo, saw to that. The old Italian, who could not walk now and could hardly speak, still ruled New England with an iron fist. He had just sent the word: Senator Keogh is not to be bothered. And that was that. Keogh understood and was appreciative. The old man had learned about the stupidity of the death of his friend Castellano. He never forgave it. It had taken a lifetime to prove it. But he understood.

Keogh spent long hours reading and, when he had telephone privileges, long minutes on the telephone with Roger Sharpe, who was running the newspaper in his absence. Amazingly, Sharpe and the newspaper were surviving. He liked Sharpe. Sharpe was basically like himself. A survivor. If nothing else, a survivor.

But Keogh really didn't care much about anything, because there was very little to care about. Who was left? Mr. Mac, long gone; Sweeney, the same way. Burke. Jesus, Burke. Not even the priest was there anymore. He would have given a lot to see that flat, handsome face again. McGavin? McGavin too had gone, stricken by a burden imposed on him by Keogh. Wilson? How could he feel bitter about a man who was angrier at himself than he was toward anyone else? Hickey? A nothing. Rose? Terrence? He had never had them anyway. But poor, misguided Wilson, a man capable of such treachery. Keogh sighed. Wilson had once been totally loyal. He had used to help him with his homework.

If anything, the days in prison were just boring. Not brutal; just boring for a man who had been used to such movement in his life, such cliff-hanging excitement. He took it all in his stride, playing an occasional game of chess with a man whom Don Raimondo had chosen to look after him.

The week before Thanksgiving, Keogh was summoned to the Deputy Warden's office. He was a big, heavily muscled man of Polish extraction. He was polite and shook hands with a quick smile.

"Senator," he formally addressed him, "you have many friends in the outside world."

Keogh nodded, not knowing why he would make the observation. The deputy continued.

"The Parole Board is sitting after Thanksgiving. I'm told they have a file four inches thick containing petitions from public and private citizens asking for your release. You obviously have a spotless record in here. Do you wish to go before the board?"

"I . . . well . . . I guess so."

Ten days later, Sean Keogh was given a single message by a smiling corrections officer, an Irishman from Boston.

"You're a free bird, Senator. Tomorrow, the first bus out at eight in the morning."

Keogh shook his hand and smiled. Funny. There was no exhilaration. He didn't even call Roger Sharpe to send a limousine to pick him up.

At eight the next morning, wearing the same tweed coat and slacks that he had worn when he entered prison ten months earlier, he passed through the bleak outer walls of Walpole. The Massachusetts winter was steel-gray and biting. Keogh simply wandered through the front clearing office, waved to a few of the lifers who ran the candy store and walked into the damp air. There were no farewells. Keogh had long since abandoned getting close to other human beings.

He wouldn't even catch the bus. He had nobody to meet, nobody to see. He would call Roger the next day. Right now he would just go into Walpole Township and have some eggs and bacon and wend his way back to Boston.

He heard a toot on a car horn, looked up to see a big old-model Cadillac. He walked over to it, first looking into the front seat to see a burly uniformed chauffeur and then into the back seat. There was a short, squat man. He opened the door, smiled. In the corner of the limousine, swathed in blankets and propped up on pillows, sat a very old man.

"Please, Senator, get in." The accent was heavy, thick, Southern European. Keogh had heard that Don Raimondo had lately surrounded himself only with native-born Sicilians.

The old man was tiny. It had been many years since Sean had physically seen him. During the campaign he had heard from him often, but never seen him.

The old man nodded and managed a weak smile. Don Raimondo made no attempt to talk. The man with the thick accent did it for him.

"We will drive you home, Senator. To Carson Beach?"

"That would be fine. Don Raimondo, many thanks for many things."

The old man nodded his head. He must be only months from death.

The man with the accent spoke again. "Don Raimondo wants you to know he has much sorrow in his heart for what has happened to you."

Keogh smiled. He nodded in acknowledgment to the old man as the limousine sped toward Boston. The old man again smiled weakly and nodded.

"Don Raimondo," said the man with the accent, "also says that he thinks you have acted with much honor and your people must be very proud of you."

Keogh nodded.

"And he hopes you will be successful in your endeavors. He asks what are your endeavors?"

Former Senator Keogh turned toward Don Raimondo and, speaking slowly for the benefit of the old man who was called "Sox" on Federal Hill in Providence, he said simply, "I will go back into business. I still have my newspaper, the *Clarion*. Obviously there is no alternative."

"Don Raimondo believes that is best for you, and he wishes to offer any help he can. Financing, of course, if you need it."

Keogh shook his head. "Many thanks, and I'm honored. No, financially I think we're fine."

The trip took fifty minutes before the limousine pulled up to Keogh's home in Carson Beach, the home he felt most comfortable in, the home he was proudest of. The talk during the trip was warm and inconsequential.

As the car pulled up to Keogh's home, Don Raimondo tugged at the coat sleeve of the man with the accent.

"Don Raimondo bids you farewell with the hope you will call on him if you ever need him, and he would be honored when the time comes for you to attend his funeral."

Keogh shook hands with the frail old man and simply gave his thanks.

"One other thing," said the man. "Should you ever need any help, you know Mr. Paul Castle."

"Paul Castle? Of course. He worked for me. Now he is Speaker of the House. A very able man."

The man smiled. "Don Raimondo thinks you should know that Paul Castle was once Paulo Castellano, the nephew of another Castellano whom you met many years ago."

Keogh's face registered no surprise. It wasn't supposed to. It was just that nothing really changes. He leaned over and kissed the old man on the cheek, then walked toward his house.

He opened the door. The atmosphere was musty. There was much dust. But it was home, the only real home he had ever had.

He called Roger Sharpe at the office. Sharpe bubbled with excitement.

"Are we going to celebrate? Why didn't you tell me? I would have picked you up."

"No celebrations. Just see you tomorrow morning, nine o'clock. Don't let's make a fuss. Let's pretend nothing happened."

"Whatever you want, Sean. Anything I can do?"

"One thing."

"Shoot."

"Track down Mike . . . Mike McGavin."

"We'll try. I think he's somewhere in Mexico. Somewhere."

"Okay, see you tomorrow—nine o'clock."

The next day he strode through the big lobby of the *Boston Clarion* as if he had never been away. The doorman and the receptionist were far too discreet to even register a look of surprise. Keogh nodded politely and gave them a formal smile. Nothing had changed.

But something had changed. It had changed inside Sean Keogh. No longer did he feel like a visitor in the home of a better man; no longer did he feel like a well-tailored hustler in someone's private chapel. He had run fast in the last year, and with the speed the guilt had fallen in the slipstream.

He walked onto the executive floor, past the door of the office that had been the kingdom of Sheldon Mathers and had never once been used since the dark takeover so many years before.

He strode into the small office where he had spent so many hours, thinking, planning and plotting. Roger Sharpe was there. He jumped up and shook Keogh's hand until he thought it would snap.

"Sean, Sean. It's so good."

"Come, Roger, don't let's get sentimental. Let's get down to the business of making this damn paper work and having a little old-fashioned fun doing it."

"Fine, fine."

The telephone rang.

"That might be Mike. I've tracked him down."

Keogh picked up the telephone and could hear Spanish on the other end. "Hello, hello, hello. Yes, I'll accept the call."

"Hello, hello."

"Mike?"

"Senator."

"No more of that Senator stuff."

"You're free?"

"Very. How about you? How is it going?"

"Well, sir, to be honest, I called collect."

"Well, it seems you need some money."

"No, no, no. I don't want you to give me any money."

"Who the hell is talking about giving you money? You'll work for it."

"I don't understand."

"Well, you oaf, I am publisher of a newspaper, and publishers and newspapers need newspapermen. You should be sick of that thing you're doing now. You're not a fisherman. You're a newspaperman. The best there is, incidentally. The best."

"What are you saying, Senator?"

"My name is Sean. What I'm saying . . . Are you drunk or something? . . . What I am saying is Get your tail on a plane as soon as possible and be in the office in two days with a clean shave and a clean shirt and get ready to work as you've never worked before."

Sean Keogh could have sworn he heard Mike McGavin yell with joy over the telephone.

"Yes, sir. Yes, Senator—I mean Sean. I'll be there. Two days. Damn it. I'll be there tomorrow."

"Okay, fella. See you soon and let's have some fun."

He turned to Sharpe and smiled. "Great guy, Mike."

"The best. You have good taste in friends."

"Some friends."

"No, the ones who count. . . . You have perfect judgment."

Sean Keogh grew silent for a short moment.

"Well, now to the business of work. I want all the editors immediately for a conference. Let's get this show on the road."

"Right," said Sharpe enthusiastically. "I'll get them in here immediately."

"Roger?"

"Yes."

"Not in here, old fella. I want them to assemble in the Chairman's office."

Roger Sharpe threw a quick questioning glance but said nothing.

Keogh walked out the door. He looked around and threw back over his shoulder, "I'll see you inside when the rest come up. It will be a long meeting, I think."

Roger Sharpe smiled. Keogh was going into the office. The office that once he would never violate with his presence.

Sean Keogh stopped at the heavy leather-covered door. He took a deep breath and pushed it gently. It swung open unevenly. Inside, the place had been regularly dusted, but it had the eeriness that comes only from a place where humans don't breathe. It was deathly still inside.

For a short moment, Keogh looked at the many portraits around the walls. He looked up at the one of Sheldon Mathers. Keogh nodded to the portrait almost as if it were Mathers himself.

He no longer felt an interloper. At last he felt he had a rightful place in that office. He walked to the giant desk, circled it and sat in the hand-sewn leather chair. There was no longer any guilt. He was at last a good enough man to sit in that chair. He breathed deeply of the old air and it felt good. This was now legitimately his.

There was a gentle knock on the door and the editors began to file in. Keogh stood up.

"I could talk and explain things for hours, gentlemen," he said in an authoritative but friendly tone, "but I won't. Simply, I am a free man, I am here and I am in charge. There are some people in the organization who might feel a little strange working in this relationship, considering the past. If so, speak up now. I will accept your resignations and make sure your severance pay is more than adequate. Any takers?"

Eleven men in front of him remained silent, and some even smiled that he would comment on the subject. They were glad to see him and glad to see him sitting in that chair.

Keogh looked around, and he smiled at first and even managed a chuckle. A ripple of a chuckle went through the assembled editors.

"Well, then," Keogh said at last, feeling the hand stitching and smelling the luxuriousness of the leather chair in which he was sitting, "let's get on with the business of making this the best damned newspaper in the country."

He smiled again and stole a glance at the portrait of Sheldon Mathers. I think we're friends at last, Keogh mused. Friends at last.